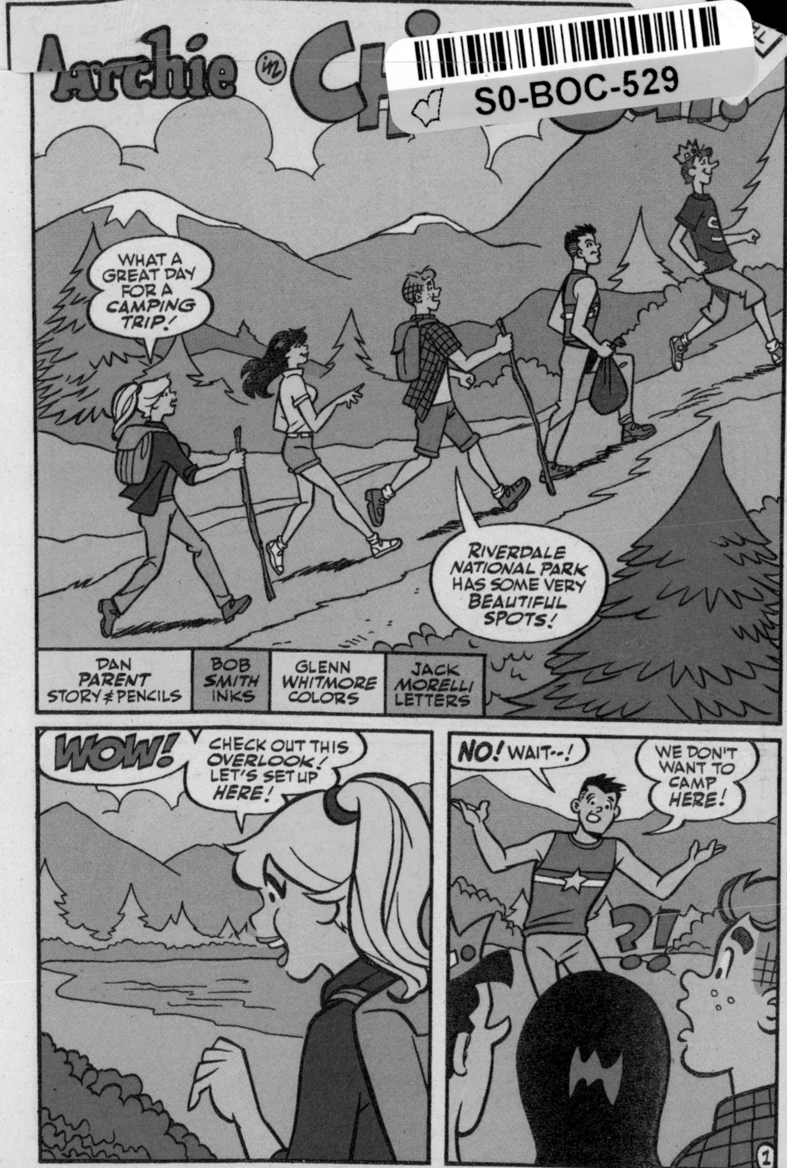
Archie in
WHAT A GREAT DAY FOR A CAMPING TRIP!
RIVERDALE NATIONAL PARK HAS SOME VERY BEAUTIFUL SPOTS!
DAN PARENT STORY & PENCILS
BOB SMITH INKS
GLENN WHITMORE COLORS
JACK MORELLI LETTERS
WOW!
CHECK OUT THIS OVERLOOK! LET'S SET UP HERE!
NO! WAIT--!
WE DON'T WANT TO CAMP HERE!
?!
1

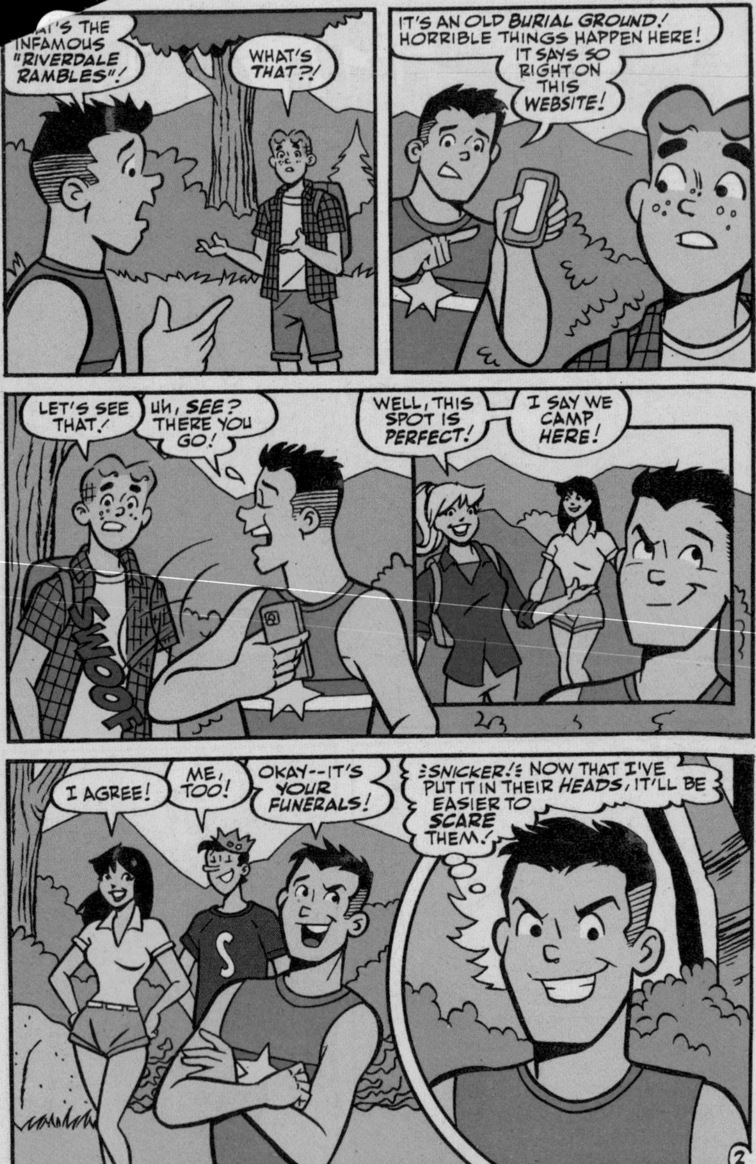

...AT'S THE INFAMOUS "RIVERDALE RAMBLES"!
WHAT'S THAT?!
IT'S AN OLD BURIAL GROUND! HORRIBLE THINGS HAPPEN HERE!
IT SAYS SO RIGHT ON THIS WEBSITE!
LET'S SEE THAT!
UH, SEE? THERE YOU GO!
SWOOF
WELL, THIS SPOT IS PERFECT!
I SAY WE CAMP HERE!
I AGREE!
ME, TOO!
OKAY--IT'S YOUR FUNERALS!
SNICKER! NOW THAT I'VE PUT IT IN THEIR HEADS, IT'LL BE EASIER TO SCARE THEM!
2

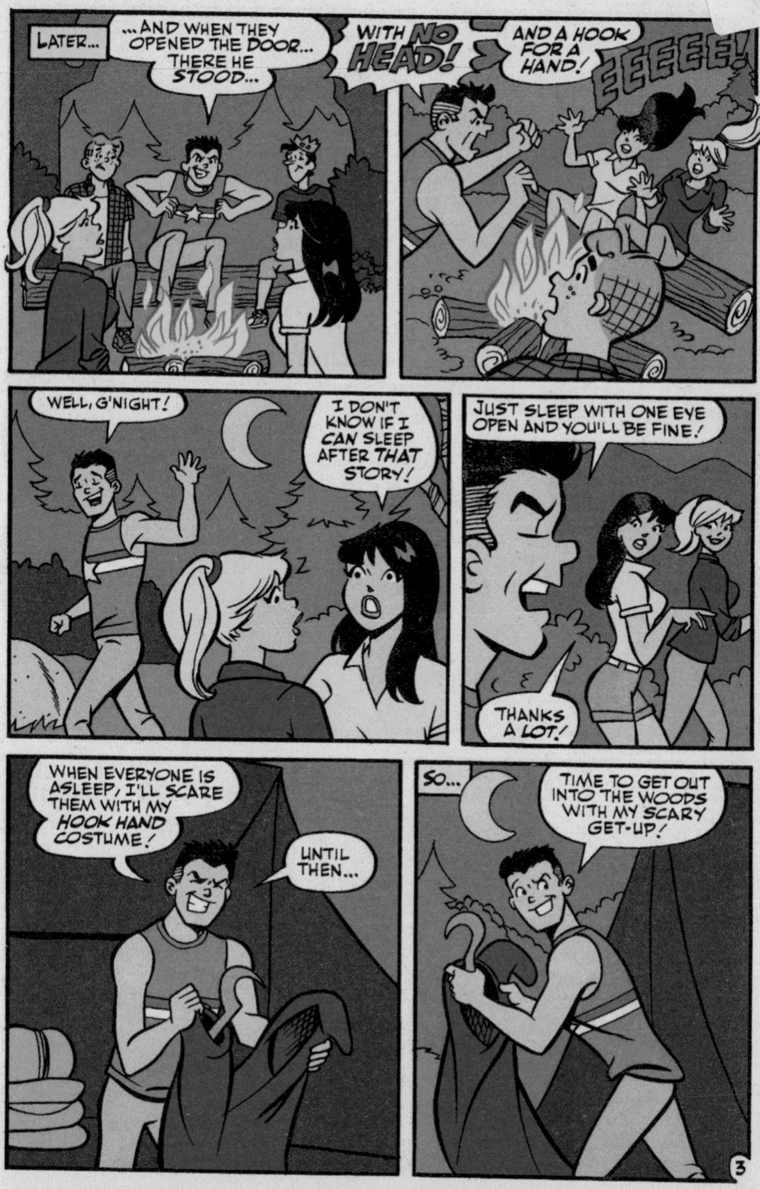
LATER...
...AND WHEN THEY OPENED THE DOOR... THERE HE STOOD...
WITH NO HEAD!
AND A HOOK FOR A HAND!
EEEEEE!
WELL, G'NIGHT!
I DON'T KNOW IF I CAN SLEEP AFTER THAT STORY!
JUST SLEEP WITH ONE EYE OPEN AND YOU'LL BE FINE!
THANKS A LOT!
WHEN EVERYONE IS ASLEEP, I'LL SCARE THEM WITH MY HOOK HAND COSTUME!
UNTIL THEN...
SO...
TIME TO GET OUT INTO THE WOODS WITH MY SCARY GET-UP!
3

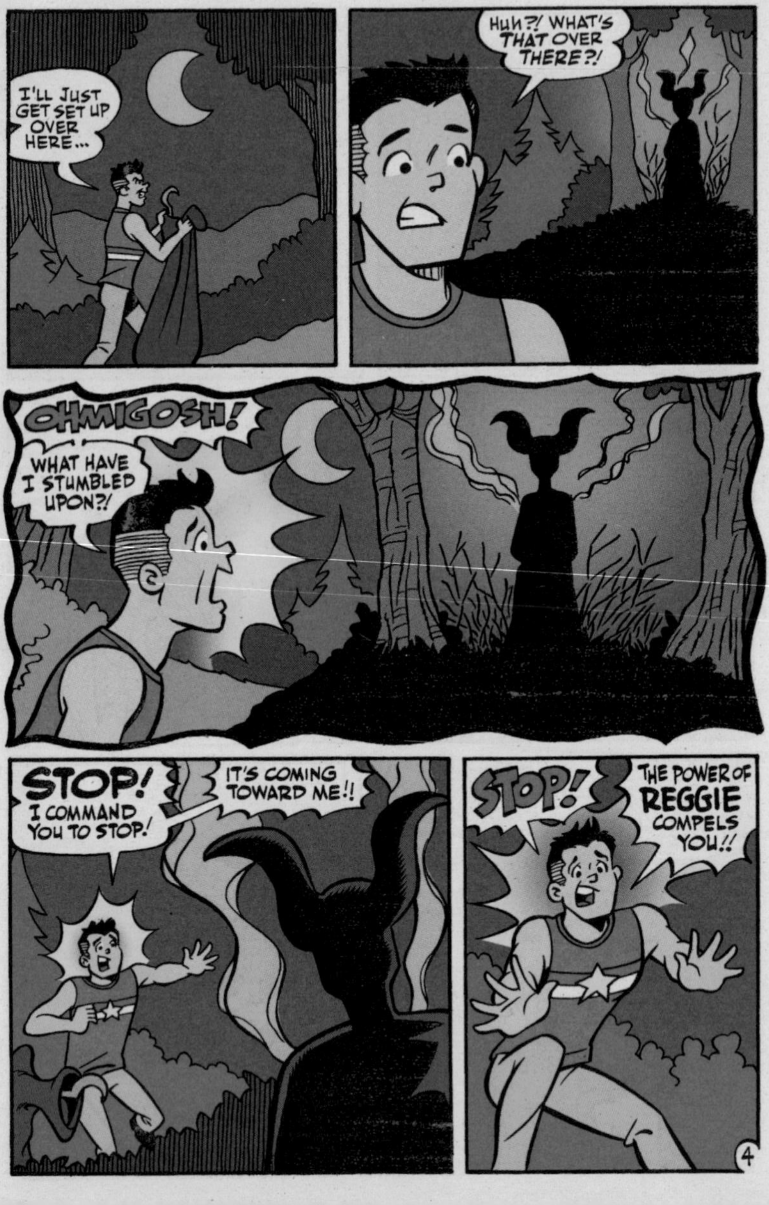
I'LL JUST GET SET UP OVER HERE...
HUH?! WHAT'S THAT OVER THERE?!
OHMIGOSH!
WHAT HAVE I STUMBLED UPON?!
STOP! I COMMAND YOU TO STOP!
IT'S COMING TOWARD ME!!
STOP!
THE POWER OF REGGIE COMPELS YOU!!
4

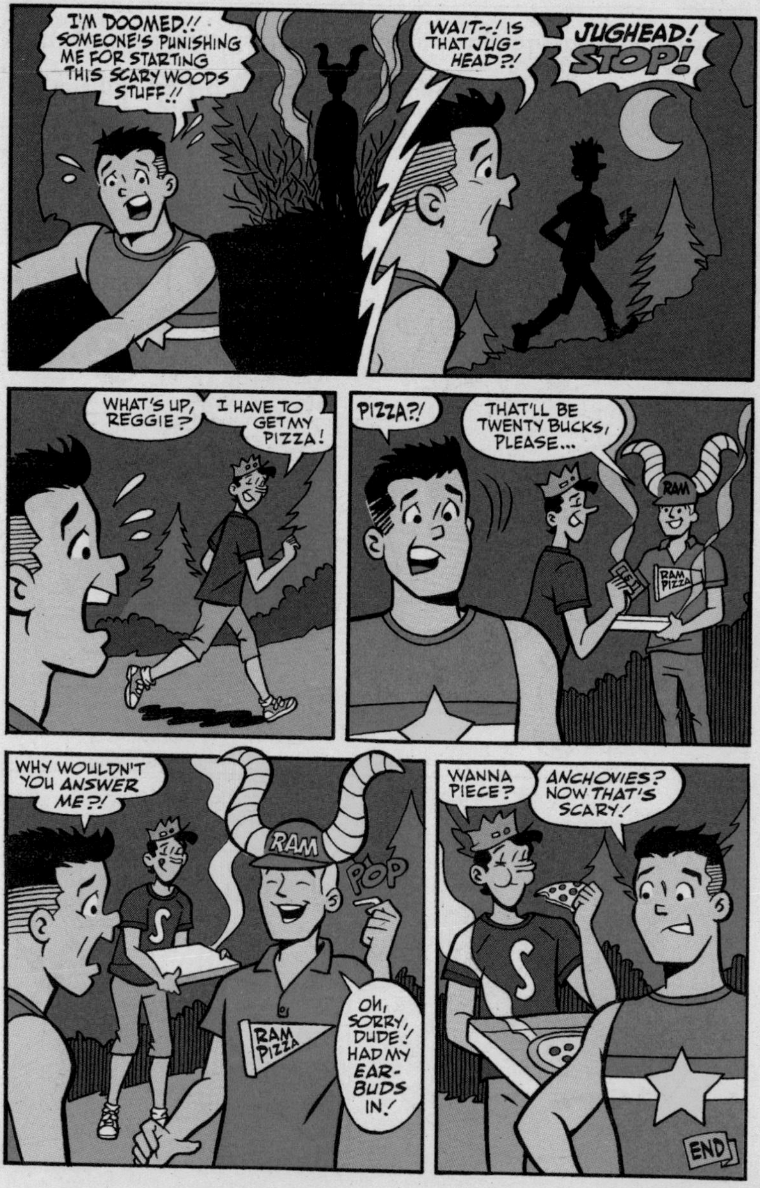
I'M DOOMED!!
SOMEONE'S PUNISHING ME FOR STARTING THIS SCARY WOODS STUFF!!
WAIT--! IS THAT JUG-HEAD?!
JUGHEAD! STOP!
WHAT'S UP, REGGIE?
I HAVE TO GET MY PIZZA!
PIZZA?!
THAT'LL BE TWENTY BUCKS, PLEASE...
RAM
RAM PIZZA
WHY WOULDN'T YOU ANSWER ME?!
RAM
POP
RAM PIZZA
OH, SORRY, DUDE! HAD MY EAR-BUDS IN!
WANNA PIECE?
ANCHOVIES? NOW THAT'S SCARY!
END

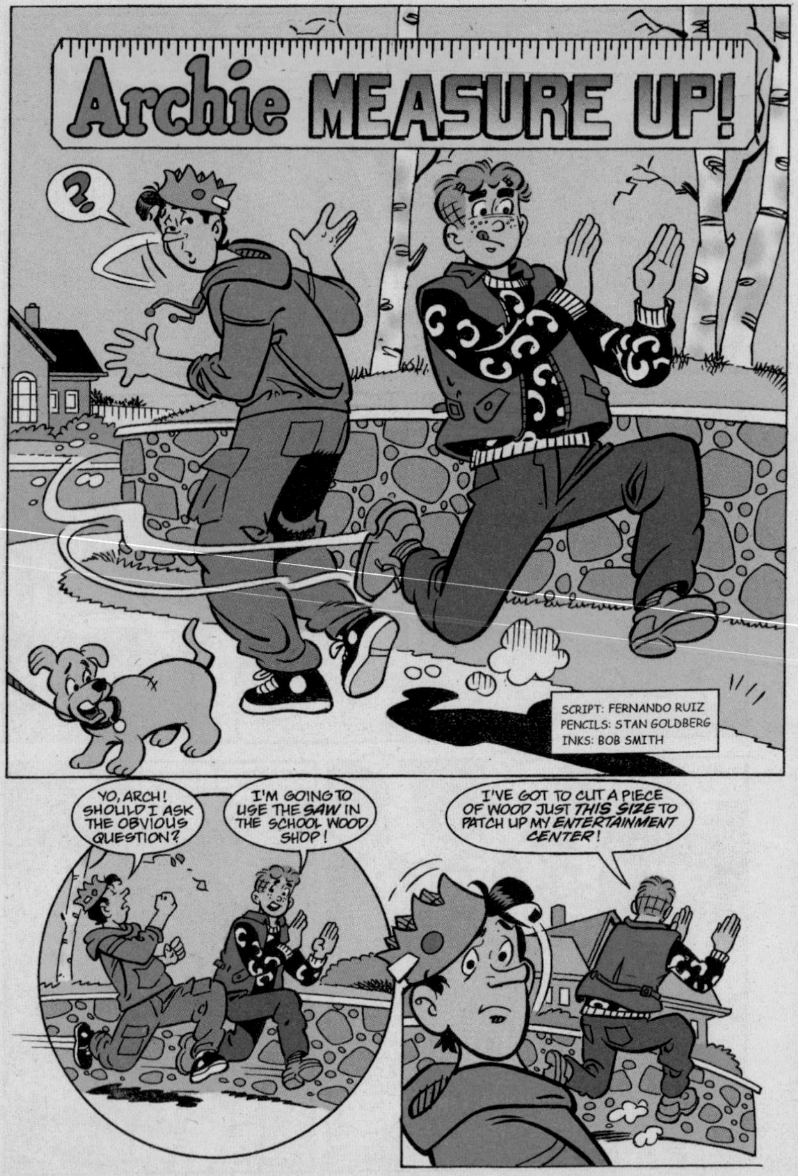

Archie MEASURE UP!
?
SCRIPT: FERNANDO RUIZ
PENCILS: STAN GOLDBERG
INKS: BOB SMITH
YO, ARCH! SHOULD I ASK THE OBVIOUS QUESTION?
I'M GOING TO USE THE SAW IN THE SCHOOL WOOD SHOP!
I'VE GOT TO CUT A PIECE OF WOOD JUST THIS SIZE TO PATCH UP MY ENTERTAINMENT CENTER!

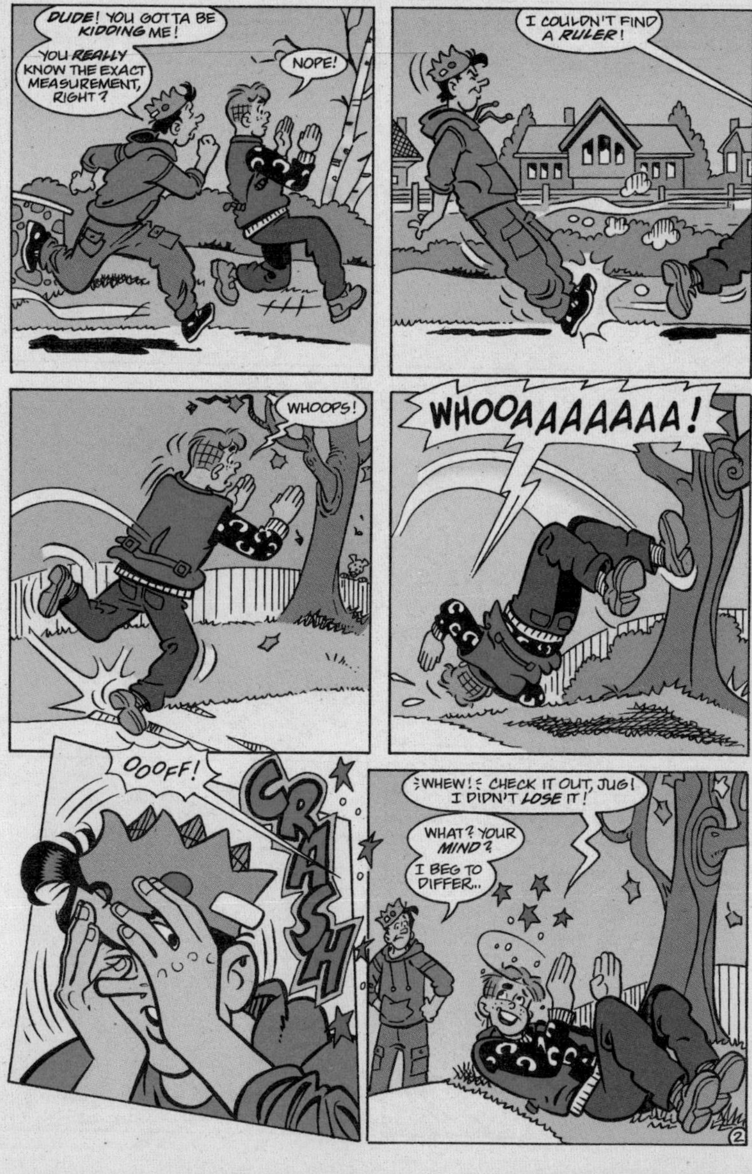
DUDE! YOU GOTTA BE KIDDING ME!
YOU REALLY KNOW THE EXACT MEASUREMENT, RIGHT?
NOPE!
I COULDN'T FIND A RULER!
WHOOPS!
WHOOAAAAAAA!
OOOFF!
CRASH
WHEW! CHECK IT OUT, JUG! I DIDN'T LOSE IT!
WHAT? YOUR MIND?
I BEG TO DIFFER...

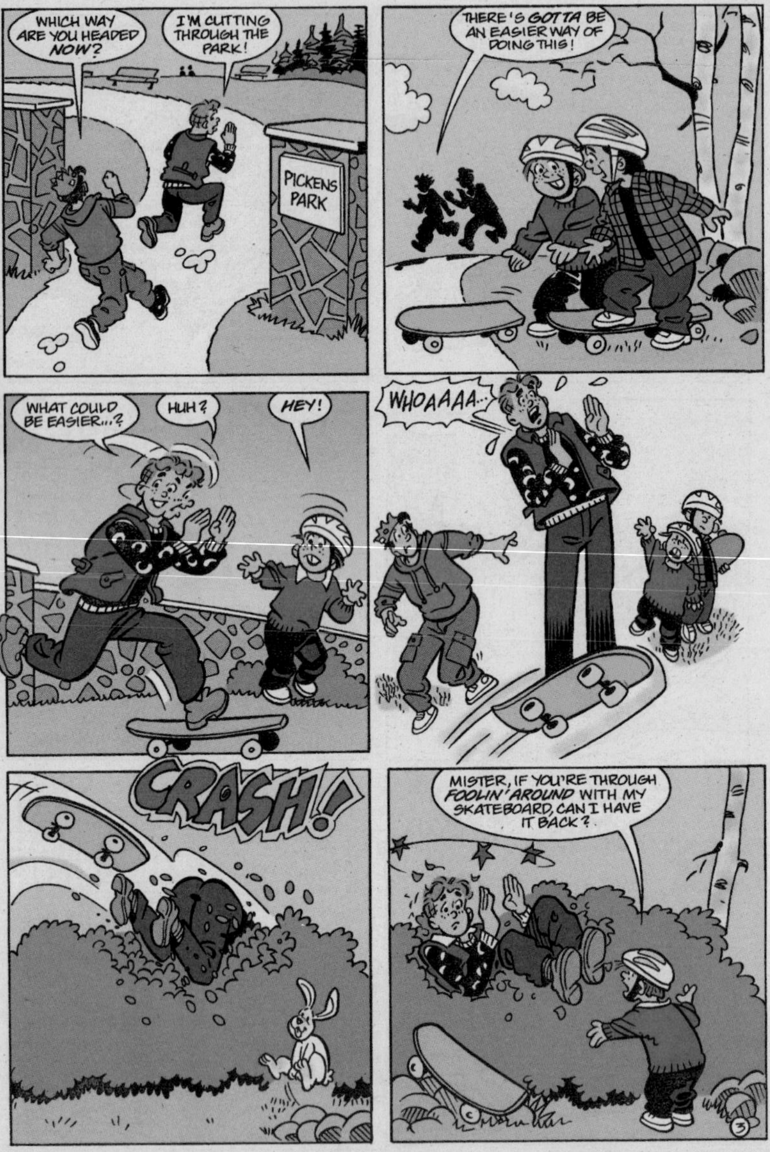
WHICH WAY ARE YOU HEADED NOW?
I'M CUTTING THROUGH THE PARK!
PICKENS PARK
THERE'S GOTTA BE AN EASIER WAY OF DOING THIS!
WHAT COULD BE EASIER...?
HUH?
HEY!
WHOAAAA...
CRASH!
MISTER, IF YOU'RE THROUGH FOOLIN' AROUND WITH MY SKATEBOARD, CAN I HAVE IT BACK?
3

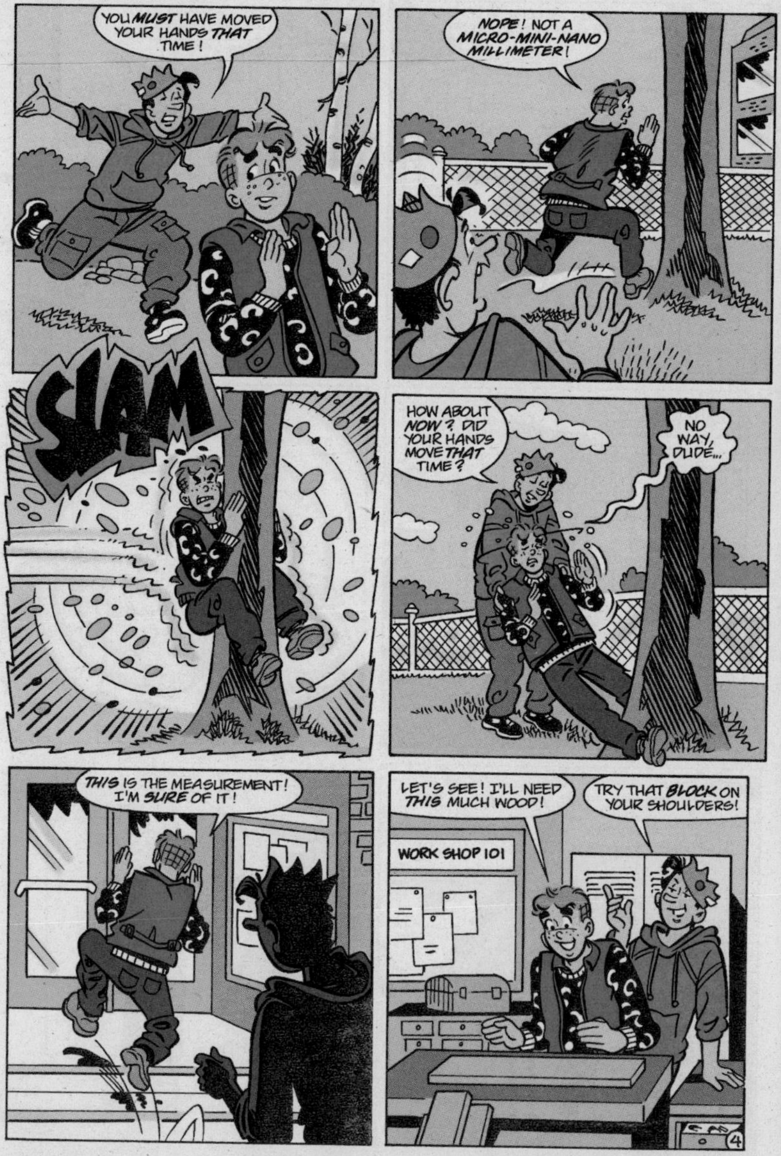
YOU MUST HAVE MOVED YOUR HANDS THAT TIME!
NOPE! NOT A MICRO-MINI-NANO MILLIMETER!
SLAM
HOW ABOUT NOW? DID YOUR HANDS MOVE THAT TIME?
NO WAY, DUDE...
THIS IS THE MEASUREMENT! I'M SURE OF IT!
LET'S SEE! I'LL NEED THIS MUCH WOOD!
TRY THAT BLOCK ON YOUR SHOULDERS!
WORK SHOP 101
4

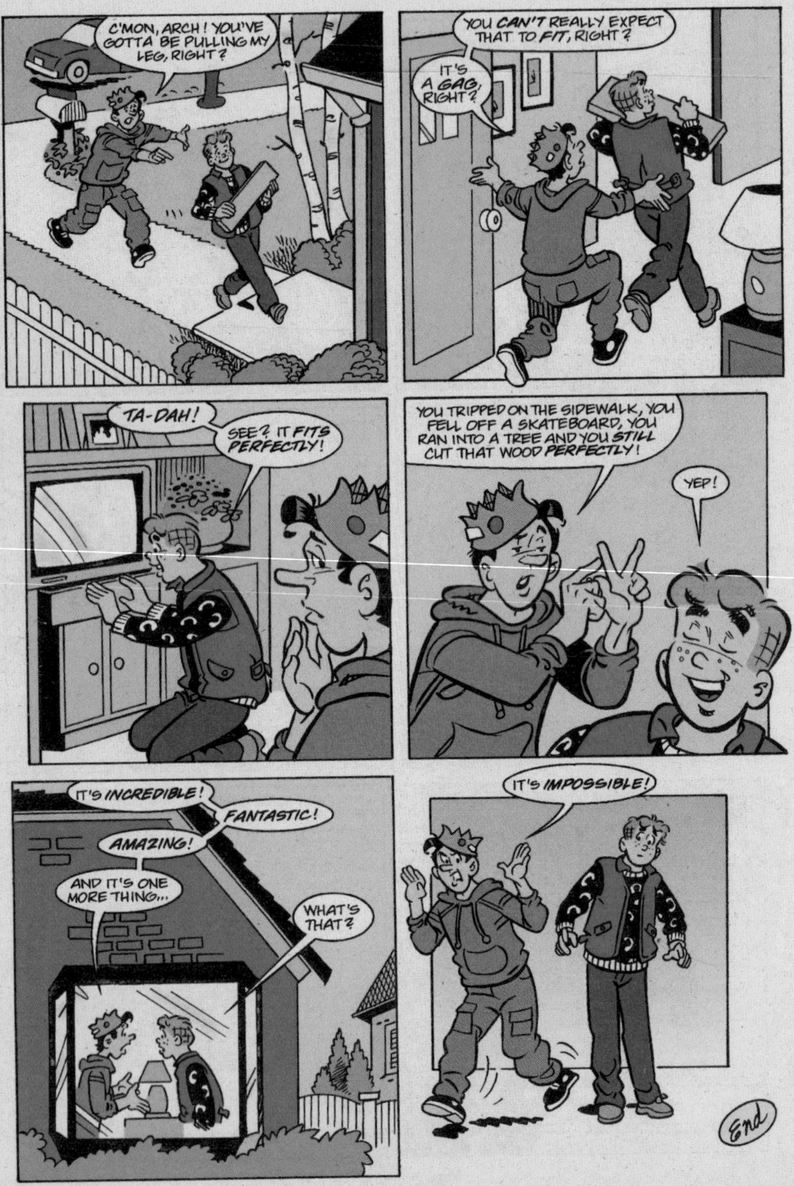

C'MON, ARCH! YOU'VE GOTTA BE PULLING MY LEG, RIGHT?
YOU CAN'T REALLY EXPECT THAT TO FIT, RIGHT?
IT'S A GAG, RIGHT?
TA-DAH!
SEE? IT FITS PERFECTLY!
YOU TRIPPED ON THE SIDEWALK, YOU FELL OFF A SKATEBOARD, YOU RAN INTO A TREE AND YOU STILL CUT THAT WOOD PERFECTLY!
YEP!
IT'S INCREDIBLE!
FANTASTIC!
AMAZING!
AND IT'S ONE MORE THING...
WHAT'S THAT?
IT'S IMPOSSIBLE!
End

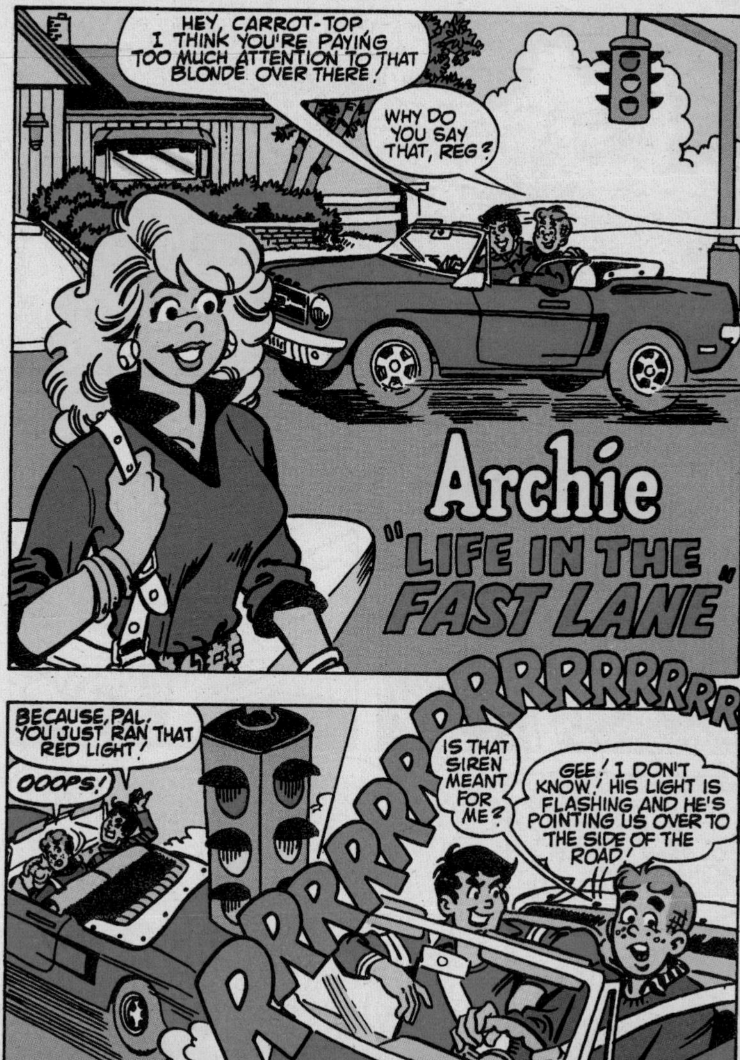
HEY, CARROT-TOP I THINK YOU'RE PAYING TOO MUCH ATTENTION TO THAT BLONDE OVER THERE!
WHY DO YOU SAY THAT, REG?
Archie
"LIFE IN THE FAST LANE"
RRRRRRRRRRRRRRRRRRRR
BECAUSE, PAL, YOU JUST RAN THAT RED LIGHT!
OOOPS!
IS THAT SIREN MEANT FOR ME?
GEE! I DON'T KNOW! HIS LIGHT IS FLASHING AND HE'S POINTING US OVER TO THE SIDE OF THE ROAD!
1

Script: Bill Golliher / Pencils: Stan Goldberg / Inks: Mike Esposito / Letters: Bill Yoshida

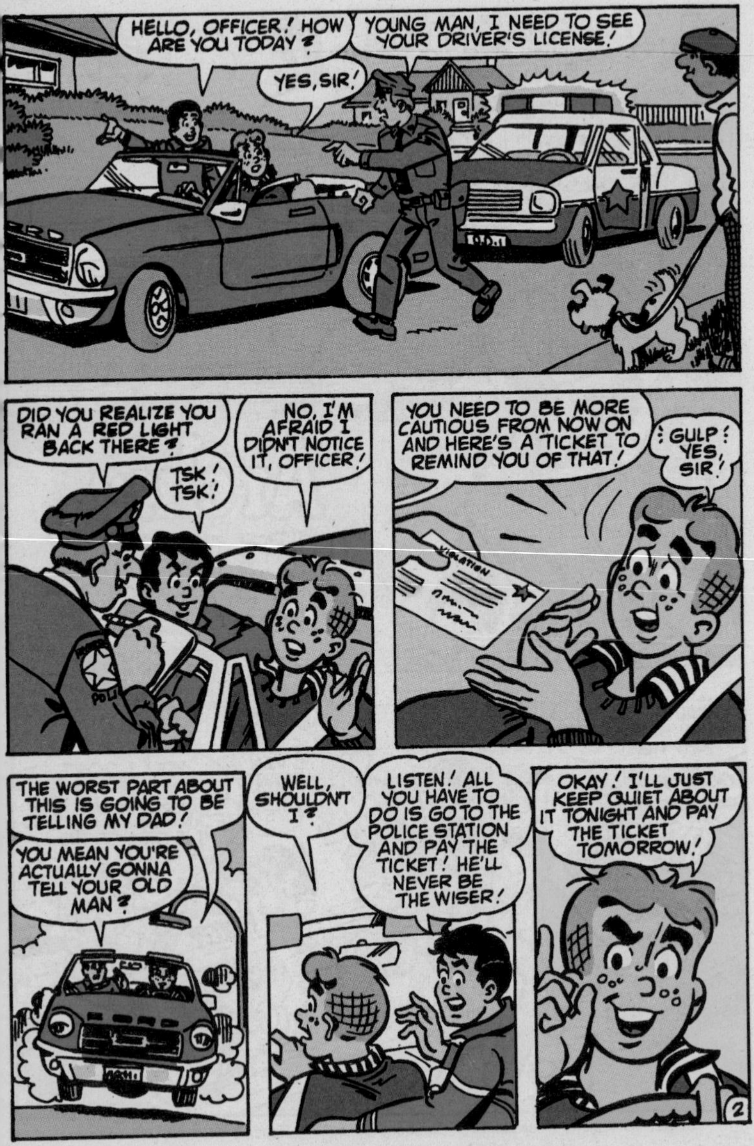
HELLO, OFFICER! HOW ARE YOU TODAY?
YOUNG MAN, I NEED TO SEE YOUR DRIVER'S LICENSE!
YES, SIR!
DID YOU REALIZE YOU RAN A RED LIGHT BACK THERE?
TSK! TSK!
NO, I'M AFRAID I DIDN'T NOTICE IT, OFFICER!
YOU NEED TO BE MORE CAUTIOUS FROM NOW ON AND HERE'S A TICKET TO REMIND YOU OF THAT!
GULP! YES, SIR!
VIOLATION
THE WORST PART ABOUT THIS IS GOING TO BE TELLING MY DAD!
YOU MEAN YOU'RE ACTUALLY GONNA TELL YOUR OLD MAN?
WELL, SHOULDN'T I?
LISTEN! ALL YOU HAVE TO DO IS GO TO THE POLICE STATION AND PAY THE TICKET! HE'LL NEVER BE THE WISER!
OKAY! I'LL JUST KEEP QUIET ABOUT IT TONIGHT AND PAY THE TICKET TOMORROW!
2

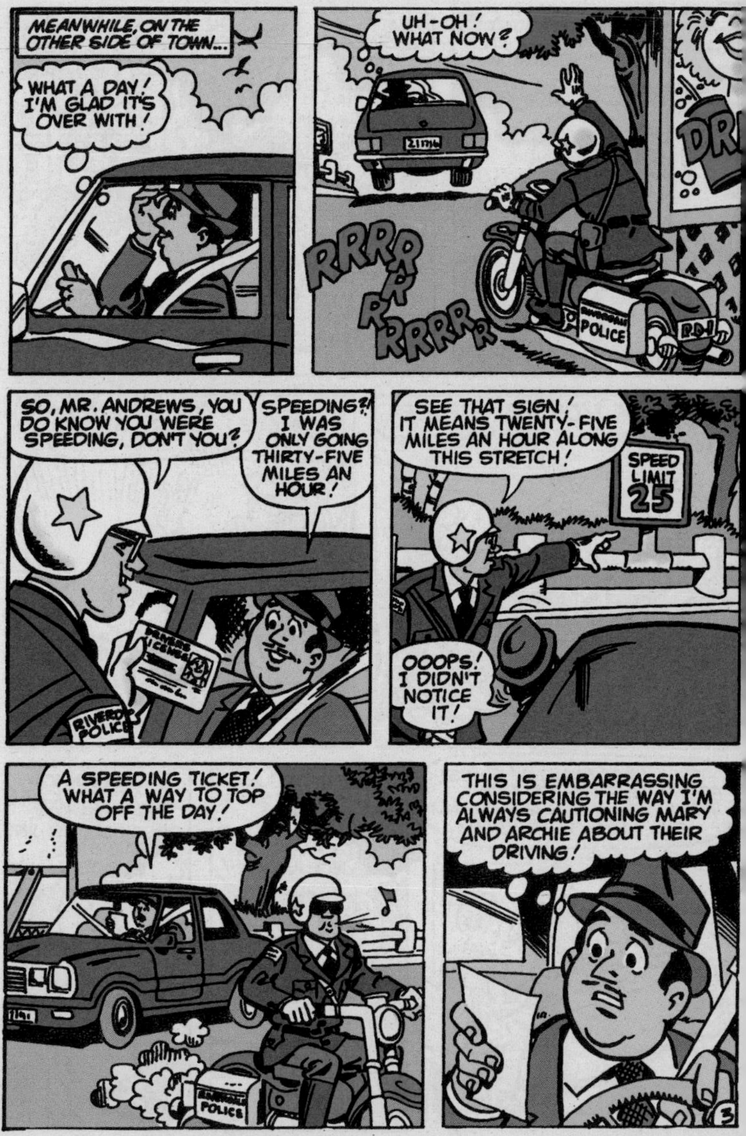

MEANWHILE, ON THE OTHER SIDE OF TOWN...
WHAT A DAY! I'M GLAD IT'S OVER WITH!
UH-OH! WHAT NOW?
RRRRRRRRRRRR
POLICE
SO, MR. ANDREWS, YOU DO KNOW YOU WERE SPEEDING, DON'T YOU?
SPEEDING?! I WAS ONLY GOING THIRTY-FIVE MILES AN HOUR!
SEE THAT SIGN! IT MEANS TWENTY-FIVE MILES AN HOUR ALONG THIS STRETCH!
SPEED LIMIT 25
OOOPS! I DIDN'T NOTICE IT!
A SPEEDING TICKET! WHAT A WAY TO TOP OFF THE DAY!
POLICE
THIS IS EMBARRASSING CONSIDERING THE WAY I'M ALWAYS CAUTIONING MARY AND ARCHIE ABOUT THEIR DRIVING!
3

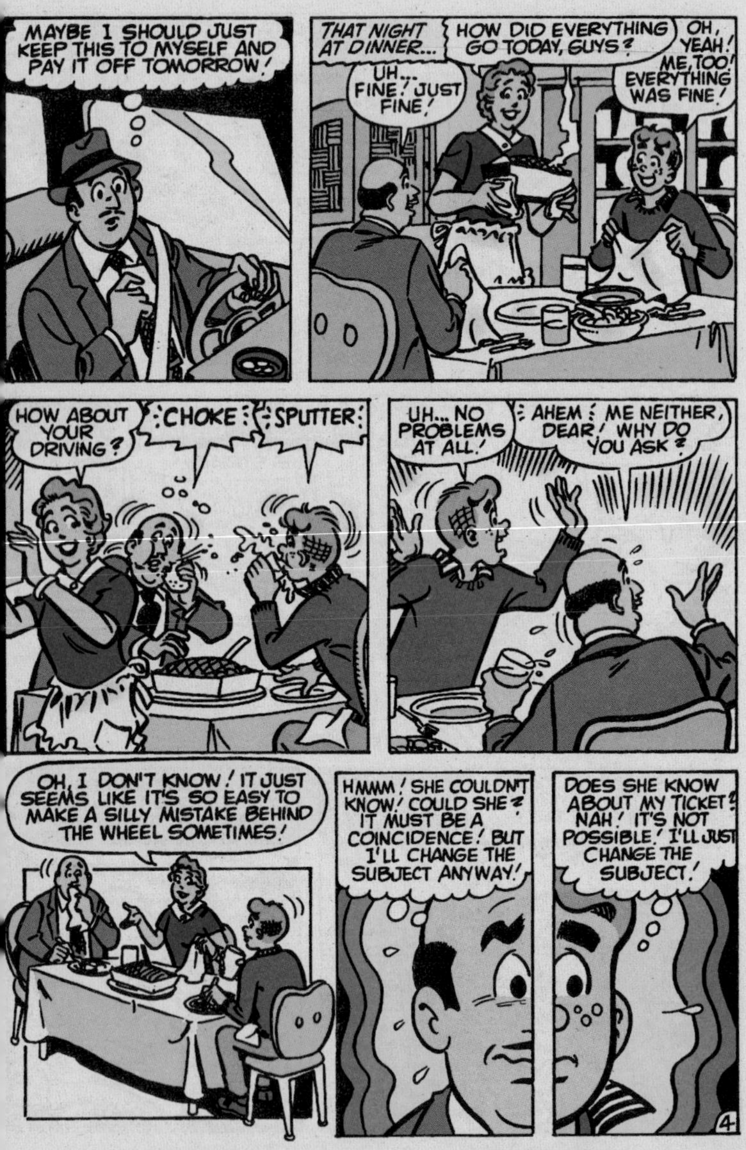
MAYBE I SHOULD JUST KEEP THIS TO MYSELF AND PAY IT OFF TOMORROW!
THAT NIGHT AT DINNER...
HOW DID EVERYTHING GO TODAY, GUYS?
UH... FINE! JUST FINE!
OH, YEAH! ME, TOO! EVERYTHING WAS FINE!
HOW ABOUT YOUR DRIVING?
CHOKE
SPUTTER
UH... NO PROBLEMS AT ALL!
AHEM! ME NEITHER, DEAR! WHY DO YOU ASK?
OH, I DON'T KNOW! IT JUST SEEMS LIKE IT'S SO EASY TO MAKE A SILLY MISTAKE BEHIND THE WHEEL SOMETIMES!
HMMM! SHE COULDN'T KNOW! COULD SHE? IT MUST BE A COINCIDENCE! BUT I'LL CHANGE THE SUBJECT ANYWAY!
DOES SHE KNOW ABOUT MY TICKET?! NAH! IT'S NOT POSSIBLE! I'LL JUST CHANGE THE SUBJECT!
4

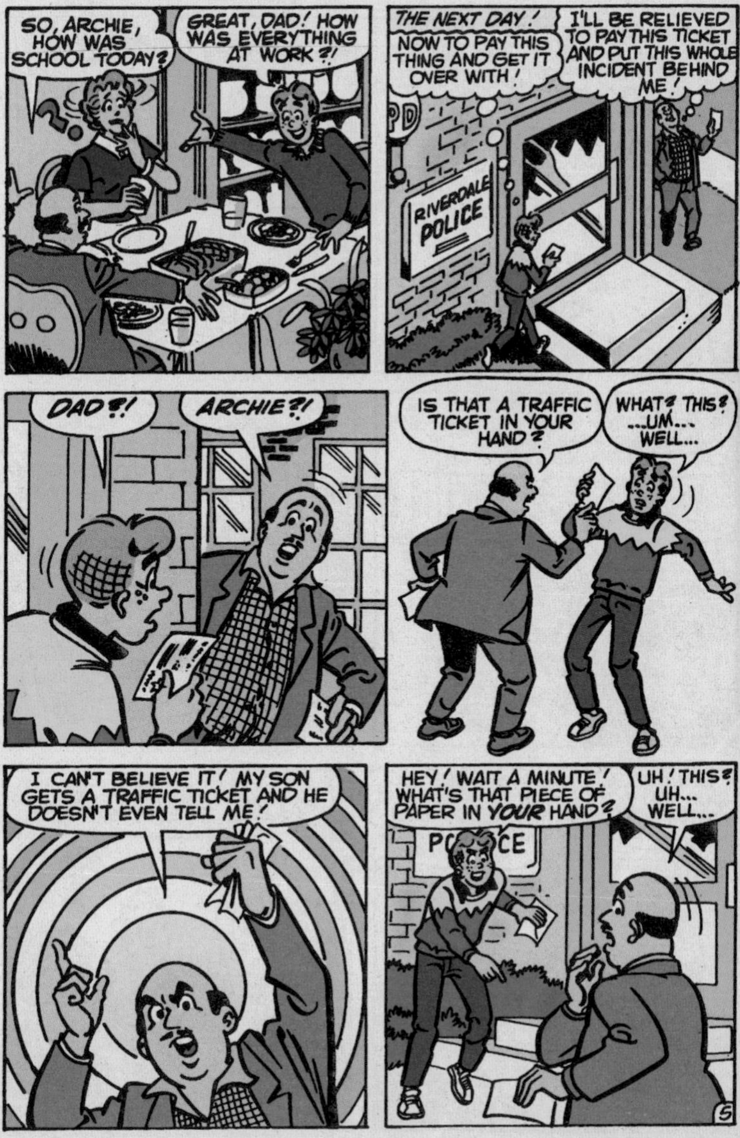
SO, ARCHIE, HOW WAS SCHOOL TODAY?
GREAT, DAD! HOW WAS EVERYTHING AT WORK?!
THE NEXT DAY!
NOW TO PAY THIS THING AND GET IT OVER WITH!
I'LL BE RELIEVED TO PAY THIS TICKET AND PUT THIS WHOLE INCIDENT BEHIND ME!
PD
RIVERDALE POLICE
DAD?!
ARCHIE?!
IS THAT A TRAFFIC TICKET IN YOUR HAND?
WHAT? THIS? ...UM... WELL...
I CAN'T BELIEVE IT! MY SON GETS A TRAFFIC TICKET AND HE DOESN'T EVEN TELL ME!
HEY! WAIT A MINUTE! WHAT'S THAT PIECE OF PAPER IN YOUR HAND?
UH! THIS? UH... WELL...
5

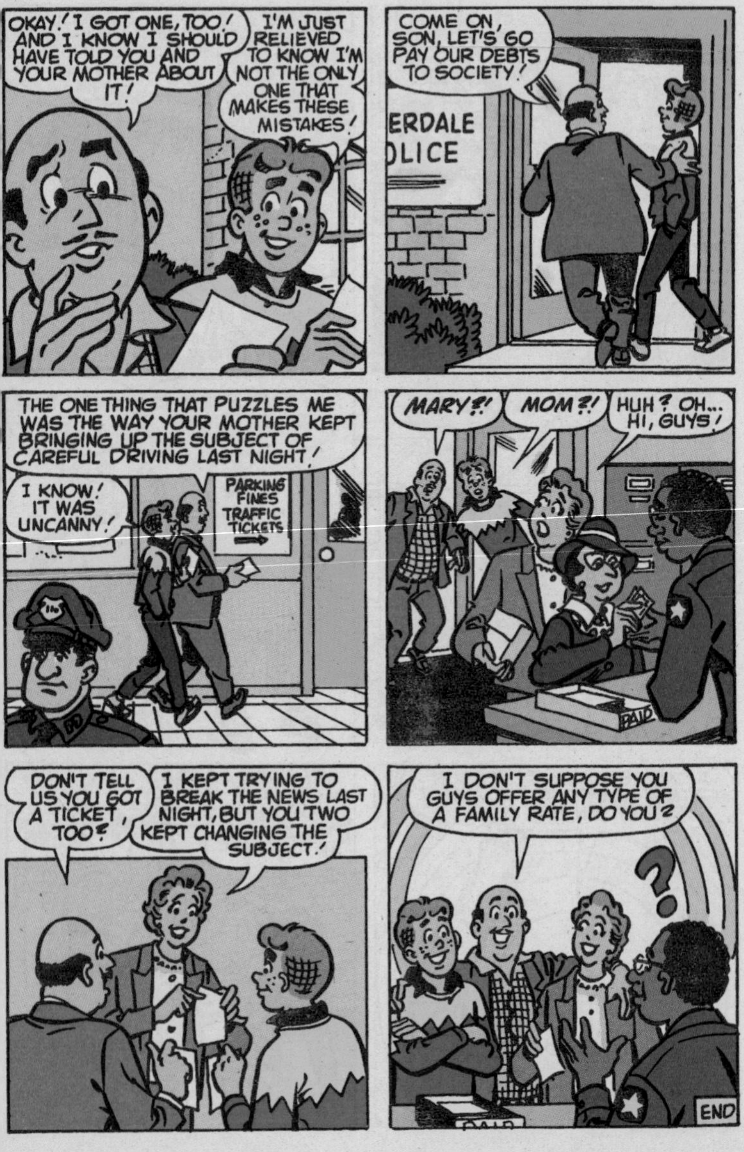
OKAY! I GOT ONE, TOO! AND I KNOW I SHOULD HAVE TOLD YOU AND YOUR MOTHER ABOUT IT!
I'M JUST RELIEVED TO KNOW I'M NOT THE ONLY ONE THAT MAKES THESE MISTAKES!
COME ON, SON, LET'S GO PAY OUR DEBTS TO SOCIETY!
ERDALE
OLICE
THE ONE THING THAT PUZZLES ME WAS THE WAY YOUR MOTHER KEPT BRINGING UP THE SUBJECT OF CAREFUL DRIVING LAST NIGHT!
I KNOW! IT WAS UNCANNY!
PARKING FINES
TRAFFIC TICKETS
MARY?!
MOM?!
HUH? OH... HI, GUYS!
PAID
DON'T TELL US YOU GOT A TICKET, TOO?
I KEPT TRYING TO BREAK THE NEWS LAST NIGHT, BUT YOU TWO KEPT CHANGING THE SUBJECT!
I DON'T SUPPOSE YOU GUYS OFFER ANY TYPE OF A FAMILY RATE, DO YOU?
END

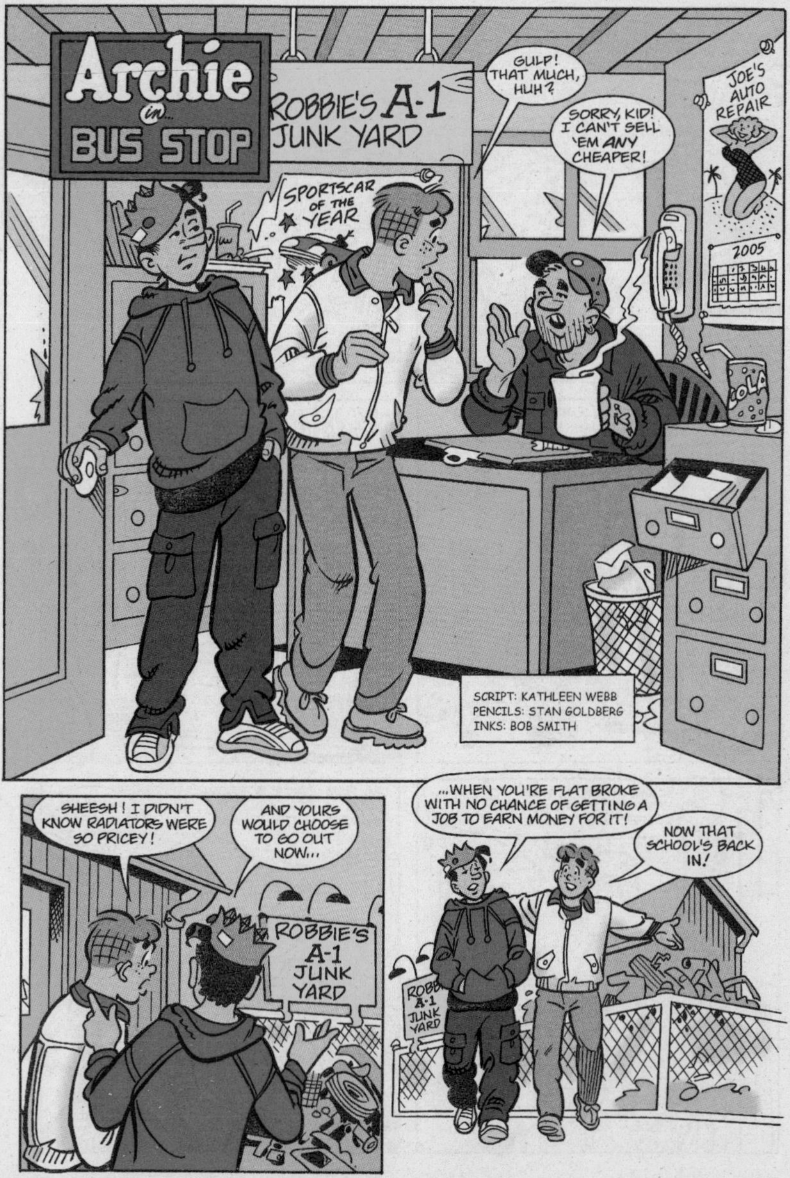
Archie in... BUS STOP
ROBBIE'S A-1 JUNK YARD
SPORTSCAR OF THE YEAR
GULP! THAT MUCH, HUH?
SORRY, KID! I CAN'T SELL 'EM ANY CHEAPER!
JOE'S AUTO REPAIR
2005
COLA
SCRIPT: KATHLEEN WEBB
PENCILS: STAN GOLDBERG
INKS: BOB SMITH
SHEESH! I DIDN'T KNOW RADIATORS WERE SO PRICEY!
AND YOURS WOULD CHOOSE TO GO OUT NOW...
ROBBIE'S A-1 JUNK YARD
...WHEN YOU'RE FLAT BROKE WITH NO CHANCE OF GETTING A JOB TO EARN MONEY FOR IT!
NOW THAT SCHOOL'S BACK IN!

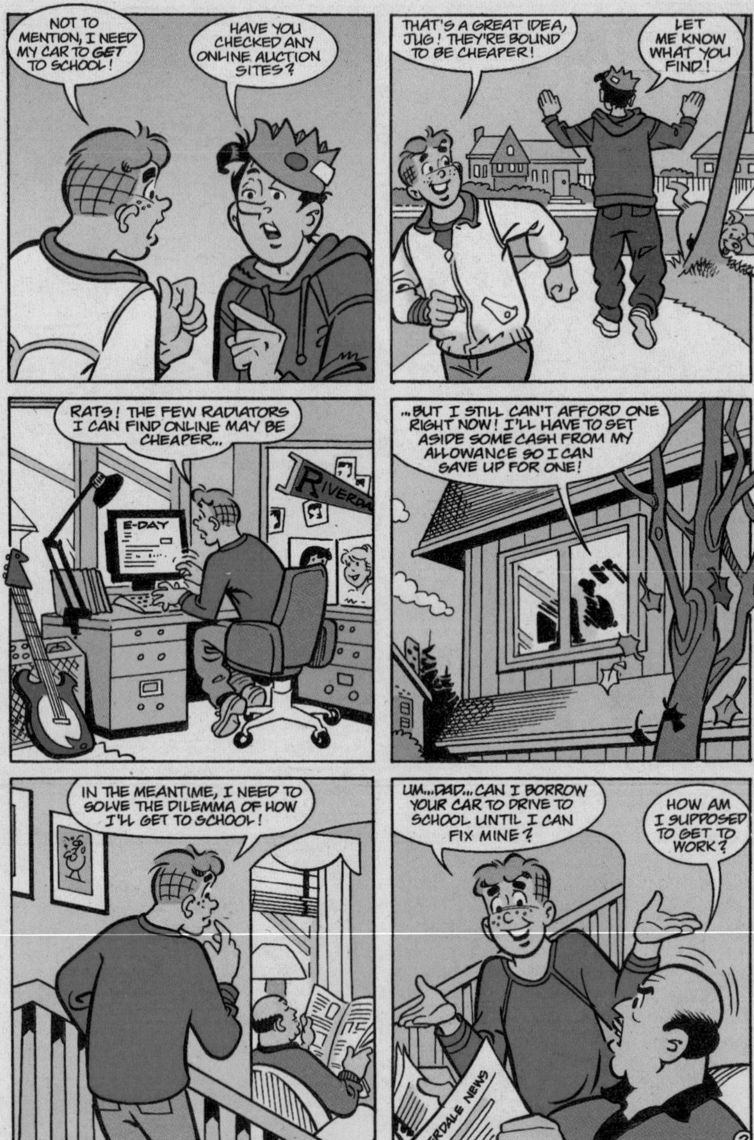

NOT TO MENTION, I NEED MY CAR TO GET TO SCHOOL!
HAVE YOU CHECKED ANY ONLINE AUCTION SITES?
THAT'S A GREAT IDEA, JUG! THEY'RE BOUND TO BE CHEAPER!
LET ME KNOW WHAT YOU FIND!
RATS! THE FEW RADIATORS I CAN FIND ONLINE MAY BE CHEAPER...
E-DAY
RIVERDA
...BUT I STILL CAN'T AFFORD ONE RIGHT NOW! I'LL HAVE TO SET ASIDE SOME CASH FROM MY ALLOWANCE SO I CAN SAVE UP FOR ONE!
IN THE MEANTIME, I NEED TO SOLVE THE DILEMMA OF HOW I'LL GET TO SCHOOL!
UM...DAD...CAN I BORROW YOUR CAR TO DRIVE TO SCHOOL UNTIL I CAN FIX MINE?
HOW AM I SUPPOSED TO GET TO WORK?
RIVERDALE NEWS
2

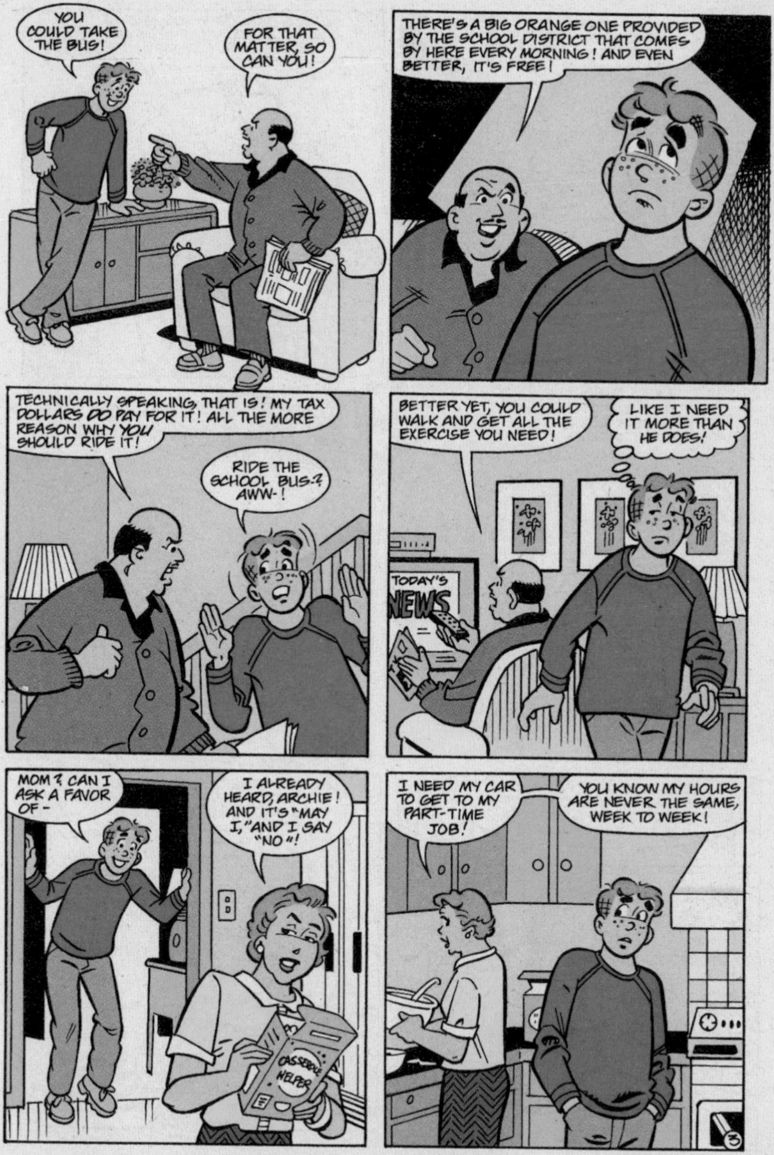
YOU COULD TAKE THE BUS!
FOR THAT MATTER, SO CAN YOU!
THERE'S A BIG ORANGE ONE PROVIDED BY THE SCHOOL DISTRICT THAT COMES BY HERE EVERY MORNING! AND EVEN BETTER, IT'S FREE!
TECHNICALLY SPEAKING, THAT IS! MY TAX DOLLARS DO PAY FOR IT! ALL THE MORE REASON WHY YOU SHOULD RIDE IT!
RIDE THE SCHOOL BUS?! AWW-!
BETTER YET, YOU COULD WALK AND GET ALL THE EXERCISE YOU NEED!
LIKE I NEED IT MORE THAN HE DOES!
TODAY'S NEWS
MOM? CAN I ASK A FAVOR OF-
I ALREADY HEARD, ARCHIE! AND IT'S "MAY I," AND I SAY "NO"!
CASSEROLE HELPER
I NEED MY CAR TO GET TO MY PART-TIME JOB!
YOU KNOW MY HOURS ARE NEVER THE SAME, WEEK TO WEEK!
3

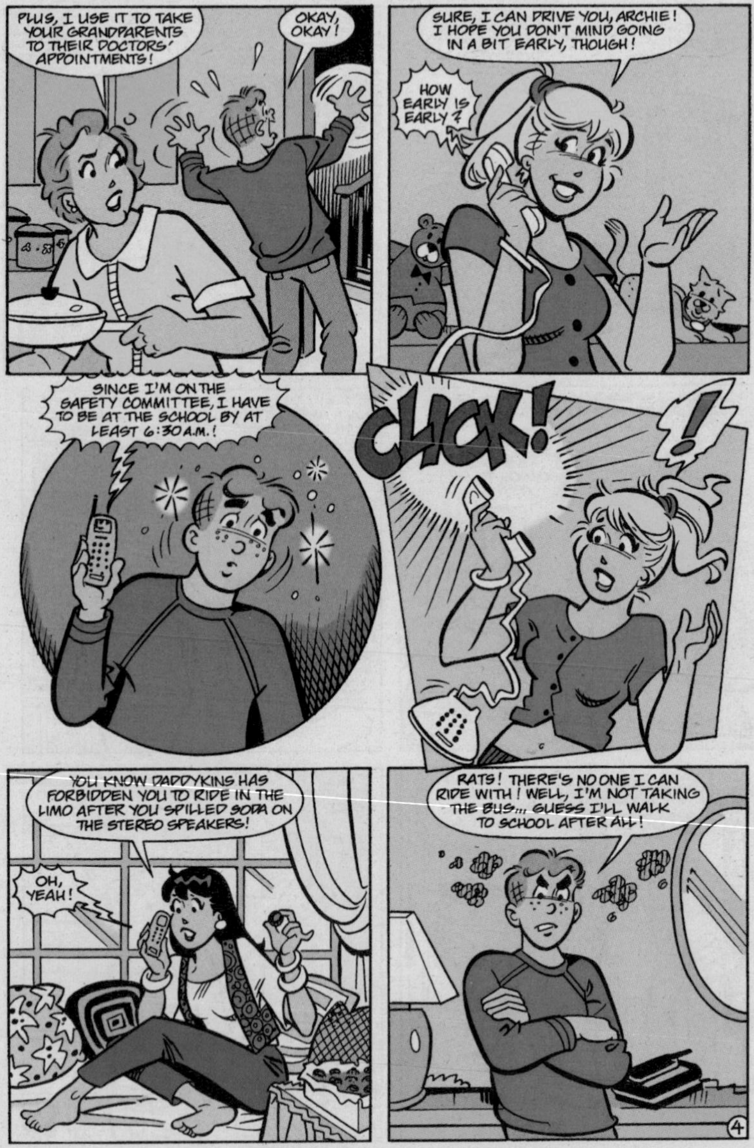
PLUS, I USE IT TO TAKE YOUR GRANDPARENTS TO THEIR DOCTORS' APPOINTMENTS!
OKAY, OKAY!
SURE, I CAN DRIVE YOU, ARCHIE! I HOPE YOU DON'T MIND GOING IN A BIT EARLY, THOUGH!
HOW EARLY IS EARLY?
SINCE I'M ON THE SAFETY COMMITTEE, I HAVE TO BE AT THE SCHOOL BY AT LEAST 6:30 A.M.!
CLICK!
!
YOU KNOW DADDYKINS HAS FORBIDDEN YOU TO RIDE IN THE LIMO AFTER YOU SPILLED SODA ON THE STEREO SPEAKERS!
OH, YEAH!
RATS! THERE'S NO ONE I CAN RIDE WITH! WELL, I'M NOT TAKING THE BUS... GUESS I'LL WALK TO SCHOOL AFTER ALL!
4

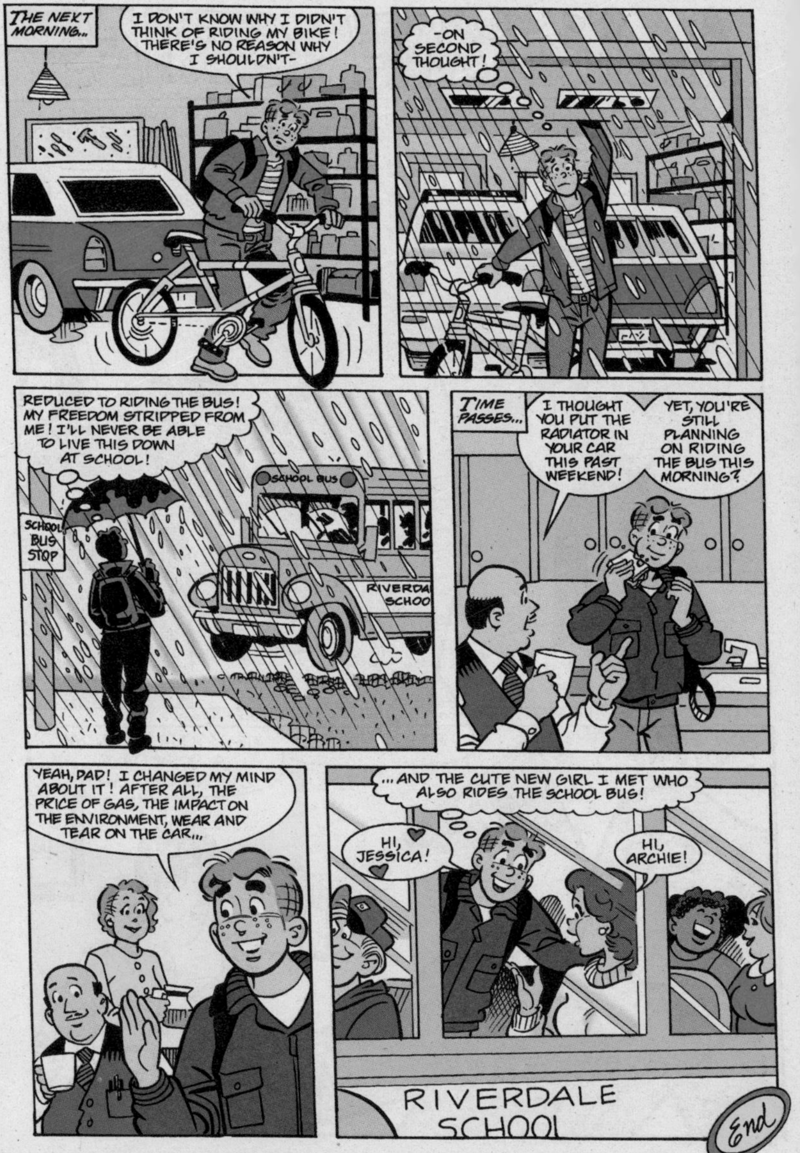
THE NEXT MORNING...
I DON'T KNOW WHY I DIDN'T THINK OF RIDING MY BIKE! THERE'S NO REASON WHY I SHOULDN'T-
-ON SECOND THOUGHT!
REDUCED TO RIDING THE BUS! MY FREEDOM STRIPPED FROM ME! I'LL NEVER BE ABLE TO LIVE THIS DOWN AT SCHOOL!
SCHOOL BUS STOP
SCHOOL BUS
TIME PASSES...
I THOUGHT YOU PUT THE RADIATOR IN YOUR CAR THIS PAST WEEKEND!
YET, YOU'RE STILL PLANNING ON RIDING THE BUS THIS MORNING?
YEAH, DAD! I CHANGED MY MIND ABOUT IT! AFTER ALL, THE PRICE OF GAS, THE IMPACT ON THE ENVIRONMENT, WEAR AND TEAR ON THE CAR...
...AND THE CUTE NEW GIRL I MET WHO ALSO RIDES THE SCHOOL BUS!
HI, JESSICA!
HI, ARCHIE!
RIVERDALE SCHOOL
End

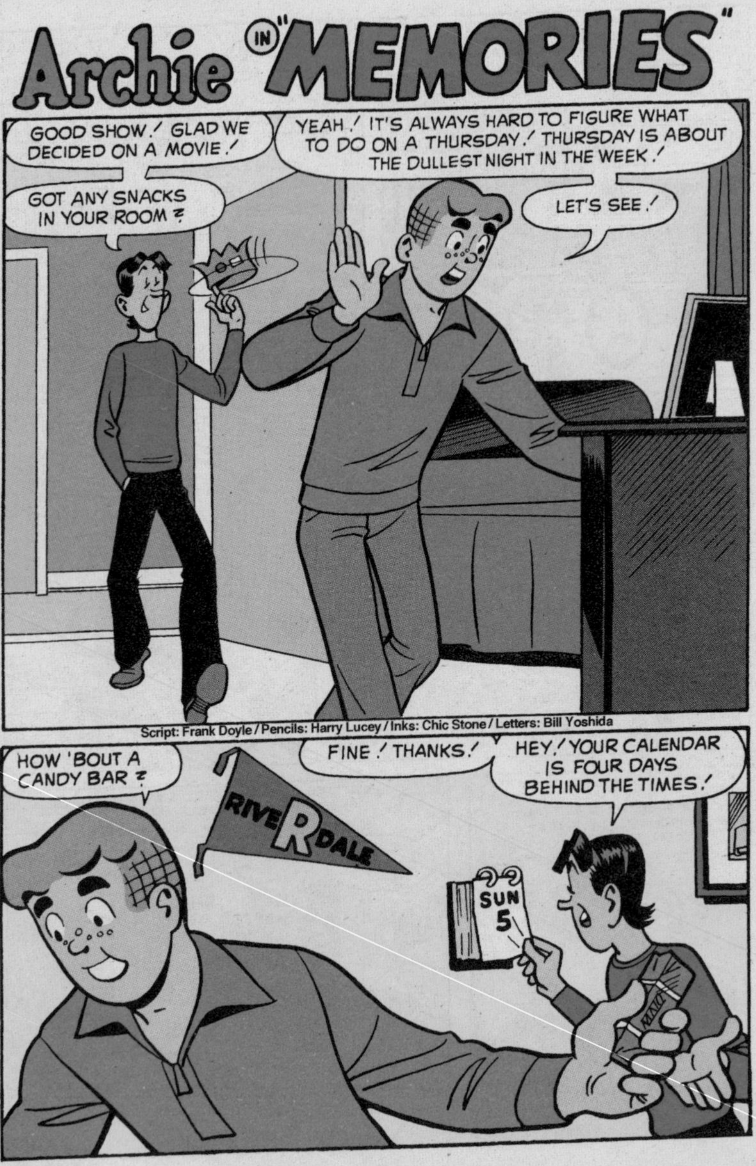
Archie in "MEMORIES"
GOOD SHOW! GLAD WE DECIDED ON A MOVIE!
GOT ANY SNACKS IN YOUR ROOM?
YEAH! IT'S ALWAYS HARD TO FIGURE WHAT TO DO ON A THURSDAY! THURSDAY IS ABOUT THE DULLEST NIGHT IN THE WEEK!
LET'S SEE!
Script: Frank Doyle / Pencils: Harry Lucey / Inks: Chic Stone / Letters: Bill Yoshida
HOW 'BOUT A CANDY BAR?
RIVERDALE
FINE! THANKS!
HEY! YOUR CALENDAR IS FOUR DAYS BEHIND THE TIMES!
SUN
5

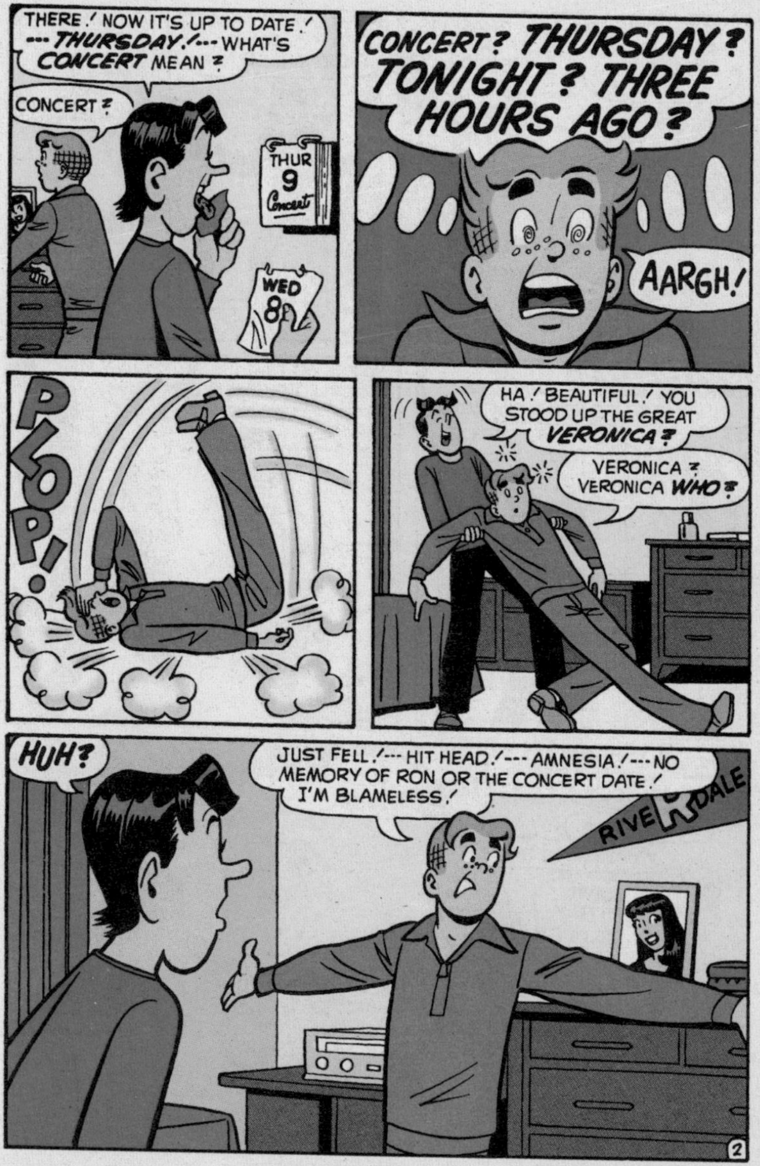
THERE.! NOW IT'S UP TO DATE.! --- THURSDAY.!--- WHAT'S CONCERT MEAN?
CONCERT?
THUR 9 Concert
WED 8
CONCERT? THURSDAY? TONIGHT? THREE HOURS AGO?
AARGH!
PLOP!
HA! BEAUTIFUL! YOU STOOD UP THE GREAT VERONICA?
VERONICA? VERONICA WHO?
HUH?
JUST FELL.!--- HIT HEAD.!--- AMNESIA.!--- NO MEMORY OF RON OR THE CONCERT DATE.! I'M BLAMELESS.!
RIVERDALE

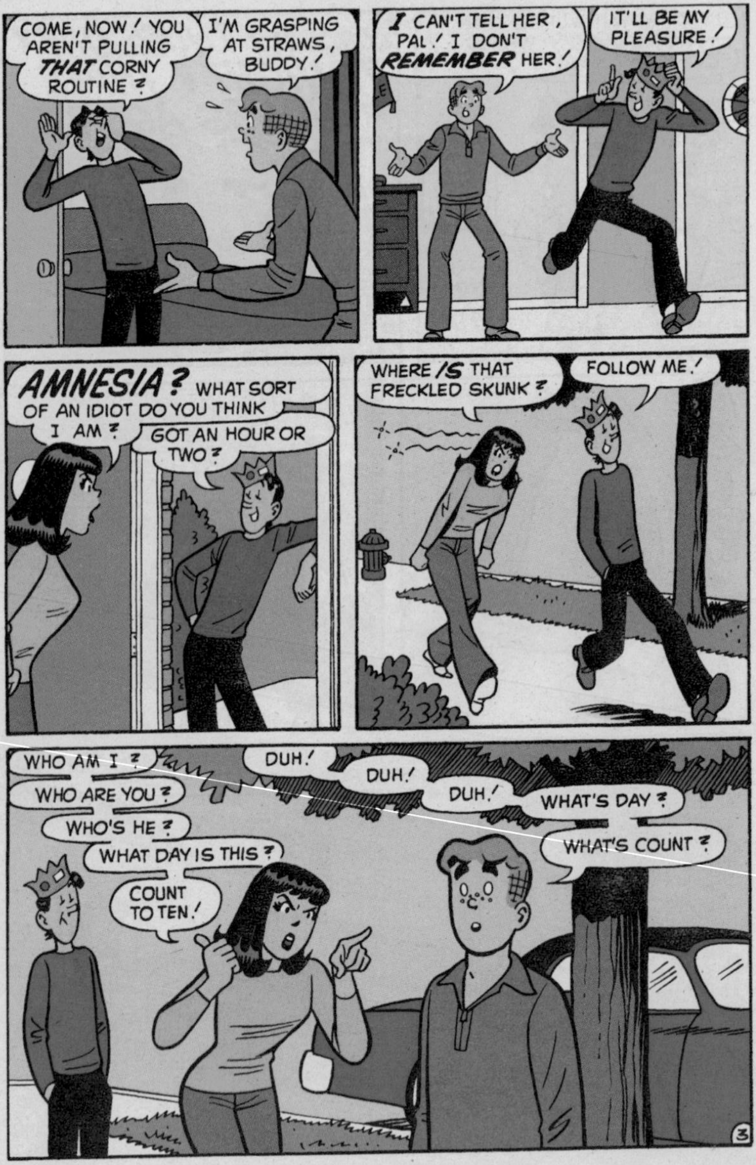

COME, NOW! YOU AREN'T PULLING THAT CORNY ROUTINE?
I'M GRASPING AT STRAWS, BUDDY!
I CAN'T TELL HER, PAL! I DON'T REMEMBER HER!
IT'LL BE MY PLEASURE!
AMNESIA? WHAT SORT OF AN IDIOT DO YOU THINK I AM?
GOT AN HOUR OR TWO?
WHERE IS THAT FRECKLED SKUNK?
FOLLOW ME!
WHO AM I?
WHO ARE YOU?
WHO'S HE?
WHAT DAY IS THIS?
COUNT TO TEN!
DUH!
DUH!
DUH!
WHAT'S DAY?
WHAT'S COUNT?
3

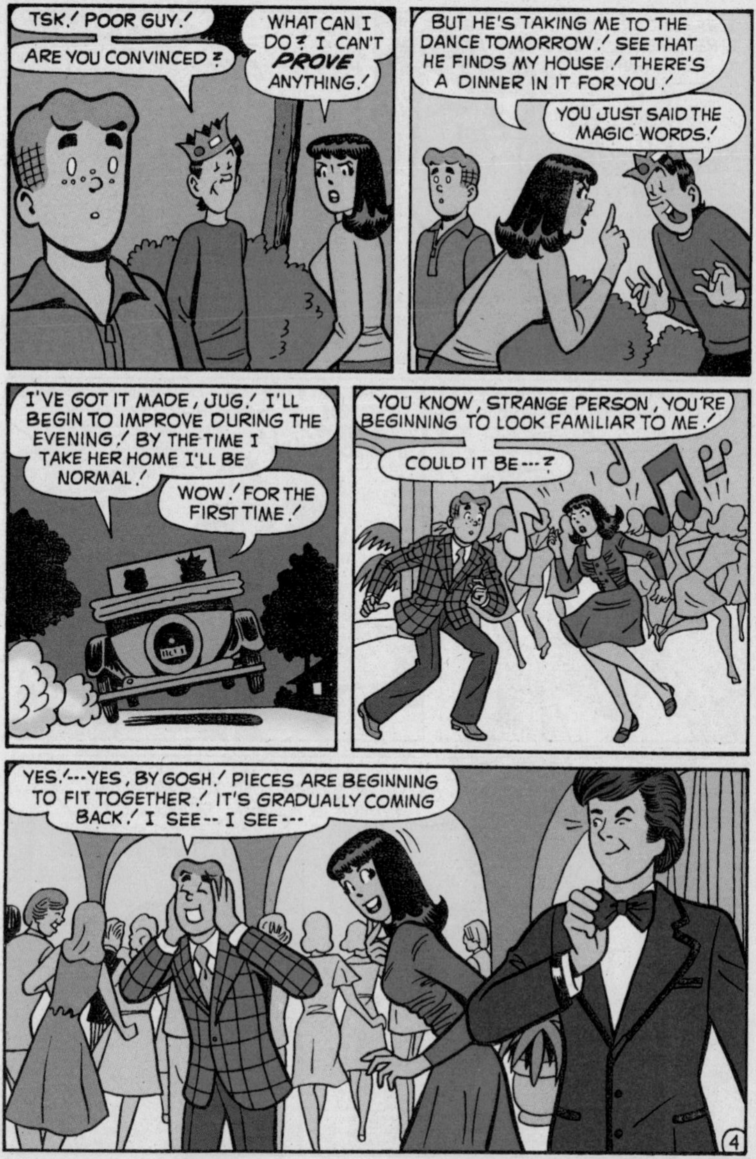
TSK.! POOR GUY.!
ARE YOU CONVINCED ?
WHAT CAN I DO ? I CAN'T PROVE ANYTHING.!
BUT HE'S TAKING ME TO THE DANCE TOMORROW.! SEE THAT HE FINDS MY HOUSE.! THERE'S A DINNER IN IT FOR YOU.!
YOU JUST SAID THE MAGIC WORDS.!
I'VE GOT IT MADE, JUG.! I'LL BEGIN TO IMPROVE DURING THE EVENING.! BY THE TIME I TAKE HER HOME I'LL BE NORMAL.!
WOW.! FOR THE FIRST TIME.!
YOU KNOW, STRANGE PERSON, YOU'RE BEGINNING TO LOOK FAMILIAR TO ME.!
COULD IT BE---?
YES.!---YES, BY GOSH.! PIECES ARE BEGINNING TO FIT TOGETHER.! IT'S GRADUALLY COMING BACK.! I SEE--I SEE---
4

Panel 1: I REMEMBER! VERONICA, I REMEMBER! I'M CURED! IT'S A MIRACLE!!

Panel 2: ? EEP! WHACK!

Panel 3: VERONICA! BABY, ARE YOU ALL RIGHT? / VERONICA?? --- WHO'S VERONICA?

Panel 4: WHERE AM I? WHO *AM* I? *DOCTOR!* I NEED YOU! / TSK! THAT BUMP SCRAMBLED HER HEAD! SHE THINKS I'M HER DOCTOR!

Panel 5: ARCHIE, HOW CAN YOU BE SO *SURE* VERONICA IS A FAKER? / IT TAKES ONE TO *KNOW* ONE, DOGGONE IT!

THE END

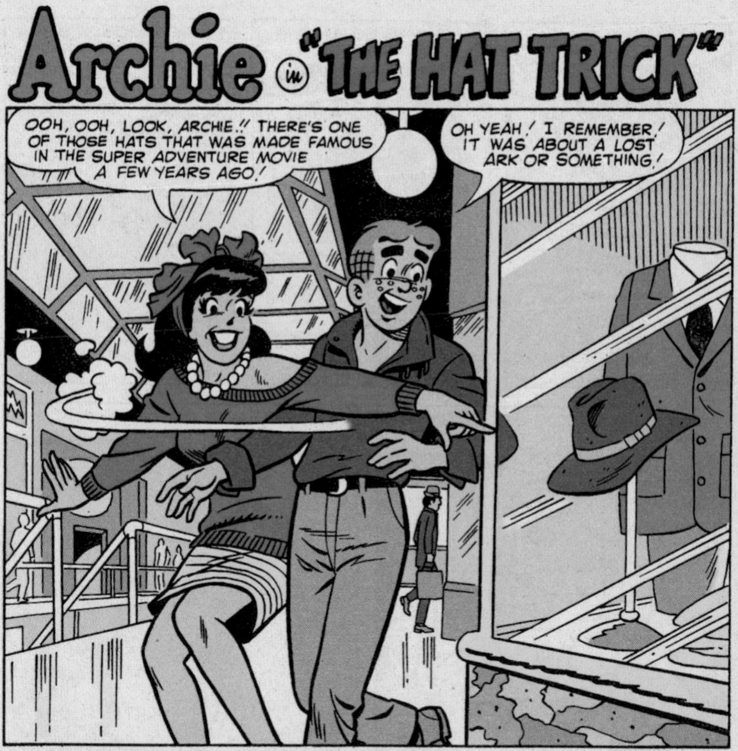
Archie in "THE HAT TRICK"
OOH, OOH, LOOK, ARCHIE.!! THERE'S ONE OF THOSE HATS THAT WAS MADE FAMOUS IN THE SUPER ADVENTURE MOVIE A FEW YEARS AGO!
OH YEAH! I REMEMBER! IT WAS ABOUT A LOST ARK OR SOMETHING!

Script: Frank Doyle / Pencils: Rex Lindsey / Inks: Jon D'Agostino / Letters: Bill Yoshida

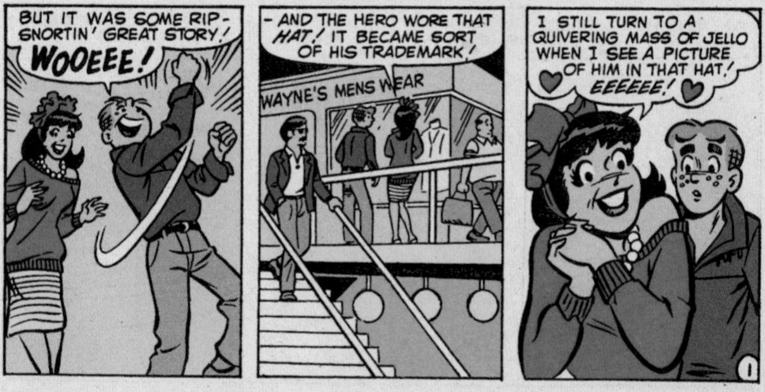
BUT IT WAS SOME RIP-SNORTIN' GREAT STORY!
WOOEEE!
-AND THE HERO WORE THAT HAT! IT BECAME SORT OF HIS TRADEMARK!
WAYNE'S MENS WEAR
I STILL TURN TO A QUIVERING MASS OF JELLO WHEN I SEE A PICTURE OF HIM IN THAT HAT! EEEEEE!
1

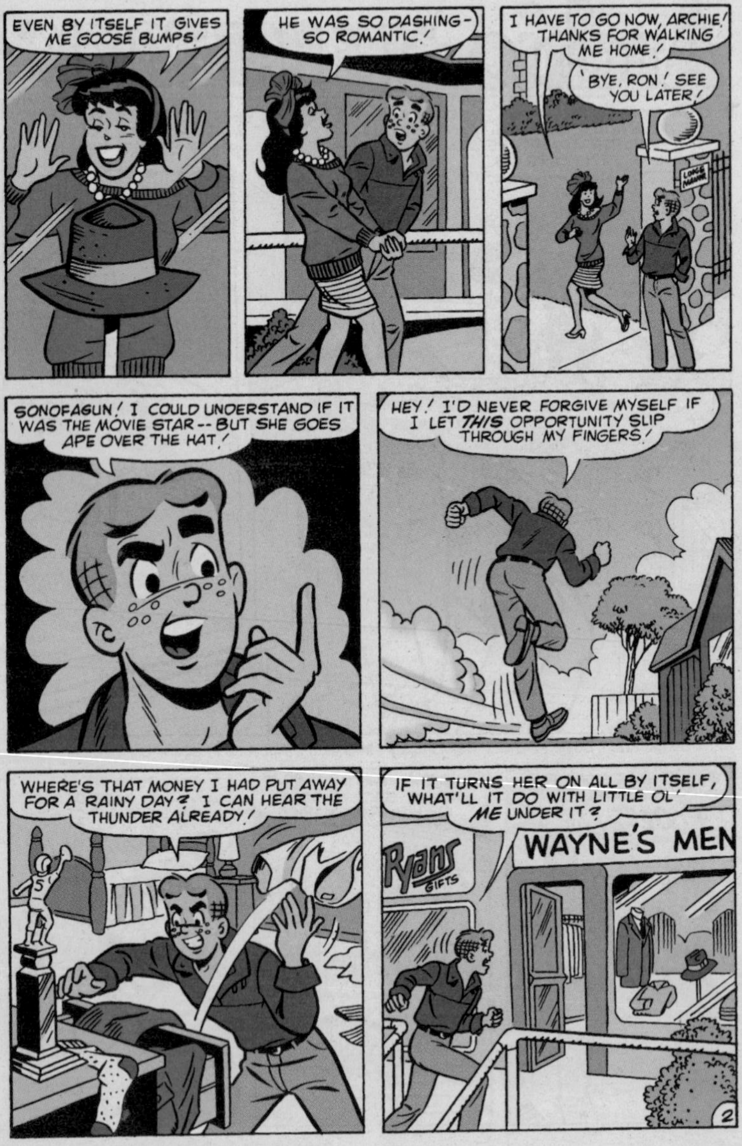
EVEN BY ITSELF IT GIVES ME GOOSE BUMPS!
HE WAS SO DASHING - SO ROMANTIC!
I HAVE TO GO NOW, ARCHIE! THANKS FOR WALKING ME HOME!
'BYE, RON! SEE YOU LATER!
LODGE MANOR
SONOFAGUN! I COULD UNDERSTAND IF IT WAS THE MOVIE STAR -- BUT SHE GOES APE OVER THE HAT!
HEY! I'D NEVER FORGIVE MYSELF IF I LET THIS OPPORTUNITY SLIP THROUGH MY FINGERS!
WHERE'S THAT MONEY I HAD PUT AWAY FOR A RAINY DAY? I CAN HEAR THE THUNDER ALREADY!
IF IT TURNS HER ON ALL BY ITSELF, WHAT'LL IT DO WITH LITTLE OL' ME UNDER IT?
Ryans GIFTS
WAYNE'S MEN
2

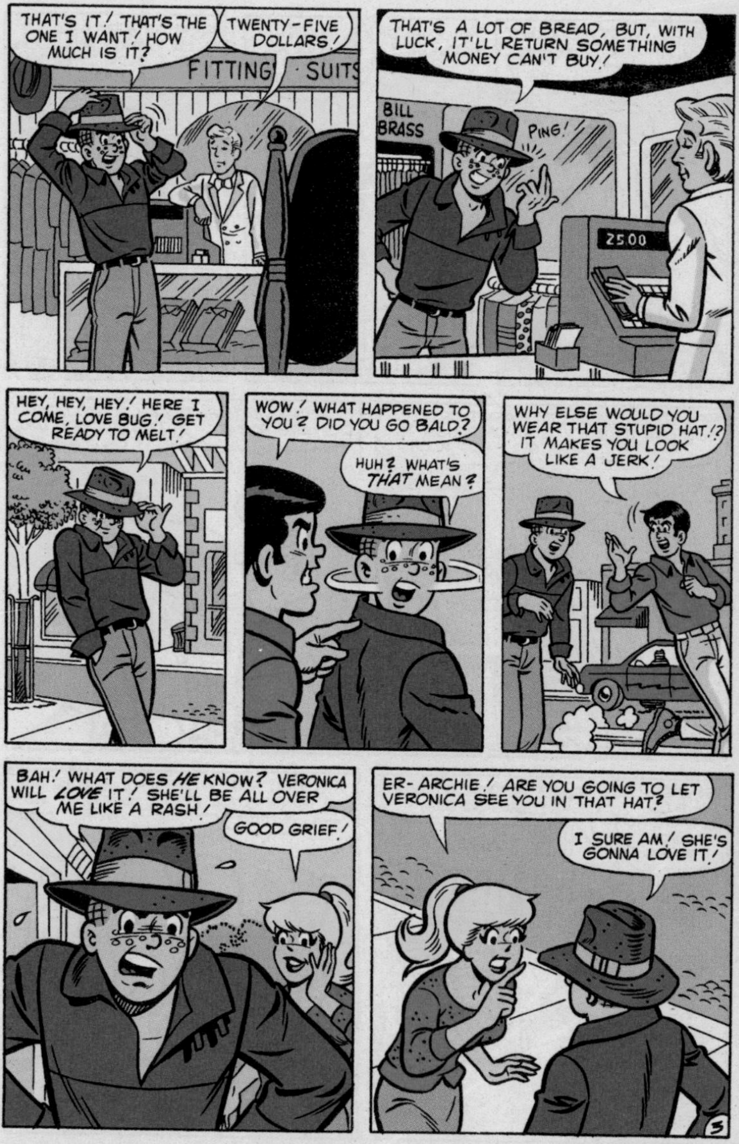
THAT'S IT! THAT'S THE ONE I WANT! HOW MUCH IS IT?
TWENTY-FIVE DOLLARS!
FITTING SUITS
THAT'S A LOT OF BREAD, BUT, WITH LUCK, IT'LL RETURN SOMETHING MONEY CAN'T BUY!
BILL BRASS
PING!
25.00
HEY, HEY, HEY! HERE I COME, LOVE BUG! GET READY TO MELT!
WOW! WHAT HAPPENED TO YOU? DID YOU GO BALD?
HUH? WHAT'S THAT MEAN?
WHY ELSE WOULD YOU WEAR THAT STUPID HAT!? IT MAKES YOU LOOK LIKE A JERK!
BAH! WHAT DOES HE KNOW? VERONICA WILL LOVE IT! SHE'LL BE ALL OVER ME LIKE A RASH!
GOOD GRIEF!
ER-ARCHIE! ARE YOU GOING TO LET VERONICA SEE YOU IN THAT HAT?
I SURE AM! SHE'S GONNA LOVE IT!
3

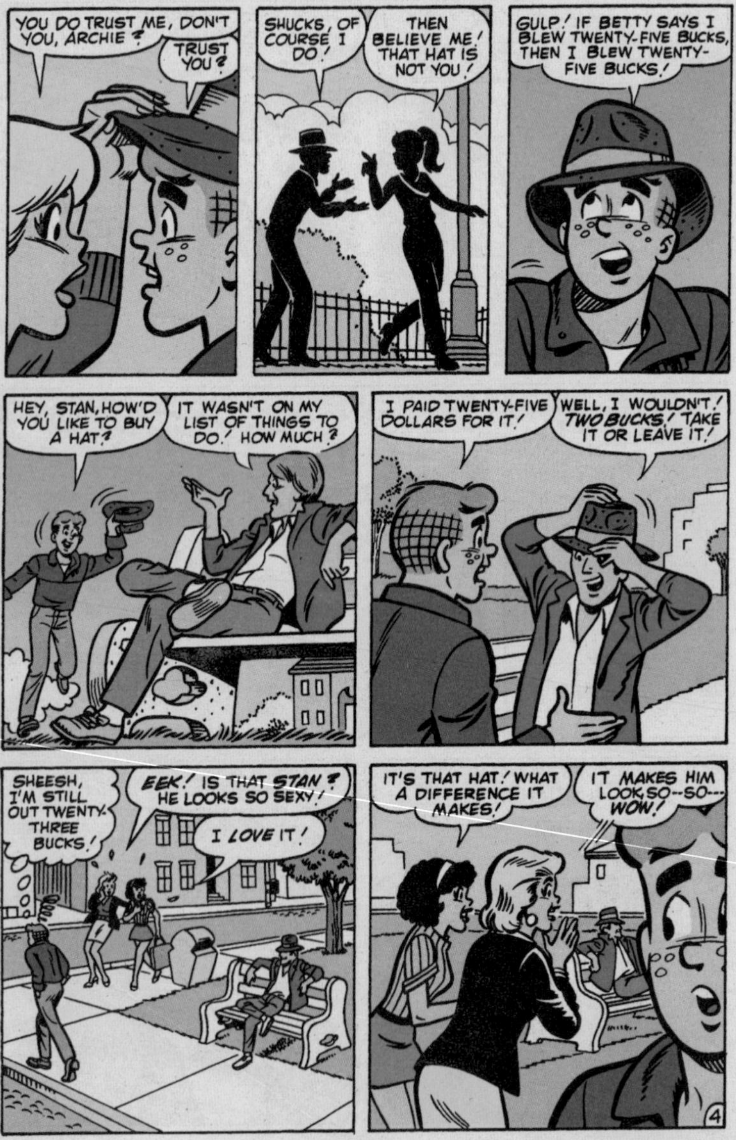

YOU DO TRUST ME, DON'T YOU, ARCHIE?
TRUST YOU?
SHUCKS, OF COURSE I DO!
THEN BELIEVE ME! THAT HAT IS NOT YOU!
GULP! IF BETTY SAYS I BLEW TWENTY-FIVE BUCKS, THEN I BLEW TWENTY-FIVE BUCKS!
HEY, STAN, HOW'D YOU LIKE TO BUY A HAT?
IT WASN'T ON MY LIST OF THINGS TO DO! HOW MUCH?
I PAID TWENTY-FIVE DOLLARS FOR IT!
WELL, I WOULDN'T! TWO BUCKS! TAKE IT OR LEAVE IT!
SHEESH, I'M STILL OUT TWENTY-THREE BUCKS!
EEK! IS THAT STAN? HE LOOKS SO SEXY!
I LOVE IT!
IT'S THAT HAT! WHAT A DIFFERENCE IT MAKES!
IT MAKES HIM LOOK SO--SO--- WOW!
4

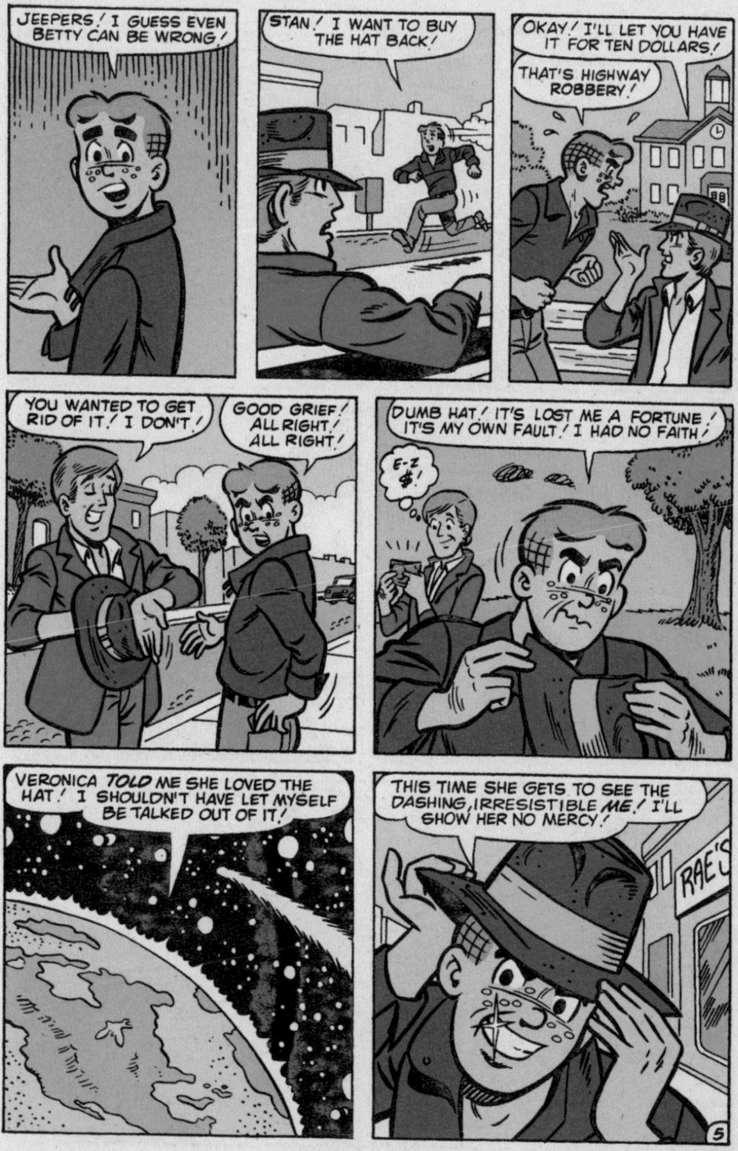
JEEPERS! I GUESS EVEN BETTY CAN BE WRONG!
STAN! I WANT TO BUY THE HAT BACK!
OKAY! I'LL LET YOU HAVE IT FOR TEN DOLLARS!
THAT'S HIGHWAY ROBBERY!
YOU WANTED TO GET RID OF IT! I DON'T!
GOOD GRIEF! ALL RIGHT! ALL RIGHT!
DUMB HAT! IT'S LOST ME A FORTUNE! IT'S MY OWN FAULT! I HAD NO FAITH!
E-Z $!
VERONICA TOLD ME SHE LOVED THE HAT! I SHOULDN'T HAVE LET MYSELF BE TALKED OUT OF IT!
THIS TIME SHE GETS TO SEE THE DASHING, IRRESISTIBLE ME! I'LL SHOW HER NO MERCY!
RAE'S

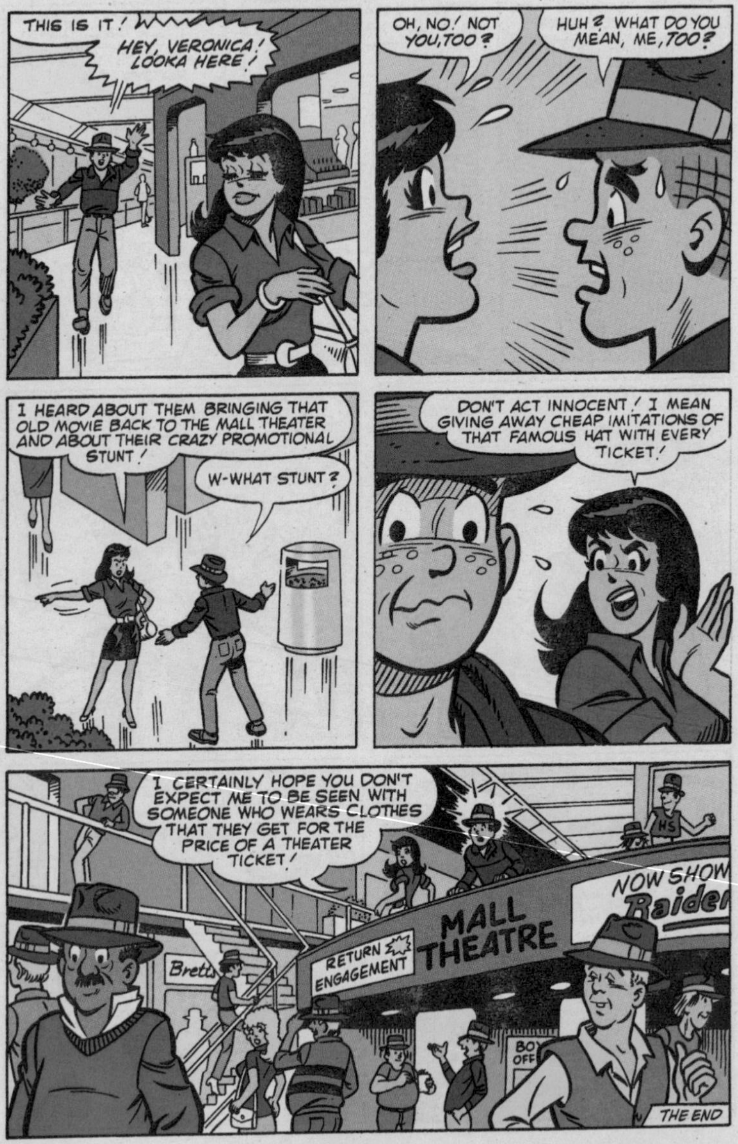
THIS IS IT!
HEY, VERONICA! LOOKA HERE!
OH, NO! NOT YOU, TOO?
HUH? WHAT DO YOU MEAN, ME, TOO?
I HEARD ABOUT THEM BRINGING THAT OLD MOVIE BACK TO THE MALL THEATER AND ABOUT THEIR CRAZY PROMOTIONAL STUNT!
W-WHAT STUNT?
DON'T ACT INNOCENT! I MEAN GIVING AWAY CHEAP IMITATIONS OF THAT FAMOUS HAT WITH EVERY TICKET!
I CERTAINLY HOPE YOU DON'T EXPECT ME TO BE SEEN WITH SOMEONE WHO WEARS CLOTHES THAT THEY GET FOR THE PRICE OF A THEATER TICKET!
NOW SHOW
Raider
MALL THEATRE
RETURN ENGAGEMENT
Bretts
HS
THE END

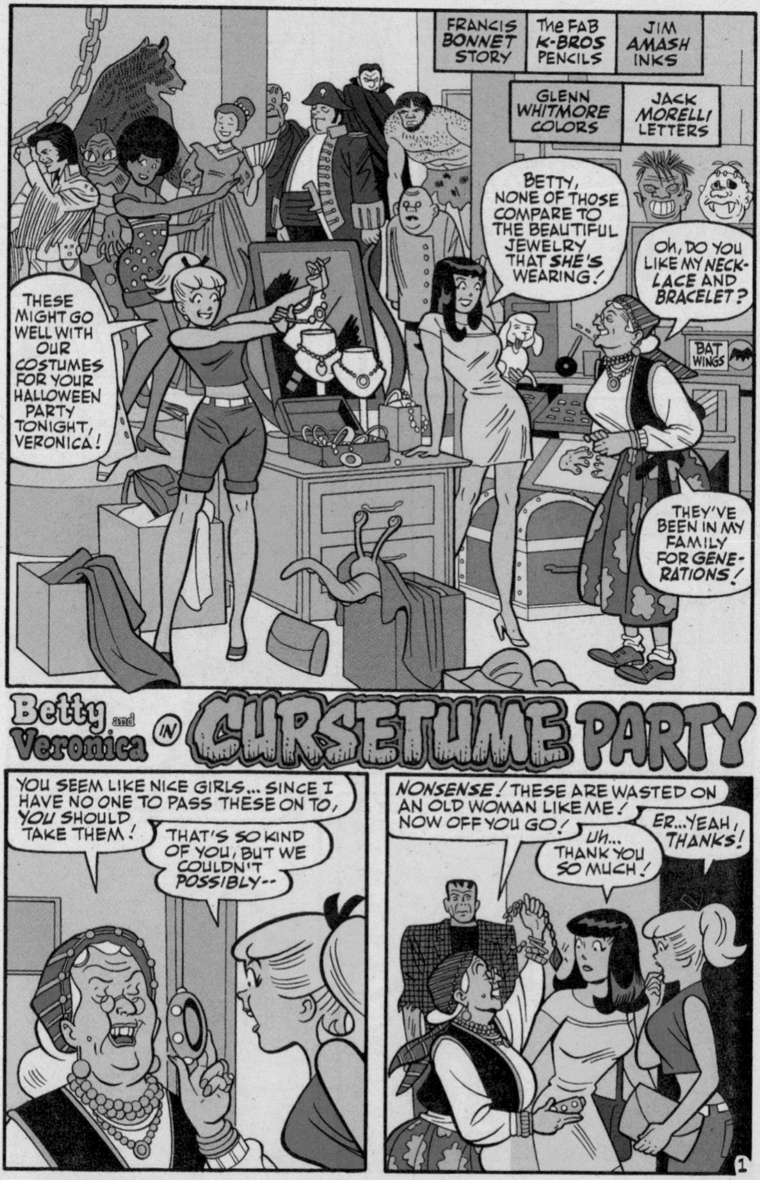
FRANCIS BONNET STORY
The FAB K-BROS PENCILS
JIM AMASH INKS
GLENN WHITMORE COLORS
JACK MORELLI LETTERS
THESE MIGHT GO WELL WITH OUR COSTUMES FOR YOUR HALLOWEEN PARTY TONIGHT, VERONICA!
BETTY, NONE OF THOSE COMPARE TO THE BEAUTIFUL JEWELRY THAT SHE'S WEARING!
Oh, DO YOU LIKE MY NECKLACE AND BRACELET?
BAT WINGS
THEY'VE BEEN IN MY FAMILY FOR GENERATIONS!
Betty and Veronica IN CURSETUME PARTY
YOU SEEM LIKE NICE GIRLS... SINCE I HAVE NO ONE TO PASS THESE ON TO, YOU SHOULD TAKE THEM!
THAT'S SO KIND OF YOU, BUT WE COULDN'T POSSIBLY--
NONSENSE! THESE ARE WASTED ON AN OLD WOMAN LIKE ME! NOW OFF YOU GO!
Uh... THANK YOU SO MUCH!
ER...YEAH, THANKS!
1

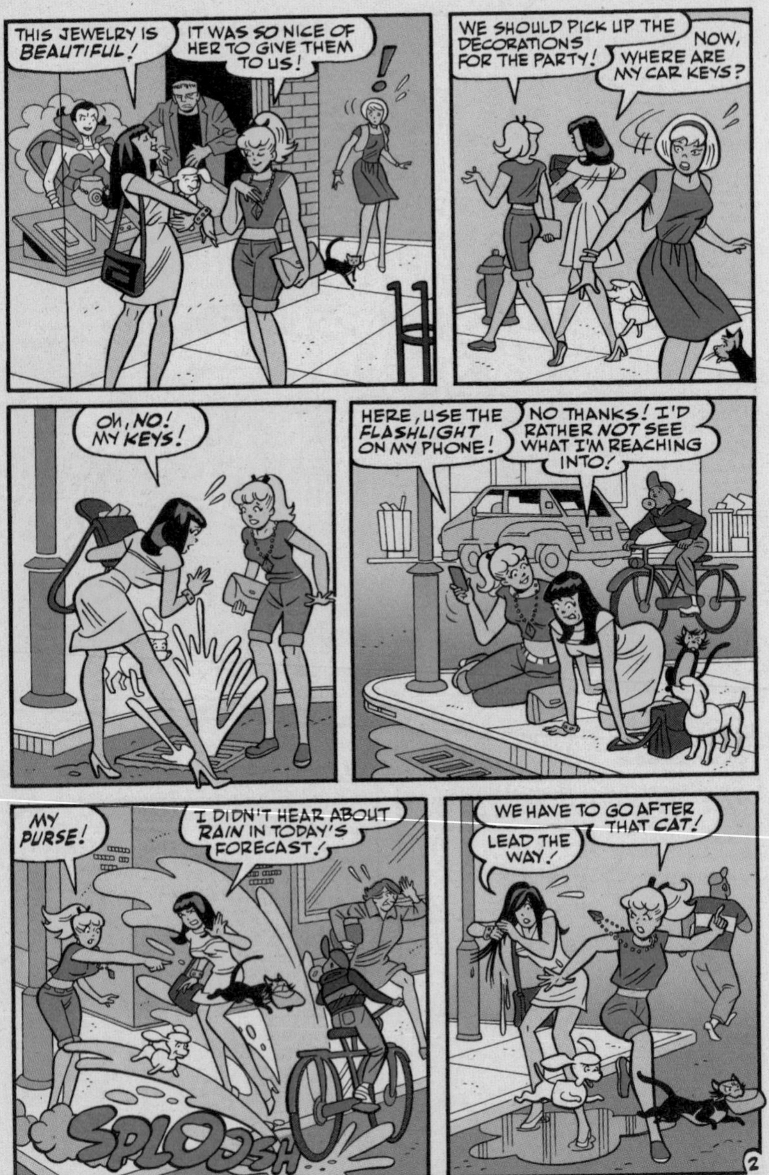
THIS JEWELRY IS BEAUTIFUL!
IT WAS SO NICE OF HER TO GIVE THEM TO US!
!
WE SHOULD PICK UP THE DECORATIONS FOR THE PARTY!
NOW, WHERE ARE MY CAR KEYS?
OH, NO! MY KEYS!
HERE, USE THE FLASHLIGHT ON MY PHONE!
NO THANKS! I'D RATHER NOT SEE WHAT I'M REACHING INTO!
MY PURSE!
I DIDN'T HEAR ABOUT RAIN IN TODAY'S FORECAST!
SPLOOSH
WE HAVE TO GO AFTER THAT CAT!
LEAD THE WAY!

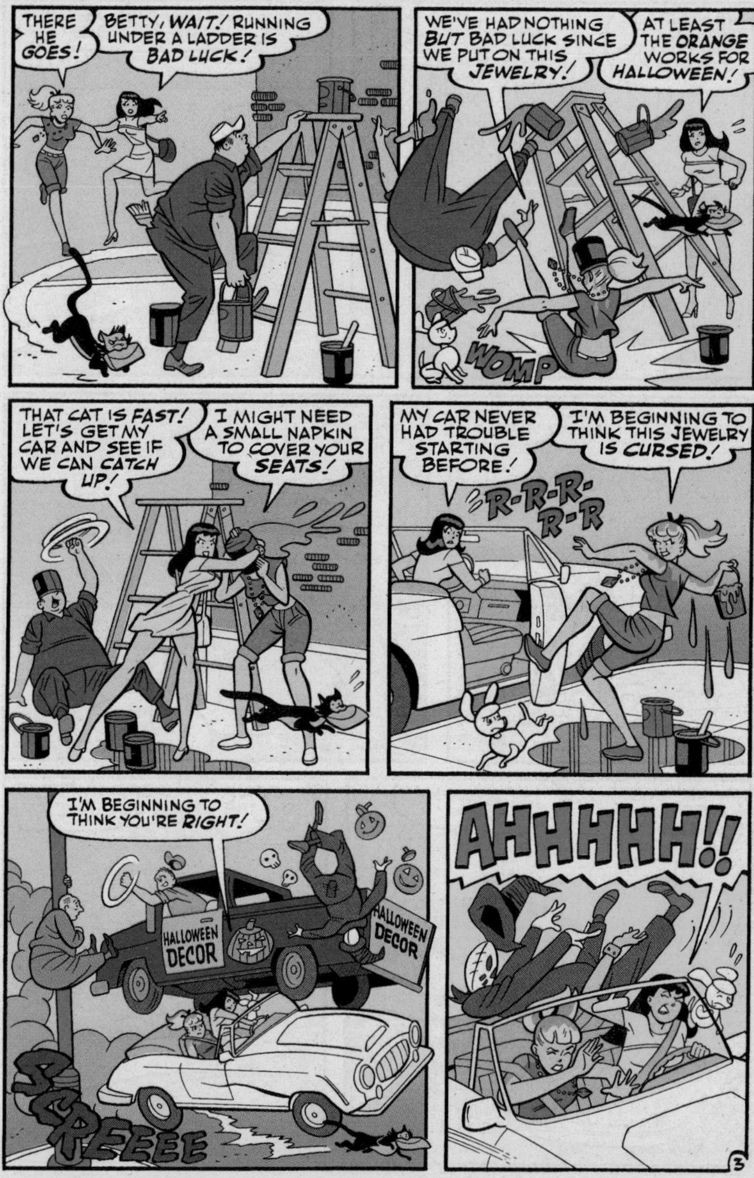
THERE HE GOES!
BETTY, WAIT! RUNNING UNDER A LADDER IS BAD LUCK!
WE'VE HAD NOTHING BUT BAD LUCK SINCE WE PUT ON THIS JEWELRY!
AT LEAST THE ORANGE WORKS FOR HALLOWEEN!
WOMP
THAT CAT IS FAST! LET'S GET MY CAR AND SEE IF WE CAN CATCH UP!
I MIGHT NEED A SMALL NAPKIN TO COVER YOUR SEATS!
MY CAR NEVER HAD TROUBLE STARTING BEFORE!
R-R-R-R-R
I'M BEGINNING TO THINK THIS JEWELRY IS CURSED!
I'M BEGINNING TO THINK YOU'RE RIGHT!
HALLOWEEN DECOR
HALLOWEEN DECOR
SCREEEEE
AHHHHH!!
3

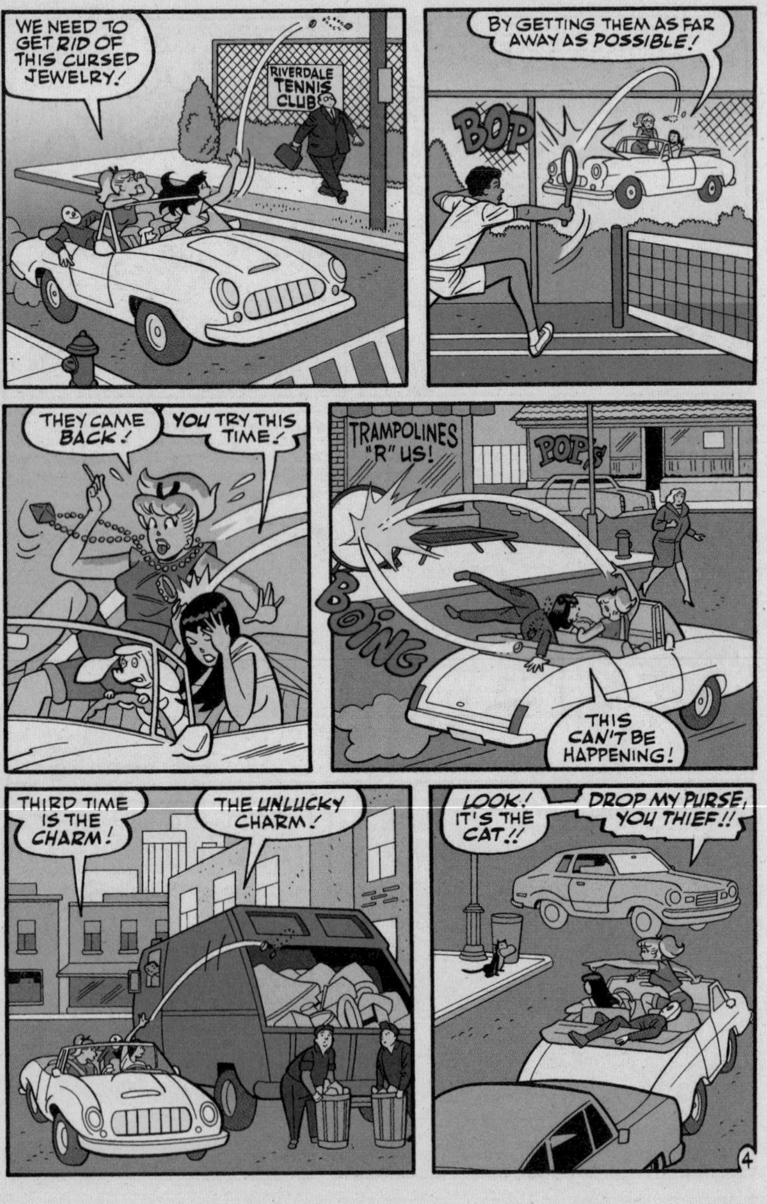

WE NEED TO GET RID OF THIS CURSED JEWELRY!
RIVERDALE TENNIS CLUB
BY GETTING THEM AS FAR AWAY AS POSSIBLE!
BOP
THEY CAME BACK!
YOU TRY THIS TIME!
TRAMPOLINES "R" US!
POP'S
BOING
THIS CAN'T BE HAPPENING!
THIRD TIME IS THE CHARM!
THE UNLUCKY CHARM!
LOOK! IT'S THE CAT!!
DROP MY PURSE, YOU THIEF!!
4

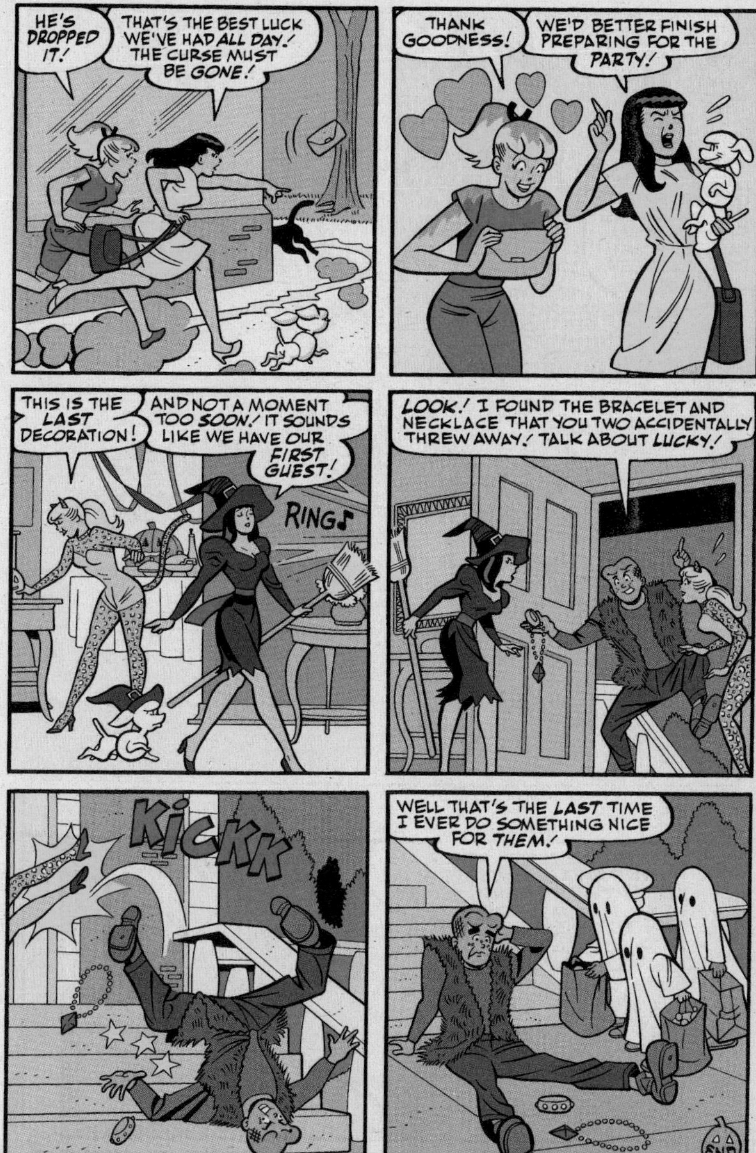
HE'S DROPPED IT!
THAT'S THE BEST LUCK WE'VE HAD ALL DAY! THE CURSE MUST BE GONE!
THANK GOODNESS!
WE'D BETTER FINISH PREPARING FOR THE PARTY!
THIS IS THE LAST DECORATION!
AND NOT A MOMENT TOO SOON! IT SOUNDS LIKE WE HAVE OUR FIRST GUEST!
RING
LOOK! I FOUND THE BRACELET AND NECKLACE THAT YOU TWO ACCIDENTALLY THREW AWAY! TALK ABOUT LUCKY!
KICKK
WELL THAT'S THE LAST TIME I EVER DO SOMETHING NICE FOR THEM!
END

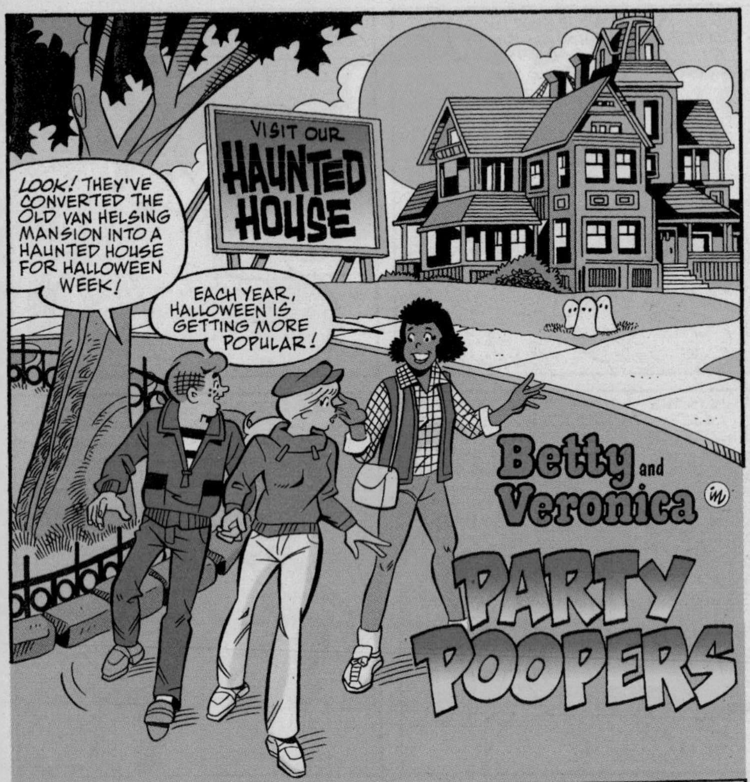
VISIT OUR HAUNTED HOUSE
LOOK! THEY'VE CONVERTED THE OLD VAN HELSING MANSION INTO A HAUNTED HOUSE FOR HALLOWEEN WEEK!
EACH YEAR, HALLOWEEN IS GETTING MORE POPULAR!
Betty and Veronica in
PARTY POOPERS

Script:	Pencils:	Inks:	Letters:	Colors:
GEORGE GLADIR	PAT KENNEDY	JIM AMASH	JACK MORELLI	BARRY GROSSMAN

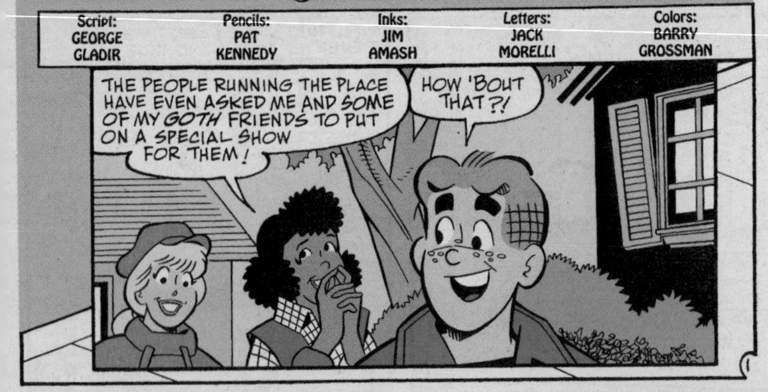
THE PEOPLE RUNNING THE PLACE HAVE EVEN ASKED ME AND SOME OF MY GOTH FRIENDS TO PUT ON A SPECIAL SHOW FOR THEM!
HOW 'BOUT THAT?!

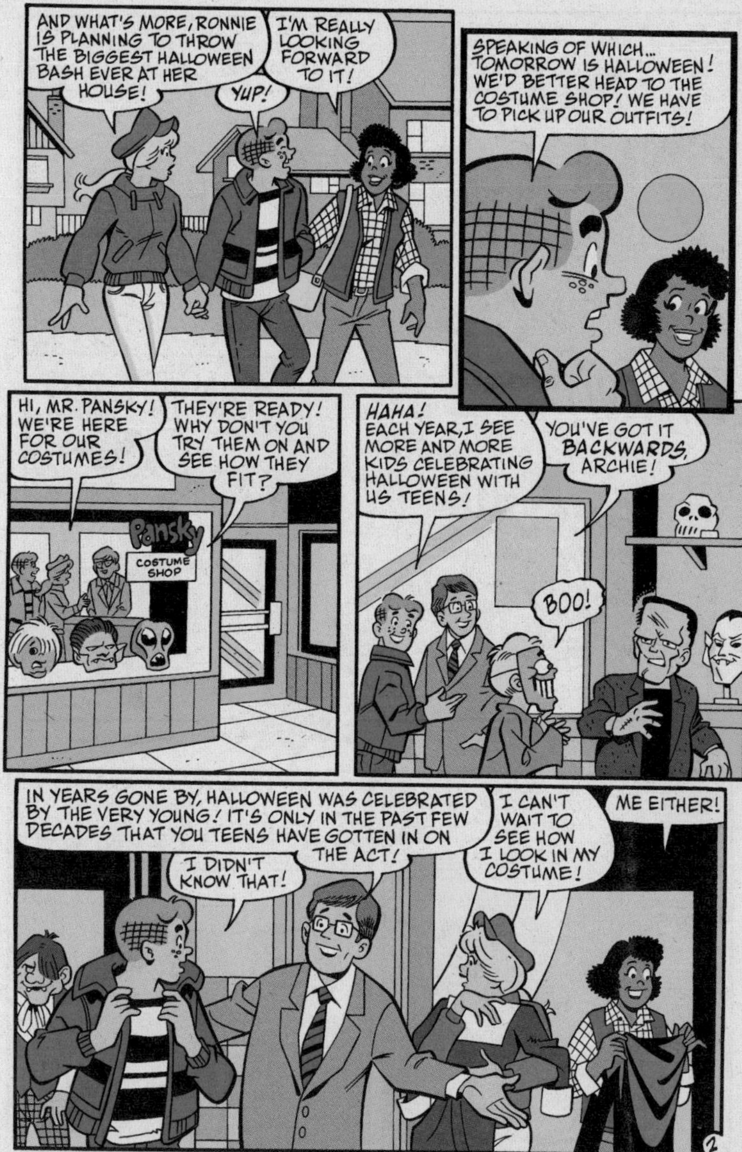
AND WHAT'S MORE, RONNIE IS PLANNING TO THROW THE BIGGEST HALLOWEEN BASH EVER AT HER HOUSE!
I'M REALLY LOOKING FORWARD TO IT!
YUP!
SPEAKING OF WHICH... TOMORROW IS HALLOWEEN! WE'D BETTER HEAD TO THE COSTUME SHOP! WE HAVE TO PICK UP OUR OUTFITS!
HI, MR. PANSKY! WE'RE HERE FOR OUR COSTUMES!
THEY'RE READY! WHY DON'T YOU TRY THEM ON AND SEE HOW THEY FIT?
PANSKY
COSTUME SHOP
HAHA! EACH YEAR, I SEE MORE AND MORE KIDS CELEBRATING HALLOWEEN WITH US TEENS!
YOU'VE GOT IT BACKWARDS, ARCHIE!
BOO!
IN YEARS GONE BY, HALLOWEEN WAS CELEBRATED BY THE VERY YOUNG! IT'S ONLY IN THE PAST FEW DECADES THAT YOU TEENS HAVE GOTTEN IN ON THE ACT!
I DIDN'T KNOW THAT!
I CAN'T WAIT TO SEE HOW I LOOK IN MY COSTUME!
ME EITHER!
2

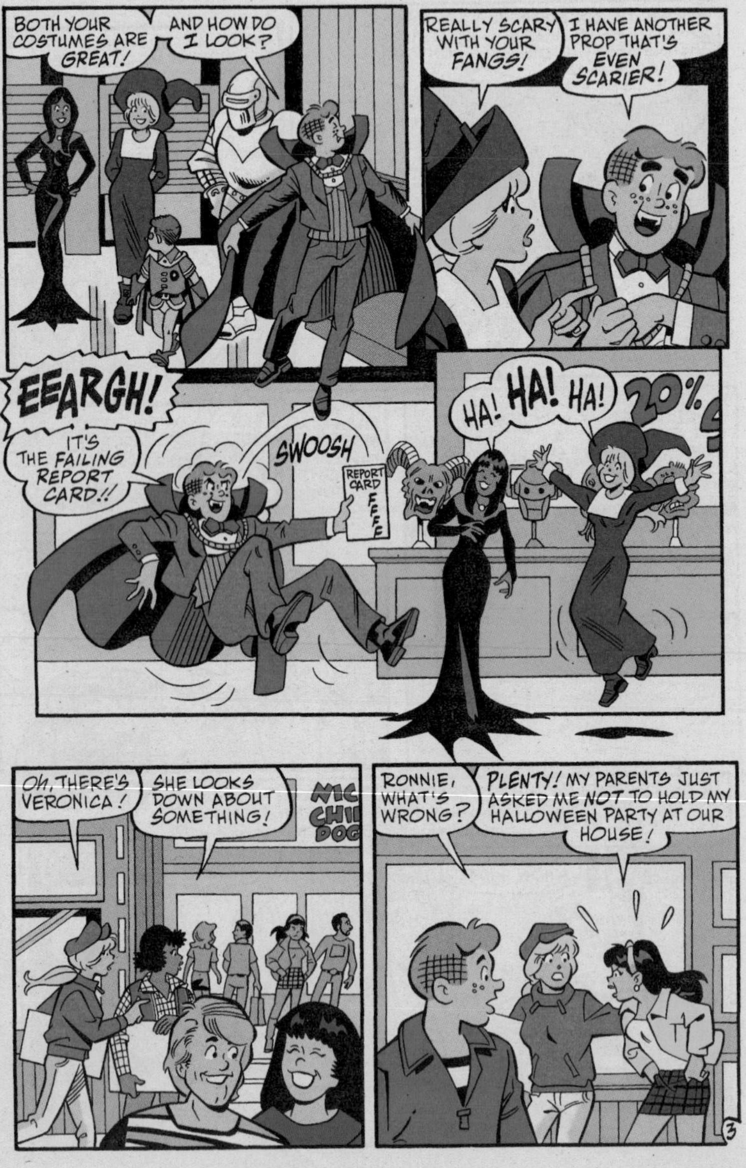

BOTH YOUR COSTUMES ARE GREAT!
AND HOW DO I LOOK?
REALLY SCARY WITH YOUR FANGS!
I HAVE ANOTHER PROP THAT'S EVEN SCARIER!
EEARGH!
IT'S THE FAILING REPORT CARD!!
SWOOSH
REPORT CARD
HA! HA! HA!
20%
Oh, THERE'S VERONICA!
SHE LOOKS DOWN ABOUT SOMETHING!
RONNIE, WHAT'S WRONG?
PLENTY! MY PARENTS JUST ASKED ME NOT TO HOLD MY HALLOWEEN PARTY AT OUR HOUSE!
3

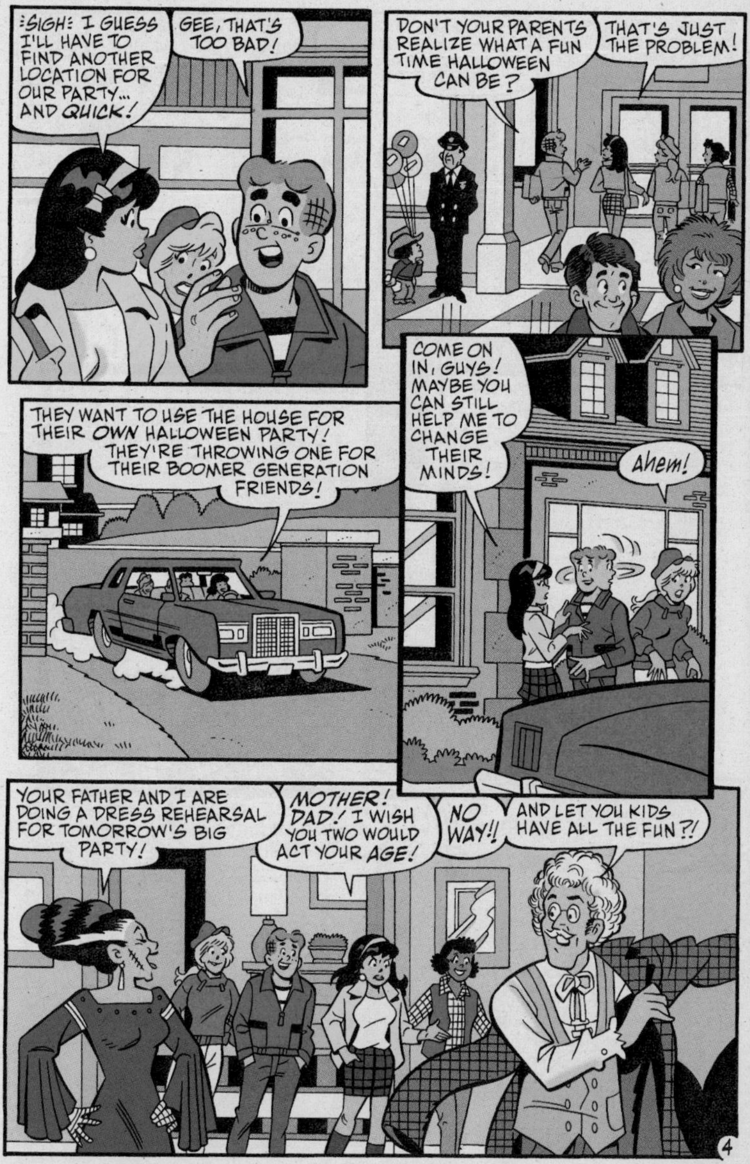

:SIGH: I GUESS I'LL HAVE TO FIND ANOTHER LOCATION FOR OUR PARTY... AND QUICK!
GEE, THAT'S TOO BAD!
DON'T YOUR PARENTS REALIZE WHAT A FUN TIME HALLOWEEN CAN BE?
THAT'S JUST THE PROBLEM!
THEY WANT TO USE THE HOUSE FOR THEIR OWN HALLOWEEN PARTY!
THEY'RE THROWING ONE FOR THEIR BOOMER GENERATION FRIENDS!
COME ON IN, GUYS! MAYBE YOU CAN STILL HELP ME TO CHANGE THEIR MINDS!
Ahem!
YOUR FATHER AND I ARE DOING A DRESS REHEARSAL FOR TOMORROW'S BIG PARTY!
MOTHER! DAD! I WISH YOU TWO WOULD ACT YOUR AGE!
NO WAY!!
AND LET YOU KIDS HAVE ALL THE FUN?!

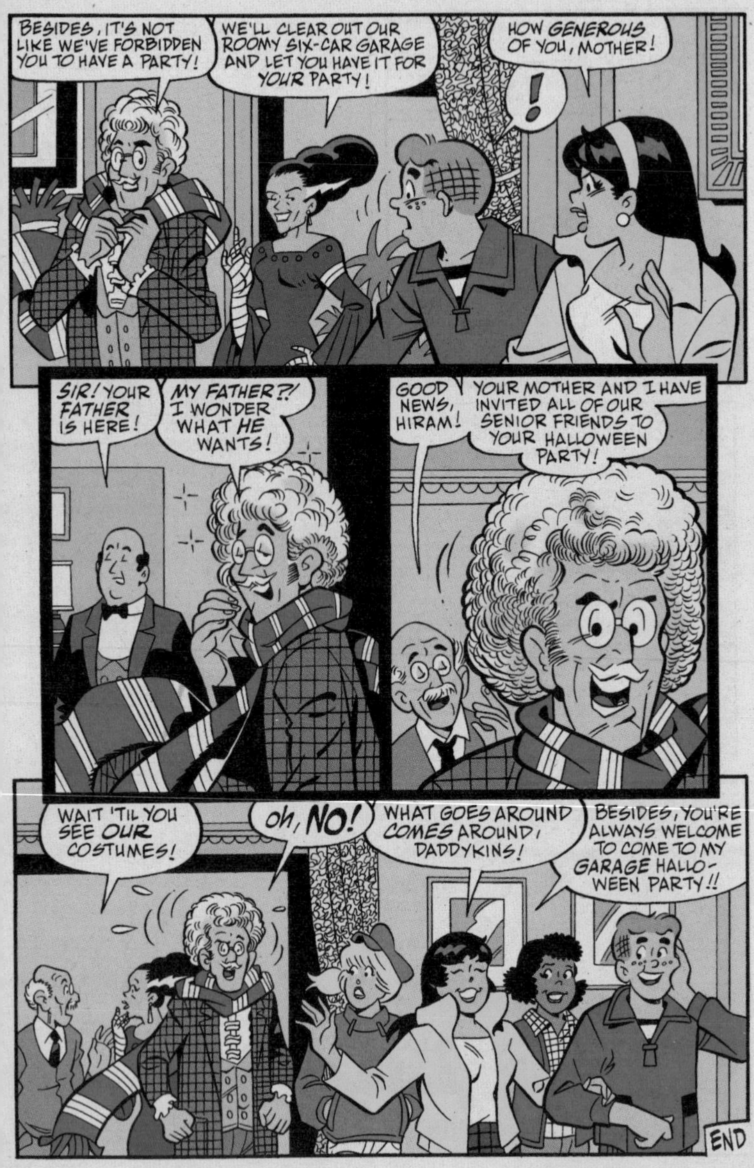
BESIDES, IT'S NOT LIKE WE'VE FORBIDDEN YOU TO HAVE A PARTY!
WE'LL CLEAR OUT OUR ROOMY SIX-CAR GARAGE AND LET YOU HAVE IT FOR YOUR PARTY!
!
HOW GENEROUS OF YOU, MOTHER!
SIR! YOUR FATHER IS HERE!
MY FATHER?! I WONDER WHAT HE WANTS!
GOOD NEWS, HIRAM!
YOUR MOTHER AND I HAVE INVITED ALL OF OUR SENIOR FRIENDS TO YOUR HALLOWEEN PARTY!
WAIT 'TIL YOU SEE OUR COSTUMES!
oh, NO!
WHAT GOES AROUND COMES AROUND, DADDYKINS!
BESIDES, YOU'RE ALWAYS WELCOME TO COME TO MY GARAGE HALLOWEEN PARTY!!
END

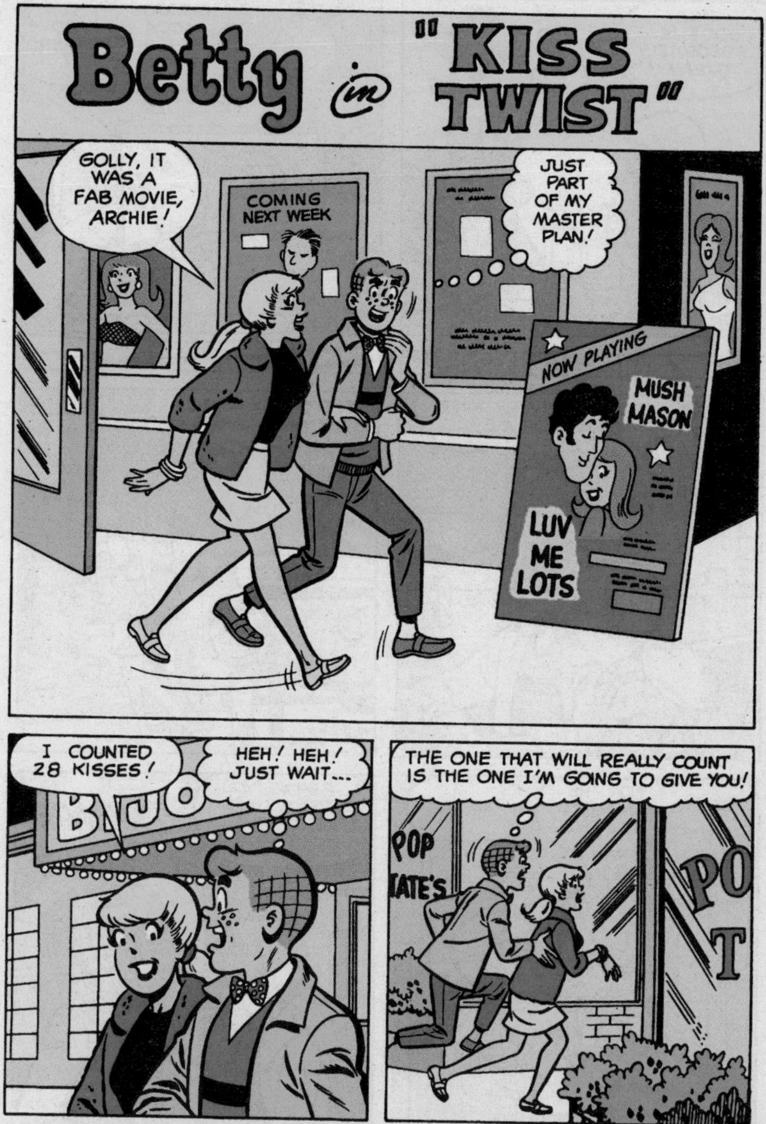
Betty in "KISS TWIST"
GOLLY, IT WAS A FAB MOVIE, ARCHIE!
JUST PART OF MY MASTER PLAN!
COMING NEXT WEEK
NOW PLAYING
MUSH MASON
LUV ME LOTS
I COUNTED 28 KISSES!
HEH! HEH! JUST WAIT...
THE ONE THAT WILL REALLY COUNT IS THE ONE I'M GOING TO GIVE YOU!
POP
TATE'S

Script & Pencils: Al Hartley / Inks: Jon D'Agostino / Letters: Bill Yoshida

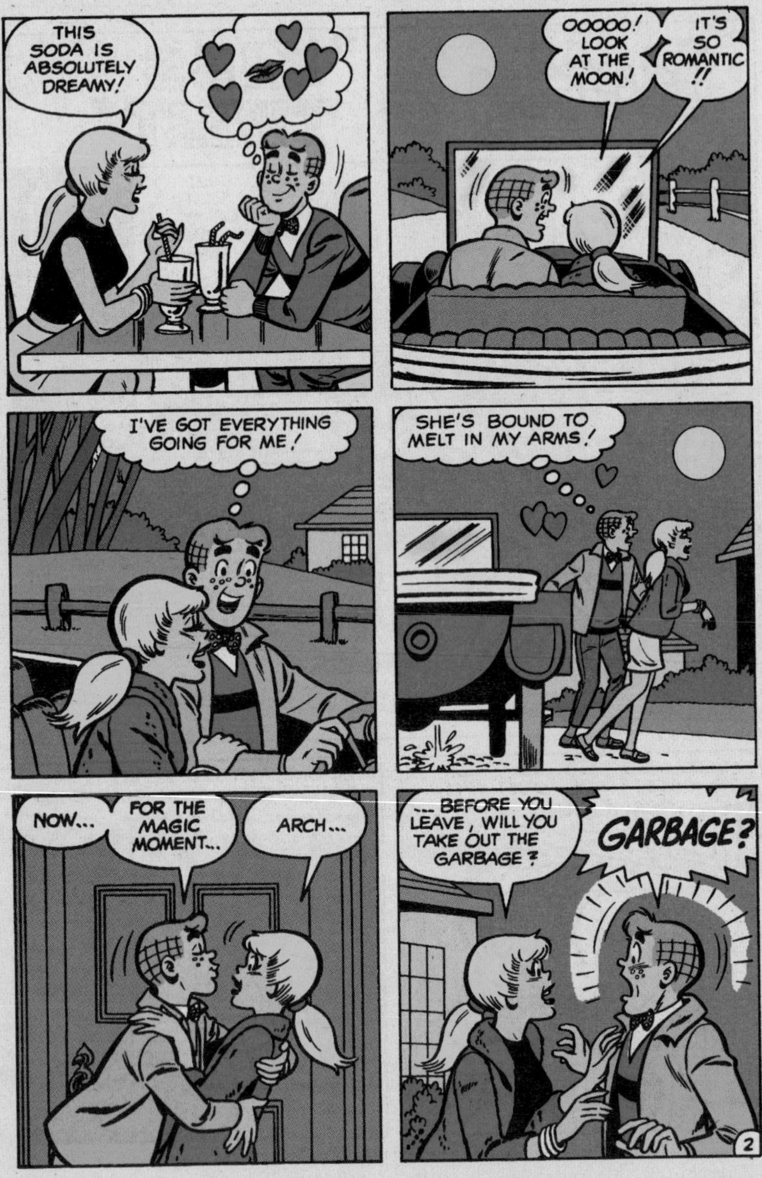
THIS SODA IS ABSOLUTELY DREAMY!
OOOOO! LOOK AT THE MOON!
IT'S SO ROMANTIC !!
I'VE GOT EVERYTHING GOING FOR ME!
SHE'S BOUND TO MELT IN MY ARMS!
NOW...
FOR THE MAGIC MOMENT...
ARCH...
... BEFORE YOU LEAVE, WILL YOU TAKE OUT THE GARBAGE?
GARBAGE?
2

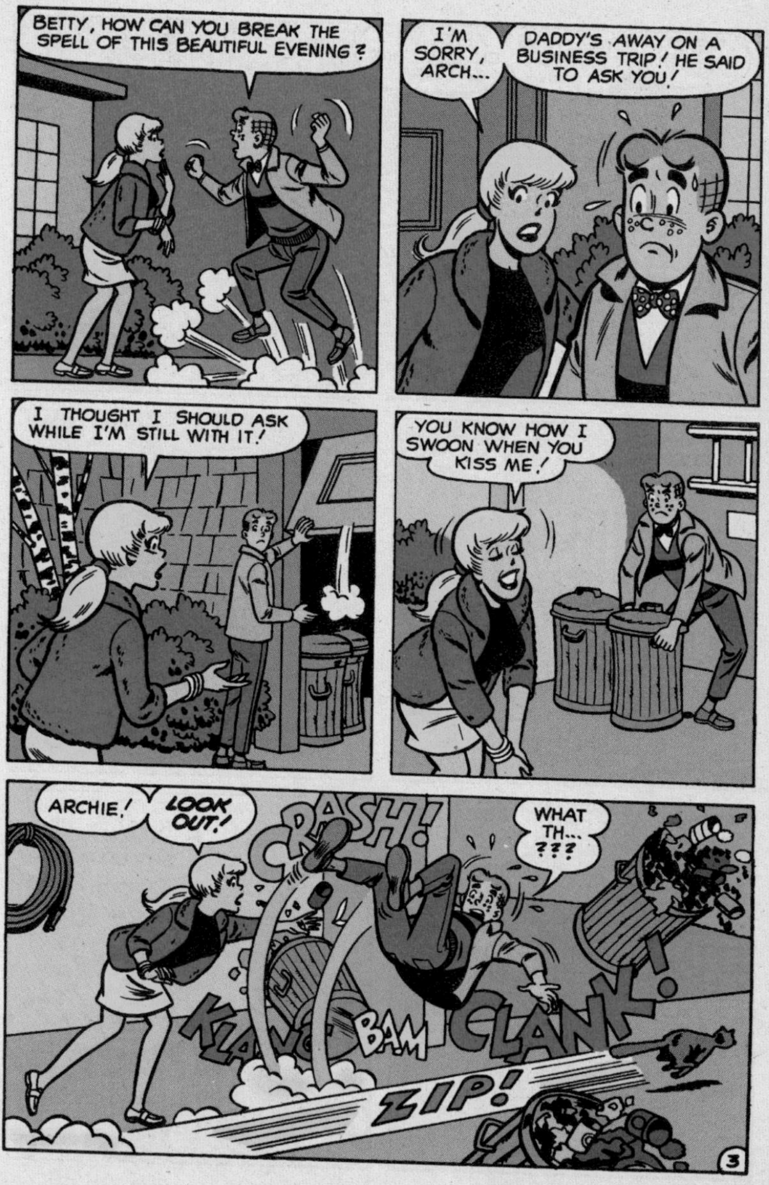
BETTY, HOW CAN YOU BREAK THE SPELL OF THIS BEAUTIFUL EVENING ?
I'M SORRY, ARCH...
DADDY'S AWAY ON A BUSINESS TRIP! HE SAID TO ASK YOU!
I THOUGHT I SHOULD ASK WHILE I'M STILL WITH IT!
YOU KNOW HOW I SWOON WHEN YOU KISS ME!
ARCHIE!
LOOK OUT!
CRASH!
WHAT TH... ???
KLANG
BAM
CLANK!
ZIP!
3

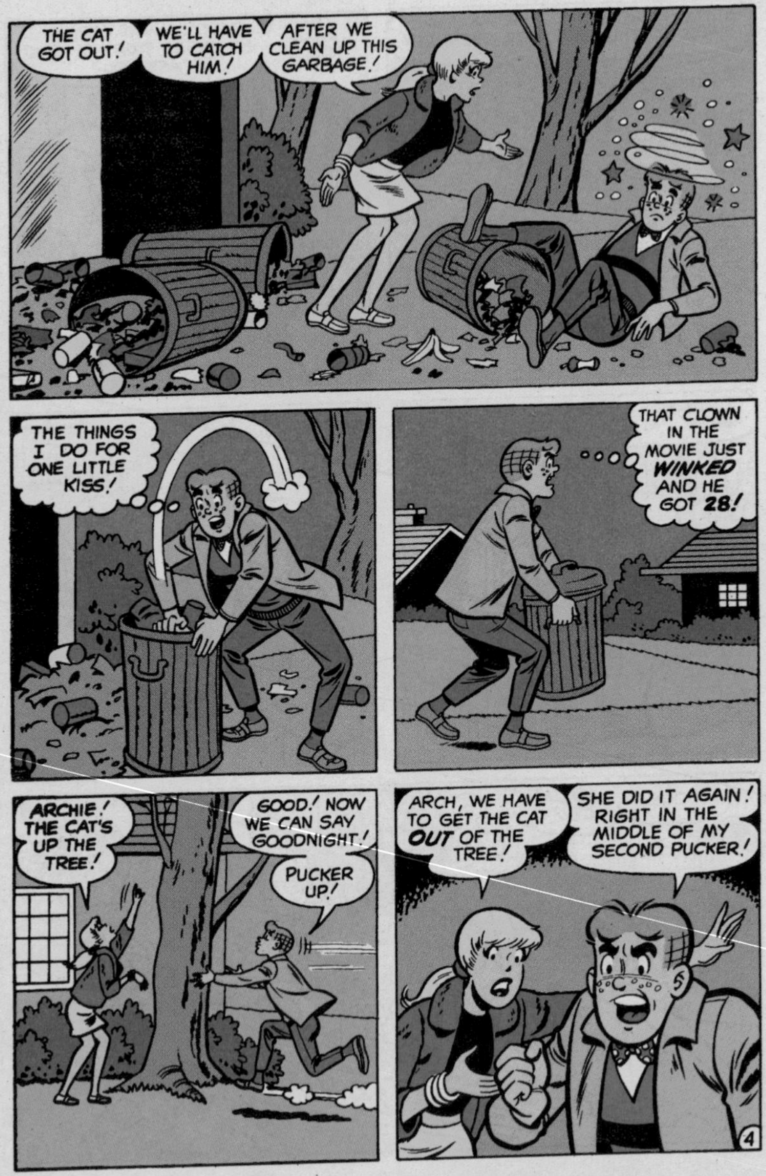
THE CAT GOT OUT!
WE'LL HAVE TO CATCH HIM!
AFTER WE CLEAN UP THIS GARBAGE!
THE THINGS I DO FOR ONE LITTLE KISS!
THAT CLOWN IN THE MOVIE JUST WINKED AND HE GOT 28!
ARCHIE! THE CAT'S UP THE TREE!
GOOD! NOW WE CAN SAY GOODNIGHT!
PUCKER UP!
ARCH, WE HAVE TO GET THE CAT OUT OF THE TREE!
SHE DID IT AGAIN! RIGHT IN THE MIDDLE OF MY SECOND PUCKER!
4

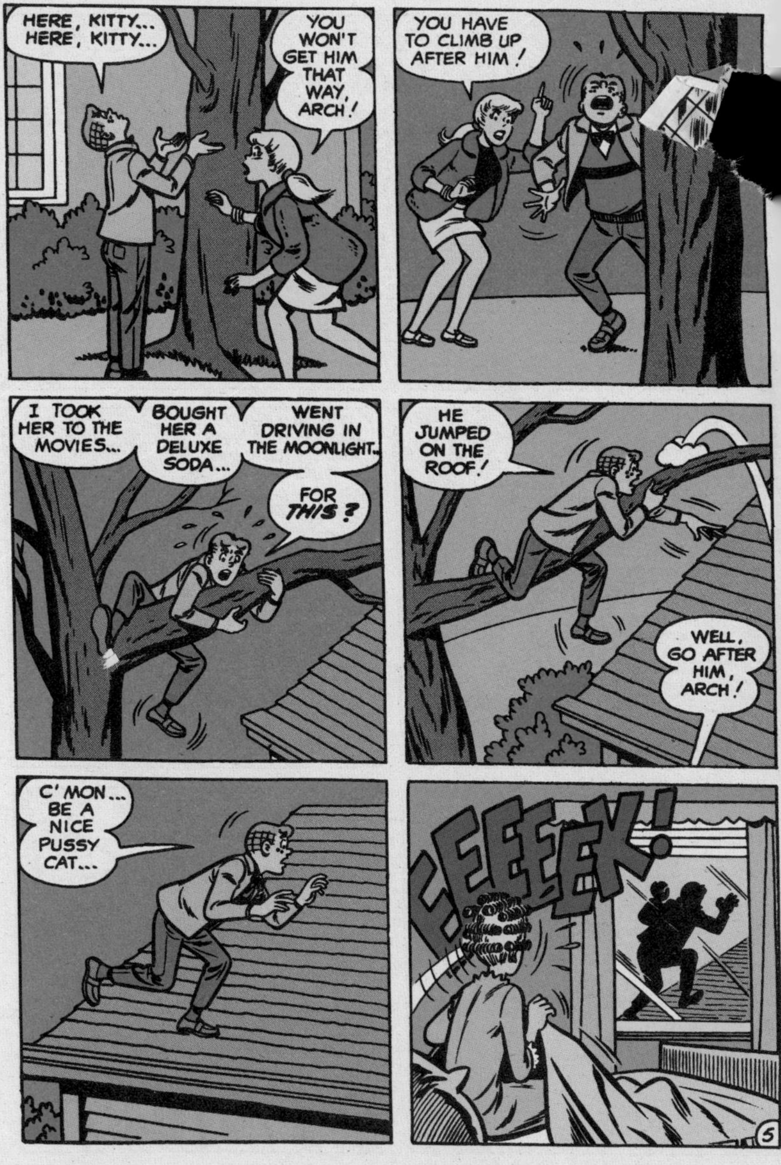
HERE, KITTY... HERE, KITTY...
YOU WON'T GET HIM THAT WAY, ARCH!
YOU HAVE TO CLIMB UP AFTER HIM!
I TOOK HER TO THE MOVIES...
BOUGHT HER A DELUXE SODA...
WENT DRIVING IN THE MOONLIGHT...
FOR THIS?
HE JUMPED ON THE ROOF!
WELL, GO AFTER HIM, ARCH!
C'MON... BE A NICE PUSSY CAT...
EEEEK!

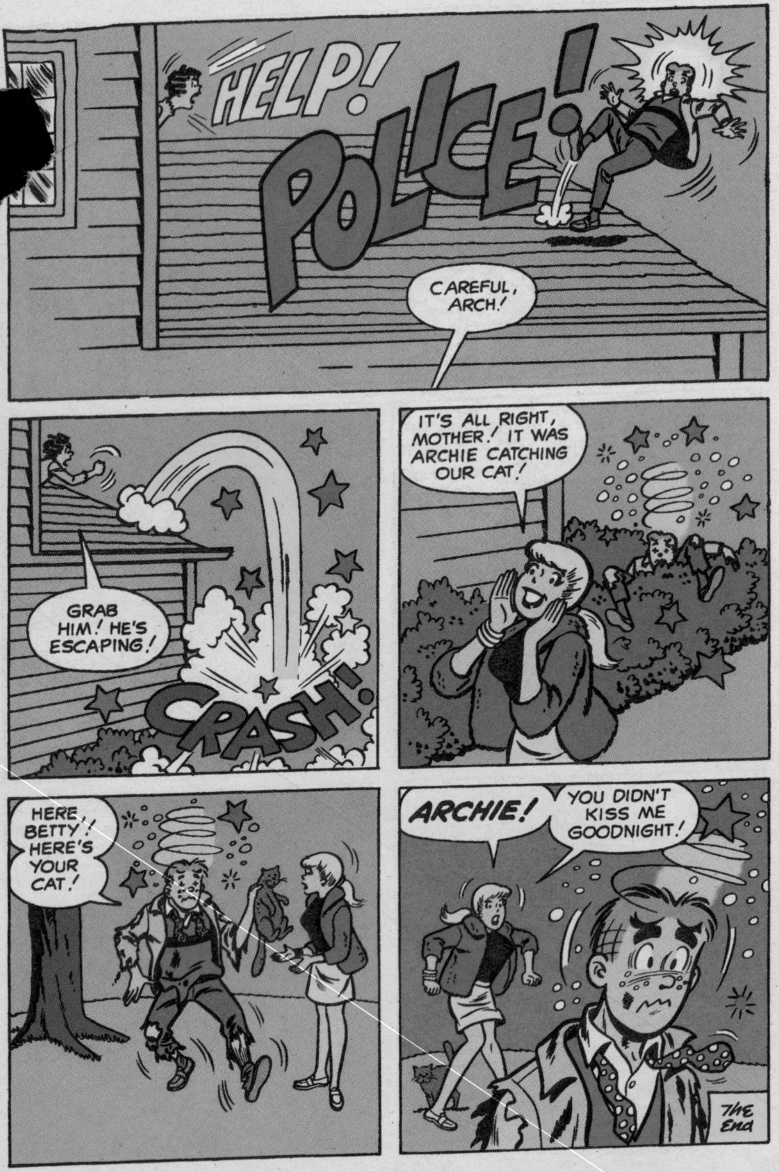
HELP!
POLICE!
CAREFUL, ARCH!
GRAB HIM! HE'S ESCAPING!
CRASH!
IT'S ALL RIGHT, MOTHER! IT WAS ARCHIE CATCHING OUR CAT!
HERE BETTY! HERE'S YOUR CAT!
ARCHIE!
YOU DIDN'T KISS ME GOODNIGHT!
THE End

Veronica in "THE CRUELEST CUT"

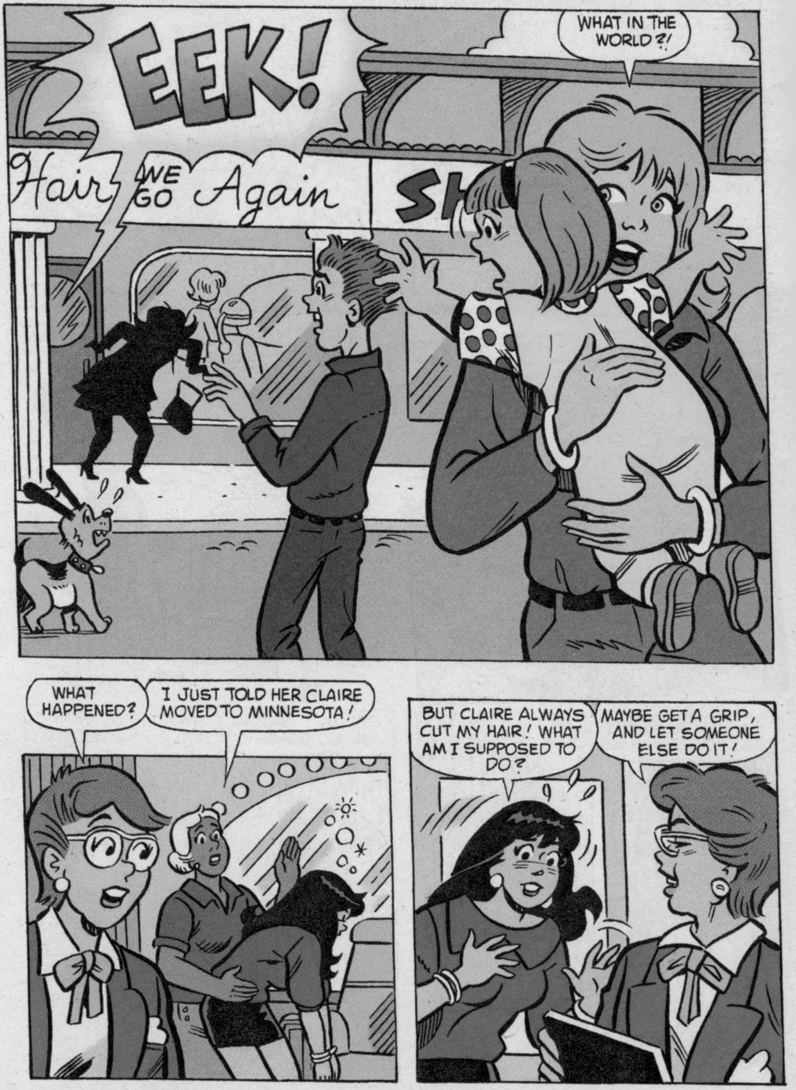
EEK!
WHAT IN THE WORLD?!
Hair WE GO Again
WHAT HAPPENED?
I JUST TOLD HER CLAIRE MOVED TO MINNESOTA!
BUT CLAIRE ALWAYS CUT MY HAIR! WHAT AM I SUPPOSED TO DO?
MAYBE GET A GRIP, AND LET SOMEONE ELSE DO IT!

Script: Bill Golliher / Pencils: Tim Kennedy / Inks: Rudy Lapick / Letters: Bill Yoshida

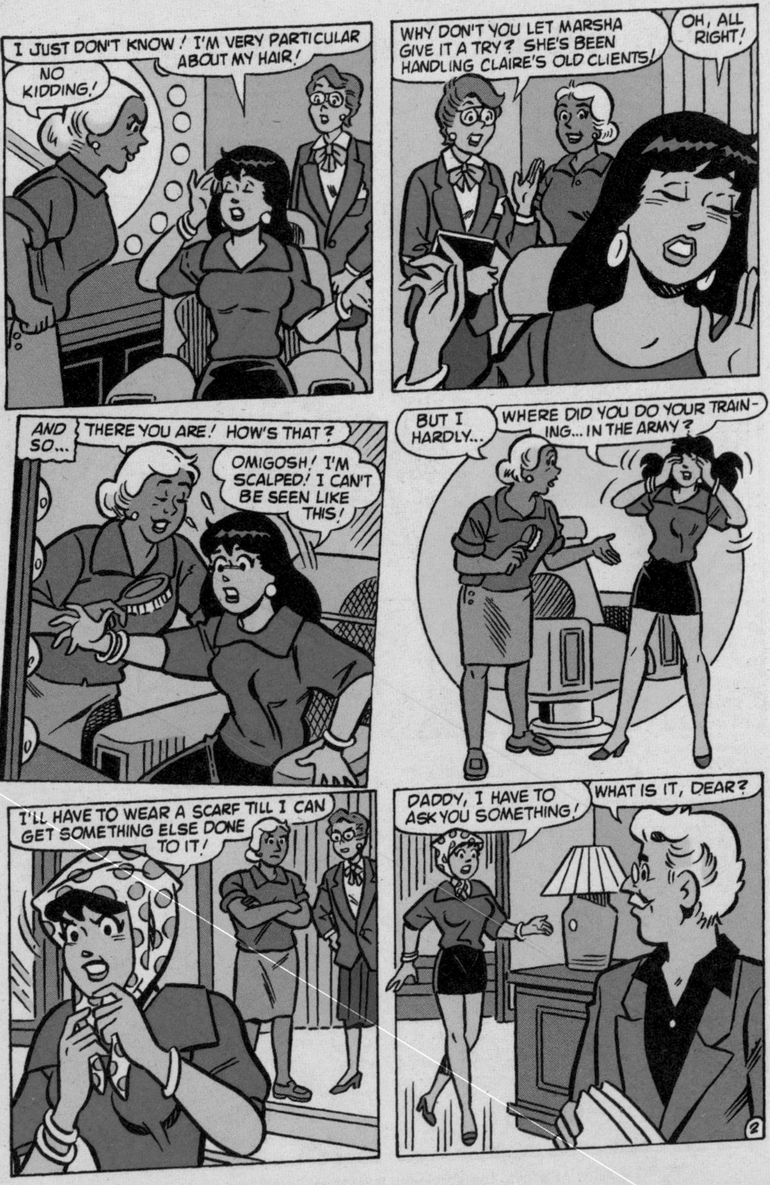
I JUST DON'T KNOW! I'M VERY PARTICULAR ABOUT MY HAIR!
NO KIDDING!
WHY DON'T YOU LET MARSHA GIVE IT A TRY? SHE'S BEEN HANDLING CLAIRE'S OLD CLIENTS!
OH, ALL RIGHT!
AND SO...
THERE YOU ARE! HOW'S THAT?
OMIGOSH! I'M SCALPED! I CAN'T BE SEEN LIKE THIS!
BUT I HARDLY...
WHERE DID YOU DO YOUR TRAINING... IN THE ARMY?
I'LL HAVE TO WEAR A SCARF TILL I CAN GET SOMETHING ELSE DONE TO IT!
DADDY, I HAVE TO ASK YOU SOMETHING!
WHAT IS IT, DEAR?
2

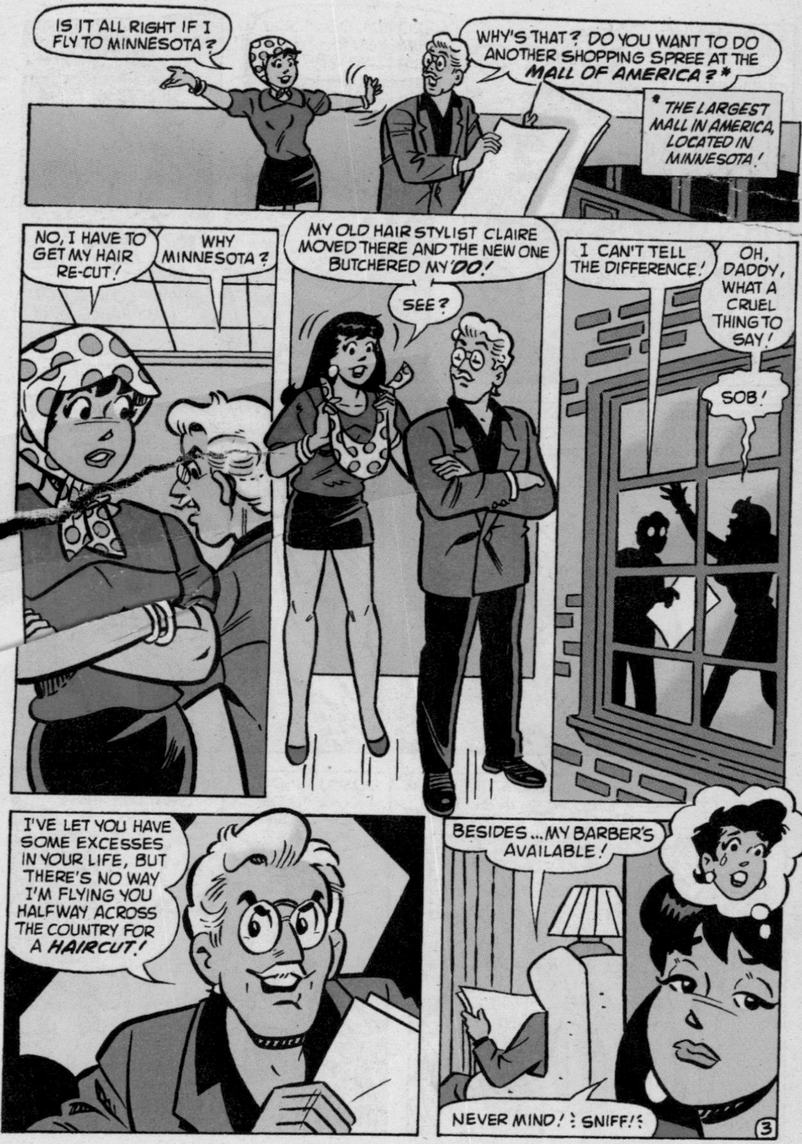
IS IT ALL RIGHT IF I FLY TO MINNESOTA?
WHY'S THAT? DO YOU WANT TO DO ANOTHER SHOPPING SPREE AT THE MALL OF AMERICA?*
* THE LARGEST MALL IN AMERICA, LOCATED IN MINNESOTA!
NO, I HAVE TO GET MY HAIR RE-CUT!
WHY MINNESOTA?
MY OLD HAIR STYLIST CLAIRE MOVED THERE AND THE NEW ONE BUTCHERED MY 'DO!
SEE?
I CAN'T TELL THE DIFFERENCE!
OH, DADDY, WHAT A CRUEL THING TO SAY!
SOB!
I'VE LET YOU HAVE SOME EXCESSES IN YOUR LIFE, BUT THERE'S NO WAY I'M FLYING YOU HALFWAY ACROSS THE COUNTRY FOR A HAIRCUT!
BESIDES... MY BARBER'S AVAILABLE!
NEVER MIND! SNIFF!
3

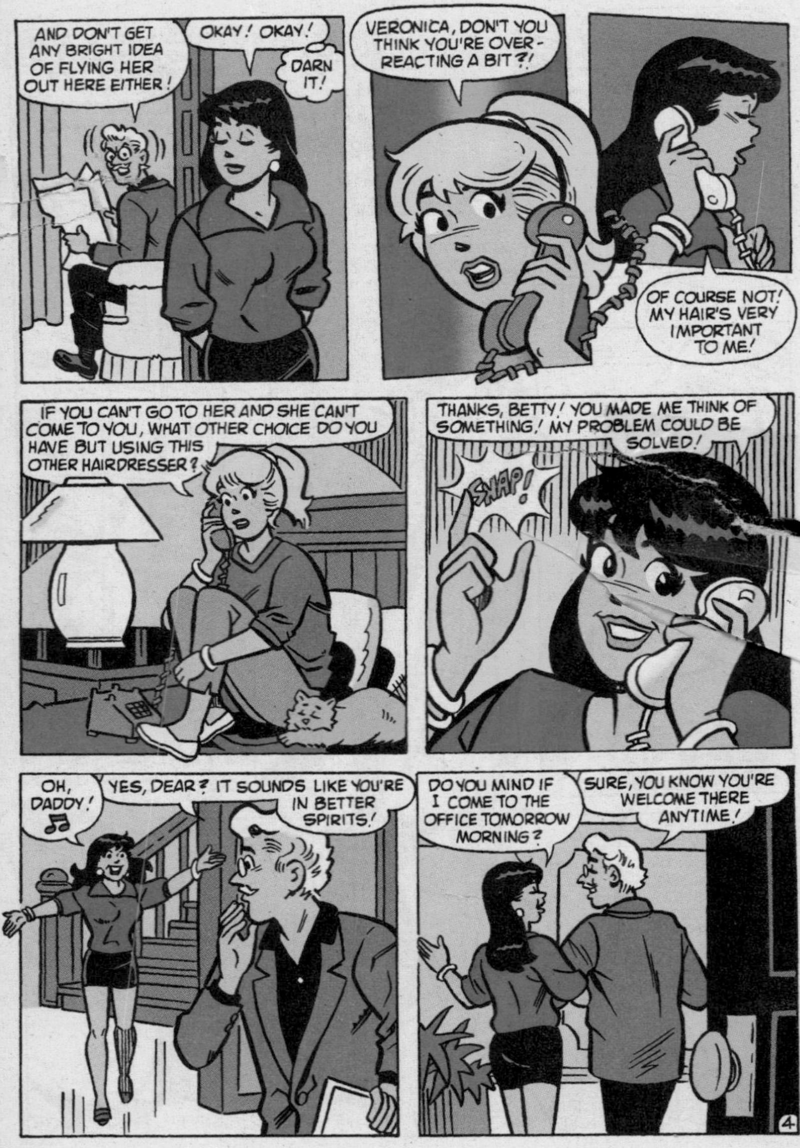

AND DON'T GET ANY BRIGHT IDEA OF FLYING HER OUT HERE EITHER!
OKAY! OKAY!
DARN IT!
VERONICA, DON'T YOU THINK YOU'RE OVER-REACTING A BIT?!
OF COURSE NOT! MY HAIR'S VERY IMPORTANT TO ME!
IF YOU CAN'T GO TO HER AND SHE CAN'T COME TO YOU, WHAT OTHER CHOICE DO YOU HAVE BUT USING THIS OTHER HAIRDRESSER?
THANKS, BETTY! YOU MADE ME THINK OF SOMETHING! MY PROBLEM COULD BE SOLVED!
SNAP!
OH, DADDY!
YES, DEAR? IT SOUNDS LIKE YOU'RE IN BETTER SPIRITS!
DO YOU MIND IF I COME TO THE OFFICE TOMORROW MORNING?
SURE, YOU KNOW YOU'RE WELCOME THERE ANYTIME!
4

HMM! SHE'S INTERESTED IN THE OFFICE?! MAYBE SHE REALIZED HOW SILLY THIS WHOLE THING WAS AND SHE'S BEGINNING TO GROW UP!

NEXT MORNING...

GOOD MORNING, MR. ALBERTS! READY FOR OUR MEETING WITH ZIRCON INDUSTRIES?

YOUR SECRETARY TELLS ME THIS ROOM IS OCCUPIED!

OCCUPIED? WE'VE HAD THE ROOM RESERVED FOR WEEKS!

BUT, SIR, SHE SAID IT WAS AN EMERGENCY!

LODGE INDUSTRIES

LODGE INDUSTRIES

SHE?! I'LL GET TO THE BOTTOM OF THIS!

TELE-CONFERENCE ROOM

THAT'S GREAT! AND MAYBE ANOTHER INCH OFF THE TOP!

HI, DAD! MEET CLAIRE! AREN'T MODERN CONVENIENCES WONDERFUL?

END

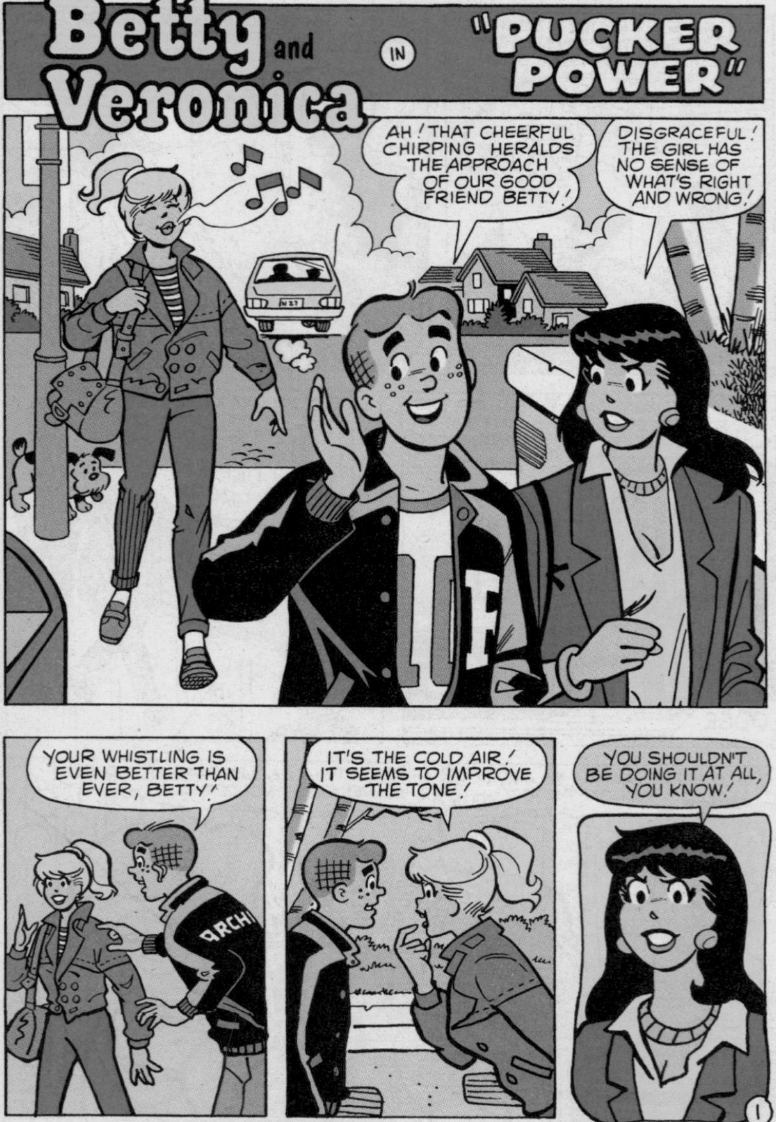
Betty and Veronica
IN
"PUCKER POWER"
AH! THAT CHEERFUL CHIRPING HERALDS THE APPROACH OF OUR GOOD FRIEND BETTY!
DISGRACEFUL! THE GIRL HAS NO SENSE OF WHAT'S RIGHT AND WRONG!
YOUR WHISTLING IS EVEN BETTER THAN EVER, BETTY!
IT'S THE COLD AIR! IT SEEMS TO IMPROVE THE TONE!
YOU SHOULDN'T BE DOING IT AT ALL, YOU KNOW!
1

Script: Frank Doyle / Pencils: Stan Goldberg / Inks: Hy Eisman / Letters: Bill Yoshida

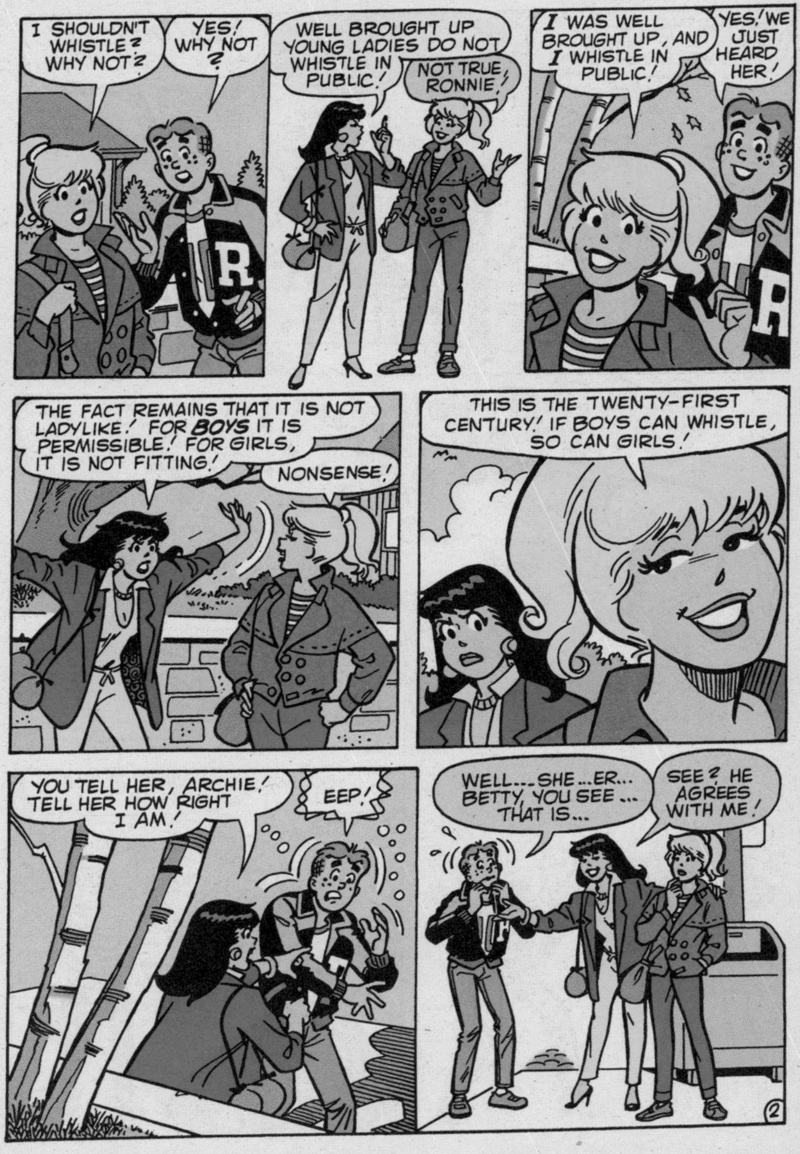
I SHOULDN'T WHISTLE? WHY NOT?
YES! WHY NOT?
WELL BROUGHT UP YOUNG LADIES DO NOT WHISTLE IN PUBLIC!
NOT TRUE, RONNIE!
I WAS WELL BROUGHT UP, AND I WHISTLE IN PUBLIC!
YES! WE JUST HEARD HER!
THE FACT REMAINS THAT IT IS NOT LADYLIKE! FOR BOYS IT IS PERMISSIBLE! FOR GIRLS, IT IS NOT FITTING!
NONSENSE!
THIS IS THE TWENTY-FIRST CENTURY! IF BOYS CAN WHISTLE, SO CAN GIRLS!
YOU TELL HER, ARCHIE! TELL HER HOW RIGHT I AM!
EEP!
WELL... SHE... ER... BETTY, YOU SEE... THAT IS...
SEE? HE AGREES WITH ME!
2

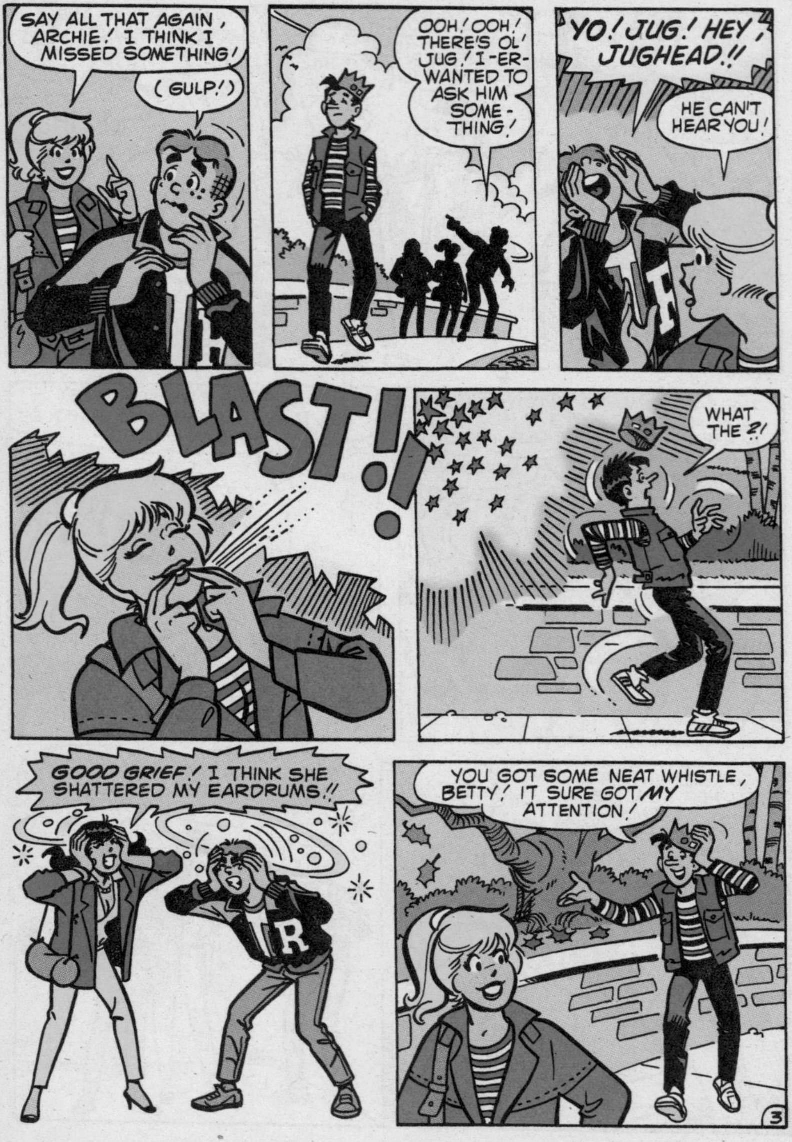

SAY ALL THAT AGAIN, ARCHIE! I THINK I MISSED SOMETHING!
(GULP!)
OOH! OOH! THERE'S OL' JUG! I-ER-WANTED TO ASK HIM SOME-THING!
YO! JUG! HEY, JUGHEAD!!
HE CAN'T HEAR YOU!
BLAST!!
WHAT THE ?!
GOOD GRIEF! I THINK SHE SHATTERED MY EARDRUMS!!
YOU GOT SOME NEAT WHISTLE, BETTY! IT SURE GOT MY ATTENTION!
3

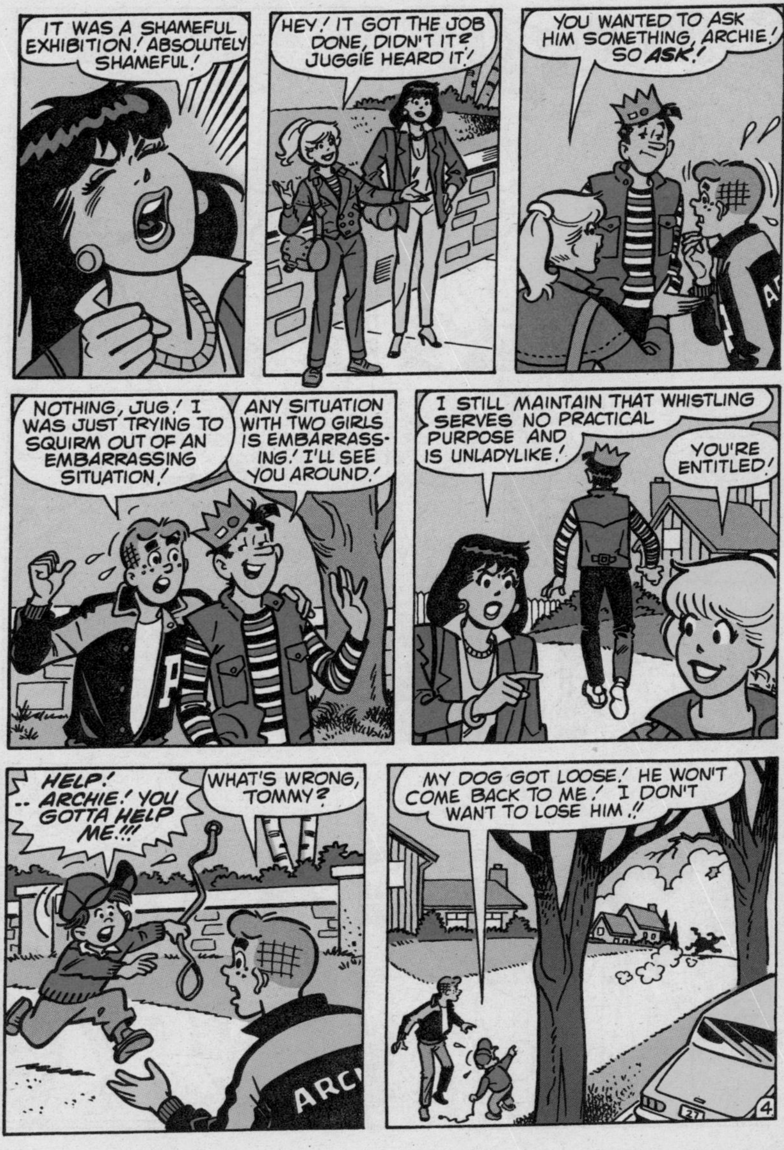
IT WAS A SHAMEFUL EXHIBITION! ABSOLUTELY SHAMEFUL!
HEY! IT GOT THE JOB DONE, DIDN'T IT? JUGGIE HEARD IT!
YOU WANTED TO ASK HIM SOMETHING, ARCHIE! SO ASK!
NOTHING, JUG! I WAS JUST TRYING TO SQUIRM OUT OF AN EMBARRASSING SITUATION!
ANY SITUATION WITH TWO GIRLS IS EMBARRASSING! I'LL SEE YOU AROUND!
I STILL MAINTAIN THAT WHISTLING SERVES NO PRACTICAL PURPOSE AND IS UNLADYLIKE!
YOU'RE ENTITLED!
HELP! .. ARCHIE! YOU GOTTA HELP ME!!!
WHAT'S WRONG, TOMMY?
ARCH
MY DOG GOT LOOSE! HE WON'T COME BACK TO ME! I DON'T WANT TO LOSE HIM!!
4

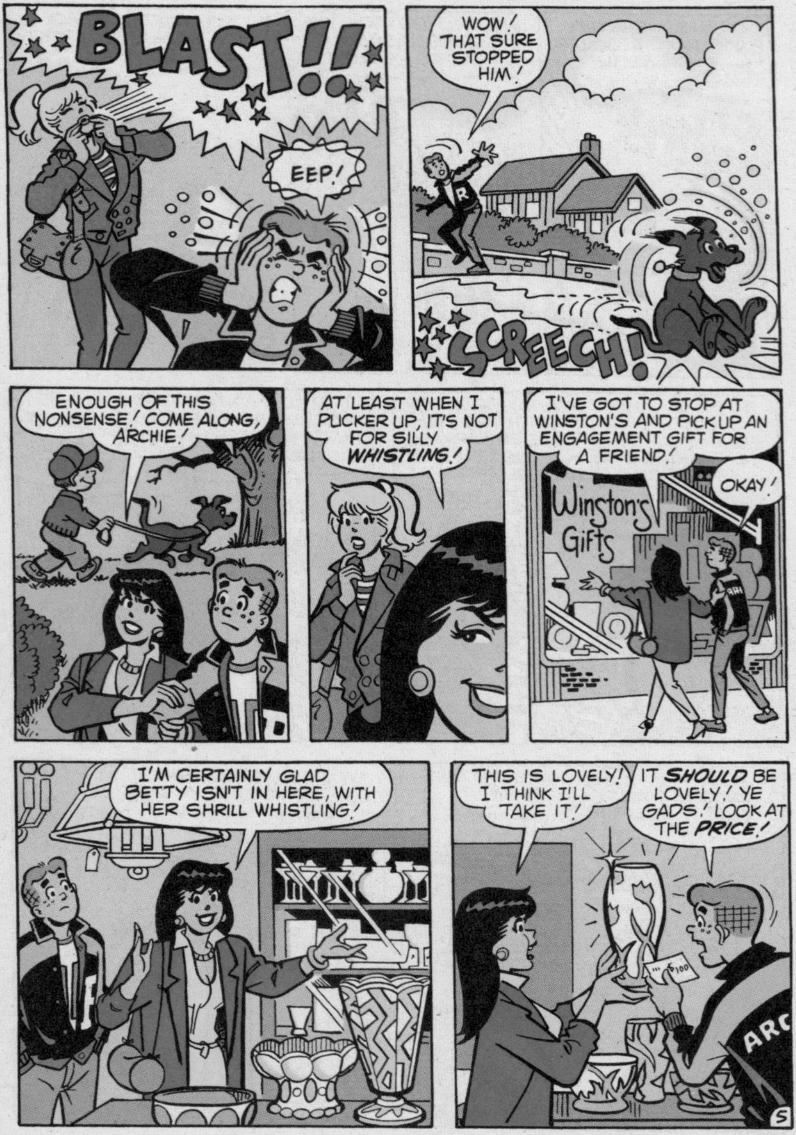
BLAST!!
EEP!
WOW! THAT SURE STOPPED HIM!
SCREECH!
ENOUGH OF THIS NONSENSE! COME ALONG, ARCHIE!
AT LEAST WHEN I PUCKER UP, IT'S NOT FOR SILLY WHISTLING!
I'VE GOT TO STOP AT WINSTON'S AND PICK UP AN ENGAGEMENT GIFT FOR A FRIEND!
Winston's Gifts
OKAY!
I'M CERTAINLY GLAD BETTY ISN'T IN HERE, WITH HER SHRILL WHISTLING!
THIS IS LOVELY! I THINK I'LL TAKE IT!
IT SHOULD BE LOVELY! YE GADS! LOOK AT THE PRICE!
$100
5

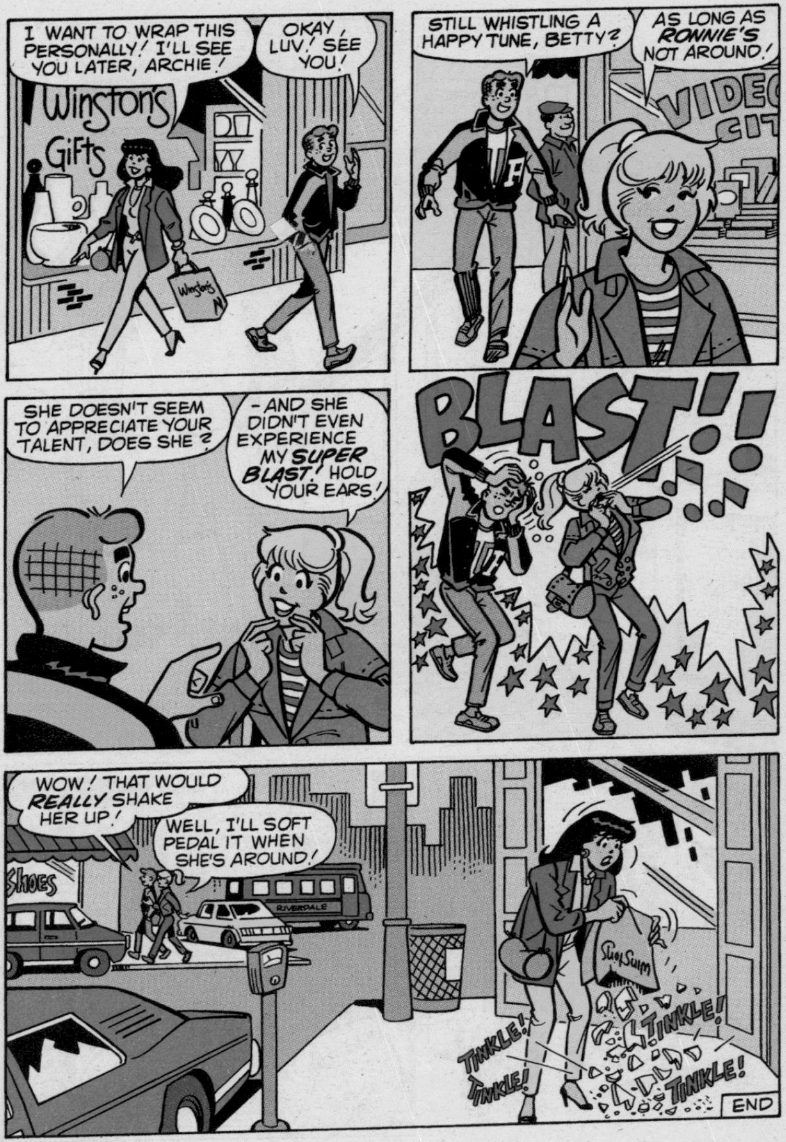
I WANT TO WRAP THIS PERSONALLY! I'LL SEE YOU LATER, ARCHIE!
OKAY, LUV! SEE YOU!
Winston's Gifts
STILL WHISTLING A HAPPY TUNE, BETTY?
AS LONG AS RONNIE'S NOT AROUND!
VIDEO CITY
SHE DOESN'T SEEM TO APPRECIATE YOUR TALENT, DOES SHE?
- AND SHE DIDN'T EVEN EXPERIENCE MY SUPER BLAST! HOLD YOUR EARS!
BLAST!!
WOW! THAT WOULD REALLY SHAKE HER UP!
WELL, I'LL SOFT PEDAL IT WHEN SHE'S AROUND!
SHOES
RIVERDALE
TINKLE!
TINKLE!
TINKLE!
TINKLE!
END

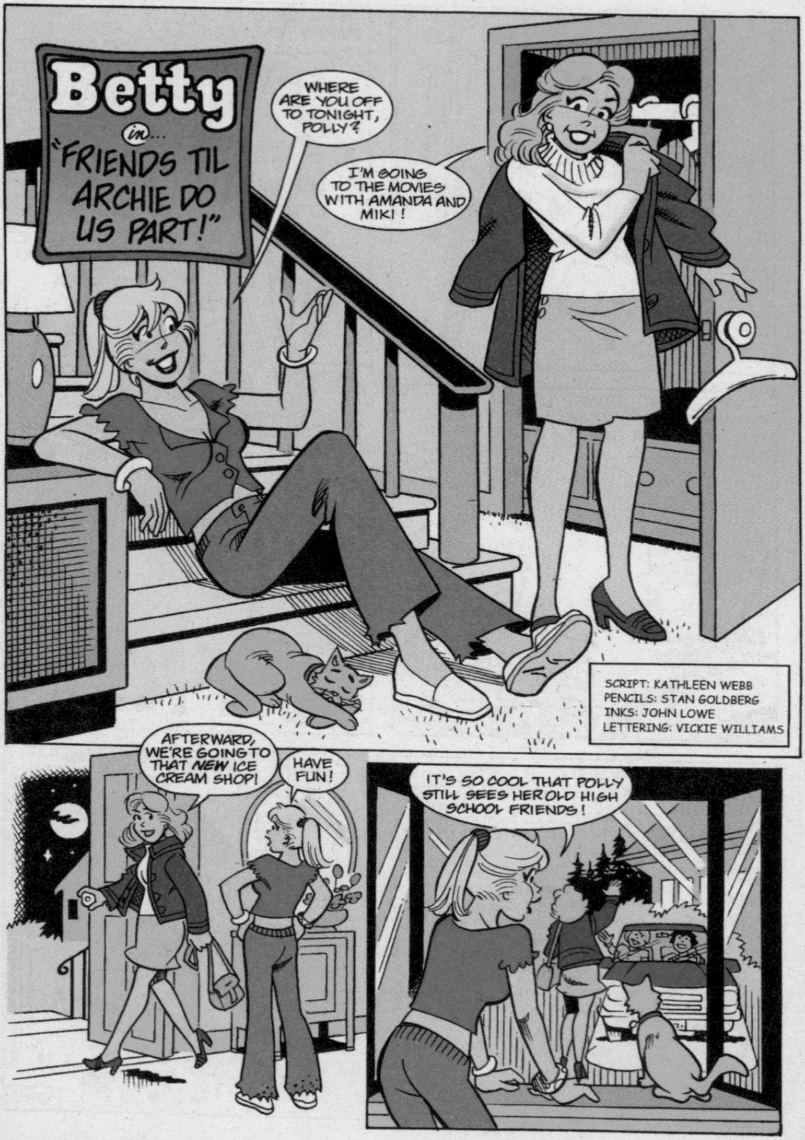
Betty
in...
"FRIENDS TIL ARCHIE DO US PART!"
WHERE ARE YOU OFF TO TONIGHT, POLLY?
I'M GOING TO THE MOVIES WITH AMANDA AND MIKI!
SCRIPT: KATHLEEN WEBB
PENCILS: STAN GOLDBERG
INKS: JOHN LOWE
LETTERING: VICKIE WILLIAMS
AFTERWARD, WE'RE GOING TO THAT NEW ICE CREAM SHOP!
HAVE FUN!
IT'S SO COOL THAT POLLY STILL SEES HER OLD HIGH SCHOOL FRIENDS!

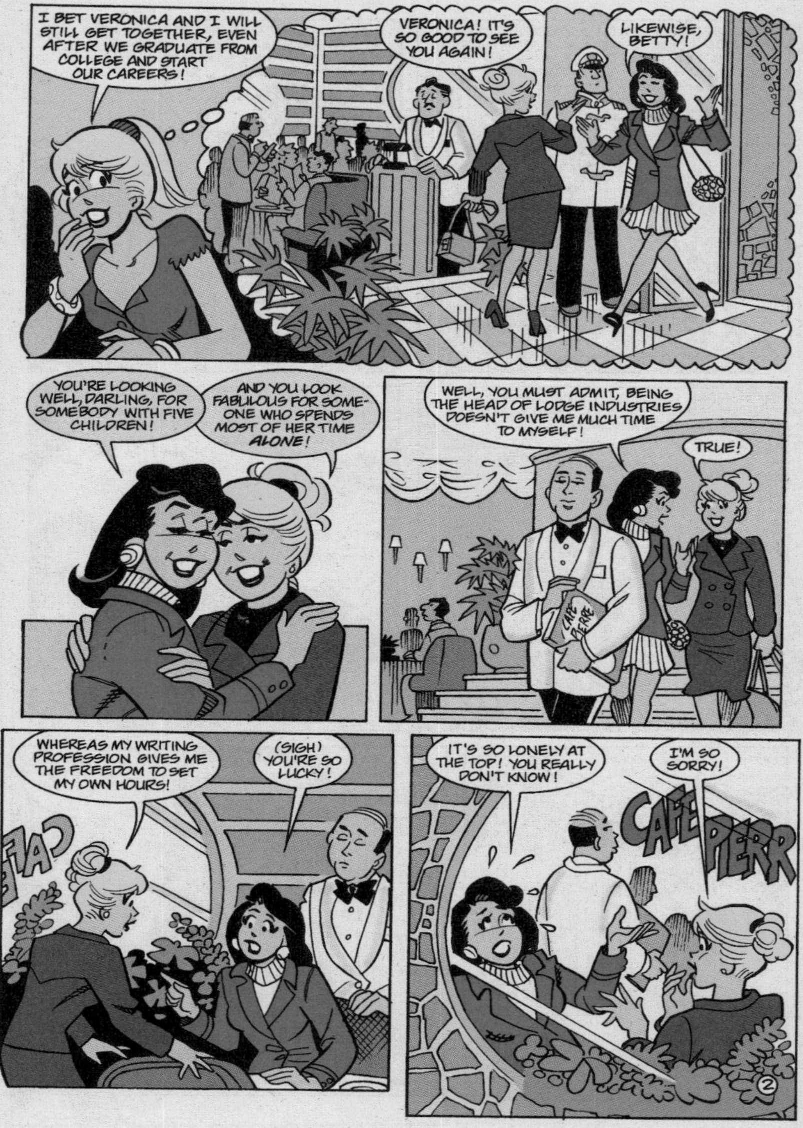

I BET VERONICA AND I WILL STILL GET TOGETHER, EVEN AFTER WE GRADUATE FROM COLLEGE AND START OUR CAREERS!
VERONICA! IT'S SO GOOD TO SEE YOU AGAIN!
LIKEWISE, BETTY!
YOU'RE LOOKING WELL, DARLING, FOR SOMEBODY WITH FIVE CHILDREN!
AND YOU LOOK FABULOUS FOR SOMEONE WHO SPENDS MOST OF HER TIME ALONE!
WELL, YOU MUST ADMIT, BEING THE HEAD OF LODGE INDUSTRIES DOESN'T GIVE ME MUCH TIME TO MYSELF!
TRUE!
CAFE PIERRE
WHEREAS MY WRITING PROFESSION GIVES ME THE FREEDOM TO SET MY OWN HOURS!
(SIGH) YOU'RE SO LUCKY!
IT'S SO LONELY AT THE TOP! YOU REALLY DON'T KNOW!
I'M SO SORRY!
CAFE PIERR

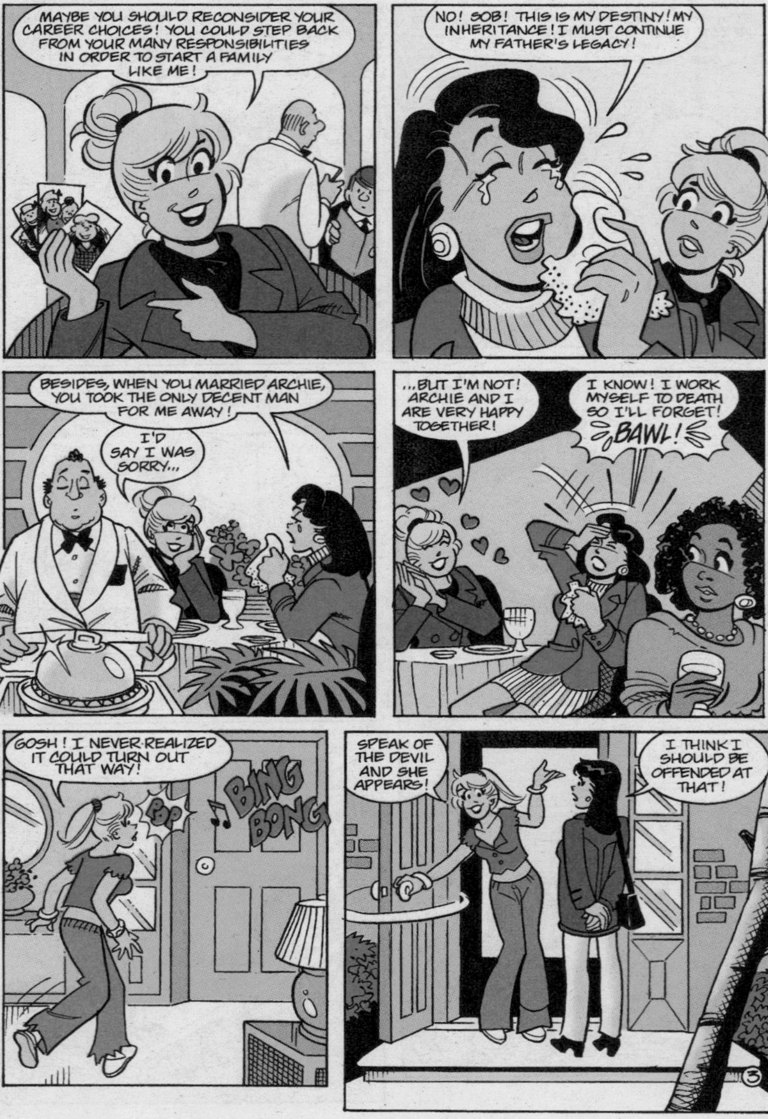
MAYBE YOU SHOULD RECONSIDER YOUR CAREER CHOICES! YOU COULD STEP BACK FROM YOUR MANY RESPONSIBILITIES IN ORDER TO START A FAMILY LIKE ME!
NO! SOB! THIS IS MY DESTINY! MY INHERITANCE! I MUST CONTINUE MY FATHER'S LEGACY!
BESIDES, WHEN YOU MARRIED ARCHIE, YOU TOOK THE ONLY DECENT MAN FOR ME AWAY!
I'D SAY I WAS SORRY...
...BUT I'M NOT! ARCHIE AND I ARE VERY HAPPY TOGETHER!
I KNOW! I WORK MYSELF TO DEATH SO I'LL FORGET!
BAWL!
GOSH! I NEVER REALIZED IT COULD TURN OUT THAT WAY!
BING BONG
SPEAK OF THE DEVIL AND SHE APPEARS!
I THINK I SHOULD BE OFFENDED AT THAT!
3

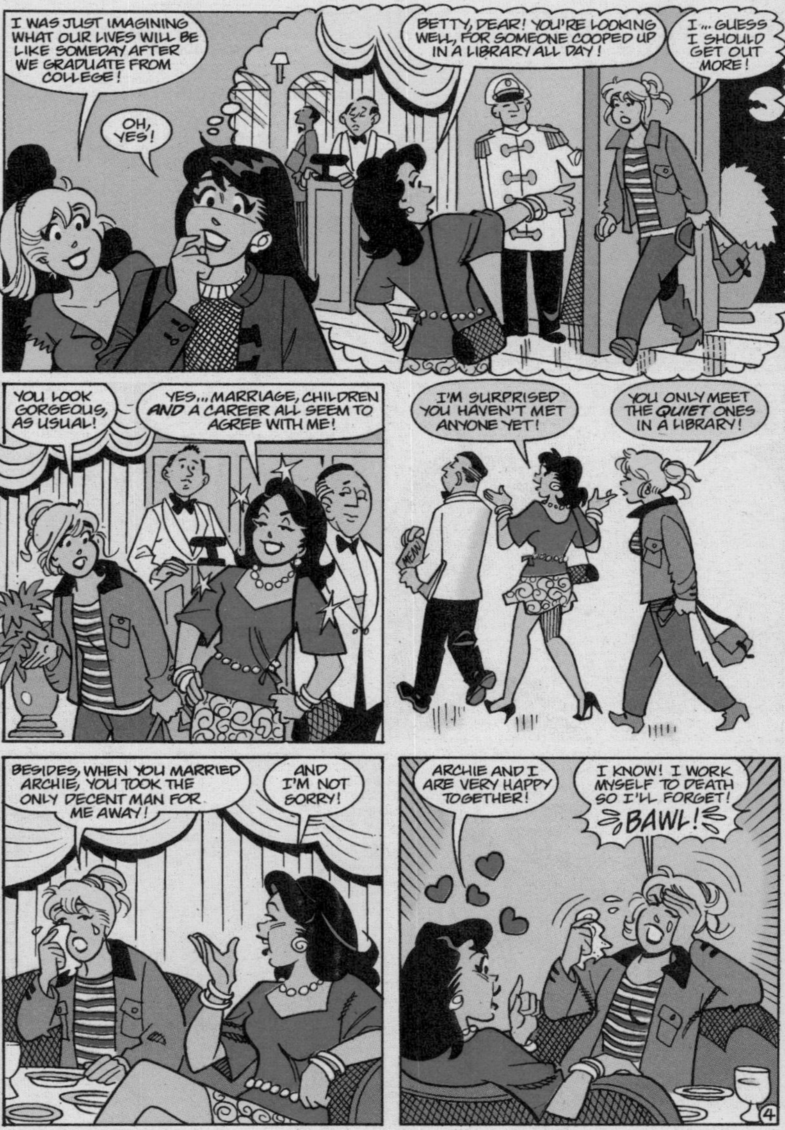
I WAS JUST IMAGINING WHAT OUR LIVES WILL BE LIKE SOMEDAY AFTER WE GRADUATE FROM COLLEGE!
OH, YES!
BETTY, DEAR! YOU'RE LOOKING WELL, FOR SOMEONE COOPED UP IN A LIBRARY ALL DAY!
I... GUESS I SHOULD GET OUT MORE!
YOU LOOK GORGEOUS, AS USUAL!
YES... MARRIAGE, CHILDREN AND A CAREER ALL SEEM TO AGREE WITH ME!
I'M SURPRISED YOU HAVEN'T MET ANYONE YET!
YOU ONLY MEET THE QUIET ONES IN A LIBRARY!
BESIDES, WHEN YOU MARRIED ARCHIE, YOU TOOK THE ONLY DECENT MAN FOR ME AWAY!
AND I'M NOT SORRY!
ARCHIE AND I ARE VERY HAPPY TOGETHER!
I KNOW! I WORK MYSELF TO DEATH SO I'LL FORGET!
BAWL!
4

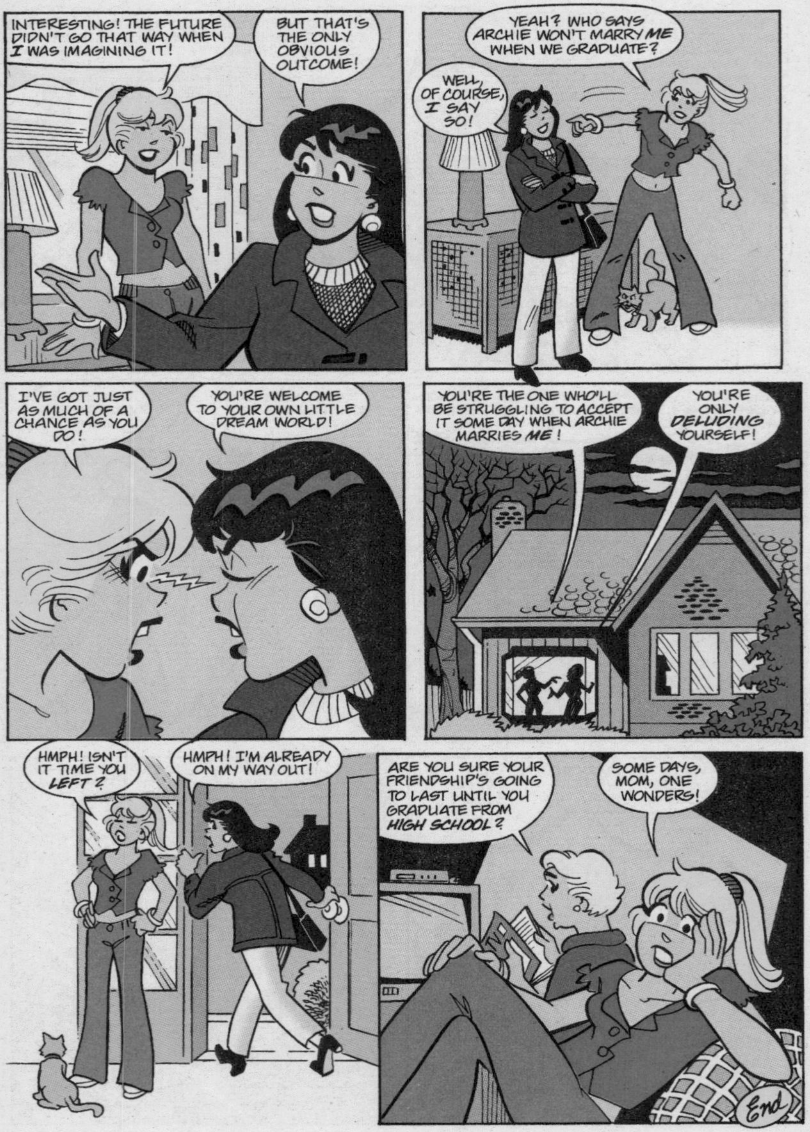
INTERESTING! THE FUTURE DIDN'T GO THAT WAY WHEN I WAS IMAGINING IT!
BUT THAT'S THE ONLY OBVIOUS OUTCOME!
YEAH? WHO SAYS ARCHIE WON'T MARRY ME WHEN WE GRADUATE?
WELL, OF COURSE, I SAY SO!
I'VE GOT JUST AS MUCH OF A CHANCE AS YOU DO!
YOU'RE WELCOME TO YOUR OWN LITTLE DREAM WORLD!
YOU'RE THE ONE WHO'LL BE STRUGGLING TO ACCEPT IT SOME DAY WHEN ARCHIE MARRIES ME!
YOU'RE ONLY DELUDING YOURSELF!
HMPH! ISN'T IT TIME YOU LEFT?
HMPH! I'M ALREADY ON MY WAY OUT!
ARE YOU SURE YOUR FRIENDSHIP'S GOING TO LAST UNTIL YOU GRADUATE FROM HIGH SCHOOL?
SOME DAYS, MOM, ONE WONDERS!
End

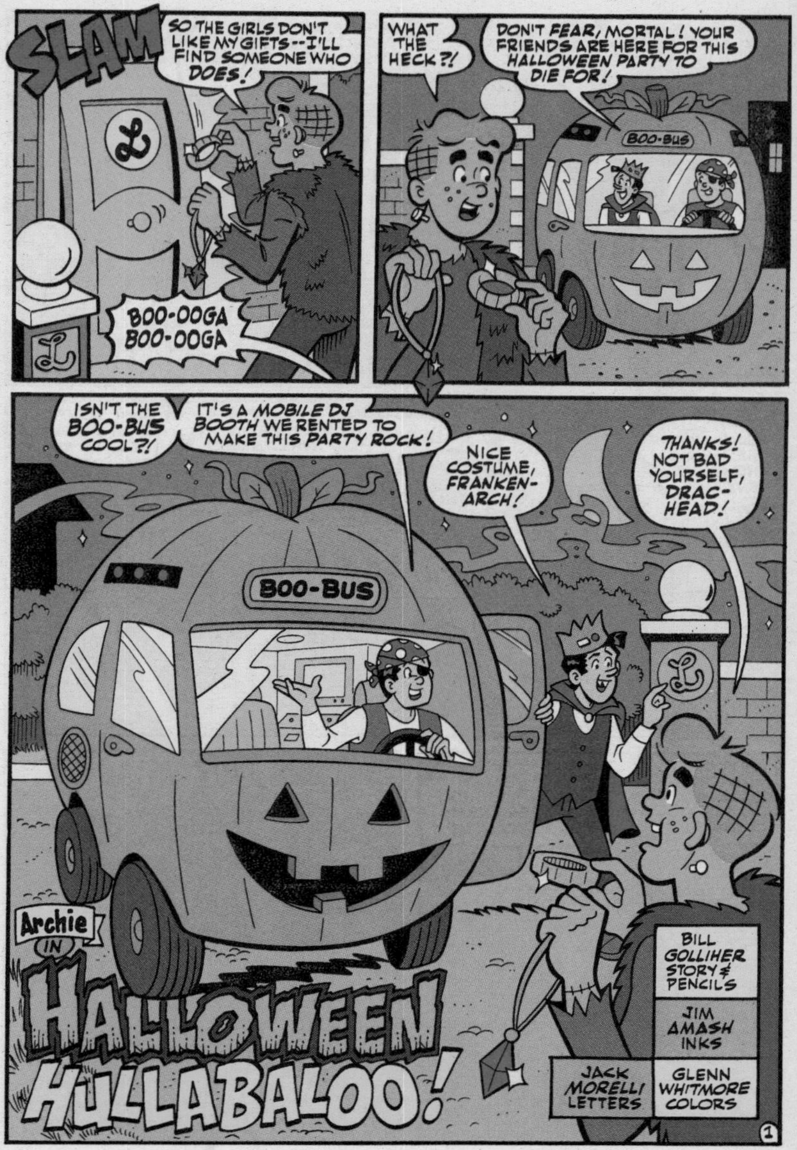
SLAM
SO THE GIRLS DON'T LIKE MY GIFTS--I'LL FIND SOMEONE WHO DOES!
BOO-OOGA BOO-OOGA
WHAT THE HECK?!
DON'T FEAR, MORTAL! YOUR FRIENDS ARE HERE FOR THIS HALLOWEEN PARTY TO DIE FOR!
BOO-BUS
ISN'T THE BOO-BUS COOL?!
IT'S A MOBILE DJ BOOTH WE RENTED TO MAKE THIS PARTY ROCK!
NICE COSTUME, FRANKEN-ARCH!
THANKS! NOT BAD YOURSELF, DRAC-HEAD!
BOO-BUS
Archie IN
HALLOWEEN HULLABALOO!
BILL GOLLIHER STORY & PENCILS
JIM AMASH INKS
JACK MORELLI LETTERS
GLENN WHITMORE COLORS
1

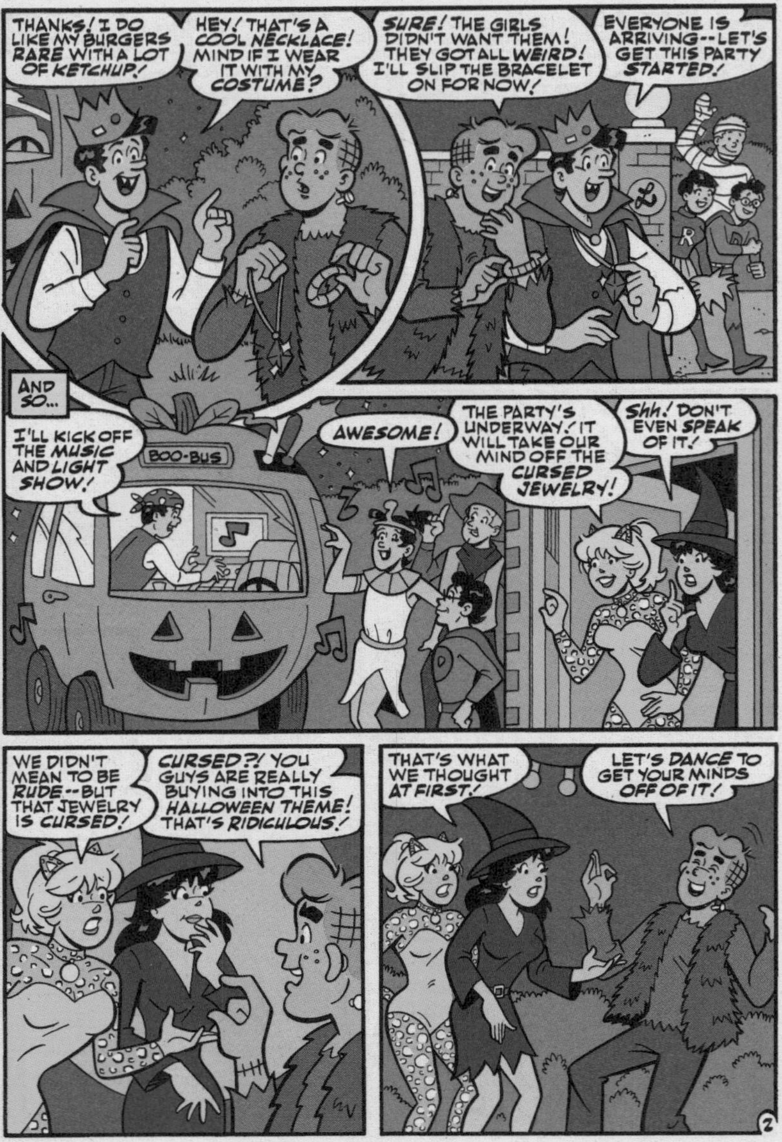
THANKS! I DO LIKE MY BURGERS RARE WITH A LOT OF KETCHUP!
HEY! THAT'S A COOL NECKLACE! MIND IF I WEAR IT WITH MY COSTUME?
SURE! THE GIRLS DIDN'T WANT THEM! THEY GOT ALL WEIRD! I'LL SLIP THE BRACELET ON FOR NOW!
EVERYONE IS ARRIVING--LET'S GET THIS PARTY STARTED!
AND SO...
I'LL KICK OFF THE MUSIC AND LIGHT SHOW!
BOO-BUS
AWESOME!
THE PARTY'S UNDERWAY! IT WILL TAKE OUR MIND OFF THE CURSED JEWELRY!
Shh! DON'T EVEN SPEAK OF IT!
WE DIDN'T MEAN TO BE RUDE--BUT THAT JEWELRY IS CURSED!
CURSED?! YOU GUYS ARE REALLY BUYING INTO THIS HALLOWEEN THEME! THAT'S RIDICULOUS!
THAT'S WHAT WE THOUGHT AT FIRST!
LET'S DANCE TO GET YOUR MINDS OFF OF IT!
2

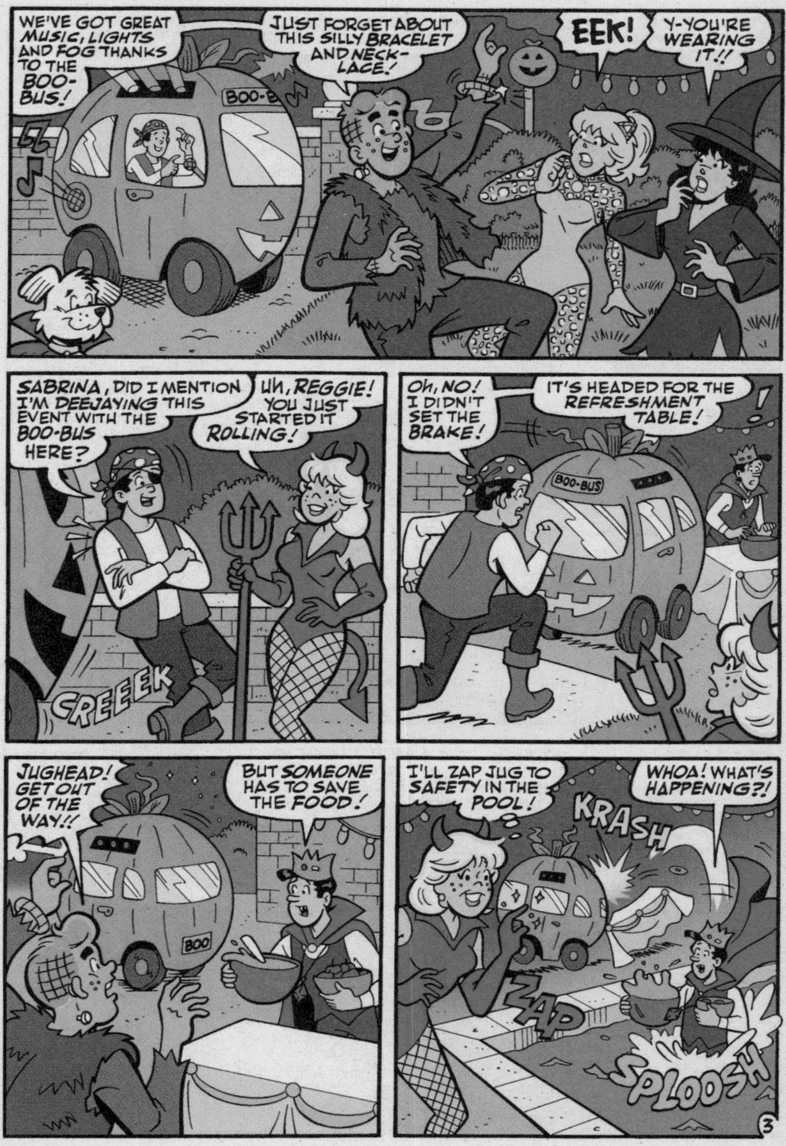
WE'VE GOT GREAT MUSIC, LIGHTS AND FOG THANKS TO THE BOO-BUS!
JUST FORGET ABOUT THIS SILLY BRACELET AND NECK-LACE!
EEK!
Y-YOU'RE WEARING IT!!
BOO-B
SABRINA, DID I MENTION I'M DEEJAYING THIS EVENT WITH THE BOO-BUS HERE?
UH, REGGIE! YOU JUST STARTED IT ROLLING!
CREEEEK
OH, NO! I DIDN'T SET THE BRAKE!
IT'S HEADED FOR THE REFRESHMENT TABLE!
!
BOO-BUS
JUGHEAD! GET OUT OF THE WAY!!
BUT SOMEONE HAS TO SAVE THE FOOD!
BOO
I'LL ZAP JUG TO SAFETY IN THE POOL!
WHOA! WHAT'S HAPPENING?!
KRASH
ZAP
SPLOOSH

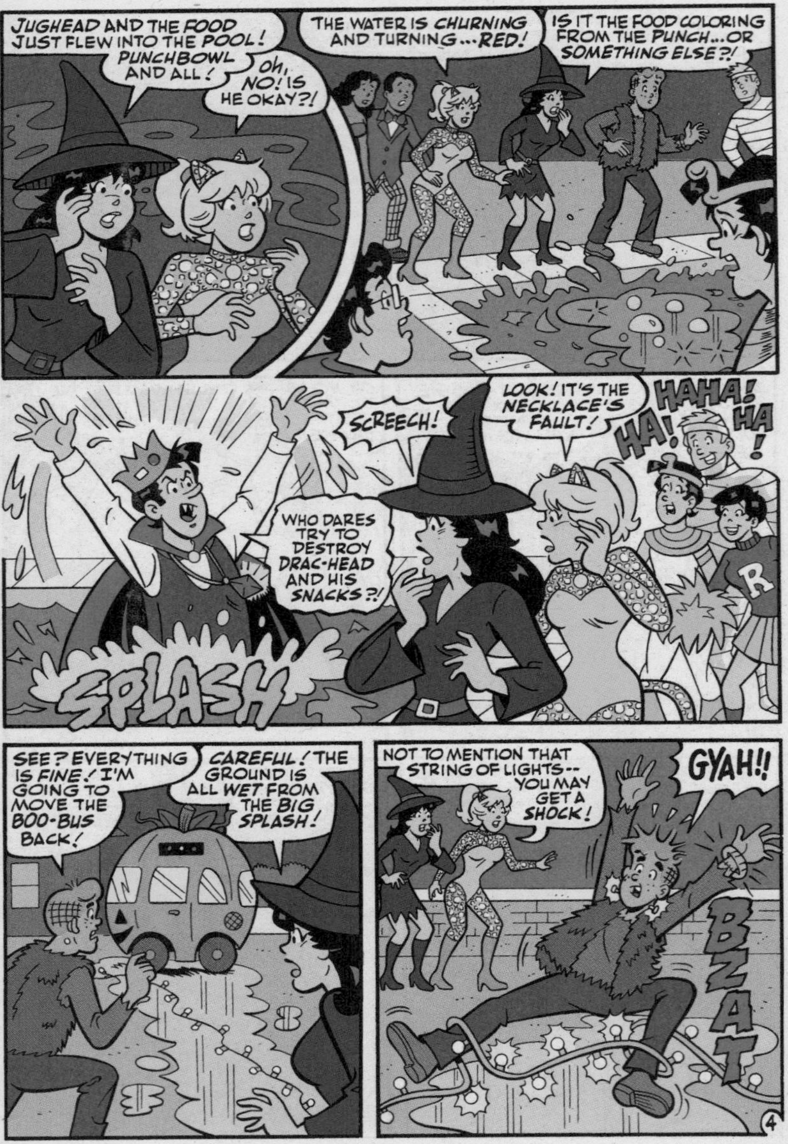
JUGHEAD AND THE FOOD JUST FLEW INTO THE POOL!
PUNCHBOWL AND ALL!
OH, NO! IS HE OKAY?!
THE WATER IS CHURNING AND TURNING... RED!
IS IT THE FOOD COLORING FROM THE PUNCH... OR SOMETHING ELSE?!
SCREECH!
LOOK! IT'S THE NECKLACE'S FAULT!
HAHA! HA! HA!
WHO DARES TRY TO DESTROY DRAC-HEAD AND HIS SNACKS?!
SPLASH
SEE? EVERYTHING IS FINE! I'M GOING TO MOVE THE BOO-BUS BACK!
CAREFUL! THE GROUND IS ALL WET FROM THE BIG SPLASH!
NOT TO MENTION THAT STRING OF LIGHTS-- YOU MAY GET A SHOCK!
GYAH!!
BZZAT

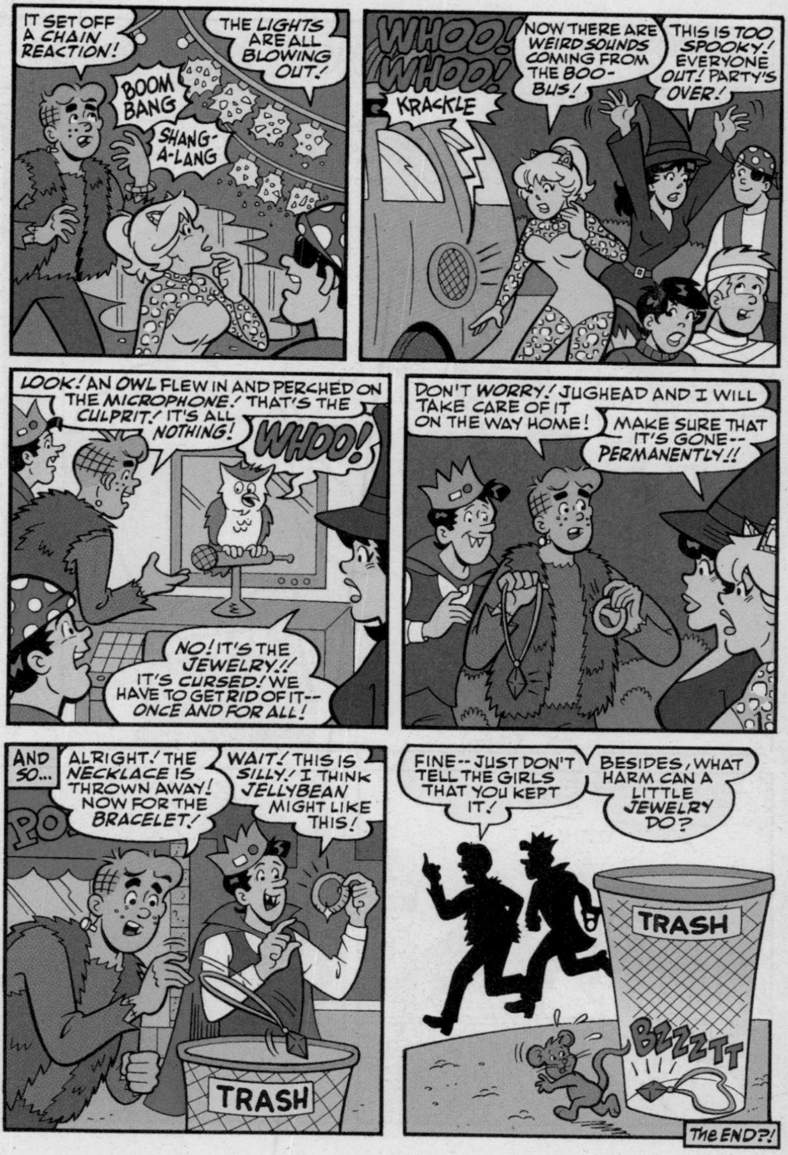

IT SET OFF A CHAIN REACTION!
THE LIGHTS ARE ALL BLOWING OUT!
BOOM BANG
SHANG-A-LANG
WHOO! WHOO!
KRACKLE
NOW THERE ARE WEIRD SOUNDS COMING FROM THE BOO-BUS!
THIS IS TOO SPOOKY! EVERYONE OUT! PARTY'S OVER!
LOOK! AN OWL FLEW IN AND PERCHED ON THE MICROPHONE! THAT'S THE CULPRIT! IT'S ALL NOTHING!
WHOO!
NO! IT'S THE JEWELRY!! IT'S CURSED! WE HAVE TO GET RID OF IT-- ONCE AND FOR ALL!
DON'T WORRY! JUGHEAD AND I WILL TAKE CARE OF IT ON THE WAY HOME!
MAKE SURE THAT IT'S GONE-- PERMANENTLY!!
AND SO...
ALRIGHT! THE NECKLACE IS THROWN AWAY! NOW FOR THE BRACELET!
WAIT! THIS IS SILLY! I THINK JELLYBEAN MIGHT LIKE THIS!
TRASH
FINE-- JUST DON'T TELL THE GIRLS THAT YOU KEPT IT!
BESIDES, WHAT HARM CAN A LITTLE JEWELRY DO?
TRASH
BZZZTT
THE END?!

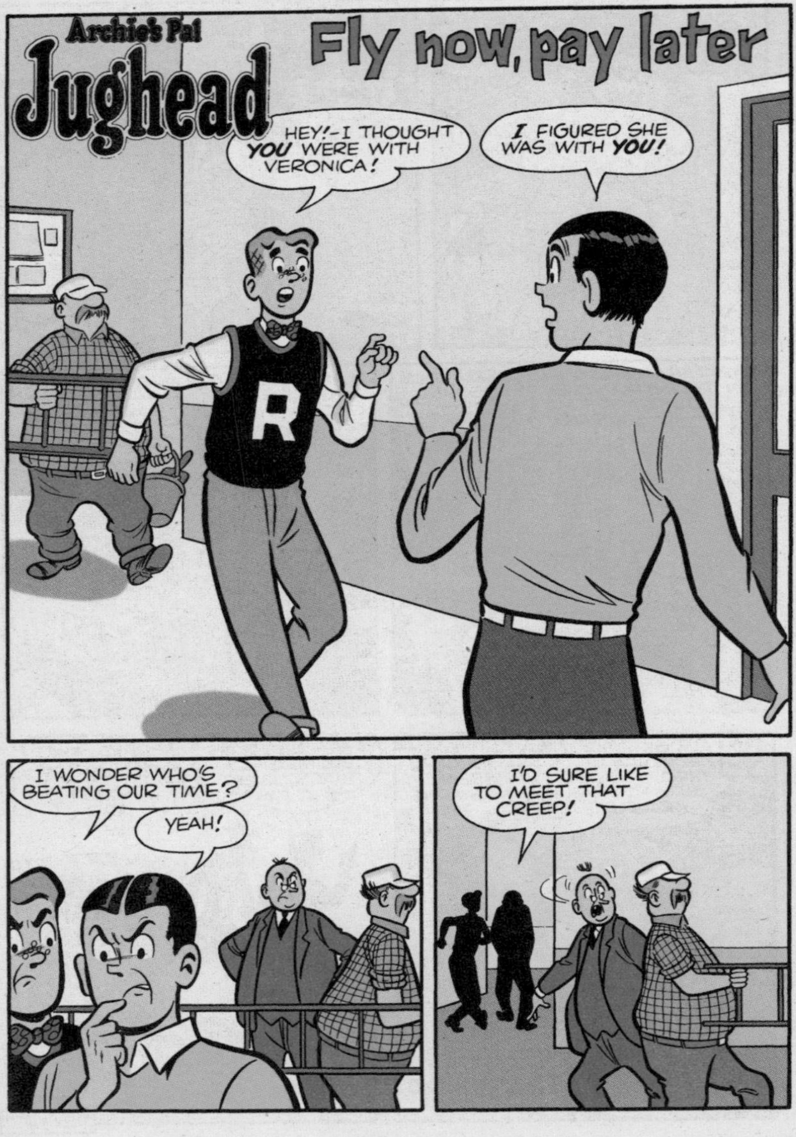
Archie's Pal
Jughead
Fly now, pay later
HEY!-I THOUGHT YOU WERE WITH VERONICA!
I FIGURED SHE WAS WITH YOU!
I WONDER WHO'S BEATING OUR TIME?
YEAH!
I'D SURE LIKE TO MEET THAT CREEP!

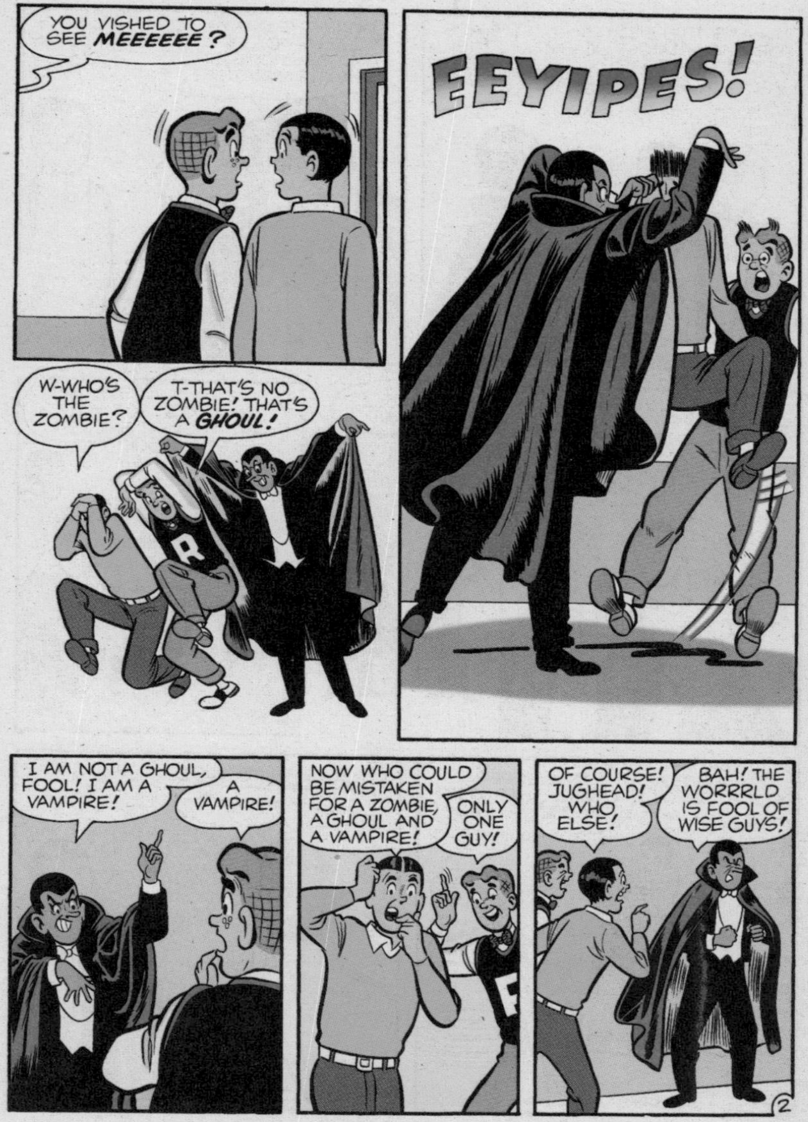
YOU VISHED TO SEE MEEEEEE?
EEYIPES!
W-WHO'S THE ZOMBIE?
T-THAT'S NO ZOMBIE! THAT'S A GHOUL!
I AM NOT A GHOUL, FOOL! I AM A VAMPIRE!
A VAMPIRE!
NOW WHO COULD BE MISTAKEN FOR A ZOMBIE, A GHOUL AND A VAMPIRE!
ONLY ONE GUY!
OF COURSE! JUGHEAD! WHO ELSE!
BAH! THE WORRRLD IS FOOL OF WISE GUYS!
2

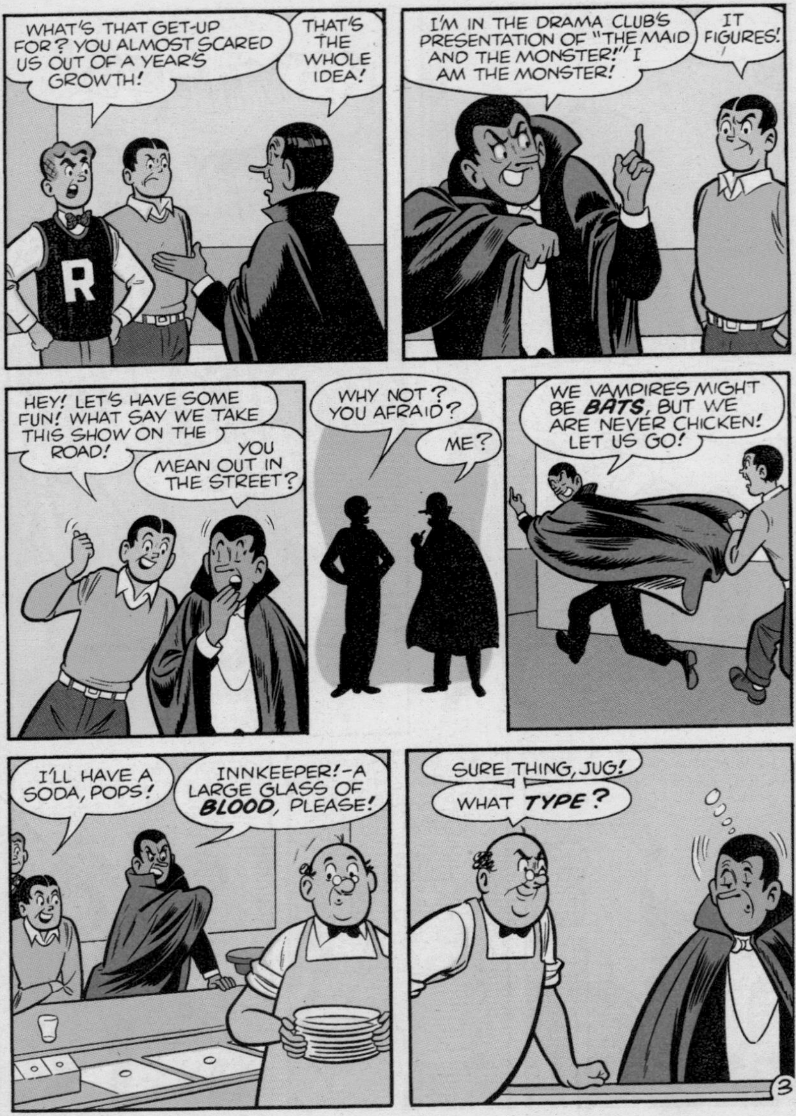

WHAT'S THAT GET-UP FOR? YOU ALMOST SCARED US OUT OF A YEAR'S GROWTH!
THAT'S THE WHOLE IDEA!
I'M IN THE DRAMA CLUB'S PRESENTATION OF "THE MAID AND THE MONSTER!" I AM THE MONSTER!
IT FIGURES!
HEY! LET'S HAVE SOME FUN! WHAT SAY WE TAKE THIS SHOW ON THE ROAD!
YOU MEAN OUT IN THE STREET?
WHY NOT? YOU AFRAID?
ME?
WE VAMPIRES MIGHT BE BATS, BUT WE ARE NEVER CHICKEN! LET US GO!
I'LL HAVE A SODA, POPS!
INNKEEPER!-A LARGE GLASS OF BLOOD, PLEASE!
SURE THING, JUG!
WHAT TYPE?

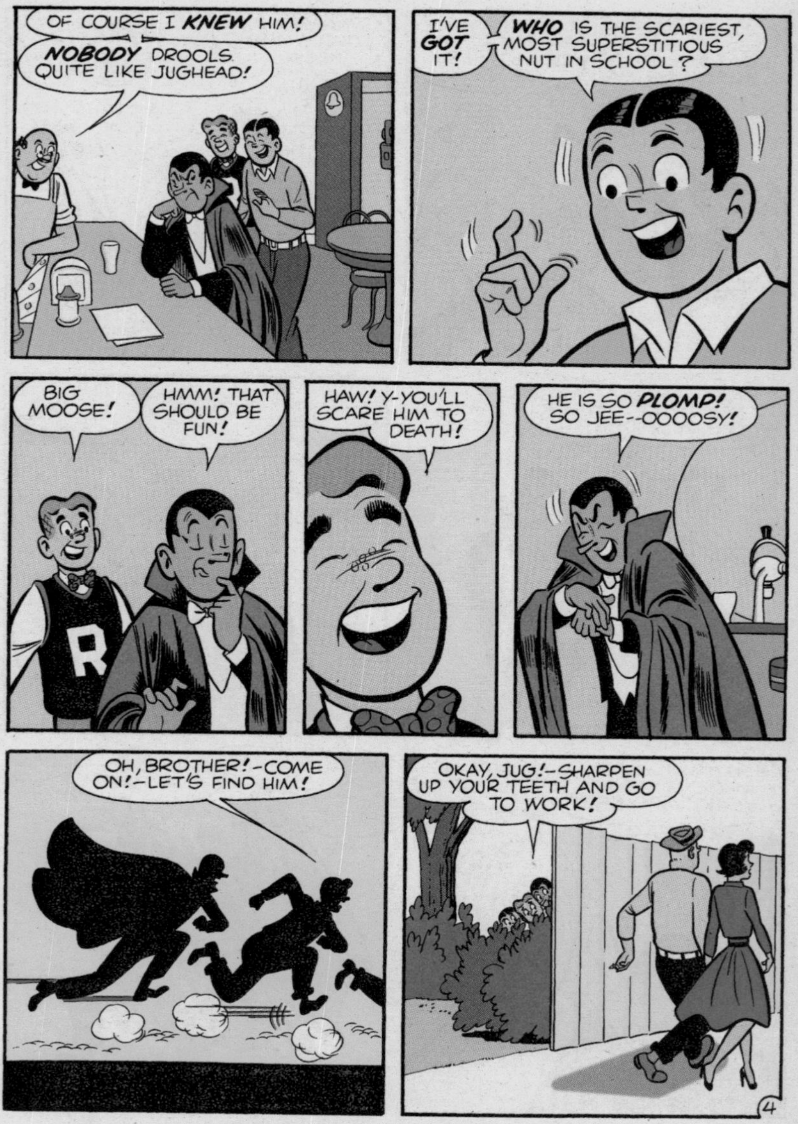

OF COURSE I KNEW HIM!
NOBODY DROOLS QUITE LIKE JUGHEAD!
I'VE GOT IT!
WHO IS THE SCARIEST, MOST SUPERSTITIOUS NUT IN SCHOOL?
BIG MOOSE!
HMM! THAT SHOULD BE FUN!
HAW! Y-YOU'LL SCARE HIM TO DEATH!
HE IS SO PLOMP! SO JEE--OOOOSY!
OH, BROTHER!-COME ON!-LET'S FIND HIM!
OKAY, JUG!-SHARPEN UP YOUR TEETH AND GO TO WORK!

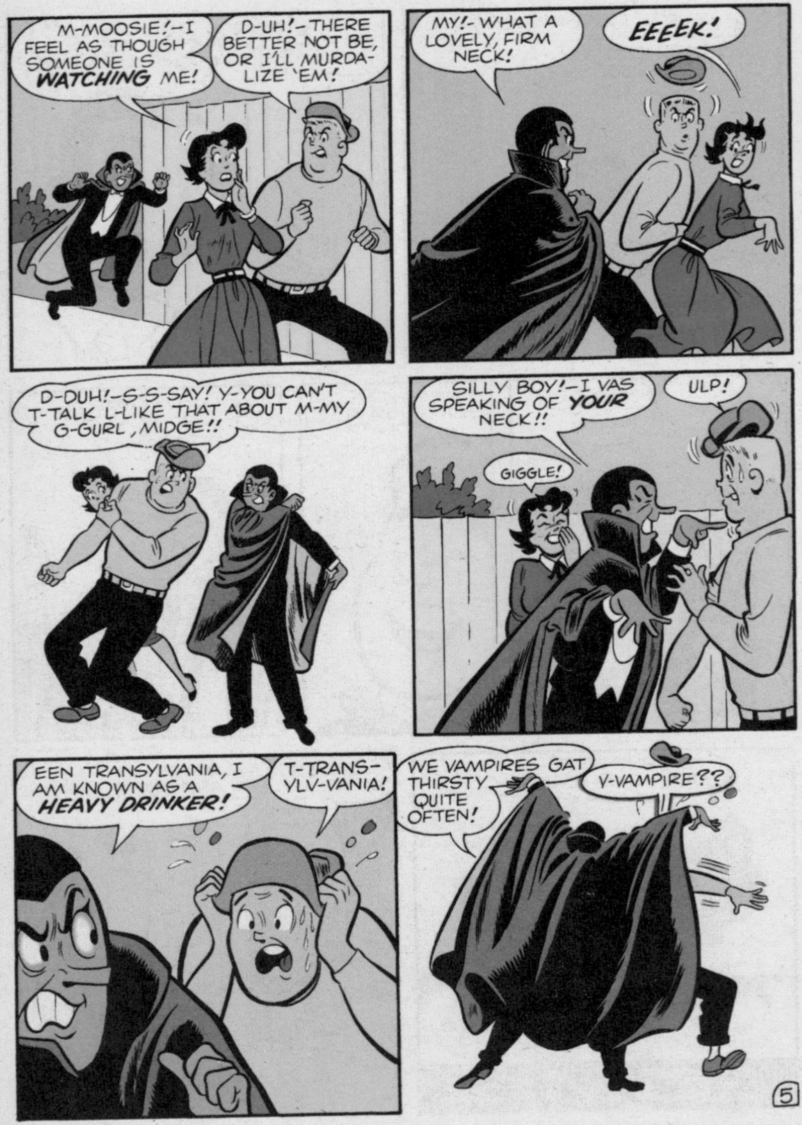

M-MOOSIE!–I FEEL AS THOUGH SOMEONE IS WATCHING ME!
D-UH!–THERE BETTER NOT BE, OR I'LL MURDA-LIZE 'EM!
MY!- WHAT A LOVELY, FIRM NECK!
EEEEK!
D-DUH!–S-S-SAY! Y-YOU CAN'T T-TALK L-LIKE THAT ABOUT M-MY G-GURL, MIDGE!!
SILLY BOY!–I VAS SPEAKING OF YOUR NECK!!
ULP!
GIGGLE!
EEN TRANSYLVANIA, I AM KNOWN AS A HEAVY DRINKER!
T-TRANS-YLV-VANIA!
WE VAMPIRES GAT THIRSTY QUITE OFTEN!
V-VAMPIRE??

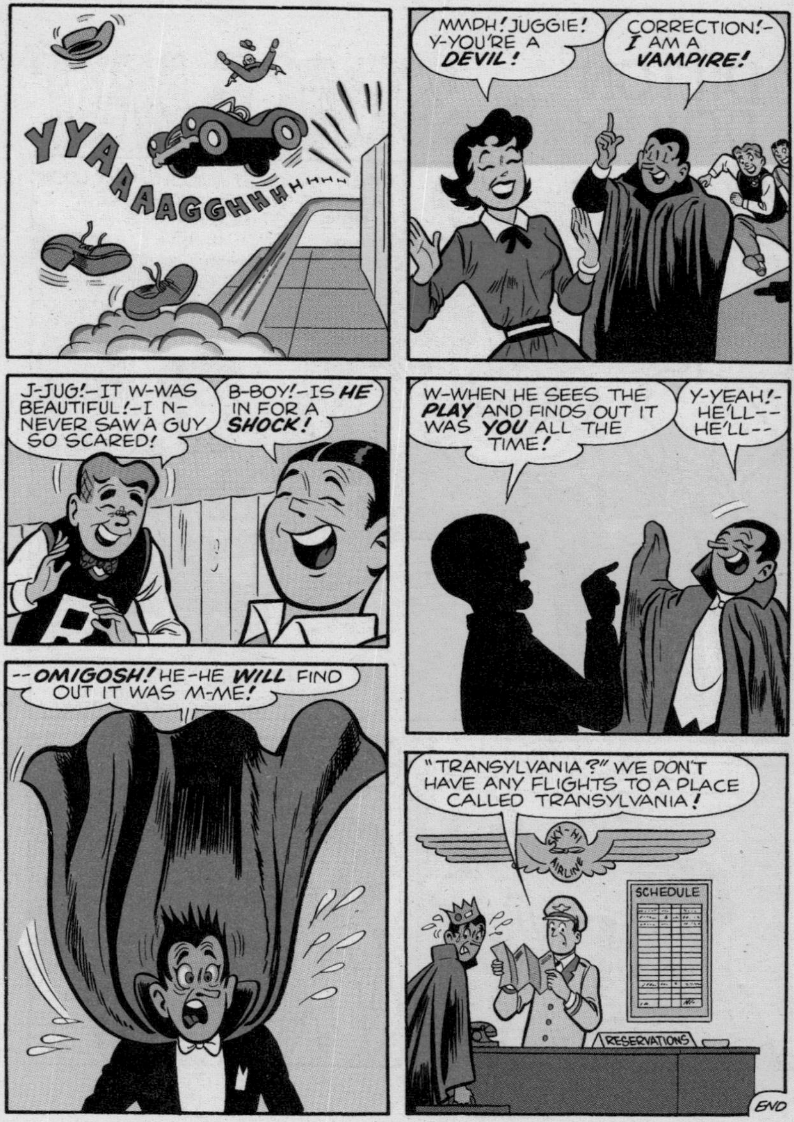
YYAAAAAGGHHHHHHHH
MMPH! JUGGIE! Y-YOU'RE A DEVIL!
CORRECTION!- I AM A VAMPIRE!
J-JUG!-IT W-WAS BEAUTIFUL!-I N-NEVER SAW A GUY SO SCARED!
B-BOY!-IS HE IN FOR A SHOCK!
W-WHEN HE SEES THE PLAY AND FINDS OUT IT WAS YOU ALL THE TIME!
Y-YEAH!- HE'LL-- HE'LL--
--OMIGOSH! HE-HE WILL FIND OUT IT WAS M-ME!
"TRANSYLVANIA?" WE DON'T HAVE ANY FLIGHTS TO A PLACE CALLED TRANSYLVANIA!
SKY-HI AIRLINE
SCHEDULE
RESERVATIONS
END

DILTON DOILEY IN "SPACE NUT"

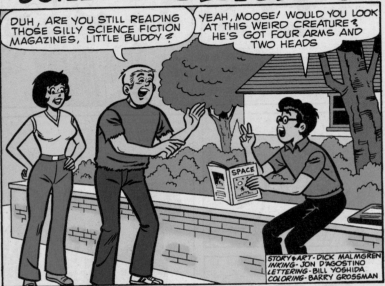

DUH, ARE YOU STILL READING THOSE SILLY SCIENCE FICTION MAGAZINES, LITTLE BUDDY?

YEAH, MOOSE! WOULD YOU LOOK AT THIS WEIRD CREATURE? HE'S GOT FOUR ARMS AND TWO HEADS

SPACE

STORY & ART - DICK MALMGREN
INKING - JON D'AGOSTINO
LETTERING - BILL YOSHIDA
COLORING - BARRY GROSSMAN

I WOULDN'T WANT TO RUN INTO HIM IN A DARK ALLEY!

LOOK AT WHAT DILTON'S AFRAID OF, MIDGE! HEE! HEE! HA!

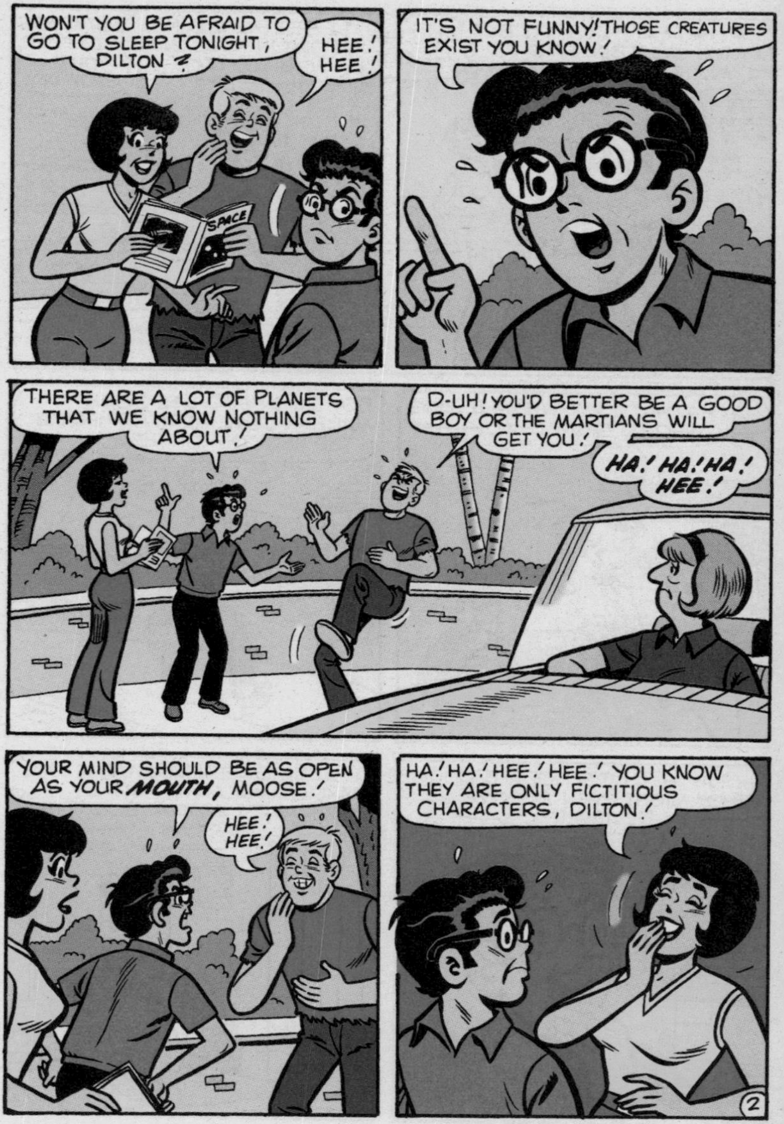
WON'T YOU BE AFRAID TO GO TO SLEEP TONIGHT, DILTON?
HEE! HEE!
SPACE
IT'S NOT FUNNY! THOSE CREATURES EXIST YOU KNOW!
THERE ARE A LOT OF PLANETS THAT WE KNOW NOTHING ABOUT!
D-UH! YOU'D BETTER BE A GOOD BOY OR THE MARTIANS WILL GET YOU!
HA! HA! HA! HEE!
YOUR MIND SHOULD BE AS OPEN AS YOUR MOUTH, MOOSE!
HEE! HEE!
HA! HA! HEE! HEE! YOU KNOW THEY ARE ONLY FICTITIOUS CHARACTERS, DILTON!
2

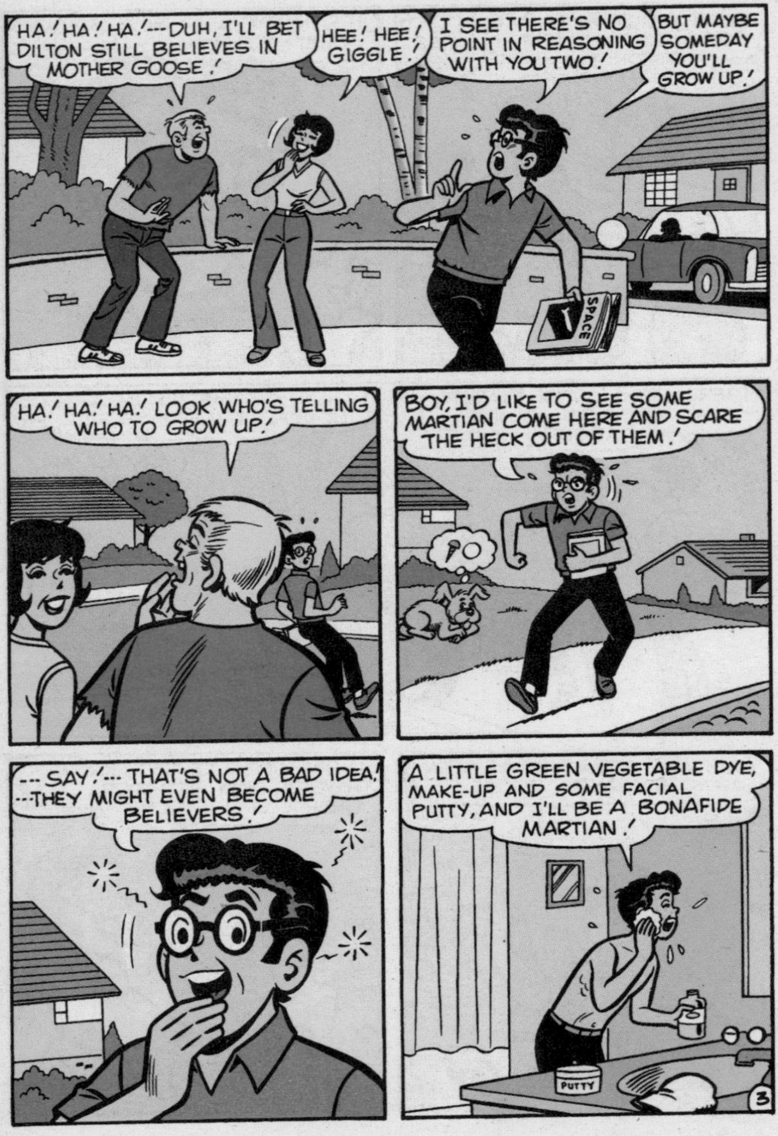
HA! HA! HA!---DUH, I'LL BET DILTON STILL BELIEVES IN MOTHER GOOSE!
HEE! HEE! GIGGLE!
I SEE THERE'S NO POINT IN REASONING WITH YOU TWO!
BUT MAYBE SOMEDAY YOU'LL GROW UP!
SPACE
HA! HA! HA! LOOK WHO'S TELLING WHO TO GROW UP!
BOY, I'D LIKE TO SEE SOME MARTIAN COME HERE AND SCARE THE HECK OUT OF THEM!
---SAY!--- THAT'S NOT A BAD IDEA! --THEY MIGHT EVEN BECOME BELIEVERS!
A LITTLE GREEN VEGETABLE DYE, MAKE-UP AND SOME FACIAL PUTTY, AND I'LL BE A BONAFIDE MARTIAN!
PUTTY
3

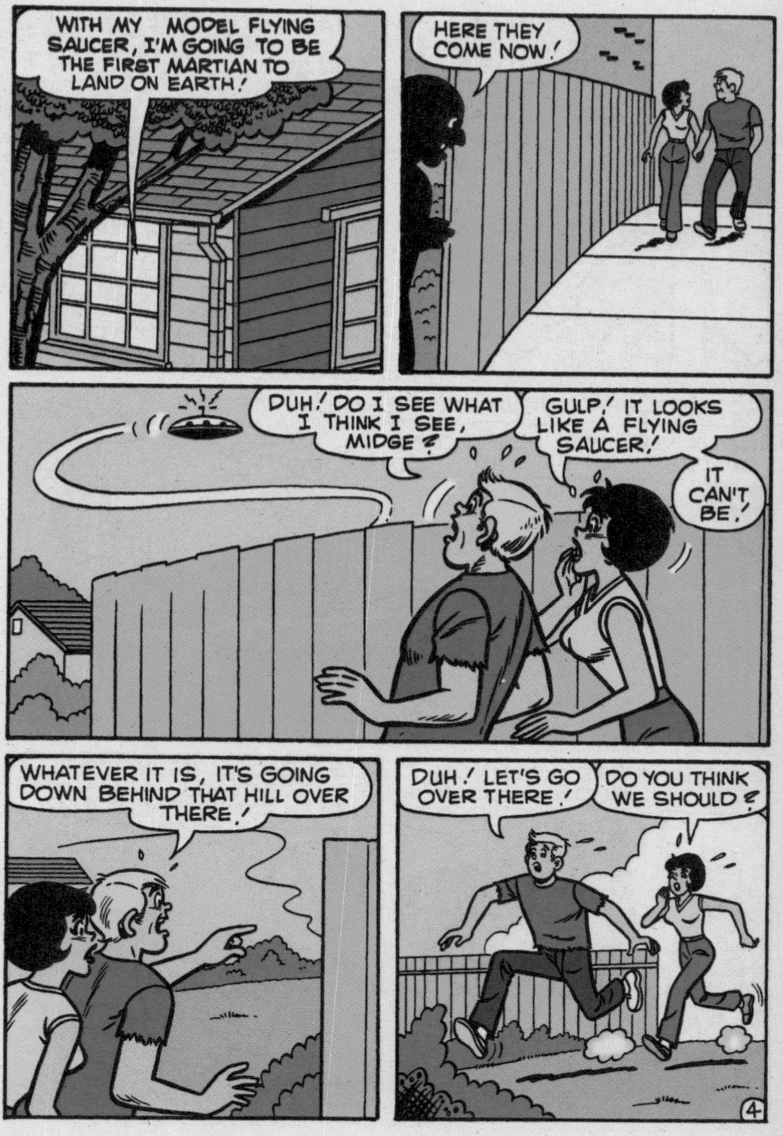
WITH MY MODEL FLYING SAUCER, I'M GOING TO BE THE FIRST MARTIAN TO LAND ON EARTH!
HERE THEY COME NOW!
DUH! DO I SEE WHAT I THINK I SEE, MIDGE?
GULP! IT LOOKS LIKE A FLYING SAUCER!
IT CAN'T BE!
WHATEVER IT IS, IT'S GOING DOWN BEHIND THAT HILL OVER THERE!
DUH! LET'S GO OVER THERE!
DO YOU THINK WE SHOULD?
4

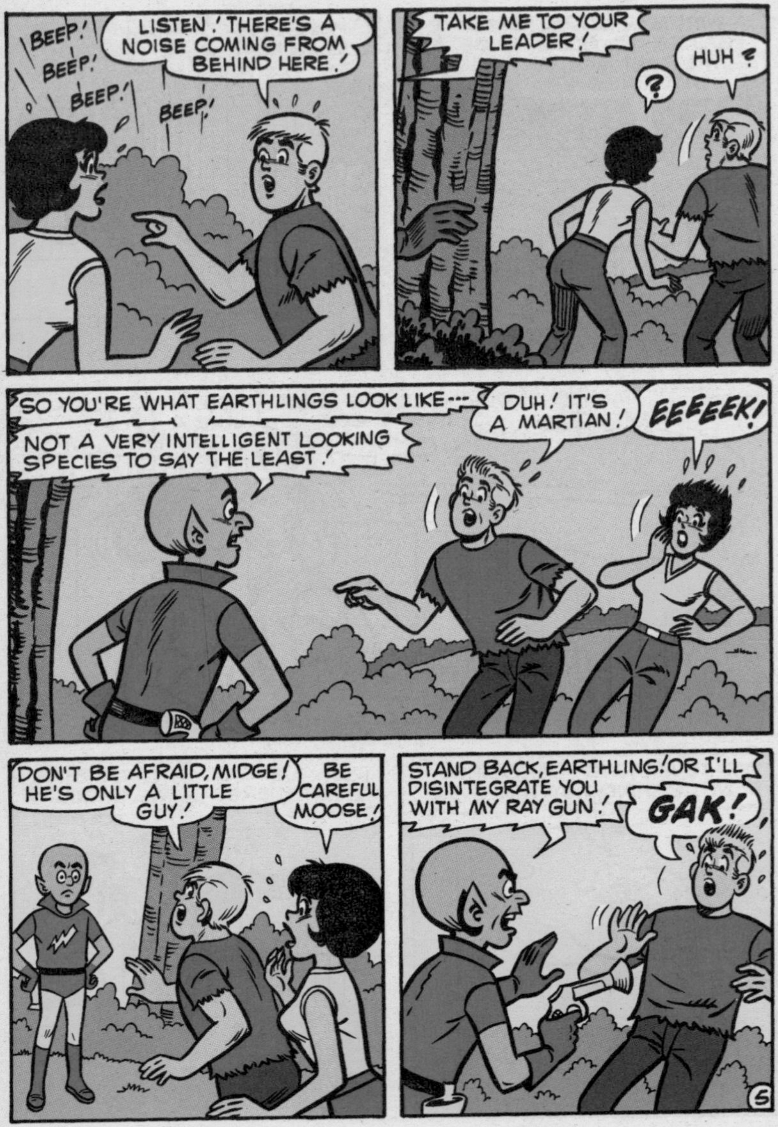
BEEP! BEEP! BEEP! BEEP!
LISTEN! THERE'S A NOISE COMING FROM BEHIND HERE!
TAKE ME TO YOUR LEADER!
?
HUH ?
SO YOU'RE WHAT EARTHLINGS LOOK LIKE---
NOT A VERY INTELLIGENT LOOKING SPECIES TO SAY THE LEAST!
DUH! IT'S A MARTIAN!
EEEEEK!
DON'T BE AFRAID, MIDGE! HE'S ONLY A LITTLE GUY!
BE CAREFUL MOOSE!
STAND BACK, EARTHLING! OR I'LL DISINTEGRATE YOU WITH MY RAY GUN!
GAK!
5

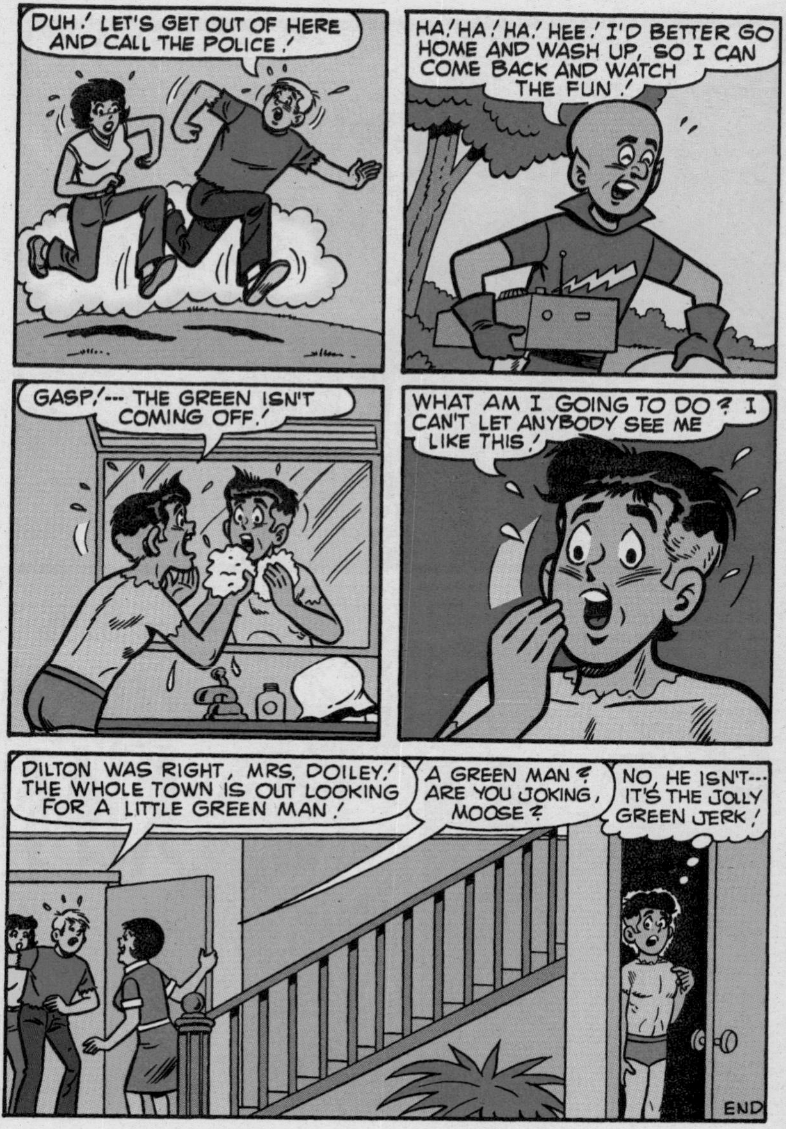
DUH! LET'S GET OUT OF HERE AND CALL THE POLICE!
HA! HA! HA! HEE! I'D BETTER GO HOME AND WASH UP, SO I CAN COME BACK AND WATCH THE FUN!
GASP! --- THE GREEN ISN'T COMING OFF!
WHAT AM I GOING TO DO? I CAN'T LET ANYBODY SEE ME LIKE THIS!
DILTON WAS RIGHT, MRS. DOILEY! THE WHOLE TOWN IS OUT LOOKING FOR A LITTLE GREEN MAN!
A GREEN MAN? ARE YOU JOKING, MOOSE?
NO, HE ISN'T--- IT'S THE JOLLY GREEN JERK!
END

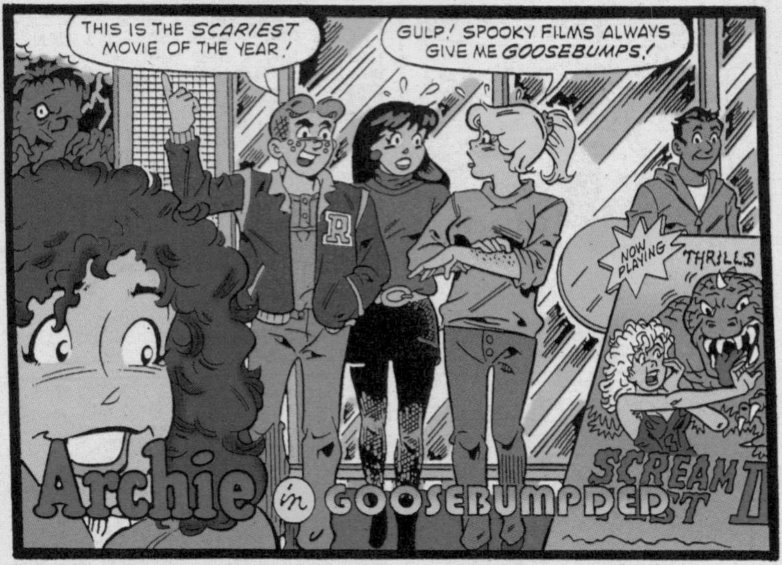
THIS IS THE SCARIEST MOVIE OF THE YEAR!
GULP! SPOOKY FILMS ALWAYS GIVE ME GOOSEBUMPS!
NOW PLAYING
THRILLS
SCREAM FEST II
Archie in GOOSEBUMPDED

Script: Mike Pellowski / Pencils: Fernando Ruiz / Inks: Ken Selig / Letters: Bill Yoshida

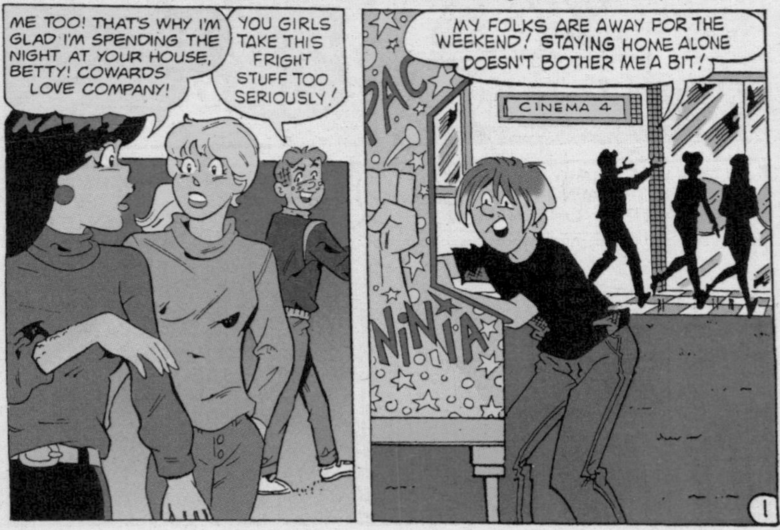
ME TOO! THAT'S WHY I'M GLAD I'M SPENDING THE NIGHT AT YOUR HOUSE, BETTY! COWARDS LOVE COMPANY!
YOU GIRLS TAKE THIS FRIGHT STUFF TOO SERIOUSLY!
MY FOLKS ARE AWAY FOR THE WEEKEND! STAYING HOME ALONE DOESN'T BOTHER ME A BIT!
CINEMA 4
NINJA
1

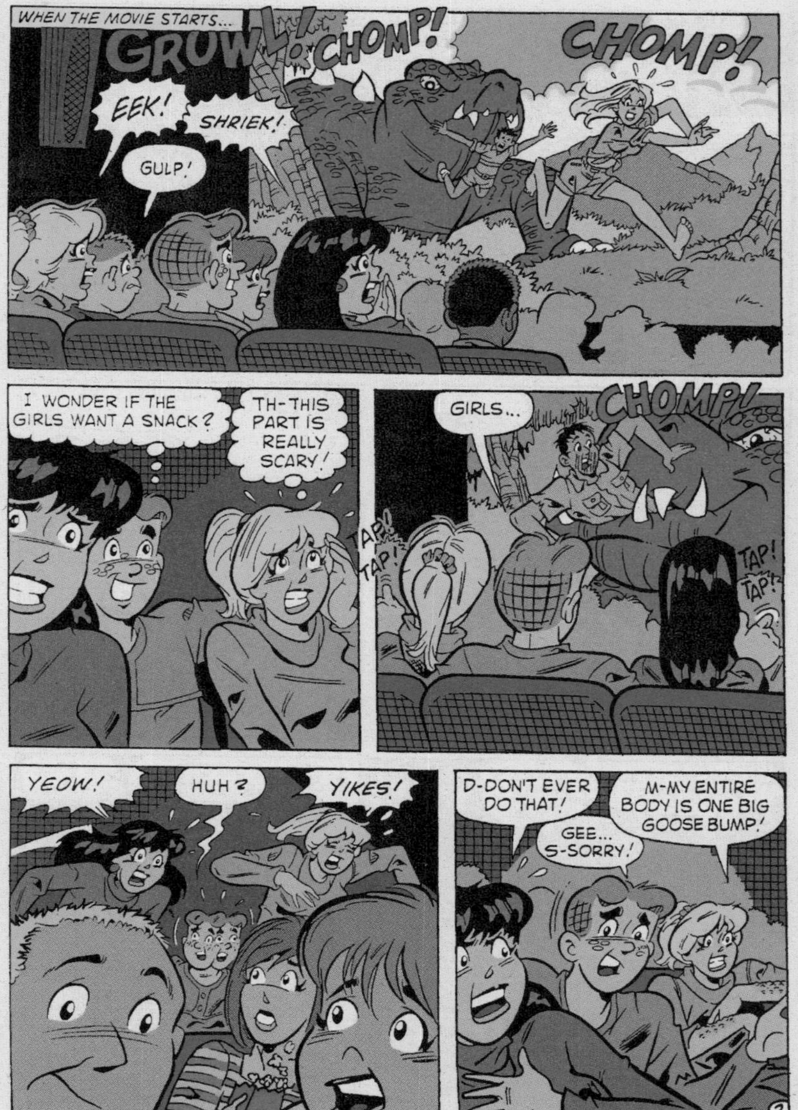

WHEN THE MOVIE STARTS...
GRUWL!
CHOMP!
CHOMP!
EEK!
SHRIEK!
GULP!
I WONDER IF THE GIRLS WANT A SNACK?
TH-THIS PART IS REALLY SCARY!
TAP! TAP!
GIRLS...
CHOMP!
TAP! TAP!
YEOW!
HUH?
YIKES!
D-DON'T EVER DO THAT!
GEE... S-SORRY!
M-MY ENTIRE BODY IS ONE BIG GOOSE BUMP!
2

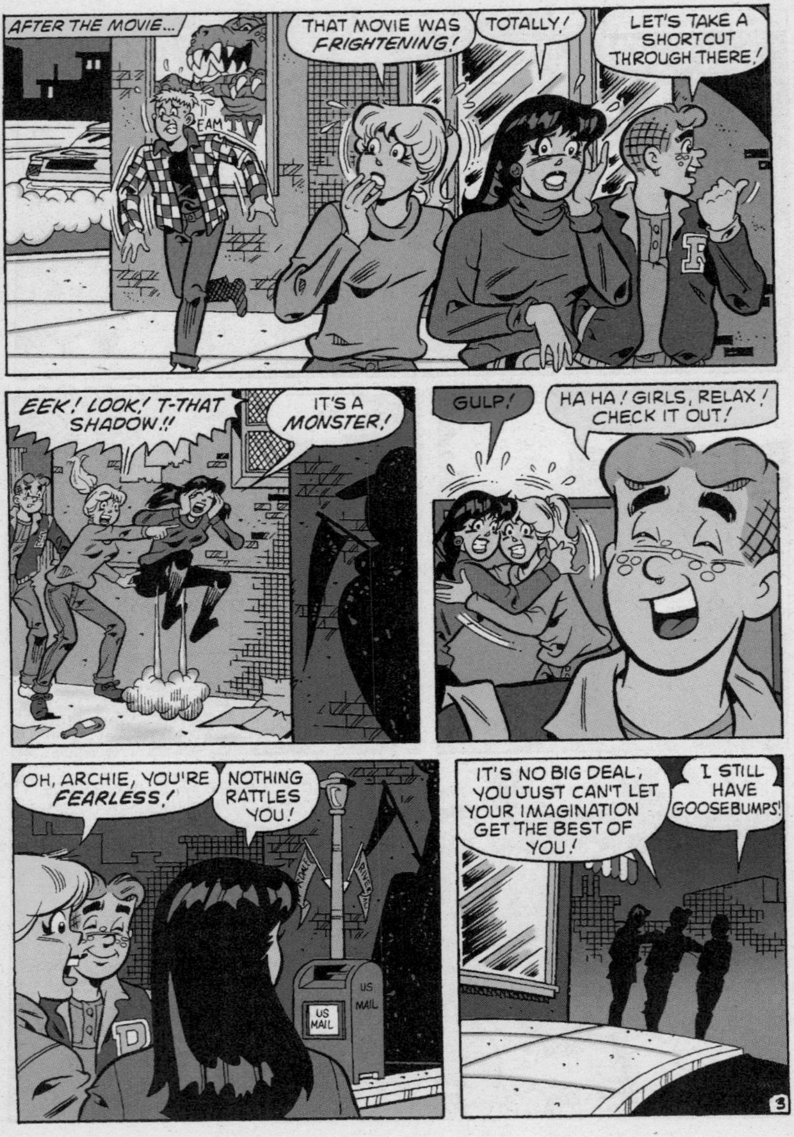

AFTER THE MOVIE...
THAT MOVIE WAS FRIGHTENING!
TOTALLY!
LET'S TAKE A SHORTCUT THROUGH THERE!
EAM TV
EEK! LOOK! T-THAT SHADOW!!
IT'S A MONSTER!
GULP!
HA HA! GIRLS, RELAX! CHECK IT OUT!
OH, ARCHIE, YOU'RE FEARLESS!
NOTHING RATTLES YOU!
US MAIL
US MAIL
IT'S NO BIG DEAL, YOU JUST CAN'T LET YOUR IMAGINATION GET THE BEST OF YOU!
I STILL HAVE GOOSEBUMPS!

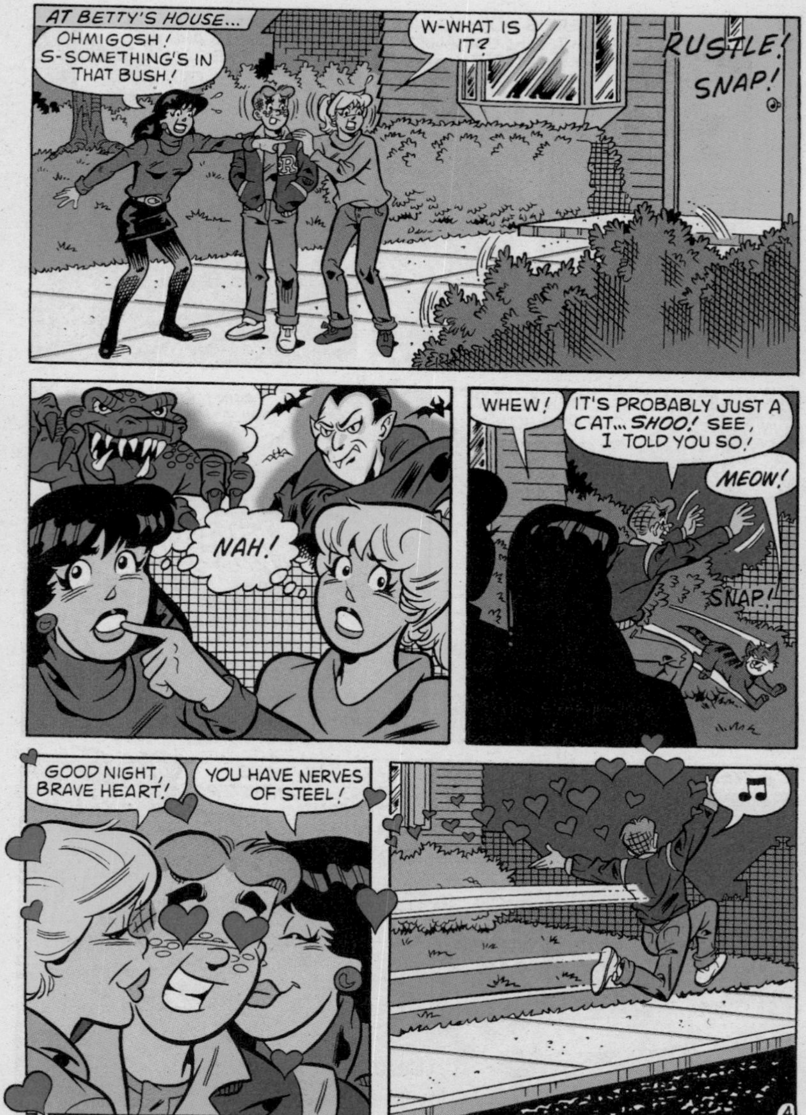
AT BETTY'S HOUSE...
OHMIGOSH! S-SOMETHING'S IN THAT BUSH!
W-WHAT IS IT?
RUSTLE!
SNAP!
NAH!
WHEW!
IT'S PROBABLY JUST A CAT... SHOO! SEE, I TOLD YOU SO!
MEOW!
SNAP!
GOOD NIGHT, BRAVE HEART!
YOU HAVE NERVES OF STEEL!
4

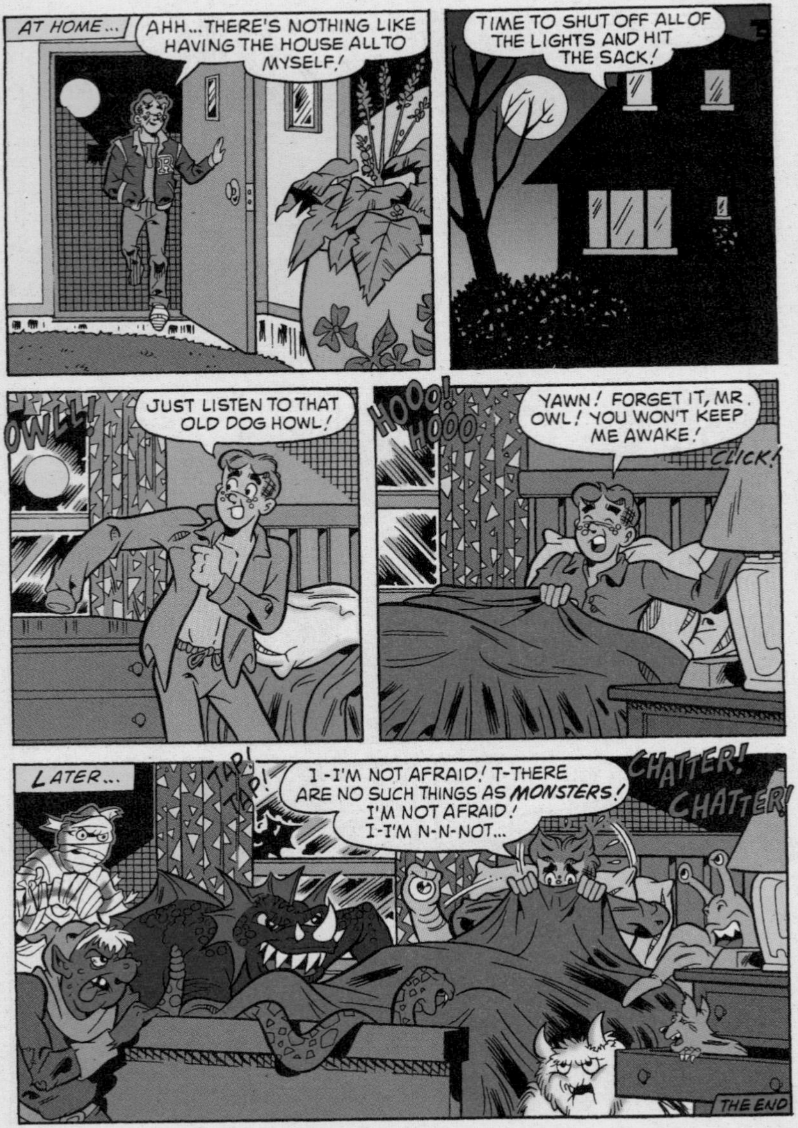
AT HOME...
AHH...THERE'S NOTHING LIKE HAVING THE HOUSE ALL TO MYSELF!
TIME TO SHUT OFF ALL OF THE LIGHTS AND HIT THE SACK!
OWLL!
JUST LISTEN TO THAT OLD DOG HOWL!
HOOO! HOOO
YAWN! FORGET IT, MR. OWL! YOU WON'T KEEP ME AWAKE!
CLICK!
LATER...
TAP! TAP!
I-I'M NOT AFRAID! T-THERE ARE NO SUCH THINGS AS MONSTERS! I'M NOT AFRAID! I-I'M N-N-NOT...
CHATTER! CHATTER!
THE END

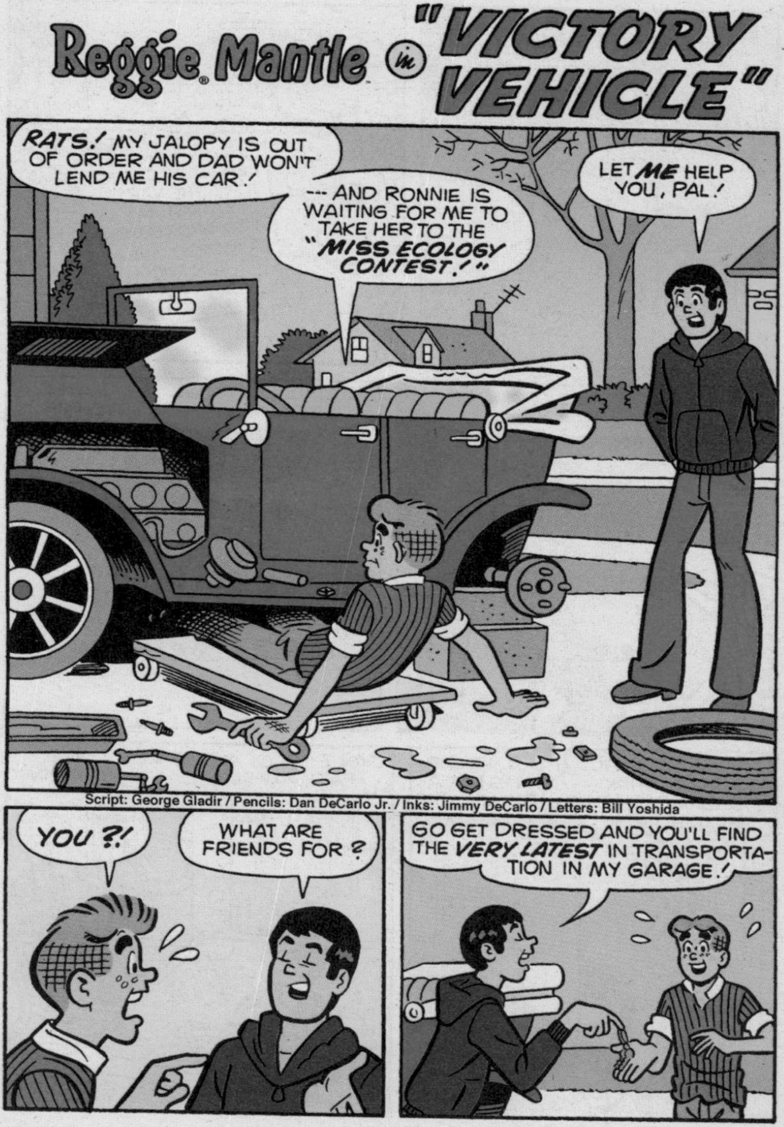
Reggie Mantle in "VICTORY VEHICLE"
RATS.! MY JALOPY IS OUT OF ORDER AND DAD WON'T LEND ME HIS CAR.!
--- AND RONNIE IS WAITING FOR ME TO TAKE HER TO THE "MISS ECOLOGY CONTEST.!"
LET ME HELP YOU, PAL.!
Script: George Gladir / Pencils: Dan DeCarlo Jr. / Inks: Jimmy DeCarlo / Letters: Bill Yoshida
YOU ?!
WHAT ARE FRIENDS FOR ?
GO GET DRESSED AND YOU'LL FIND THE VERY LATEST IN TRANSPORTATION IN MY GARAGE.!

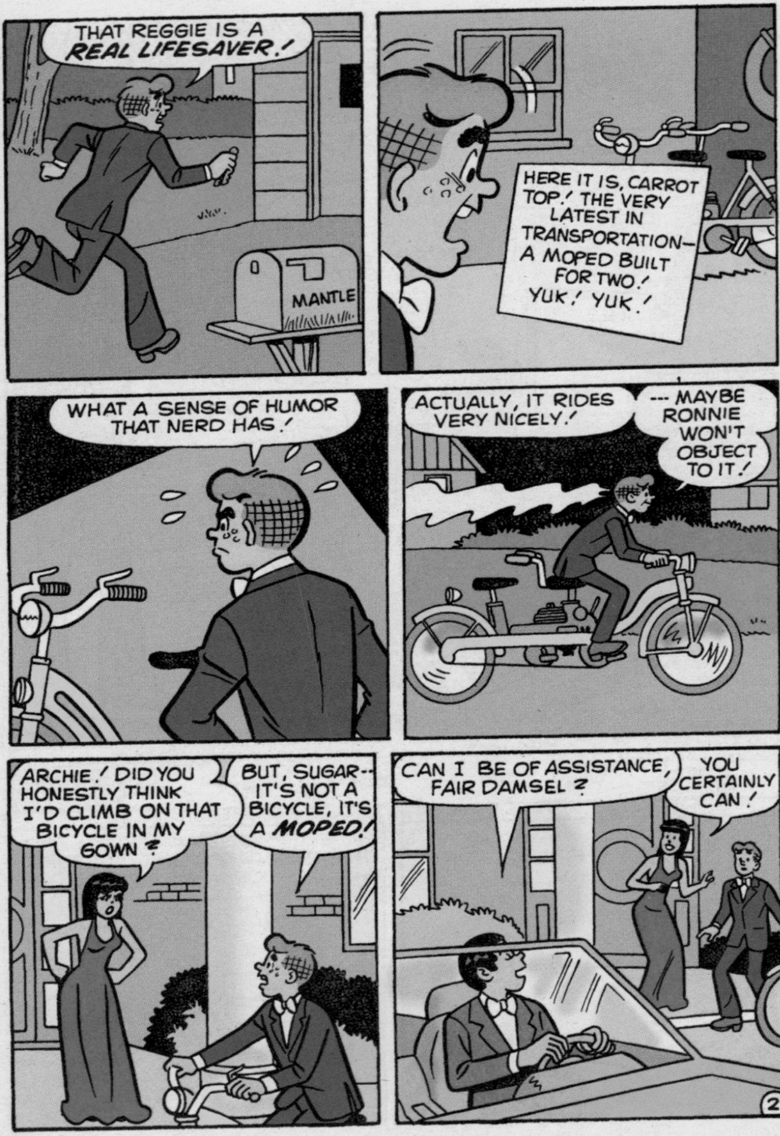
THAT REGGIE IS A REAL LIFESAVER.!
MANTLE
HERE IT IS, CARROT TOP! THE VERY LATEST IN TRANSPORTATION— A MOPED BUILT FOR TWO! YUK! YUK!
WHAT A SENSE OF HUMOR THAT NERD HAS!
ACTUALLY, IT RIDES VERY NICELY!
--- MAYBE RONNIE WON'T OBJECT TO IT!
ARCHIE! DID YOU HONESTLY THINK I'D CLIMB ON THAT BICYCLE IN MY GOWN?
BUT, SUGAR-- IT'S NOT A BICYCLE, IT'S A MOPED!
CAN I BE OF ASSISTANCE, FAIR DAMSEL?
YOU CERTAINLY CAN!
2

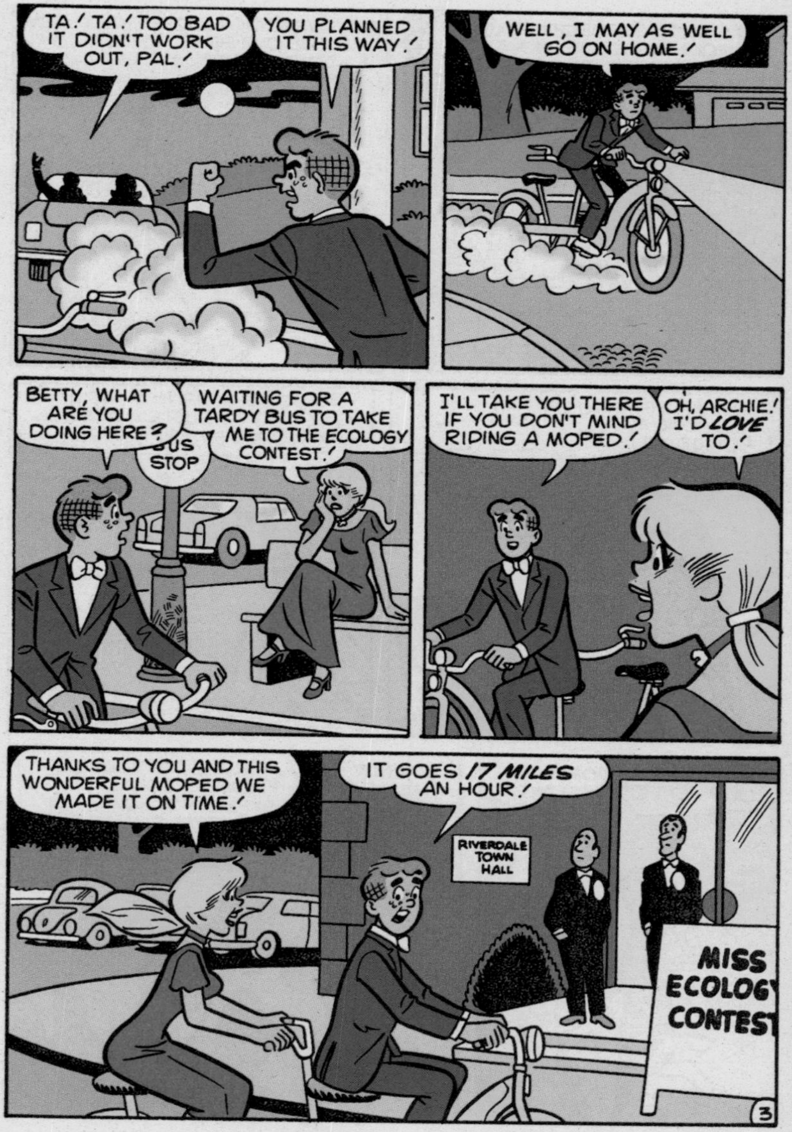
TA! TA! TOO BAD IT DIDN'T WORK OUT, PAL!
YOU PLANNED IT THIS WAY!
WELL, I MAY AS WELL GO ON HOME!
BETTY, WHAT ARE YOU DOING HERE?
BUS STOP
WAITING FOR A TARDY BUS TO TAKE ME TO THE ECOLOGY CONTEST!
I'LL TAKE YOU THERE IF YOU DON'T MIND RIDING A MOPED!
OH, ARCHIE! I'D LOVE TO!
THANKS TO YOU AND THIS WONDERFUL MOPED WE MADE IT ON TIME!
IT GOES 17 MILES AN HOUR!
RIVERDALE TOWN HALL
MISS ECOLOGY CONTEST
3

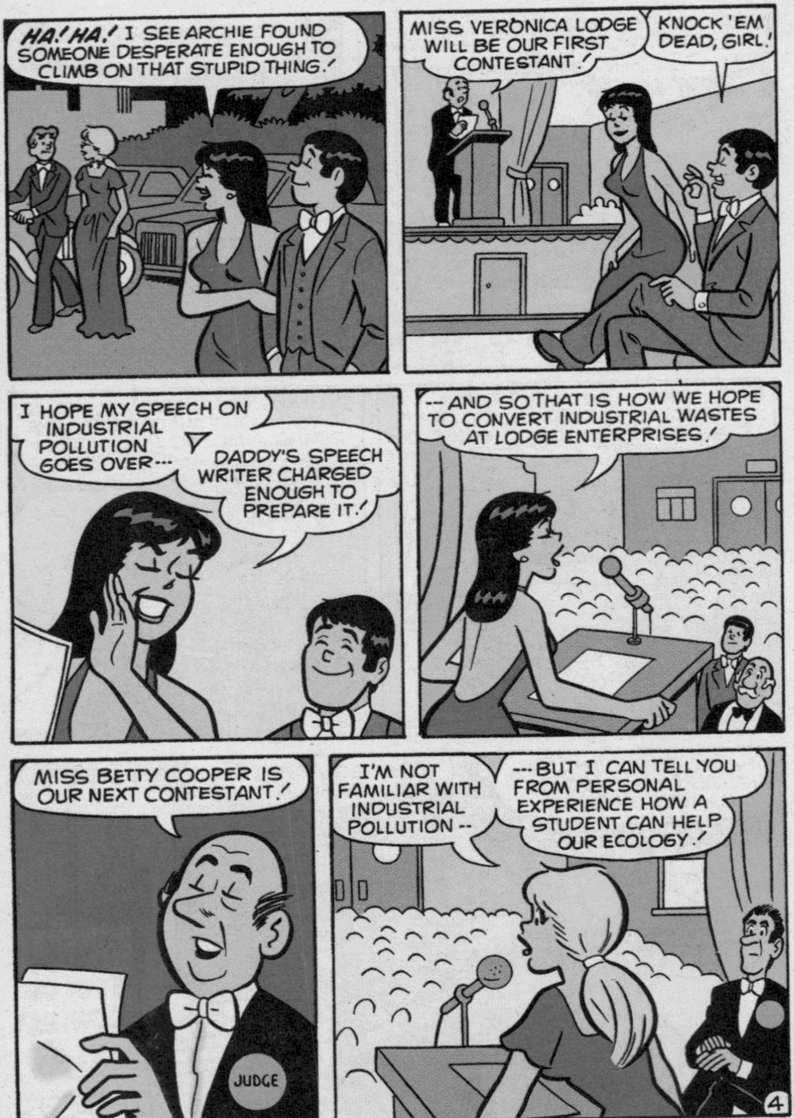
HA! HA! I SEE ARCHIE FOUND SOMEONE DESPERATE ENOUGH TO CLIMB ON THAT STUPID THING!
MISS VERONICA LODGE WILL BE OUR FIRST CONTESTANT!
KNOCK 'EM DEAD, GIRL!
I HOPE MY SPEECH ON INDUSTRIAL POLLUTION GOES OVER---
DADDY'S SPEECH WRITER CHARGED ENOUGH TO PREPARE IT!
---AND SO THAT IS HOW WE HOPE TO CONVERT INDUSTRIAL WASTES AT LODGE ENTERPRISES!
MISS BETTY COOPER IS OUR NEXT CONTESTANT!
JUDGE
I'M NOT FAMILIAR WITH INDUSTRIAL POLLUTION --
---BUT I CAN TELL YOU FROM PERSONAL EXPERIENCE HOW A STUDENT CAN HELP OUR ECOLOGY!
4

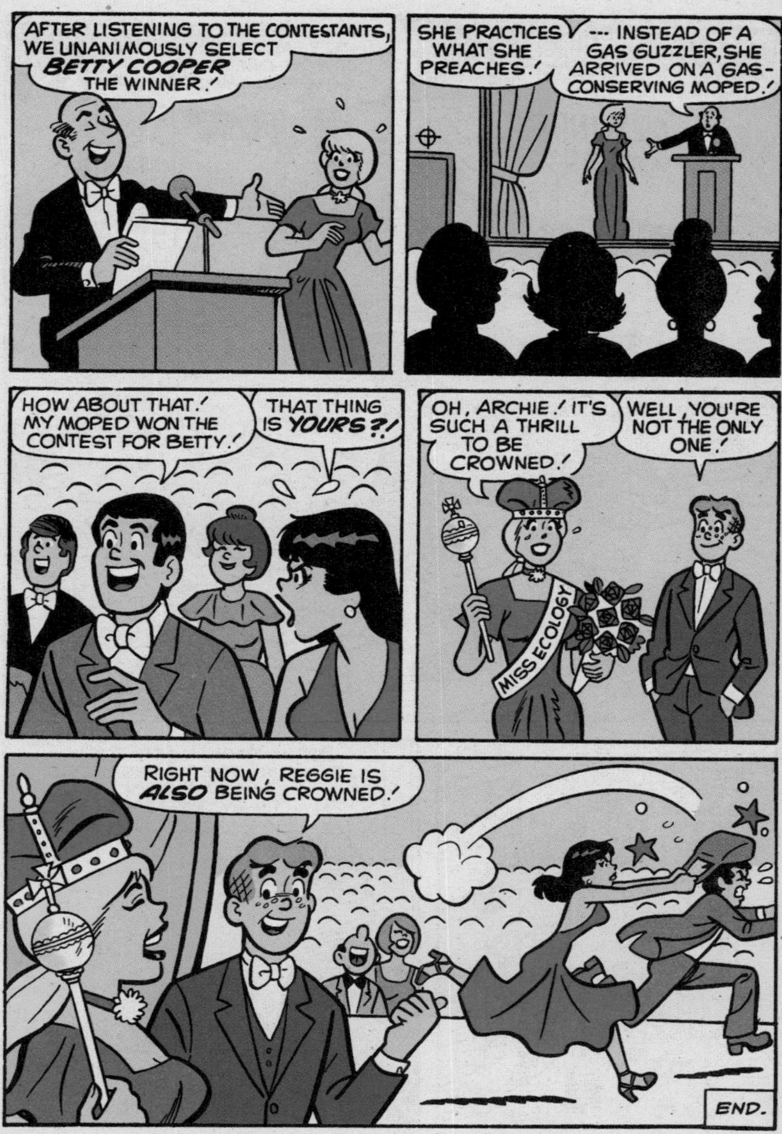
AFTER LISTENING TO THE CONTESTANTS, WE UNANIMOUSLY SELECT BETTY COOPER THE WINNER!
SHE PRACTICES WHAT SHE PREACHES!
--- INSTEAD OF A GAS GUZZLER, SHE ARRIVED ON A GAS-CONSERVING MOPED!
HOW ABOUT THAT! MY MOPED WON THE CONTEST FOR BETTY!
THAT THING IS YOURS?!
OH, ARCHIE! IT'S SUCH A THRILL TO BE CROWNED!
WELL, YOU'RE NOT THE ONLY ONE!
MISS ECOLOGY
RIGHT NOW, REGGIE IS ALSO BEING CROWNED!
END.

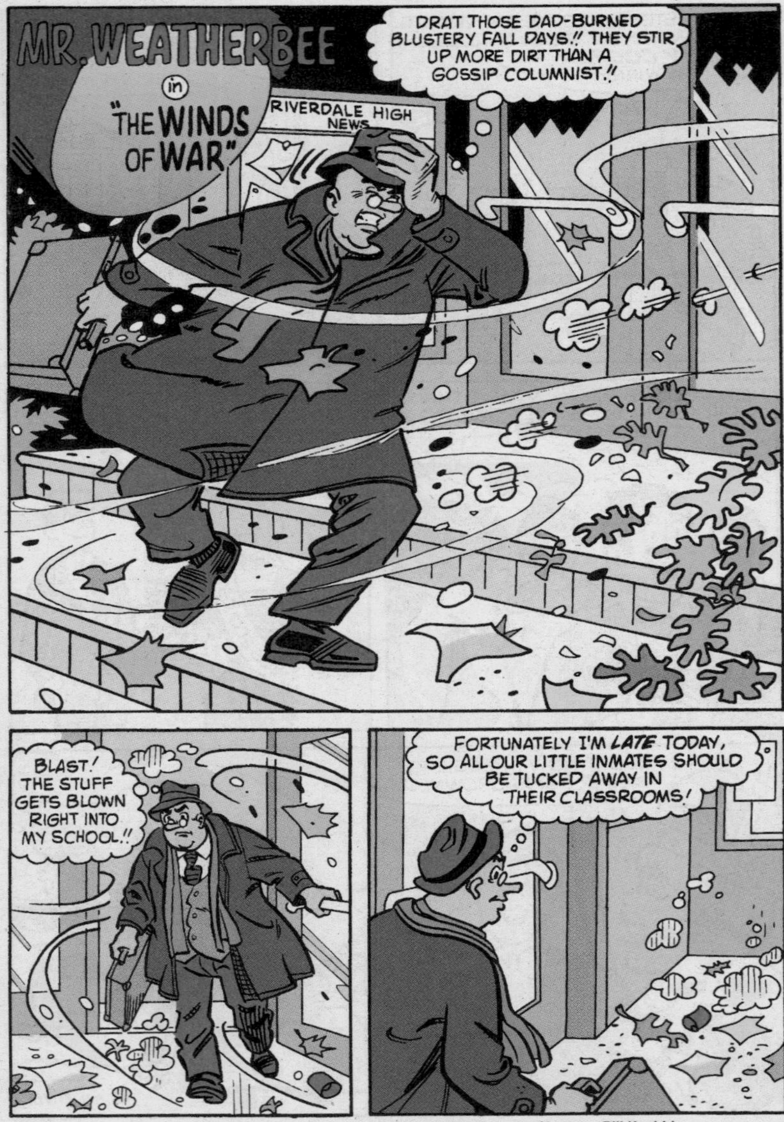
MR. WEATHERBEE
in
"THE WINDS OF WAR"
DRAT THOSE DAD-BURNED BLUSTERY FALL DAYS!! THEY STIR UP MORE DIRT THAN A GOSSIP COLUMNIST!!
RIVERDALE HIGH NEWS
BLAST! THE STUFF GETS BLOWN RIGHT INTO MY SCHOOL!!
FORTUNATELY I'M *LATE* TODAY, SO ALL OUR LITTLE INMATES SHOULD BE TUCKED AWAY IN THEIR CLASSROOMS!

Script: Frank Doyle / Pencils: Stan Goldberg / Inks: Mike Esposito / Letters: Bill Yoshida

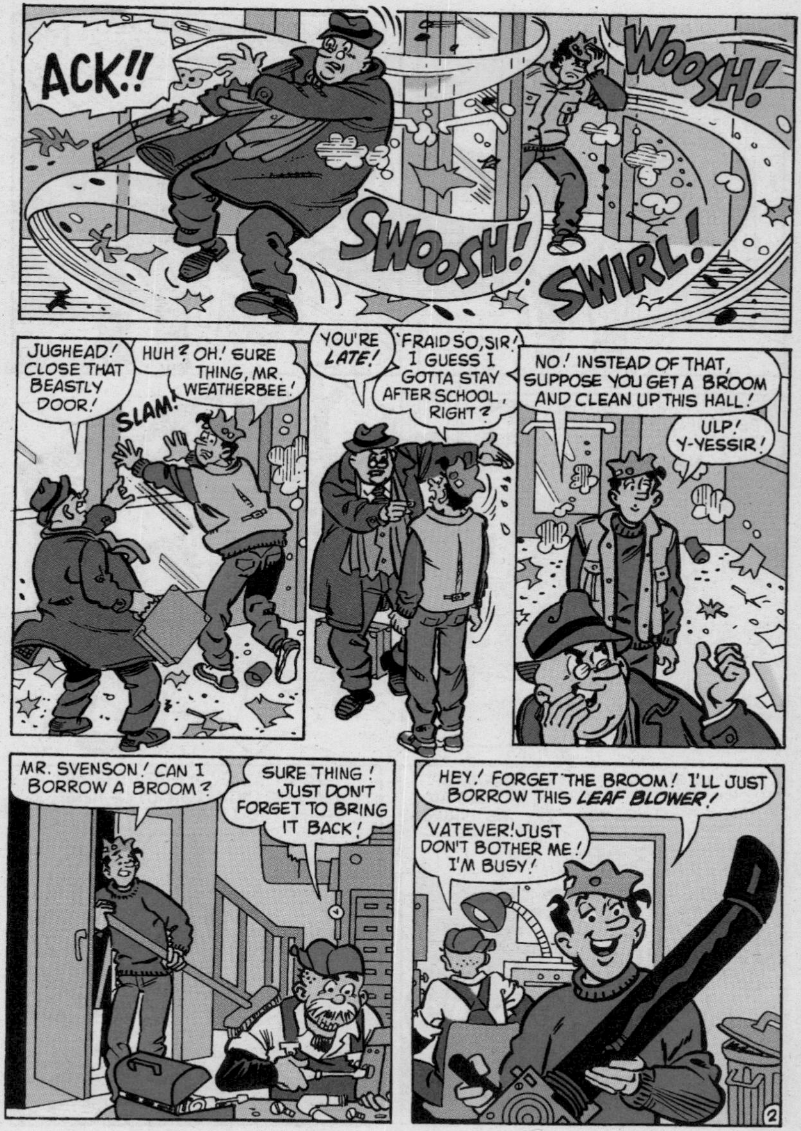
ACK!!
WOOSH!
SWOOSH!
SWIRL!
JUGHEAD! CLOSE THAT BEASTLY DOOR!
HUH? OH! SURE THING, MR. WEATHERBEE!
SLAM!
YOU'RE LATE!
'FRAID SO, SIR! I GUESS I GOTTA STAY AFTER SCHOOL, RIGHT?
NO! INSTEAD OF THAT, SUPPOSE YOU GET A BROOM AND CLEAN UP THIS HALL!
ULP! Y-YESSIR!
MR. SVENSON! CAN I BORROW A BROOM?
SURE THING! JUST DON'T FORGET TO BRING IT BACK!
HEY! FORGET THE BROOM! I'LL JUST BORROW THIS LEAF BLOWER!
VATEVER! JUST DON'T BOTHER ME! I'M BUSY!
2

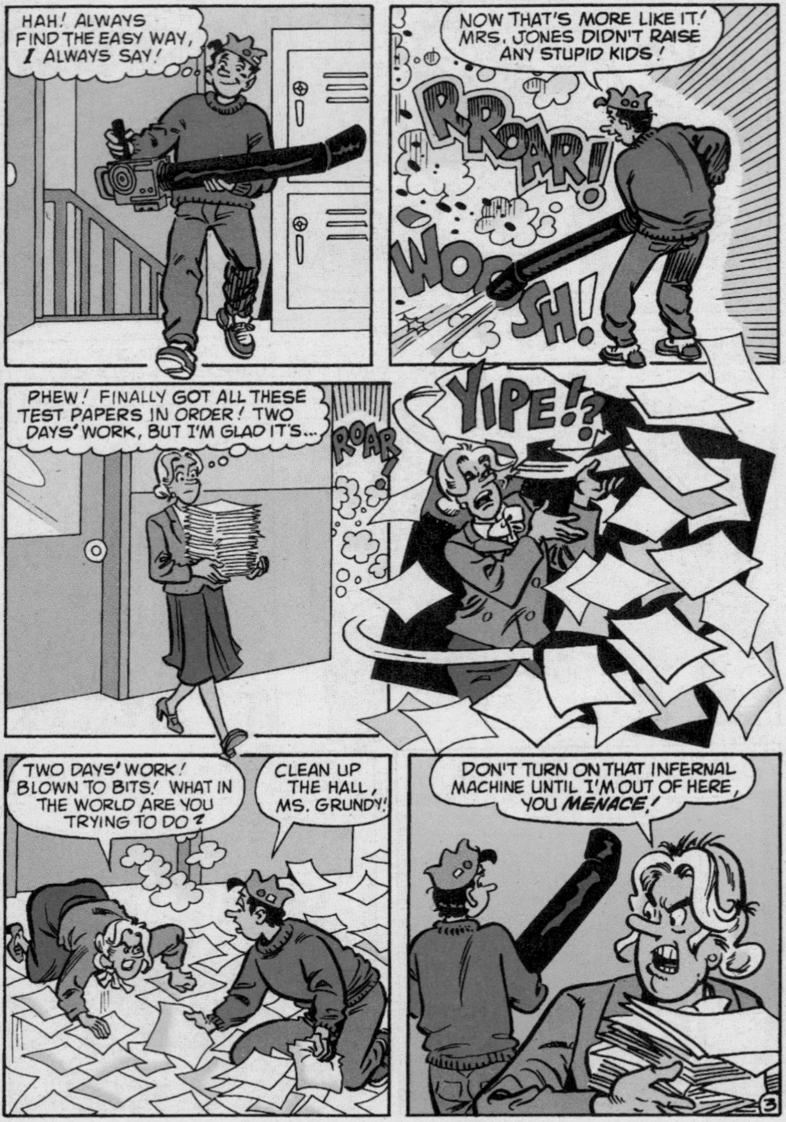
HAH! ALWAYS FIND THE EASY WAY, I ALWAYS SAY!
NOW THAT'S MORE LIKE IT! MRS. JONES DIDN'T RAISE ANY STUPID KIDS!
RROAR!
WOOSH!
PHEW! FINALLY GOT ALL THESE TEST PAPERS IN ORDER! TWO DAYS' WORK, BUT I'M GLAD IT'S...
ROAR!
YIPE!?
TWO DAYS' WORK! BLOWN TO BITS! WHAT IN THE WORLD ARE YOU TRYING TO DO?
CLEAN UP THE HALL, MS. GRUNDY!
DON'T TURN ON THAT INFERNAL MACHINE UNTIL I'M OUT OF HERE, YOU MENACE!
3

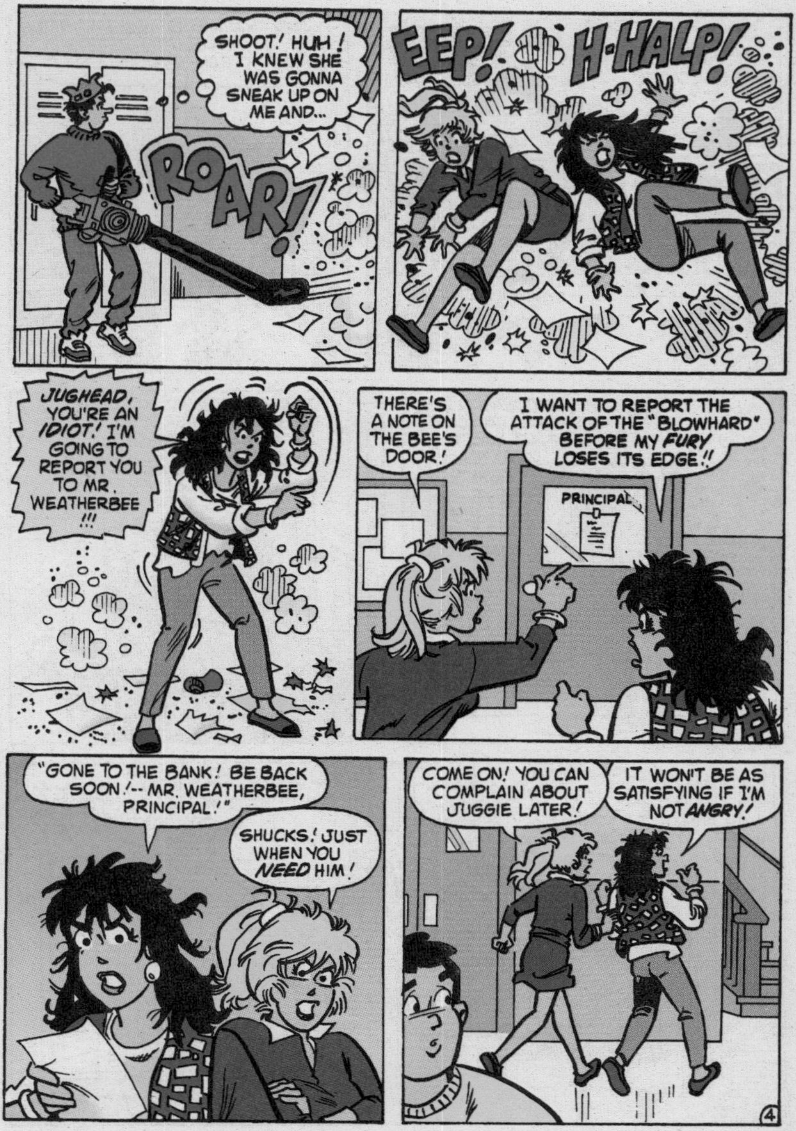
SHOOT! HUH! I KNEW SHE WAS GONNA SNEAK UP ON ME AND...
ROAR!
EEP!
H-HALP!
JUGHEAD, YOU'RE AN IDIOT! I'M GOING TO REPORT YOU TO MR. WEATHERBEE!!!
THERE'S A NOTE ON THE BEE'S DOOR!
I WANT TO REPORT THE ATTACK OF THE "BLOWHARD" BEFORE MY FURY LOSES ITS EDGE!!
PRINCIPAL
"GONE TO THE BANK! BE BACK SOON!-- MR. WEATHERBEE, PRINCIPAL!"
SHUCKS! JUST WHEN YOU NEED HIM!
COME ON! YOU CAN COMPLAIN ABOUT JUGGIE LATER!
IT WON'T BE AS SATISFYING IF I'M NOT ANGRY!
4

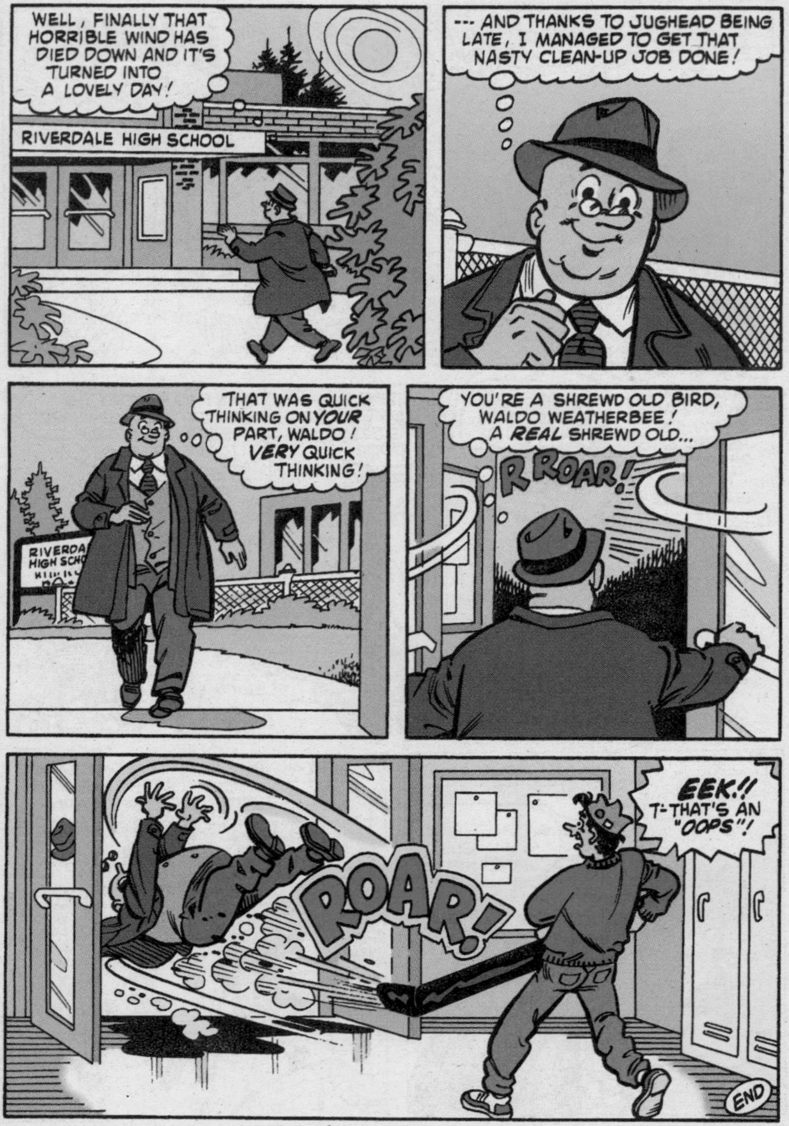
WELL, FINALLY THAT HORRIBLE WIND HAS DIED DOWN AND IT'S TURNED INTO A LOVELY DAY!
RIVERDALE HIGH SCHOOL
--- AND THANKS TO JUGHEAD BEING LATE, I MANAGED TO GET THAT NASTY CLEAN-UP JOB DONE!
THAT WAS QUICK THINKING ON YOUR PART, WALDO! VERY QUICK THINKING!
YOU'RE A SHREWD OLD BIRD, WALDO WEATHERBEE! A REAL SHREWD OLD...
R ROAR!
ROAR!
EEK!! T-THAT'S AN "OOPS"!
END

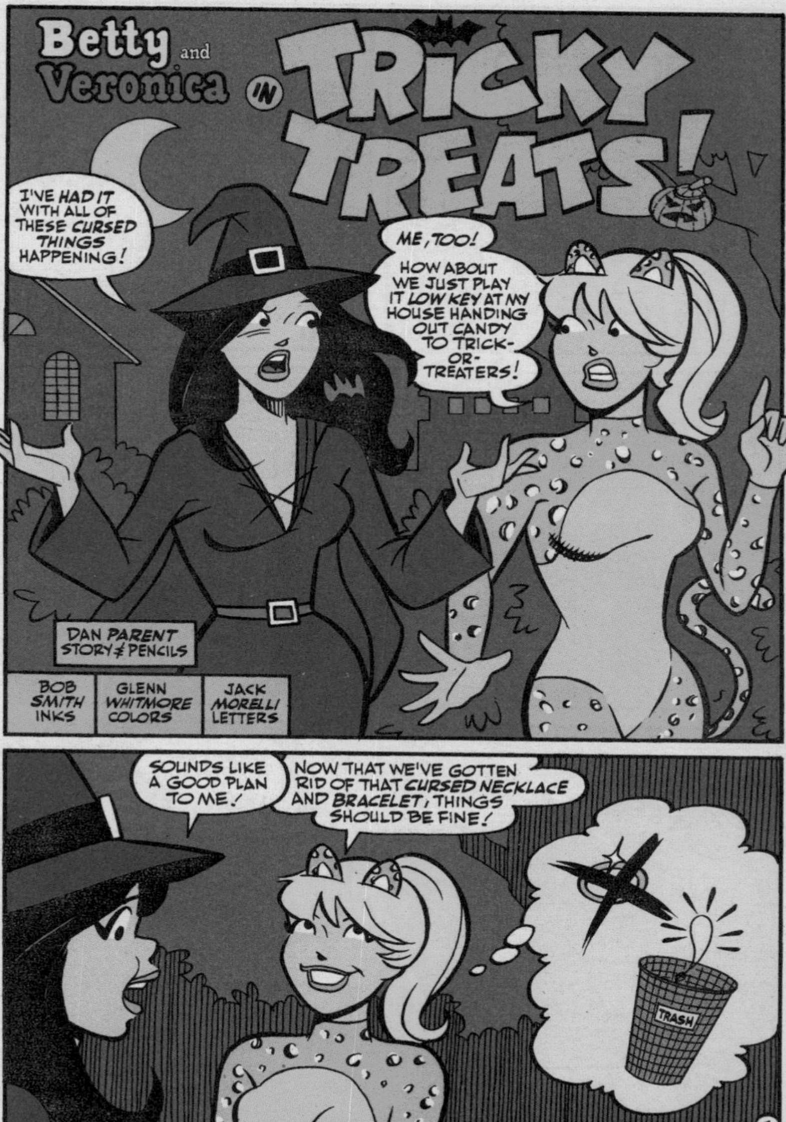
Betty and Veronica IN TRICKY TREATS!
I'VE HAD IT WITH ALL OF THESE CURSED THINGS HAPPENING!
ME, TOO!
HOW ABOUT WE JUST PLAY IT LOW KEY AT MY HOUSE HANDING OUT CANDY TO TRICK-OR-TREATERS!
DAN PARENT STORY & PENCILS
BOB SMITH INKS
GLENN WHITMORE COLORS
JACK MORELLI LETTERS
SOUNDS LIKE A GOOD PLAN TO ME!
NOW THAT WE'VE GOTTEN RID OF THAT CURSED NECKLACE AND BRACELET, THINGS SHOULD BE FINE!
TRASH

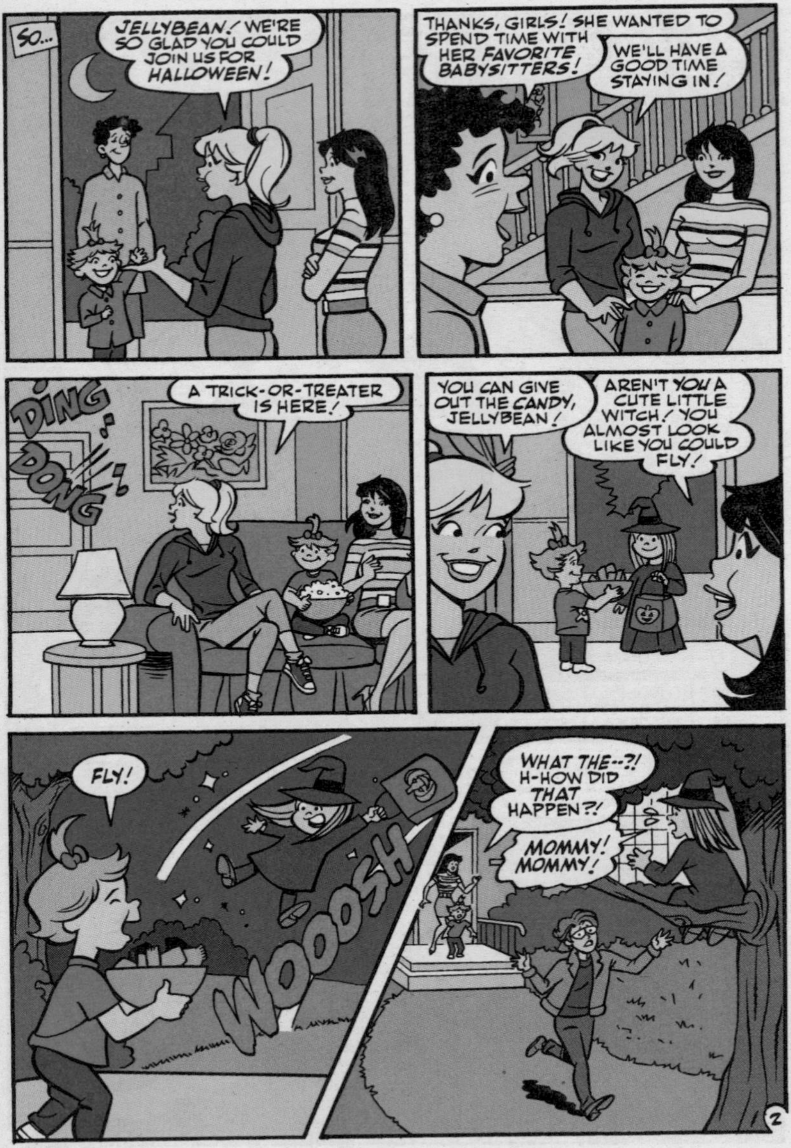
SO...
JELLYBEAN! WE'RE SO GLAD YOU COULD JOIN US FOR HALLOWEEN!
THANKS, GIRLS! SHE WANTED TO SPEND TIME WITH HER FAVORITE BABYSITTERS!
WE'LL HAVE A GOOD TIME STAYING IN!
DING DONG
A TRICK-OR-TREATER IS HERE!
YOU CAN GIVE OUT THE CANDY, JELLYBEAN!
AREN'T YOU A CUTE LITTLE WITCH! YOU ALMOST LOOK LIKE YOU COULD FLY!
FLY!
WOOOSH
WHAT THE--?! H-HOW DID THAT HAPPEN?!
MOMMY! MOMMY!

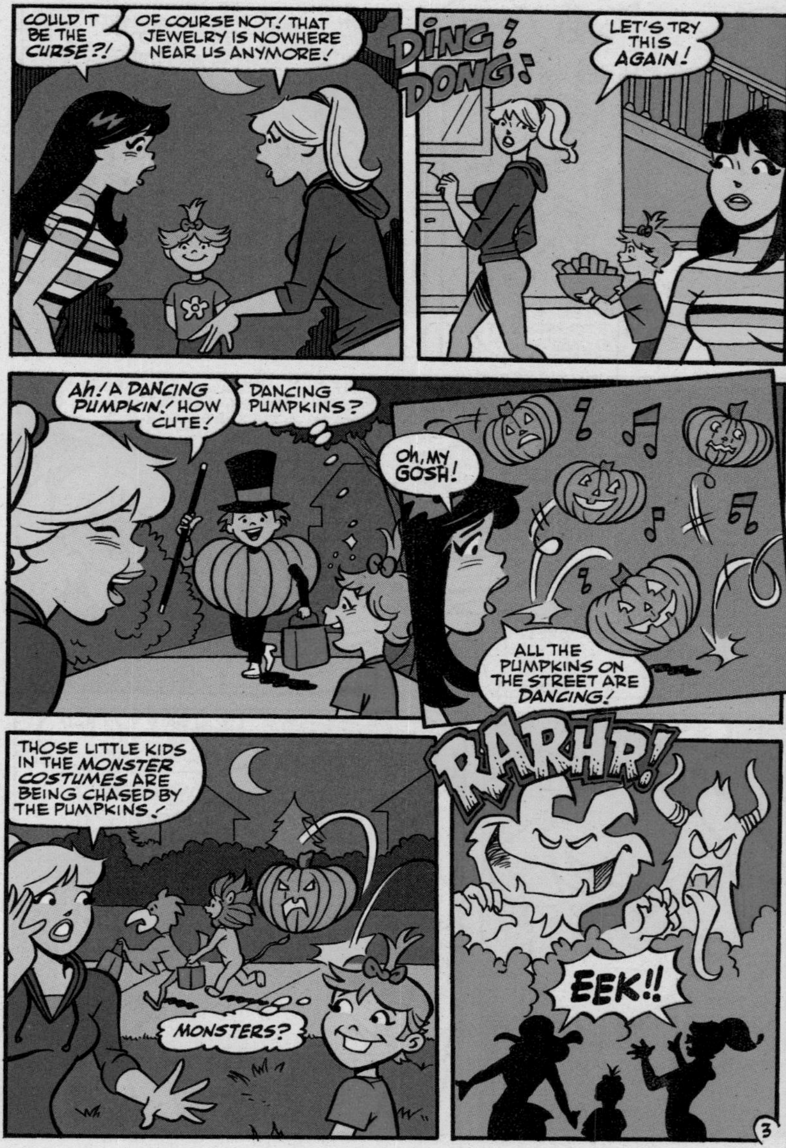

COULD IT BE THE CURSE?!
OF COURSE NOT! THAT JEWELRY IS NOWHERE NEAR US ANYMORE!
DING DONG
LET'S TRY THIS AGAIN!
Ah! A DANCING PUMPKIN! HOW CUTE!
DANCING PUMPKINS?
Oh, MY GOSH!
ALL THE PUMPKINS ON THE STREET ARE DANCING!
THOSE LITTLE KIDS IN THE MONSTER COSTUMES ARE BEING CHASED BY THE PUMPKINS!
MONSTERS?
RARHR!
EEK!!

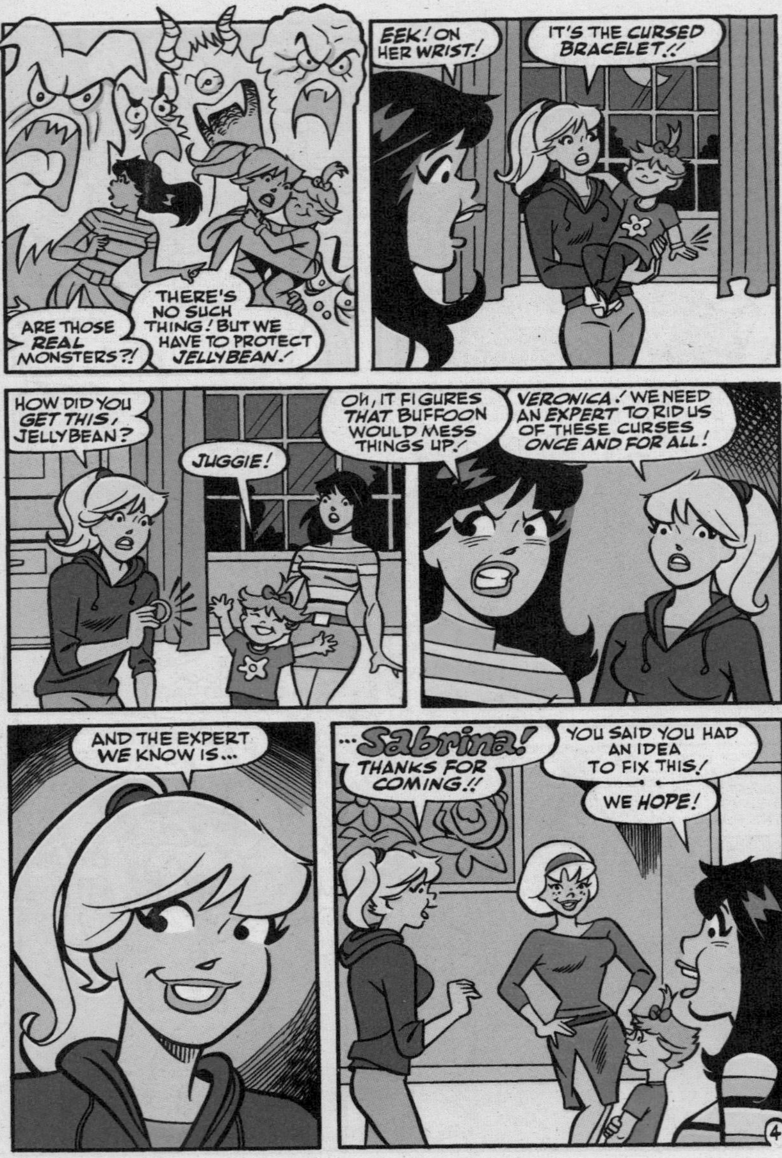
ARE THOSE REAL MONSTERS?!
THERE'S NO SUCH THING! BUT WE HAVE TO PROTECT JELLYBEAN!
EEK! ON HER WRIST!
IT'S THE CURSED BRACELET!!
HOW DID YOU GET THIS, JELLYBEAN?
JUGGIE!
OH, IT FIGURES THAT BUFFOON WOULD MESS THINGS UP!
VERONICA! WE NEED AN EXPERT TO RID US OF THESE CURSES ONCE AND FOR ALL!
AND THE EXPERT WE KNOW IS...
...Sabrina! THANKS FOR COMING!!
YOU SAID YOU HAD AN IDEA TO FIX THIS!
WE HOPE!
4

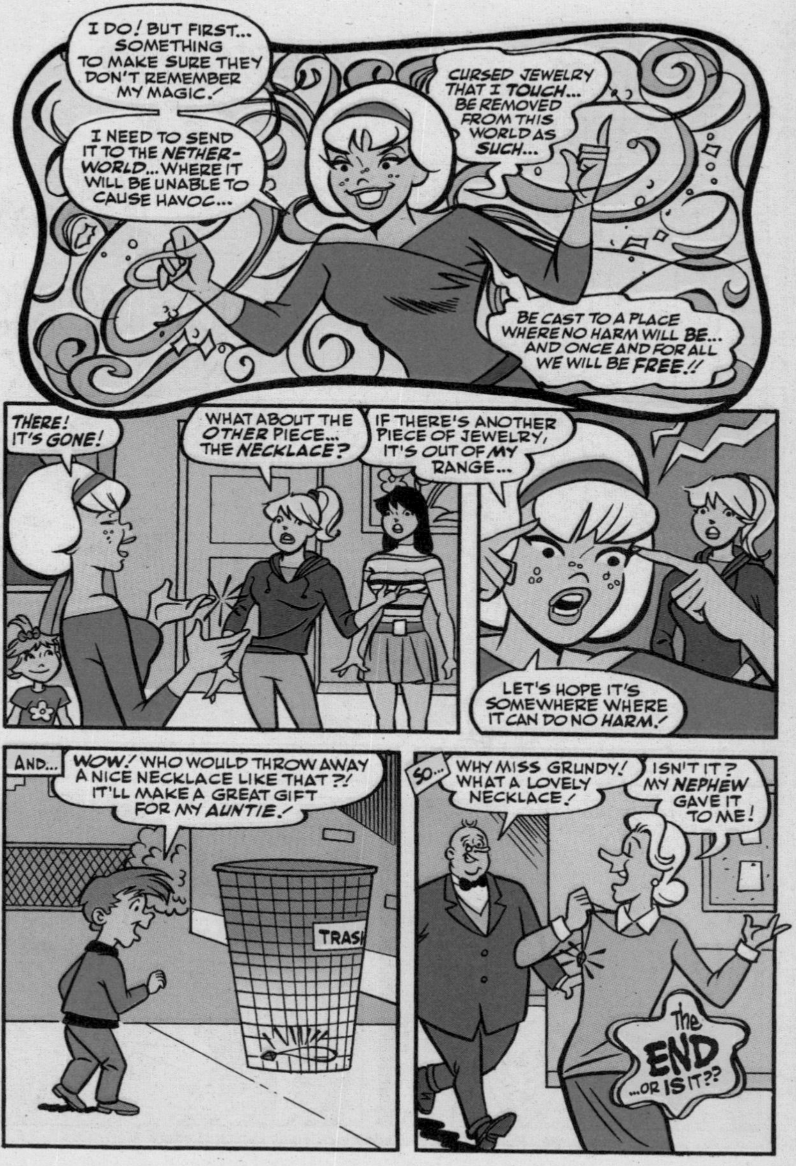

I DO! BUT FIRST... SOMETHING TO MAKE SURE THEY DON'T REMEMBER MY MAGIC.!
I NEED TO SEND IT TO THE NETHER-WORLD... WHERE IT WILL BE UNABLE TO CAUSE HAVOC...
CURSED JEWELRY THAT I TOUCH... BE REMOVED FROM THIS WORLD AS SUCH...
BE CAST TO A PLACE WHERE NO HARM WILL BE... AND ONCE AND FOR ALL WE WILL BE FREE!!
THERE! IT'S GONE!
WHAT ABOUT THE OTHER PIECE... THE NECKLACE?
IF THERE'S ANOTHER PIECE OF JEWELRY, IT'S OUT OF MY RANGE...
LET'S HOPE IT'S SOMEWHERE WHERE IT CAN DO NO HARM.!
AND...
WOW! WHO WOULD THROW AWAY A NICE NECKLACE LIKE THAT?! IT'LL MAKE A GREAT GIFT FOR MY AUNTIE.!
TRASH
SO...
WHY MISS GRUNDY! WHAT A LOVELY NECKLACE!
ISN'T IT? MY NEPHEW GAVE IT TO ME!
The END ...OR IS IT??

Betty and Veronica in CHILLER DILLER

OOOH! THAT WAS GOOD!

I ALWAYS ENJOY A REAL THRILLER!

NOW PLAYING

DEMONS after DARK

STARRING VINCENT BORIS PETER

NOW! EMONS DARK

ULP! BUT--BUT NEXT TIME WE'D BETTER GO IN THE DAYTIME!

EEP! I SEE WHAT YOU MEAN!

Script: Frank Doyle / Pencils: Dan DeCarlo / Inks: Rudy Lapick / Letters: Marty Epp

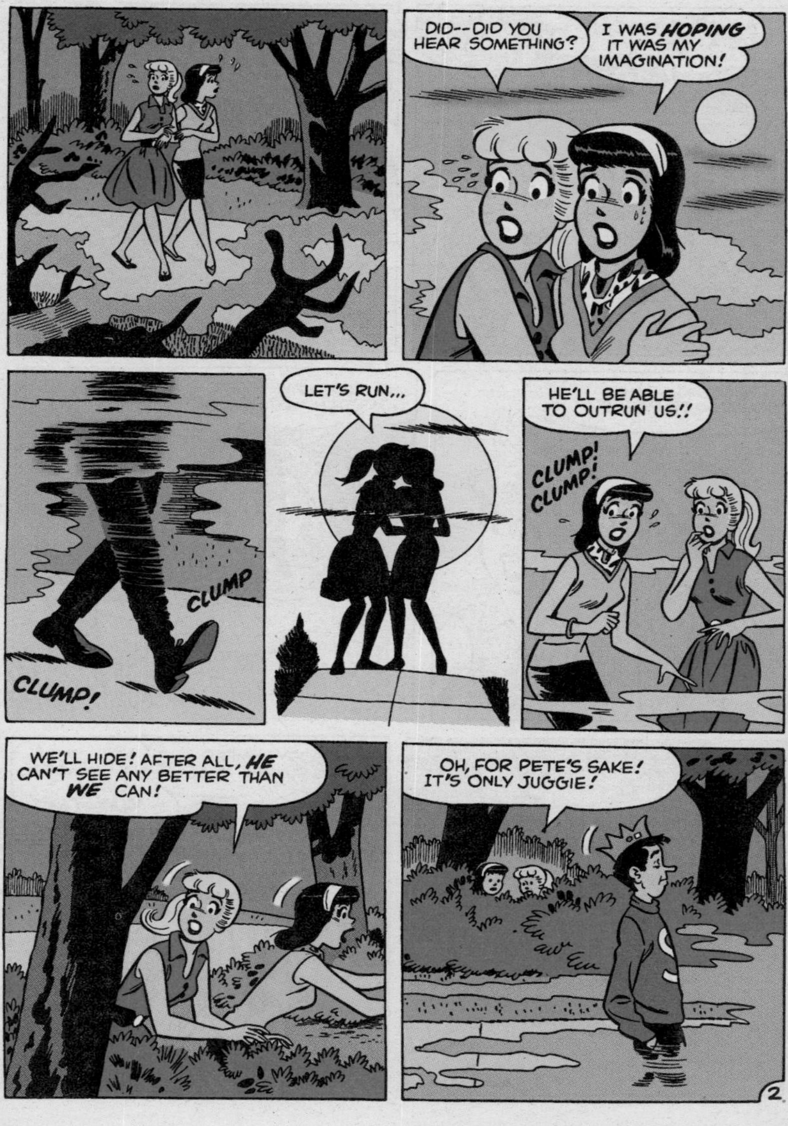
DID--DID YOU HEAR SOMETHING?
I WAS HOPING IT WAS MY IMAGINATION!
CLUMP
CLUMP!
LET'S RUN...
HE'LL BE ABLE TO OUTRUN US!!
CLUMP! CLUMP!
WE'LL HIDE! AFTER ALL, HE CAN'T SEE ANY BETTER THAN WE CAN!
OH, FOR PETE'S SAKE! IT'S ONLY JUGGIE!

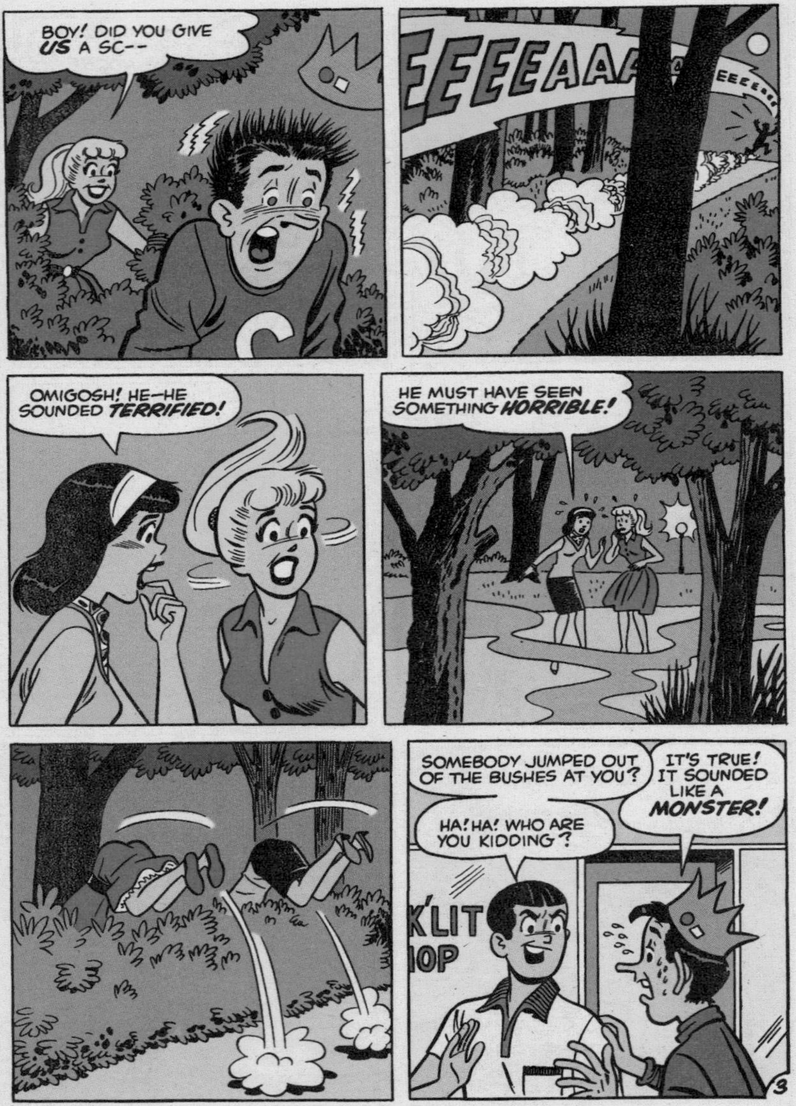
BOY! DID YOU GIVE US A SC--
EEEEAAA
EEEEEEEE
OMIGOSH! HE—HE SOUNDED TERRIFIED!
HE MUST HAVE SEEN SOMETHING HORRIBLE!
SOMEBODY JUMPED OUT OF THE BUSHES AT YOU?
HA! HA! WHO ARE YOU KIDDING?
IT'S TRUE! IT SOUNDED LIKE A MONSTER!
K'LIT
IOP
3

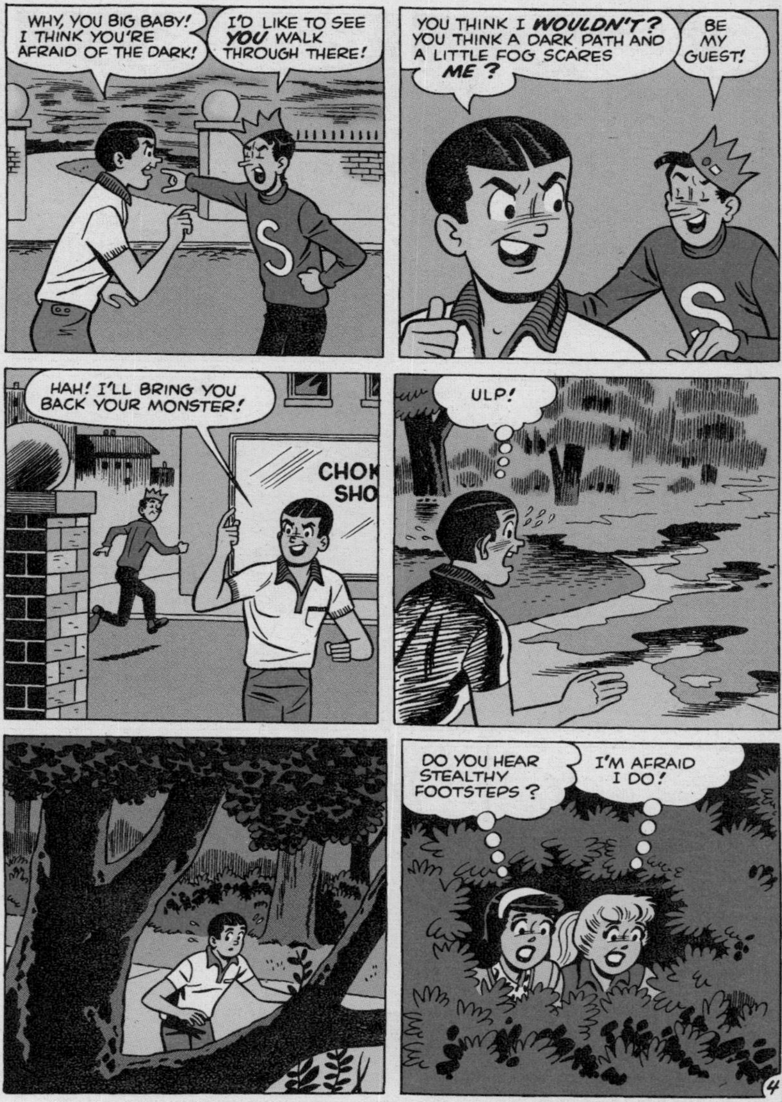
WHY, YOU BIG BABY! I THINK YOU'RE AFRAID OF THE DARK!
I'D LIKE TO SEE YOU WALK THROUGH THERE!
YOU THINK I WOULDN'T? YOU THINK A DARK PATH AND A LITTLE FOG SCARES ME?
BE MY GUEST!
HAH! I'LL BRING YOU BACK YOUR MONSTER!
CHOK
SHO
ULP!
DO YOU HEAR STEALTHY FOOTSTEPS?
I'M AFRAID I DO!
4

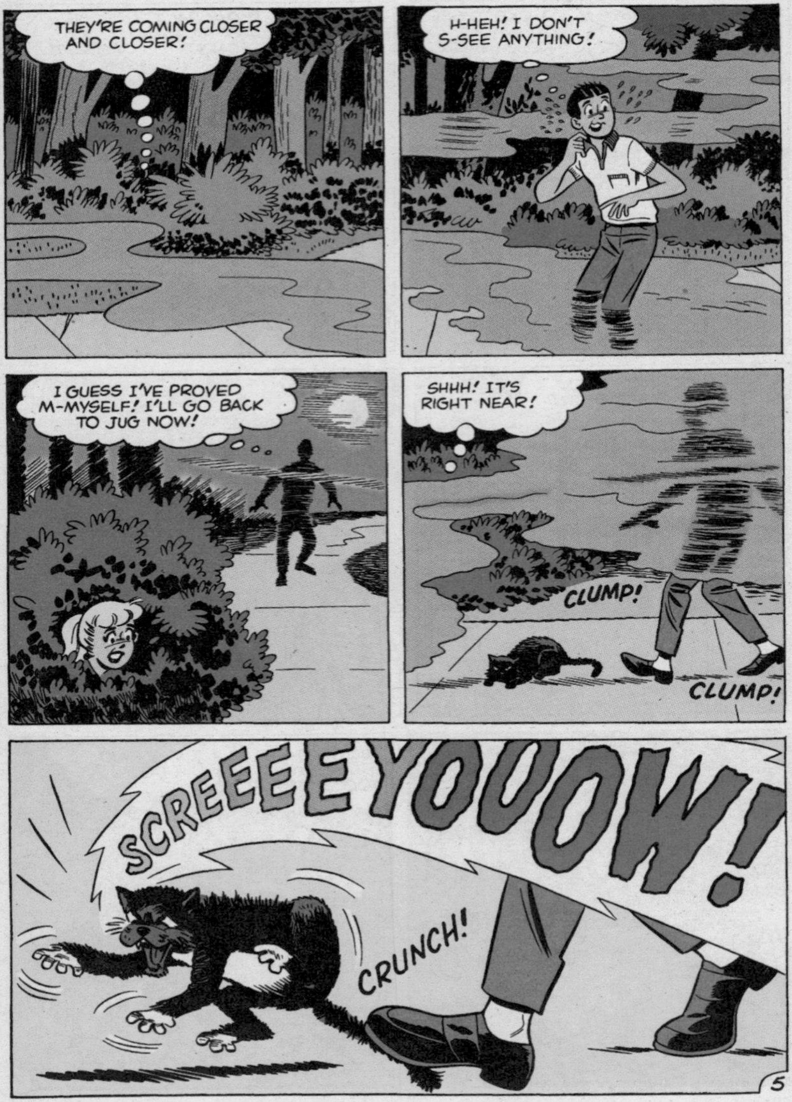

THEY'RE COMING CLOSER AND CLOSER!
H-HEH! I DON'T S-SEE ANYTHING!
I GUESS I'VE PROVED M-MYSELF! I'LL GO BACK TO JUG NOW!
SHHH! IT'S RIGHT NEAR!
CLUMP!
CLUMP!
SCREEEEYOOOW!
CRUNCH!

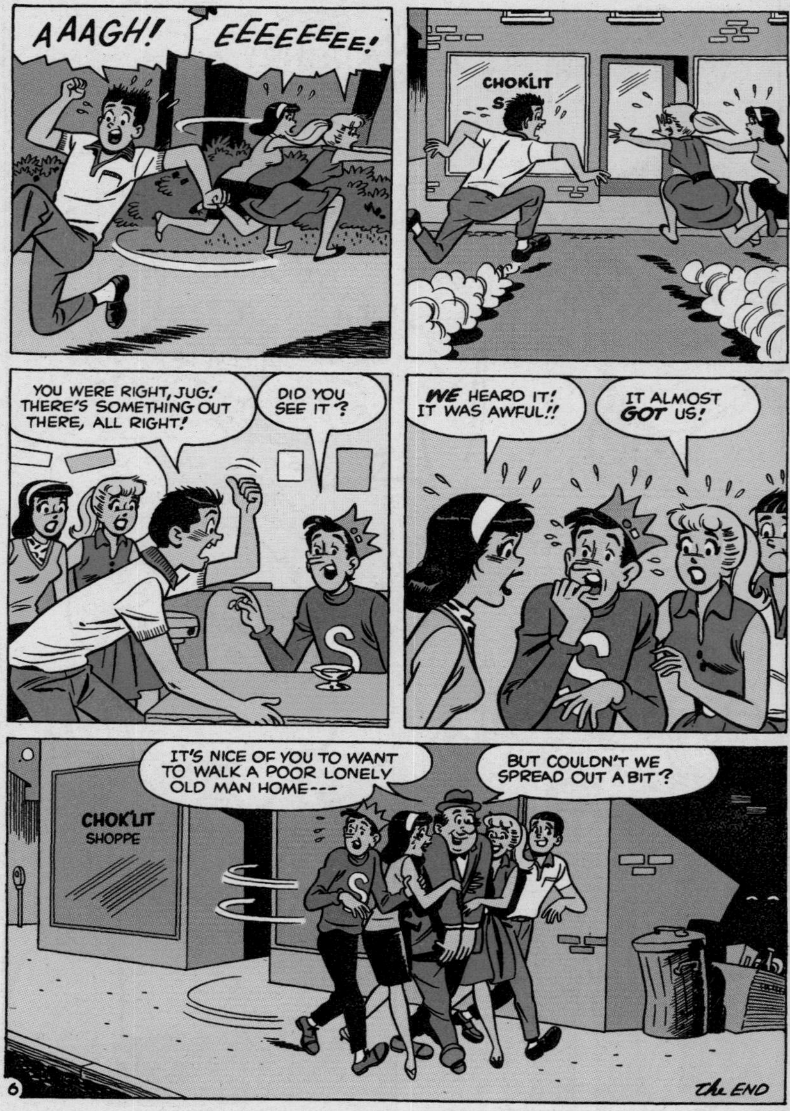
AAAGH!
EEEEEEEEE!
CHOKLIT S
YOU WERE RIGHT, JUG! THERE'S SOMETHING OUT THERE, ALL RIGHT!
DID YOU SEE IT?
WE HEARD IT! IT WAS AWFUL!!
IT ALMOST GOT US!
IT'S NICE OF YOU TO WANT TO WALK A POOR LONELY OLD MAN HOME---
BUT COULDN'T WE SPREAD OUT A BIT?
CHOK'LIT SHOPPE
the END

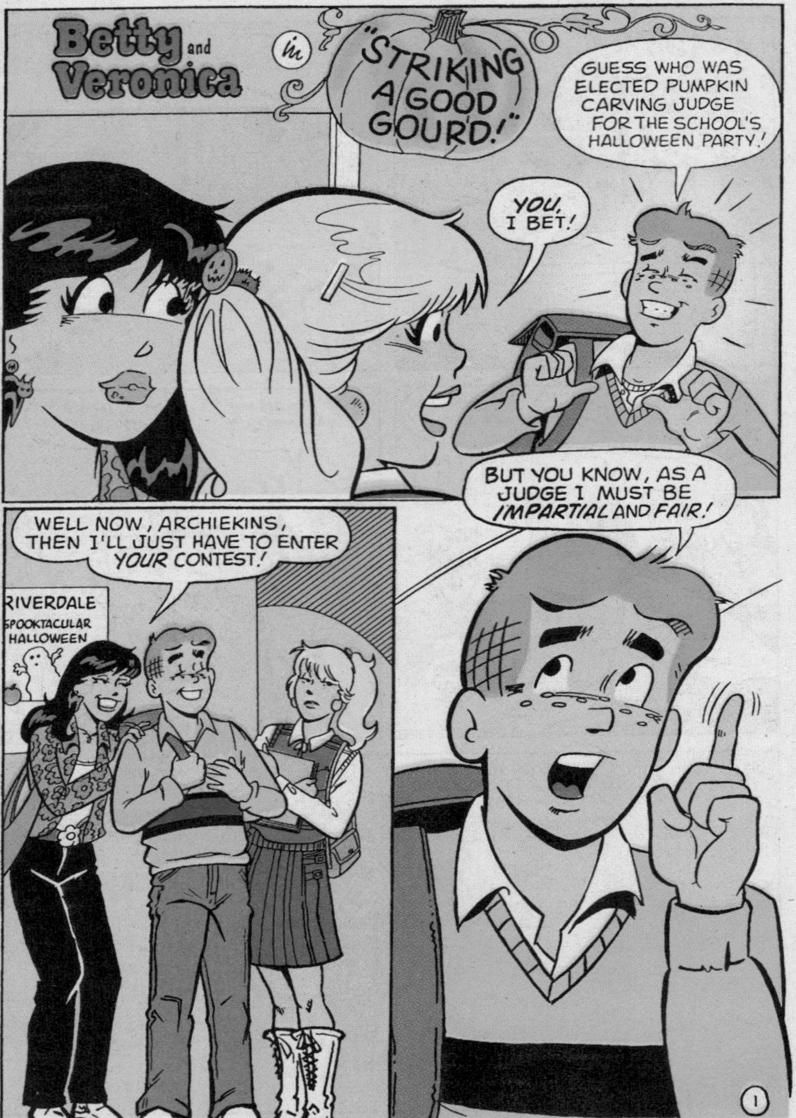
Betty and Veronica
in
"STRIKING A GOOD GOURD!"
GUESS WHO WAS ELECTED PUMPKIN CARVING JUDGE FOR THE SCHOOL'S HALLOWEEN PARTY!
YOU, I BET!
BUT YOU KNOW, AS A JUDGE I MUST BE IMPARTIAL AND FAIR!
WELL NOW, ARCHIEKINS, THEN I'LL JUST HAVE TO ENTER YOUR CONTEST!
RIVERDALE SPOOKTACULAR HALLOWEEN

Script & Art: Holly G! / Letters: Bill Yoshida

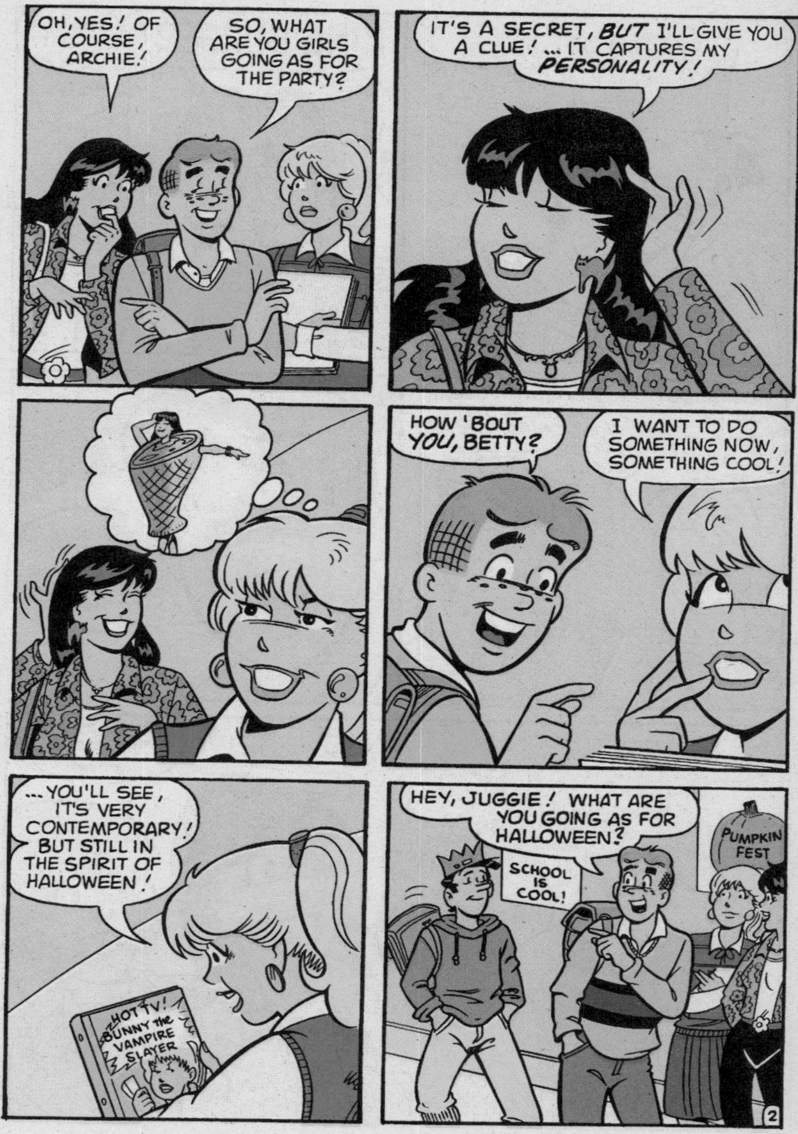
OH, YES! OF COURSE, ARCHIE!
SO, WHAT ARE YOU GIRLS GOING AS FOR THE PARTY?
IT'S A SECRET, BUT I'LL GIVE YOU A CLUE! ... IT CAPTURES MY PERSONALITY!
HOW 'BOUT YOU, BETTY?
I WANT TO DO SOMETHING NOW, SOMETHING COOL!
... YOU'LL SEE, IT'S VERY CONTEMPORARY! BUT STILL IN THE SPIRIT OF HALLOWEEN!
HOT TV! BUNNY the VAMPIRE SLAYER
HEY, JUGGIE! WHAT ARE YOU GOING AS FOR HALLOWEEN?
SCHOOL IS COOL!
PUMPKIN FEST
2

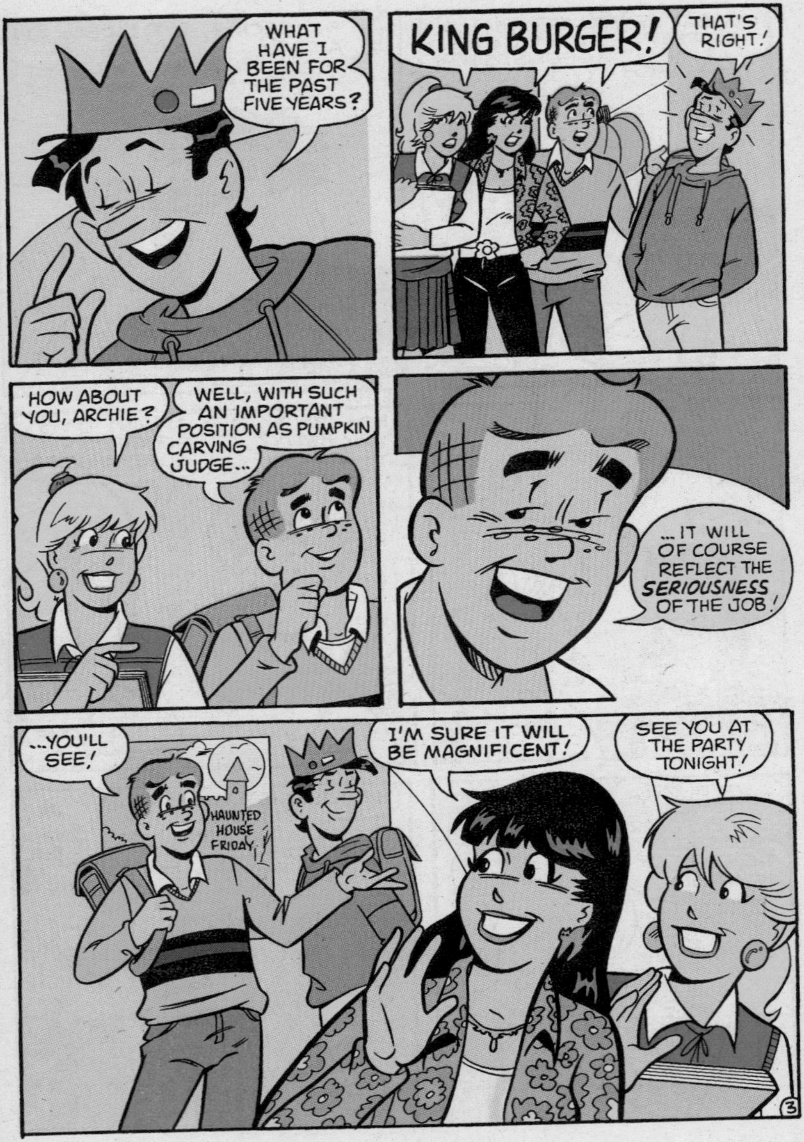
WHAT HAVE I BEEN FOR THE PAST FIVE YEARS?
KING BURGER!
THAT'S RIGHT!
HOW ABOUT YOU, ARCHIE?
WELL, WITH SUCH AN IMPORTANT POSITION AS PUMPKIN CARVING JUDGE...
...IT WILL OF COURSE REFLECT THE SERIOUSNESS OF THE JOB!
...YOU'LL SEE!
HAUNTED HOUSE FRIDAY
I'M SURE IT WILL BE MAGNIFICENT!
SEE YOU AT THE PARTY TONIGHT!
3

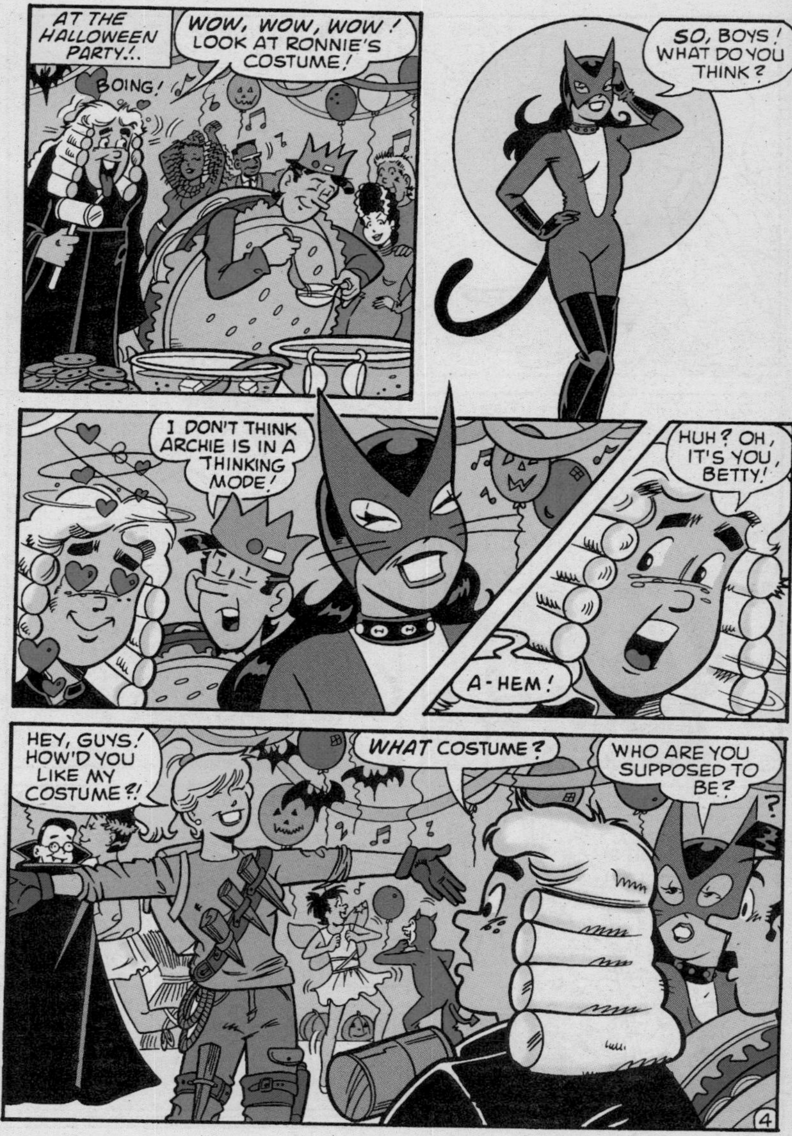
AT THE HALLOWEEN PARTY!..
WOW, WOW, WOW! LOOK AT RONNIE'S COSTUME!
BOING!
SO, BOYS! WHAT DO YOU THINK?
I DON'T THINK ARCHIE IS IN A THINKING MODE!
HUH? OH, IT'S YOU, BETTY!
A-HEM!
HEY, GUYS! HOW'D YOU LIKE MY COSTUME?!
WHAT COSTUME?
WHO ARE YOU SUPPOSED TO BE?
?
4

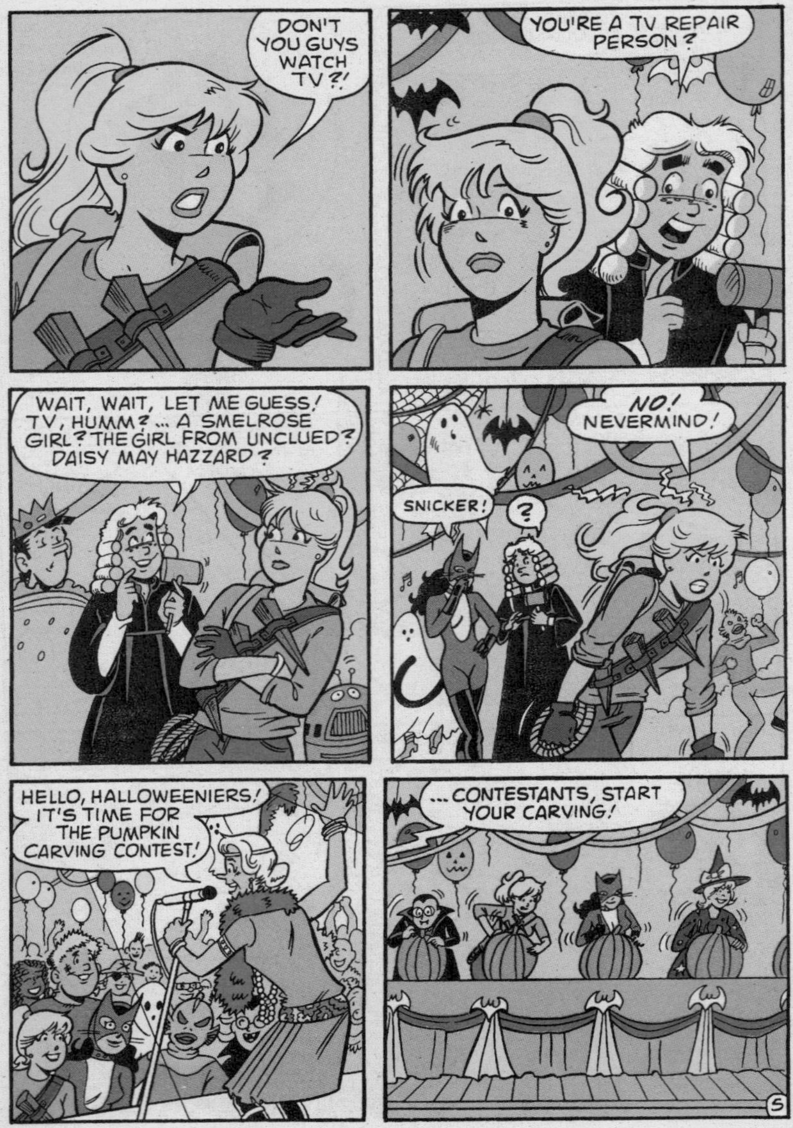
DON'T YOU GUYS WATCH TV?!
YOU'RE A TV REPAIR PERSON?
WAIT, WAIT, LET ME GUESS! TV, HUMM? ... A SMELROSE GIRL? THE GIRL FROM UNCLUED? DAISY MAY HAZZARD?
NO! NEVERMIND!
SNICKER!
?
HELLO, HALLOWEENIERS! IT'S TIME FOR THE PUMPKIN CARVING CONTEST!
... CONTESTANTS, START YOUR CARVING!
5

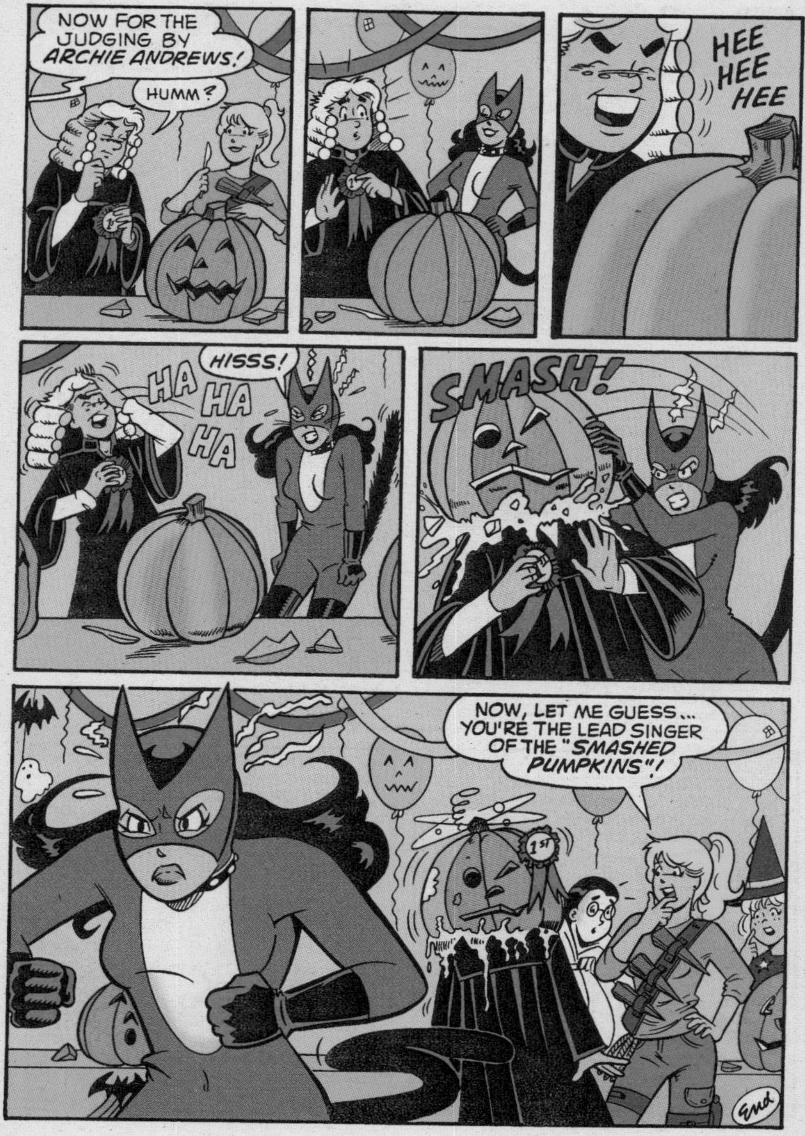

NOW FOR THE JUDGING BY ARCHIE ANDREWS!
HUMM?
HEE HEE HEE
HISSS!
HA HA HA
SMASH!
NOW, LET ME GUESS... YOU'RE THE LEAD SINGER OF THE "SMASHED PUMPKINS"!
1ST
End

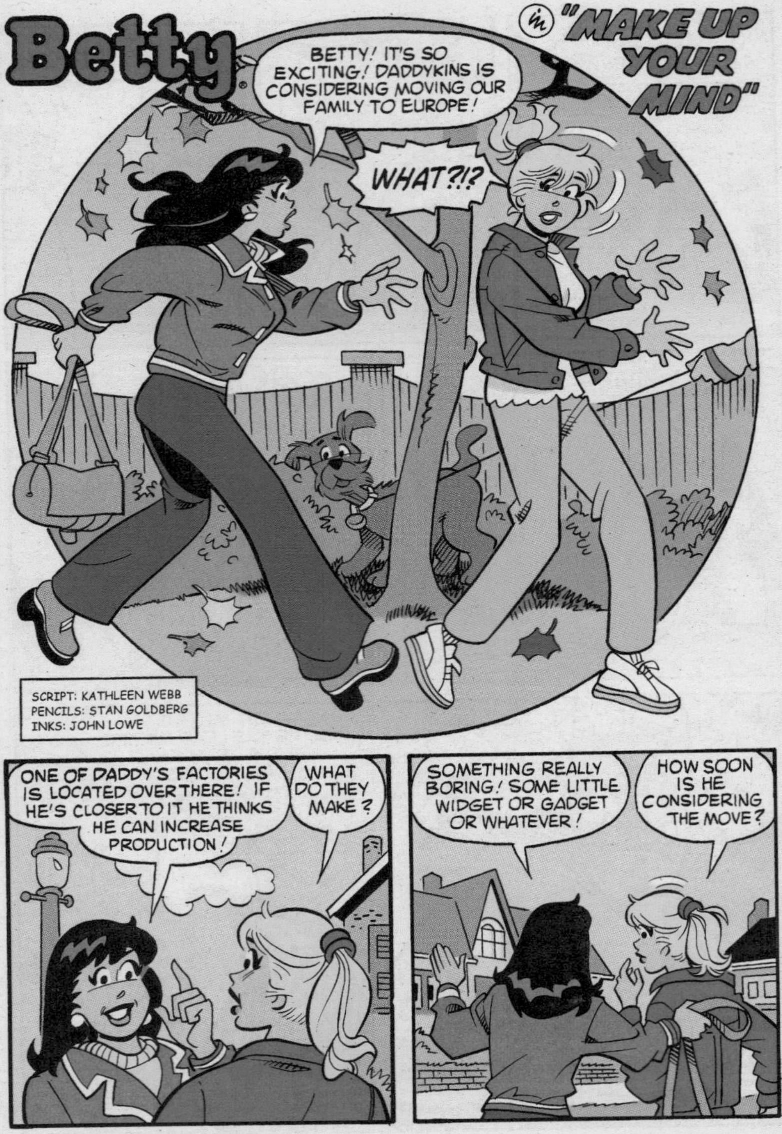

Betty
in "MAKE UP YOUR MIND"
BETTY! IT'S SO EXCITING! DADDYKINS IS CONSIDERING MOVING OUR FAMILY TO EUROPE!
WHAT?!?
SCRIPT: KATHLEEN WEBB
PENCILS: STAN GOLDBERG
INKS: JOHN LOWE
ONE OF DADDY'S FACTORIES IS LOCATED OVER THERE! IF HE'S CLOSER TO IT HE THINKS HE CAN INCREASE PRODUCTION!
WHAT DO THEY MAKE?
SOMETHING REALLY BORING! SOME LITTLE WIDGET OR GADGET OR WHATEVER!
HOW SOON IS HE CONSIDERING THE MOVE?

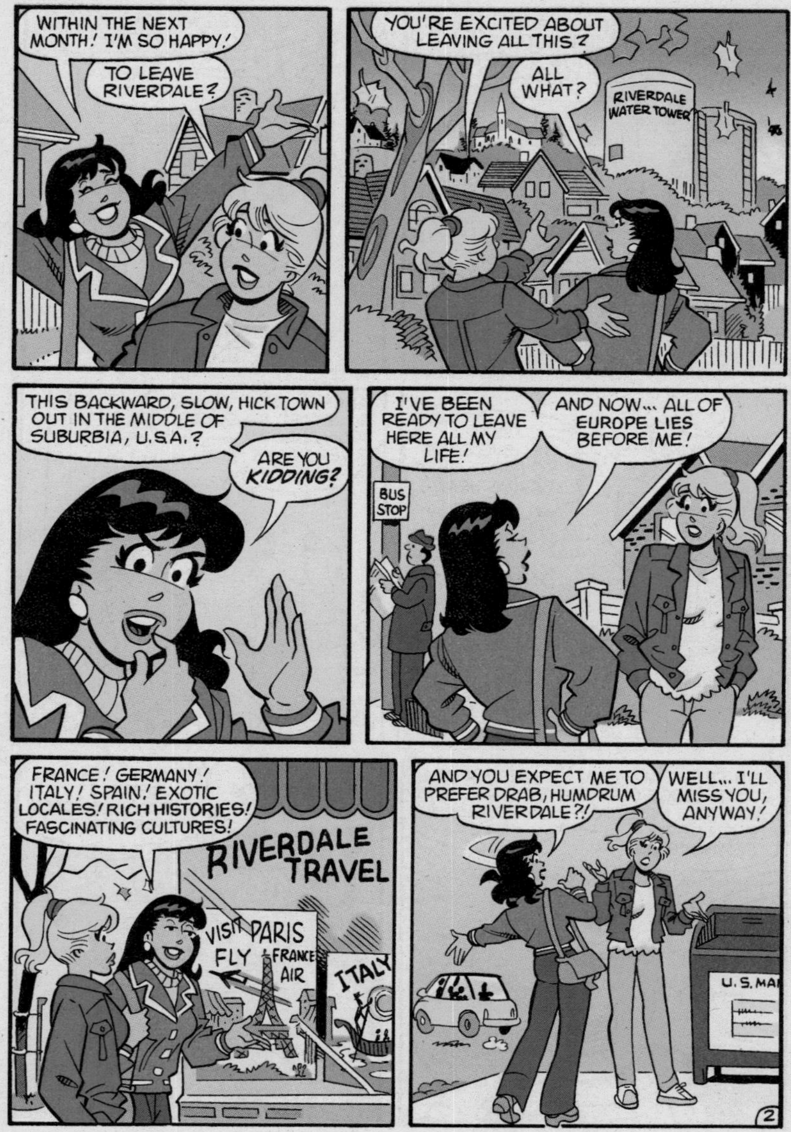

WITHIN THE NEXT MONTH! I'M SO HAPPY!
TO LEAVE RIVERDALE?
YOU'RE EXCITED ABOUT LEAVING ALL THIS?
ALL WHAT?
RIVERDALE WATER TOWER
THIS BACKWARD, SLOW, HICK TOWN OUT IN THE MIDDLE OF SUBURBIA, U.S.A.?
ARE YOU *KIDDING?*
I'VE BEEN READY TO LEAVE HERE ALL MY LIFE!
AND NOW... ALL OF EUROPE LIES BEFORE ME!
BUS STOP
FRANCE! GERMANY! ITALY! SPAIN! EXOTIC LOCALES! RICH HISTORIES! FASCINATING CULTURES!
RIVERDALE TRAVEL
VISIT PARIS
FLY FRANCE AIR
ITALY
AND YOU EXPECT ME TO PREFER DRAB, HUMDRUM RIVERDALE?!
WELL... I'LL MISS YOU, ANYWAY!
U.S. MA

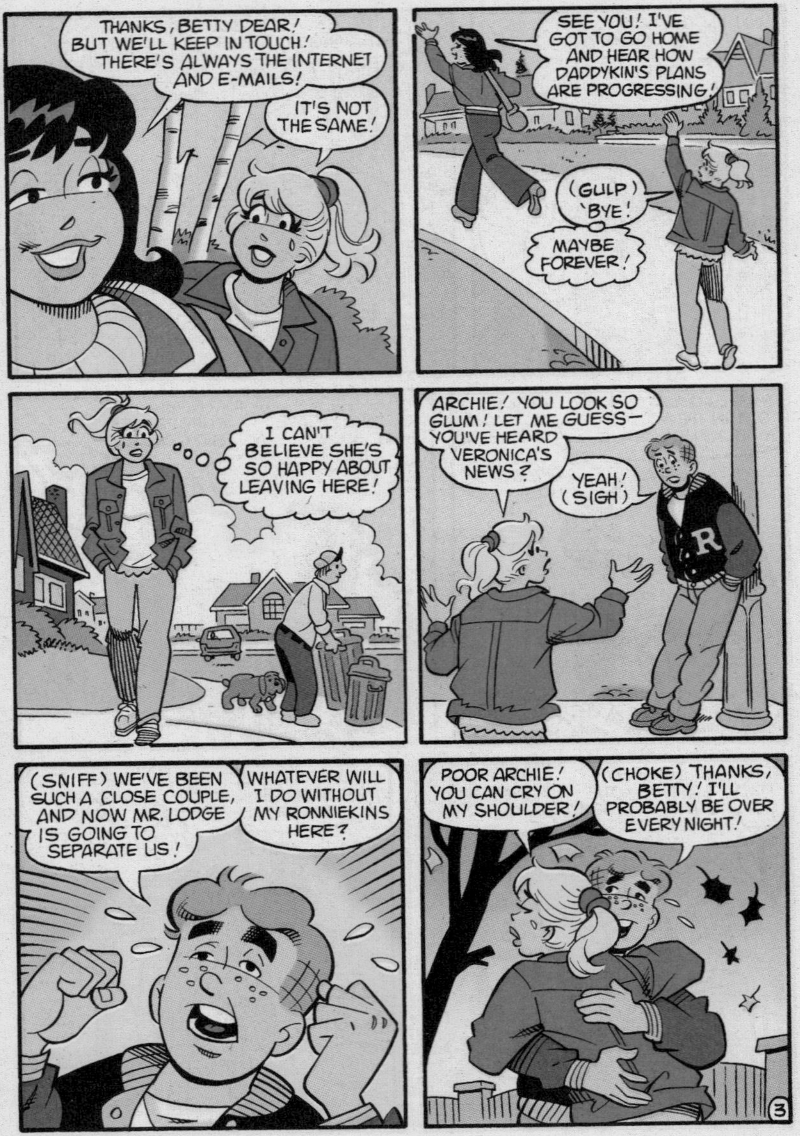
THANKS, BETTY DEAR! BUT WE'LL KEEP IN TOUCH! THERE'S ALWAYS THE INTERNET AND E-MAILS!
IT'S NOT THE SAME!
SEE YOU! I'VE GOT TO GO HOME AND HEAR HOW DADDYKIN'S PLANS ARE PROGRESSING!
(GULP) 'BYE!
MAYBE FOREVER!
I CAN'T BELIEVE SHE'S SO HAPPY ABOUT LEAVING HERE!
ARCHIE! YOU LOOK SO GLUM! LET ME GUESS— YOU'VE HEARD VERONICA'S NEWS?
YEAH! (SIGH)
(SNIFF) WE'VE BEEN SUCH A CLOSE COUPLE, AND NOW MR. LODGE IS GOING TO SEPARATE US!
WHATEVER WILL I DO WITHOUT MY RONNIEKINS HERE?
POOR ARCHIE! YOU CAN CRY ON MY SHOULDER!
(CHOKE) THANKS, BETTY! I'LL PROBABLY BE OVER EVERY NIGHT!
3

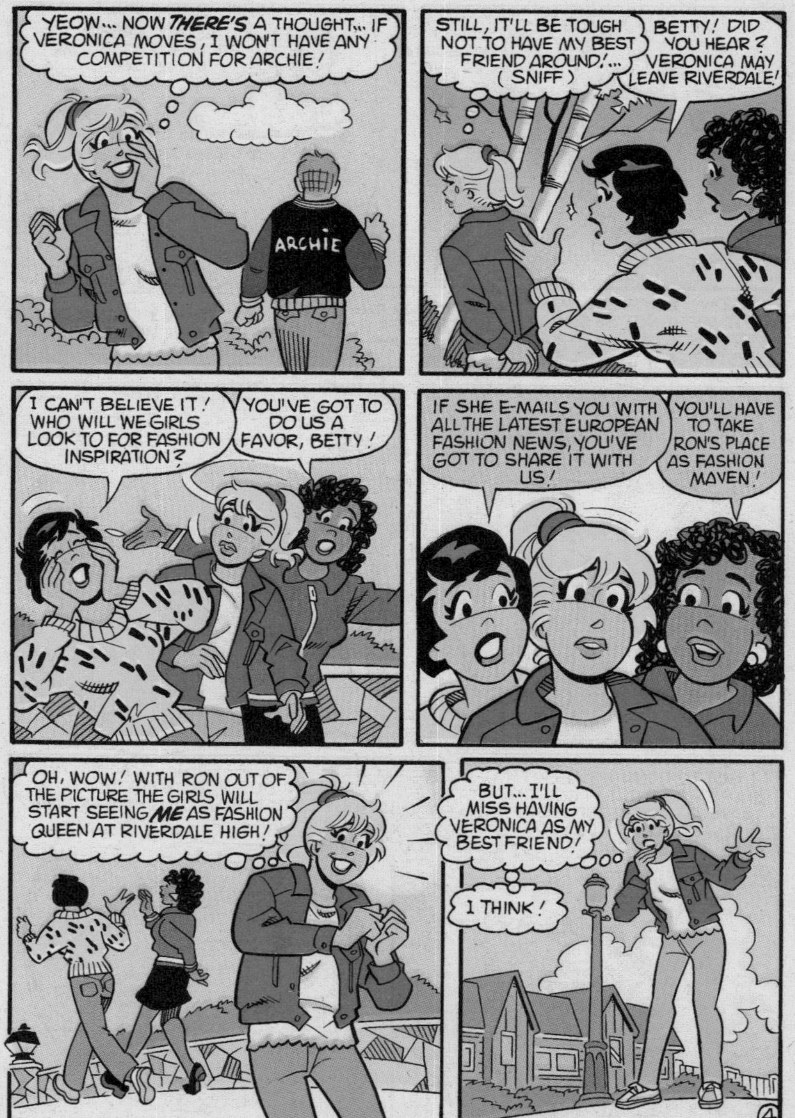
YEOW... NOW THERE'S A THOUGHT... IF VERONICA MOVES, I WON'T HAVE ANY COMPETITION FOR ARCHIE!
ARCHIE
STILL, IT'LL BE TOUGH NOT TO HAVE MY BEST FRIEND AROUND!... (SNIFF)
BETTY! DID YOU HEAR? VERONICA MAY LEAVE RIVERDALE!
I CAN'T BELIEVE IT! WHO WILL WE GIRLS LOOK TO FOR FASHION INSPIRATION?
YOU'VE GOT TO DO US A FAVOR, BETTY!
IF SHE E-MAILS YOU WITH ALL THE LATEST EUROPEAN FASHION NEWS, YOU'VE GOT TO SHARE IT WITH US!
YOU'LL HAVE TO TAKE RON'S PLACE AS FASHION MAVEN!
OH, WOW! WITH RON OUT OF THE PICTURE THE GIRLS WILL START SEEING ME AS FASHION QUEEN AT RIVERDALE HIGH!
BUT... I'LL MISS HAVING VERONICA AS MY BEST FRIEND!
I THINK!
4

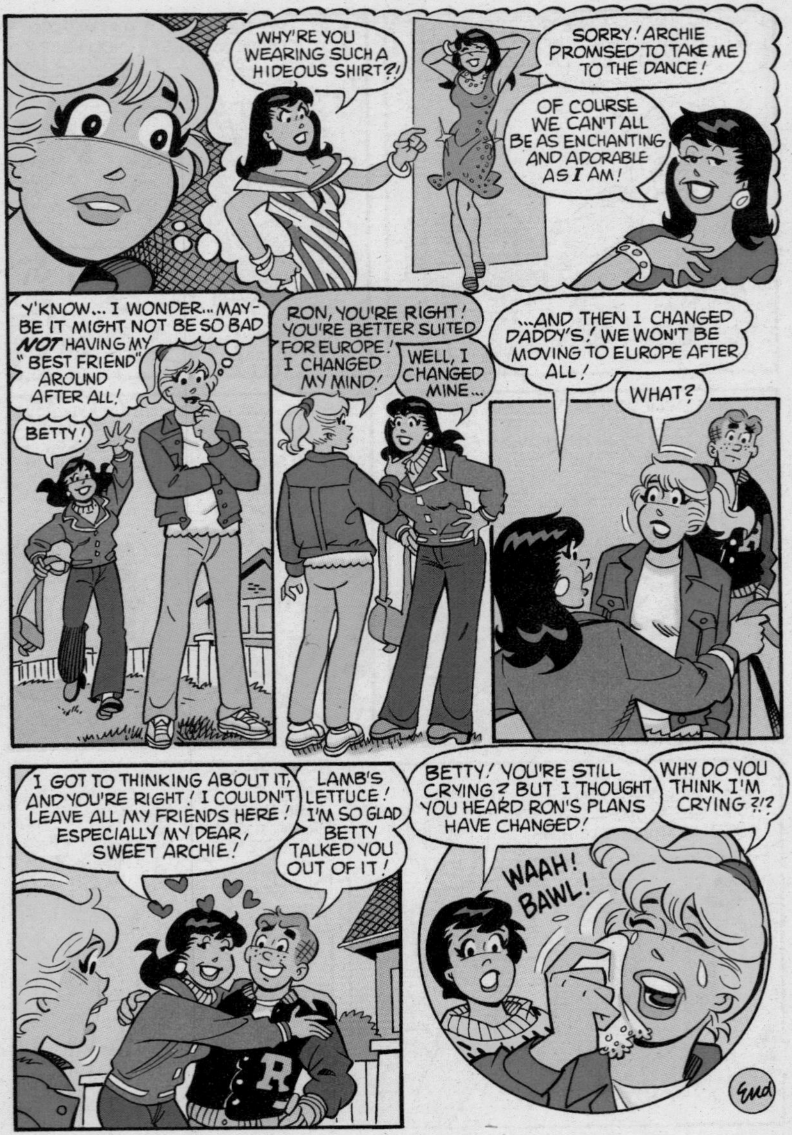
WHY'RE YOU WEARING SUCH A HIDEOUS SHIRT?!
SORRY! ARCHIE PROMISED TO TAKE ME TO THE DANCE!
OF COURSE WE CAN'T ALL BE AS ENCHANTING AND ADORABLE AS I AM!
Y'KNOW... I WONDER... MAY-BE IT MIGHT NOT BE SO BAD NOT HAVING MY "BEST FRIEND" AROUND AFTER ALL!
BETTY!
RON, YOU'RE RIGHT! YOU'RE BETTER SUITED FOR EUROPE! I CHANGED MY MIND!
WELL, I CHANGED MINE...
...AND THEN I CHANGED DADDY'S! WE WON'T BE MOVING TO EUROPE AFTER ALL!
WHAT?
I GOT TO THINKING ABOUT IT, AND YOU'RE RIGHT! I COULDN'T LEAVE ALL MY FRIENDS HERE! ESPECIALLY MY DEAR, SWEET ARCHIE!
LAMB'S LETTUCE! I'M SO GLAD BETTY TALKED YOU OUT OF IT!
BETTY! YOU'RE STILL CRYING? BUT I THOUGHT YOU HEARD RON'S PLANS HAVE CHANGED!
WHY DO YOU THINK I'M CRYING ?!?
WAAH! BAWL!
End

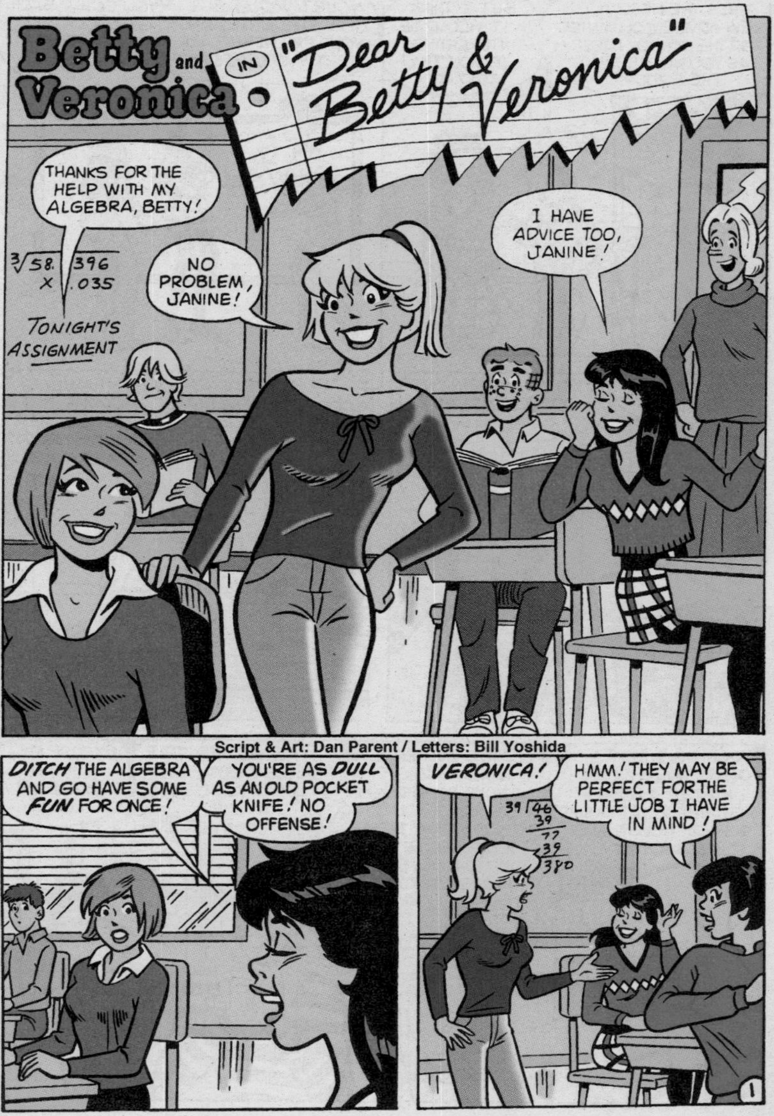
Betty and Veronica
IN
"Dear Betty & Veronica"
THANKS FOR THE HELP WITH MY ALGEBRA, BETTY!
NO PROBLEM, JANINE!
I HAVE ADVICE TOO, JANINE!
TONIGHT'S ASSIGNMENT
Script & Art: Dan Parent / Letters: Bill Yoshida
DITCH THE ALGEBRA AND GO HAVE SOME FUN FOR ONCE!
YOU'RE AS DULL AS AN OLD POCKET KNIFE! NO OFFENSE!
VERONICA!
HMM! THEY MAY BE PERFECT FOR THE LITTLE JOB I HAVE IN MIND!
1

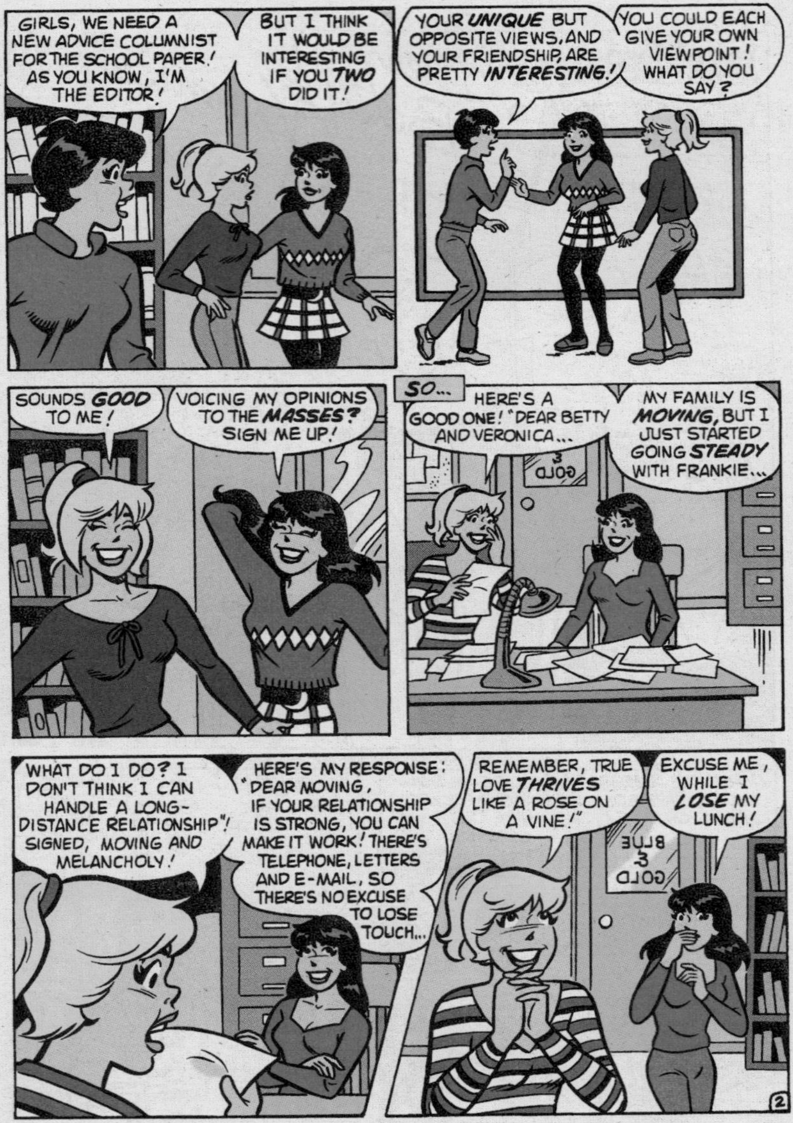

GIRLS, WE NEED A NEW ADVICE COLUMNIST FOR THE SCHOOL PAPER! AS YOU KNOW, I'M THE EDITOR!
BUT I THINK IT WOULD BE INTERESTING IF YOU TWO DID IT!
YOUR UNIQUE BUT OPPOSITE VIEWS, AND YOUR FRIENDSHIP, ARE PRETTY INTERESTING!
YOU COULD EACH GIVE YOUR OWN VIEWPOINT! WHAT DO YOU SAY?
SOUNDS GOOD TO ME!
VOICING MY OPINIONS TO THE MASSES? SIGN ME UP!
SO...
HERE'S A GOOD ONE! "DEAR BETTY AND VERONICA...
MY FAMILY IS MOVING, BUT I JUST STARTED GOING STEADY WITH FRANKIE...
WHAT DO I DO? I DON'T THINK I CAN HANDLE A LONG-DISTANCE RELATIONSHIP"! SIGNED, MOVING AND MELANCHOLY!
HERE'S MY RESPONSE: "DEAR MOVING, IF YOUR RELATIONSHIP IS STRONG, YOU CAN MAKE IT WORK! THERE'S TELEPHONE, LETTERS AND E-MAIL, SO THERE'S NO EXCUSE TO LOSE TOUCH...
REMEMBER, TRUE LOVE THRIVES LIKE A ROSE ON A VINE!"
EXCUSE ME, WHILE I LOSE MY LUNCH!
2

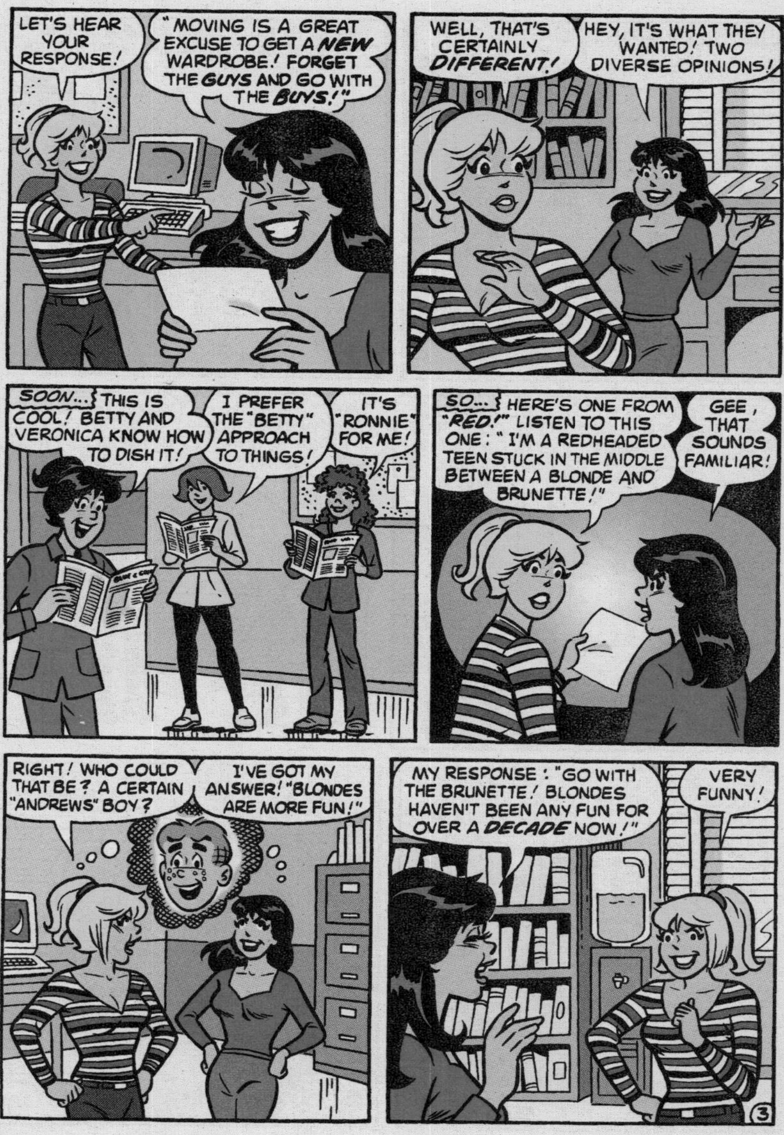
LET'S HEAR YOUR RESPONSE!
"MOVING IS A GREAT EXCUSE TO GET A NEW WARDROBE! FORGET THE GUYS AND GO WITH THE BUYS!"
WELL, THAT'S CERTAINLY DIFFERENT!
HEY, IT'S WHAT THEY WANTED! TWO DIVERSE OPINIONS!
SOON...
THIS IS COOL! BETTY AND VERONICA KNOW HOW TO DISH IT!
I PREFER THE "BETTY" APPROACH TO THINGS!
IT'S "RONNIE" FOR ME!
SO...
HERE'S ONE FROM "RED!" LISTEN TO THIS ONE: "I'M A REDHEADED TEEN STUCK IN THE MIDDLE BETWEEN A BLONDE AND BRUNETTE!"
GEE, THAT SOUNDS FAMILIAR!
RIGHT! WHO COULD THAT BE? A CERTAIN "ANDREWS" BOY?
I'VE GOT MY ANSWER! "BLONDES ARE MORE FUN!"
MY RESPONSE: "GO WITH THE BRUNETTE! BLONDES HAVEN'T BEEN ANY FUN FOR OVER A DECADE NOW!"
VERY FUNNY!
3

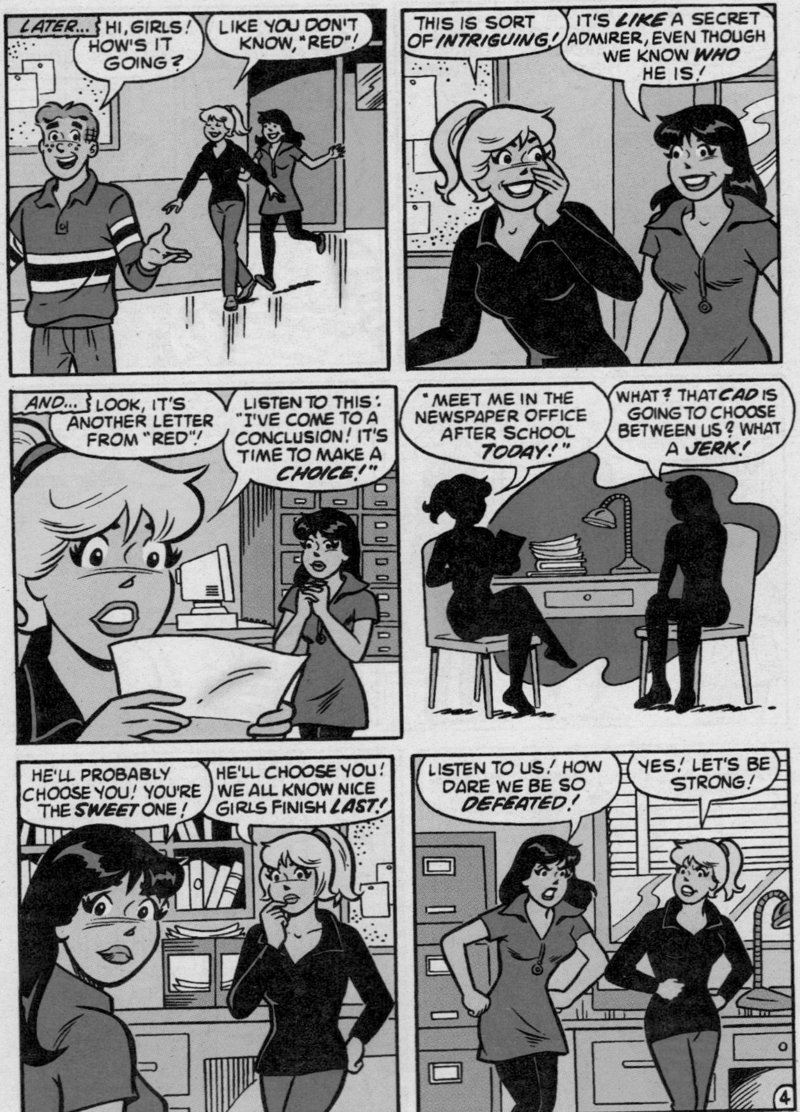
LATER...
HI, GIRLS! HOW'S IT GOING?
LIKE YOU DON'T KNOW, "RED"!
THIS IS SORT OF INTRIGUING!
IT'S LIKE A SECRET ADMIRER, EVEN THOUGH WE KNOW WHO HE IS!
AND...
LOOK, IT'S ANOTHER LETTER FROM "RED"!
LISTEN TO THIS: "I'VE COME TO A CONCLUSION! IT'S TIME TO MAKE A CHOICE!"
"MEET ME IN THE NEWSPAPER OFFICE AFTER SCHOOL TODAY!"
WHAT? THAT CAD IS GOING TO CHOOSE BETWEEN US? WHAT A JERK!
HE'LL PROBABLY CHOOSE YOU! YOU'RE THE SWEET ONE!
HE'LL CHOOSE YOU! WE ALL KNOW NICE GIRLS FINISH LAST!
LISTEN TO US! HOW DARE WE BE SO DEFEATED!
YES! LET'S BE STRONG!
4

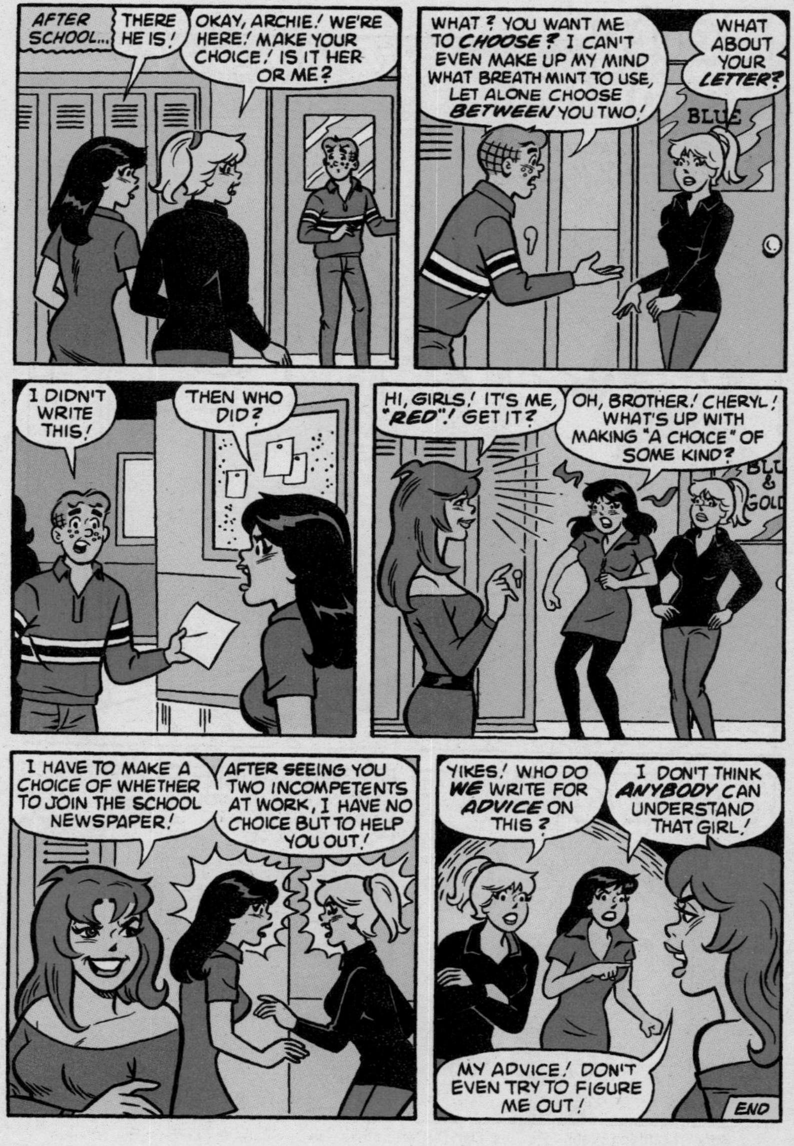

AFTER SCHOOL...
THERE HE IS!
OKAY, ARCHIE! WE'RE HERE! MAKE YOUR CHOICE! IS IT HER OR ME?
WHAT? YOU WANT ME TO CHOOSE? I CAN'T EVEN MAKE UP MY MIND WHAT BREATH MINT TO USE, LET ALONE CHOOSE BETWEEN YOU TWO!
WHAT ABOUT YOUR LETTER?
BLUE
I DIDN'T WRITE THIS!
THEN WHO DID?
HI, GIRLS! IT'S ME, "RED"! GET IT?
OH, BROTHER! CHERYL! WHAT'S UP WITH MAKING "A CHOICE" OF SOME KIND?
BLUE & GOLD
I HAVE TO MAKE A CHOICE OF WHETHER TO JOIN THE SCHOOL NEWSPAPER!
AFTER SEEING YOU TWO INCOMPETENTS AT WORK, I HAVE NO CHOICE BUT TO HELP YOU OUT!
YIKES! WHO DO WE WRITE FOR ADVICE ON THIS?
I DON'T THINK ANYBODY CAN UNDERSTAND THAT GIRL!
MY ADVICE! DON'T EVEN TRY TO FIGURE ME OUT!
END

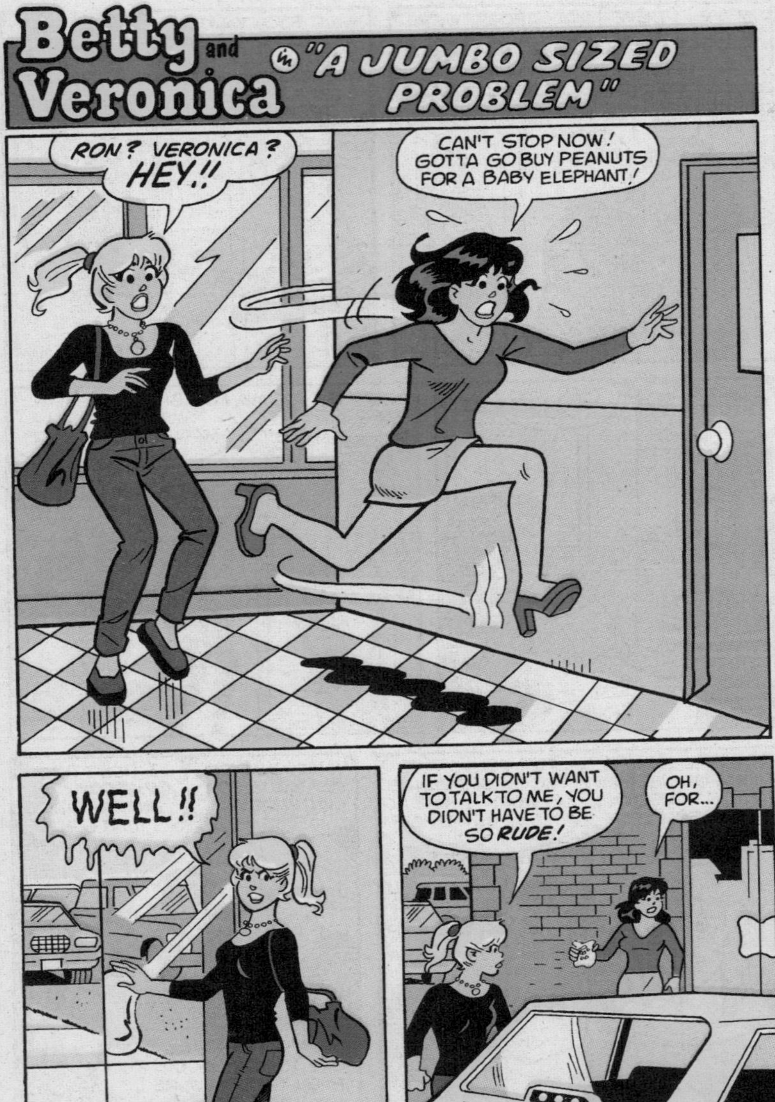
Betty and Veronica
in "A JUMBO SIZED PROBLEM"
RON? VERONICA? HEY!!
CAN'T STOP NOW! GOTTA GO BUY PEANUTS FOR A BABY ELEPHANT!
WELL!!
IF YOU DIDN'T WANT TO TALK TO ME, YOU DIDN'T HAVE TO BE SO RUDE!
OH, FOR...

Script: Kathleen Webb / Pencils: Dan DeCarlo / Inks: Henry Scarpelli / Letters: Bill Yoshida

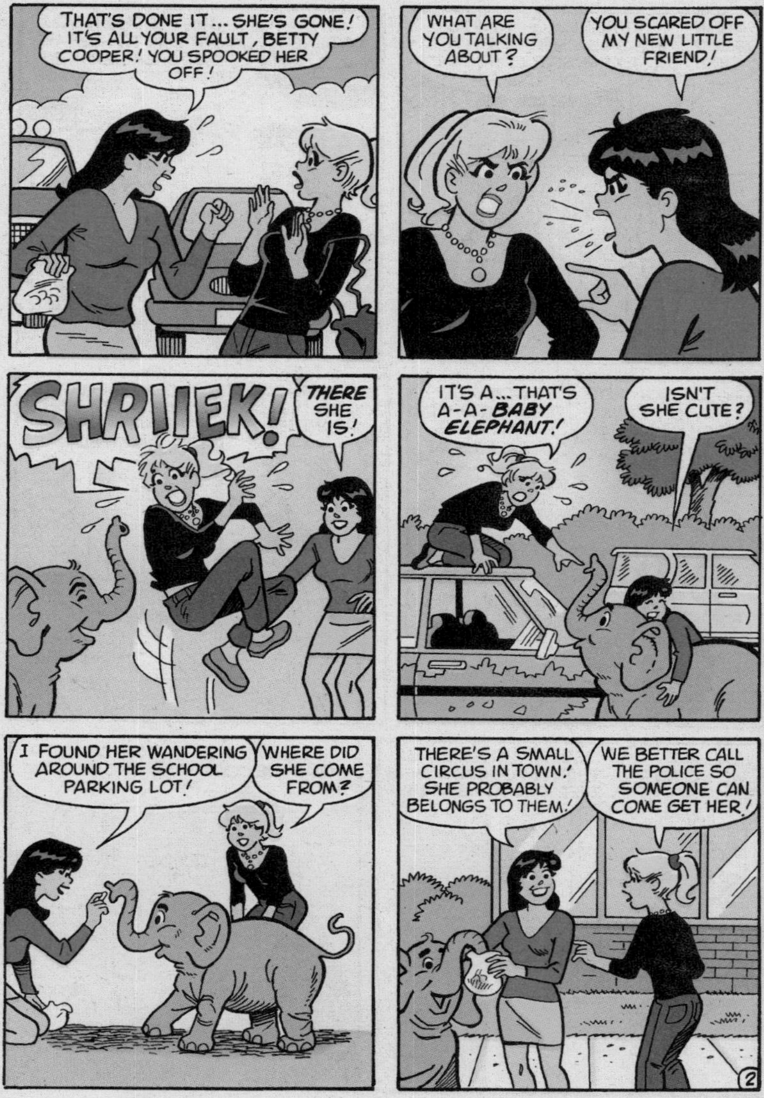
THAT'S DONE IT ... SHE'S GONE! IT'S ALL YOUR FAULT, BETTY COOPER! YOU SPOOKED HER OFF!
WHAT ARE YOU TALKING ABOUT?
YOU SCARED OFF MY NEW LITTLE FRIEND!
SHRIIEK!
THERE SHE IS!
IT'S A...THAT'S A-A-BABY ELEPHANT!
ISN'T SHE CUTE?
I FOUND HER WANDERING AROUND THE SCHOOL PARKING LOT!
WHERE DID SHE COME FROM?
THERE'S A SMALL CIRCUS IN TOWN! SHE PROBABLY BELONGS TO THEM!
WE BETTER CALL THE POLICE SO SOMEONE CAN COME GET HER!
2

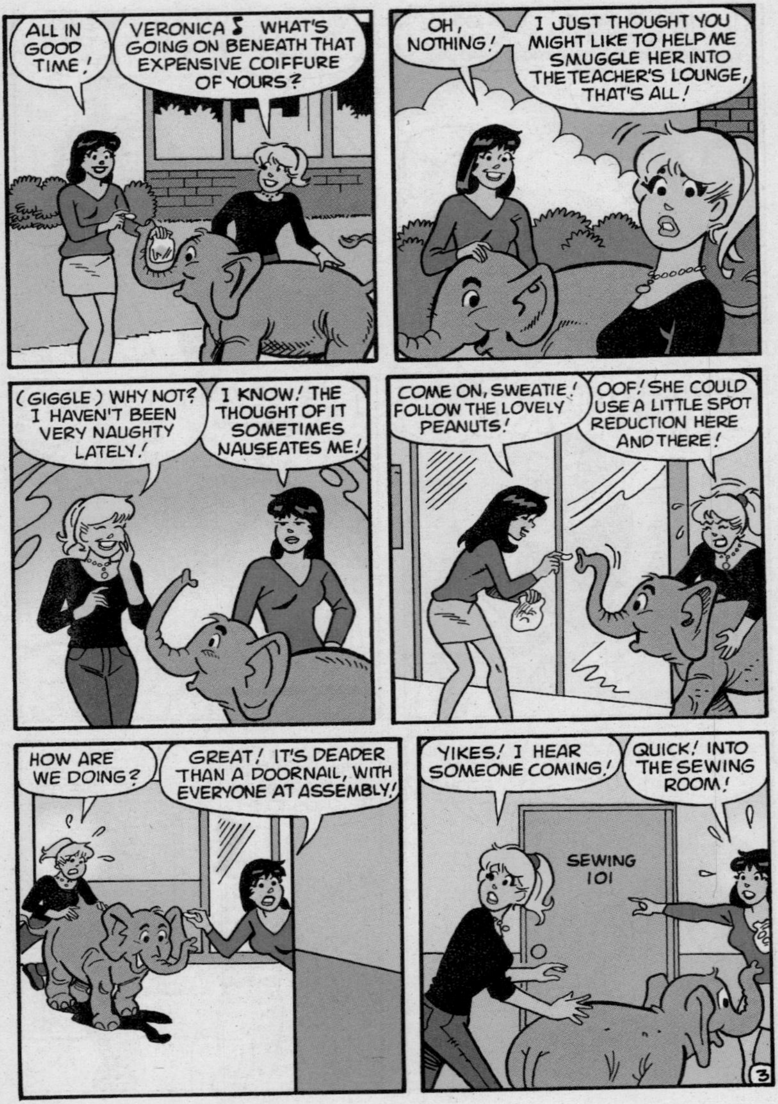
ALL IN GOOD TIME!
VERONICA! WHAT'S GOING ON BENEATH THAT EXPENSIVE COIFFURE OF YOURS?
OH, NOTHING!
I JUST THOUGHT YOU MIGHT LIKE TO HELP ME SMUGGLE HER INTO THE TEACHER'S LOUNGE, THAT'S ALL!
(GIGGLE) WHY NOT? I HAVEN'T BEEN VERY NAUGHTY LATELY!
I KNOW! THE THOUGHT OF IT SOMETIMES NAUSEATES ME!
COME ON, SWEATIE! FOLLOW THE LOVELY PEANUTS!
OOF! SHE COULD USE A LITTLE SPOT REDUCTION HERE AND THERE!
HOW ARE WE DOING?
GREAT! IT'S DEADER THAN A DOORNAIL, WITH EVERYONE AT ASSEMBLY!
YIKES! I HEAR SOMEONE COMING!
QUICK! INTO THE SEWING ROOM!
SEWING 101
3

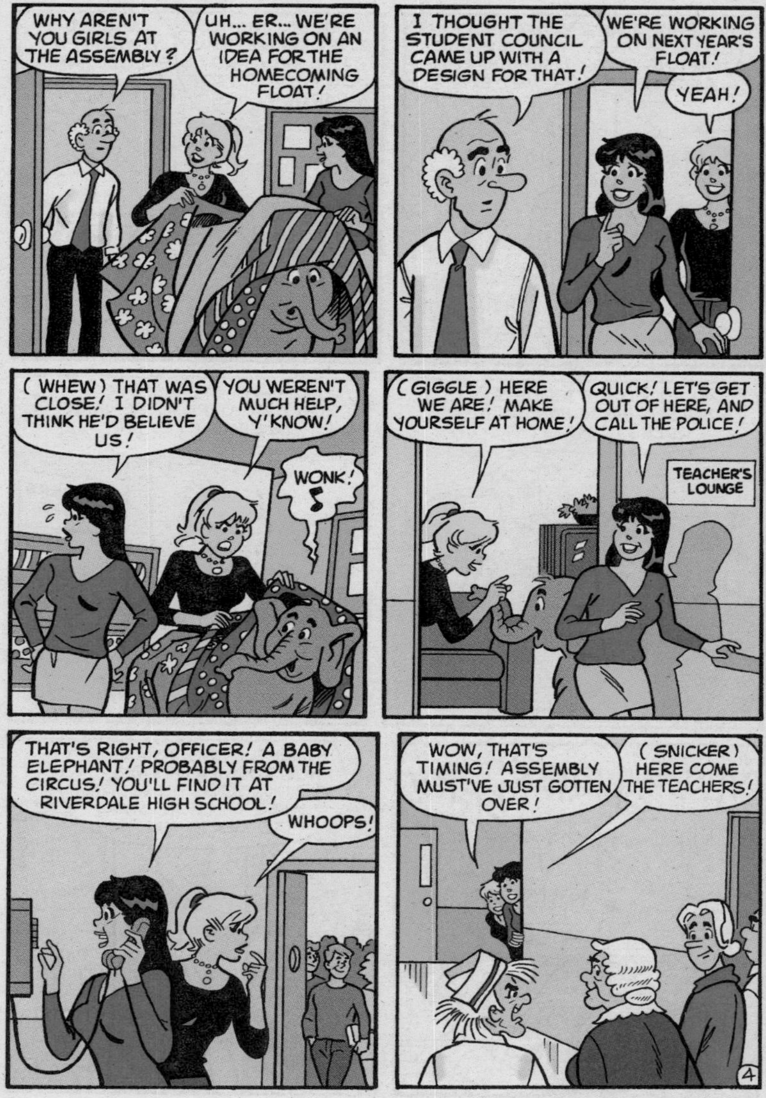
WHY AREN'T YOU GIRLS AT THE ASSEMBLY?
UH... ER... WE'RE WORKING ON AN IDEA FOR THE HOMECOMING FLOAT!
I THOUGHT THE STUDENT COUNCIL CAME UP WITH A DESIGN FOR THAT!
WE'RE WORKING ON NEXT YEAR'S FLOAT!
YEAH!
(WHEW) THAT WAS CLOSE! I DIDN'T THINK HE'D BELIEVE US!
YOU WEREN'T MUCH HELP, Y'KNOW!
WONK!
(GIGGLE) HERE WE ARE! MAKE YOURSELF AT HOME!
QUICK! LET'S GET OUT OF HERE, AND CALL THE POLICE!
TEACHER'S LOUNGE
THAT'S RIGHT, OFFICER! A BABY ELEPHANT! PROBABLY FROM THE CIRCUS! YOU'LL FIND IT AT RIVERDALE HIGH SCHOOL!
WHOOPS!
WOW, THAT'S TIMING! ASSEMBLY MUST'VE JUST GOTTEN OVER!
(SNICKER) HERE COME THE TEACHERS!
4

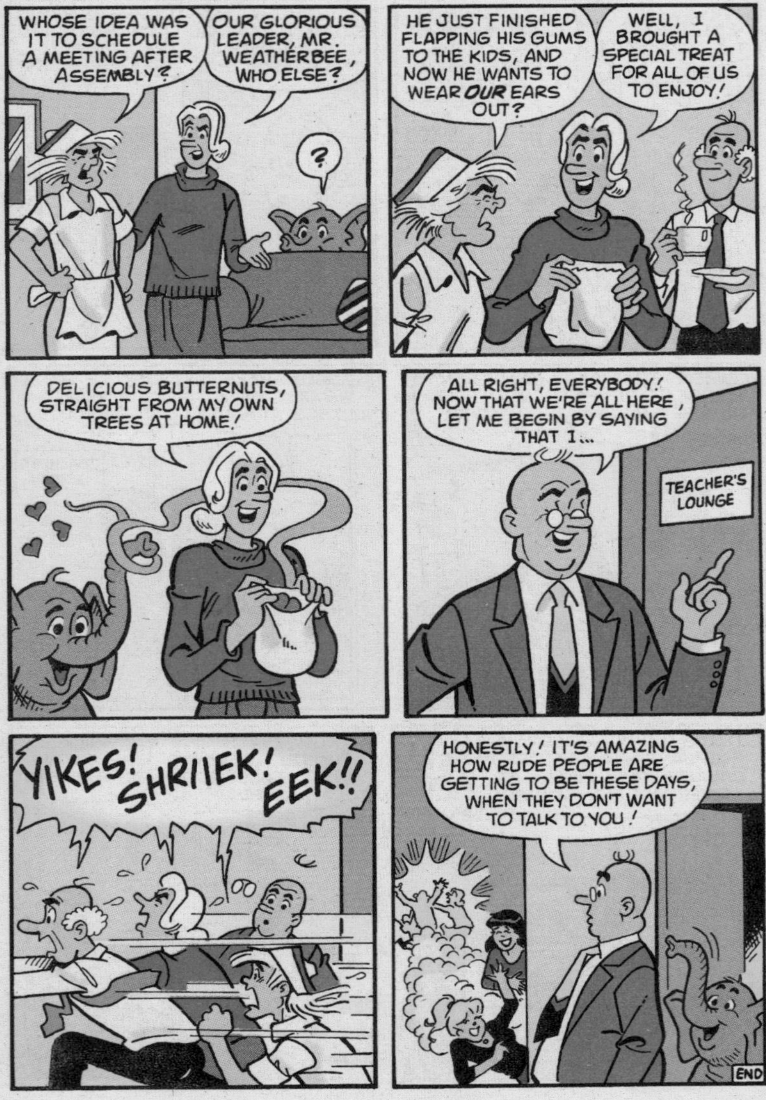
WHOSE IDEA WAS IT TO SCHEDULE A MEETING AFTER ASSEMBLY?
OUR GLORIOUS LEADER, MR. WEATHERBEE, WHO ELSE?
?
HE JUST FINISHED FLAPPING HIS GUMS TO THE KIDS, AND NOW HE WANTS TO WEAR OUR EARS OUT?
WELL, I BROUGHT A SPECIAL TREAT FOR ALL OF US TO ENJOY!
DELICIOUS BUTTERNUTS, STRAIGHT FROM MY OWN TREES AT HOME!
ALL RIGHT, EVERYBODY! NOW THAT WE'RE ALL HERE, LET ME BEGIN BY SAYING THAT I...
TEACHER'S LOUNGE
YIKES! SHRIIEK! EEK!!
HONESTLY! IT'S AMAZING HOW RUDE PEOPLE ARE GETTING TO BE THESE DAYS, WHEN THEY DON'T WANT TO TALK TO YOU!
END

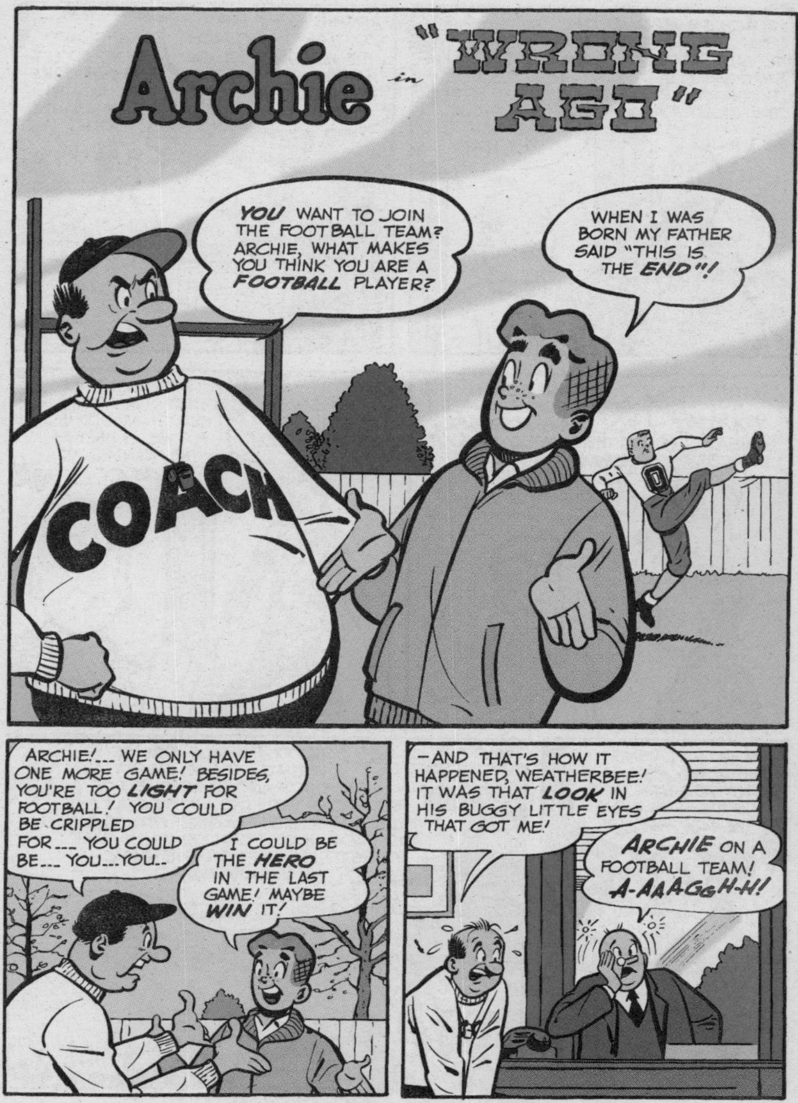
Archie in "WRONG AGI"
YOU WANT TO JOIN THE FOOTBALL TEAM? ARCHIE, WHAT MAKES YOU THINK YOU ARE A FOOTBALL PLAYER?
WHEN I WAS BORN MY FATHER SAID "THIS IS THE END"!
COACH
ARCHIE!... WE ONLY HAVE ONE MORE GAME! BESIDES, YOU'RE TOO LIGHT FOR FOOTBALL! YOU COULD BE CRIPPLED FOR... YOU COULD BE... YOU...YOU..
I COULD BE THE HERO IN THE LAST GAME! MAYBE WIN IT!
-AND THAT'S HOW IT HAPPENED, WEATHERBEE! IT WAS THAT LOOK IN HIS BUGGY LITTLE EYES THAT GOT ME!
ARCHIE ON A FOOTBALL TEAM! A-AAAGGH-H!

Script: Frank Doyle / Art: Harry Lucey

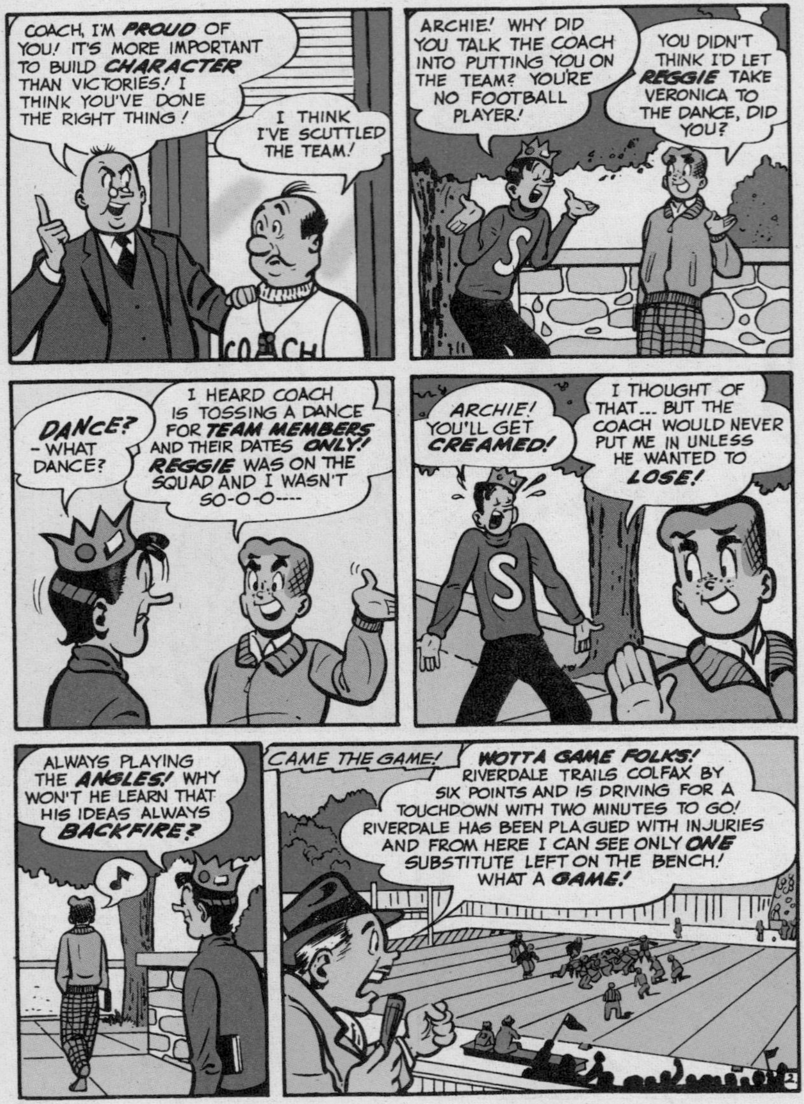
COACH, I'M PROUD OF YOU! IT'S MORE IMPORTANT TO BUILD CHARACTER THAN VICTORIES! I THINK YOU'VE DONE THE RIGHT THING!
I THINK I'VE SCUTTLED THE TEAM!
COACH
ARCHIE! WHY DID YOU TALK THE COACH INTO PUTTING YOU ON THE TEAM? YOU'RE NO FOOTBALL PLAYER!
YOU DIDN'T THINK I'D LET REGGIE TAKE VERONICA TO THE DANCE, DID YOU?
DANCE? - WHAT DANCE?
I HEARD COACH IS TOSSING A DANCE FOR TEAM MEMBERS AND THEIR DATES ONLY! REGGIE WAS ON THE SQUAD AND I WASN'T SO-O-O----
ARCHIE! YOU'LL GET CREAMED!
I THOUGHT OF THAT... BUT THE COACH WOULD NEVER PUT ME IN UNLESS HE WANTED TO LOSE!
ALWAYS PLAYING THE ANGLES! WHY WON'T HE LEARN THAT HIS IDEAS ALWAYS BACKFIRE?
CAME THE GAME!
WOTTA GAME FOLKS! RIVERDALE TRAILS COLFAX BY SIX POINTS AND IS DRIVING FOR A TOUCHDOWN WITH TWO MINUTES TO GO! RIVERDALE HAS BEEN PLAGUED WITH INJURIES AND FROM HERE I CAN SEE ONLY ONE SUBSTITUTE LEFT ON THE BENCH! WHAT A GAME!
2

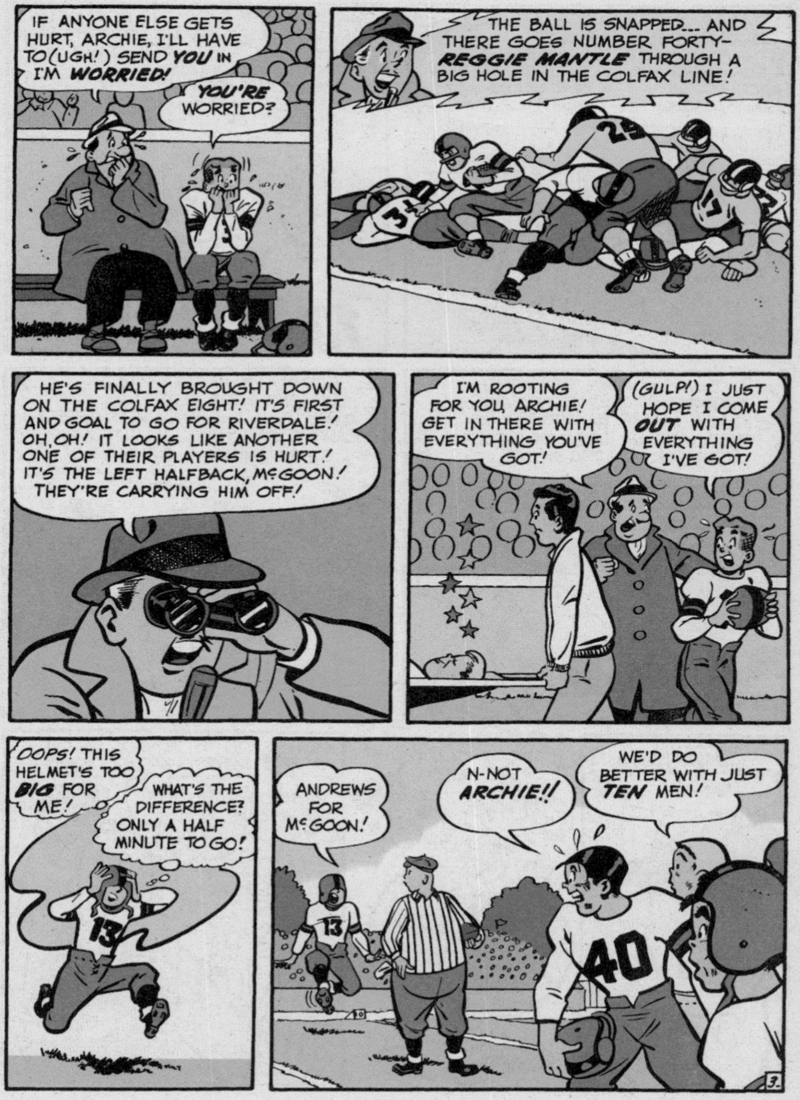
IF ANYONE ELSE GETS HURT, ARCHIE, I'LL HAVE TO (UGH!) SEND YOU IN I'M WORRIED!
YOU'RE WORRIED?
THE BALL IS SNAPPED... AND THERE GOES NUMBER FORTY- REGGIE MANTLE THROUGH A BIG HOLE IN THE COLFAX LINE!
HE'S FINALLY BROUGHT DOWN ON THE COLFAX EIGHT! IT'S FIRST AND GOAL TO GO FOR RIVERDALE! OH, OH! IT LOOKS LIKE ANOTHER ONE OF THEIR PLAYERS IS HURT! IT'S THE LEFT HALFBACK, McGOON! THEY'RE CARRYING HIM OFF!
I'M ROOTING FOR YOU, ARCHIE! GET IN THERE WITH EVERYTHING YOU'VE GOT!
(GULP!) I JUST HOPE I COME OUT WITH EVERYTHING I'VE GOT!
OOPS! THIS HELMET'S TOO BIG FOR ME!
WHAT'S THE DIFFERENCE? ONLY A HALF MINUTE TO GO!
ANDREWS FOR McGOON!
N-NOT ARCHIE!!
WE'D DO BETTER WITH JUST TEN MEN!
3.

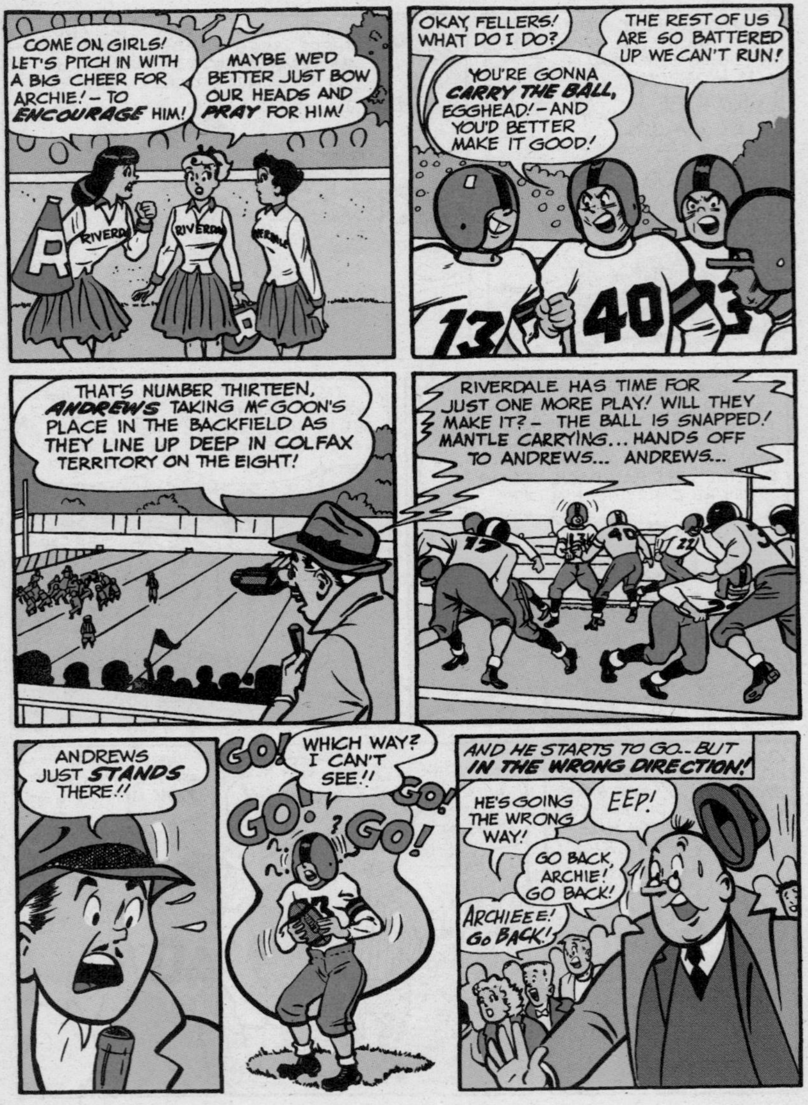

COME ON, GIRLS! LET'S PITCH IN WITH A BIG CHEER FOR ARCHIE! – TO ENCOURAGE HIM!
MAYBE WE'D BETTER JUST BOW OUR HEADS AND PRAY FOR HIM!
OKAY, FELLERS! WHAT DO I DO?
YOU'RE GONNA CARRY THE BALL, EGGHEAD! – AND YOU'D BETTER MAKE IT GOOD!
THE REST OF US ARE SO BATTERED UP WE CAN'T RUN!
THAT'S NUMBER THIRTEEN, ANDREWS TAKING McGOON'S PLACE IN THE BACKFIELD AS THEY LINE UP DEEP IN COLFAX TERRITORY ON THE EIGHT!
RIVERDALE HAS TIME FOR JUST ONE MORE PLAY! WILL THEY MAKE IT? – THE BALL IS SNAPPED! MANTLE CARRYING... HANDS OFF TO ANDREWS... ANDREWS...
ANDREWS JUST STANDS THERE!!
GO!
WHICH WAY? I CAN'T SEE!!
GO!
GO!
GO!
AND HE STARTS TO GO.. BUT IN THE WRONG DIRECTION!
HE'S GOING THE WRONG WAY!
EEP!
GO BACK, ARCHIE! GO BACK!
ARCHIEEE! GO BACK!

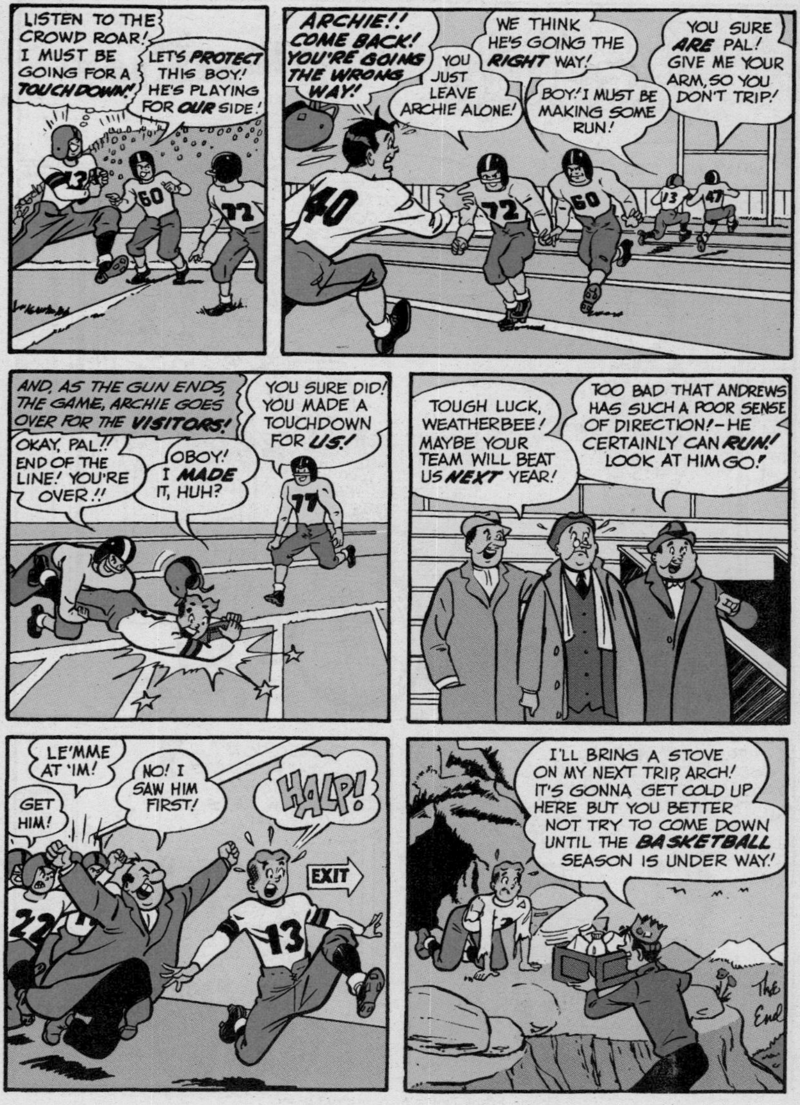

LISTEN TO THE CROWD ROAR! I MUST BE GOING FOR A TOUCHDOWN!
LET'S PROTECT THIS BOY! HE'S PLAYING FOR OUR SIDE!
ARCHIE!! COME BACK! YOU'RE GOING THE WRONG WAY!
YOU JUST LEAVE ARCHIE ALONE!
WE THINK HE'S GOING THE RIGHT WAY!
BOY! I MUST BE MAKING SOME RUN!
YOU SURE ARE PAL! GIVE ME YOUR ARM, SO YOU DON'T TRIP!
AND, AS THE GUN ENDS THE GAME, ARCHIE GOES OVER FOR THE VISITORS!
OKAY, PAL!! END OF THE LINE! YOU'RE OVER!!
OBOY! I MADE IT, HUH?
YOU SURE DID! YOU MADE A TOUCHDOWN FOR US!
TOUGH LUCK, WEATHERBEE! MAYBE YOUR TEAM WILL BEAT US NEXT YEAR!
TOO BAD THAT ANDREWS HAS SUCH A POOR SENSE OF DIRECTION!—HE CERTAINLY CAN RUN! LOOK AT HIM GO!
LE'MME AT 'IM!
GET HIM!
NO! I SAW HIM FIRST!
HALP!
EXIT
I'LL BRING A STOVE ON MY NEXT TRIP, ARCH! IT'S GONNA GET COLD UP HERE BUT YOU BETTER NOT TRY TO COME DOWN UNTIL THE BASKETBALL SEASON IS UNDER WAY!
The End

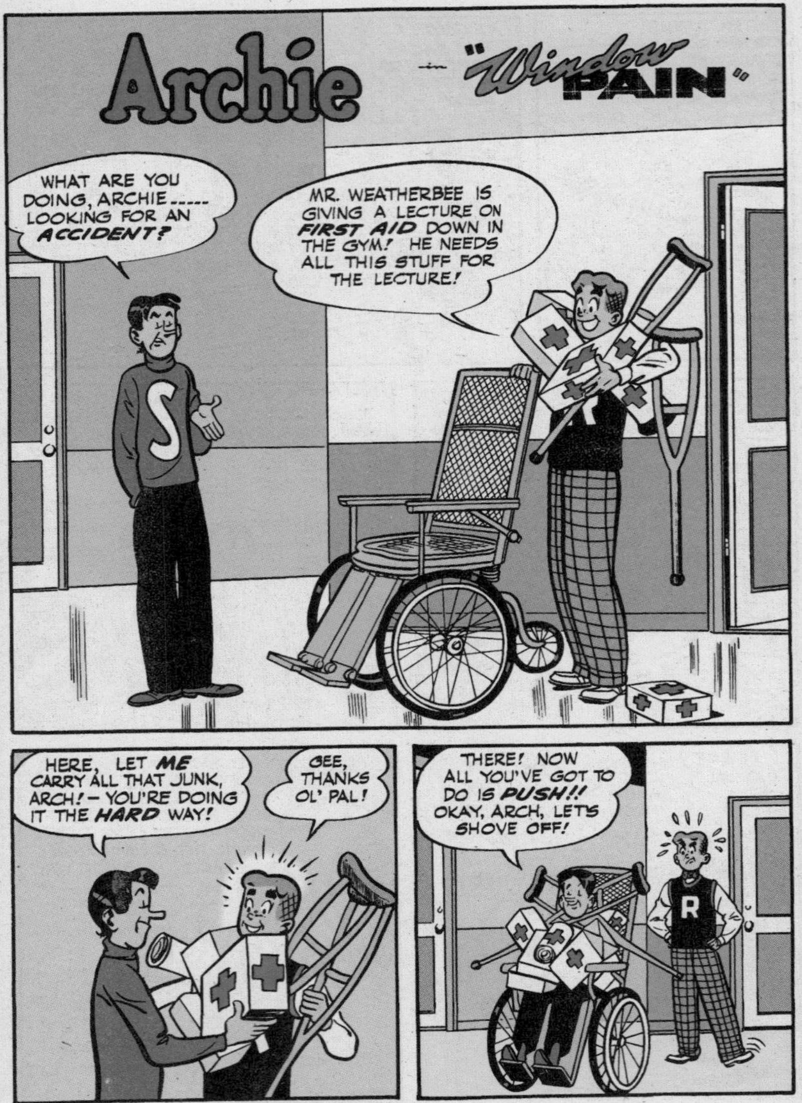
Archie
-in- "Window PAIN"
WHAT ARE YOU DOING, ARCHIE...... LOOKING FOR AN ACCIDENT?
MR. WEATHERBEE IS GIVING A LECTURE ON FIRST AID DOWN IN THE GYM! HE NEEDS ALL THIS STUFF FOR THE LECTURE!
HERE, LET ME CARRY ALL THAT JUNK, ARCH! – YOU'RE DOING IT THE HARD WAY!
GEE, THANKS OL' PAL!
THERE! NOW ALL YOU'VE GOT TO DO IS PUSH!! OKAY, ARCH, LET'S SHOVE OFF!
R

Script: Frank Doyle / Art: Harry Lucey

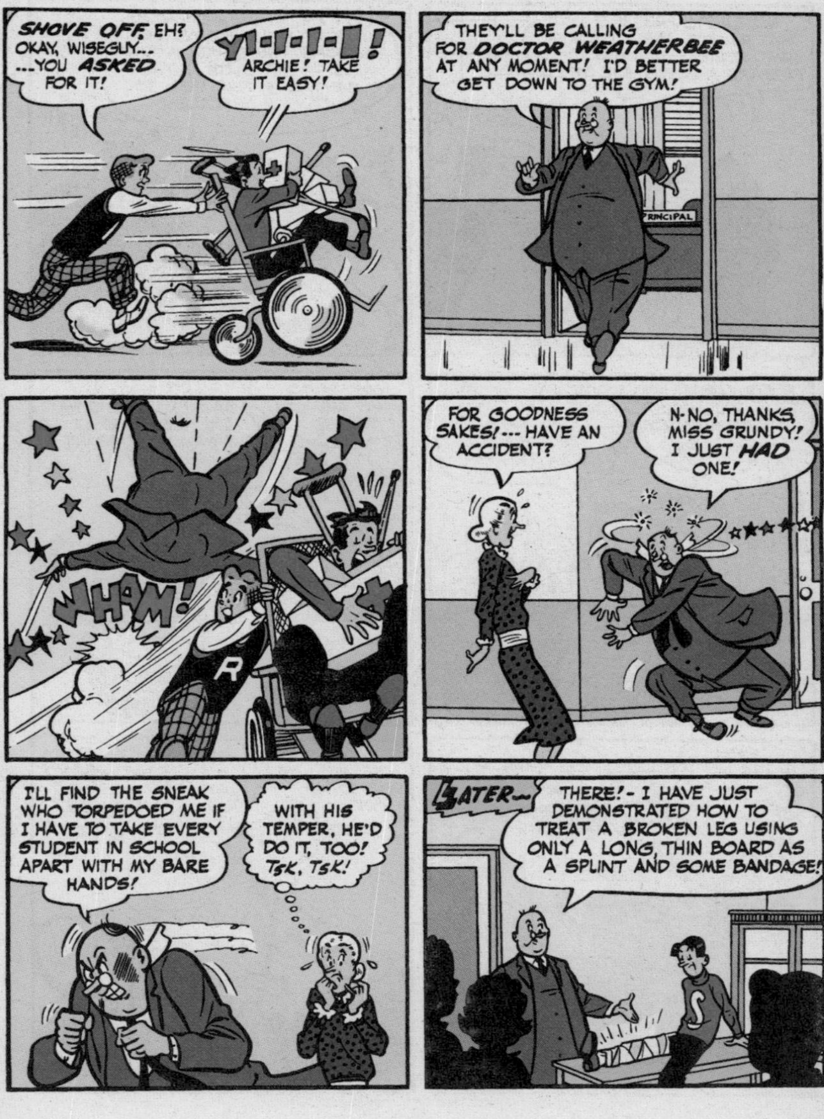
SHOVE OFF, EH? OKAY, WISEGUY... ...YOU ASKED FOR IT!
YI-I-I-I-I!
ARCHIE! TAKE IT EASY!
THEY'LL BE CALLING FOR DOCTOR WEATHERBEE AT ANY MOMENT! I'D BETTER GET DOWN TO THE GYM!
PRINCIPAL
WHAM!
FOR GOODNESS SAKES! --- HAVE AN ACCIDENT?
N-NO, THANKS, MISS GRUNDY! I JUST HAD ONE!
I'LL FIND THE SNEAK WHO TORPEDOED ME IF I HAVE TO TAKE EVERY STUDENT IN SCHOOL APART WITH MY BARE HANDS!
WITH HIS TEMPER, HE'D DO IT, TOO! TSK, TSK!
LATER--
THERE! - I HAVE JUST DEMONSTRATED HOW TO TREAT A BROKEN LEG USING ONLY A LONG, THIN BOARD AS A SPLINT AND SOME BANDAGE!

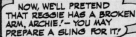

NOW, WE'LL PRETEND THAT REGGIE HAS A BROKEN ARM, ARCHIE! — YOU MAY PREPARE A SLING FOR IT!

I'D SOONER BREAK THE ARM!

YIPE!! --- VERONICA! IF YOU WOULD REMOVE BETTY'S EARRING FIRST, YOU WOULDN'T HAVE TO CUT SLITS IN THE BANDAGES FOR THEM TO DANGLE THROUGH!

REGGIE!! YOU NEVER TIE A TOURNIQUET AROUND ANYONE'S NECK!

NO? IT'S NOT A BAD IDEA, THOUGH!

JUGHEAD!! WHAT ARE YOU DOING?

I CAN'T BEND MY BROKEN LEG THE WAY YOU FIXED IT SO I'M SAWING THE SPLINT IN HALF!

THIS IS IT!

EVERYBODY DANCE!!

LAST STOP!

THE OLD GOAT ACTS LIKE HE'S POPPED HIS CORK!

GOOD HEAVENS! I HOPE HE HASN'T HARMED ANY OF THE STUDENTS!

3.

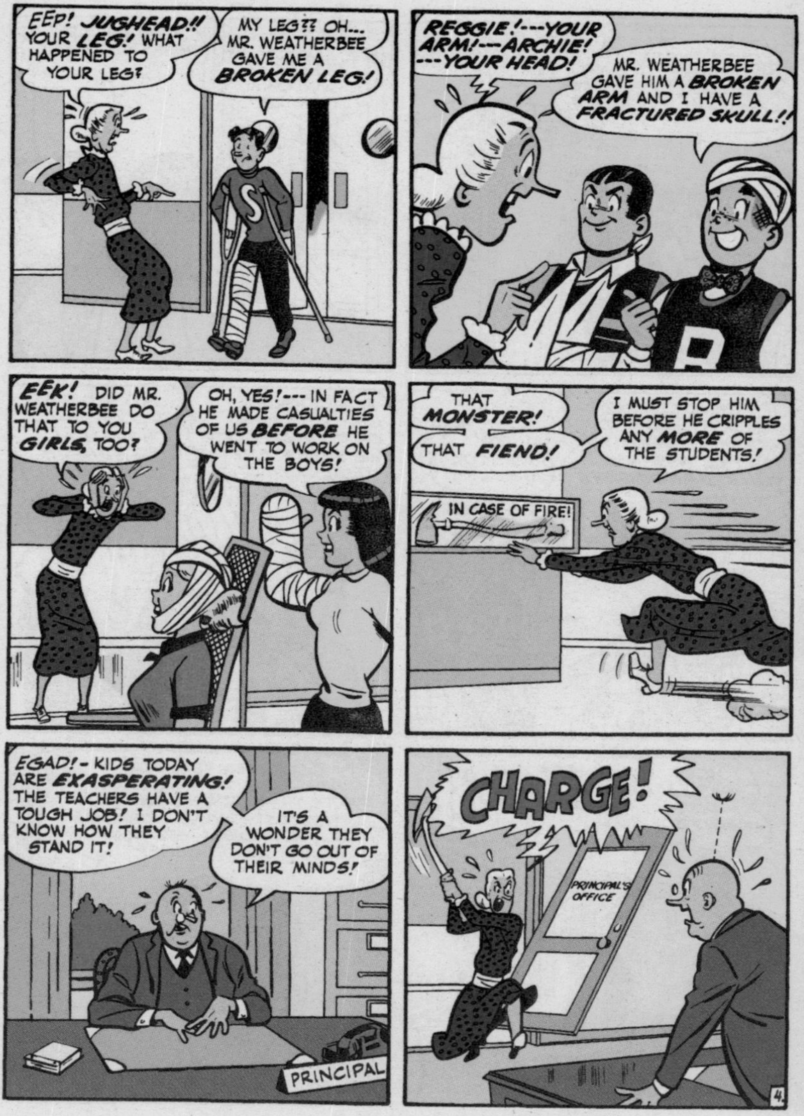
EEp! JUGHEAD!! YOUR LEG! WHAT HAPPENED TO YOUR LEG?
MY LEG?? OH... MR. WEATHERBEE GAVE ME A BROKEN LEG!
REGGIE!---YOUR ARM!---ARCHIE! ---YOUR HEAD!
MR. WEATHERBEE GAVE HIM A BROKEN ARM AND I HAVE A FRACTURED SKULL!!
EEK! DID MR. WEATHERBEE DO THAT TO YOU GIRLS, TOO?
OH, YES!--- IN FACT HE MADE CASUALTIES OF US BEFORE HE WENT TO WORK ON THE BOYS!
THAT MONSTER!
THAT FIEND!
I MUST STOP HIM BEFORE HE CRIPPLES ANY MORE OF THE STUDENTS!
IN CASE OF FIRE!
EGAD! - KIDS TODAY ARE EXASPERATING! THE TEACHERS HAVE A TOUGH JOB! I DON'T KNOW HOW THEY STAND IT!
IT'S A WONDER THEY DON'T GO OUT OF THEIR MINDS!
PRINCIPAL
CHARGE!
PRINCIPAL'S OFFICE
4

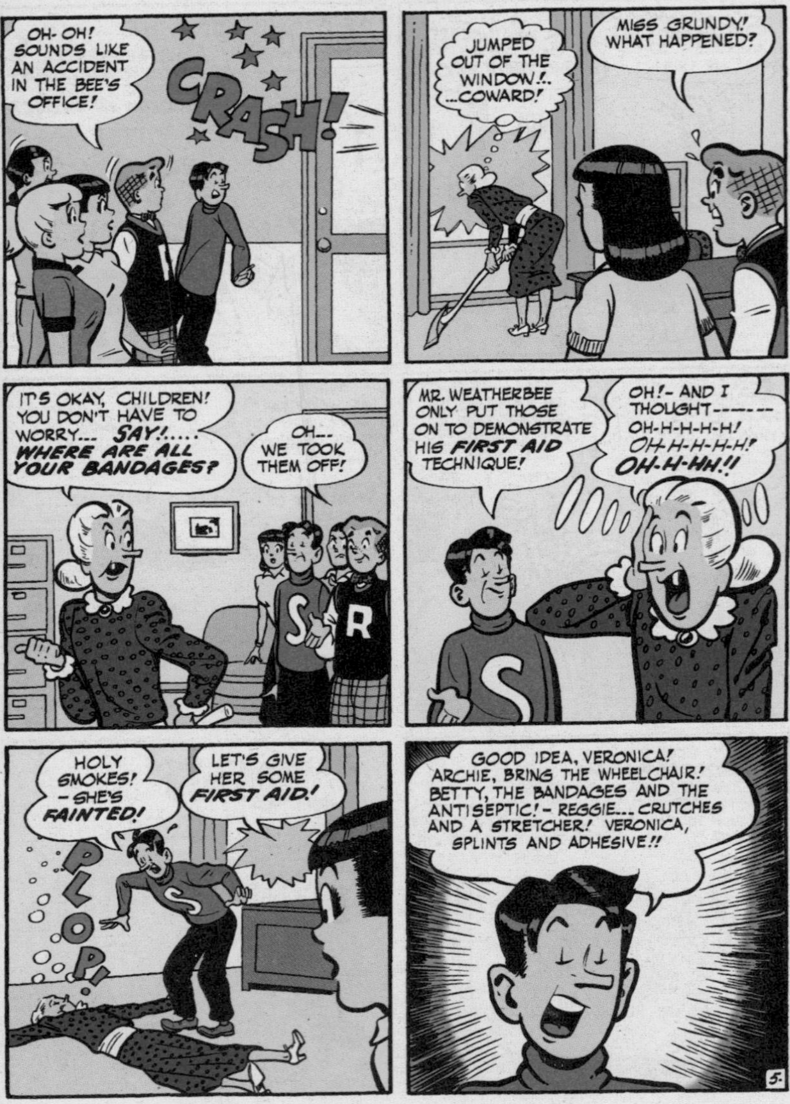
OH- OH! SOUNDS LIKE AN ACCIDENT IN THE BEE'S OFFICE!
CRASH!
MISS GRUNDY! WHAT HAPPENED?
JUMPED OUT OF THE WINDOW!.. ...COWARD!
IT'S OKAY, CHILDREN! YOU DON'T HAVE TO WORRY... SAY!.... WHERE ARE ALL YOUR BANDAGES?
OH... WE TOOK THEM OFF!
MR. WEATHERBEE ONLY PUT THOSE ON TO DEMONSTRATE HIS FIRST AID TECHNIQUE!
OH!- AND I THOUGHT------- OH-H-H-H-H! OH-H-H-H-H! OH-H-HH!!
HOLY SMOKES! - SHE'S FAINTED!
LET'S GIVE HER SOME FIRST AID!
PLOP!
GOOD IDEA, VERONICA! ARCHIE, BRING THE WHEELCHAIR! BETTY, THE BANDAGES AND THE ANTISEPTIC! - REGGIE... CRUTCHES AND A STRETCHER! VERONICA, SPLINTS AND ADHESIVE!!
5-

Panel 1: AREN'T YOU SUPPOSED TO BEND THE HEAD *BACKWARDS?*

NO! — YOU'RE SUPPOSED TO PUSH IT *FORWARD!* --I THINK!

RAISING THE FEET IS GOOD, TOO! --OR IS THAT JUST FOR SOMEONE WHO FALLS DOWN AN ELEVATOR SHAFT?

Panel 2: CLANGITY! CLANG! GANGWAY! — LET A COUPLE OF *REAL* FIRST-AIDERS GO TO WORK!

HAVE YOU CHECKED HER *ARTIFICIAL RESPIRATION?*

Panel 3: I WONDER IF SHE HAD A *STROKE!*

MAYBE SHE HAD A *HEART ATTACK!*

....OR A *CONCLUSION!*

IS SHE STILL *BREATHING*

Panel 4: OH-OH! *HERE'S* THE TROUBLE! — SHE HAS A TINY *CUT* ON HER FINGER!

Panel 5: SHE MUST HAVE BEEN NICKED BY A PIECE OF FLYING GLASS WHEN THE WINDOW BROKE!

I WONDER WHO BROKE IT!?

Panel 6: WE'RE TAKING MISS GRUNDY HOME, MISTER WEATHERBEE!

SHE WAS INJURED WHEN SOME DOPE BROKE YOUR WINDOW!

The End

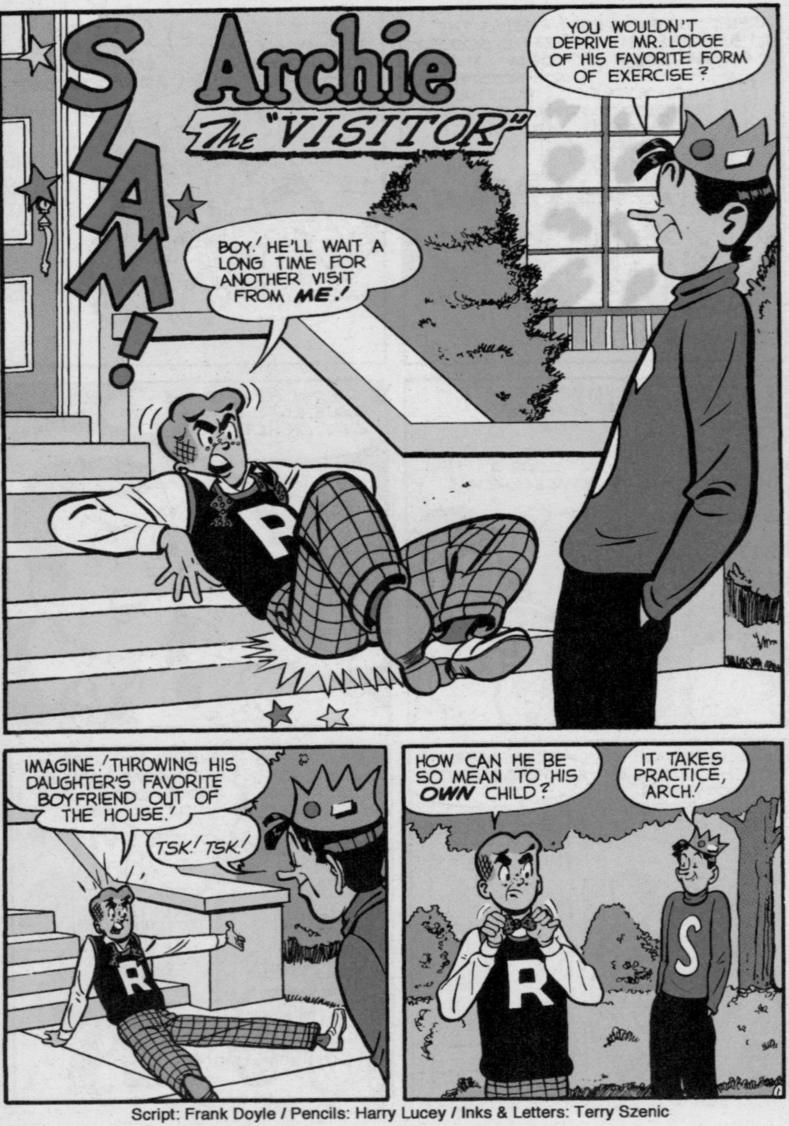
Archie
The "VISITOR"
SLAM!
YOU WOULDN'T DEPRIVE MR. LODGE OF HIS FAVORITE FORM OF EXERCISE?
BOY! HE'LL WAIT A LONG TIME FOR ANOTHER VISIT FROM ME!
IMAGINE! THROWING HIS DAUGHTER'S FAVORITE BOYFRIEND OUT OF THE HOUSE!
TSK! TSK!
HOW CAN HE BE SO MEAN TO HIS OWN CHILD?
IT TAKES PRACTICE, ARCH!

Script: Frank Doyle / Pencils: Harry Lucey / Inks & Letters: Terry Szenic

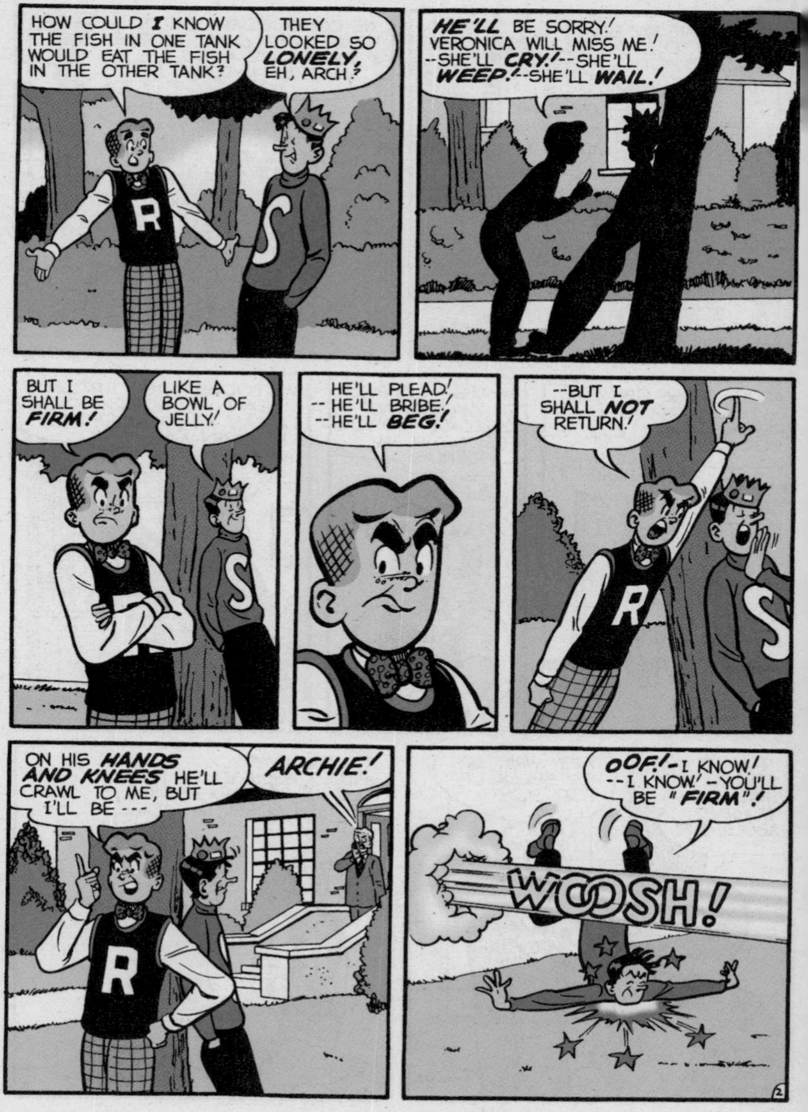
HOW COULD I KNOW THE FISH IN ONE TANK WOULD EAT THE FISH IN THE OTHER TANK?
THEY LOOKED SO LONELY, EH, ARCH?
HE'LL BE SORRY! VERONICA WILL MISS ME! --SHE'LL CRY!--SHE'LL WEEP!--SHE'LL WAIL!
BUT I SHALL BE FIRM!
LIKE A BOWL OF JELLY!
HE'LL PLEAD! --HE'LL BRIBE! --HE'LL BEG!
--BUT I SHALL NOT RETURN!
ON HIS HANDS AND KNEES HE'LL CRAWL TO ME, BUT I'LL BE ---
ARCHIE!
OOF!--I KNOW! --I KNOW! --YOU'LL BE "FIRM"!
WOOSH!
2

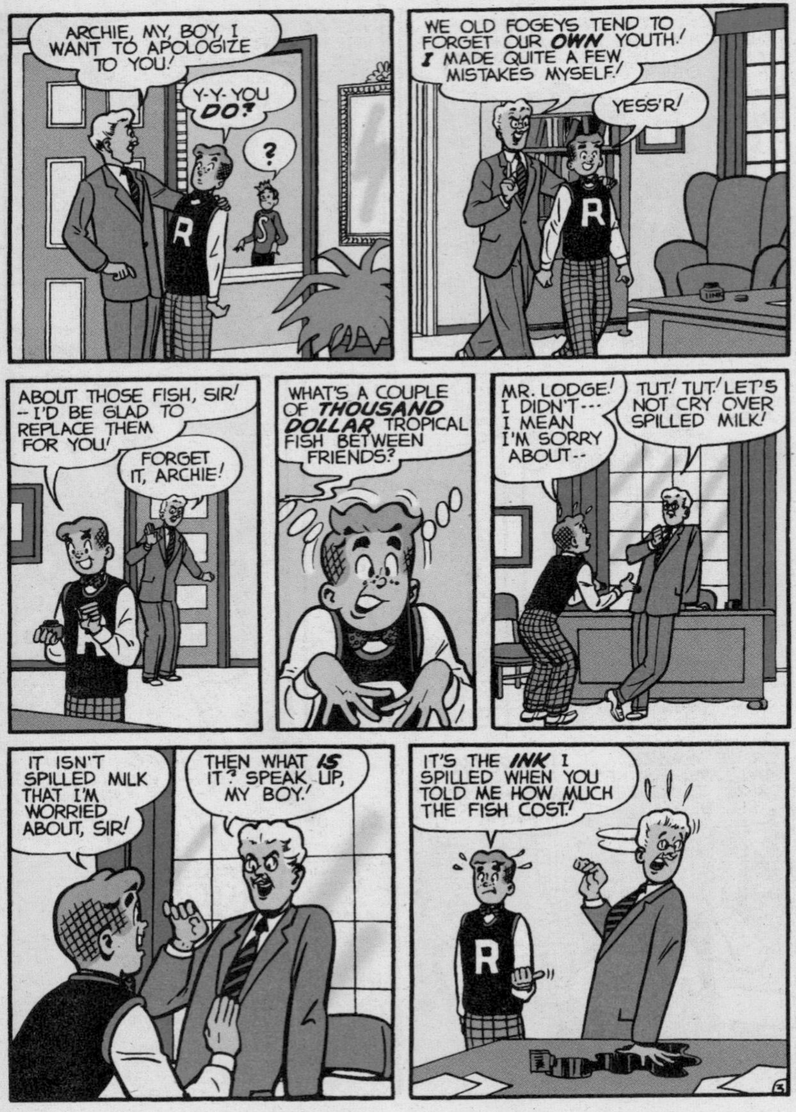
ARCHIE, MY, BOY, I WANT TO APOLOGIZE TO YOU!
Y-Y- YOU DO?
?
WE OLD FOGEYS TEND TO FORGET OUR OWN YOUTH! I MADE QUITE A FEW MISTAKES MYSELF!
YESS'R!
ABOUT THOSE FISH, SIR! --I'D BE GLAD TO REPLACE THEM FOR YOU!
FORGET IT, ARCHIE!
WHAT'S A COUPLE OF THOUSAND DOLLAR TROPICAL FISH BETWEEN FRIENDS?
MR. LODGE! I DIDN'T--- I MEAN I'M SORRY ABOUT--
TUT! TUT! LET'S NOT CRY OVER SPILLED MILK!
IT ISN'T SPILLED MILK THAT I'M WORRIED ABOUT, SIR!
THEN WHAT IS IT? SPEAK UP, MY BOY!
IT'S THE INK I SPILLED WHEN YOU TOLD ME HOW MUCH THE FISH COST!
INK
3

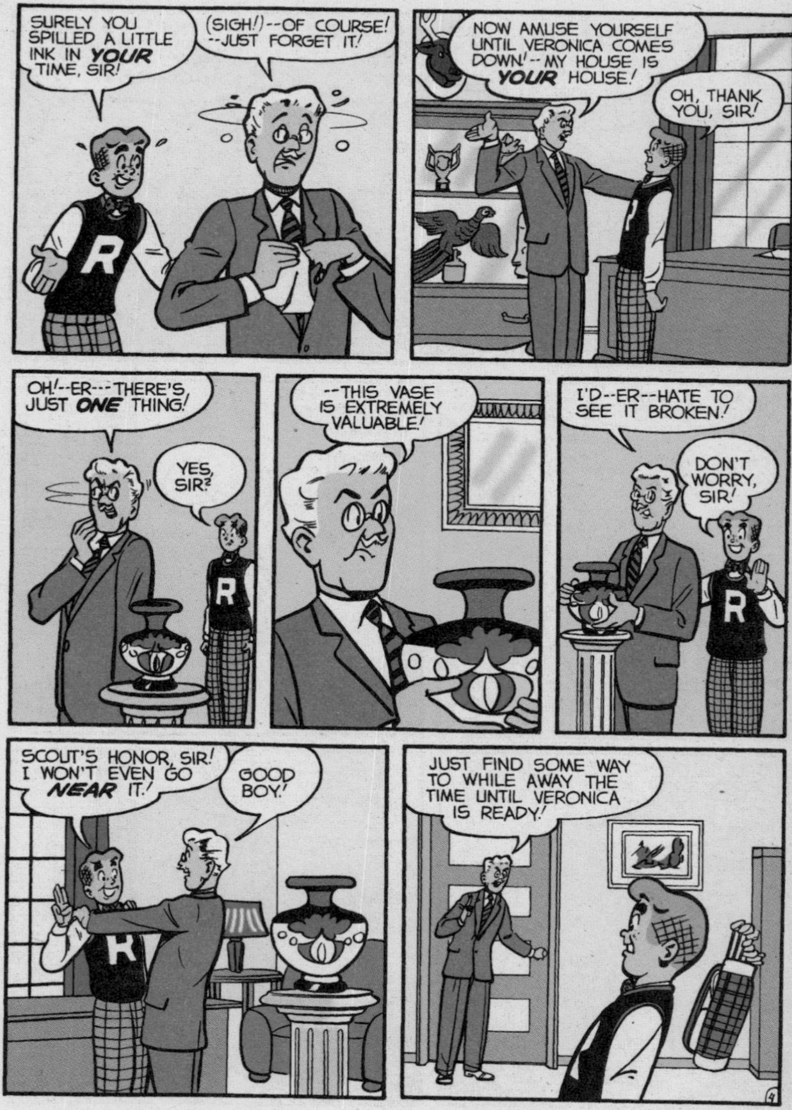

SURELY YOU SPILLED A LITTLE INK IN YOUR TIME, SIR!
(SIGH!)--OF COURSE! --JUST FORGET IT!
NOW AMUSE YOURSELF UNTIL VERONICA COMES DOWN!--MY HOUSE IS YOUR HOUSE!
OH, THANK YOU, SIR!
OH!--ER---THERE'S JUST ONE THING!
YES, SIR?
--THIS VASE IS EXTREMELY VALUABLE!
I'D--ER--HATE TO SEE IT BROKEN!
DON'T WORRY, SIR!
SCOUT'S HONOR, SIR! I WON'T EVEN GO NEAR IT!
GOOD BOY!
JUST FIND SOME WAY TO WHILE AWAY THE TIME UNTIL VERONICA IS READY!
4

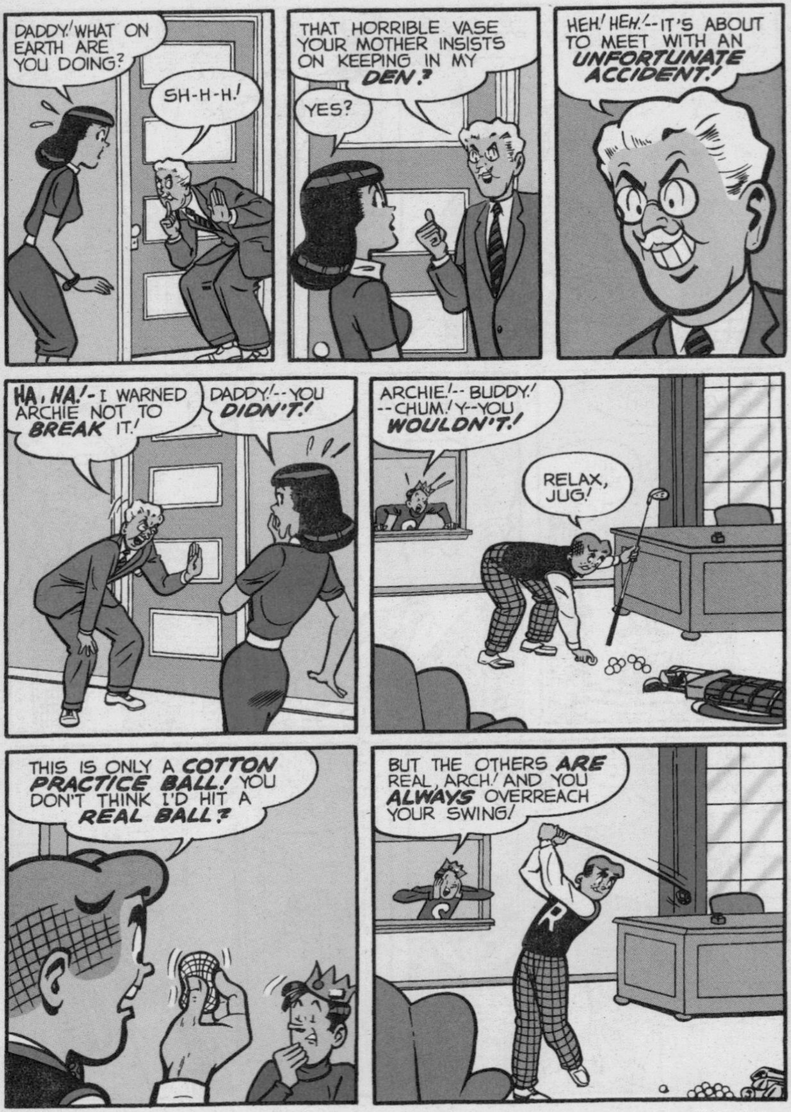

DADDY! WHAT ON EARTH ARE YOU DOING?
SH-H-H!
THAT HORRIBLE VASE YOUR MOTHER INSISTS ON KEEPING IN MY DEN?
YES?
HEH! HEH!--IT'S ABOUT TO MEET WITH AN UNFORTUNATE ACCIDENT!
HA, HA!-I WARNED ARCHIE NOT TO BREAK IT!
DADDY!--YOU DIDN'T!
ARCHIE!--BUDDY! --CHUM! Y--YOU WOULDN'T!
RELAX, JUG!
THIS IS ONLY A COTTON PRACTICE BALL! YOU DON'T THINK I'D HIT A REAL BALL?
BUT THE OTHERS ARE REAL, ARCH! AND YOU ALWAYS OVERREACH YOUR SWING!

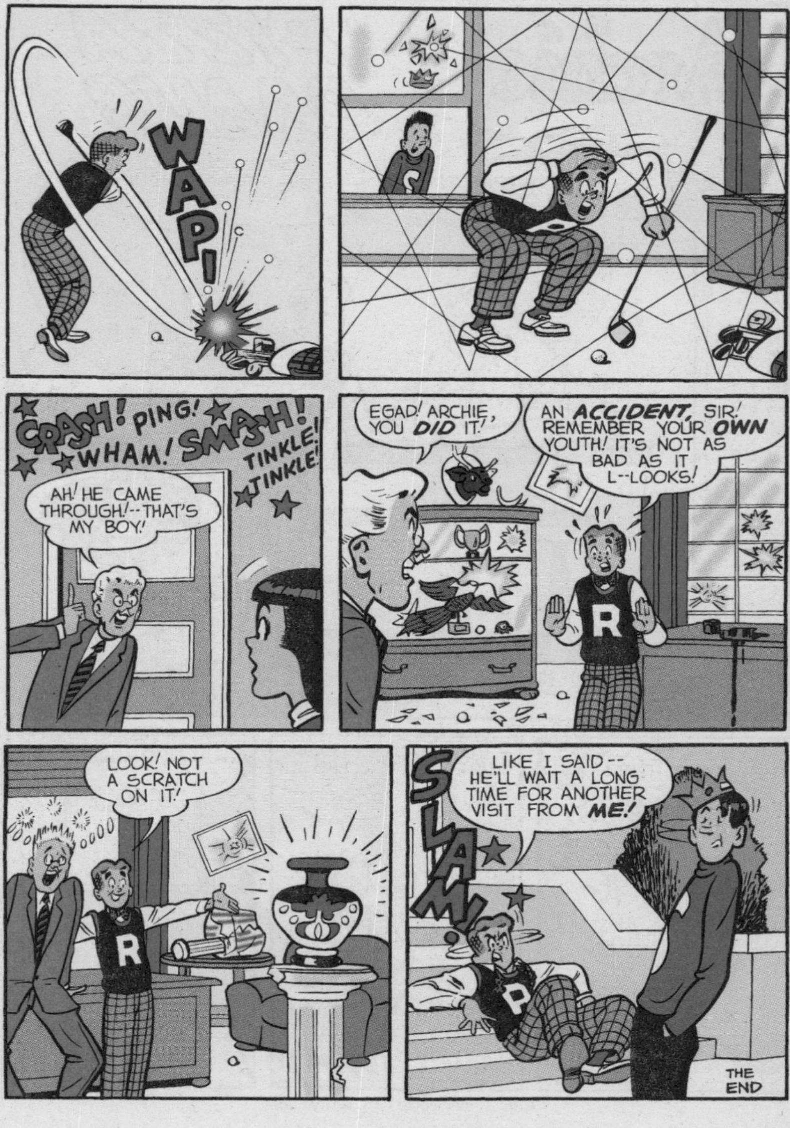

WAP!
CRASH! PING! SMASH!
WHAM!
TINKLE! TINKLE!
AH! HE CAME THROUGH!--THAT'S MY BOY!
EGAD! ARCHIE, YOU DID IT!
AN ACCIDENT, SIR! REMEMBER YOUR OWN YOUTH! IT'S NOT AS BAD AS IT L--LOOKS!
LOOK! NOT A SCRATCH ON IT!
SLAM!
LIKE I SAID -- HE'LL WAIT A LONG TIME FOR ANOTHER VISIT FROM ME!
THE END

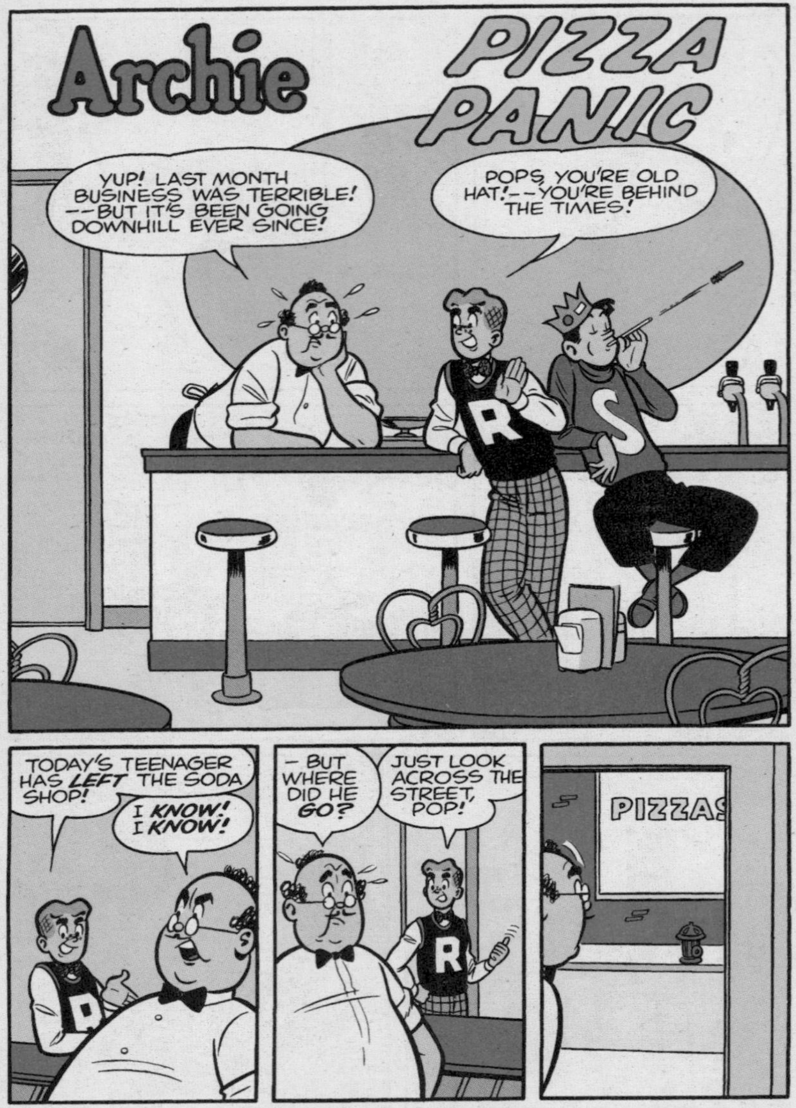
Archie
PIZZA PANIC
YUP! LAST MONTH BUSINESS WAS TERRIBLE! --BUT IT'S BEEN GOING DOWNHILL EVER SINCE!
POPS, YOU'RE OLD HAT!--YOU'RE BEHIND THE TIMES!
TODAY'S TEENAGER HAS *LEFT* THE SODA SHOP!
I *KNOW!* I *KNOW!*
– BUT WHERE DID HE *GO?*
JUST LOOK ACROSS THE STREET, POP!
PIZZAS

Script: Frank Doyle / Art: Harry Lucey

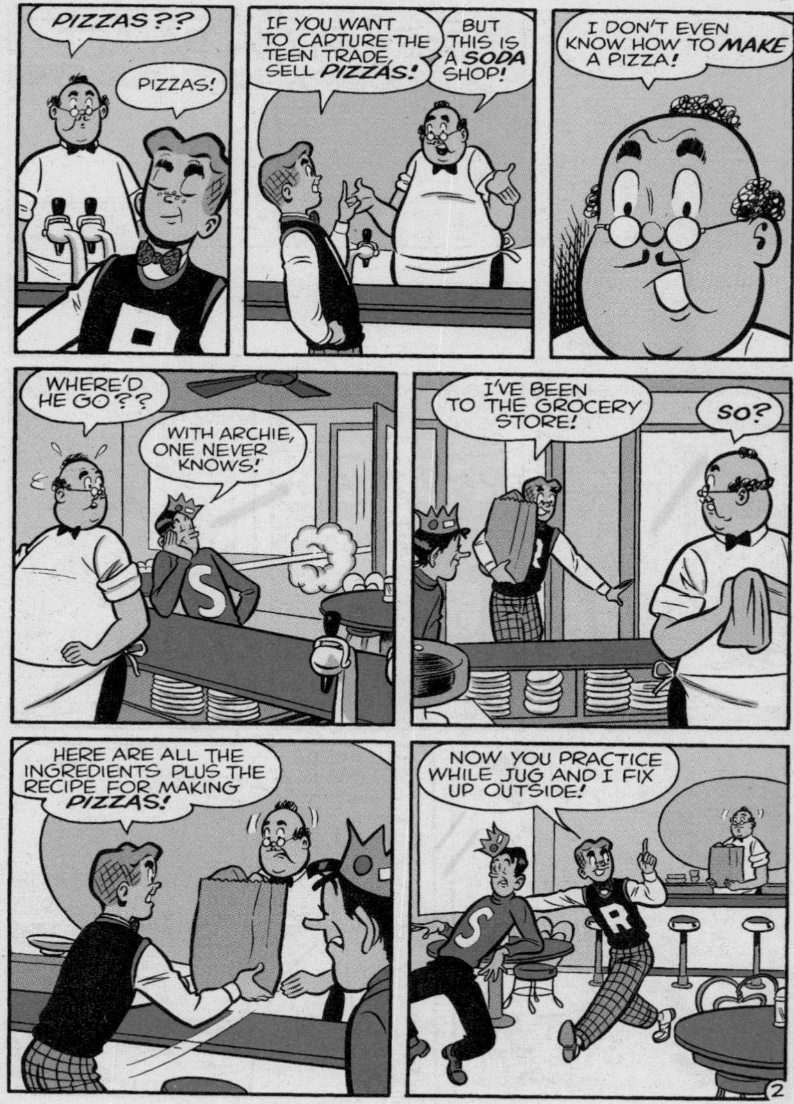
PIZZAS??
PIZZAS!
IF YOU WANT TO CAPTURE THE TEEN TRADE, SELL PIZZAS!
BUT THIS IS A SODA SHOP!
I DON'T EVEN KNOW HOW TO MAKE A PIZZA!
WHERE'D HE GO??
WITH ARCHIE, ONE NEVER KNOWS!
I'VE BEEN TO THE GROCERY STORE!
SO?
HERE ARE ALL THE INGREDIENTS PLUS THE RECIPE FOR MAKING PIZZAS!
NOW YOU PRACTICE WHILE JUG AND I FIX UP OUTSIDE!
2

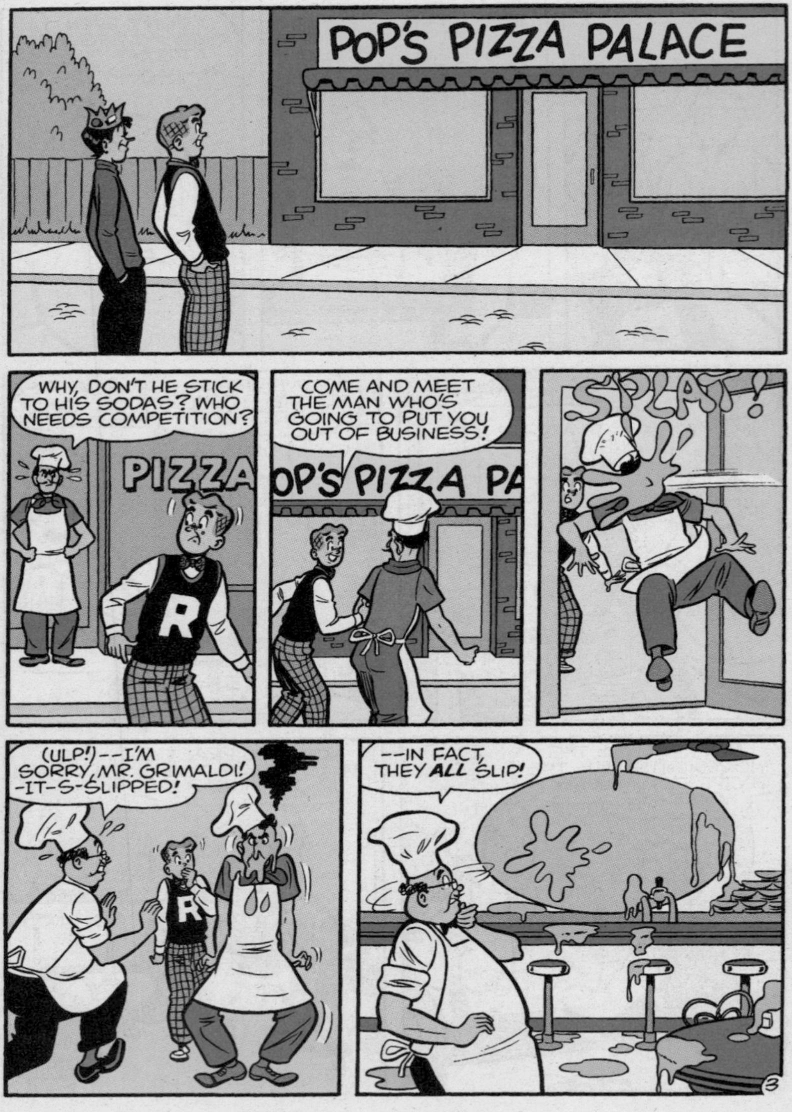
POP'S PIZZA PALACE
WHY, DON'T HE STICK TO HIS SODAS? WHO NEEDS COMPETITION?
PIZZA
COME AND MEET THE MAN WHO'S GOING TO PUT YOU OUT OF BUSINESS!
OP'S PIZZA PA
SPLAT!
(ULP!)--I'M SORRY, MR. GRIMALDI! -IT-S-SLIPPED!
--IN FACT, THEY ALL SLIP!
3

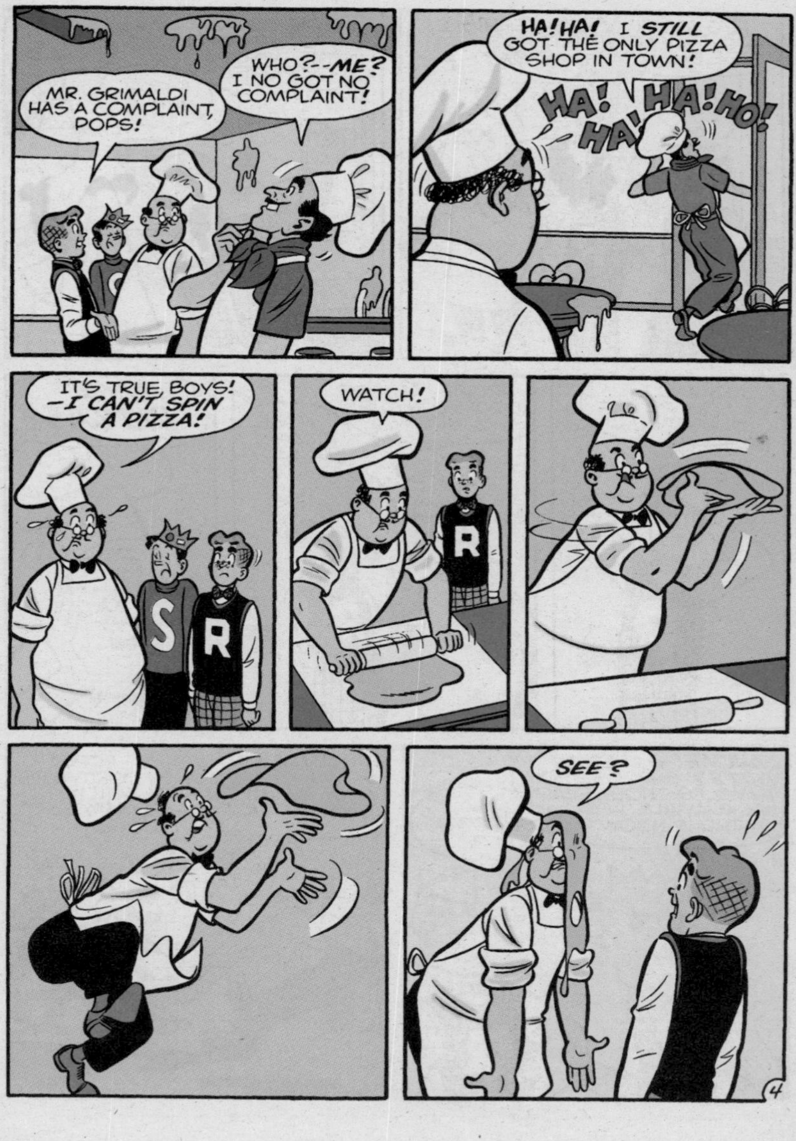
MR. GRIMALDI HAS A COMPLAINT, POPS!
WHO?--ME? I NO GOT NO COMPLAINT!
HA! HA! I STILL GOT THE ONLY PIZZA SHOP IN TOWN!
HA! HA! HA! HA! HO!
IT'S TRUE, BOYS! —I CAN'T SPIN A PIZZA!
WATCH!
SEE?
4

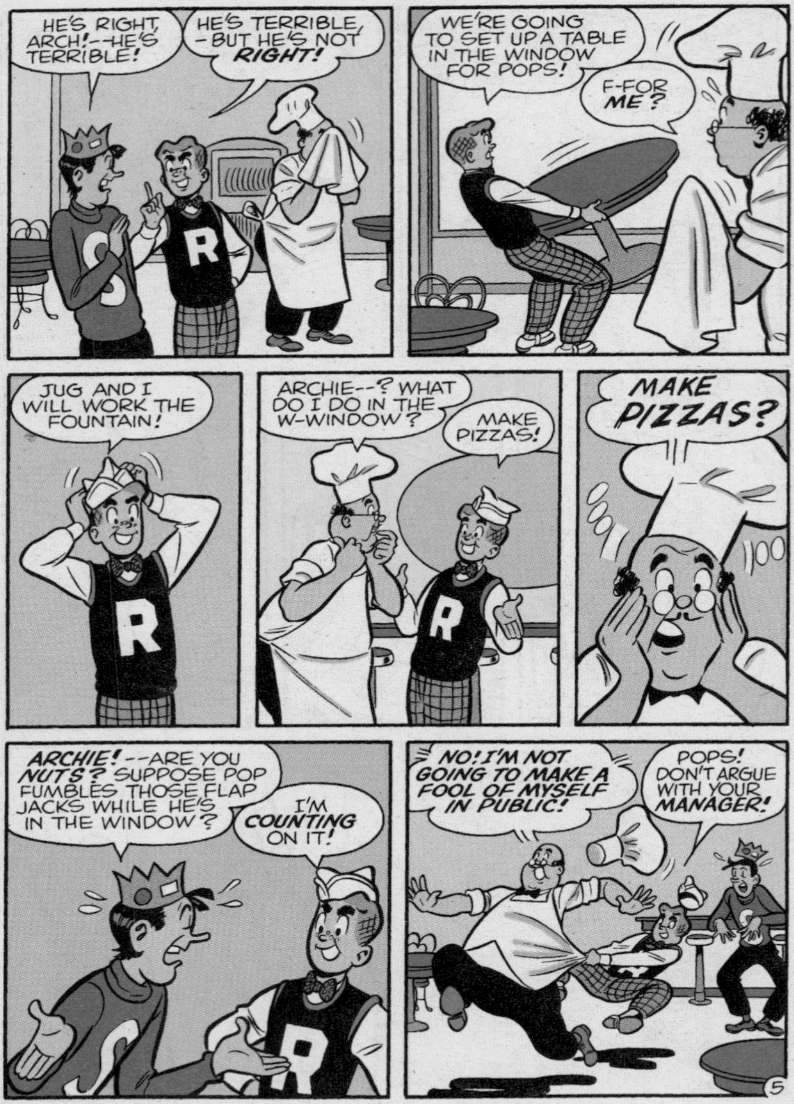
HE'S RIGHT, ARCH!--HE'S TERRIBLE!
HE'S TERRIBLE, -BUT HE'S NOT RIGHT!
WE'RE GOING TO SET UP A TABLE IN THE WINDOW FOR POPS!
F-FOR ME?
JUG AND I WILL WORK THE FOUNTAIN!
ARCHIE--? WHAT DO I DO IN THE W-WINDOW?
MAKE PIZZAS!
MAKE PIZZAS?
ARCHIE!--ARE YOU NUTS? SUPPOSE POP FUMBLES THOSE FLAP JACKS WHILE HE'S IN THE WINDOW?
I'M COUNTING ON IT!
NO! I'M NOT GOING TO MAKE A FOOL OF MYSELF IN PUBLIC!
POPS! DON'T ARGUE WITH YOUR MANAGER!
5

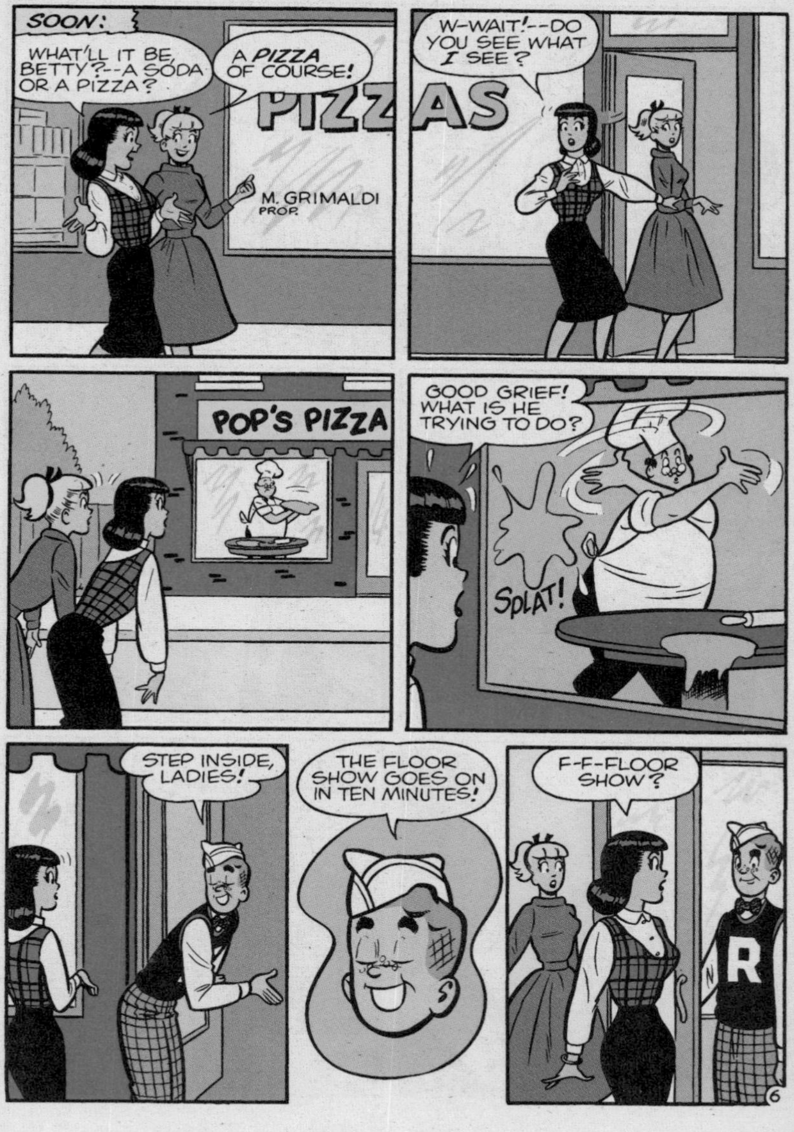
SOON:
WHAT'LL IT BE, BETTY?--A SODA OR A PIZZA?
A PIZZA OF COURSE!
PIZZAS
M. GRIMALDI PROP.
W-WAIT!--DO YOU SEE WHAT I SEE?
POP'S PIZZA
GOOD GRIEF! WHAT IS HE TRYING TO DO?
SPLAT!
STEP INSIDE, LADIES!
THE FLOOR SHOW GOES ON IN TEN MINUTES!
F-F-FLOOR SHOW?
R

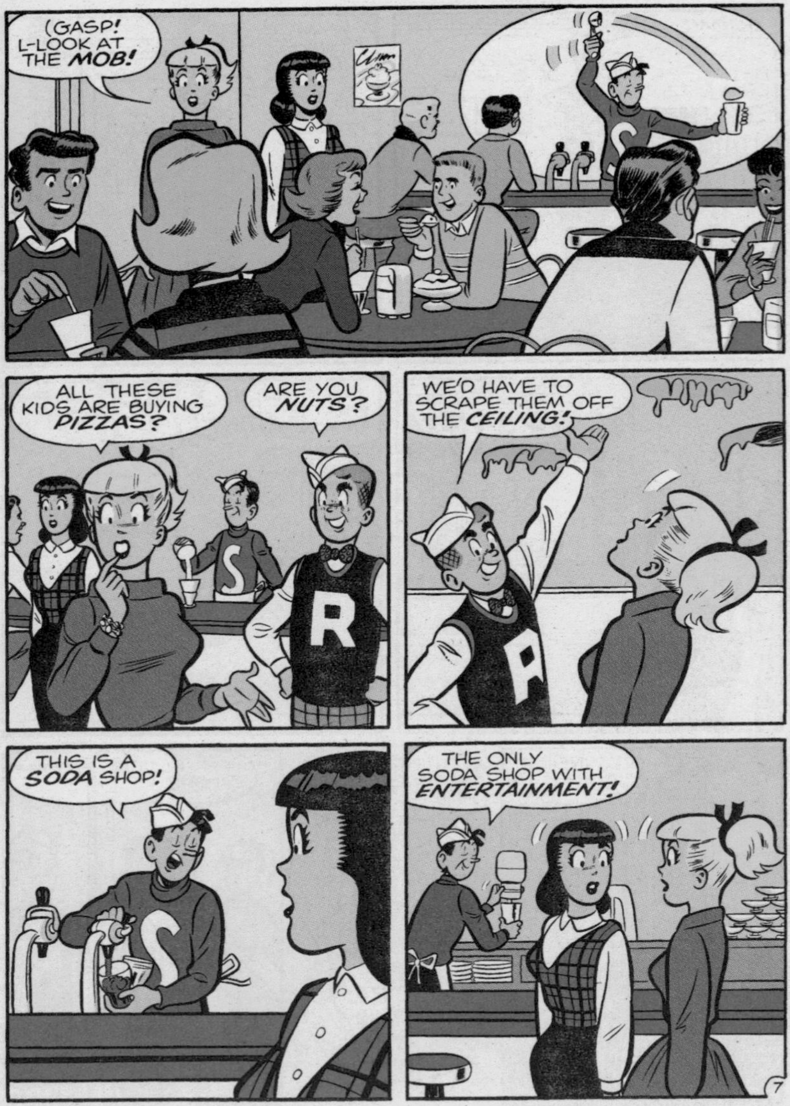
(GASP! L-LOOK AT THE MOB!
ALL THESE KIDS ARE BUYING PIZZAS?
ARE YOU NUTS?
WE'D HAVE TO SCRAPE THEM OFF THE CEILING!
THIS IS A SODA SHOP!
THE ONLY SODA SHOP WITH ENTERTAINMENT!
7

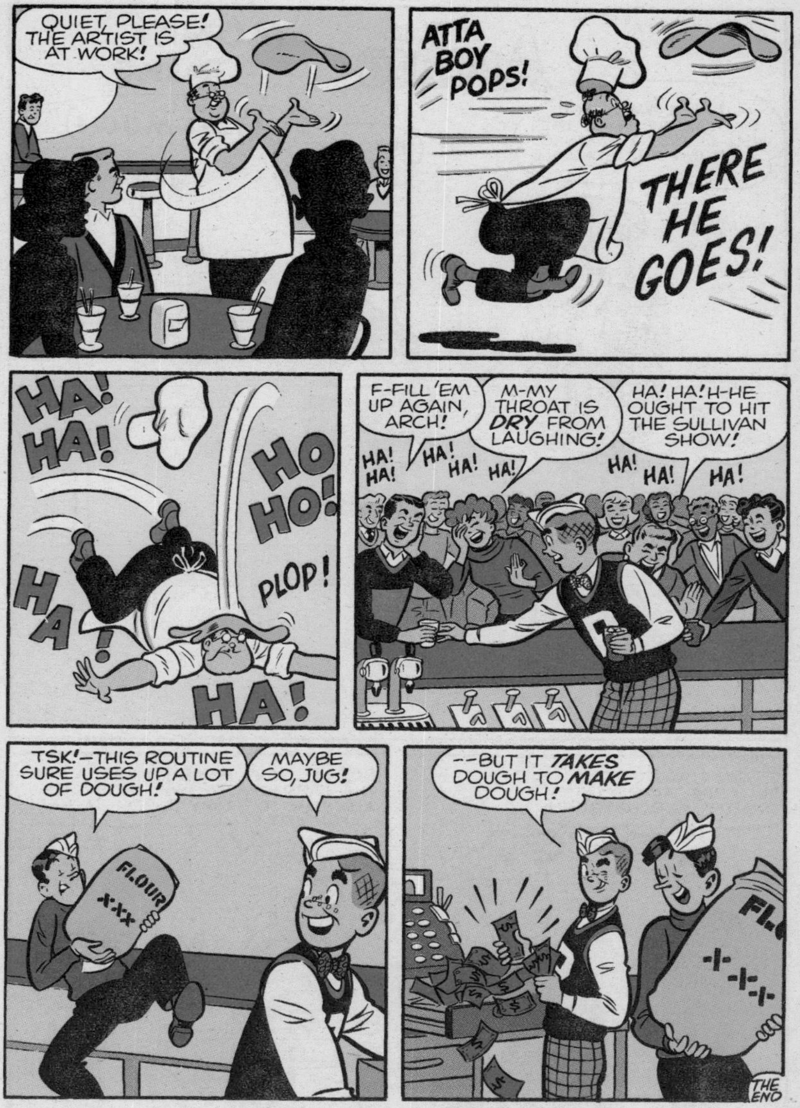
QUIET, PLEASE! THE ARTIST IS AT WORK!
ATTA BOY POPS!
THERE HE GOES!
HA! HA!
HO HO!
PLOP!
HA!
HA!
F-FILL 'EM UP AGAIN, ARCH!
M-MY THROAT IS DRY FROM LAUGHING!
HA! HA! H-HE OUGHT TO HIT THE SULLIVAN SHOW!
HA! HA!
HA! HA! HA!
HA! HA! HA!
TSK!—THIS ROUTINE SURE USES UP A LOT OF DOUGH!
MAYBE SO, JUG!
FLOUR XXX
--BUT IT TAKES DOUGH TO MAKE DOUGH!
THE END

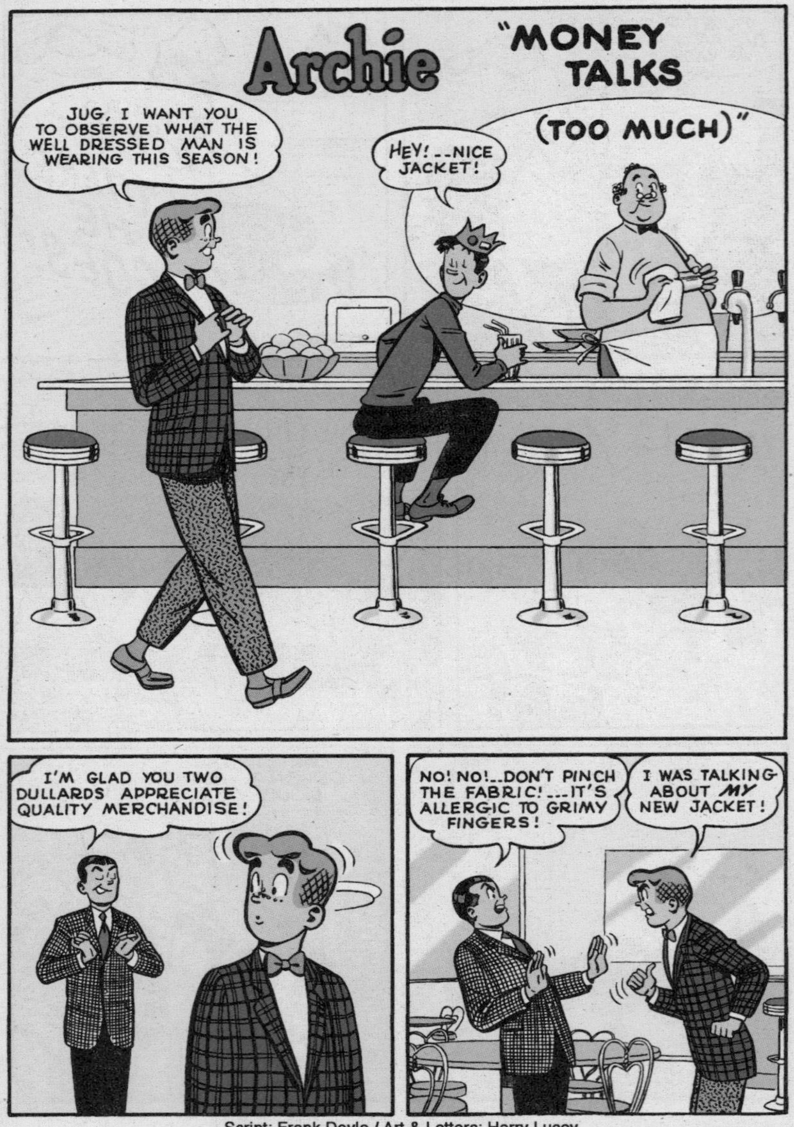
Archie
"MONEY TALKS (TOO MUCH)"
JUG, I WANT YOU TO OBSERVE WHAT THE WELL DRESSED MAN IS WEARING THIS SEASON!
HEY! --NICE JACKET!
I'M GLAD YOU TWO DULLARDS APPRECIATE QUALITY MERCHANDISE!
NO! NO!--DON'T PINCH THE FABRIC! ---IT'S ALLERGIC TO GRIMY FINGERS!
I WAS TALKING ABOUT MY NEW JACKET!

Script: Frank Doyle / Art & Letters: Harry Lucey

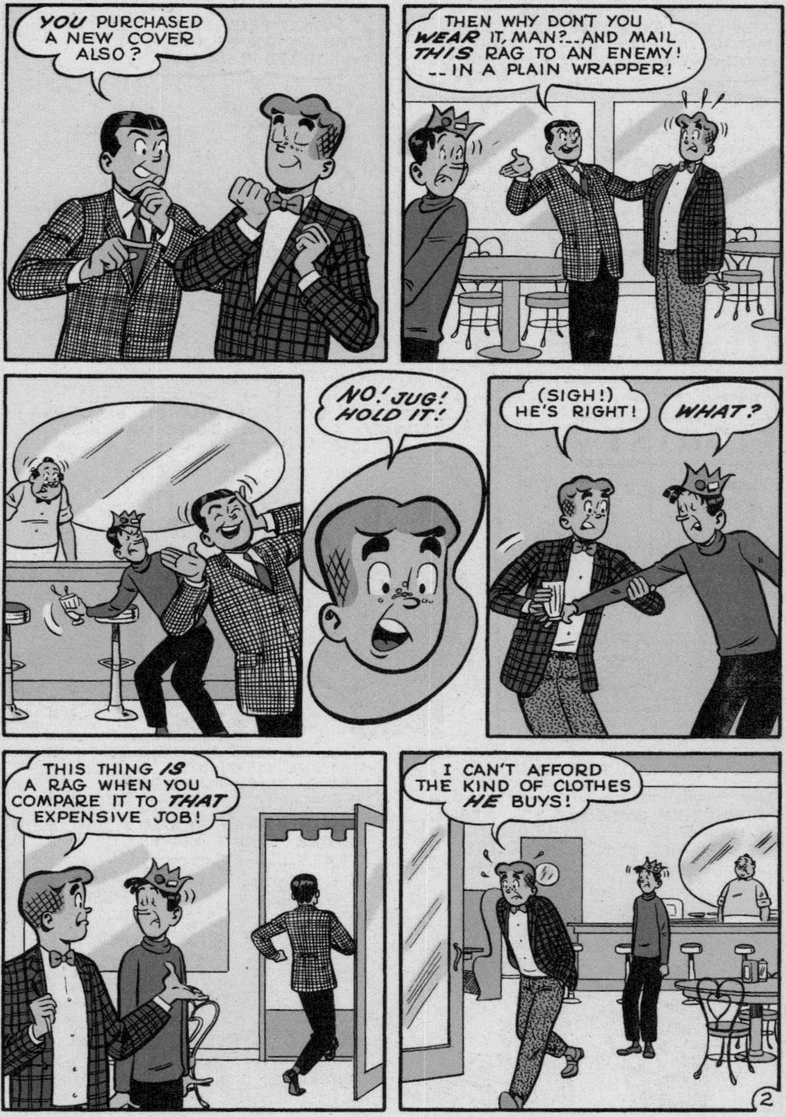
YOU PURCHASED A NEW COVER ALSO?
THEN WHY DON'T YOU WEAR IT, MAN?..AND MAIL THIS RAG TO AN ENEMY! --IN A PLAIN WRAPPER!
NO! JUG! HOLD IT!
(SIGH!) HE'S RIGHT!
WHAT?
THIS THING IS A RAG WHEN YOU COMPARE IT TO THAT EXPENSIVE JOB!
I CAN'T AFFORD THE KIND OF CLOTHES HE BUYS!
2

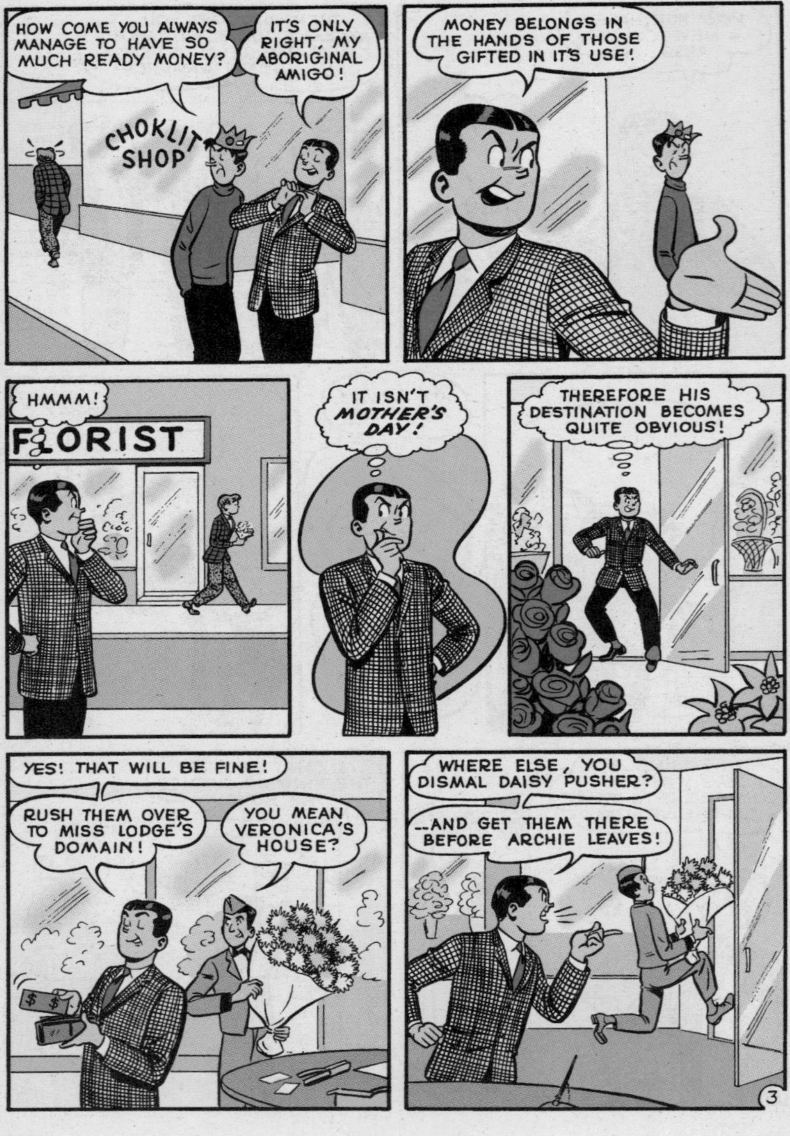

HOW COME YOU ALWAYS MANAGE TO HAVE SO MUCH READY MONEY?
IT'S ONLY RIGHT, MY ABORIGINAL AMIGO!
CHOKLIT SHOP
MONEY BELONGS IN THE HANDS OF THOSE GIFTED IN IT'S USE!
HMMM!
FLORIST
IT ISN'T MOTHER'S DAY!
THEREFORE HIS DESTINATION BECOMES QUITE OBVIOUS!
YES! THAT WILL BE FINE!
RUSH THEM OVER TO MISS LODGE'S DOMAIN!
YOU MEAN VERONICA'S HOUSE?
WHERE ELSE, YOU DISMAL DAISY PUSHER?
--AND GET THEM THERE BEFORE ARCHIE LEAVES!
3

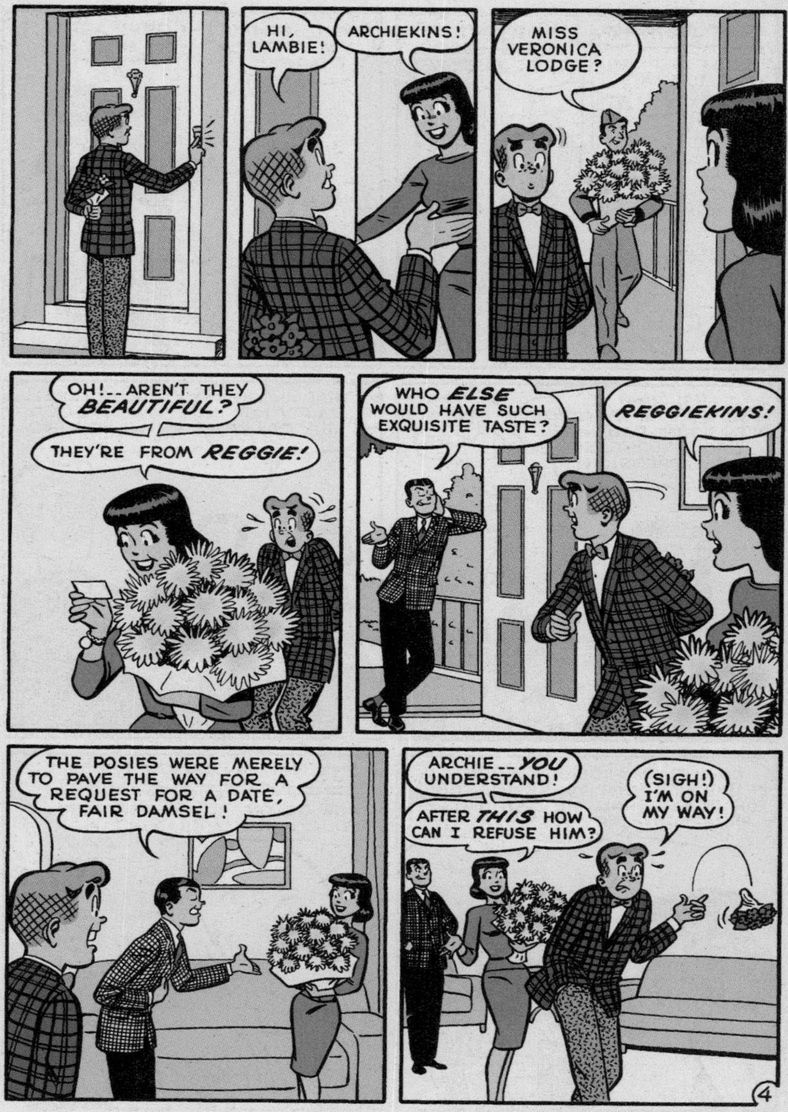
HI, LAMBIE!
ARCHIEKINS!
MISS VERONICA LODGE?
OH!-- AREN'T THEY BEAUTIFUL?
THEY'RE FROM REGGIE!
WHO ELSE WOULD HAVE SUCH EXQUISITE TASTE?
REGGIEKINS!
THE POSIES WERE MERELY TO PAVE THE WAY FOR A REQUEST FOR A DATE, FAIR DAMSEL!
ARCHIE-- YOU UNDERSTAND!
AFTER THIS HOW CAN I REFUSE HIM?
(SIGH!) I'M ON MY WAY!

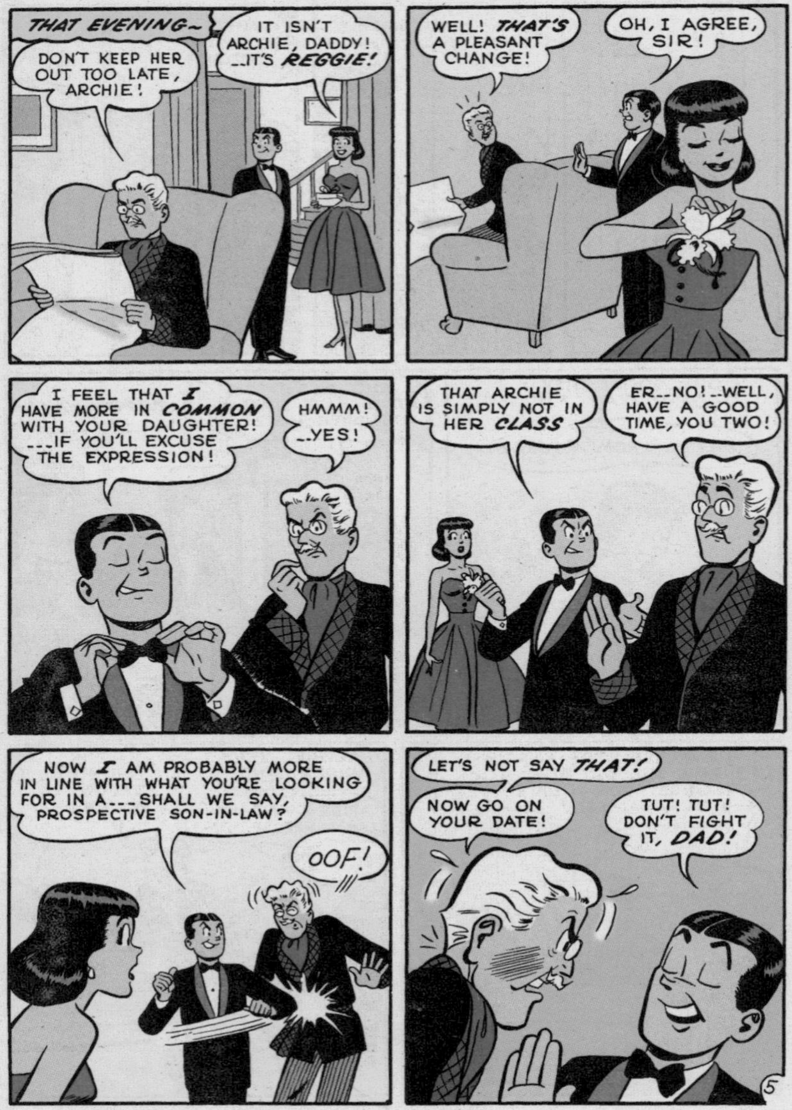
THAT EVENING~
DON'T KEEP HER OUT TOO LATE, ARCHIE!
IT ISN'T ARCHIE, DADDY! ..IT'S REGGIE!
WELL! THAT'S A PLEASANT CHANGE!
OH, I AGREE, SIR!
I FEEL THAT I HAVE MORE IN COMMON WITH YOUR DAUGHTER! ...IF YOU'LL EXCUSE THE EXPRESSION!
HMMM! ..YES!
THAT ARCHIE IS SIMPLY NOT IN HER CLASS
ER..NO! ..WELL, HAVE A GOOD TIME, YOU TWO!
NOW I AM PROBABLY MORE IN LINE WITH WHAT YOU'RE LOOKING FOR IN A... SHALL WE SAY, PROSPECTIVE SON-IN-LAW?
OOF!
LET'S NOT SAY THAT!
NOW GO ON YOUR DATE!
TUT! TUT! DON'T FIGHT IT, DAD!
5

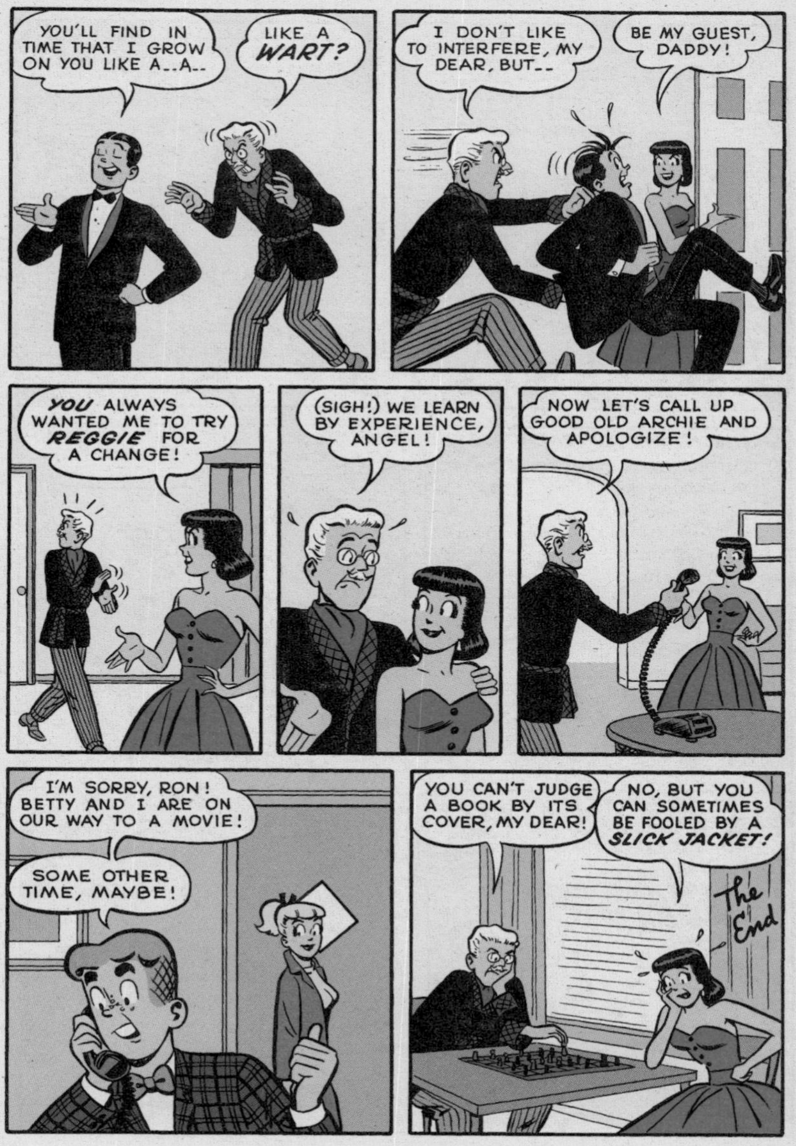
YOU'LL FIND IN TIME THAT I GROW ON YOU LIKE A--A--
LIKE A WART?
I DON'T LIKE TO INTERFERE, MY DEAR, BUT--
BE MY GUEST, DADDY!
YOU ALWAYS WANTED ME TO TRY REGGIE FOR A CHANGE!
(SIGH!) WE LEARN BY EXPERIENCE, ANGEL!
NOW LET'S CALL UP GOOD OLD ARCHIE AND APOLOGIZE!
I'M SORRY, RON! BETTY AND I ARE ON OUR WAY TO A MOVIE!
SOME OTHER TIME, MAYBE!
YOU CAN'T JUDGE A BOOK BY ITS COVER, MY DEAR!
NO, BUT YOU CAN SOMETIMES BE FOOLED BY A SLICK JACKET!
The End

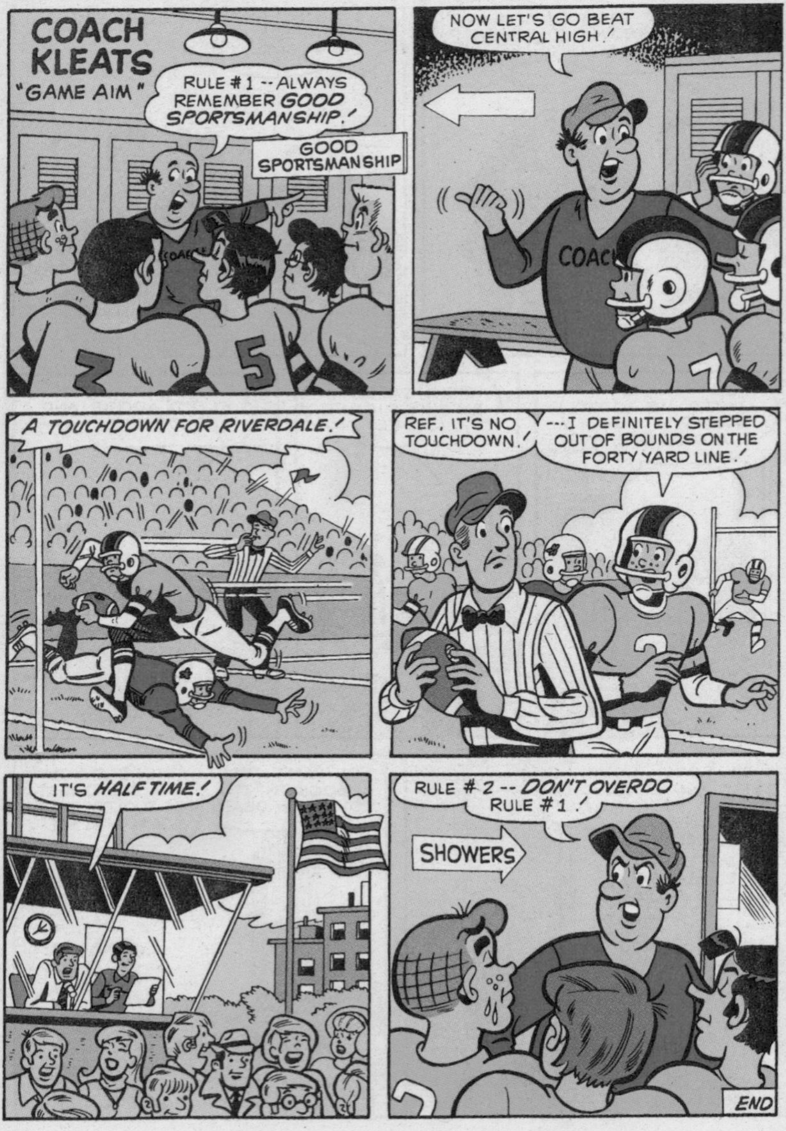

COACH KLEATS
"GAME AIM"
RULE #1 -- ALWAYS REMEMBER GOOD SPORTSMANSHIP!
GOOD SPORTSMANSHIP
NOW LET'S GO BEAT CENTRAL HIGH!
A TOUCHDOWN FOR RIVERDALE!
REF, IT'S NO TOUCHDOWN!
---I DEFINITELY STEPPED OUT OF BOUNDS ON THE FORTY YARD LINE!
IT'S HALF TIME!
RULE # 2 -- DON'T OVERDO RULE #1!
SHOWERS
END

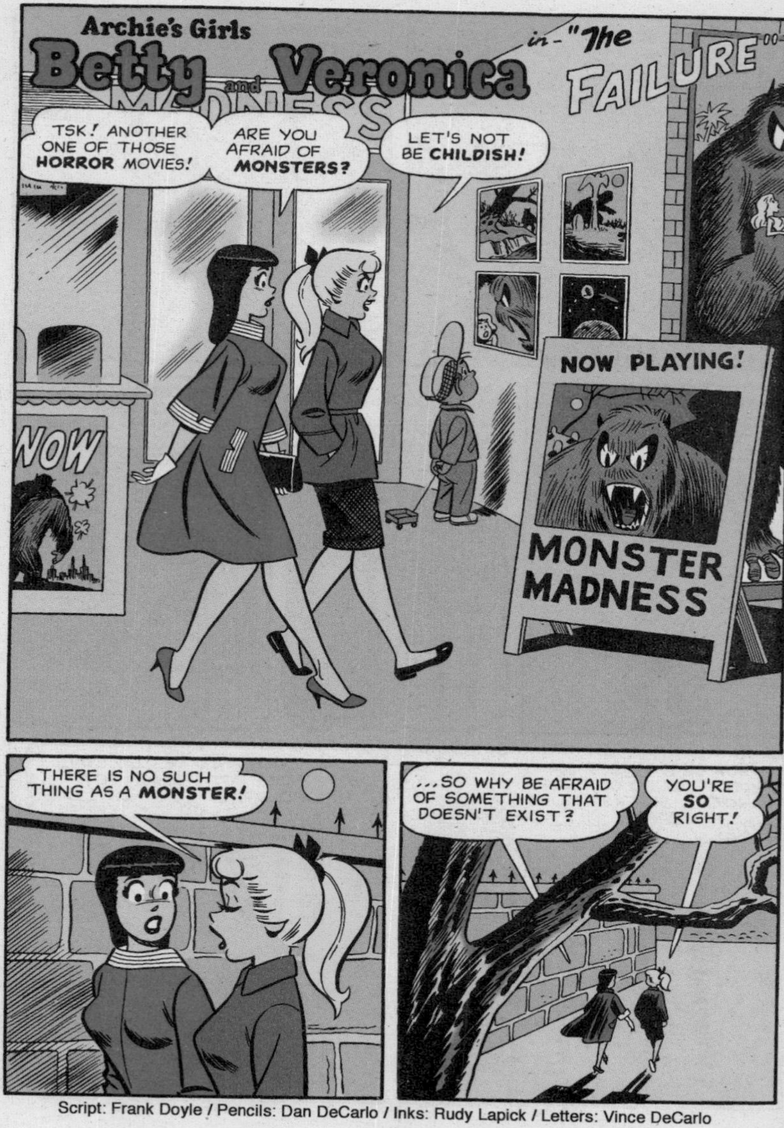
Archie's Girls
Betty and Veronica
in- "The FAILURE"
MADNESS
TSK! ANOTHER ONE OF THOSE HORROR MOVIES!
ARE YOU AFRAID OF MONSTERS?
LET'S NOT BE CHILDISH!
NOW
NOW PLAYING!
MONSTER MADNESS
THERE IS NO SUCH THING AS A MONSTER!
...SO WHY BE AFRAID OF SOMETHING THAT DOESN'T EXIST?
YOU'RE SO RIGHT!

Script: Frank Doyle / Pencils: Dan DeCarlo / Inks: Rudy Lapick / Letters: Vince DeCarlo

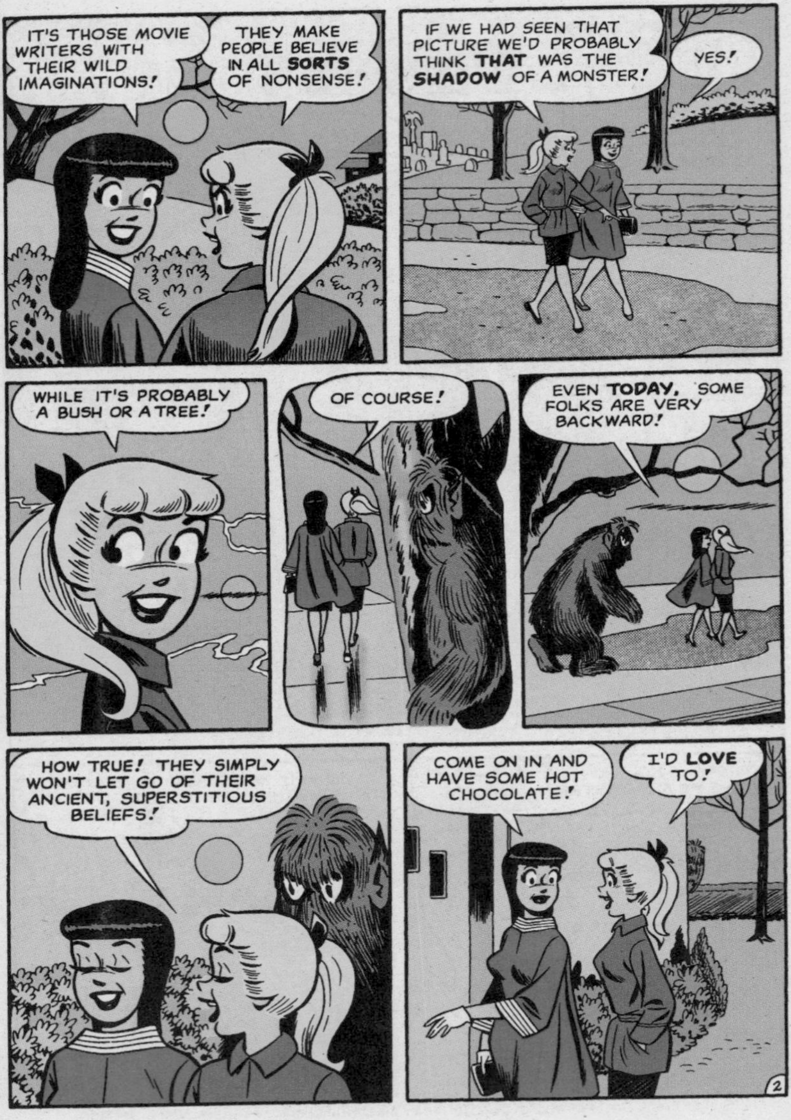
IT'S THOSE MOVIE WRITERS WITH THEIR WILD IMAGINATIONS!
THEY MAKE PEOPLE BELIEVE IN ALL SORTS OF NONSENSE!
IF WE HAD SEEN THAT PICTURE WE'D PROBABLY THINK THAT WAS THE SHADOW OF A MONSTER!
YES!
WHILE IT'S PROBABLY A BUSH OR A TREE!
OF COURSE!
EVEN TODAY, SOME FOLKS ARE VERY BACKWARD!
HOW TRUE! THEY SIMPLY WON'T LET GO OF THEIR ANCIENT, SUPERSTITIOUS BELIEFS!
COME ON IN AND HAVE SOME HOT CHOCOLATE!
I'D LOVE TO!
2

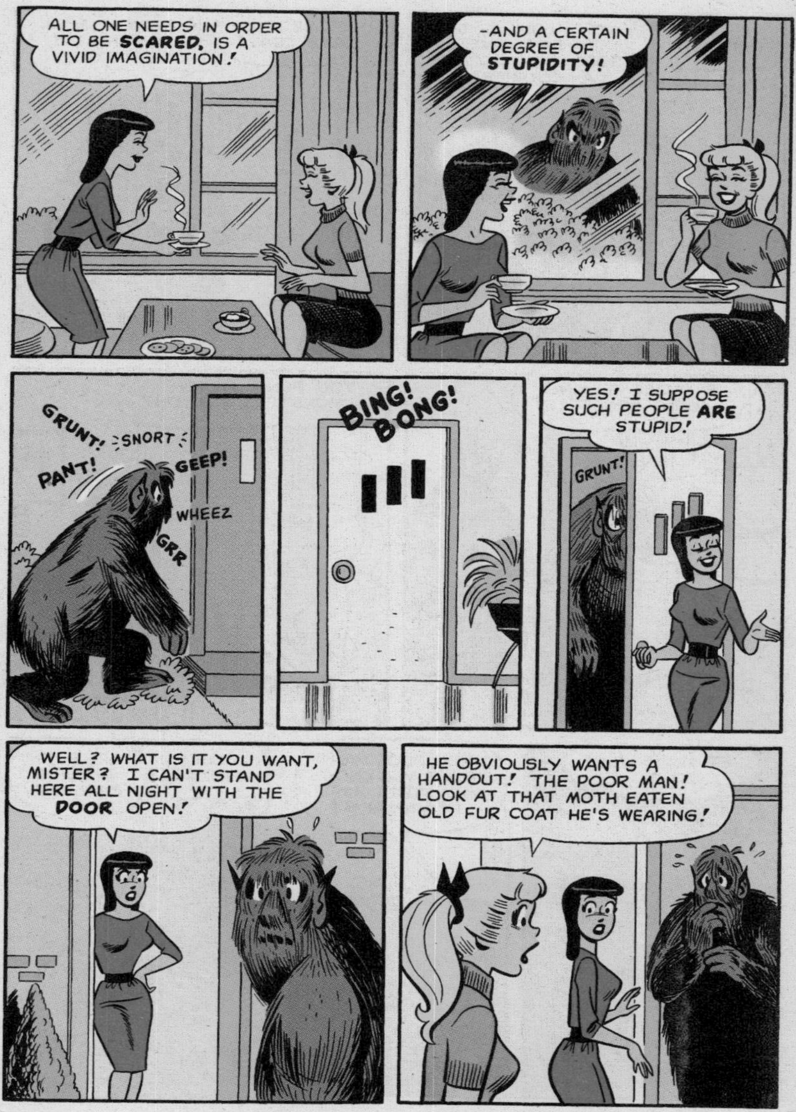
ALL ONE NEEDS IN ORDER TO BE **SCARED**, IS A VIVID IMAGINATION!
-AND A CERTAIN DEGREE OF **STUPIDITY**!
GRUNT! SNORT
PANT! GEEP!
WHEEZ
GRR
BING! BONG!
YES! I SUPPOSE SUCH PEOPLE **ARE** STUPID!
GRUNT!
WELL? WHAT IS IT YOU WANT, MISTER? I CAN'T STAND HERE ALL NIGHT WITH THE **DOOR** OPEN!
HE OBVIOUSLY WANTS A HANDOUT! THE POOR MAN! LOOK AT THAT MOTH EATEN OLD FUR COAT HE'S WEARING!

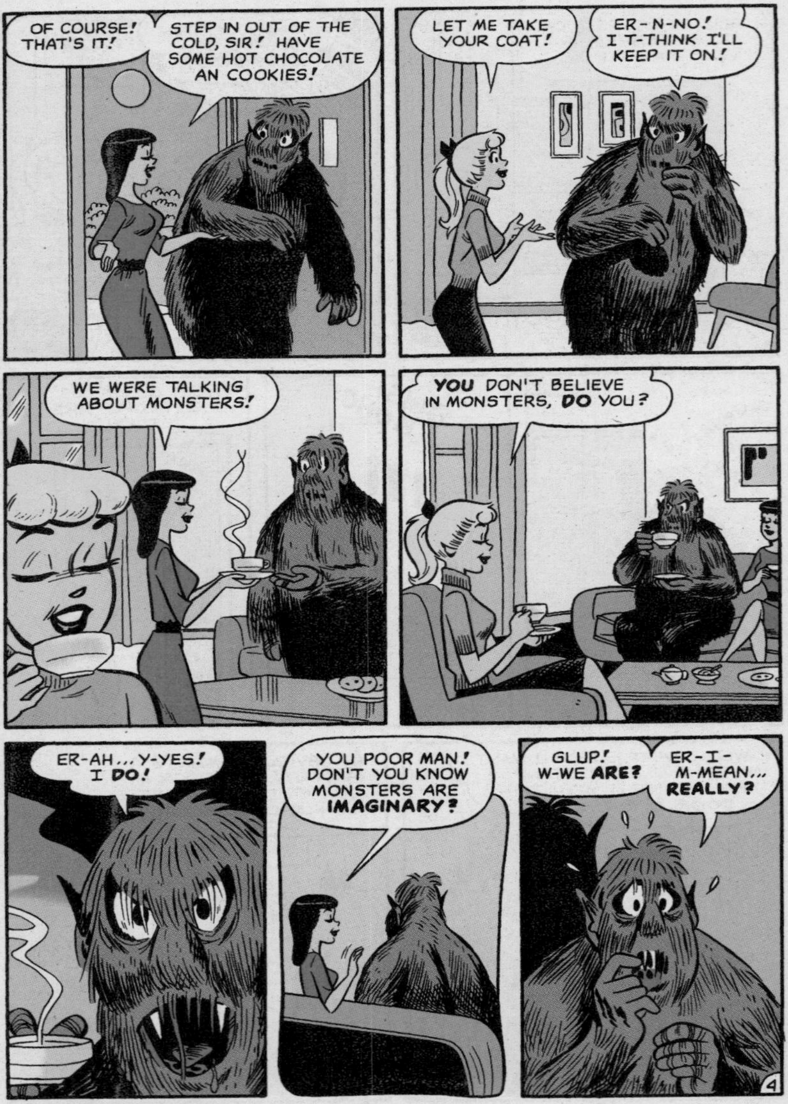

OF COURSE! THAT'S IT!
STEP IN OUT OF THE COLD, SIR! HAVE SOME HOT CHOCOLATE AN COOKIES!
LET ME TAKE YOUR COAT!
ER-N-NO! I T-THINK I'LL KEEP IT ON!
WE WERE TALKING ABOUT MONSTERS!
YOU DON'T BELIEVE IN MONSTERS, DO YOU?
ER-AH... Y-YES! I DO!
YOU POOR MAN! DON'T YOU KNOW MONSTERS ARE IMAGINARY?
GLUP! W-WE ARE?
ER-I- M-MEAN... REALLY?
4

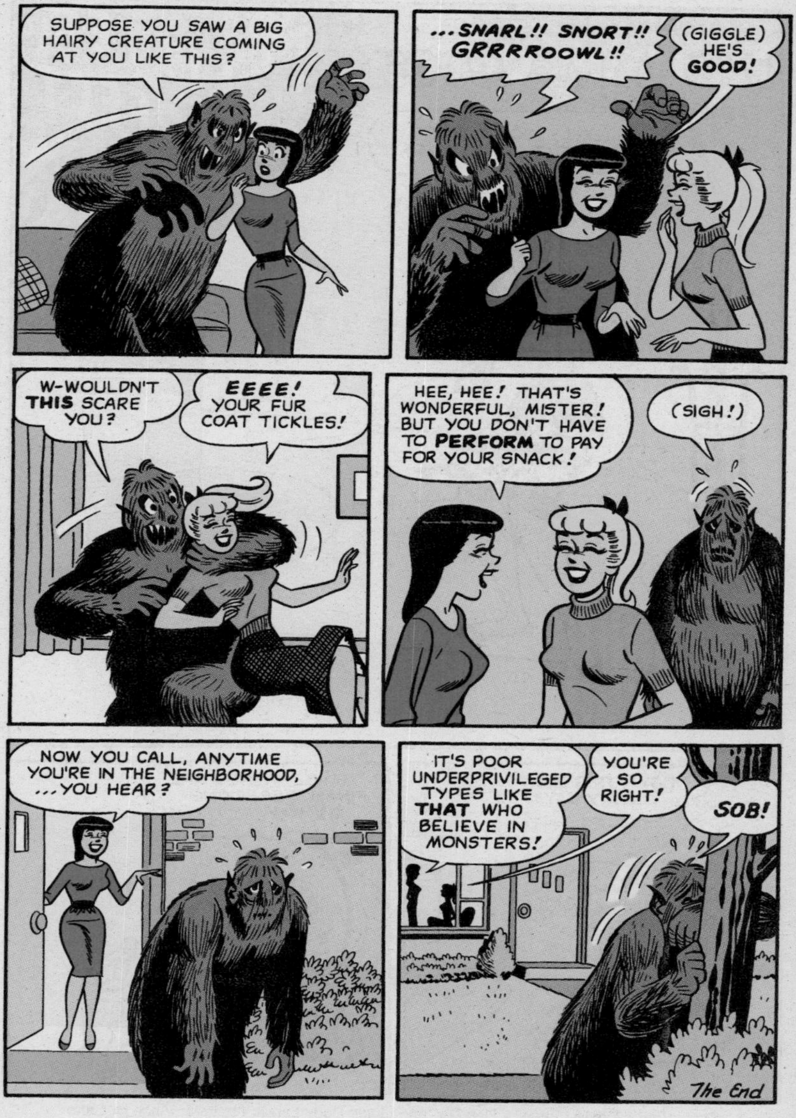

SUPPOSE YOU SAW A BIG HAIRY CREATURE COMING AT YOU LIKE THIS?
...SNARL!! SNORT!! GRRRROOWL!!
(GIGGLE) HE'S GOOD!
W-WOULDN'T THIS SCARE YOU?
EEEE! YOUR FUR COAT TICKLES!
HEE, HEE! THAT'S WONDERFUL, MISTER! BUT YOU DON'T HAVE TO PERFORM TO PAY FOR YOUR SNACK!
(SIGH!)
NOW YOU CALL, ANYTIME YOU'RE IN THE NEIGHBORHOOD, ...YOU HEAR?
IT'S POOR UNDERPRIVILEGED TYPES LIKE THAT WHO BELIEVE IN MONSTERS!
YOU'RE SO RIGHT!
SOB!
The End

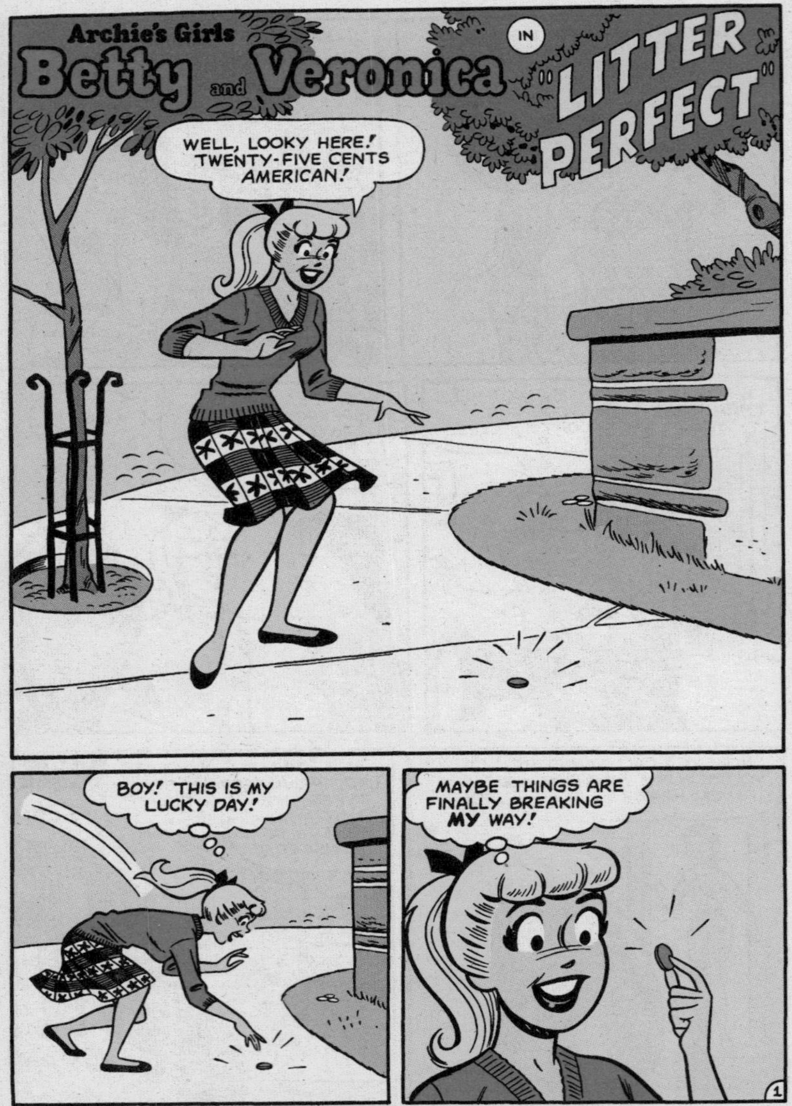
Archie's Girls
Betty and Veronica
IN
"LITTER PERFECT"
WELL, LOOKY HERE! TWENTY-FIVE CENTS AMERICAN!
BOY! THIS IS MY LUCKY DAY!
MAYBE THINGS ARE FINALLY BREAKING MY WAY!
1

Script: Frank Doyle / Pencils: Dan DeCarlo / Inks: Rudy Lapick / Letters: Vince DeCarlo

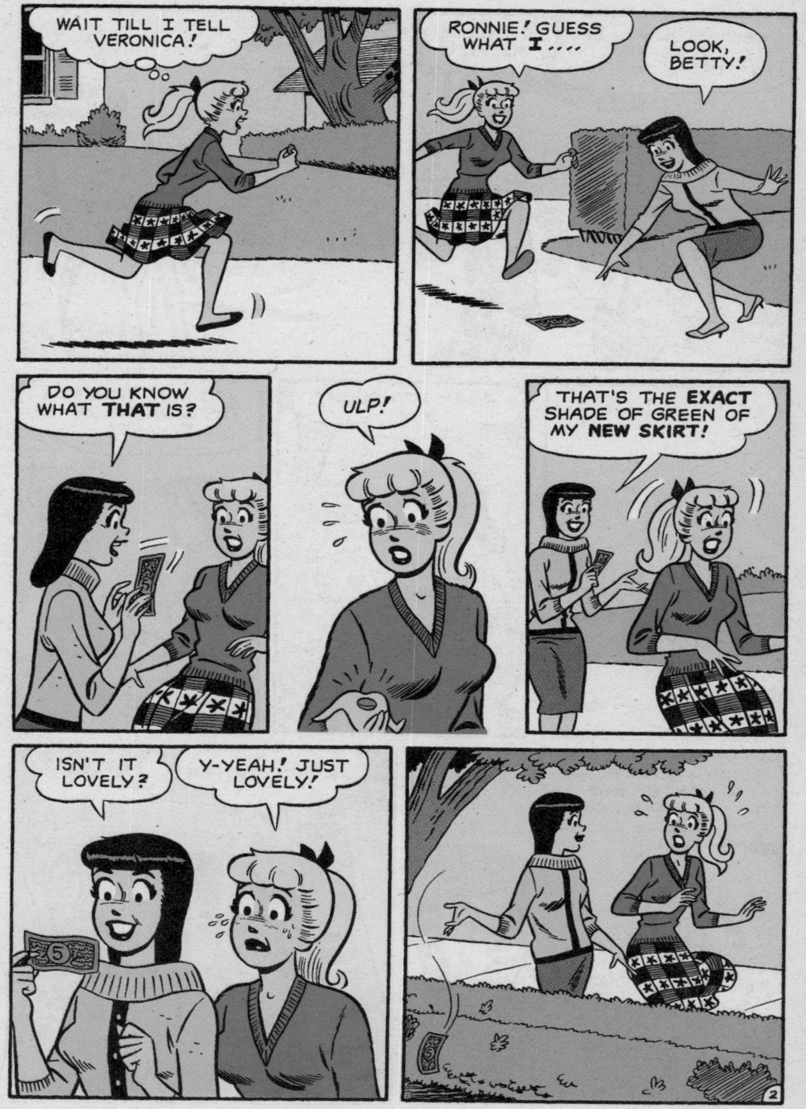
WAIT TILL I TELL VERONICA!
RONNIE! GUESS WHAT I....
LOOK, BETTY!
DO YOU KNOW WHAT THAT IS?
ULP!
THAT'S THE EXACT SHADE OF GREEN OF MY NEW SKIRT!
ISN'T IT LOVELY?
Y-YEAH! JUST LOVELY!
2

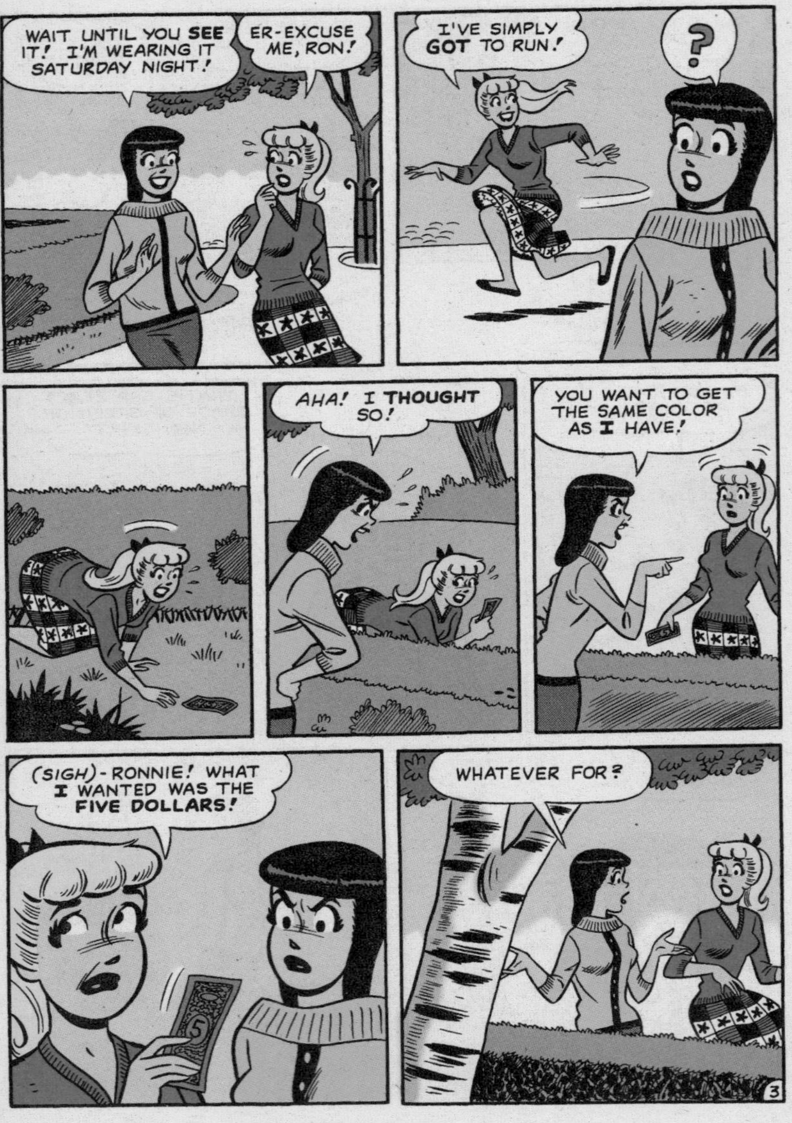
WAIT UNTIL YOU **SEE** IT! I'M WEARING IT SATURDAY NIGHT!
ER-EXCUSE ME, RON!
I'VE SIMPLY **GOT** TO RUN!
?
AHA! I **THOUGHT** SO!
YOU WANT TO GET THE SAME COLOR AS **I** HAVE!
(SIGH)-RONNIE! WHAT **I** WANTED WAS THE **FIVE DOLLARS**!
WHATEVER FOR?
3

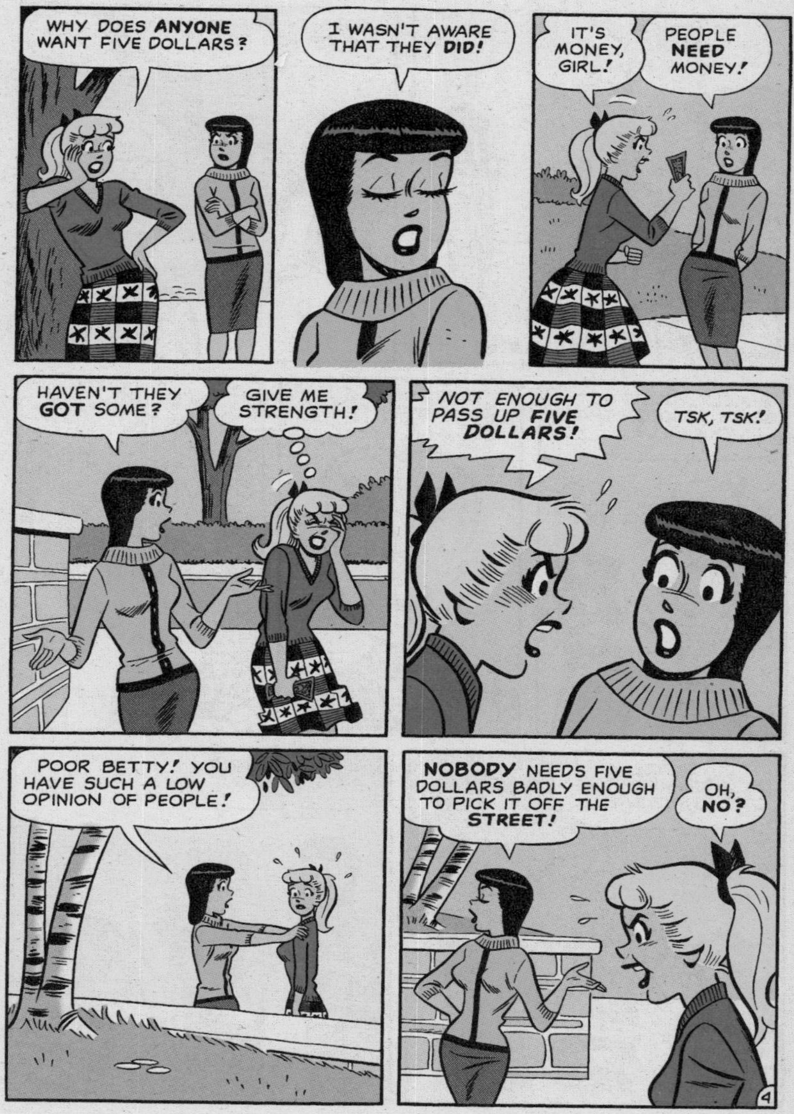

WHY DOES **ANYONE** WANT FIVE DOLLARS?
I WASN'T AWARE THAT THEY **DID!**
IT'S MONEY, GIRL!
PEOPLE **NEED** MONEY!
HAVEN'T THEY **GOT** SOME?
GIVE ME STRENGTH!
NOT ENOUGH TO PASS UP **FIVE DOLLARS!**
TSK, TSK!
POOR BETTY! YOU HAVE SUCH A LOW OPINION OF PEOPLE!
NOBODY NEEDS FIVE DOLLARS BADLY ENOUGH TO PICK IT OFF THE **STREET!**
OH, **NO?**
4

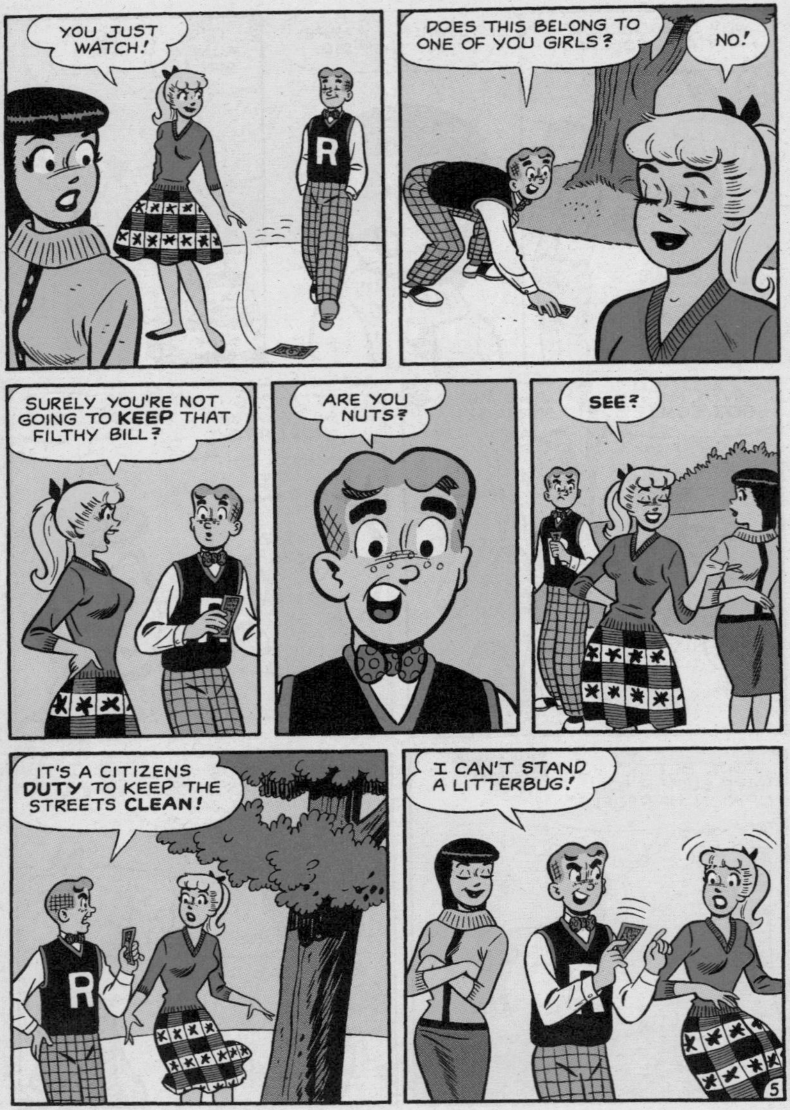
YOU JUST WATCH!
DOES THIS BELONG TO ONE OF YOU GIRLS?
NO!
SURELY YOU'RE NOT GOING TO KEEP THAT FILTHY BILL?
ARE YOU NUTS?
SEE?
IT'S A CITIZENS DUTY TO KEEP THE STREETS CLEAN!
I CAN'T STAND A LITTERBUG!
5

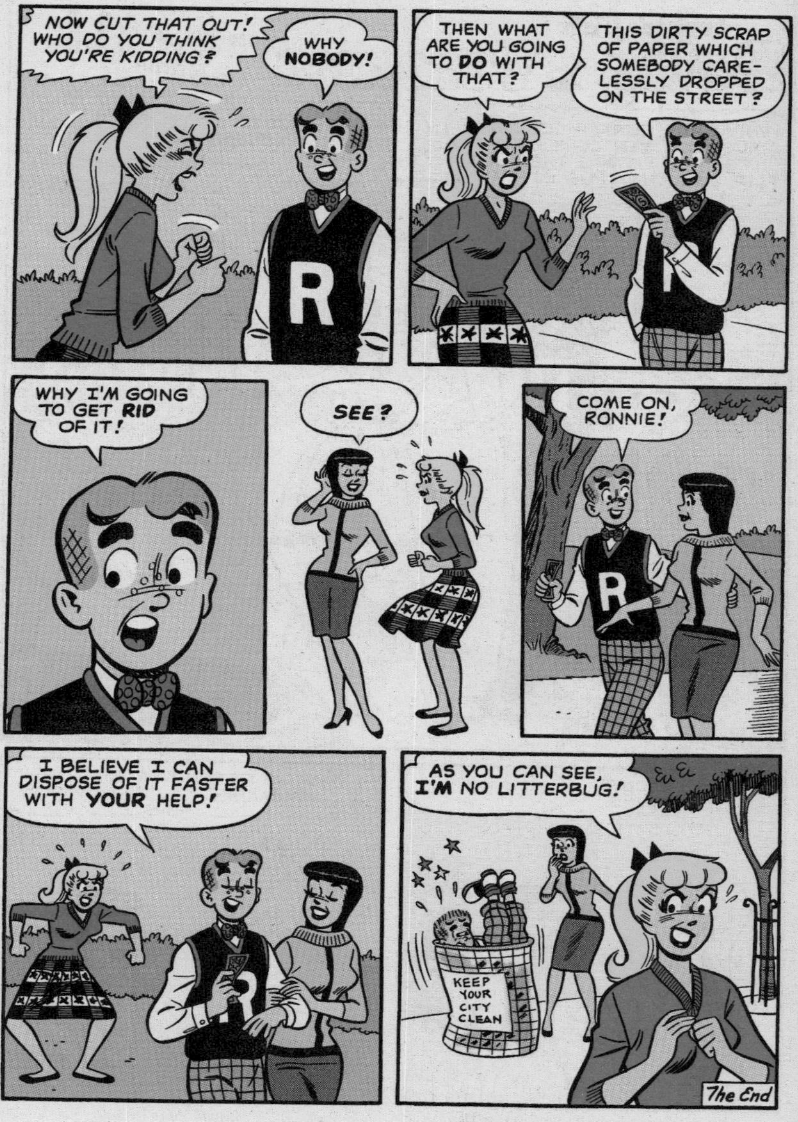
NOW CUT THAT OUT! WHO DO YOU THINK YOU'RE KIDDING?
WHY NOBODY!
THEN WHAT ARE YOU GOING TO DO WITH THAT?
THIS DIRTY SCRAP OF PAPER WHICH SOMEBODY CARE-LESSLY DROPPED ON THE STREET?
WHY I'M GOING TO GET RID OF IT!
SEE?
COME ON, RONNIE!
I BELIEVE I CAN DISPOSE OF IT FASTER WITH YOUR HELP!
AS YOU CAN SEE, I'M NO LITTERBUG!
KEEP YOUR CITY CLEAN
The End

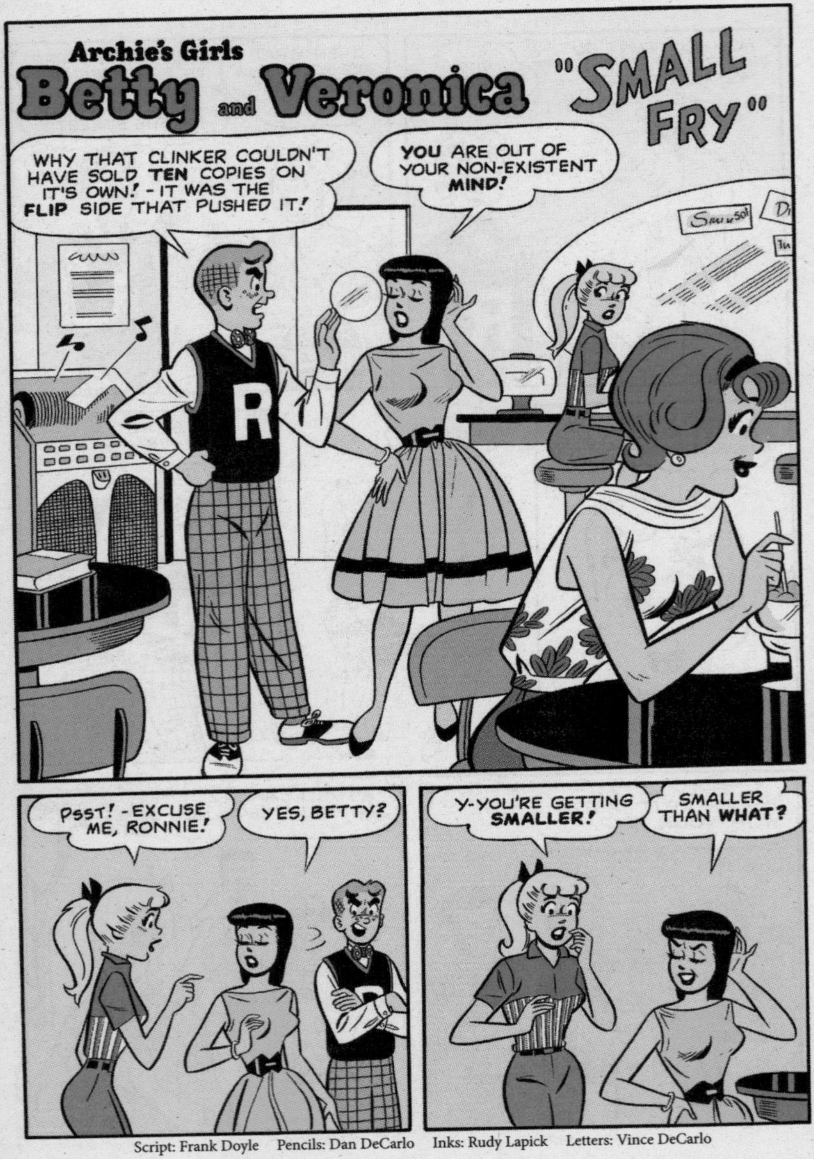
Archie's Girls
Betty and Veronica
"SMALL FRY"
WHY THAT CLINKER COULDN'T HAVE SOLD TEN COPIES ON IT'S OWN! - IT WAS THE FLIP SIDE THAT PUSHED IT!
YOU ARE OUT OF YOUR NON-EXISTENT MIND!
PSST! - EXCUSE ME, RONNIE!
YES, BETTY?
Y-YOU'RE GETTING SMALLER!
SMALLER THAN WHAT?

Script: Frank Doyle Pencils: Dan DeCarlo Inks: Rudy Lapick Letters: Vince DeCarlo

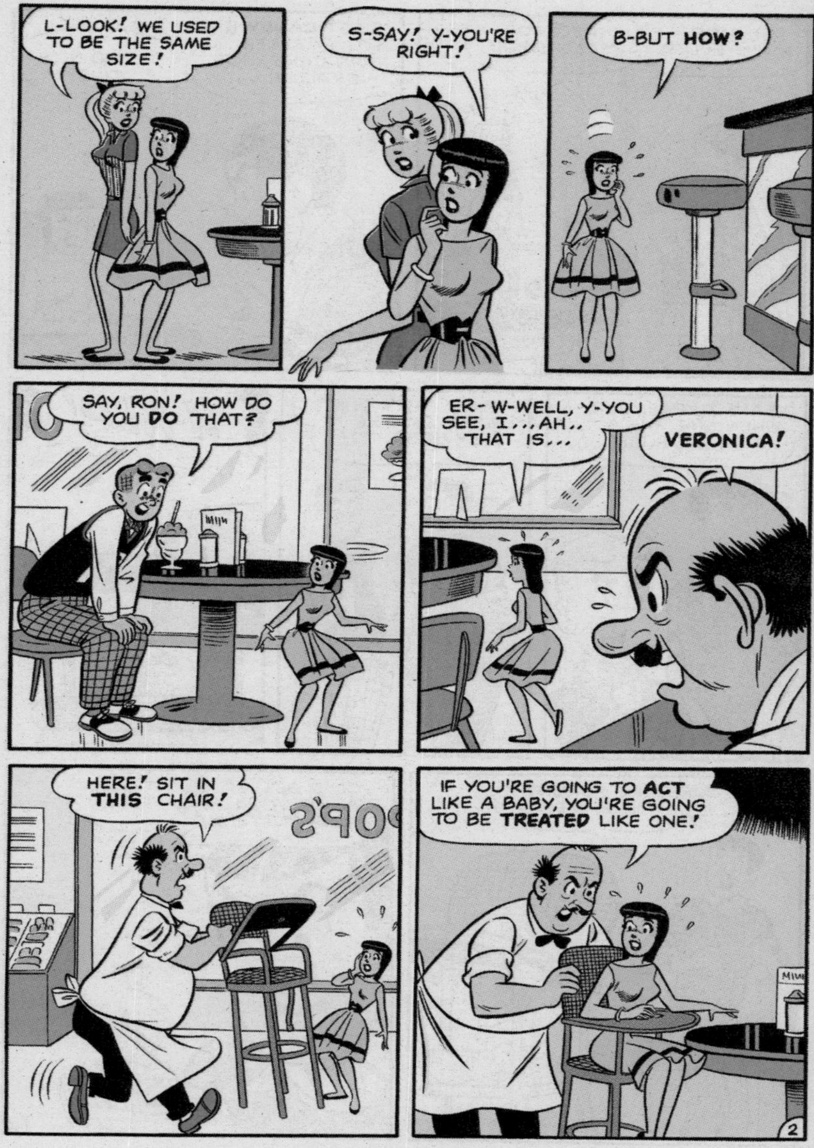
L-LOOK! WE USED TO BE THE SAME SIZE!
S-SAY! Y-YOU'RE RIGHT!
B-BUT HOW?
SAY, RON! HOW DO YOU DO THAT?
ER- W-WELL, Y-YOU SEE, I...AH.. THAT IS...
VERONICA!
HERE! SIT IN THIS CHAIR!
POP'S
IF YOU'RE GOING TO ACT LIKE A BABY, YOU'RE GOING TO BE TREATED LIKE ONE!
2

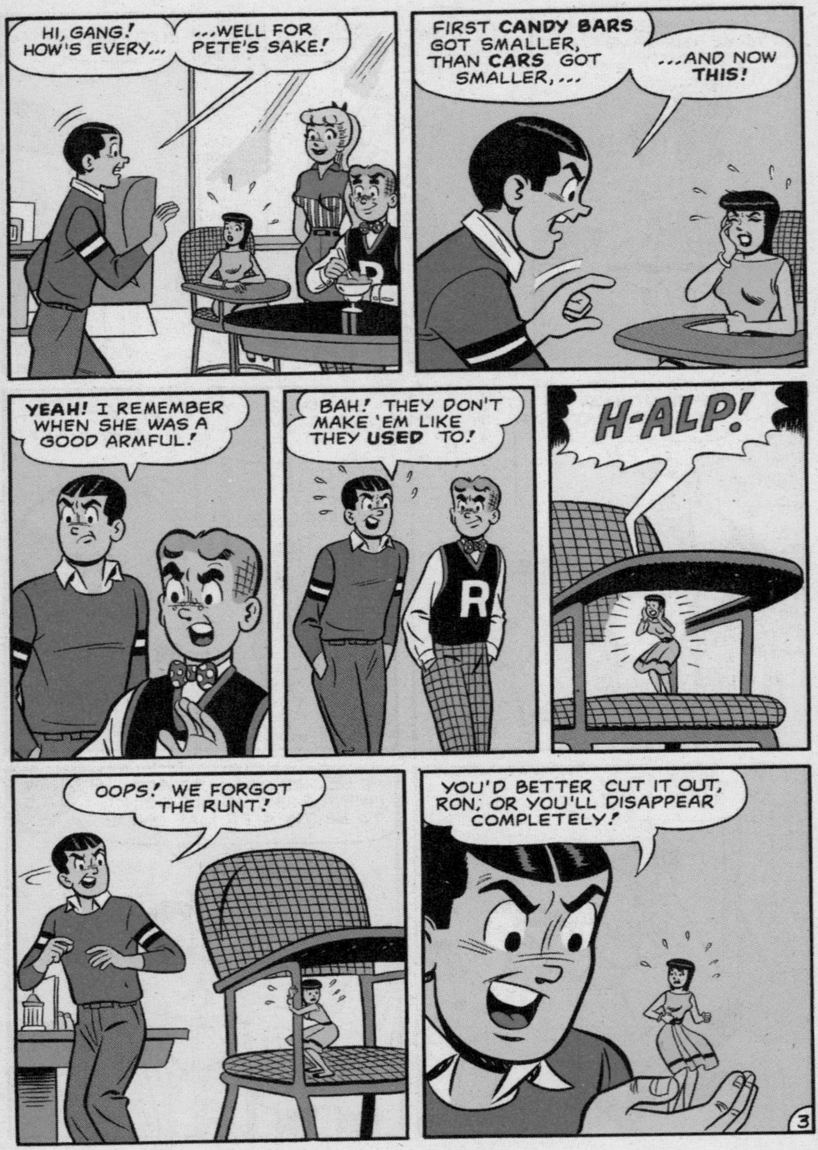
HI, GANG! HOW'S EVERY...
...WELL FOR PETE'S SAKE!
FIRST CANDY BARS GOT SMALLER, THAN CARS GOT SMALLER, ...
...AND NOW THIS!
YEAH! I REMEMBER WHEN SHE WAS A GOOD ARMFUL!
BAH! THEY DON'T MAKE 'EM LIKE THEY USED TO!
H-ALP!
OOPS! WE FORGOT THE RUNT!
YOU'D BETTER CUT IT OUT, RON, OR YOU'LL DISAPPEAR COMPLETELY!
3

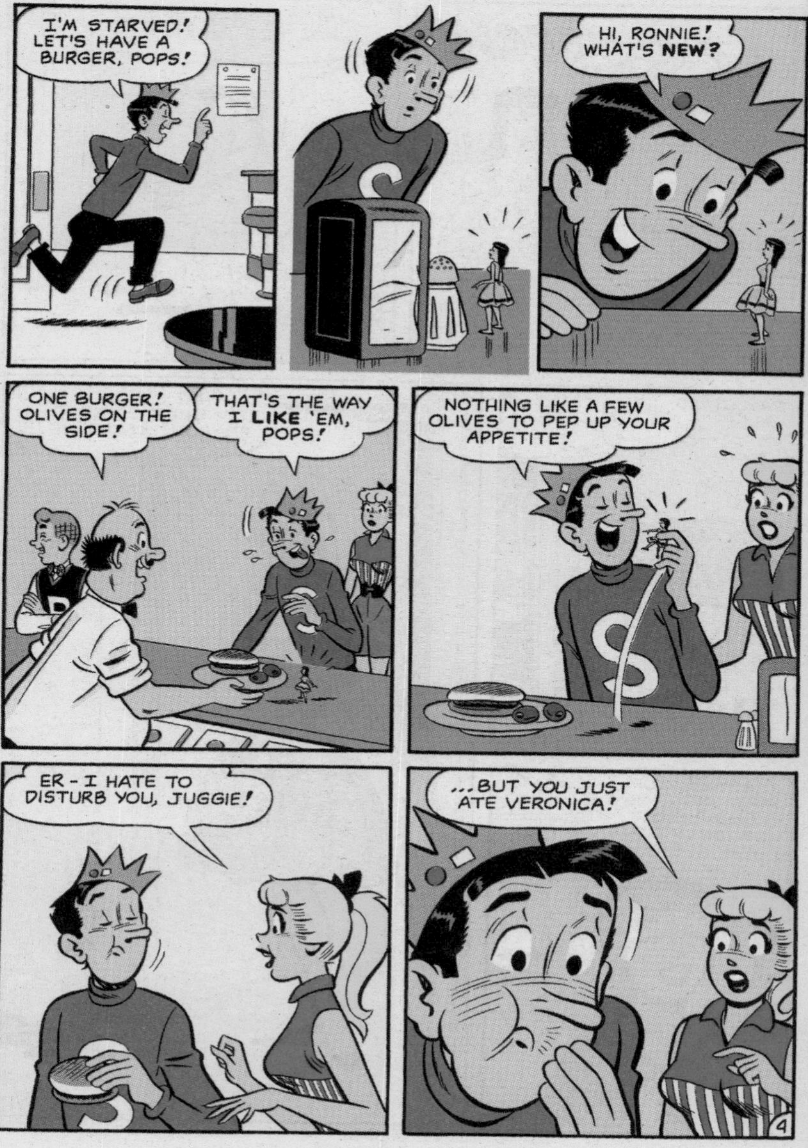
I'M STARVED! LET'S HAVE A BURGER, POPS!
HI, RONNIE! WHAT'S NEW?
ONE BURGER! OLIVES ON THE SIDE!
THAT'S THE WAY I LIKE 'EM, POPS!
NOTHING LIKE A FEW OLIVES TO PEP UP YOUR APPETITE!
ER - I HATE TO DISTURB YOU, JUGGIE!
...BUT YOU JUST ATE VERONICA!
4

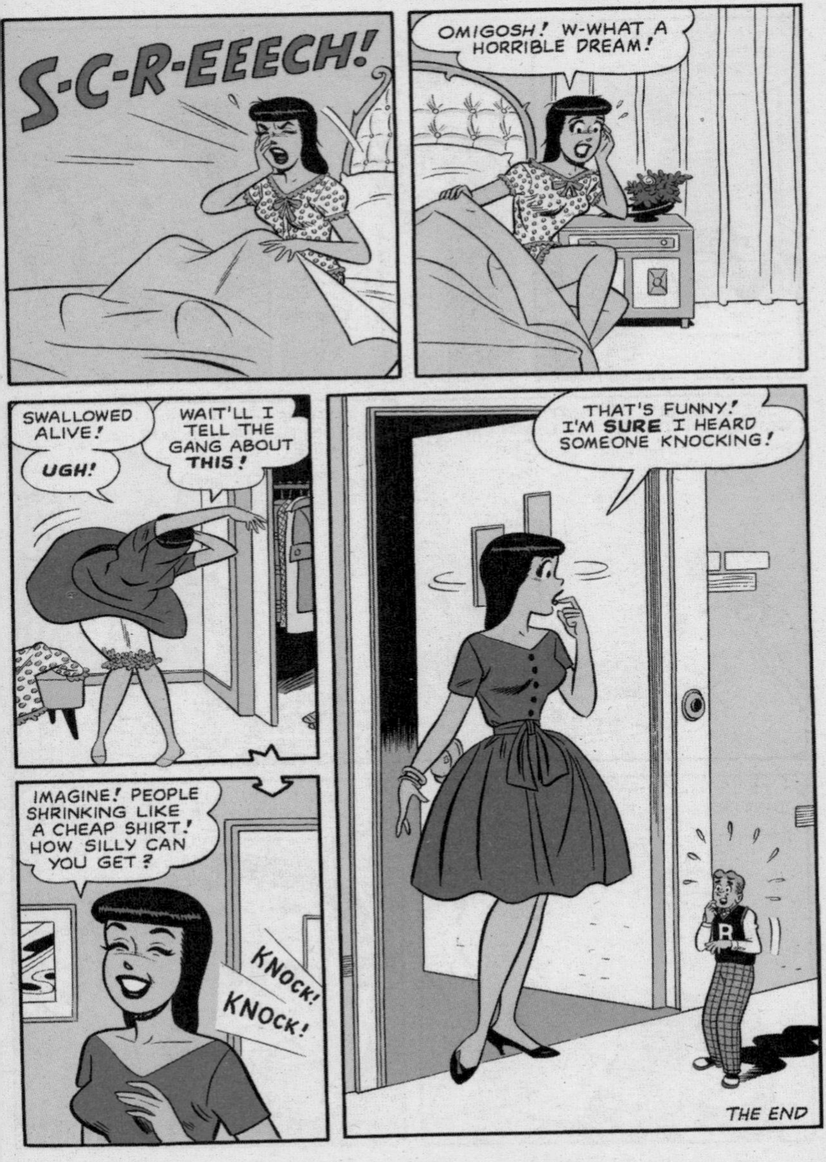
S-C-R-EEECH!
OMIGOSH! W-WHAT A HORRIBLE DREAM!
SWALLOWED ALIVE!
UGH!
WAIT'LL I TELL THE GANG ABOUT THIS!
IMAGINE! PEOPLE SHRINKING LIKE A CHEAP SHIRT! HOW SILLY CAN YOU GET?
KNOCK!
KNOCK!
THAT'S FUNNY! I'M SURE I HEARD SOMEONE KNOCKING!
R
THE END

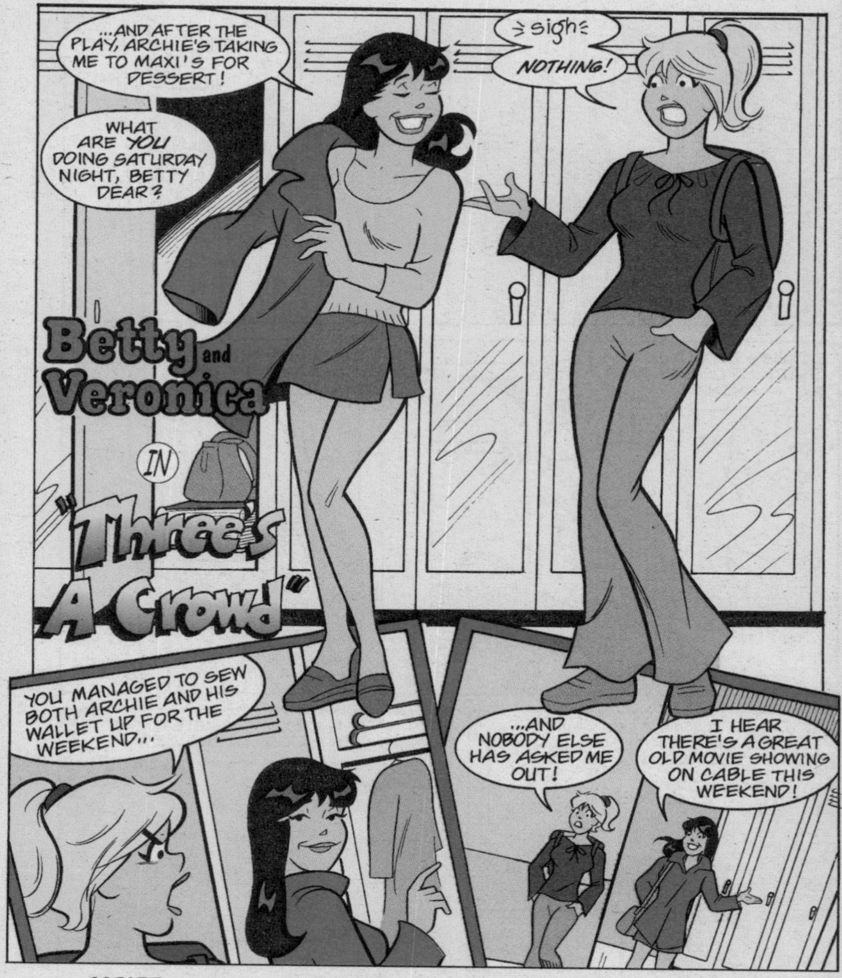
...AND AFTER THE PLAY, ARCHIE'S TAKING ME TO MAXI'S FOR DESSERT!
WHAT ARE YOU DOING SATURDAY NIGHT, BETTY DEAR?
sigh
NOTHING!
Betty and Veronica
IN
"Three's A Crowd"
YOU MANAGED TO SEW BOTH ARCHIE AND HIS WALLET UP FOR THE WEEKEND...
...AND NOBODY ELSE HAS ASKED ME OUT!
I HEAR THERE'S A GREAT OLD MOVIE SHOWING ON CABLE THIS WEEKEND!

SCRIPT: KATHLEEN WEBB PENCILS: DAN PARENT INKS: RICH KOSLOWSKI
LETTERS: VICKIE WILLIAMS COLORS: BARRY GROSSMAN

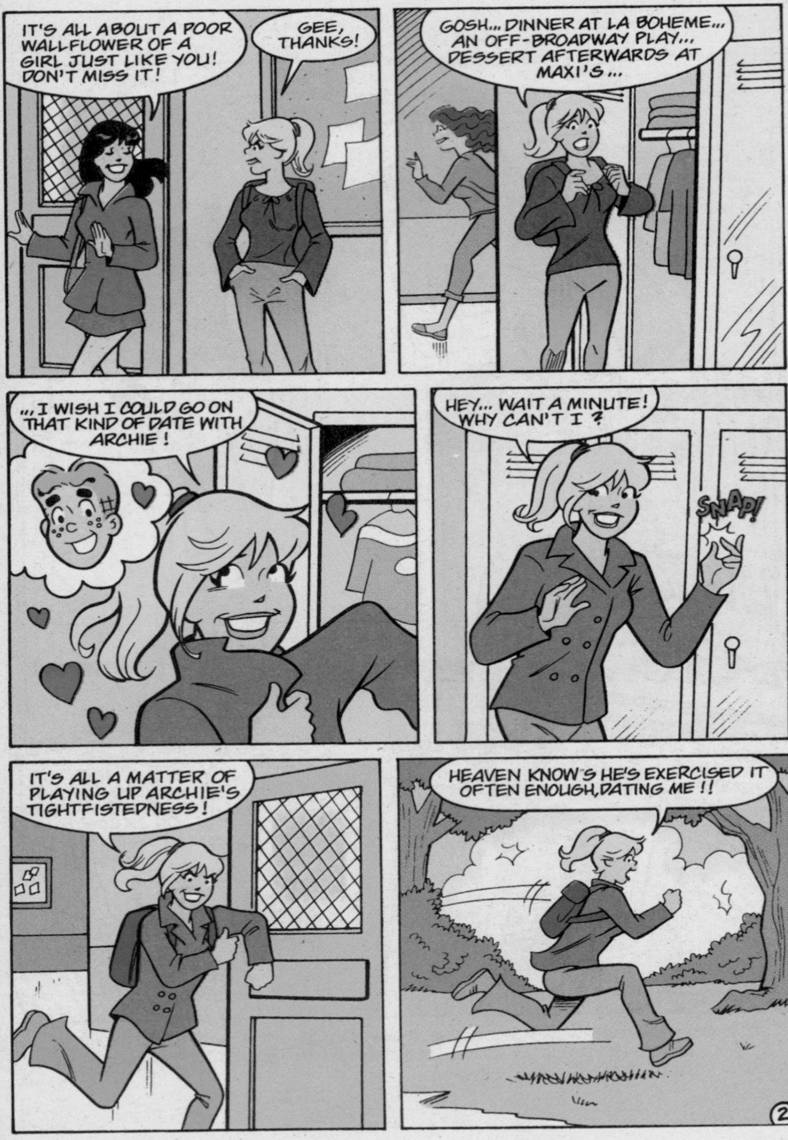
IT'S ALL ABOUT A POOR WALLFLOWER OF A GIRL JUST LIKE YOU! DON'T MISS IT!
GEE, THANKS!
GOSH... DINNER AT LA BOHEME... AN OFF-BROADWAY PLAY... DESSERT AFTERWARDS AT MAXI'S...
...I WISH I COULD GO ON THAT KIND OF DATE WITH ARCHIE!
HEY... WAIT A MINUTE! WHY CAN'T I ?
SNAP!
IT'S ALL A MATTER OF PLAYING UP ARCHIE'S TIGHTFISTEDNESS!
HEAVEN KNOW'S HE'S EXERCISED IT OFTEN ENOUGH, DATING ME!!
2

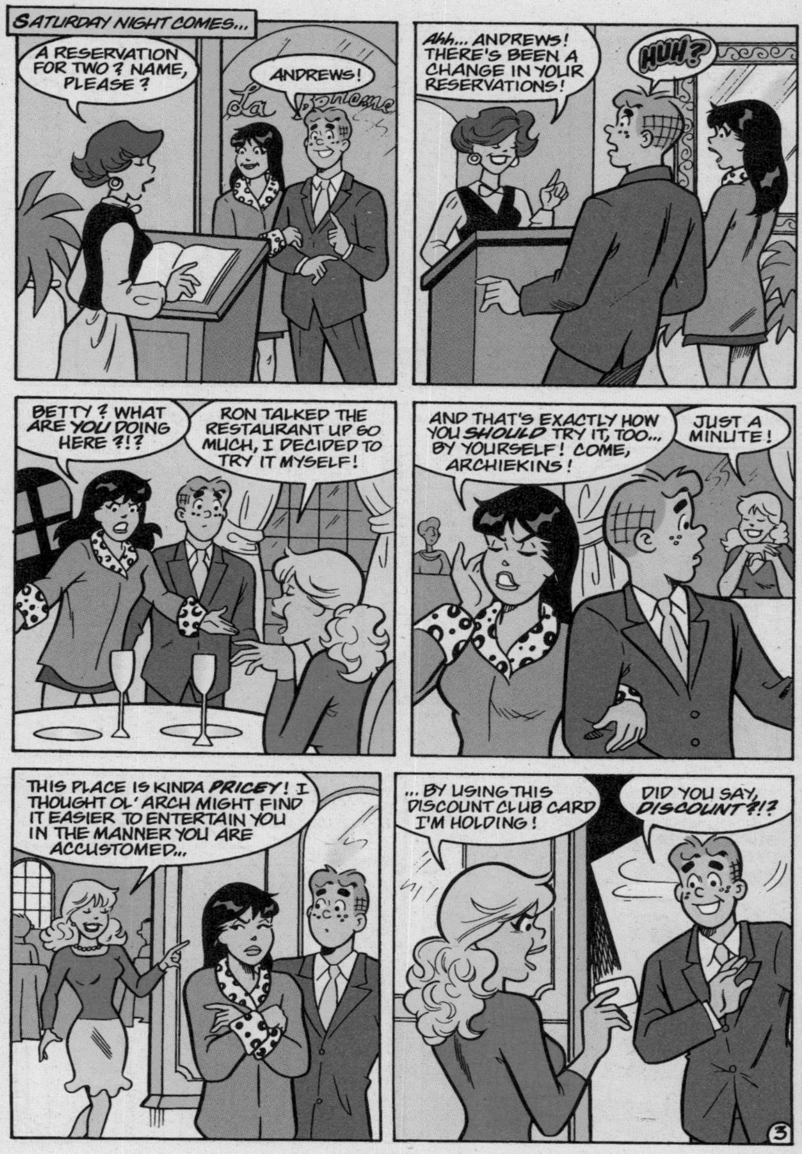
SATURDAY NIGHT COMES...
A RESERVATION FOR TWO? NAME, PLEASE?
ANDREWS!
La Boheme
Ahh... ANDREWS! THERE'S BEEN A CHANGE IN YOUR RESERVATIONS!
HUH?
BETTY? WHAT ARE YOU DOING HERE?!?
RON TALKED THE RESTAURANT UP SO MUCH, I DECIDED TO TRY IT MYSELF!
AND THAT'S EXACTLY HOW YOU SHOULD TRY IT, TOO... BY YOURSELF! COME, ARCHIEKINS!
JUST A MINUTE!
THIS PLACE IS KINDA PRICEY! I THOUGHT OL' ARCH MIGHT FIND IT EASIER TO ENTERTAIN YOU IN THE MANNER YOU ARE ACCUSTOMED...
... BY USING THIS DISCOUNT CLUB CARD I'M HOLDING!
DID YOU SAY, DISCOUNT?!?
3

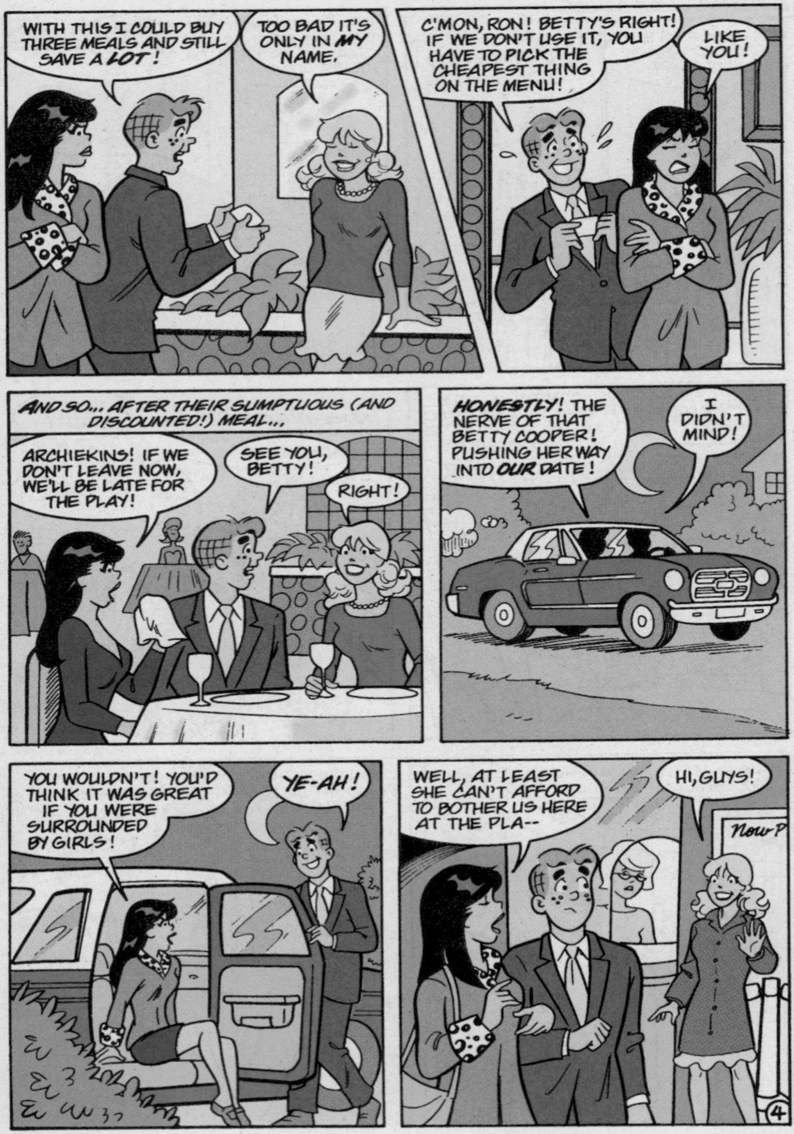
WITH THIS I COULD BUY THREE MEALS AND STILL SAVE A LOT!
TOO BAD IT'S ONLY IN MY NAME.
C'MON, RON! BETTY'S RIGHT! IF WE DON'T USE IT, YOU HAVE TO PICK THE CHEAPEST THING ON THE MENU!
LIKE YOU!
AND SO... AFTER THEIR SUMPTUOUS (AND DISCOUNTED!) MEAL...
ARCHIEKINS! IF WE DON'T LEAVE NOW, WE'LL BE LATE FOR THE PLAY!
SEE YOU, BETTY!
RIGHT!
HONESTLY! THE NERVE OF THAT BETTY COOPER! PUSHING HER WAY INTO OUR DATE!
I DIDN'T MIND!
YOU WOULDN'T! YOU'D THINK IT WAS GREAT IF YOU WERE SURROUNDED BY GIRLS!
YE-AH!
WELL, AT LEAST SHE CAN'T AFFORD TO BOTHER US HERE AT THE PLA--
HI, GUYS!
4

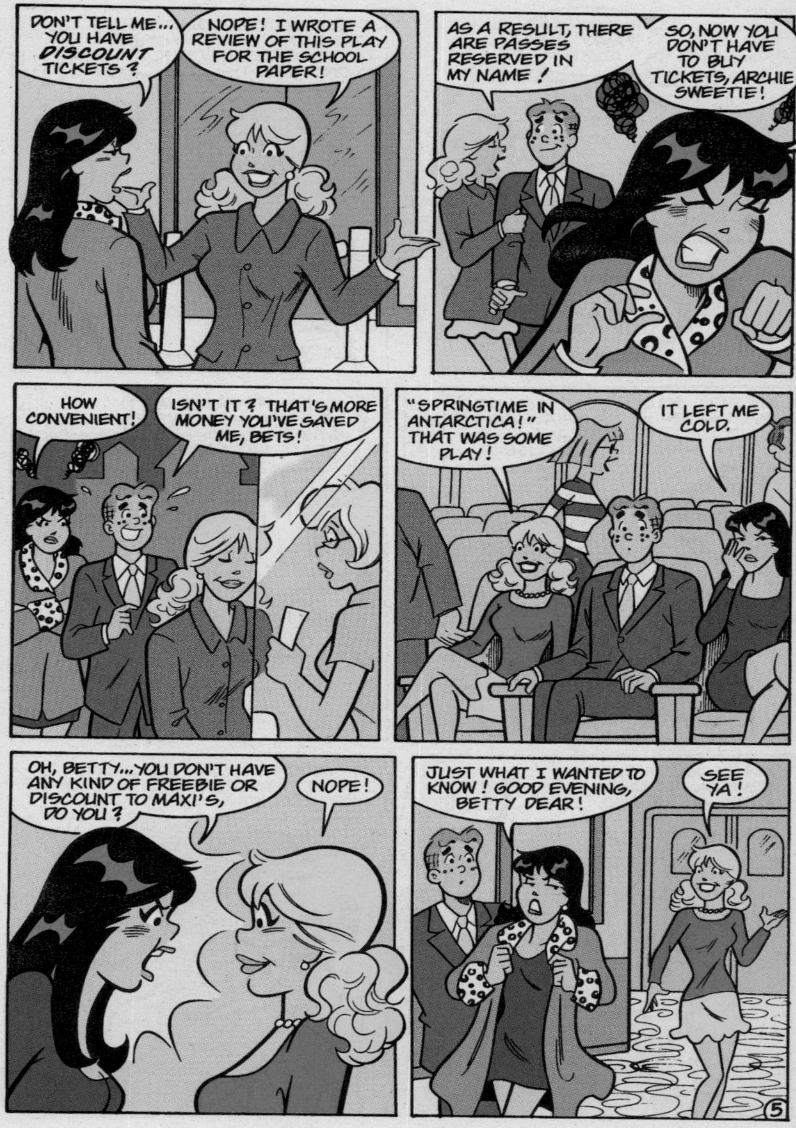
DON'T TELL ME... YOU HAVE DISCOUNT TICKETS ?
NOPE! I WROTE A REVIEW OF THIS PLAY FOR THE SCHOOL PAPER!
AS A RESULT, THERE ARE PASSES RESERVED IN MY NAME !
SO, NOW YOU DON'T HAVE TO BUY TICKETS, ARCHIE SWEETIE!
HOW CONVENIENT!
ISN'T IT ? THAT'S MORE MONEY YOU'VE SAVED ME, BETS!
"SPRINGTIME IN ANTARCTICA!" THAT WAS SOME PLAY!
IT LEFT ME COLD.
OH, BETTY... YOU DON'T HAVE ANY KIND OF FREEBIE OR DISCOUNT TO MAXI'S, DO YOU ?
NOPE!
JUST WHAT I WANTED TO KNOW ! GOOD EVENING, BETTY DEAR!
SEE YA !
5

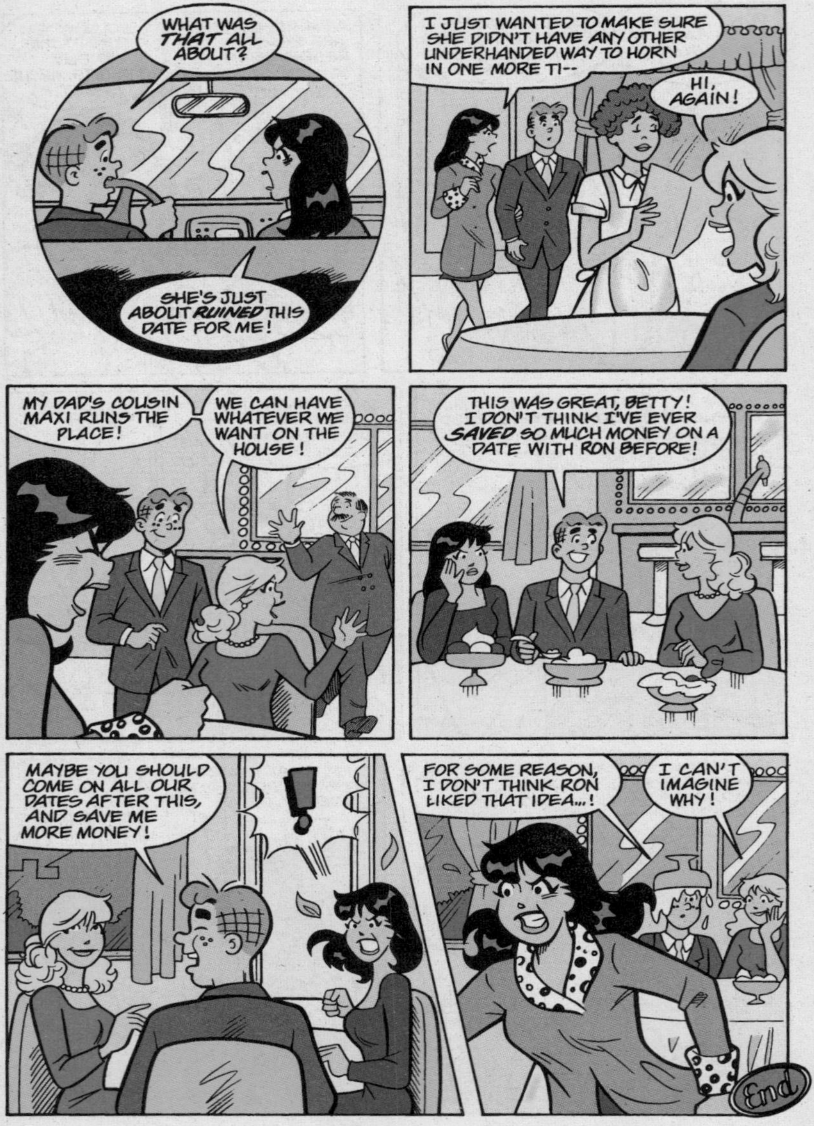
WHAT WAS THAT ALL ABOUT?
SHE'S JUST ABOUT RUINED THIS DATE FOR ME!
I JUST WANTED TO MAKE SURE SHE DIDN'T HAVE ANY OTHER UNDERHANDED WAY TO HORN IN ONE MORE TI--
HI, AGAIN!
MY DAD'S COUSIN MAXI RUNS THE PLACE!
WE CAN HAVE WHATEVER WE WANT ON THE HOUSE!
THIS WAS GREAT, BETTY! I DON'T THINK I'VE EVER SAVED SO MUCH MONEY ON A DATE WITH RON BEFORE!
MAYBE YOU SHOULD COME ON ALL OUR DATES AFTER THIS, AND SAVE ME MORE MONEY!
!
FOR SOME REASON, I DON'T THINK RON LIKED THAT IDEA...!
I CAN'T IMAGINE WHY!
End

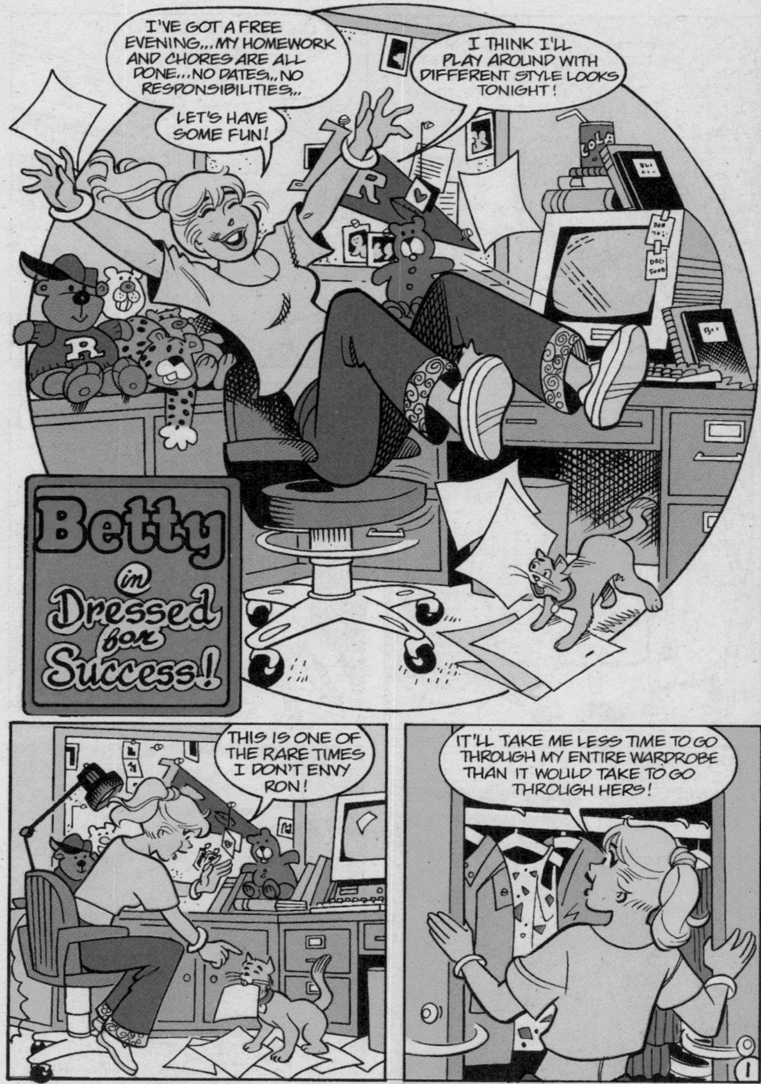
I'VE GOT A FREE EVENING... MY HOMEWORK AND CHORES ARE ALL DONE... NO DATES... NO RESPONSIBILITIES...
LET'S HAVE SOME FUN!
I THINK I'LL PLAY AROUND WITH DIFFERENT STYLE LOOKS TONIGHT!
Betty in Dressed for Success!
THIS IS ONE OF THE RARE TIMES I DON'T ENVY RON!
IT'LL TAKE ME LESS TIME TO GO THROUGH MY ENTIRE WARDROBE THAN IT WOULD TAKE TO GO THROUGH HERS!
1

Script: Kathleen Webb / Pencils: Stan Goldberg / Inks: Jon Lowe / Letters: Vickie Williams

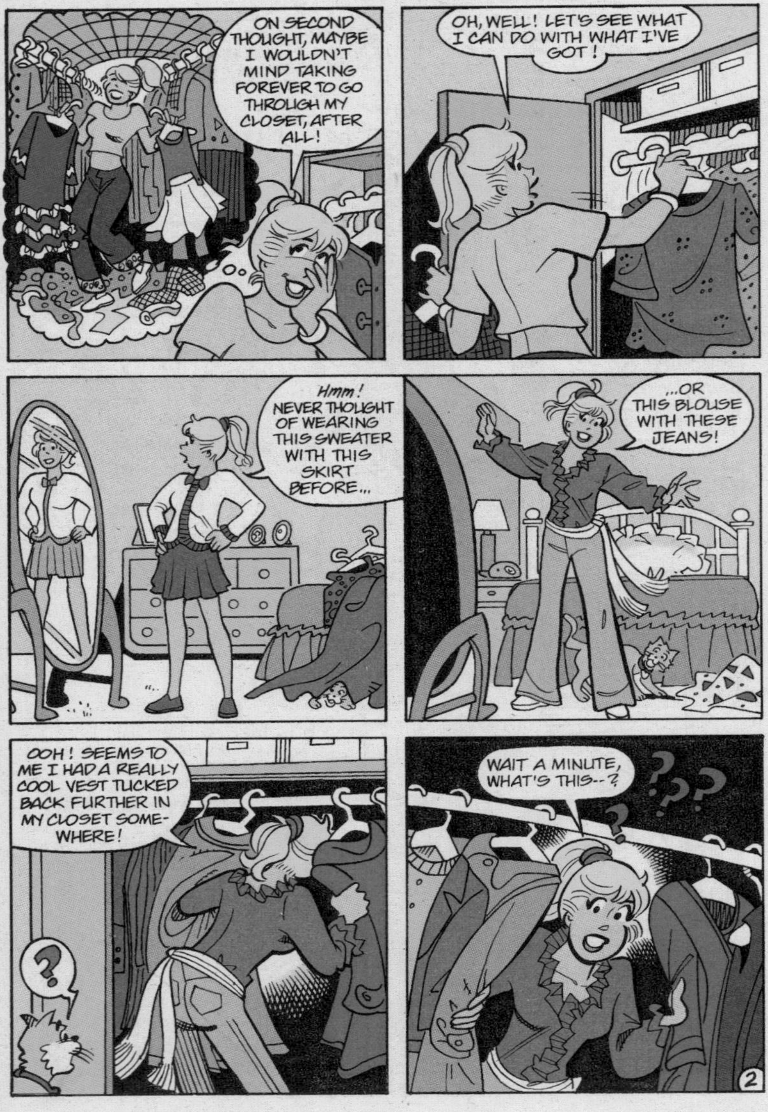
ON SECOND THOUGHT, MAYBE I WOULDN'T MIND TAKING FOREVER TO GO THROUGH MY CLOSET, AFTER ALL!
OH, WELL! LET'S SEE WHAT I CAN DO WITH WHAT I'VE GOT!
Hmm! NEVER THOUGHT OF WEARING THIS SWEATER WITH THIS SKIRT BEFORE...
...OR THIS BLOUSE WITH THESE JEANS!
OOH! SEEMS TO ME I HAD A REALLY COOL VEST TUCKED BACK FURTHER IN MY CLOSET SOME-WHERE!
?
WAIT A MINUTE, WHAT'S THIS--?
???
?
2

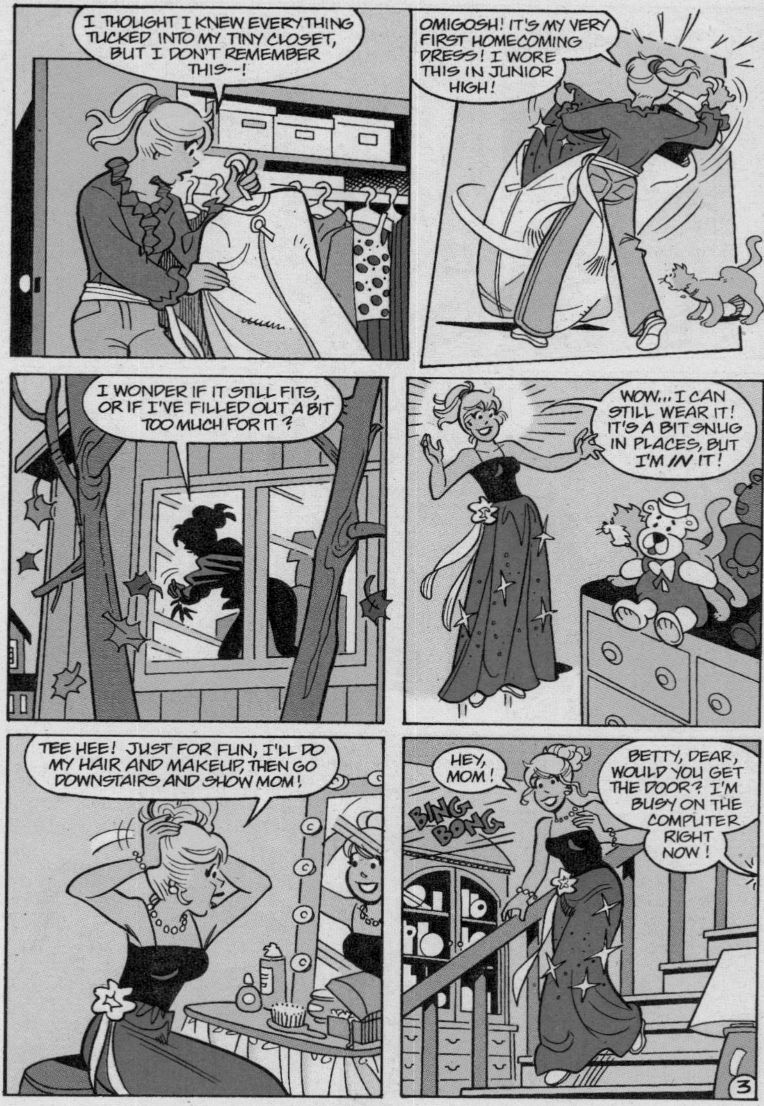
I THOUGHT I KNEW EVERYTHING TUCKED INTO MY TINY CLOSET, BUT I DON'T REMEMBER THIS--!
OMIGOSH! IT'S MY VERY FIRST HOMECOMING DRESS! I WORE THIS IN JUNIOR HIGH!
I WONDER IF IT STILL FITS, OR IF I'VE FILLED OUT A BIT TOO MUCH FOR IT?
WOW... I CAN STILL WEAR IT! IT'S A BIT SNUG IN PLACES, BUT I'M IN IT!
TEE HEE! JUST FOR FUN, I'LL DO MY HAIR AND MAKEUP, THEN GO DOWNSTAIRS AND SHOW MOM!
HEY, MOM!
BING BONG
BETTY, DEAR, WOULD YOU GET THE DOOR? I'M BUSY ON THE COMPUTER RIGHT NOW!
3

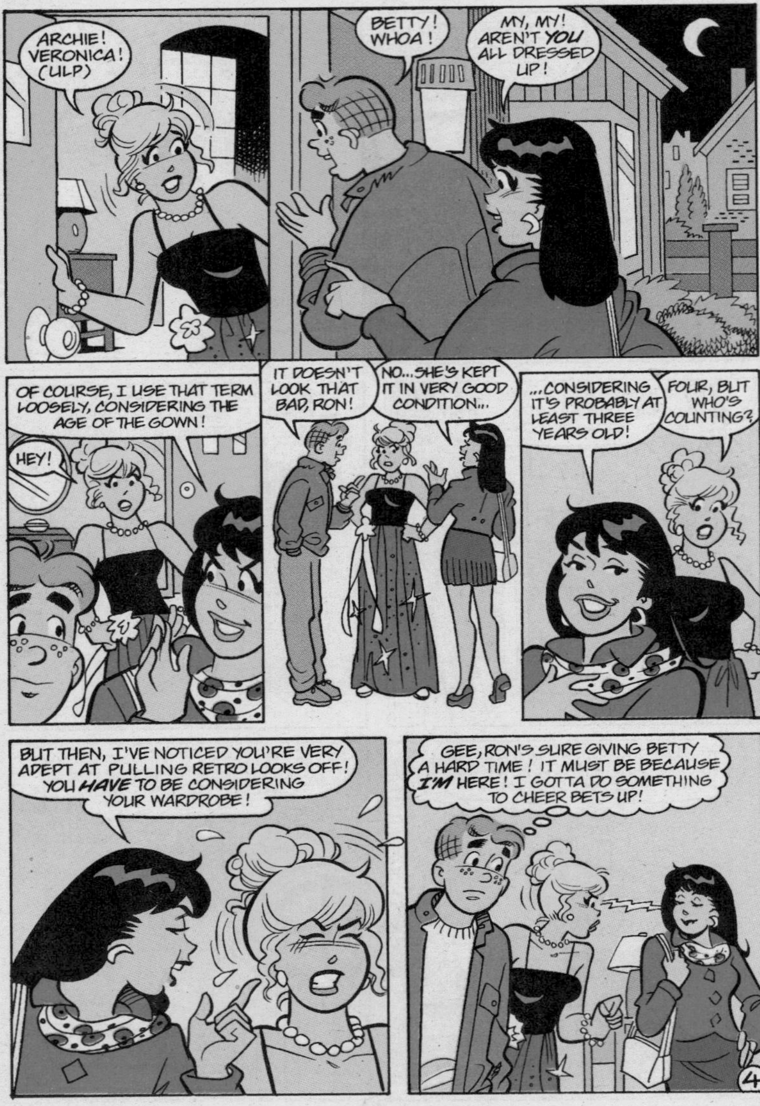
ARCHIE! VERONICA! (ULP)
BETTY! WHOA!
MY, MY! AREN'T YOU ALL DRESSED UP!
OF COURSE, I USE THAT TERM LOOSELY, CONSIDERING THE AGE OF THE GOWN!
HEY!
IT DOESN'T LOOK THAT BAD, RON!
NO... SHE'S KEPT IT IN VERY GOOD CONDITION...
...CONSIDERING IT'S PROBABLY AT LEAST THREE YEARS OLD!
FOUR, BUT WHO'S COUNTING?
BUT THEN, I'VE NOTICED YOU'RE VERY ADEPT AT PULLING RETRO LOOKS OFF! YOU HAVE TO BE CONSIDERING YOUR WARDROBE!
GEE, RON'S SURE GIVING BETTY A HARD TIME! IT MUST BE BECAUSE I'M HERE! I GOTTA DO SOMETHING TO CHEER BETS UP!
4

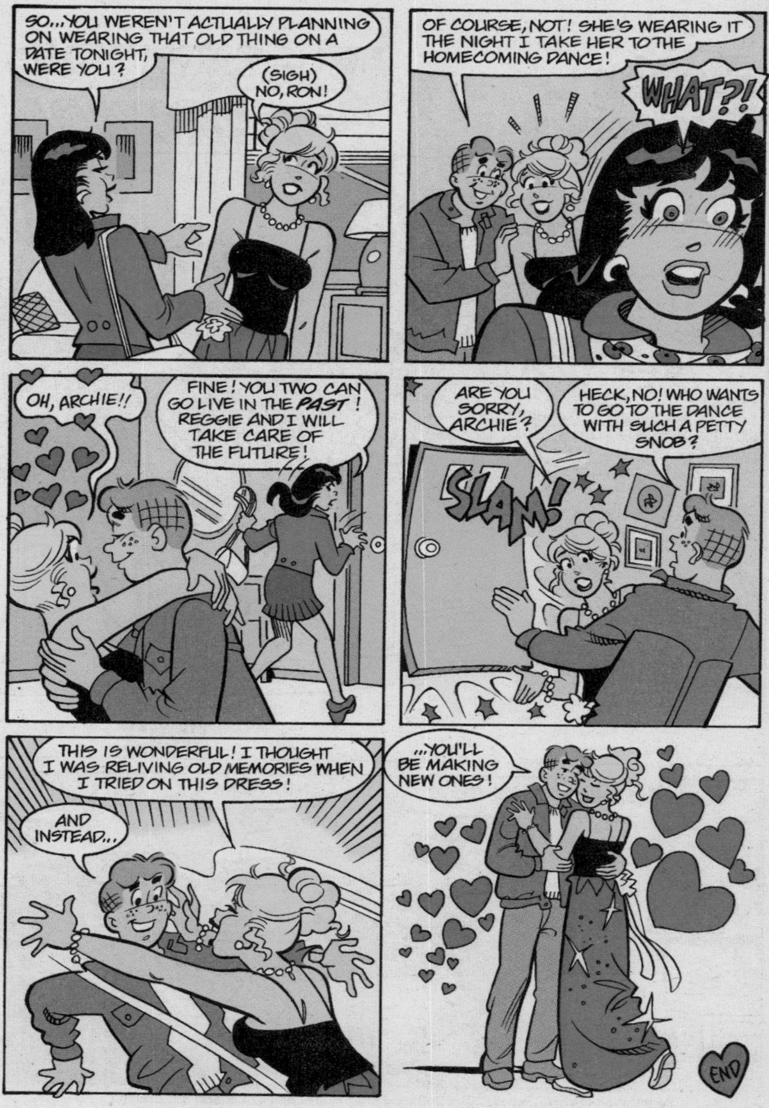
SO...YOU WEREN'T ACTUALLY PLANNING ON WEARING THAT OLD THING ON A DATE TONIGHT, WERE YOU?
(SIGH) NO, RON!
OF COURSE, NOT! SHE'S WEARING IT THE NIGHT I TAKE HER TO THE HOMECOMING DANCE!
WHAT?!
OH, ARCHIE!!
FINE! YOU TWO CAN GO LIVE IN THE PAST! REGGIE AND I WILL TAKE CARE OF THE FUTURE!
ARE YOU SORRY, ARCHIE?
HECK, NO! WHO WANTS TO GO TO THE DANCE WITH SUCH A PETTY SNOB?
SLAM!
THIS IS WONDERFUL! I THOUGHT I WAS RELIVING OLD MEMORIES WHEN I TRIED ON THIS DRESS!
AND INSTEAD...
...YOU'LL BE MAKING NEW ONES!
END

Betty and Veronica in 'Backward and Forward'

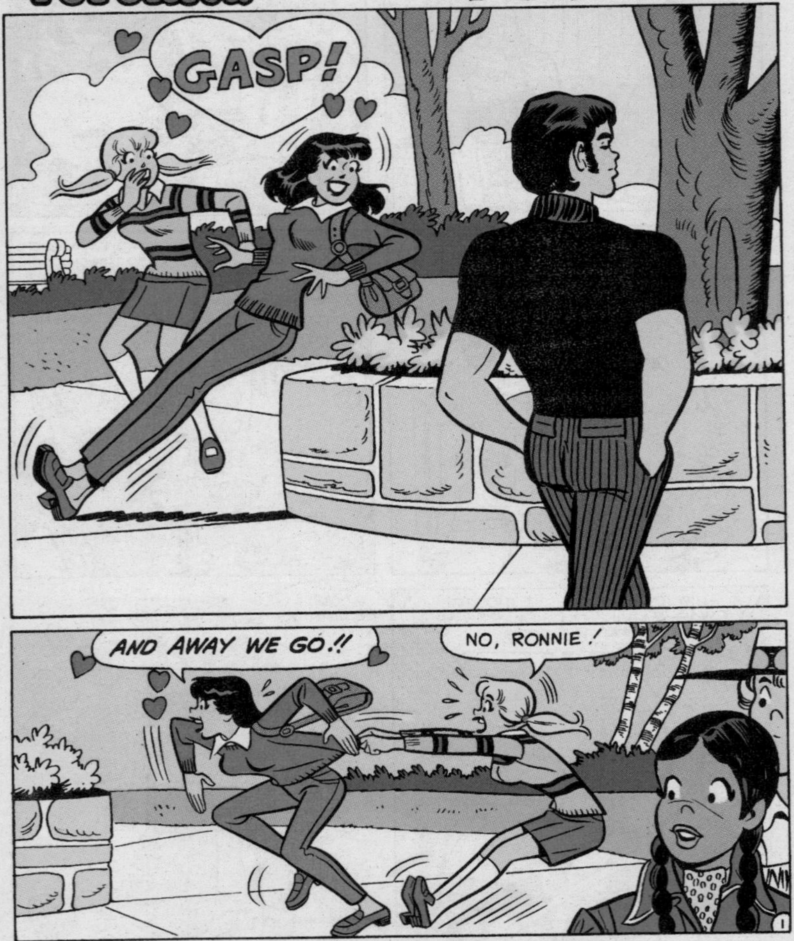
GASP!
AND AWAY WE GO.!!
NO, RONNIE!
1

Script: Frank Doyle / Pencils: Dan DeCarlo / Inks: Rudy Lapick / Letters: Bill Yoshida

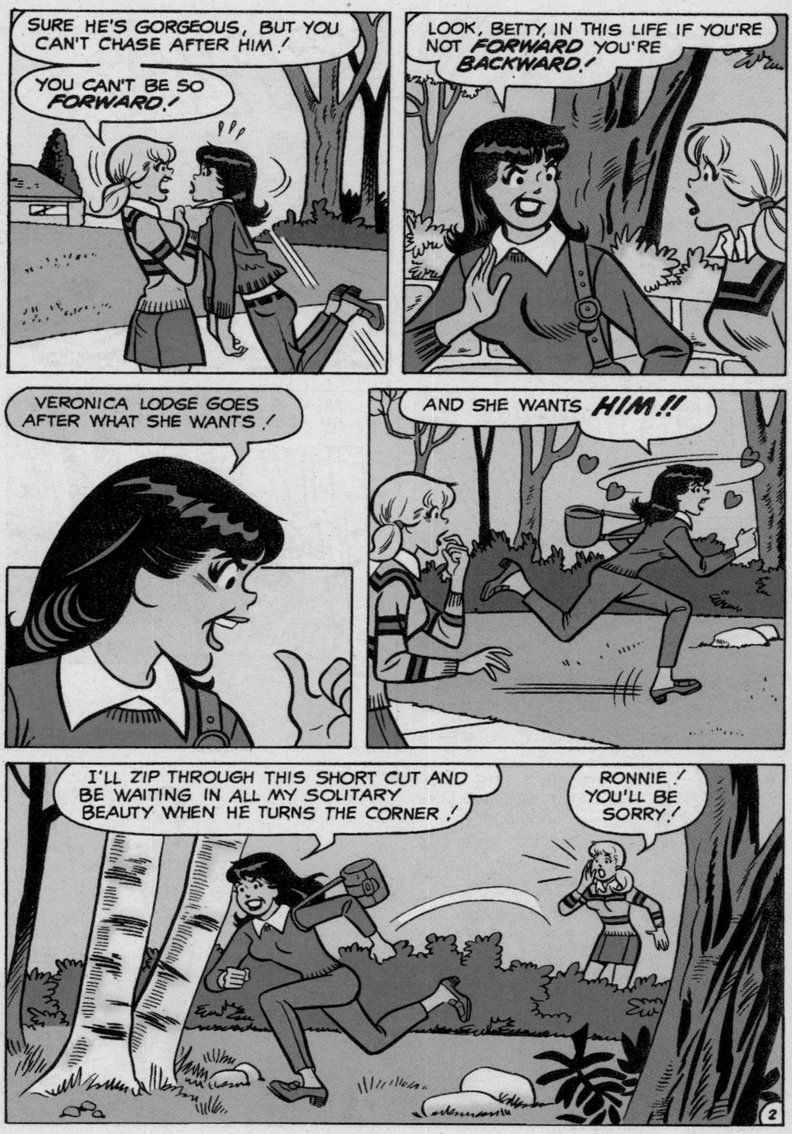
SURE HE'S GORGEOUS, BUT YOU CAN'T CHASE AFTER HIM!
YOU CAN'T BE SO FORWARD!
LOOK, BETTY, IN THIS LIFE IF YOU'RE NOT FORWARD YOU'RE BACKWARD!
VERONICA LODGE GOES AFTER WHAT SHE WANTS!
AND SHE WANTS HIM!!
I'LL ZIP THROUGH THIS SHORT CUT AND BE WAITING IN ALL MY SOLITARY BEAUTY WHEN HE TURNS THE CORNER!
RONNIE! YOU'LL BE SORRY!
2

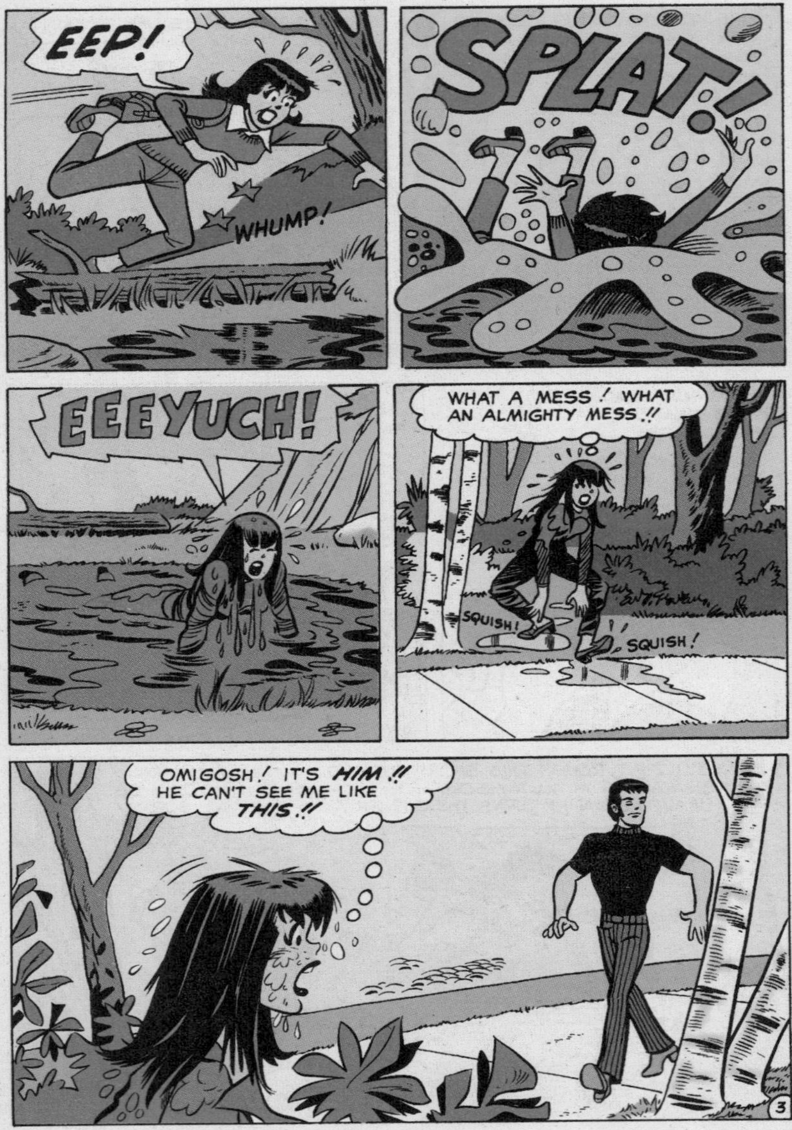
EEP!
WHUMP!
SPLAT!
EEEYUCH!
WHAT A MESS! WHAT AN ALMIGHTY MESS!!
SQUISH!
SQUISH!
OMIGOSH! IT'S HIM!! HE CAN'T SEE ME LIKE THIS!!
3

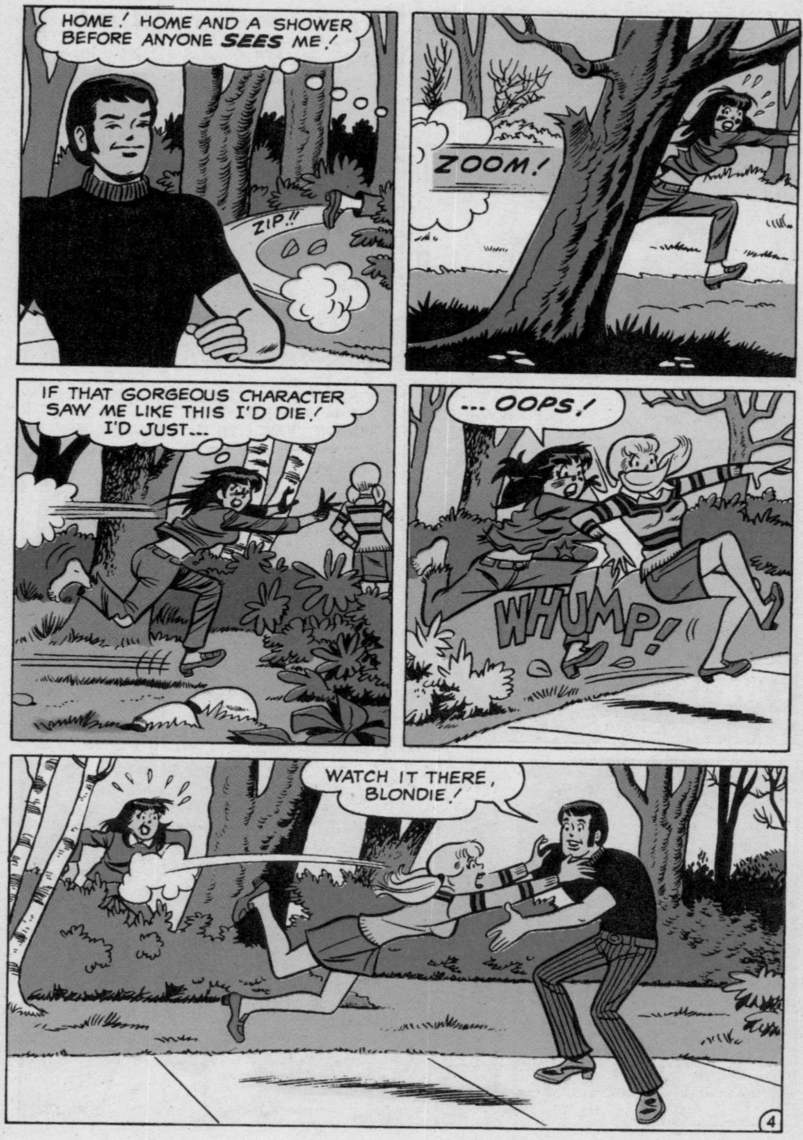
HOME! HOME AND A SHOWER BEFORE ANYONE SEES ME!
ZIP!!
ZOOM!
IF THAT GORGEOUS CHARACTER SAW ME LIKE THIS I'D DIE! I'D JUST...
... OOPS!
WHUMP!
WATCH IT THERE, BLONDIE!
4

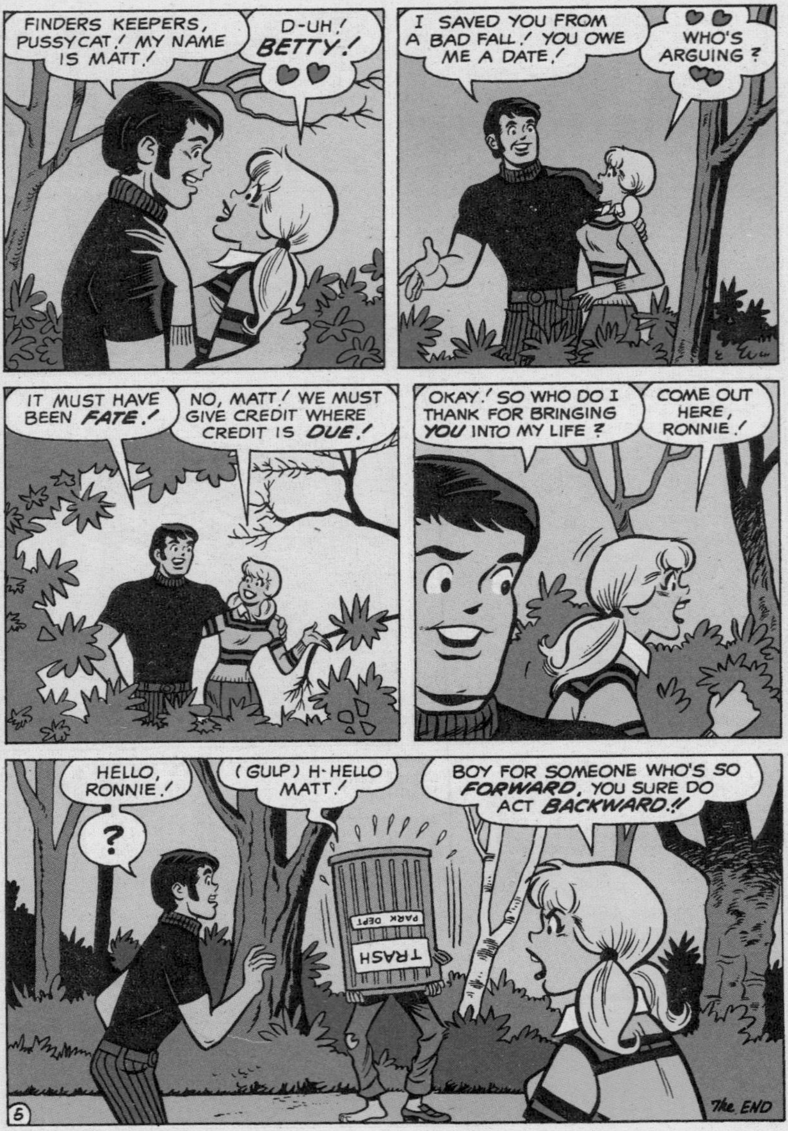
FINDERS KEEPERS, PUSSYCAT! MY NAME IS MATT!
D-UH! BETTY!
I SAVED YOU FROM A BAD FALL! YOU OWE ME A DATE!
WHO'S ARGUING?
IT MUST HAVE BEEN FATE!
NO, MATT! WE MUST GIVE CREDIT WHERE CREDIT IS DUE!
OKAY! SO WHO DO I THANK FOR BRINGING YOU INTO MY LIFE?
COME OUT HERE, RONNIE!
HELLO, RONNIE!
?
(GULP) H-HELLO MATT!
BOY FOR SOMEONE WHO'S SO FORWARD, YOU SURE DO ACT BACKWARD!!
TRASH
PARK DEPT
5
The END

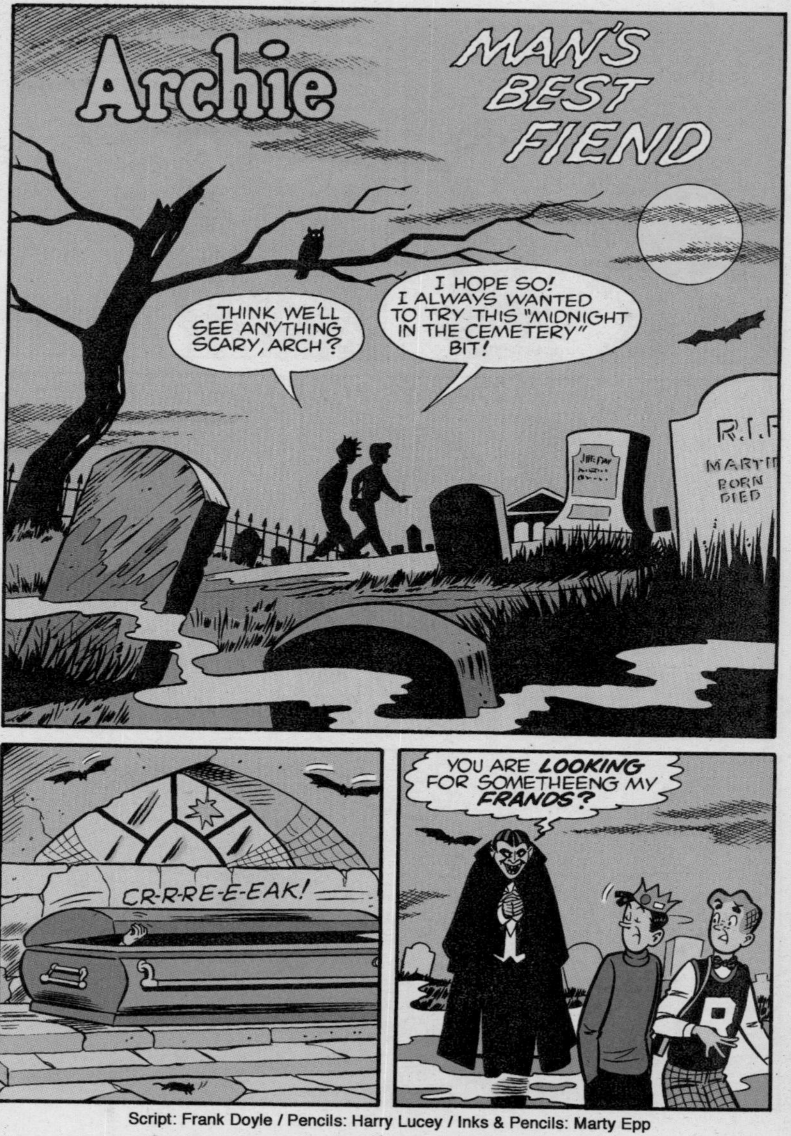
Archie
MAN'S BEST FIEND
THINK WE'LL SEE ANYTHING SCARY, ARCH?
I HOPE SO! I ALWAYS WANTED TO TRY THIS "MIDNIGHT IN THE CEMETERY" BIT!
R.I.P
CR-R-RE-E-EAK!
YOU ARE LOOKING FOR SOMETHEENG MY FRANDS?

Script: Frank Doyle / Pencils: Harry Lucey / Inks & Pencils: Marty Epp

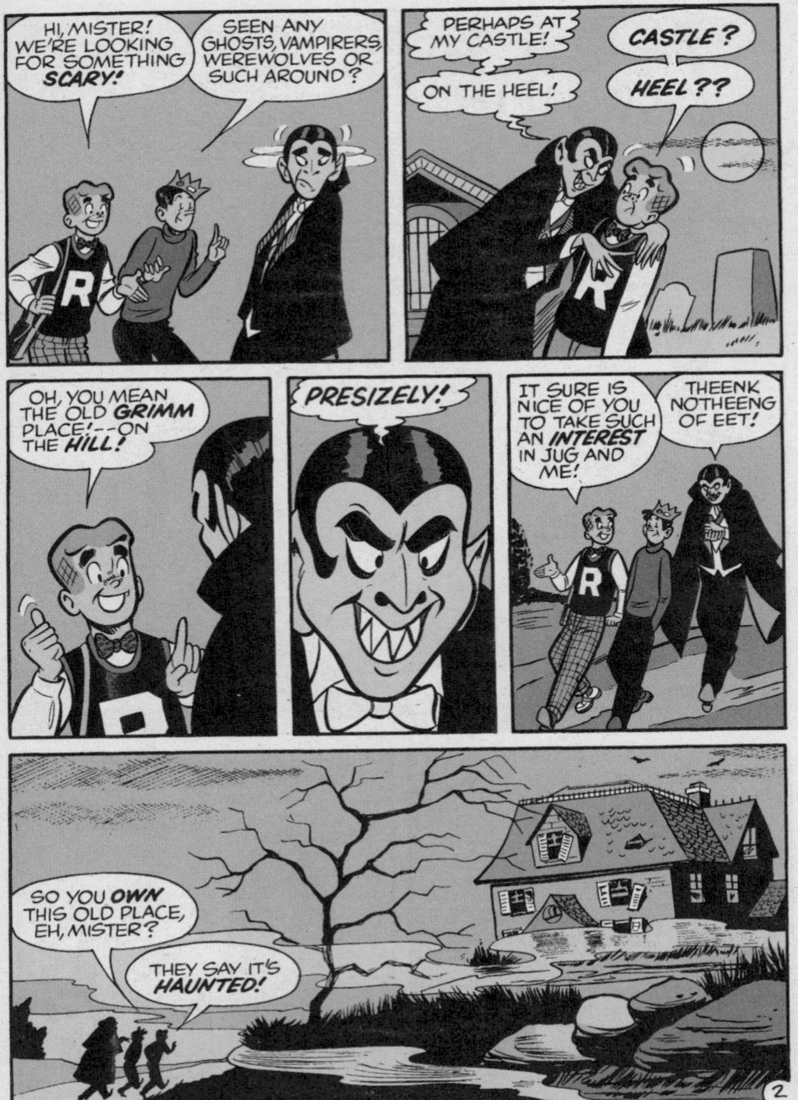
HI, MISTER! WE'RE LOOKING FOR SOMETHING SCARY!
SEEN ANY GHOSTS, VAMPIRERS, WEREWOLVES OR SUCH AROUND?
PERHAPS AT MY CASTLE!
ON THE HEEL!
CASTLE?
HEEL??
OH, YOU MEAN THE OLD GRIMM PLACE!--ON THE HILL!
PRESIZELY!
IT SURE IS NICE OF YOU TO TAKE SUCH AN INTEREST IN JUG AND ME!
THEENK NOTHEENG OF EET!
SO YOU OWN THIS OLD PLACE, EH, MISTER?
THEY SAY IT'S HAUNTED!
2

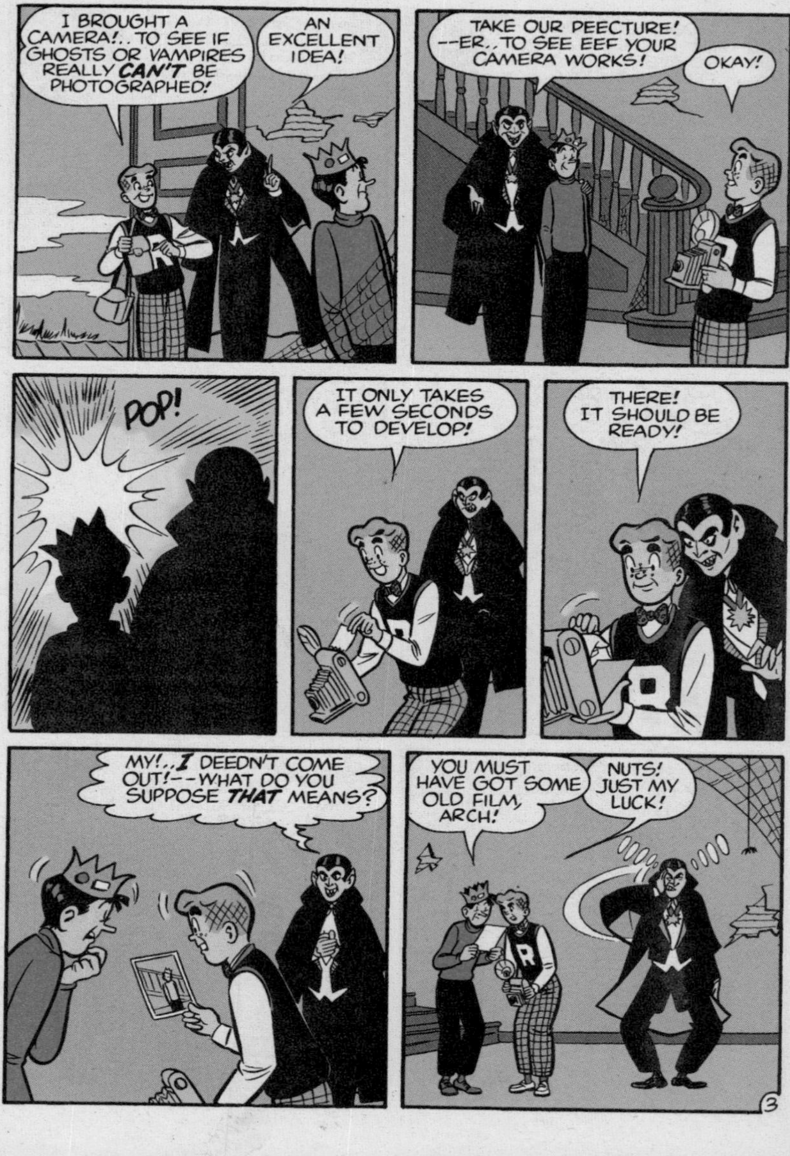
I BROUGHT A CAMERA!.. TO SEE IF GHOSTS OR VAMPIRES REALLY CAN'T BE PHOTOGRAPHED!
AN EXCELLENT IDEA!
TAKE OUR PEECTURE! --ER., TO SEE EEF YOUR CAMERA WORKS!
OKAY!
POP!
IT ONLY TAKES A FEW SECONDS TO DEVELOP!
THERE! IT SHOULD BE READY!
MY!..I DEEDN'T COME OUT!--WHAT DO YOU SUPPOSE THAT MEANS?
YOU MUST HAVE GOT SOME OLD FILM, ARCH!
NUTS! JUST MY LUCK!
3

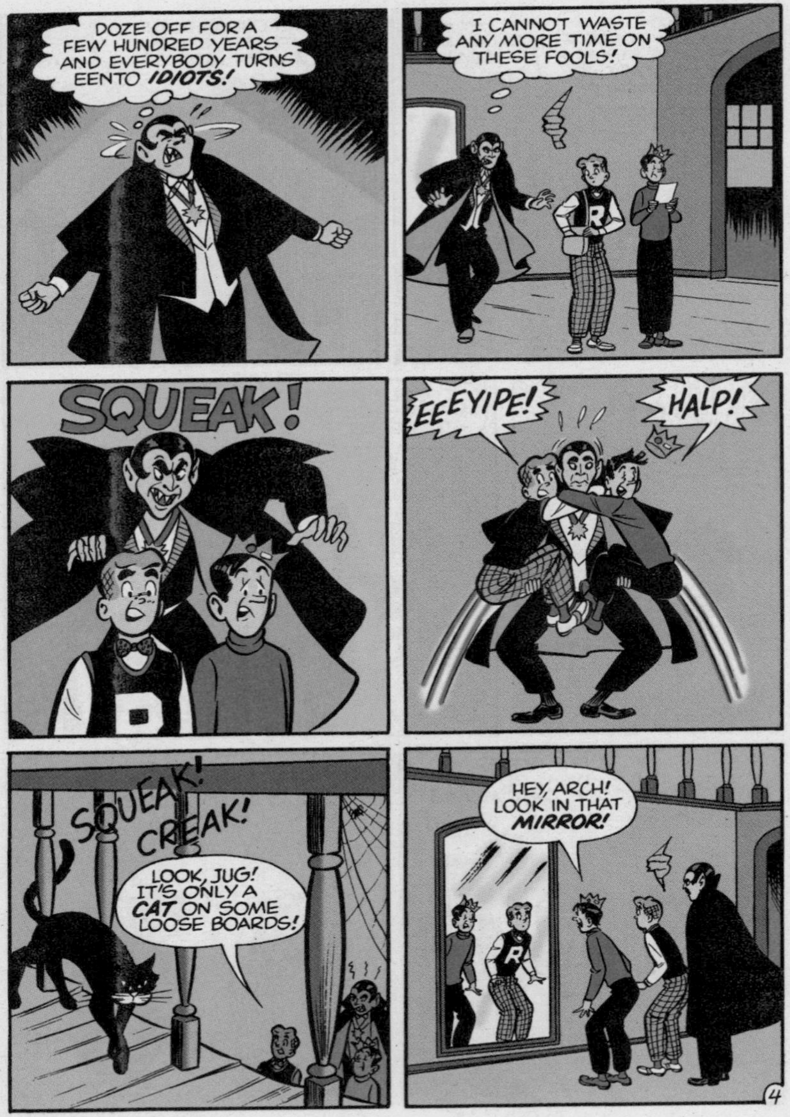

DOZE OFF FOR A FEW HUNDRED YEARS AND EVERYBODY TURNS EENTO IDIOTS!
I CANNOT WASTE ANY MORE TIME ON THESE FOOLS!
SQUEAK!
EEEYIPE!
HALP!
SQUEAK!
CREAK!
LOOK, JUG! IT'S ONLY A CAT ON SOME LOOSE BOARDS!
HEY, ARCH! LOOK IN THAT MIRROR!
4

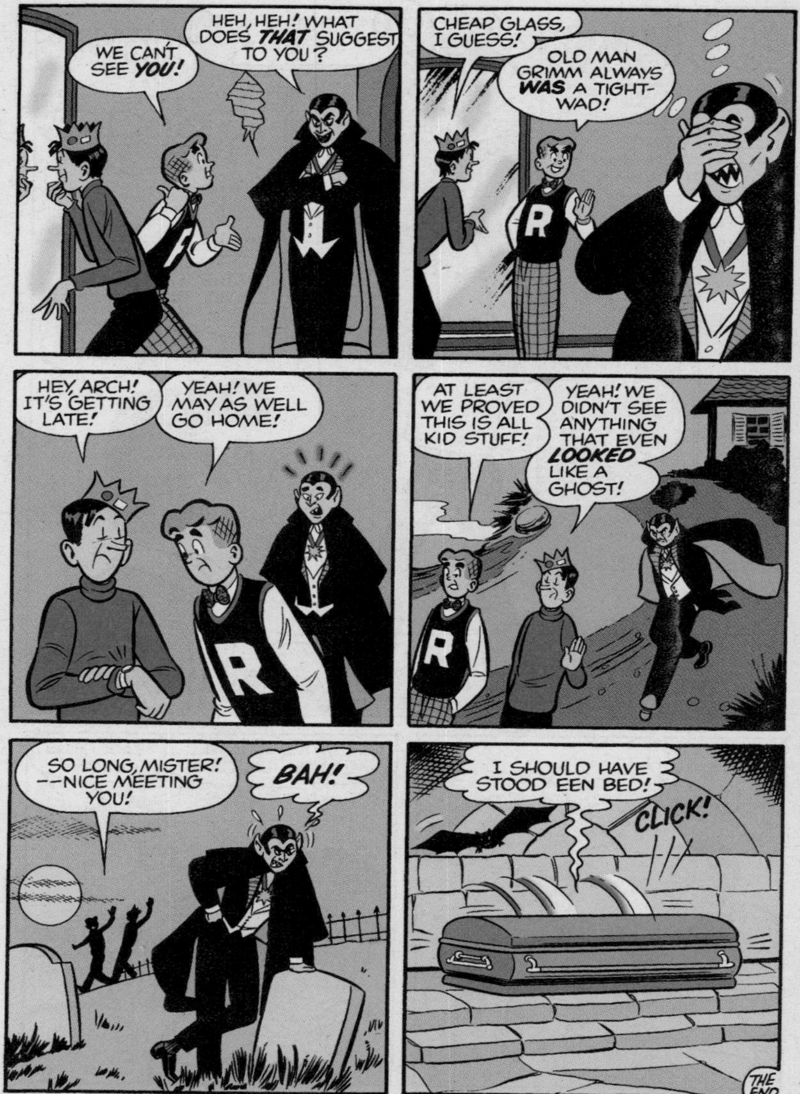
WE CAN'T SEE YOU!
HEH, HEH! WHAT DOES THAT SUGGEST TO YOU?
CHEAP GLASS, I GUESS!
OLD MAN GRIMM ALWAYS WAS A TIGHT-WAD!
HEY, ARCH! IT'S GETTING LATE!
YEAH! WE MAY AS WELL GO HOME!
AT LEAST WE PROVED THIS IS ALL KID STUFF!
YEAH! WE DIDN'T SEE ANYTHING THAT EVEN LOOKED LIKE A GHOST!
SO LONG, MISTER! --NICE MEETING YOU!
BAH!
I SHOULD HAVE STOOD EEN BED!
CLICK!
THE END

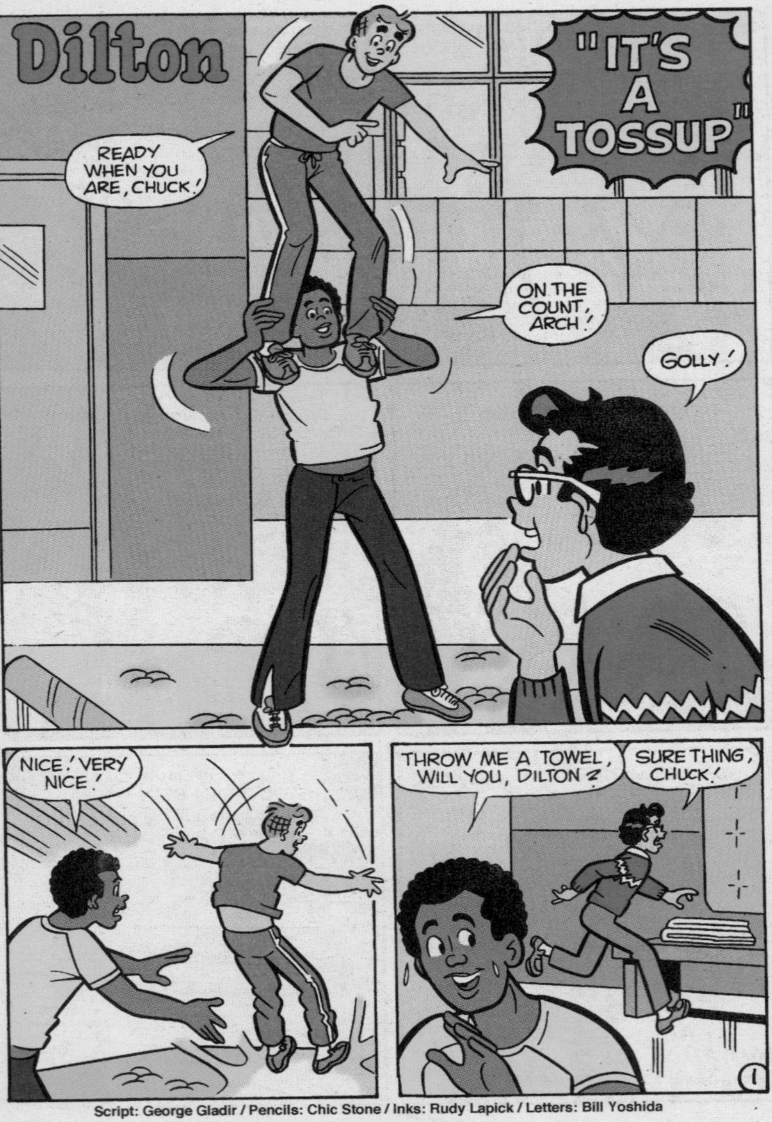
Dilton
"IT'S A TOSSUP"
READY WHEN YOU ARE, CHUCK!
ON THE COUNT, ARCH!
GOLLY!
NICE! VERY NICE!
THROW ME A TOWEL, WILL YOU, DILTON?
SURE THING, CHUCK!
1

Script: George Gladir / Pencils: Chic Stone / Inks: Rudy Lapick / Letters: Bill Yoshida

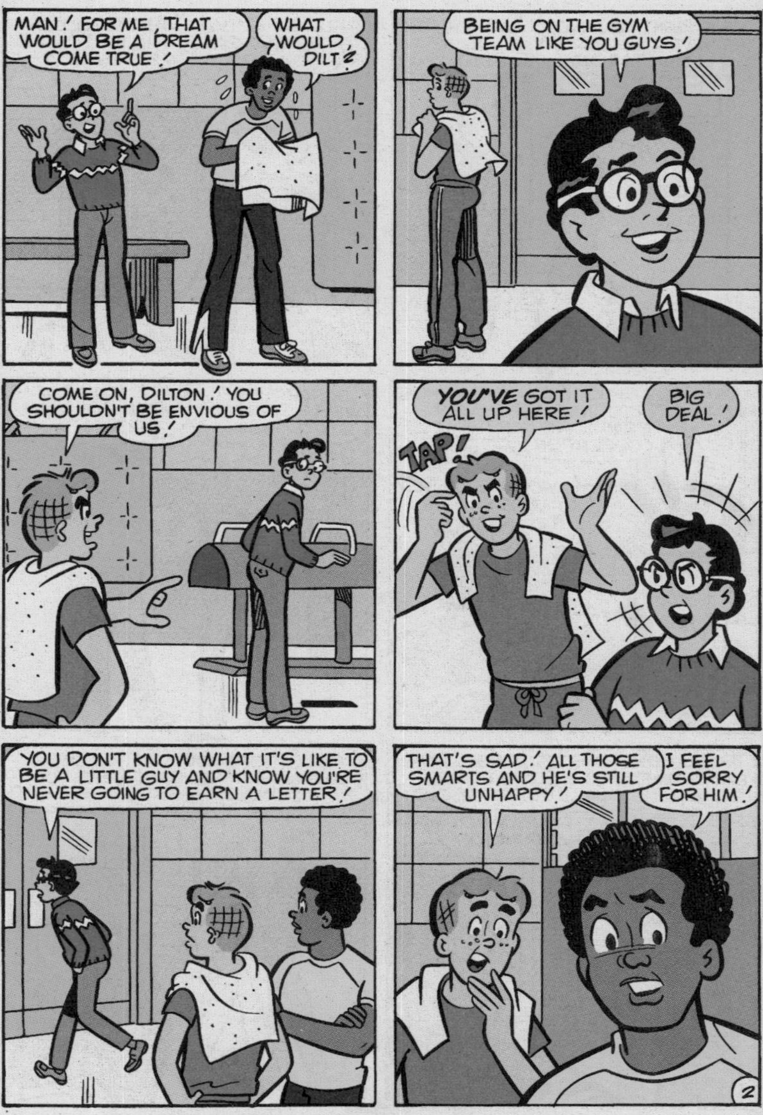
MAN! FOR ME, THAT WOULD BE A DREAM COME TRUE!
WHAT WOULD, DILT?
BEING ON THE GYM TEAM LIKE YOU GUYS!
COME ON, DILTON! YOU SHOULDN'T BE ENVIOUS OF US!
YOU'VE GOT IT ALL UP HERE!
TAP!
BIG DEAL!
YOU DON'T KNOW WHAT IT'S LIKE TO BE A LITTLE GUY AND KNOW YOU'RE NEVER GOING TO EARN A LETTER!
THAT'S SAD! ALL THOSE SMARTS AND HE'S STILL UNHAPPY!
I FEEL SORRY FOR HIM!
2

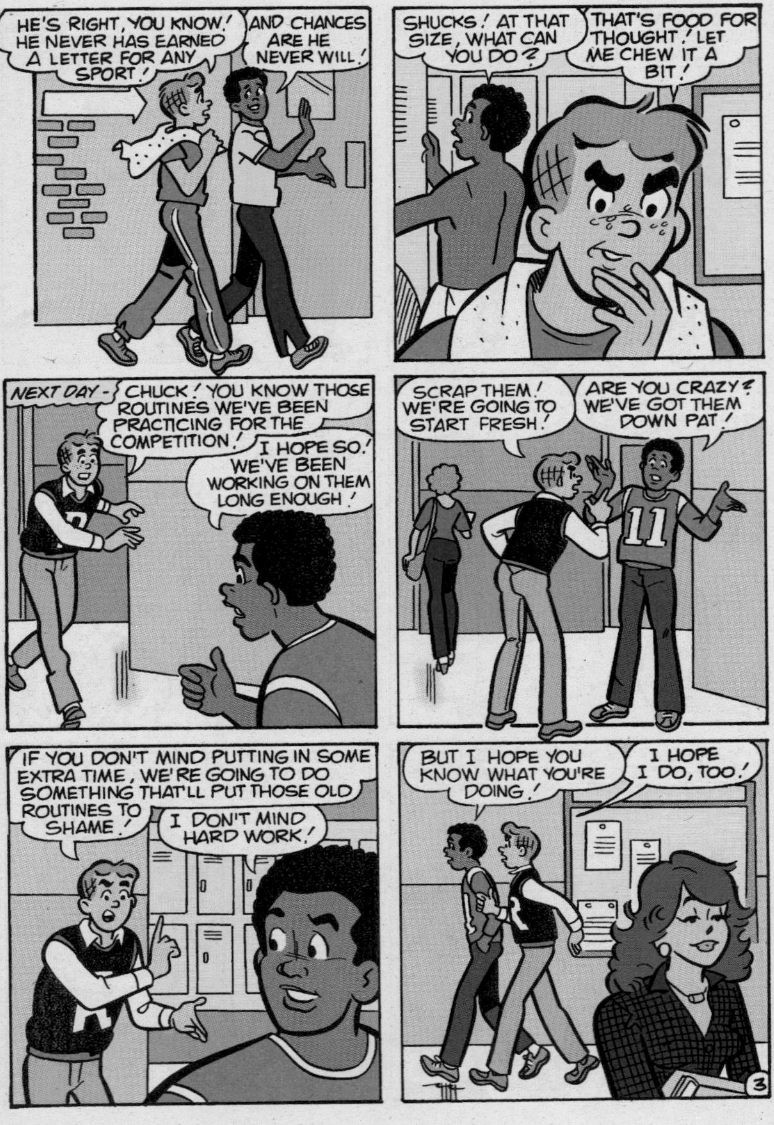

HE'S RIGHT, YOU KNOW! HE NEVER HAS EARNED A LETTER FOR ANY SPORT!
AND CHANCES ARE HE NEVER WILL!
SHUCKS! AT THAT SIZE, WHAT CAN YOU DO?
THAT'S FOOD FOR THOUGHT! LET ME CHEW IT A BIT!
NEXT DAY -
CHUCK! YOU KNOW THOSE ROUTINES WE'VE BEEN PRACTICING FOR THE COMPETITION!
I HOPE SO! WE'VE BEEN WORKING ON THEM LONG ENOUGH!
SCRAP THEM! WE'RE GOING TO START FRESH!
ARE YOU CRAZY? WE'VE GOT THEM DOWN PAT!
IF YOU DON'T MIND PUTTING IN SOME EXTRA TIME, WE'RE GOING TO DO SOMETHING THAT'LL PUT THOSE OLD ROUTINES TO SHAME!
I DON'T MIND HARD WORK!
BUT I HOPE YOU KNOW WHAT YOU'RE DOING!
I HOPE I DO, TOO!
3

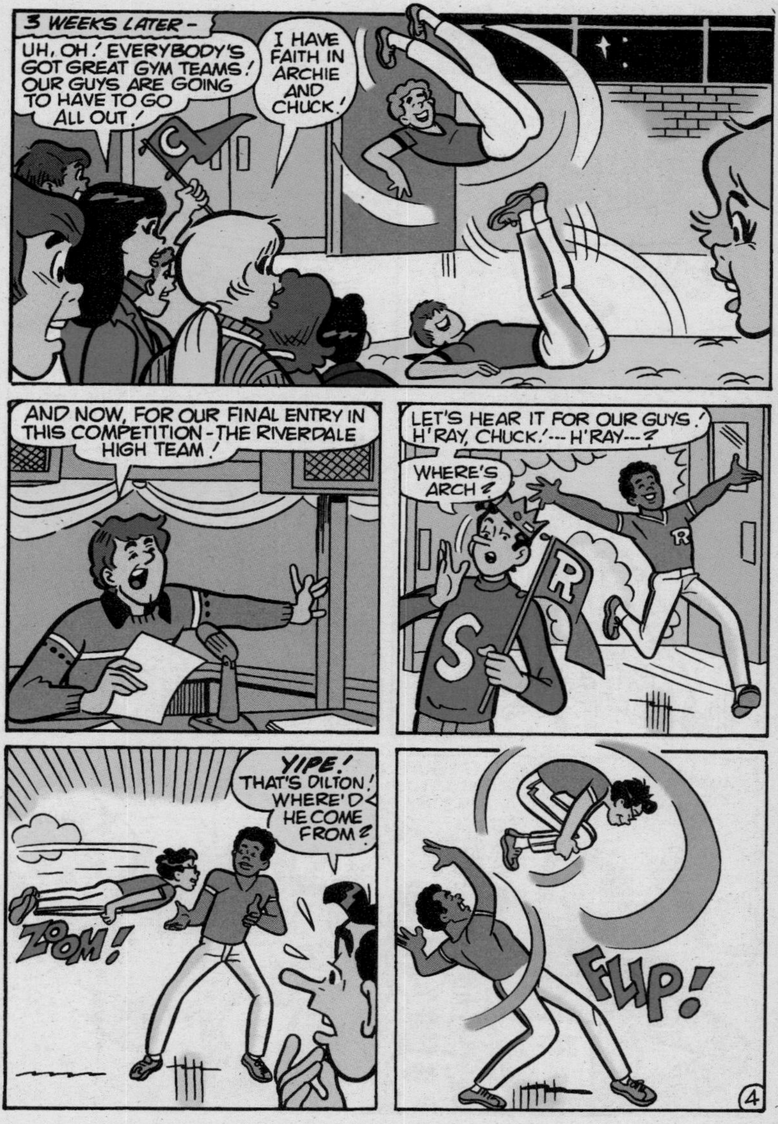
3 WEEKS LATER –
UH, OH! EVERYBODY'S GOT GREAT GYM TEAMS! OUR GUYS ARE GOING TO HAVE TO GO ALL OUT!
I HAVE FAITH IN ARCHIE AND CHUCK!
AND NOW, FOR OUR FINAL ENTRY IN THIS COMPETITION – THE RIVERDALE HIGH TEAM!
LET'S HEAR IT FOR OUR GUYS! H'RAY, CHUCK! --- H'RAY---?
WHERE'S ARCH?
YIPE! THAT'S DILTON! WHERE'D HE COME FROM?
ZOOM!
FLIP!
4

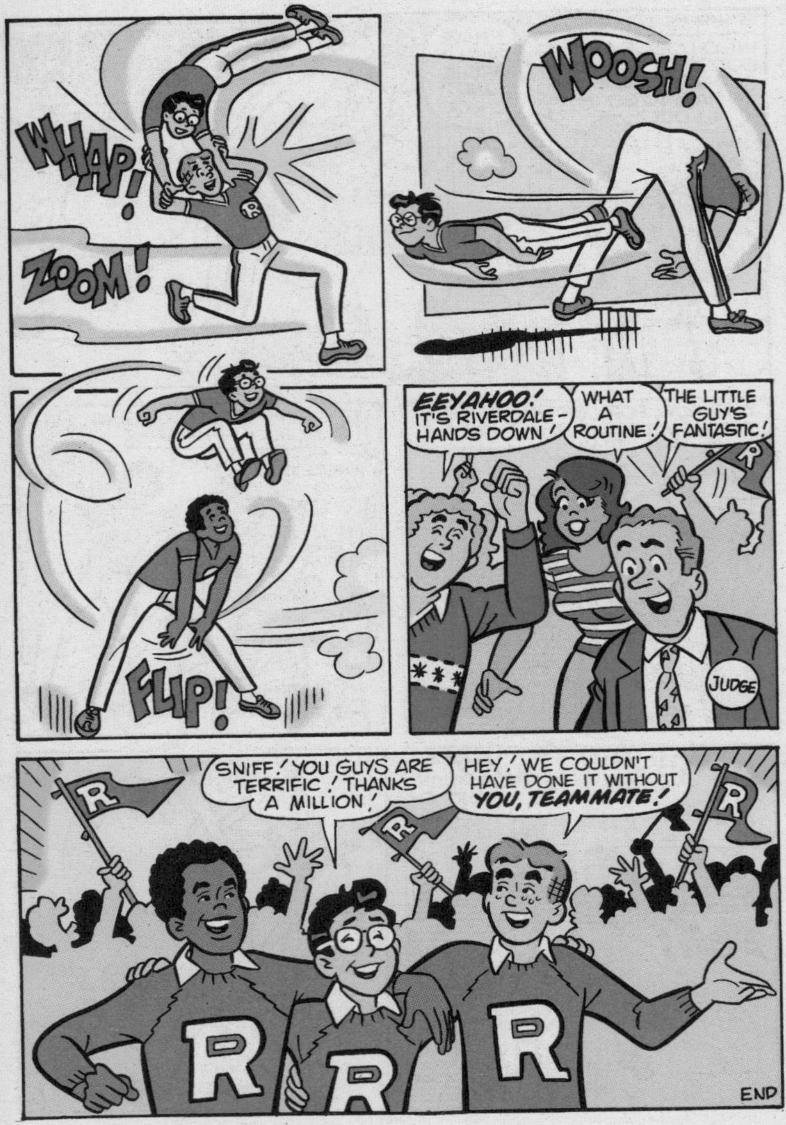
WHAP!
ZOOM!
WOOSH!
FLIP!
EEYAHOO! IT'S RIVERDALE-HANDS DOWN!
WHAT A ROUTINE!
THE LITTLE GUY'S FANTASTIC!
JUDGE
SNIFF! YOU GUYS ARE TERRIFIC! THANKS A MILLION!
HEY! WE COULDN'T HAVE DONE IT WITHOUT YOU, TEAMMATE!
END

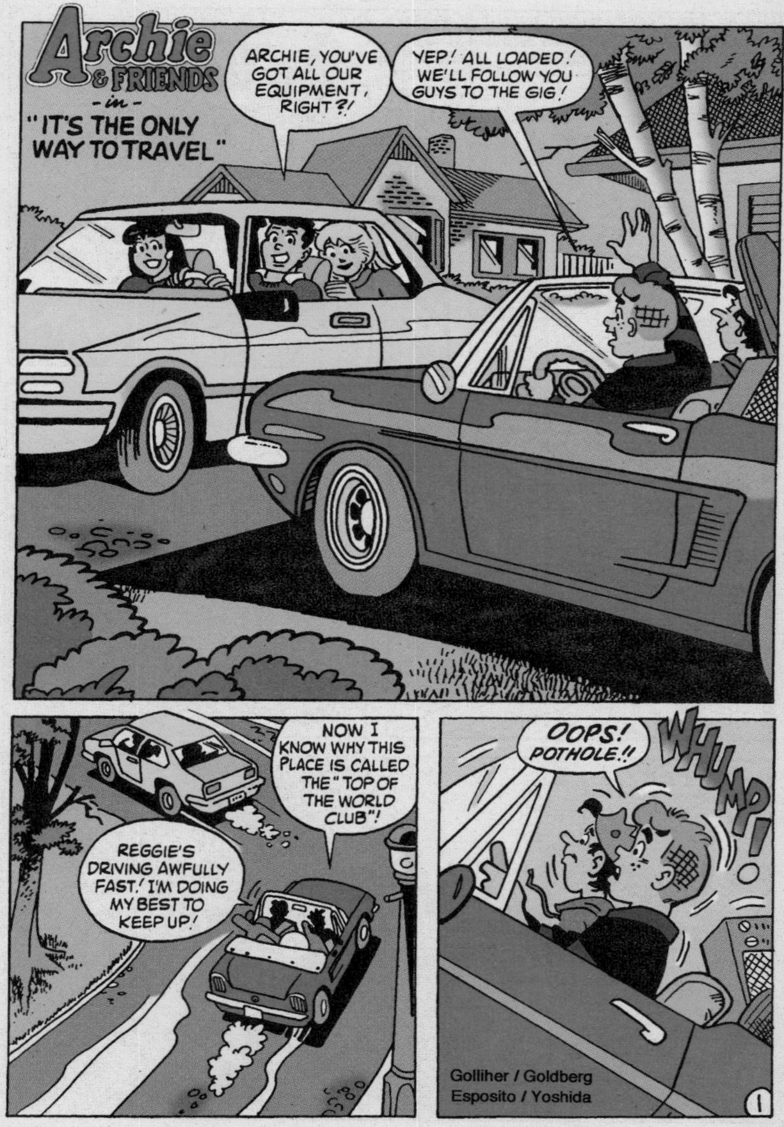
Archie & FRIENDS
-in-
"IT'S THE ONLY WAY TO TRAVEL"
ARCHIE, YOU'VE GOT ALL OUR EQUIPMENT, RIGHT?!
YEP! ALL LOADED! WE'LL FOLLOW YOU GUYS TO THE GIG!
NOW I KNOW WHY THIS PLACE IS CALLED THE "TOP OF THE WORLD CLUB"!
REGGIE'S DRIVING AWFULLY FAST! I'M DOING MY BEST TO KEEP UP!
OOPS! POTHOLE!!
WHUMP!
Golliher / Goldberg
Esposito / Yoshida
1

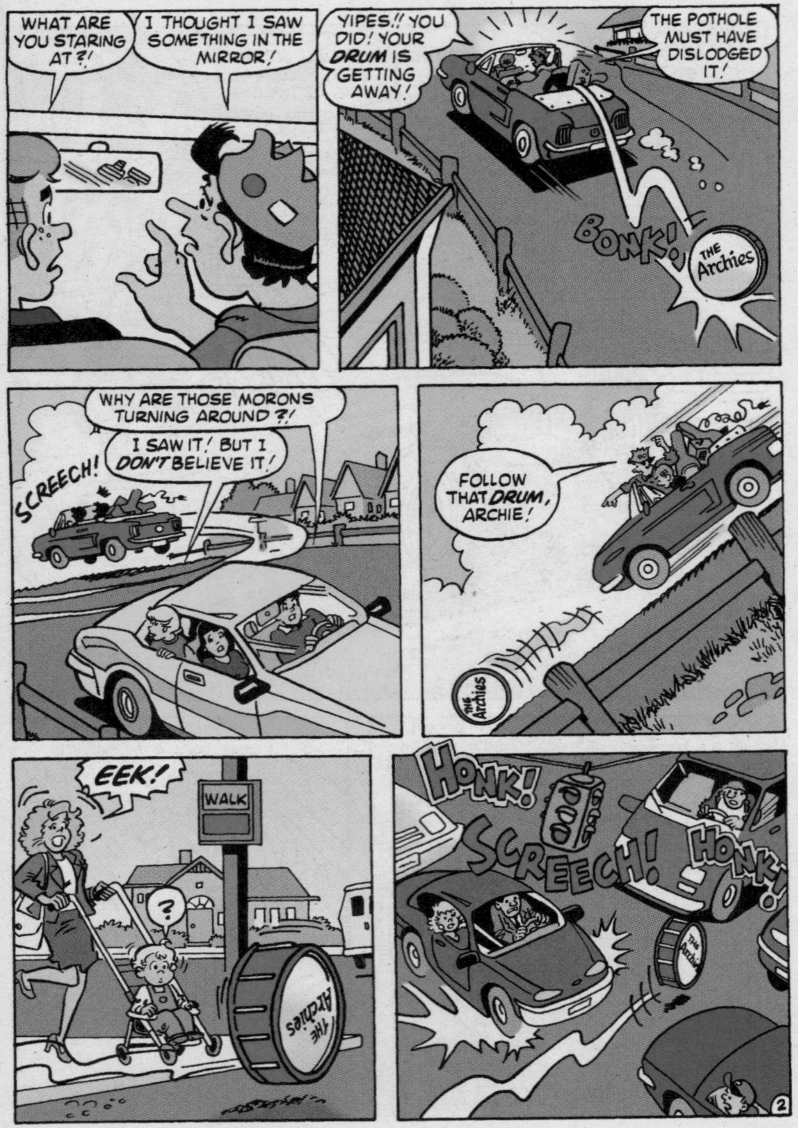
WHAT ARE YOU STARING AT?!
I THOUGHT I SAW SOMETHING IN THE MIRROR!
YIPES!! YOU DID! YOUR DRUM IS GETTING AWAY!
THE POTHOLE MUST HAVE DISLODGED IT!
BONK!
THE Archies
WHY ARE THOSE MORONS TURNING AROUND?!
SCREECH!
I SAW IT! BUT I DON'T BELIEVE IT!
FOLLOW THAT DRUM, ARCHIE!
THE Archies
EEK!
WALK
?
THE Archies
HONK!
SCREECH!
HONK!
THE Archies
2

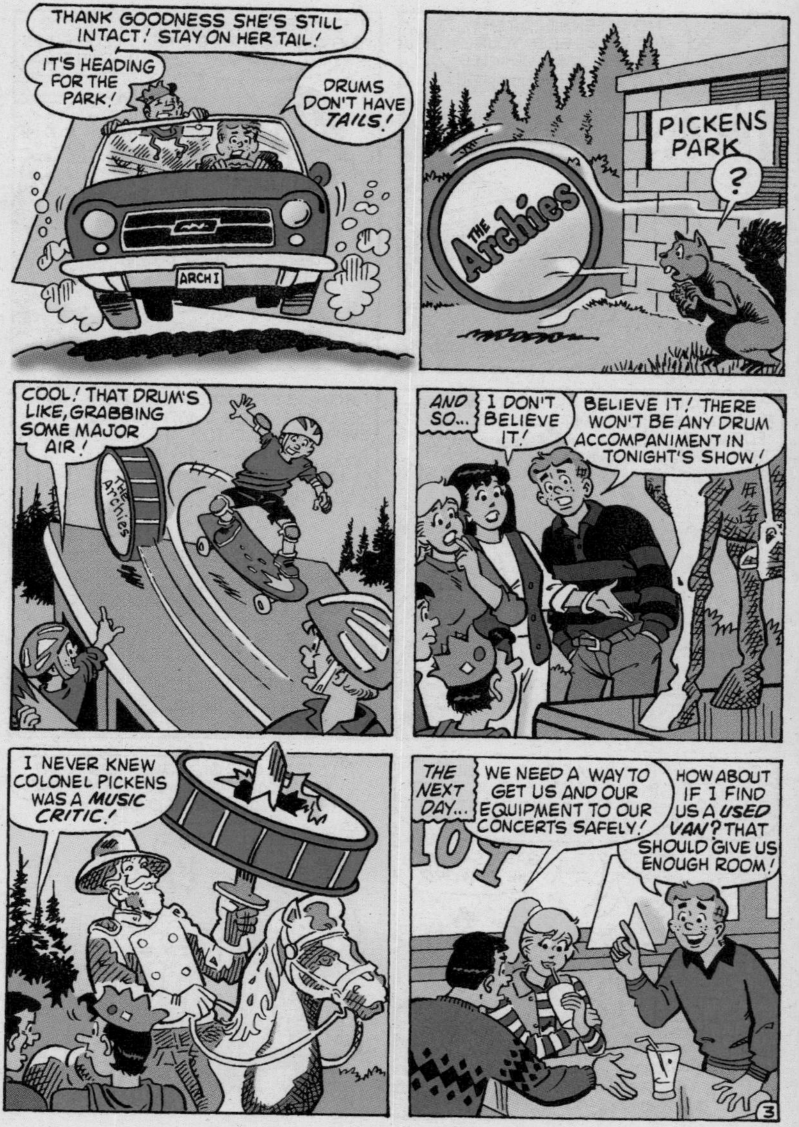
THANK GOODNESS SHE'S STILL INTACT! STAY ON HER TAIL!
IT'S HEADING FOR THE PARK!
DRUMS DON'T HAVE *TAILS*!
ARCH I
PICKENS PARK
THE Archies
?
COOL! THAT DRUM'S LIKE, GRABBING SOME MAJOR AIR!
THE Archies
AND SO...
I DON'T BELIEVE IT!
BELIEVE IT! THERE WON'T BE ANY DRUM ACCOMPANIMENT IN TONIGHT'S SHOW!
I NEVER KNEW COLONEL PICKENS WAS A *MUSIC CRITIC*!
THE NEXT DAY...
WE NEED A WAY TO GET US AND OUR EQUIPMENT TO OUR CONCERTS SAFELY!
HOW ABOUT IF I FIND US A *USED VAN*? THAT SHOULD GIVE US ENOUGH ROOM!

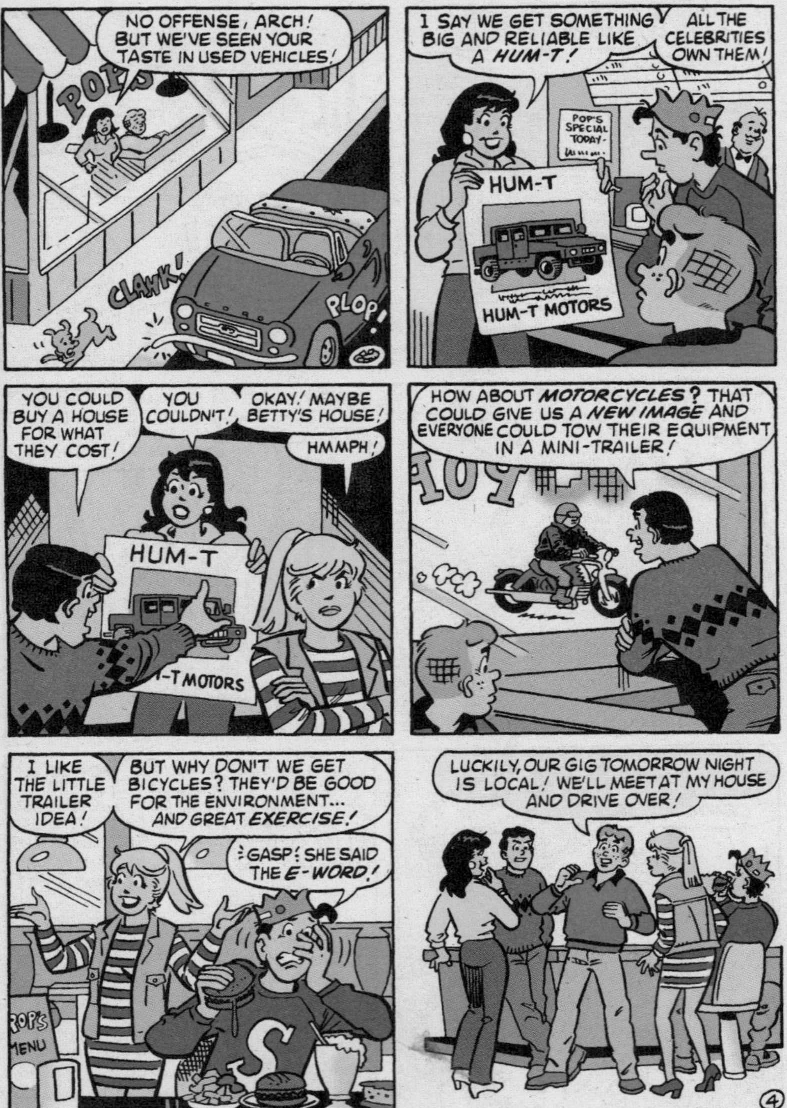

NO OFFENSE, ARCH! BUT WE'VE SEEN YOUR TASTE IN USED VEHICLES!
POP'S
CLANK!
PLOP!
I SAY WE GET SOMETHING BIG AND RELIABLE LIKE A HUM-T!
ALL THE CELEBRITIES OWN THEM!
POP'S SPECIAL TODAY
HUM-T
HUM-T MOTORS
YOU COULD BUY A HOUSE FOR WHAT THEY COST!
YOU COULDN'T!
OKAY! MAYBE BETTY'S HOUSE!
HMMPH!
HUM-T
-T MOTORS
HOW ABOUT MOTORCYCLES? THAT COULD GIVE US A NEW IMAGE AND EVERYONE COULD TOW THEIR EQUIPMENT IN A MINI-TRAILER!
I LIKE THE LITTLE TRAILER IDEA!
BUT WHY DON'T WE GET BICYCLES? THEY'D BE GOOD FOR THE ENVIRONMENT... AND GREAT EXERCISE!
GASP! SHE SAID THE E-WORD!
POP'S MENU
LUCKILY, OUR GIG TOMORROW NIGHT IS LOCAL! WE'LL MEET AT MY HOUSE AND DRIVE OVER!

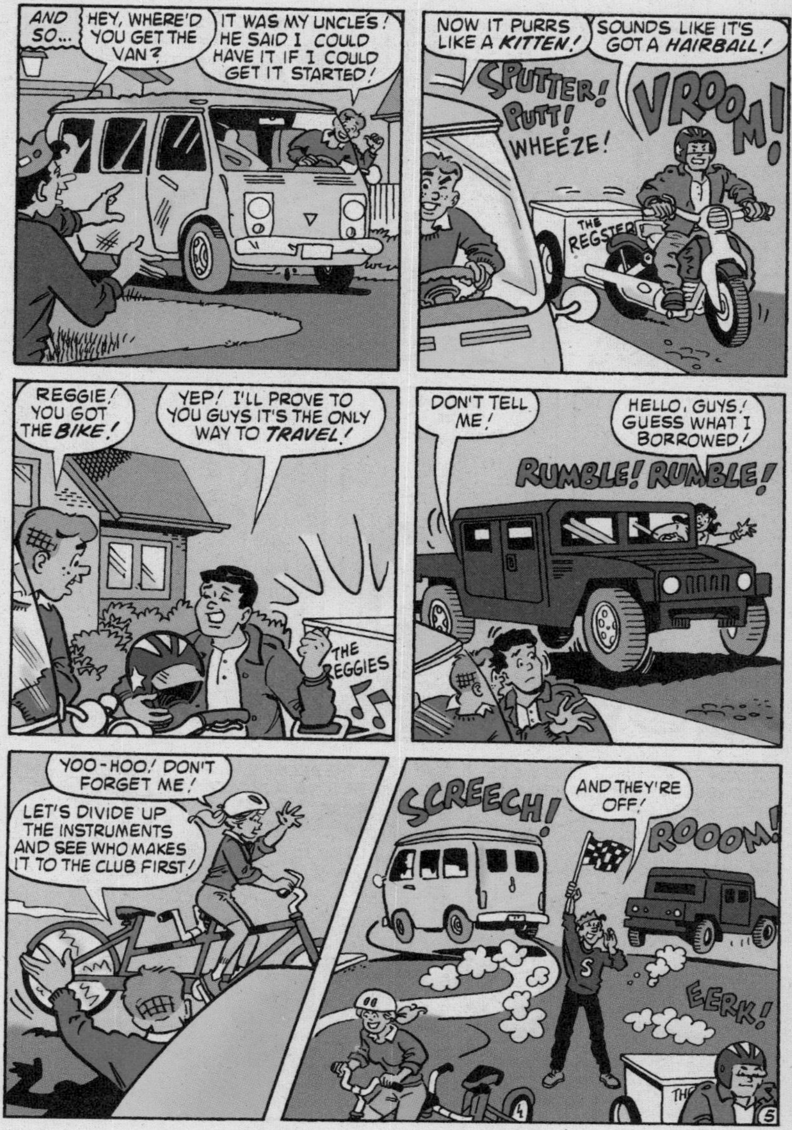
AND SO...
HEY, WHERE'D YOU GET THE VAN?
IT WAS MY UNCLE'S! HE SAID I COULD HAVE IT IF I COULD GET IT STARTED!
NOW IT PURRS LIKE A KITTEN!
SOUNDS LIKE IT'S GOT A HAIRBALL!
SPUTTER! PUTT! WHEEZE!
VROOM!
THE REGSTERS
REGGIE! YOU GOT THE BIKE!
YEP! I'LL PROVE TO YOU GUYS IT'S THE ONLY WAY TO TRAVEL!
THE REGGIES
DON'T TELL ME!
HELLO, GUYS! GUESS WHAT I BORROWED!
RUMBLE! RUMBLE!
YOO-HOO! DON'T FORGET ME!
LET'S DIVIDE UP THE INSTRUMENTS AND SEE WHO MAKES IT TO THE CLUB FIRST!
SCREECH!
AND THEY'RE OFF!
ROOOM!
EERK!
5

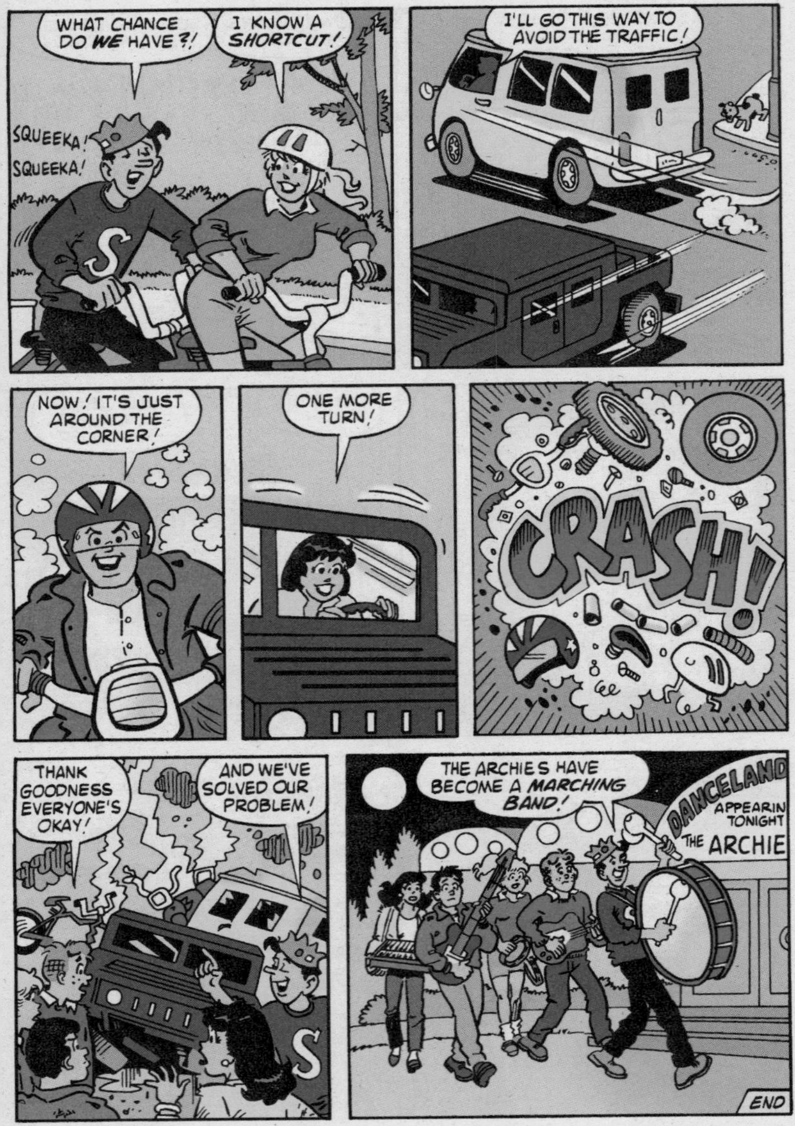

WHAT CHANCE DO *WE* HAVE ?!
I KNOW A *SHORTCUT!*
SQUEEKA! SQUEEKA!
I'LL GO THIS WAY TO AVOID THE TRAFFIC!
NOW! IT'S JUST AROUND THE CORNER!
ONE MORE TURN!
CRASH!
THANK GOODNESS EVERYONE'S OKAY!
AND WE'VE SOLVED OUR PROBLEM!
THE ARCHIES HAVE BECOME A *MARCHING BAND!*
DANCELAND
APPEARIN TONIGHT THE ARCHIE
END

Jughead A TOOTH FOR A TOOTH

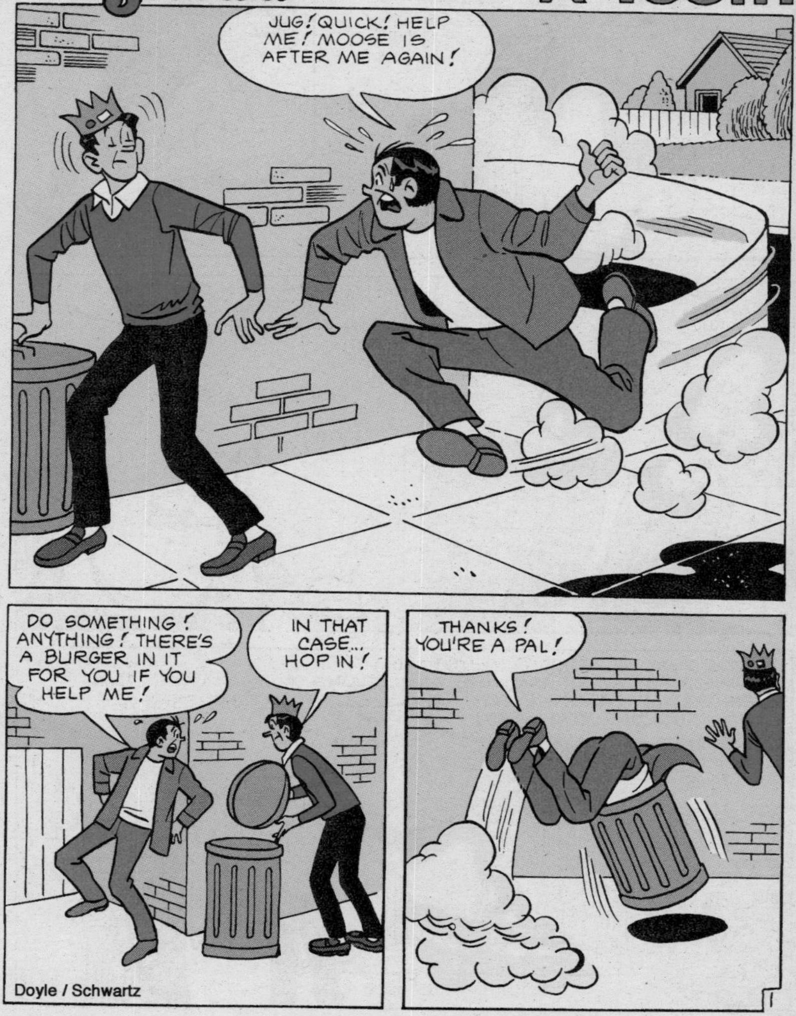
JUG! QUICK! HELP ME! MOOSE IS AFTER ME AGAIN!
DO SOMETHING! ANYTHING! THERE'S A BURGER IN IT FOR YOU IF YOU HELP ME!
IN THAT CASE... HOP IN!
THANKS! YOU'RE A PAL!
Doyle / Schwartz
1

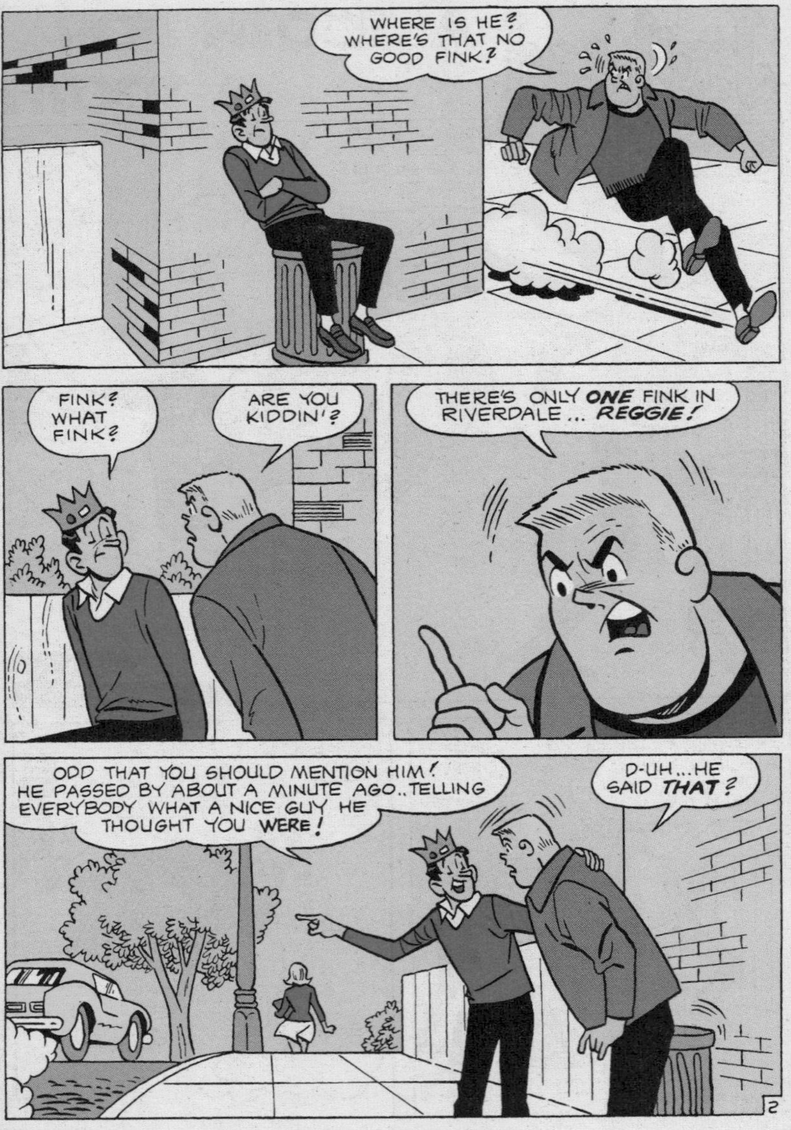
WHERE IS HE? WHERE'S THAT NO GOOD FINK?
FINK? WHAT FINK?
ARE YOU KIDDIN'?
THERE'S ONLY ONE FINK IN RIVERDALE... REGGIE!
ODD THAT YOU SHOULD MENTION HIM! HE PASSED BY ABOUT A MINUTE AGO.. TELLING EVERYBODY WHAT A NICE GUY HE THOUGHT YOU WERE!
D-UH... HE SAID THAT?
2

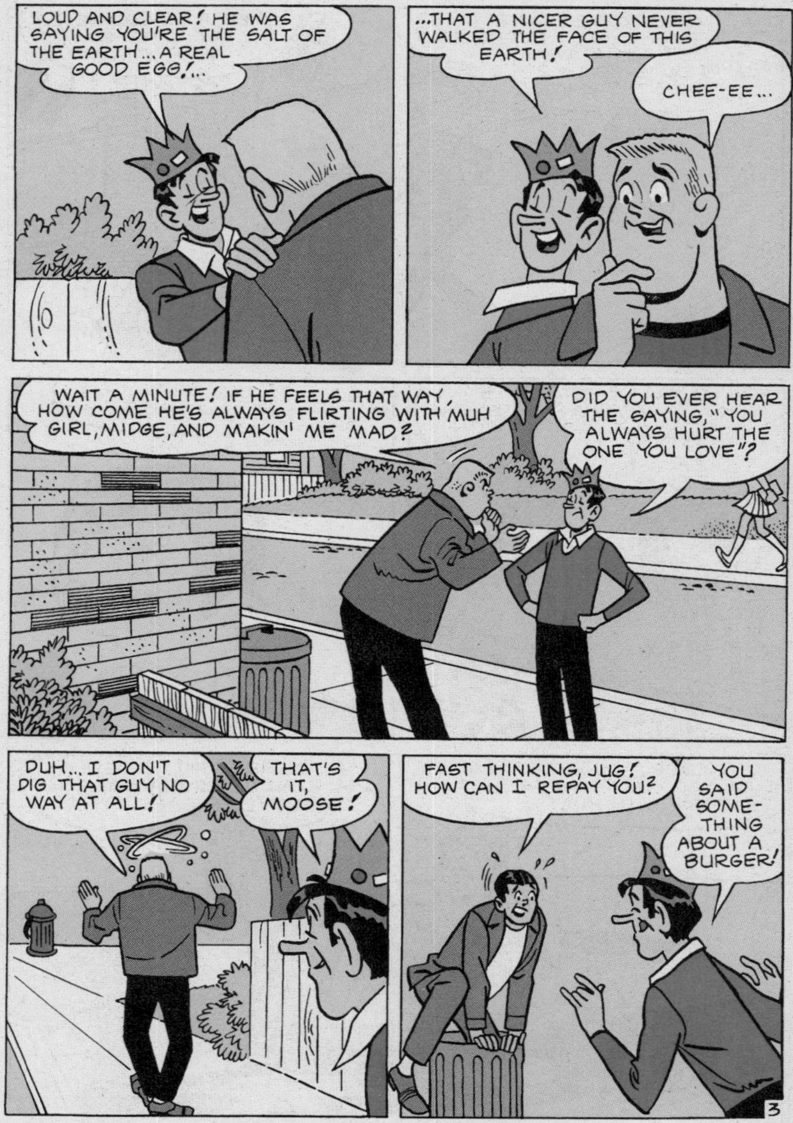
LOUD AND CLEAR! HE WAS SAYING YOU'RE THE SALT OF THE EARTH ... A REAL GOOD EGG! ...
...THAT A NICER GUY NEVER WALKED THE FACE OF THIS EARTH!
CHEE-EE...
WAIT A MINUTE! IF HE FEELS THAT WAY, HOW COME HE'S ALWAYS FLIRTING WITH MUH GIRL, MIDGE, AND MAKIN' ME MAD?
DID YOU EVER HEAR THE SAYING, "YOU ALWAYS HURT THE ONE YOU LOVE"?
DUH... I DON'T DIG THAT GUY NO WAY AT ALL!
THAT'S IT, MOOSE!
FAST THINKING, JUG! HOW CAN I REPAY YOU?
YOU SAID SOME-THING ABOUT A BURGER!
3

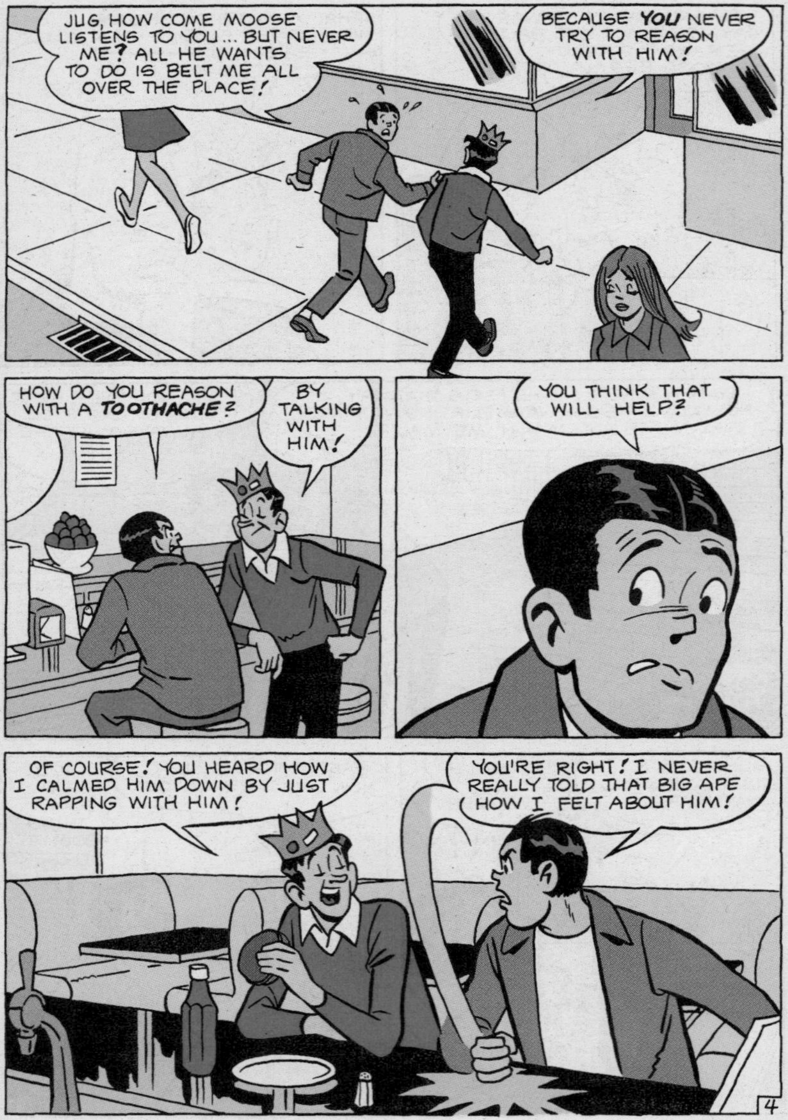
JUG, HOW COME MOOSE LISTENS TO YOU... BUT NEVER ME? ALL HE WANTS TO DO IS BELT ME ALL OVER THE PLACE!
BECAUSE YOU NEVER TRY TO REASON WITH HIM!
HOW DO YOU REASON WITH A TOOTHACHE?
BY TALKING WITH HIM!
YOU THINK THAT WILL HELP?
OF COURSE! YOU HEARD HOW I CALMED HIM DOWN BY JUST RAPPING WITH HIM!
YOU'RE RIGHT! I NEVER REALLY TOLD THAT BIG APE HOW I FELT ABOUT HIM!
4

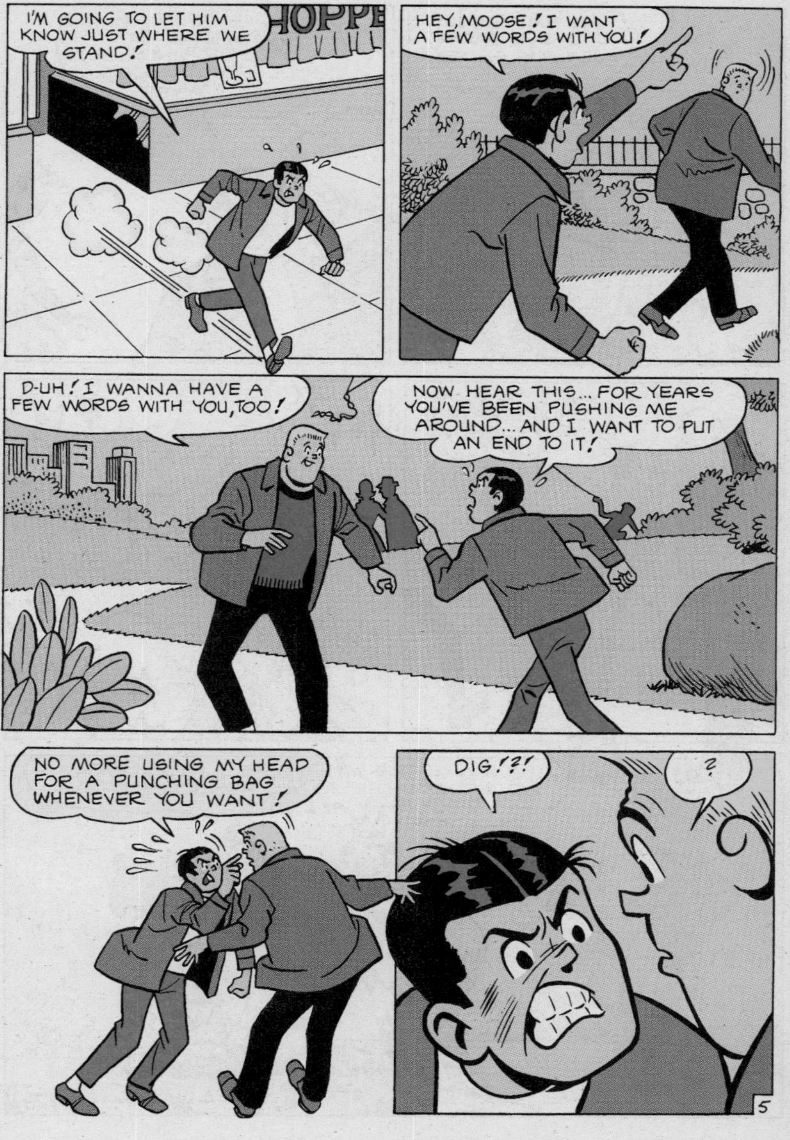

I'M GOING TO LET HIM KNOW JUST WHERE WE STAND!
HOPPE
HEY, MOOSE! I WANT A FEW WORDS WITH YOU!
D-UH! I WANNA HAVE A FEW WORDS WITH YOU, TOO!
NOW HEAR THIS... FOR YEARS YOU'VE BEEN PUSHING ME AROUND... AND I WANT TO PUT AN END TO IT!
NO MORE USING MY HEAD FOR A PUNCHING BAG WHENEVER YOU WANT!
DIG!?!
?

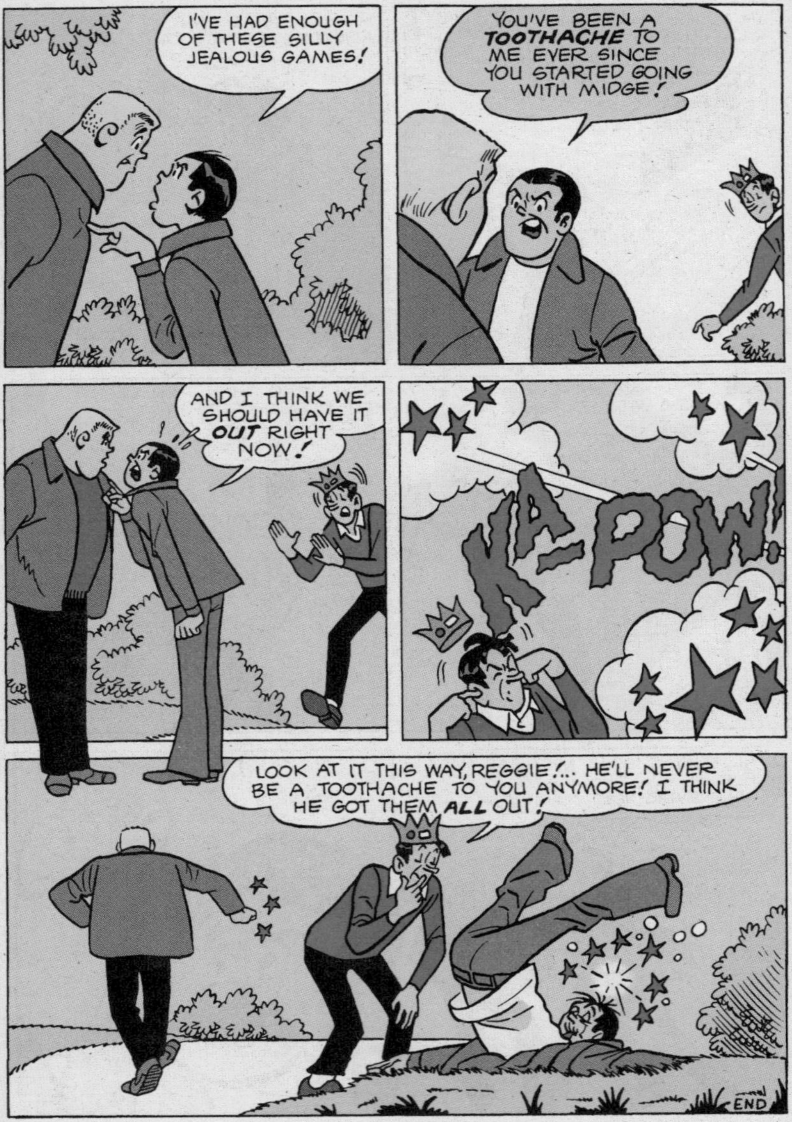
I'VE HAD ENOUGH OF THESE SILLY JEALOUS GAMES!
YOU'VE BEEN A **TOOTHACHE** TO ME EVER SINCE YOU STARTED GOING WITH MIDGE!
AND I THINK WE SHOULD HAVE IT **OUT** RIGHT NOW!
KA-POW!
LOOK AT IT THIS WAY, REGGIE!... HE'LL NEVER BE A TOOTHACHE TO YOU ANYMORE! I THINK HE GOT THEM **ALL** OUT!
END

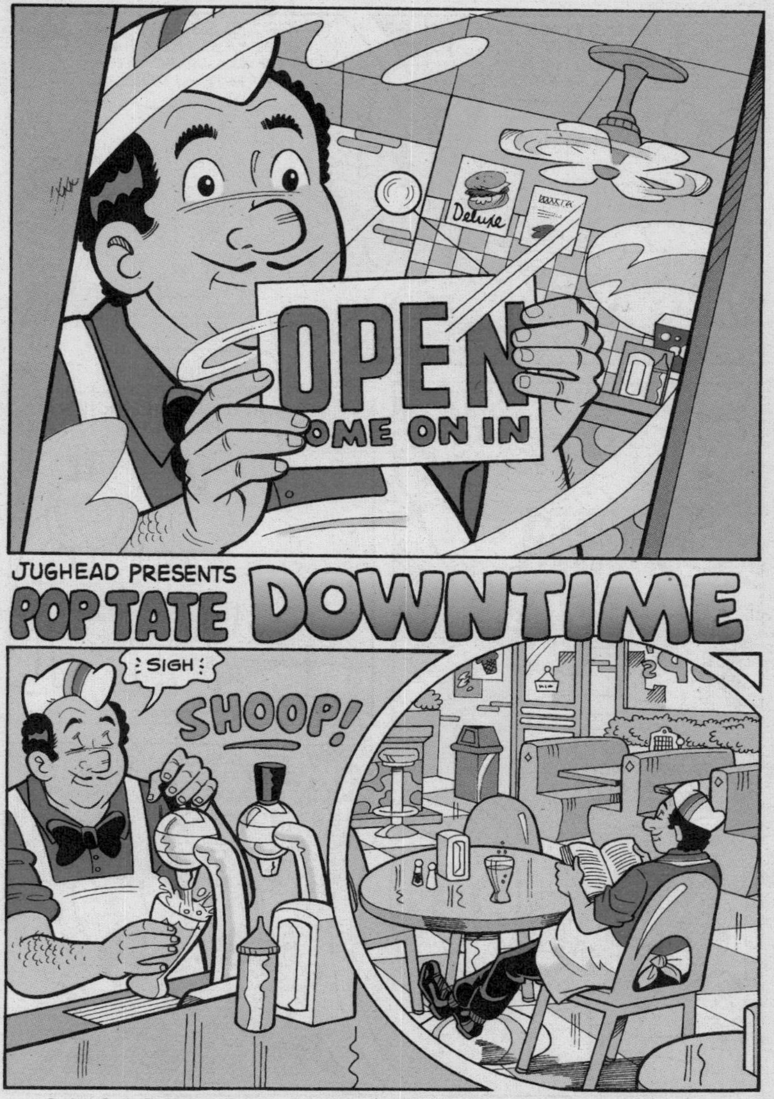
Deluxe
OPEN
OME ON IN
JUGHEAD PRESENTS
POP TATE
DOWNTIME
SIGH
SHOOP!

Script: Craig Boldman / Pencils: Rex Lindsey / Inks: Rich Koslowski / Letters: Bill Yoshida

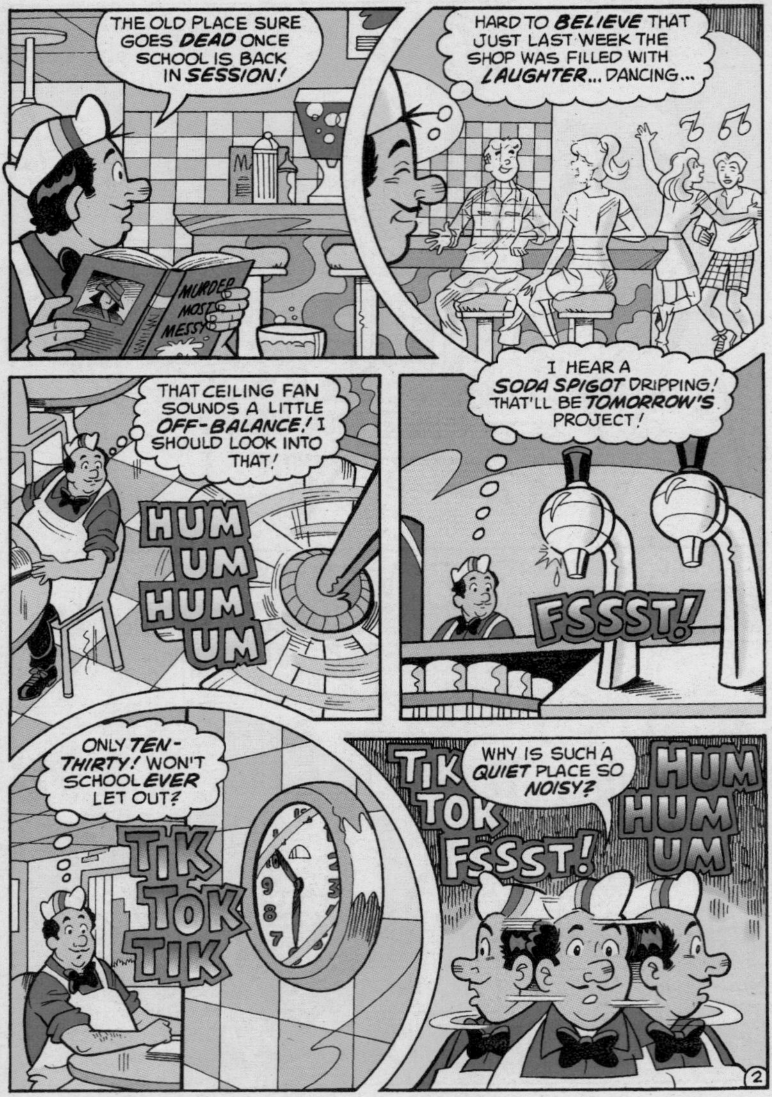
THE OLD PLACE SURE GOES DEAD ONCE SCHOOL IS BACK IN SESSION!
MURDER MOST MESSY
HARD TO BELIEVE THAT JUST LAST WEEK THE SHOP WAS FILLED WITH LAUGHTER... DANCING...
THAT CEILING FAN SOUNDS A LITTLE OFF-BALANCE! I SHOULD LOOK INTO THAT!
HUM UM HUM UM
I HEAR A SODA SPIGOT DRIPPING! THAT'LL BE TOMORROW'S PROJECT!
FSSST!
ONLY TEN-THIRTY! WON'T SCHOOL EVER LET OUT?
TIK TOK TIK
TIK TOK FSSST!
WHY IS SUCH A QUIET PLACE SO NOISY?
HUM HUM UM
2

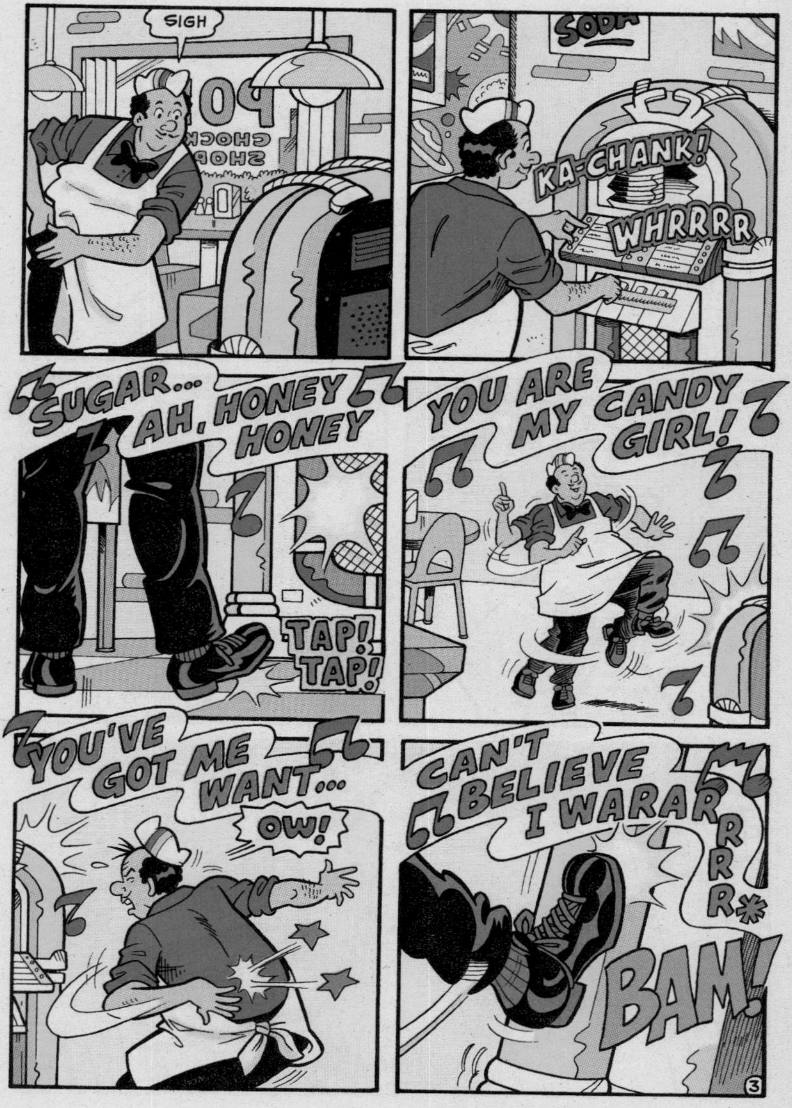
SIGH
POP
CHOCK
SHOP
SODA
KA-CHANK!
WHRRRR
SUGAR... AH, HONEY HONEY
TAP! TAP!
YOU ARE MY CANDY GIRL!
YOU'VE GOT ME WANT...
OW!
CAN'T BELIEVE I WARARRRRR*
BAM!

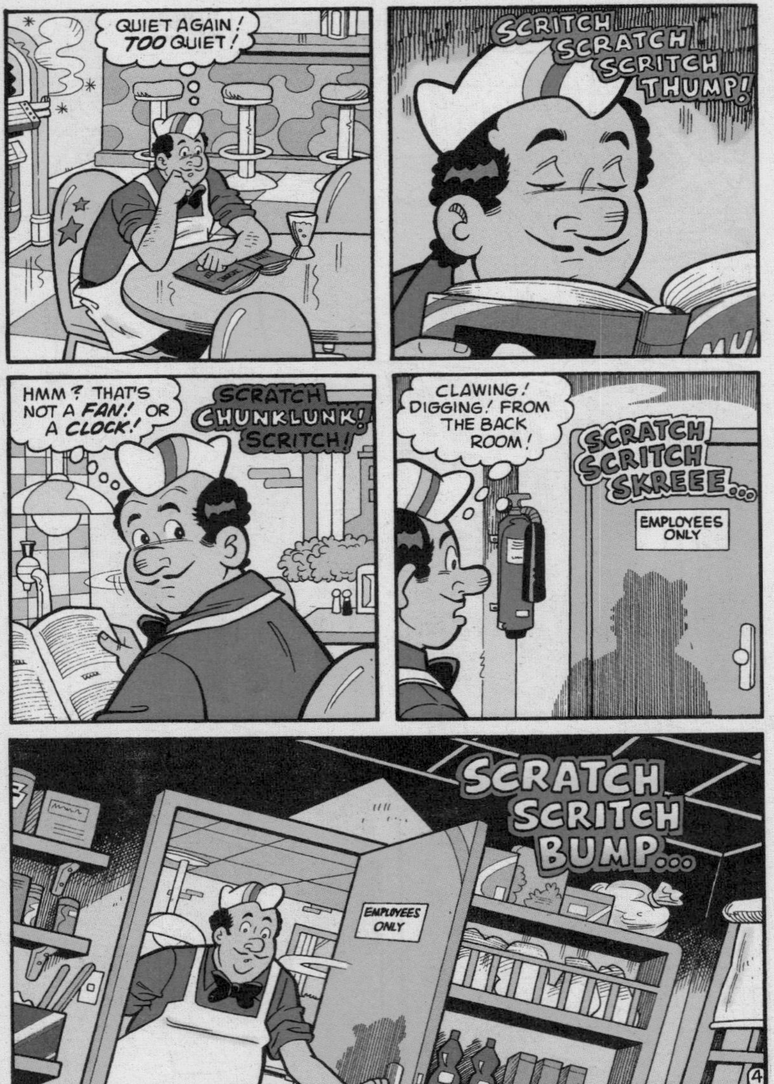
QUIET AGAIN! TOO QUIET!
SCRITCH SCRATCH SCRITCH THUMP!
HMM? THAT'S NOT A FAN! OR A CLOCK!
SCRATCH CHUNKLUNK! SCRITCH!
CLAWING! DIGGING! FROM THE BACK ROOM!
SCRATCH SCRITCH SKREEE...
EMPLOYEES ONLY
SCRATCH SCRITCH BUMP...
EMPLOYEES ONLY
4

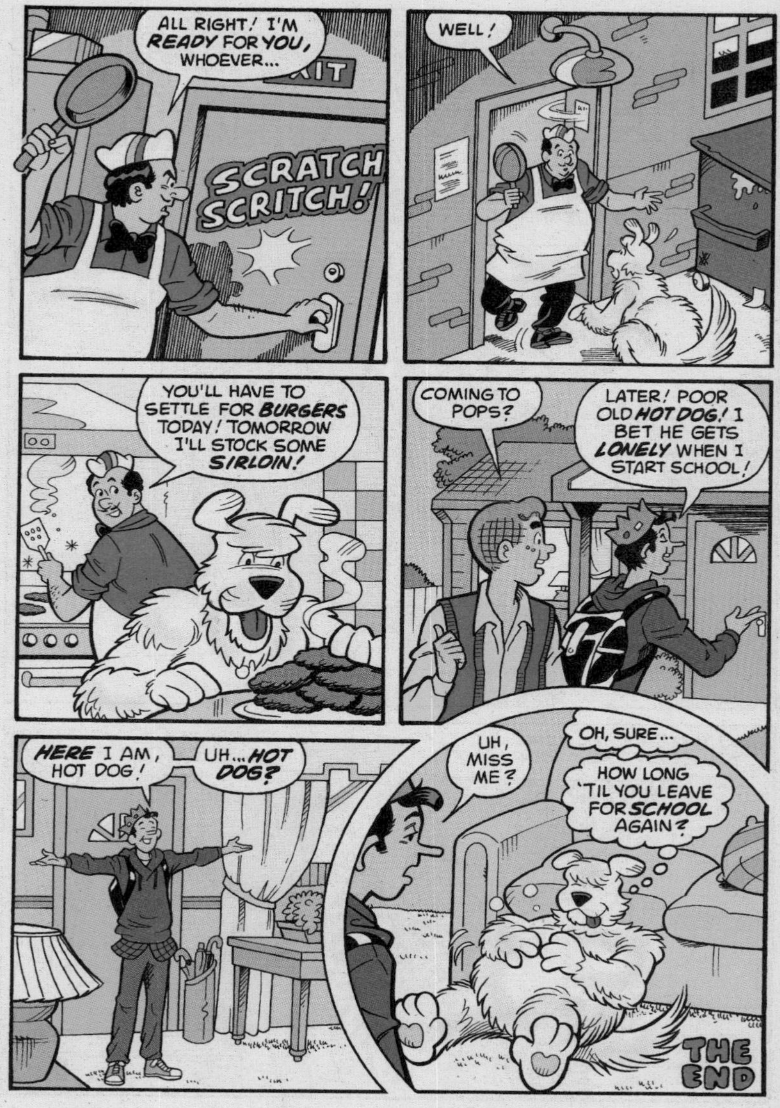
ALL RIGHT! I'M READY FOR YOU, WHOEVER...
EXIT
SCRATCH SCRITCH!
WELL!
YOU'LL HAVE TO SETTLE FOR BURGERS TODAY! TOMORROW I'LL STOCK SOME SIRLOIN!
COMING TO POPS?
LATER! POOR OLD HOT DOG! I BET HE GETS LONELY WHEN I START SCHOOL!
HERE I AM, HOT DOG!
UH... HOT DOG?
UH, MISS ME?
OH, SURE...
HOW LONG 'TIL YOU LEAVE FOR SCHOOL AGAIN?
THE END

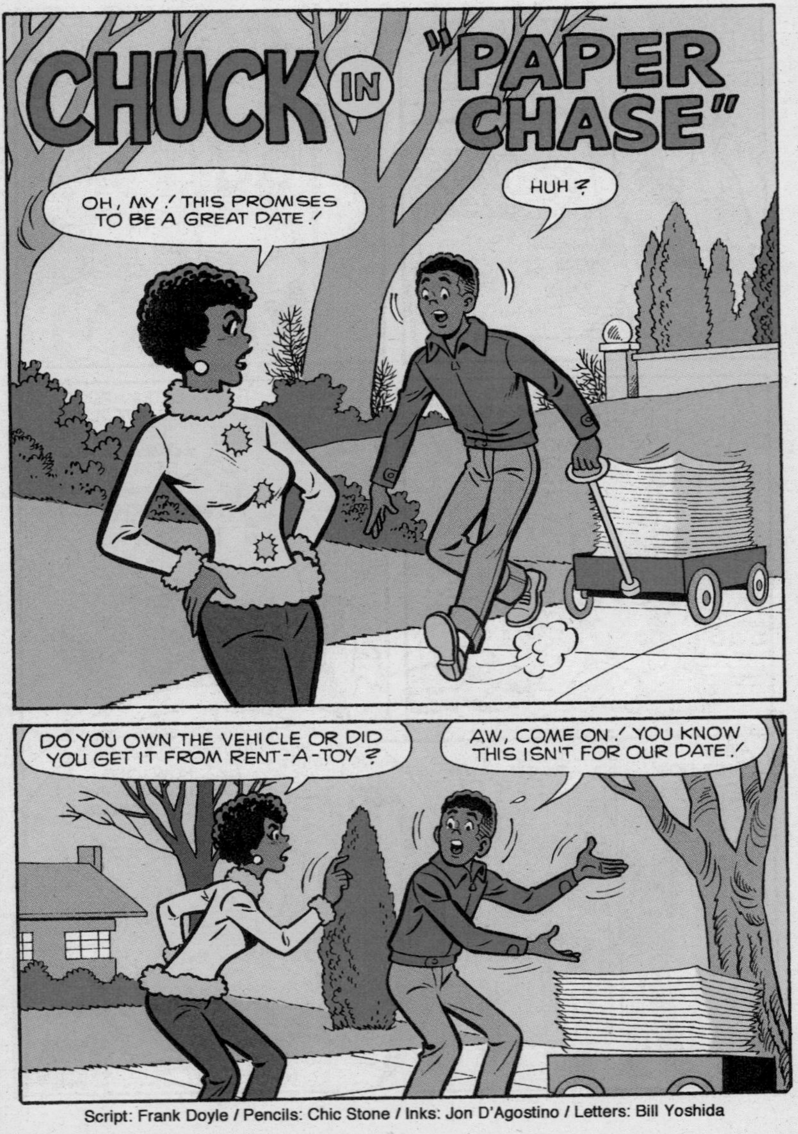
CHUCK IN "PAPER CHASE"
OH, MY! THIS PROMISES TO BE A GREAT DATE!
HUH?
DO YOU OWN THE VEHICLE OR DID YOU GET IT FROM RENT-A-TOY?
AW, COME ON! YOU KNOW THIS ISN'T FOR OUR DATE!

Script: Frank Doyle / Pencils: Chic Stone / Inks: Jon D'Agostino / Letters: Bill Yoshida

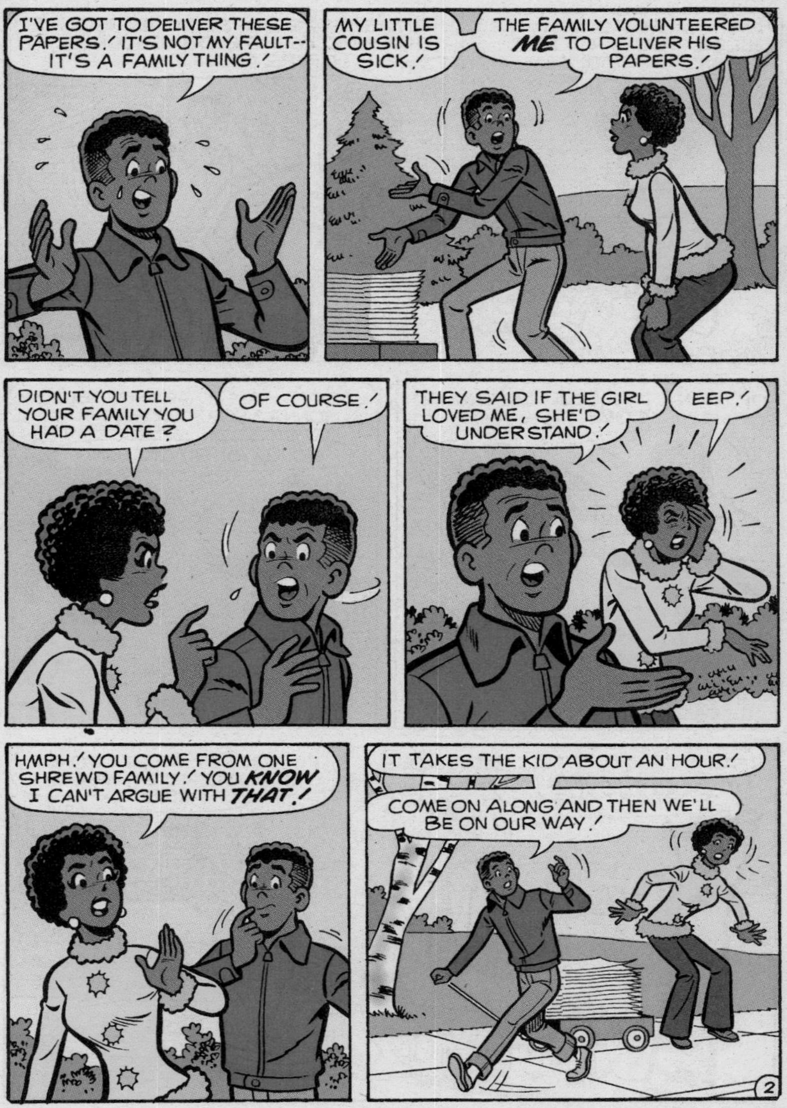
I'VE GOT TO DELIVER THESE PAPERS! IT'S NOT MY FAULT-- IT'S A FAMILY THING!
MY LITTLE COUSIN IS SICK!
THE FAMILY VOLUNTEERED ME TO DELIVER HIS PAPERS!
DIDN'T YOU TELL YOUR FAMILY YOU HAD A DATE?
OF COURSE!
THEY SAID IF THE GIRL LOVED ME, SHE'D UNDERSTAND!
EEP!
HMPH! YOU COME FROM ONE SHREWD FAMILY! YOU KNOW I CAN'T ARGUE WITH THAT!
IT TAKES THE KID ABOUT AN HOUR!
COME ON ALONG AND THEN WE'LL BE ON OUR WAY!
2

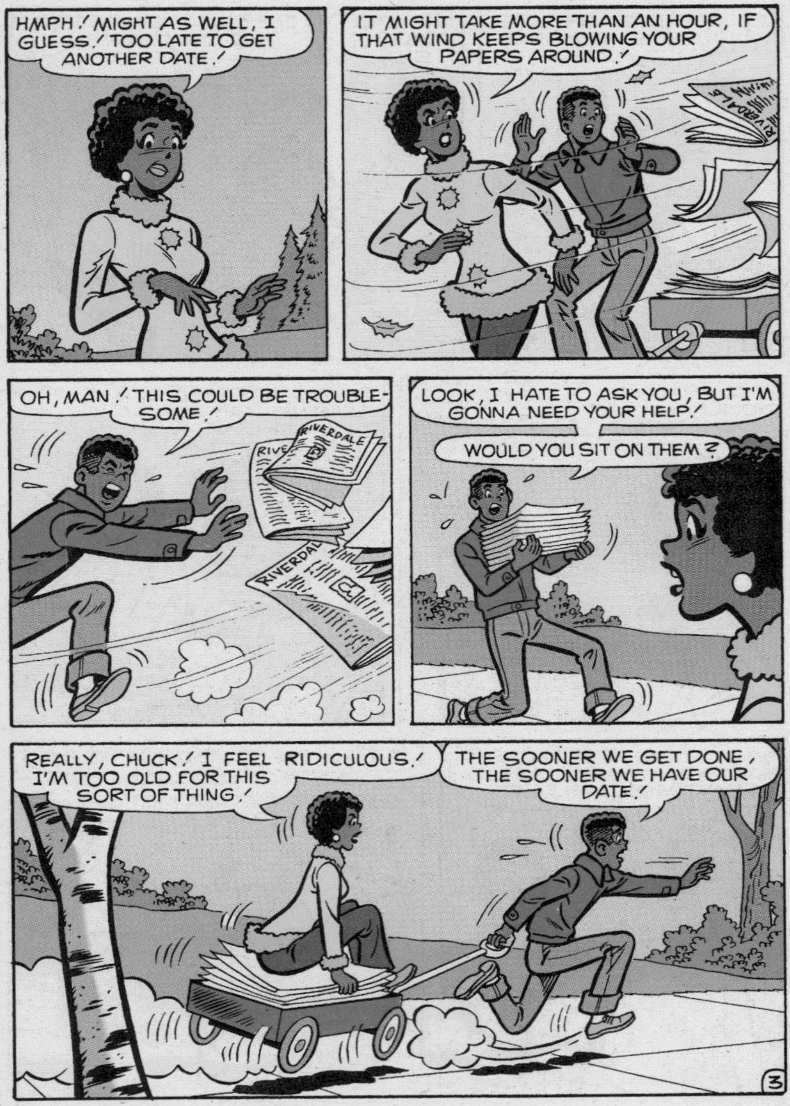
HMPH! MIGHT AS WELL, I GUESS! TOO LATE TO GET ANOTHER DATE!
IT MIGHT TAKE MORE THAN AN HOUR, IF THAT WIND KEEPS BLOWING YOUR PAPERS AROUND!
RIVERDALE
OH, MAN! THIS COULD BE TROUBLE-SOME!
RIVERDALE
RIVE
RIVERDALE
LOOK, I HATE TO ASK YOU, BUT I'M GONNA NEED YOUR HELP!
WOULD YOU SIT ON THEM?
REALLY, CHUCK! I FEEL RIDICULOUS! I'M TOO OLD FOR THIS SORT OF THING!
THE SOONER WE GET DONE, THE SOONER WE HAVE OUR DATE!
3

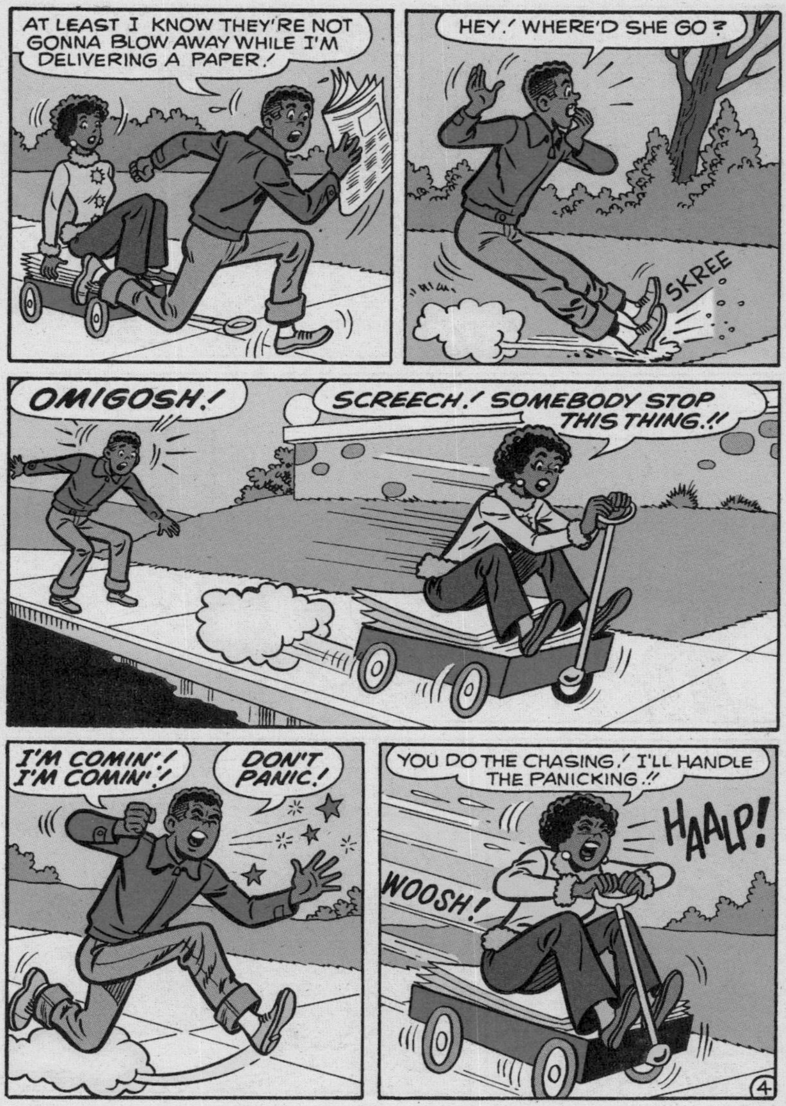
AT LEAST I KNOW THEY'RE NOT GONNA BLOW AWAY WHILE I'M DELIVERING A PAPER!
HEY! WHERE'D SHE GO?
SKREE
OMIGOSH!
SCREECH! SOMEBODY STOP THIS THING!!
I'M COMIN'! I'M COMIN'!
DON'T PANIC!
YOU DO THE CHASING! I'LL HANDLE THE PANICKING!!
HAALP!
WOOSH!

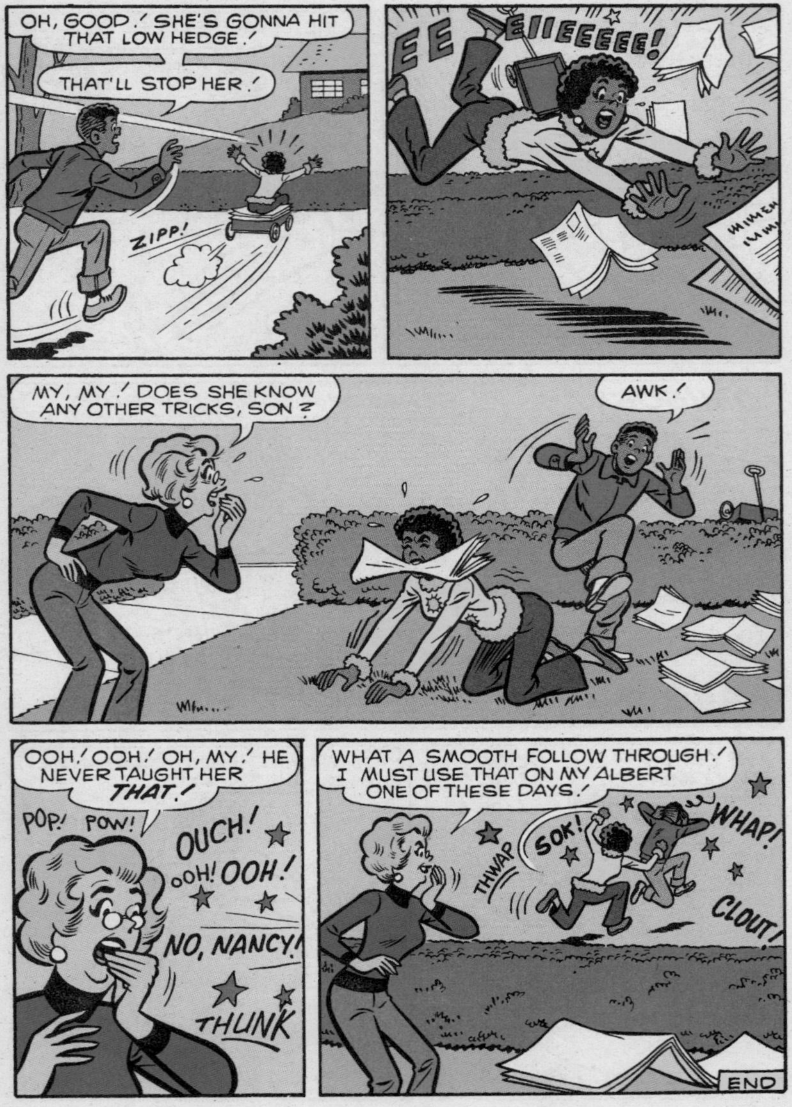
OH, GOOD.! SHE'S GONNA HIT THAT LOW HEDGE.!
THAT'LL STOP HER.!
ZIPP!
EEEIIEEEEEE!
MY, MY.! DOES SHE KNOW ANY OTHER TRICKS, SON?
AWK.!
OOH.! OOH.! OH, MY.! HE NEVER TAUGHT HER THAT.!
POP! POW!
OUCH!
OOH! OOH!
NO, NANCY!
THUNK
WHAT A SMOOTH FOLLOW THROUGH.! I MUST USE THAT ON MY ALBERT ONE OF THESE DAYS.!
THWAP
SOK!
WHAP!
CLOUT!
END

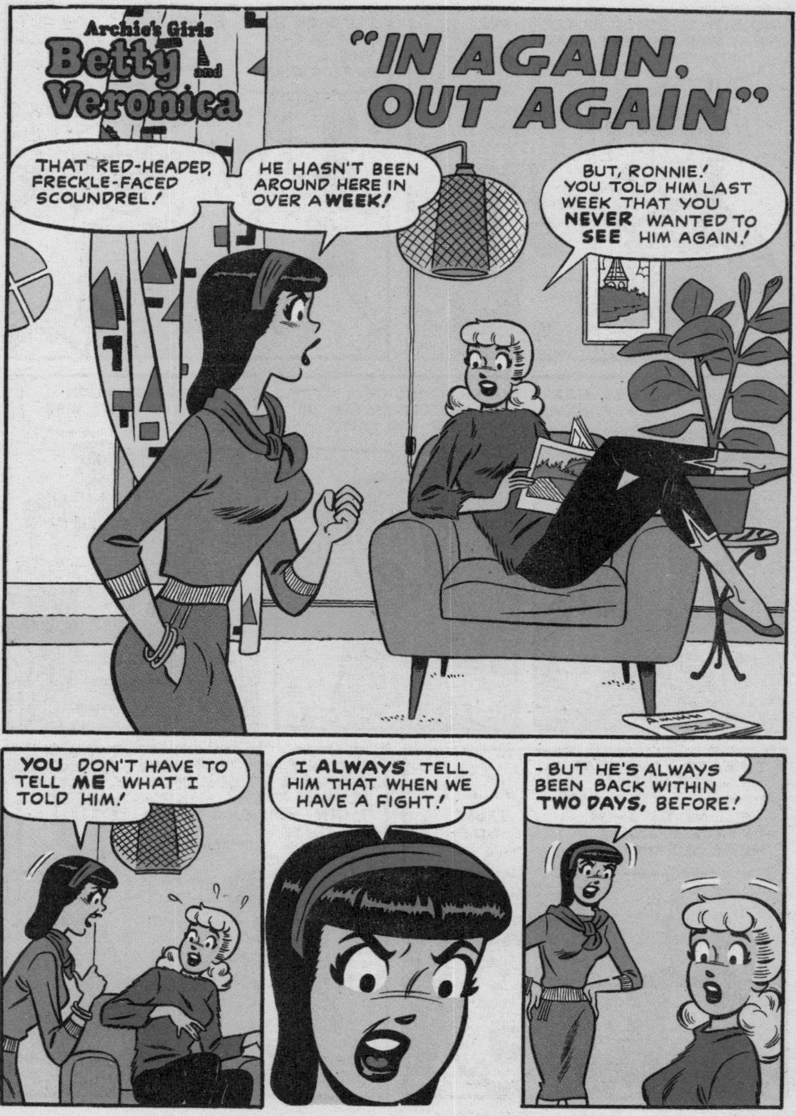
Archie's Girls Betty and Veronica
"IN AGAIN, OUT AGAIN"
THAT RED-HEADED, FRECKLE-FACED SCOUNDREL!
HE HASN'T BEEN AROUND HERE IN OVER A WEEK!
BUT, RONNIE! YOU TOLD HIM LAST WEEK THAT YOU NEVER WANTED TO SEE HIM AGAIN!
YOU DON'T HAVE TO TELL ME WHAT I TOLD HIM!
I ALWAYS TELL HIM THAT WHEN WE HAVE A FIGHT!
- BUT HE'S ALWAYS BEEN BACK WITHIN TWO DAYS, BEFORE!

Script: Frank Doyle / Art: Dan DeCarlo

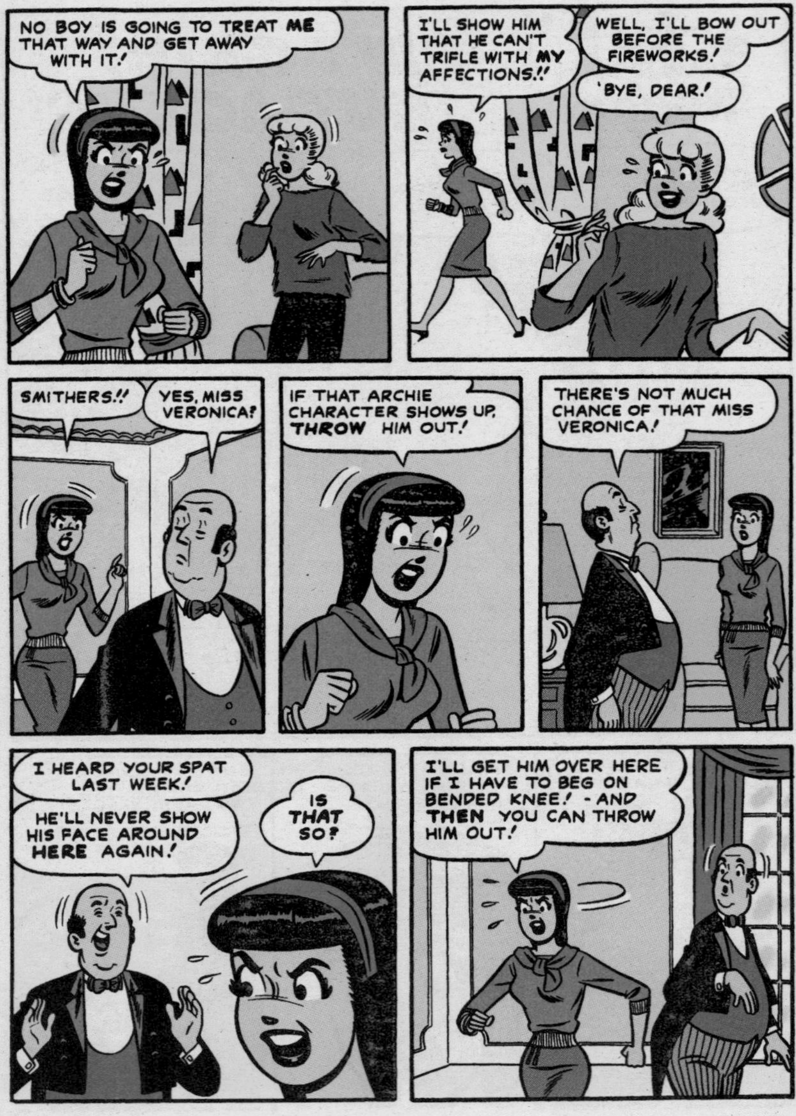

NO BOY IS GOING TO TREAT ME THAT WAY AND GET AWAY WITH IT!
I'LL SHOW HIM THAT HE CAN'T TRIFLE WITH MY AFFECTIONS!!
WELL, I'LL BOW OUT BEFORE THE FIREWORKS!
'BYE, DEAR!
SMITHERS!!
YES, MISS VERONICA?
IF THAT ARCHIE CHARACTER SHOWS UP, THROW HIM OUT!
THERE'S NOT MUCH CHANCE OF THAT MISS VERONICA!
I HEARD YOUR SPAT LAST WEEK!
HE'LL NEVER SHOW HIS FACE AROUND HERE AGAIN!
IS THAT SO?
I'LL GET HIM OVER HERE IF I HAVE TO BEG ON BENDED KNEE! - AND THEN YOU CAN THROW HIM OUT!

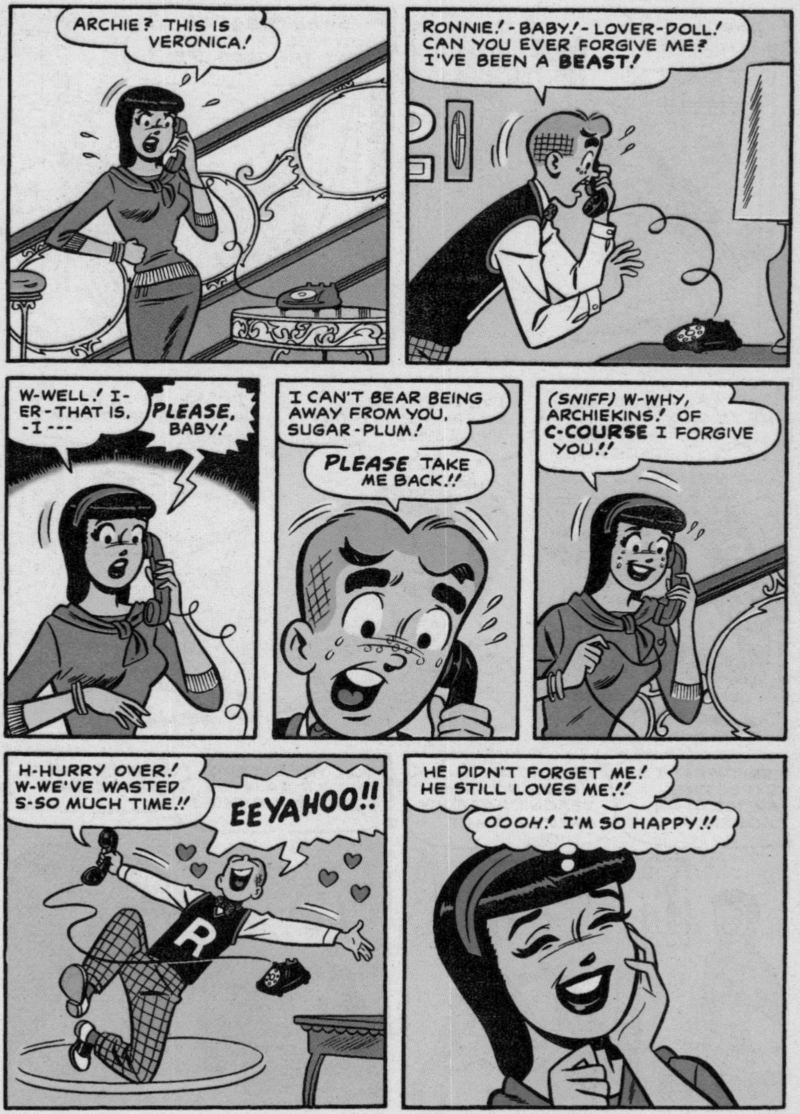
ARCHIE? THIS IS VERONICA!
RONNIE! - BABY! - LOVER-DOLL! CAN YOU EVER FORGIVE ME? I'VE BEEN A **BEAST**!
W-WELL! I- ER - THAT IS. -I ---
PLEASE, BABY!
I CAN'T BEAR BEING AWAY FROM YOU, SUGAR-PLUM!
PLEASE TAKE ME BACK!!
(SNIFF) W-WHY, ARCHIEKINS! OF **C-COURSE** I FORGIVE YOU!!
H-HURRY OVER! W-WE'VE WASTED S-SO MUCH TIME!!
EEYAHOO!!
HE DIDN'T FORGET ME! HE STILL LOVES ME!!
OOOH! I'M SO HAPPY!!

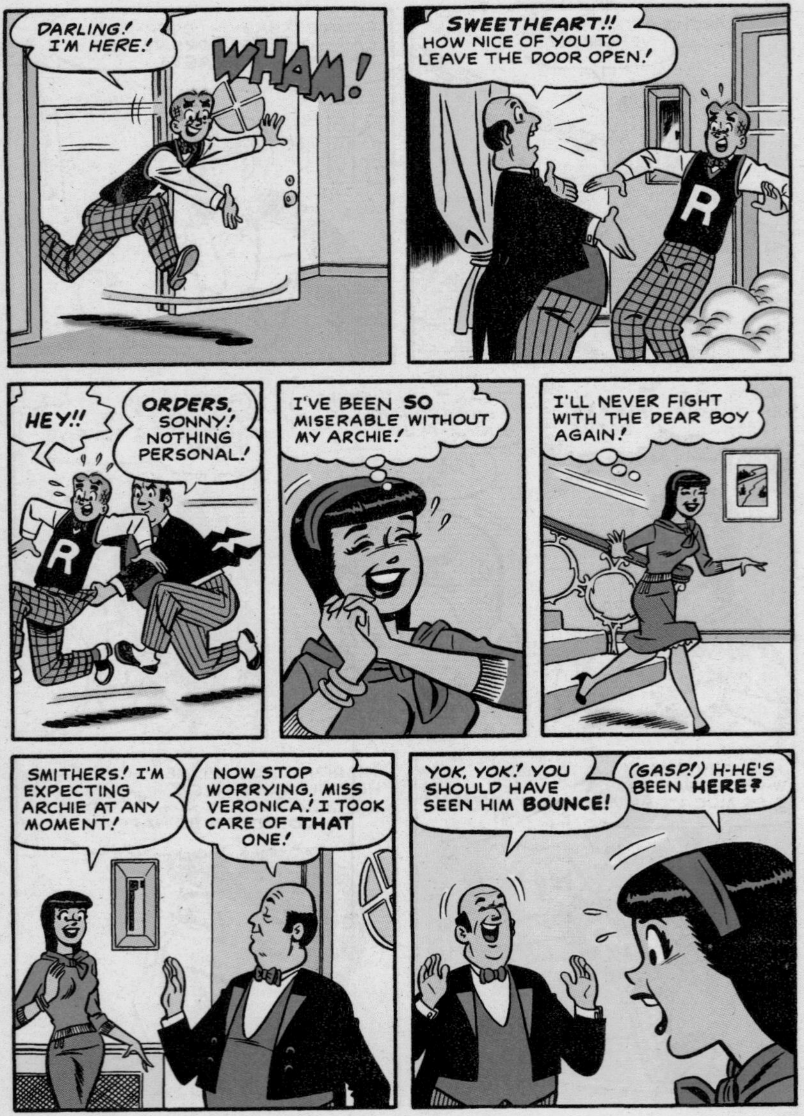
DARLING! I'M HERE!
WHAM!
SWEETHEART!! HOW NICE OF YOU TO LEAVE THE DOOR OPEN!
HEY!!
ORDERS, SONNY! NOTHING PERSONAL!
I'VE BEEN SO MISERABLE WITHOUT MY ARCHIE!
I'LL NEVER FIGHT WITH THE DEAR BOY AGAIN!
SMITHERS! I'M EXPECTING ARCHIE AT ANY MOMENT!
NOW STOP WORRYING, MISS VERONICA! I TOOK CARE OF THAT ONE!
YOK, YOK! YOU SHOULD HAVE SEEN HIM BOUNCE!
(GASP!) H-HE'S BEEN HERE?

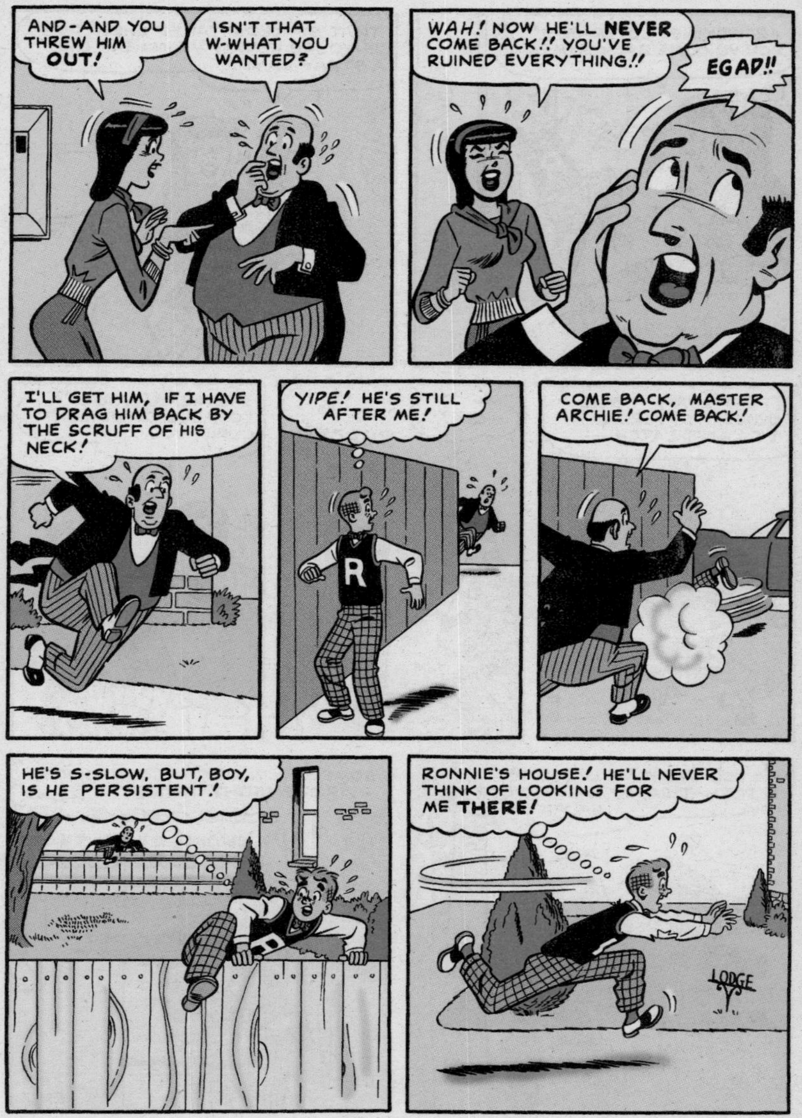
AND-AND YOU THREW HIM OUT!
ISN'T THAT W-WHAT YOU WANTED?
WAH! NOW HE'LL NEVER COME BACK!! YOU'VE RUINED EVERYTHING!!
EGAD!!
I'LL GET HIM, IF I HAVE TO DRAG HIM BACK BY THE SCRUFF OF HIS NECK!
YIPE! HE'S STILL AFTER ME!
COME BACK, MASTER ARCHIE! COME BACK!
HE'S S-SLOW, BUT, BOY, IS HE PERSISTENT!
RONNIE'S HOUSE! HE'LL NEVER THINK OF LOOKING FOR ME THERE!
LODGE

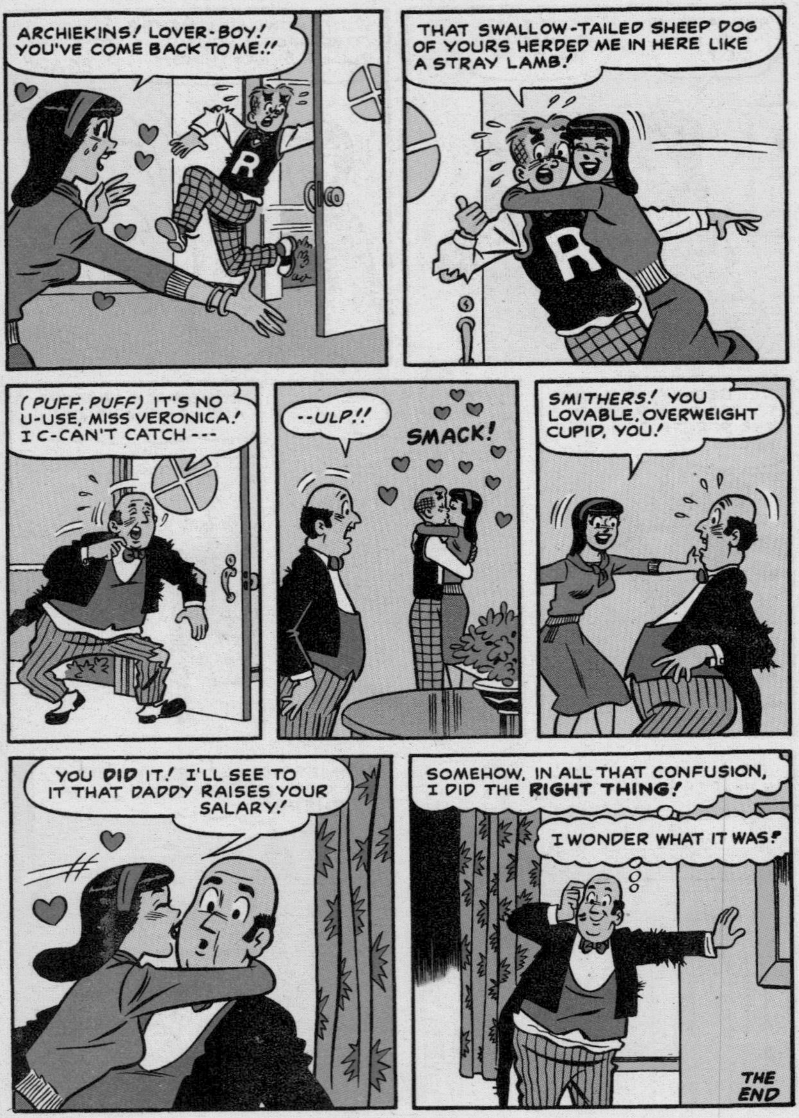
ARCHIEKINS! LOVER-BOY! YOU'VE COME BACK TO ME!!
THAT SWALLOW-TAILED SHEEP DOG OF YOURS HERDED ME IN HERE LIKE A STRAY LAMB!
(PUFF, PUFF) IT'S NO U-USE, MISS VERONICA! I C-CAN'T CATCH ---
--ULP!!
SMACK!
SMITHERS! YOU LOVABLE, OVERWEIGHT CUPID, YOU!
YOU DID IT! I'LL SEE TO IT THAT DADDY RAISES YOUR SALARY!
SOMEHOW, IN ALL THAT CONFUSION, I DID THE RIGHT THING!
I WONDER WHAT IT WAS?
THE END

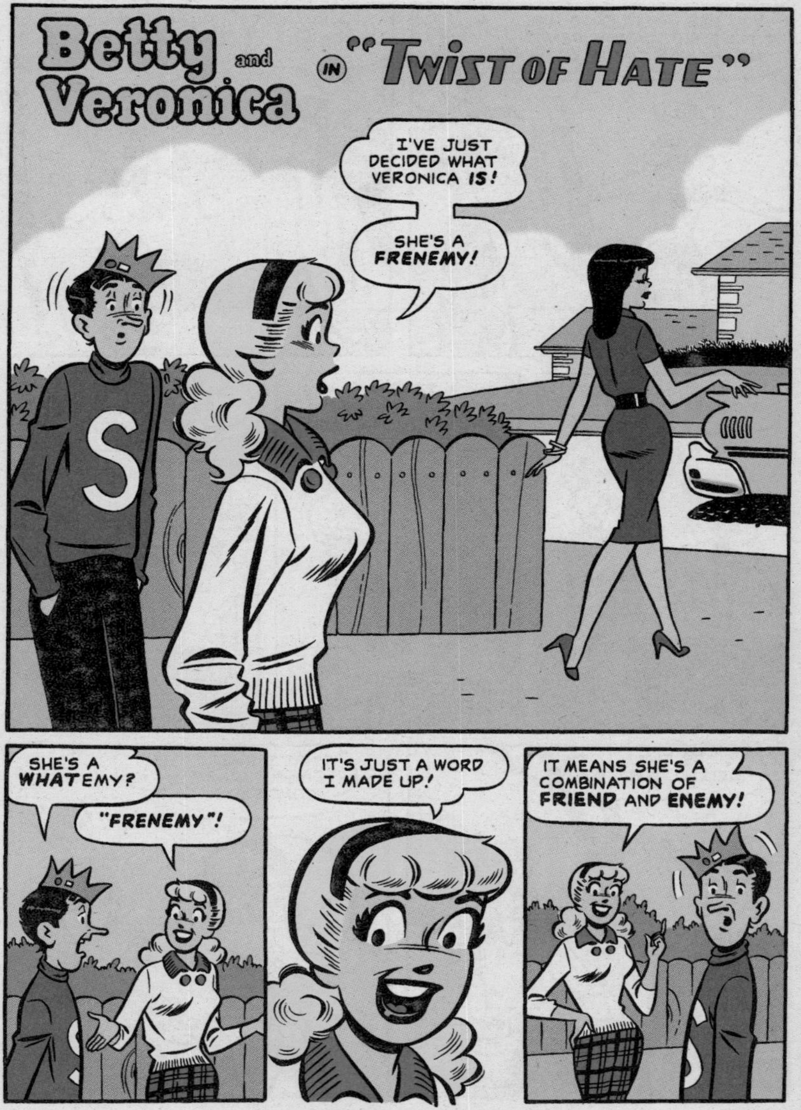
Betty and Veronica
IN "TWIST OF HATE"
I'VE JUST DECIDED WHAT VERONICA IS!
SHE'S A FRENEMY!
SHE'S A WHATEMY?
"FRENEMY"!
IT'S JUST A WORD I MADE UP!
IT MEANS SHE'S A COMBINATION OF FRIEND AND ENEMY!

Script: Frank Doyle / Art: Dan DeCarlo

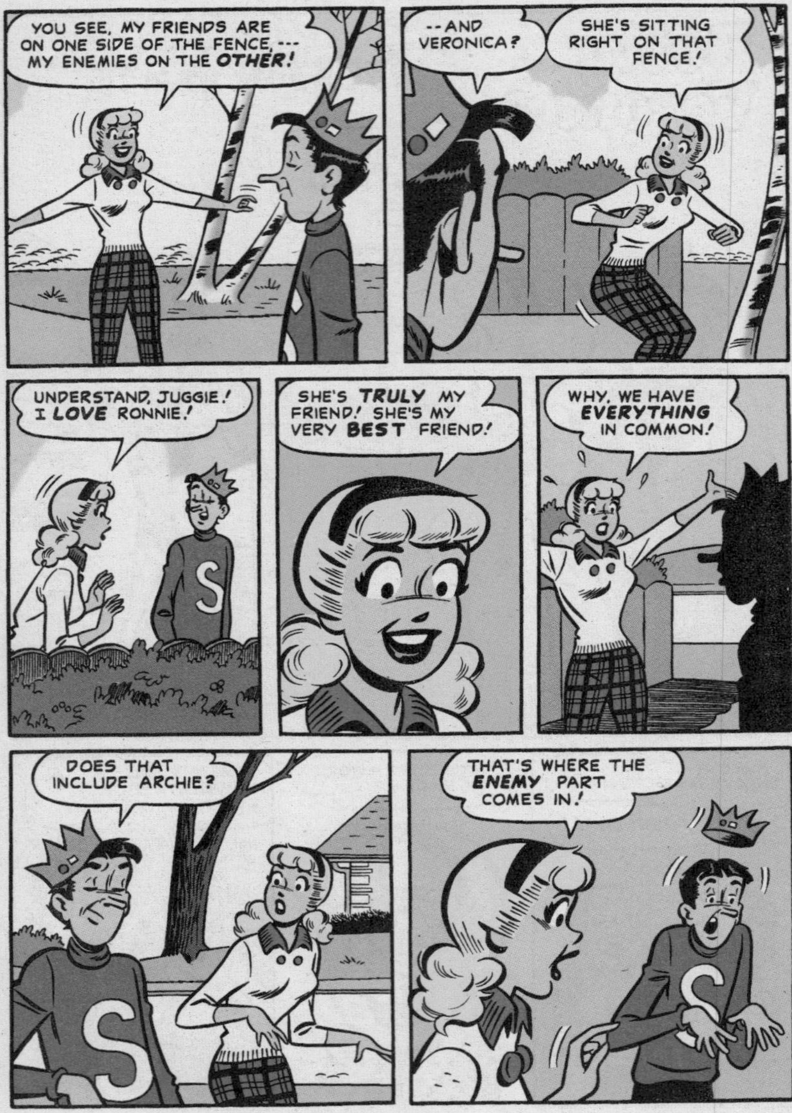

YOU SEE, MY FRIENDS ARE ON ONE SIDE OF THE FENCE, --- MY ENEMIES ON THE **OTHER**!
--AND VERONICA?
SHE'S SITTING RIGHT ON THAT FENCE!
UNDERSTAND, JUGGIE! I **LOVE** RONNIE!
SHE'S **TRULY** MY FRIEND! SHE'S MY VERY **BEST** FRIEND!
WHY, WE HAVE **EVERYTHING** IN COMMON!
DOES THAT INCLUDE ARCHIE?
THAT'S WHERE THE **ENEMY** PART COMES IN!

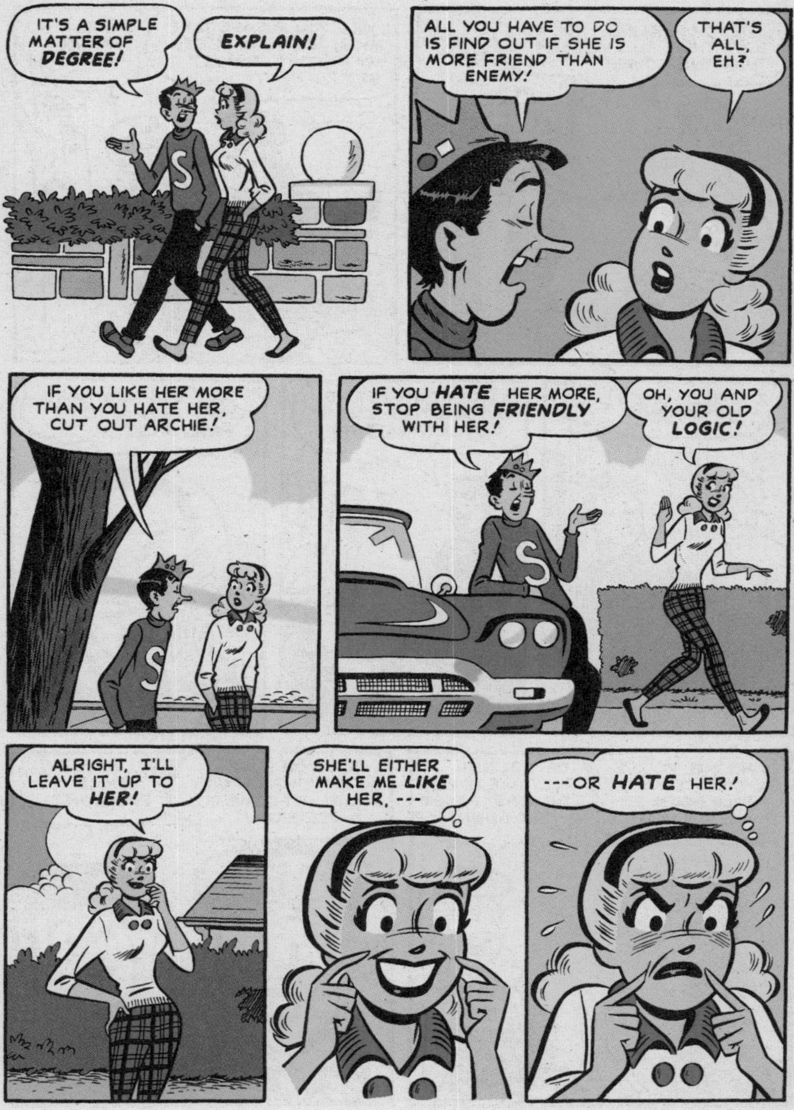
IT'S A SIMPLE MATTER OF DEGREE!
EXPLAIN!
ALL YOU HAVE TO DO IS FIND OUT IF SHE IS MORE FRIEND THAN ENEMY!
THAT'S ALL, EH?
IF YOU LIKE HER MORE THAN YOU HATE HER, CUT OUT ARCHIE!
IF YOU HATE HER MORE, STOP BEING FRIENDLY WITH HER!
OH, YOU AND YOUR OLD LOGIC!
ALRIGHT, I'LL LEAVE IT UP TO HER!
SHE'LL EITHER MAKE ME LIKE HER, ---
---OR HATE HER!

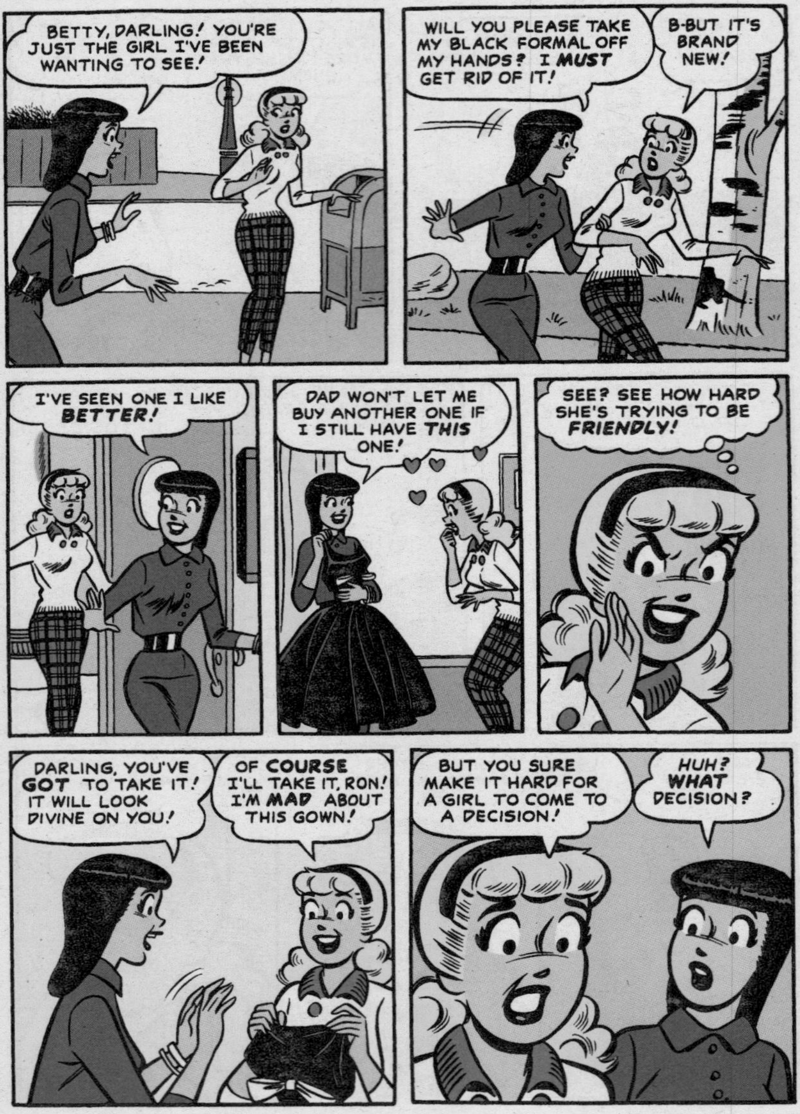
BETTY, DARLING! YOU'RE JUST THE GIRL I'VE BEEN WANTING TO SEE!
WILL YOU PLEASE TAKE MY BLACK FORMAL OFF MY HANDS? I MUST GET RID OF IT!
B-BUT IT'S BRAND NEW!
I'VE SEEN ONE I LIKE BETTER!
DAD WON'T LET ME BUY ANOTHER ONE IF I STILL HAVE THIS ONE!
SEE? SEE HOW HARD SHE'S TRYING TO BE FRIENDLY!
DARLING, YOU'VE GOT TO TAKE IT! IT WILL LOOK DIVINE ON YOU!
OF COURSE I'LL TAKE IT, RON! I'M MAD ABOUT THIS GOWN!
BUT YOU SURE MAKE IT HARD FOR A GIRL TO COME TO A DECISION!
HUH? WHAT DECISION?

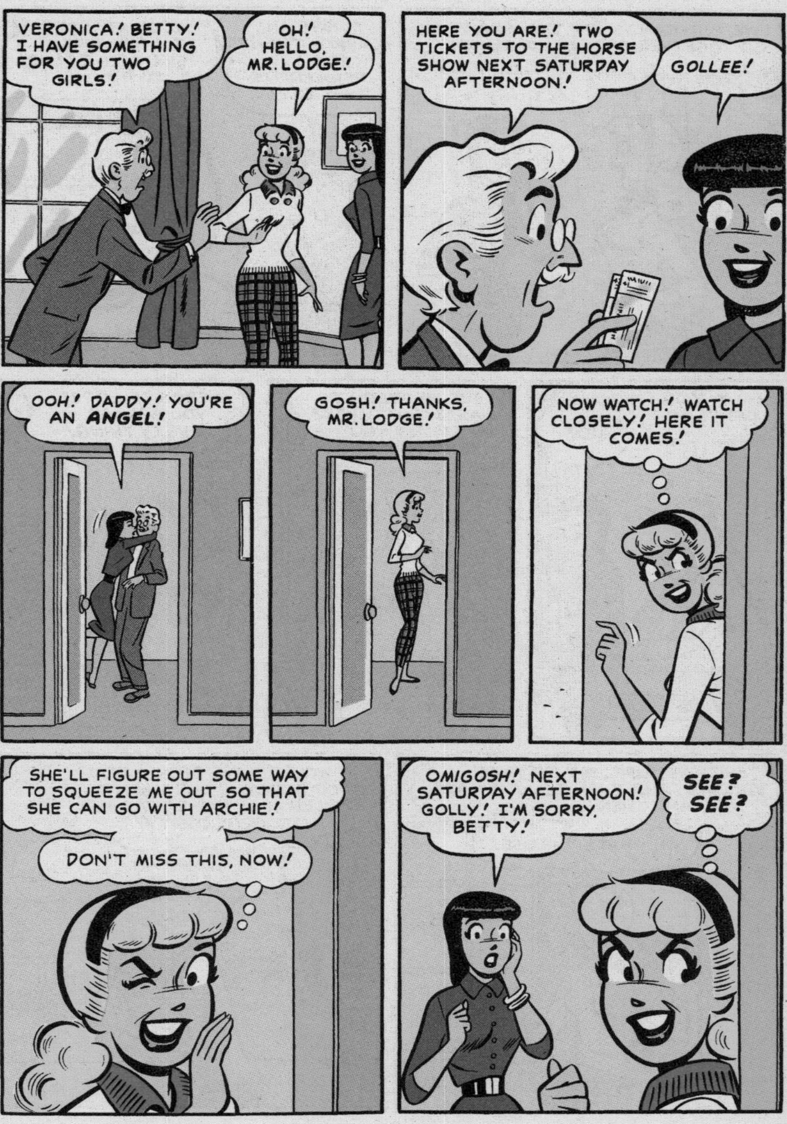
VERONICA! BETTY! I HAVE SOMETHING FOR YOU TWO GIRLS!
OH! HELLO, MR. LODGE!
HERE YOU ARE! TWO TICKETS TO THE HORSE SHOW NEXT SATURDAY AFTERNOON!
GOLLEE!
OOH! DADDY! YOU'RE AN ANGEL!
GOSH! THANKS, MR. LODGE!
NOW WATCH! WATCH CLOSELY! HERE IT COMES!
SHE'LL FIGURE OUT SOME WAY TO SQUEEZE ME OUT SO THAT SHE CAN GO WITH ARCHIE!
DON'T MISS THIS, NOW!
OMIGOSH! NEXT SATURDAY AFTERNOON! GOLLY! I'M SORRY, BETTY!
SEE? SEE?

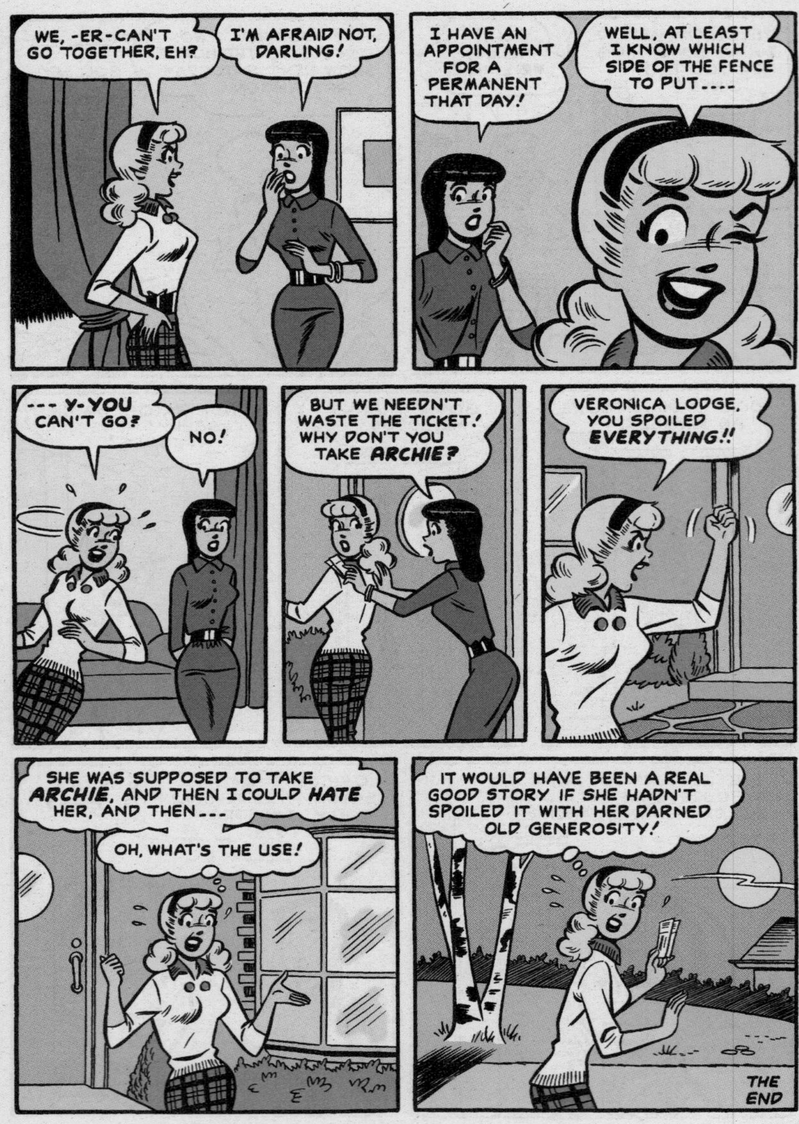
WE, -ER-CAN'T GO TOGETHER, EH?
I'M AFRAID NOT, DARLING!
I HAVE AN APPOINTMENT FOR A PERMANENT THAT DAY!
WELL, AT LEAST I KNOW WHICH SIDE OF THE FENCE TO PUT....
--- Y-YOU CAN'T GO?
NO!
BUT WE NEEDN'T WASTE THE TICKET! WHY DON'T YOU TAKE ARCHIE?
VERONICA LODGE, YOU SPOILED EVERYTHING!!
SHE WAS SUPPOSED TO TAKE ARCHIE, AND THEN I COULD HATE HER, AND THEN...
OH, WHAT'S THE USE!
IT WOULD HAVE BEEN A REAL GOOD STORY IF SHE HADN'T SPOILED IT WITH HER DARNED OLD GENEROSITY!
THE END

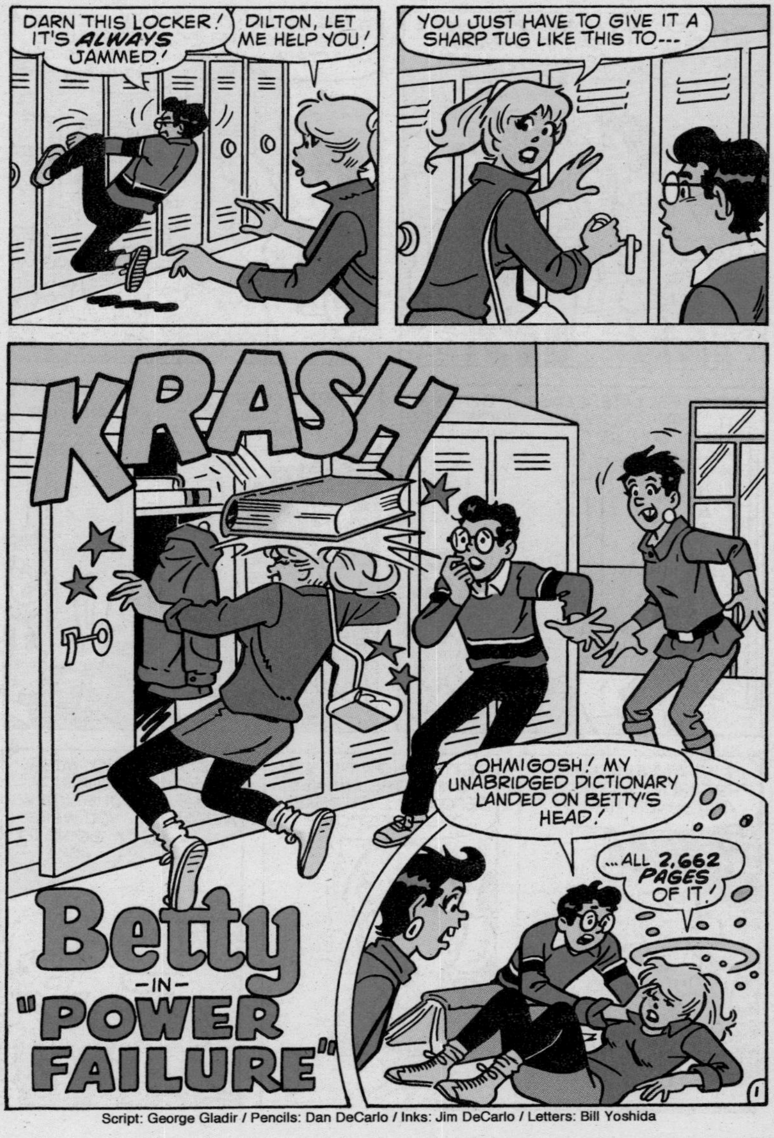
DARN THIS LOCKER! IT'S ALWAYS JAMMED!
DILTON, LET ME HELP YOU!
YOU JUST HAVE TO GIVE IT A SHARP TUG LIKE THIS TO---
KRASH
OHMIGOSH! MY UNABRIDGED DICTIONARY LANDED ON BETTY'S HEAD!
...ALL 2,662 PAGES OF IT!
Betty -IN- "POWER FAILURE"
1

Script: George Gladir / Pencils: Dan DeCarlo / Inks: Jim DeCarlo / Letters: Bill Yoshida

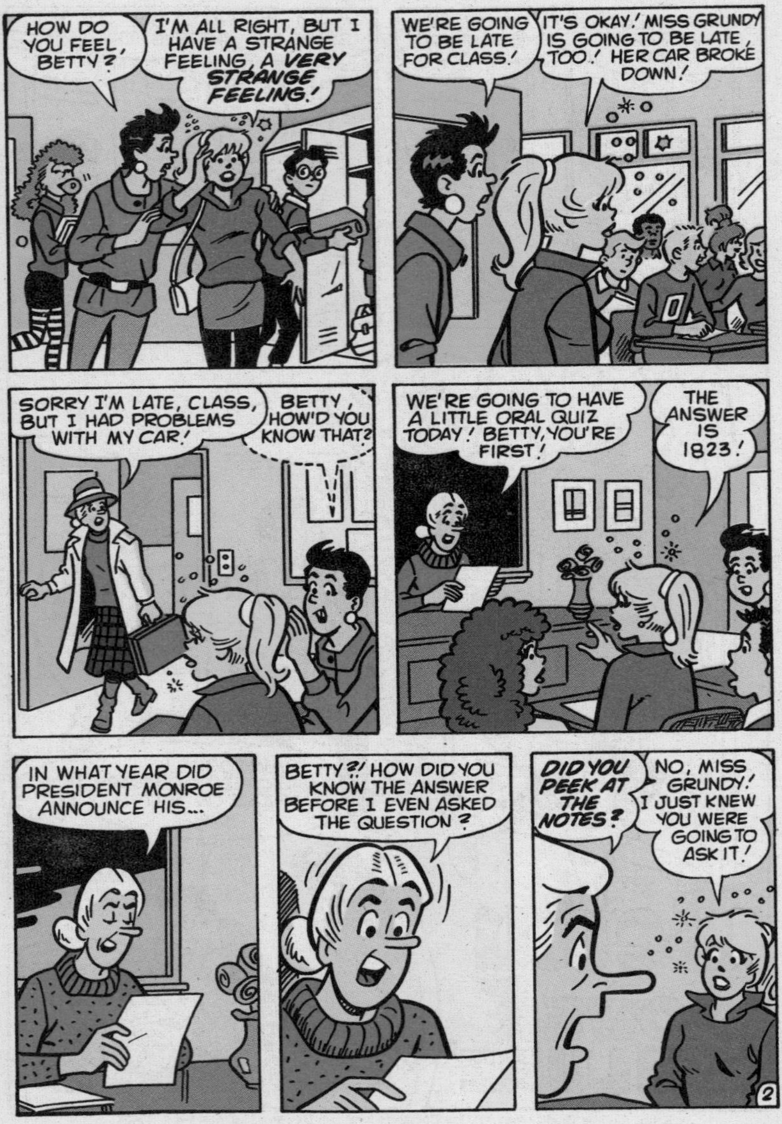
HOW DO YOU FEEL, BETTY?
I'M ALL RIGHT, BUT I HAVE A STRANGE FEELING, A VERY STRANGE FEELING!
WE'RE GOING TO BE LATE FOR CLASS!
IT'S OKAY! MISS GRUNDY IS GOING TO BE LATE, TOO! HER CAR BROKE DOWN!
SORRY I'M LATE, CLASS, BUT I HAD PROBLEMS WITH MY CAR!
BETTY, HOW'D YOU KNOW THAT?
WE'RE GOING TO HAVE A LITTLE ORAL QUIZ TODAY! BETTY, YOU'RE FIRST!
THE ANSWER IS 1823!
IN WHAT YEAR DID PRESIDENT MONROE ANNOUNCE HIS...
BETTY?! HOW DID YOU KNOW THE ANSWER BEFORE I EVEN ASKED THE QUESTION?
DID YOU PEEK AT THE NOTES?
NO, MISS GRUNDY! I JUST KNEW YOU WERE GOING TO ASK IT!
2

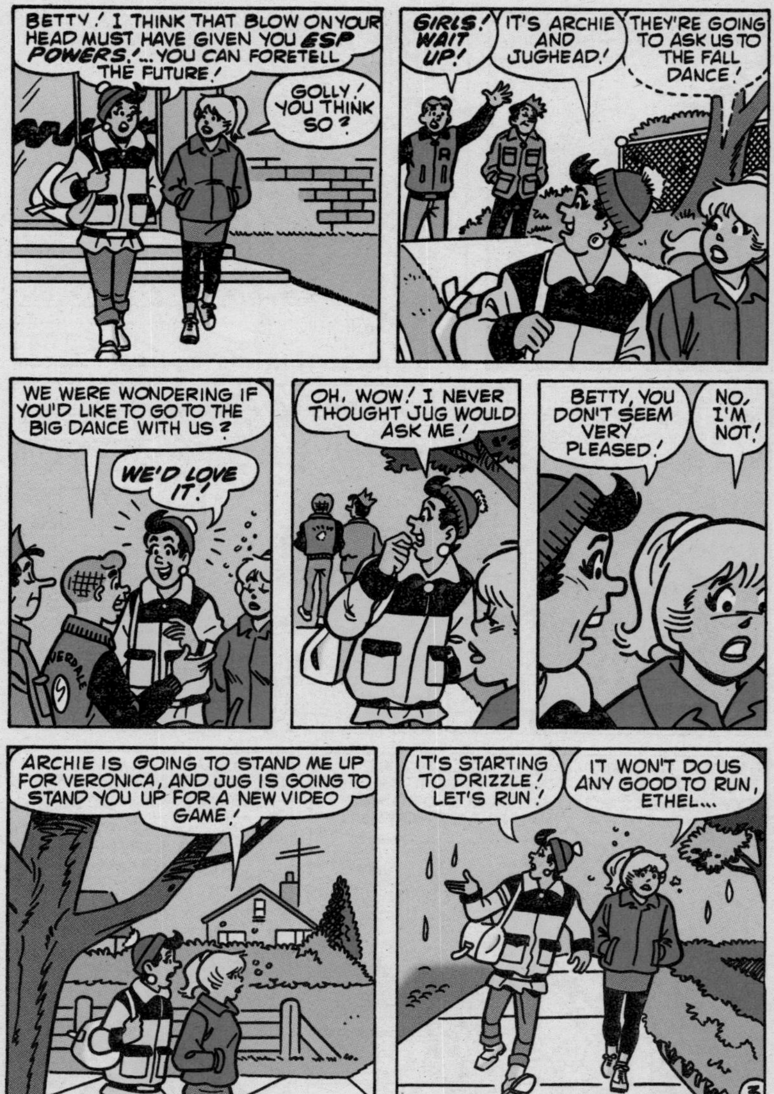
BETTY! I THINK THAT BLOW ON YOUR HEAD MUST HAVE GIVEN YOU ESP POWERS!... YOU CAN FORETELL THE FUTURE!
GOLLY! YOU THINK SO?
GIRLS! WAIT UP!
IT'S ARCHIE AND JUGHEAD!
THEY'RE GOING TO ASK US TO THE FALL DANCE!
WE WERE WONDERING IF YOU'D LIKE TO GO TO THE BIG DANCE WITH US?
WE'D LOVE IT!
OH, WOW! I NEVER THOUGHT JUG WOULD ASK ME!
BETTY, YOU DON'T SEEM VERY PLEASED!
NO, I'M NOT!
ARCHIE IS GOING TO STAND ME UP FOR VERONICA, AND JUG IS GOING TO STAND YOU UP FOR A NEW VIDEO GAME!
IT'S STARTING TO DRIZZLE! LET'S RUN!
IT WON'T DO US ANY GOOD TO RUN, ETHEL...
3

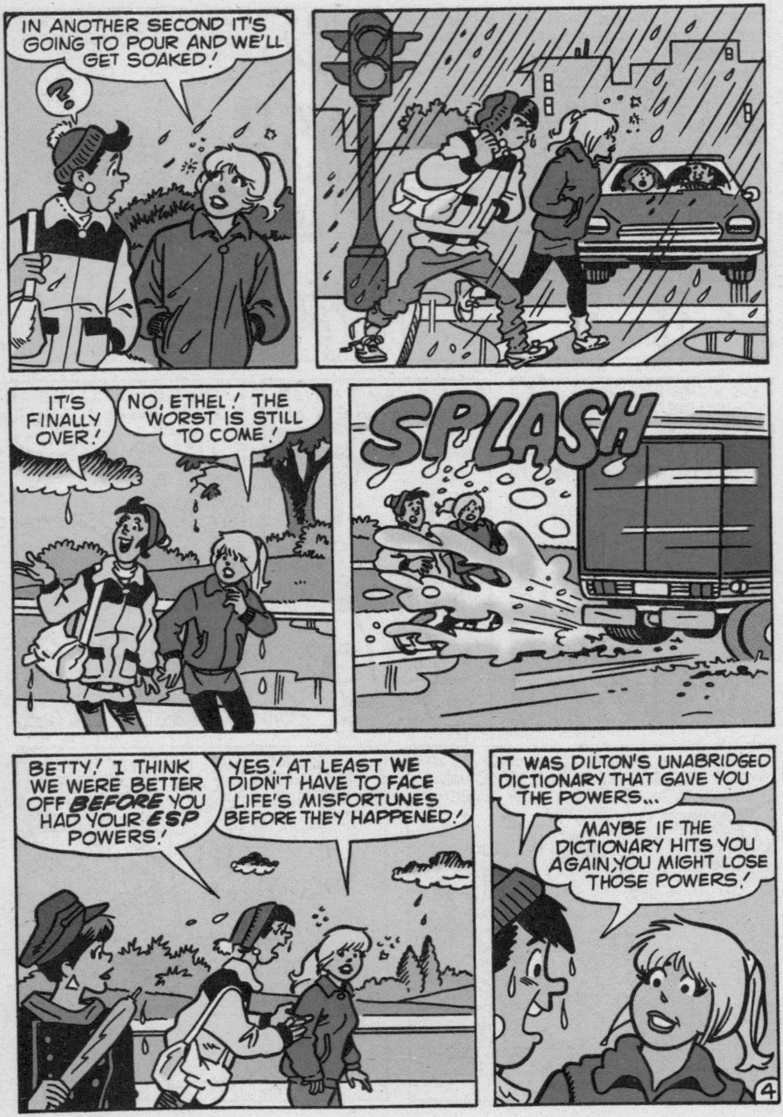
IN ANOTHER SECOND IT'S GOING TO POUR AND WE'LL GET SOAKED!
?
IT'S FINALLY OVER!
NO, ETHEL! THE WORST IS STILL TO COME!
SPLASH
BETTY! I THINK WE WERE BETTER OFF BEFORE YOU HAD YOUR ESP POWERS!
YES! AT LEAST WE DIDN'T HAVE TO FACE LIFE'S MISFORTUNES BEFORE THEY HAPPENED!
IT WAS DILTON'S UNABRIDGED DICTIONARY THAT GAVE YOU THE POWERS...
MAYBE IF THE DICTIONARY HITS YOU AGAIN, YOU MIGHT LOSE THOSE POWERS!
4

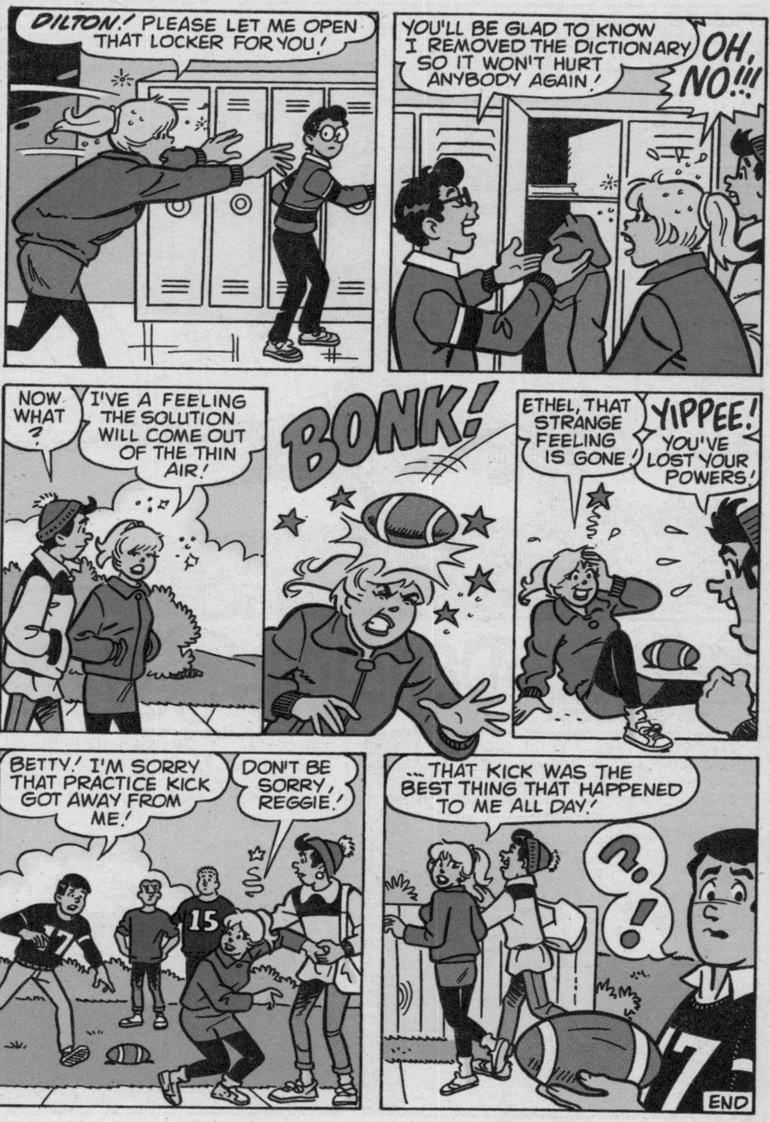
DILTON! PLEASE LET ME OPEN THAT LOCKER FOR YOU!
YOU'LL BE GLAD TO KNOW I REMOVED THE DICTIONARY SO IT WON'T HURT ANYBODY AGAIN!
OH, NO!!!
NOW WHAT ?
I'VE A FEELING THE SOLUTION WILL COME OUT OF THE THIN AIR!
BONK!
ETHEL, THAT STRANGE FEELING IS GONE!
YIPPEE! YOU'VE LOST YOUR POWERS!
BETTY! I'M SORRY THAT PRACTICE KICK GOT AWAY FROM ME!
DON'T BE SORRY, REGGIE!
...THAT KICK WAS THE BEST THING THAT HAPPENED TO ME ALL DAY!
?
!
END

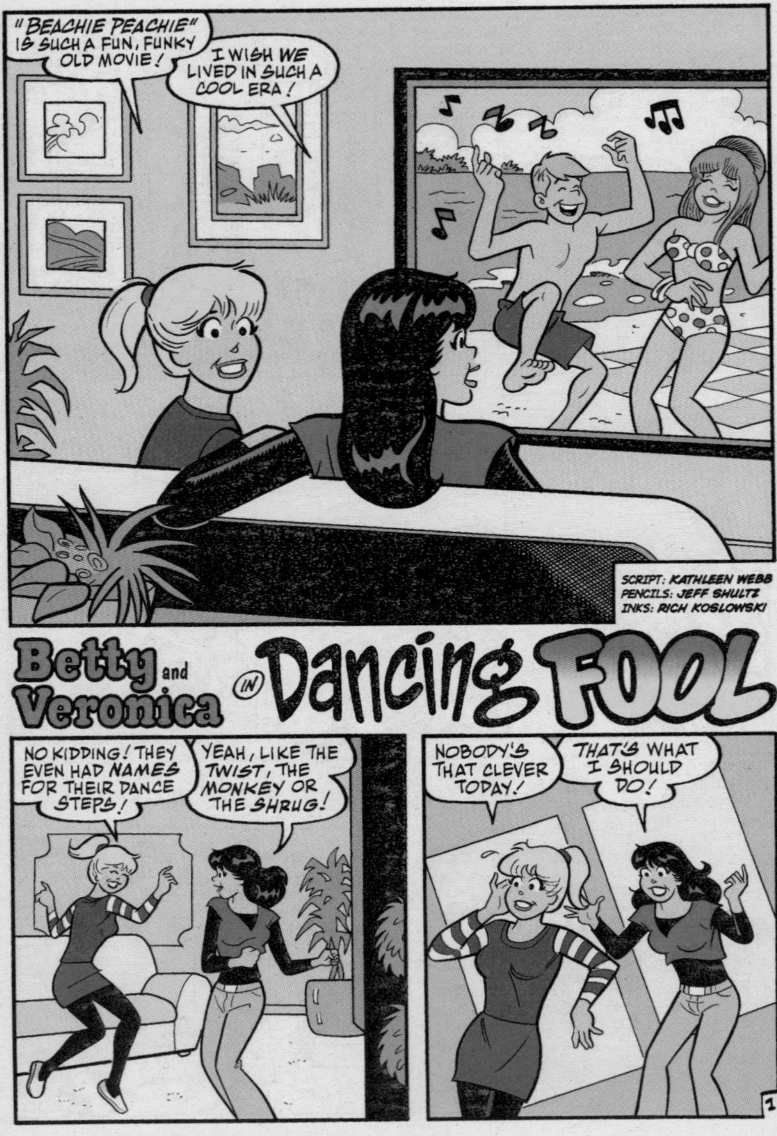
"BEACHIE PEACHIE" IS SUCH A FUN, FUNKY OLD MOVIE!
I WISH WE LIVED IN SUCH A COOL ERA!
SCRIPT: KATHLEEN WEBB
PENCILS: JEFF SHULTZ
INKS: RICH KOSLOWSKI
Betty and Veronica IN Dancing FOOL
NO KIDDING! THEY EVEN HAD NAMES FOR THEIR DANCE STEPS!
YEAH, LIKE THE TWIST, THE MONKEY OR THE SHRUG!
NOBODY'S THAT CLEVER TODAY!
THAT'S WHAT I SHOULD DO!
1

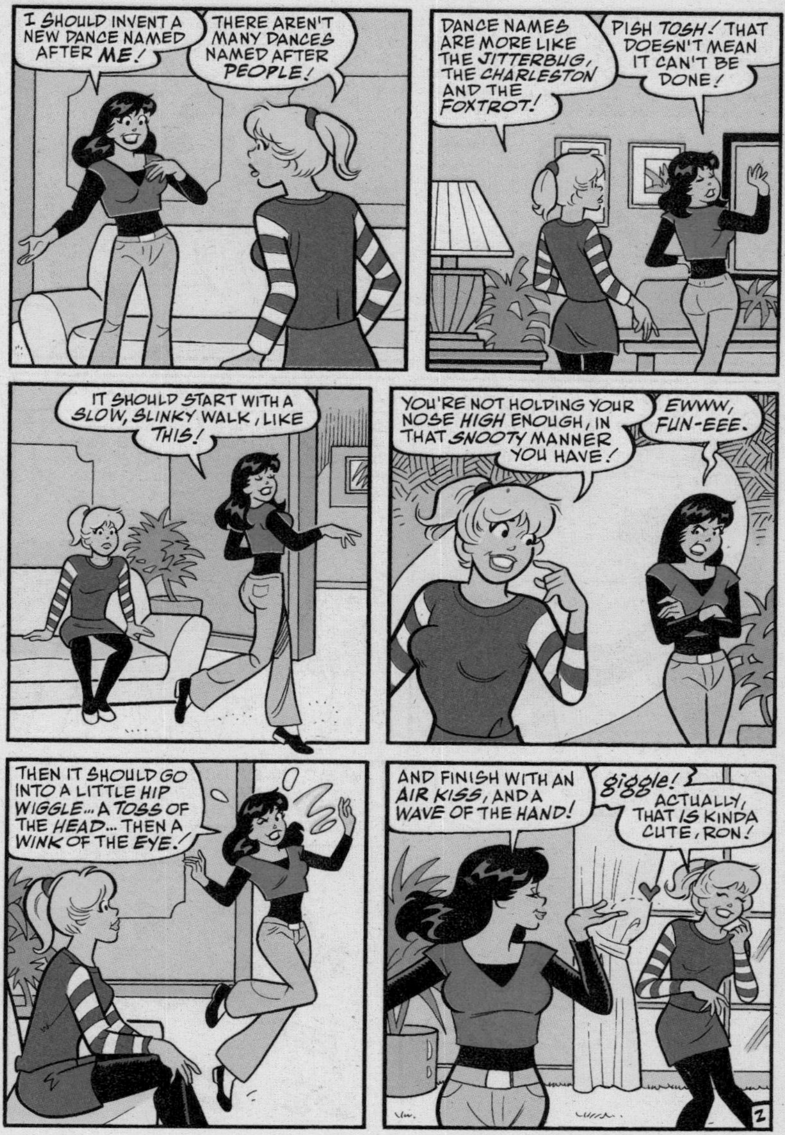
I SHOULD INVENT A NEW DANCE NAMED AFTER ME!
THERE AREN'T MANY DANCES NAMED AFTER PEOPLE!
DANCE NAMES ARE MORE LIKE THE JITTERBUG, THE CHARLESTON AND THE FOXTROT!
PISH TOSH! THAT DOESN'T MEAN IT CAN'T BE DONE!
IT SHOULD START WITH A SLOW, SLINKY WALK, LIKE THIS!
YOU'RE NOT HOLDING YOUR NOSE HIGH ENOUGH, IN THAT SNOOTY MANNER YOU HAVE!
EWWW, FUN-EEE.
THEN IT SHOULD GO INTO A LITTLE HIP WIGGLE... A TOSS OF THE HEAD... THEN A WINK OF THE EYE!
AND FINISH WITH AN AIR KISS, AND A WAVE OF THE HAND!
giggle! ACTUALLY, THAT IS KINDA CUTE, RON!
2

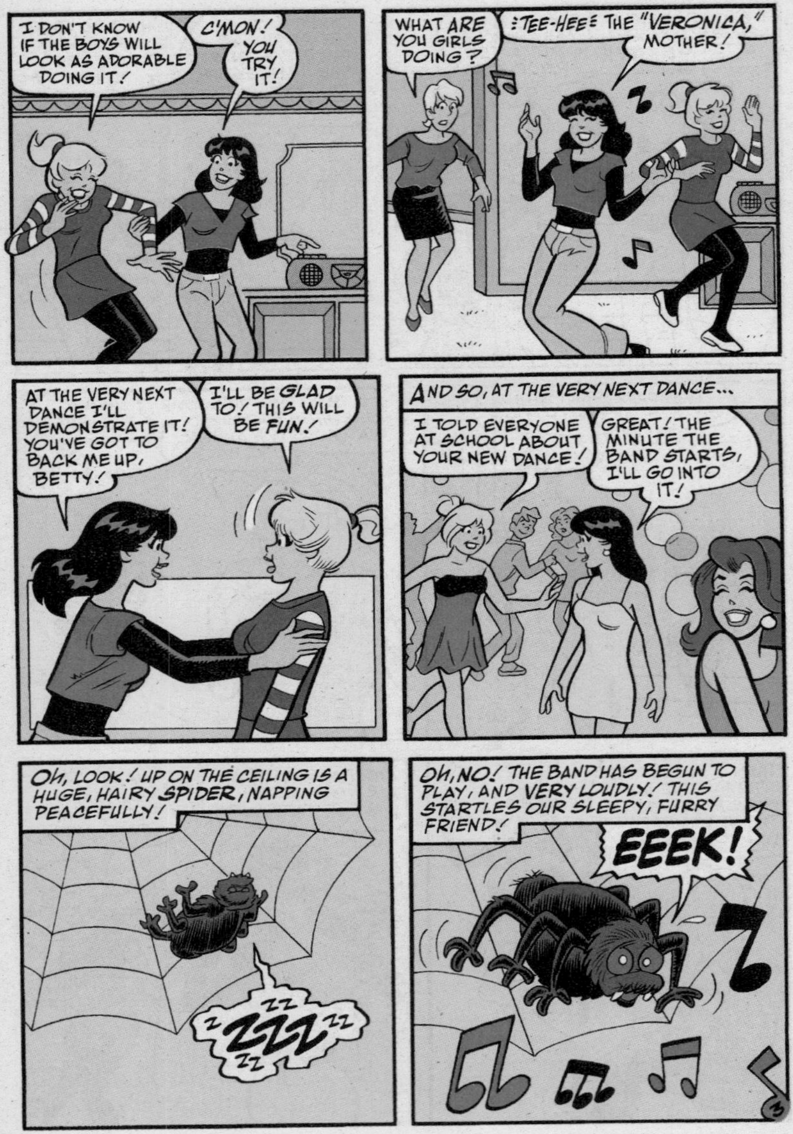
I DON'T KNOW IF THE BOYS WILL LOOK AS ADORABLE DOING IT!
C'MON! YOU TRY IT!
WHAT ARE YOU GIRLS DOING?
TEE-HEE THE "VERONICA," MOTHER!
AT THE VERY NEXT DANCE I'LL DEMONSTRATE IT! YOU'VE GOT TO BACK ME UP, BETTY!
I'LL BE GLAD TO! THIS WILL BE FUN!
AND SO, AT THE VERY NEXT DANCE...
I TOLD EVERYONE AT SCHOOL ABOUT YOUR NEW DANCE!
GREAT! THE MINUTE THE BAND STARTS, I'LL GO INTO IT!
OH, LOOK! UP ON THE CEILING IS A HUGE, HAIRY SPIDER, NAPPING PEACEFULLY!
ZZZZ
OH, NO! THE BAND HAS BEGUN TO PLAY, AND VERY LOUDLY! THIS STARTLES OUR SLEEPY, FURRY FRIEND!
EEEK!
3

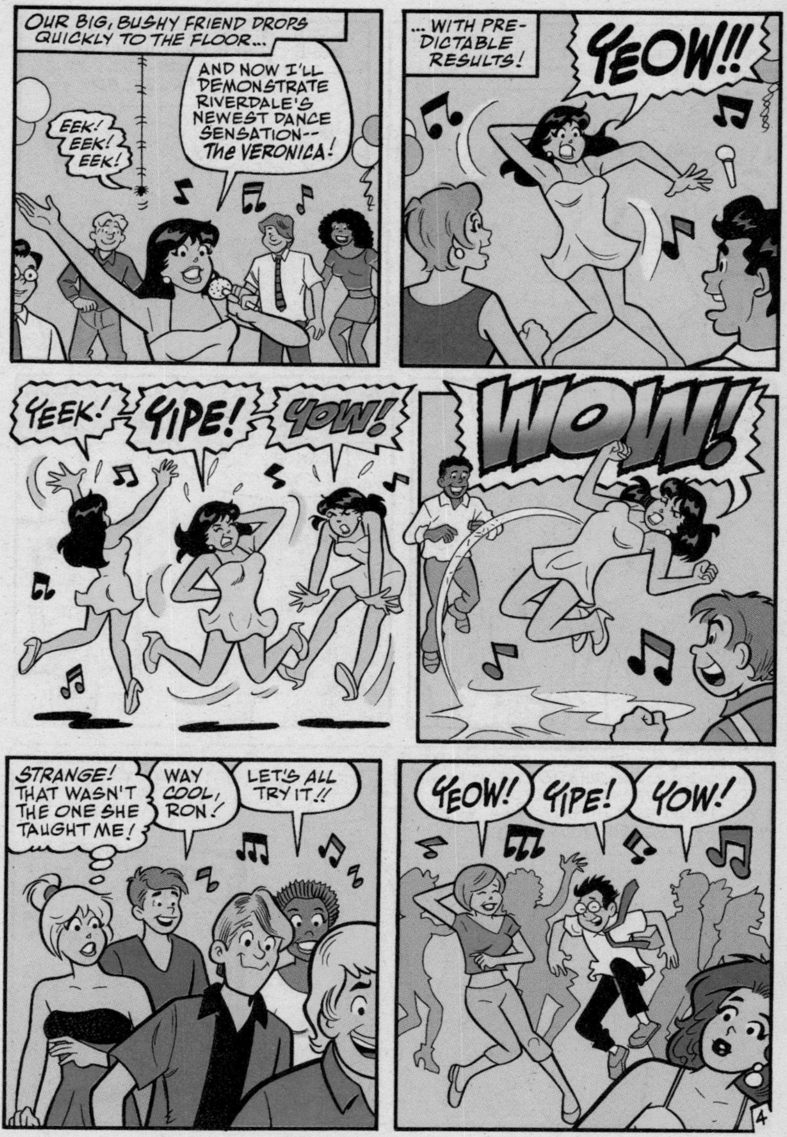
OUR BIG, BUSHY FRIEND DROPS QUICKLY TO THE FLOOR...
EEK! EEK! EEK!
AND NOW I'LL DEMONSTRATE RIVERDALE'S NEWEST DANCE SENSATION-- The VERONICA!
...WITH PRE-DICTABLE RESULTS!
YEOW!!
YEEK!
YIPE!
YOW!
WOW!
STRANGE! THAT WASN'T THE ONE SHE TAUGHT ME!
WAY COOL, RON!
LET'S ALL TRY IT!!
YEOW!
YIPE!
YOW!
4

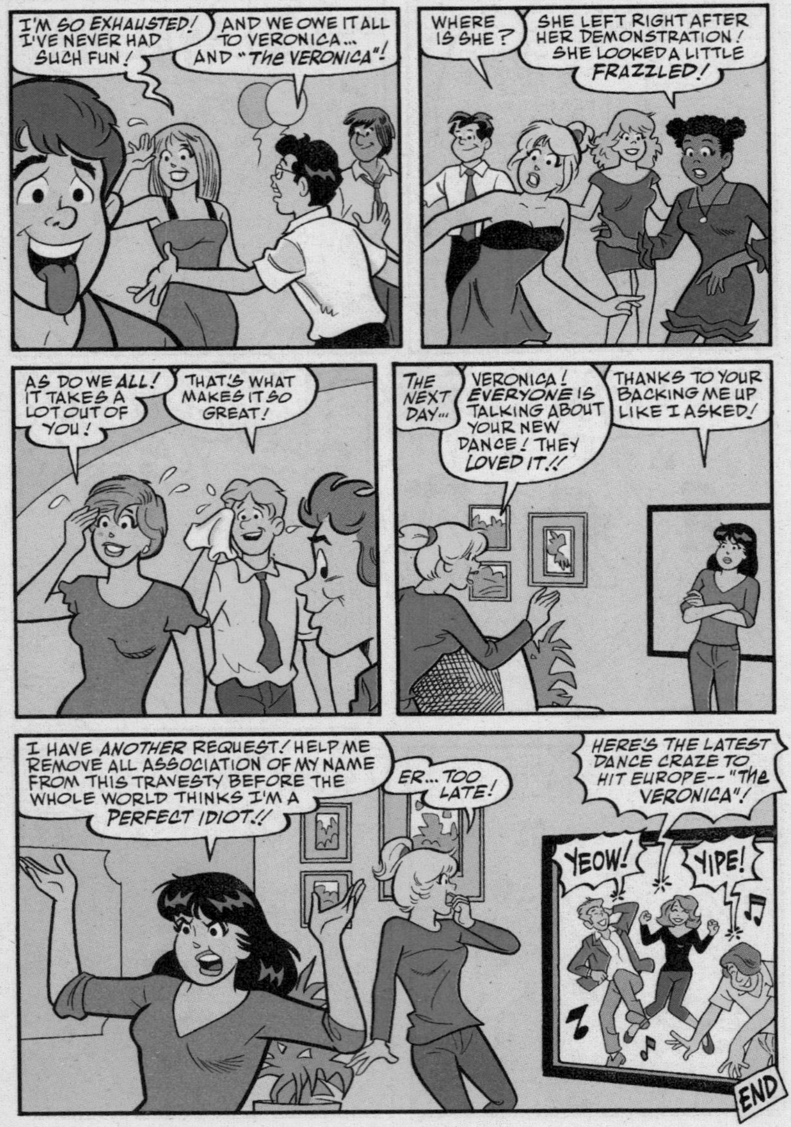
I'M SO EXHAUSTED! I'VE NEVER HAD SUCH FUN!
AND WE OWE IT ALL TO VERONICA... AND "The VERONICA"!
WHERE IS SHE?
SHE LEFT RIGHT AFTER HER DEMONSTRATION! SHE LOOKED A LITTLE FRAZZLED!
AS DO WE ALL! IT TAKES A LOT OUT OF YOU!
THAT'S WHAT MAKES IT SO GREAT!
THE NEXT DAY...
VERONICA! EVERYONE IS TALKING ABOUT YOUR NEW DANCE! THEY LOVED IT!!
THANKS TO YOUR BACKING ME UP LIKE I ASKED!
I HAVE ANOTHER REQUEST! HELP ME REMOVE ALL ASSOCIATION OF MY NAME FROM THIS TRAVESTY BEFORE THE WHOLE WORLD THINKS I'M A PERFECT IDIOT!!
ER... TOO LATE!
HERE'S THE LATEST DANCE CRAZE TO HIT EUROPE-- "The VERONICA"!
YEOW!
YIPE!
END

Veronica in "MONEY MANIA"

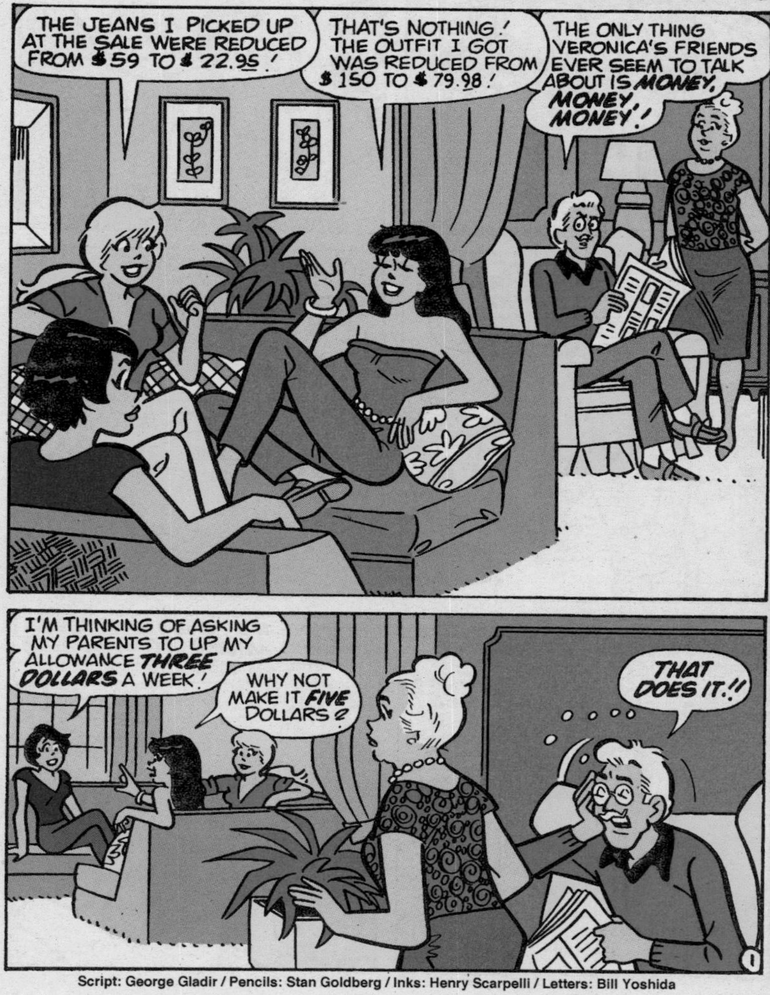
THE JEANS I PICKED UP AT THE SALE WERE REDUCED FROM $59 TO $22.95!
THAT'S NOTHING! THE OUTFIT I GOT WAS REDUCED FROM $150 TO $79.98!
THE ONLY THING VERONICA'S FRIENDS EVER SEEM TO TALK ABOUT IS MONEY, MONEY, MONEY!
I'M THINKING OF ASKING MY PARENTS TO UP MY ALLOWANCE THREE DOLLARS A WEEK!
WHY NOT MAKE IT FIVE DOLLARS?
THAT DOES IT!!
1

Script: George Gladir / Pencils: Stan Goldberg / Inks: Henry Scarpelli / Letters: Bill Yoshida

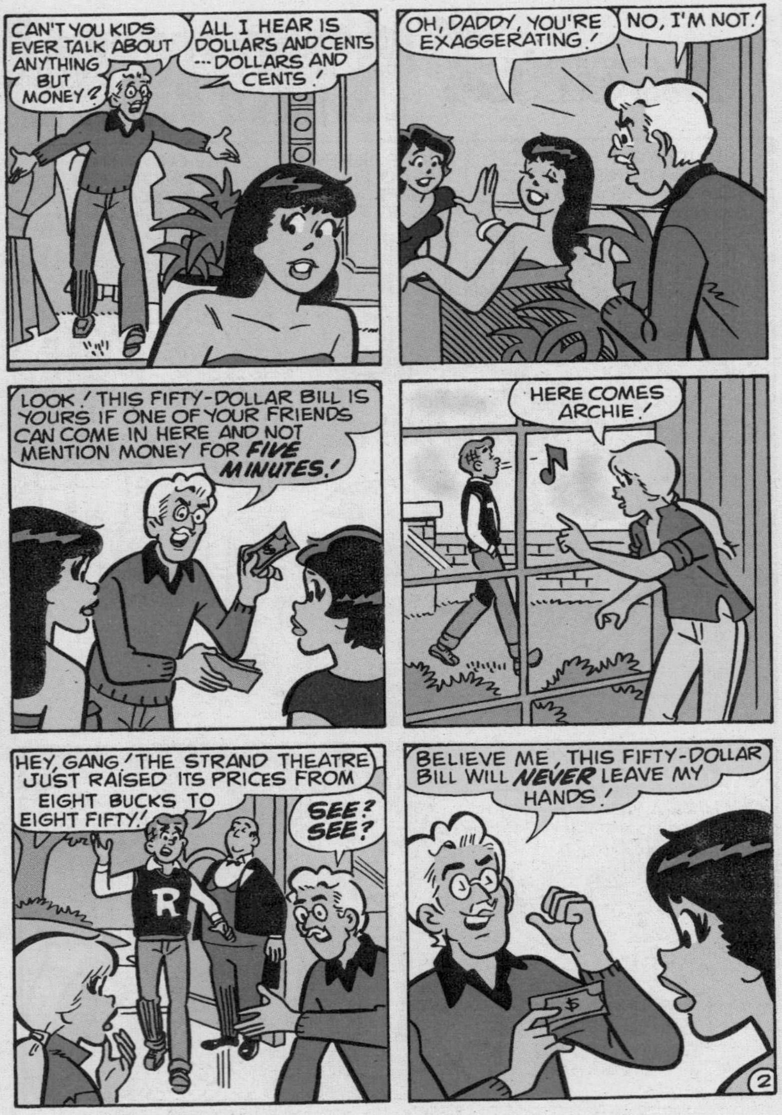

CAN'T YOU KIDS EVER TALK ABOUT ANYTHING BUT MONEY?
ALL I HEAR IS DOLLARS AND CENTS --- DOLLARS AND CENTS!
OH, DADDY, YOU'RE EXAGGERATING!
NO, I'M NOT!
LOOK! THIS FIFTY-DOLLAR BILL IS YOURS IF ONE OF YOUR FRIENDS CAN COME IN HERE AND NOT MENTION MONEY FOR FIVE MINUTES!
HERE COMES ARCHIE!
HEY, GANG! THE STRAND THEATRE JUST RAISED ITS PRICES FROM EIGHT BUCKS TO EIGHT FIFTY!
SEE? SEE?
BELIEVE ME, THIS FIFTY-DOLLAR BILL WILL NEVER LEAVE MY HANDS!
2

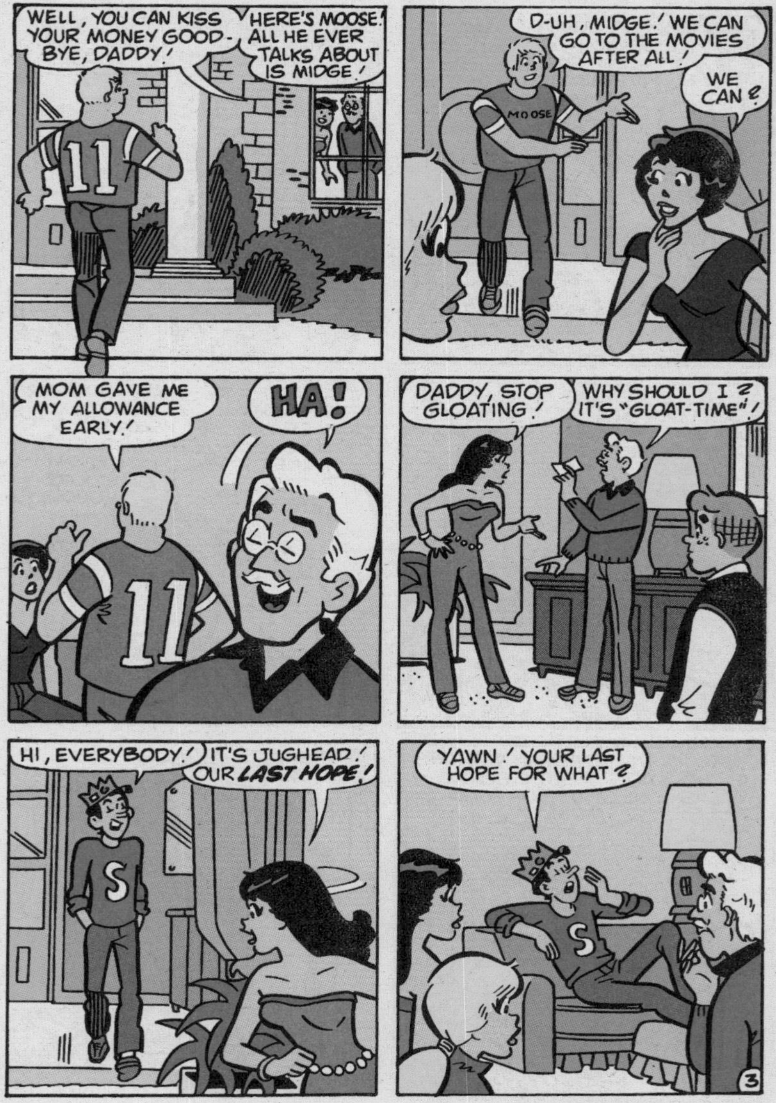
WELL, YOU CAN KISS YOUR MONEY GOOD-BYE, DADDY!
HERE'S MOOSE! ALL HE EVER TALKS ABOUT IS MIDGE!
D-UH, MIDGE! WE CAN GO TO THE MOVIES AFTER ALL!
MOOSE
WE CAN?
MOM GAVE ME MY ALLOWANCE EARLY!
HA!
DADDY, STOP GLOATING!
WHY SHOULD I? IT'S "GLOAT-TIME"!
HI, EVERYBODY!
IT'S JUGHEAD! OUR LAST HOPE!
YAWN! YOUR LAST HOPE FOR WHAT?
3

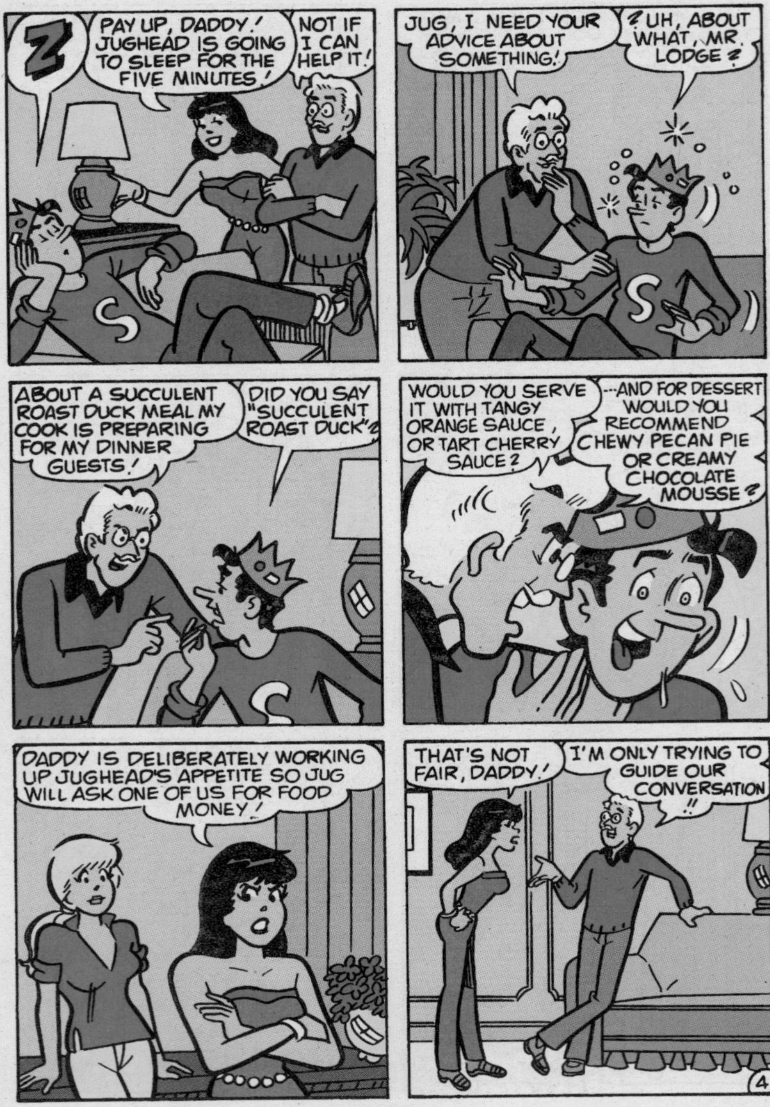

Z
PAY UP, DADDY! JUGHEAD IS GOING TO SLEEP FOR THE FIVE MINUTES!
NOT IF I CAN HELP IT!
JUG, I NEED YOUR ADVICE ABOUT SOMETHING!
? UH, ABOUT WHAT, MR. LODGE ?
ABOUT A SUCCULENT ROAST DUCK MEAL MY COOK IS PREPARING FOR MY DINNER GUESTS!
DID YOU SAY "SUCCULENT ROAST DUCK"?
WOULD YOU SERVE IT WITH TANGY ORANGE SAUCE, OR TART CHERRY SAUCE?
---AND FOR DESSERT WOULD YOU RECOMMEND CHEWY PECAN PIE OR CREAMY CHOCOLATE MOUSSE?
DADDY IS DELIBERATELY WORKING UP JUGHEAD'S APPETITE SO JUG WILL ASK ONE OF US FOR FOOD MONEY!
THAT'S NOT FAIR, DADDY!
I'M ONLY TRYING TO GUIDE OUR CONVERSATION!!
4

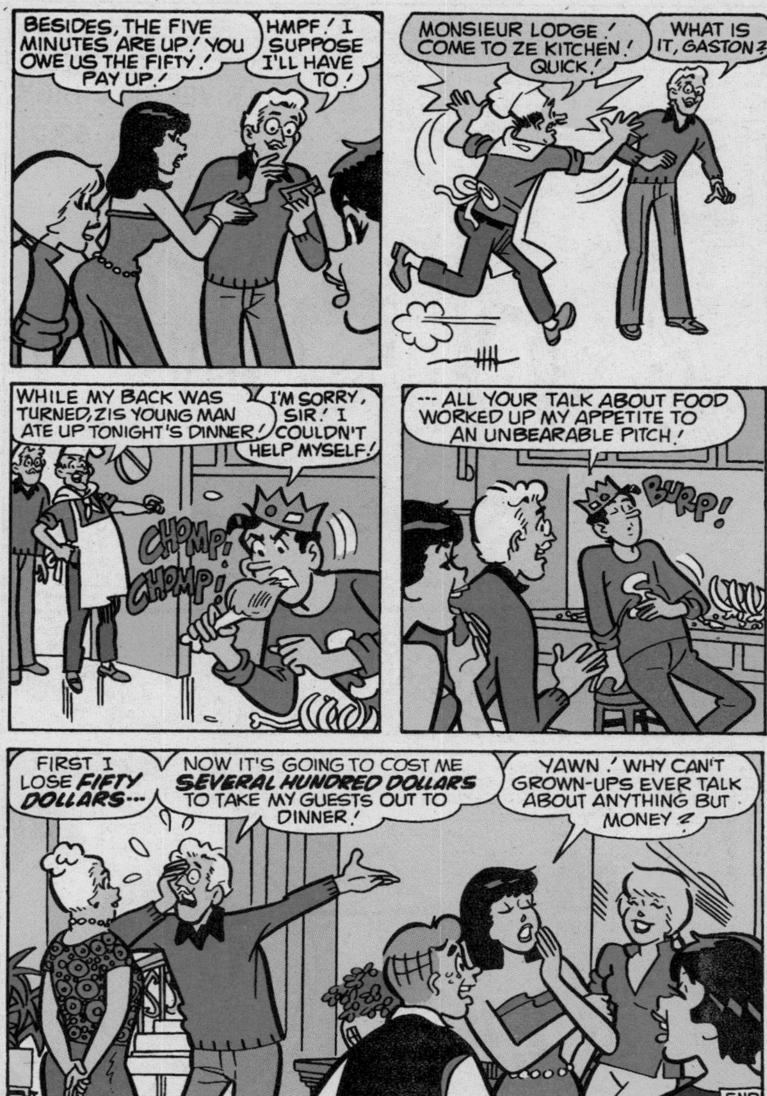
BESIDES, THE FIVE MINUTES ARE UP! YOU OWE US THE FIFTY! PAY UP!
HMPF! I SUPPOSE I'LL HAVE TO!
MONSIEUR LODGE! COME TO ZE KITCHEN! QUICK!
WHAT IS IT, GASTON?
WHILE MY BACK WAS TURNED, ZIS YOUNG MAN ATE UP TONIGHT'S DINNER!
I'M SORRY, SIR! I COULDN'T HELP MYSELF!
CHOMP! CHOMP!
--- ALL YOUR TALK ABOUT FOOD WORKED UP MY APPETITE TO AN UNBEARABLE PITCH!
BURP!
FIRST I LOSE FIFTY DOLLARS---
NOW IT'S GOING TO COST ME SEVERAL HUNDRED DOLLARS TO TAKE MY GUESTS OUT TO DINNER!
YAWN! WHY CAN'T GROWN-UPS EVER TALK ABOUT ANYTHING BUT MONEY?
END

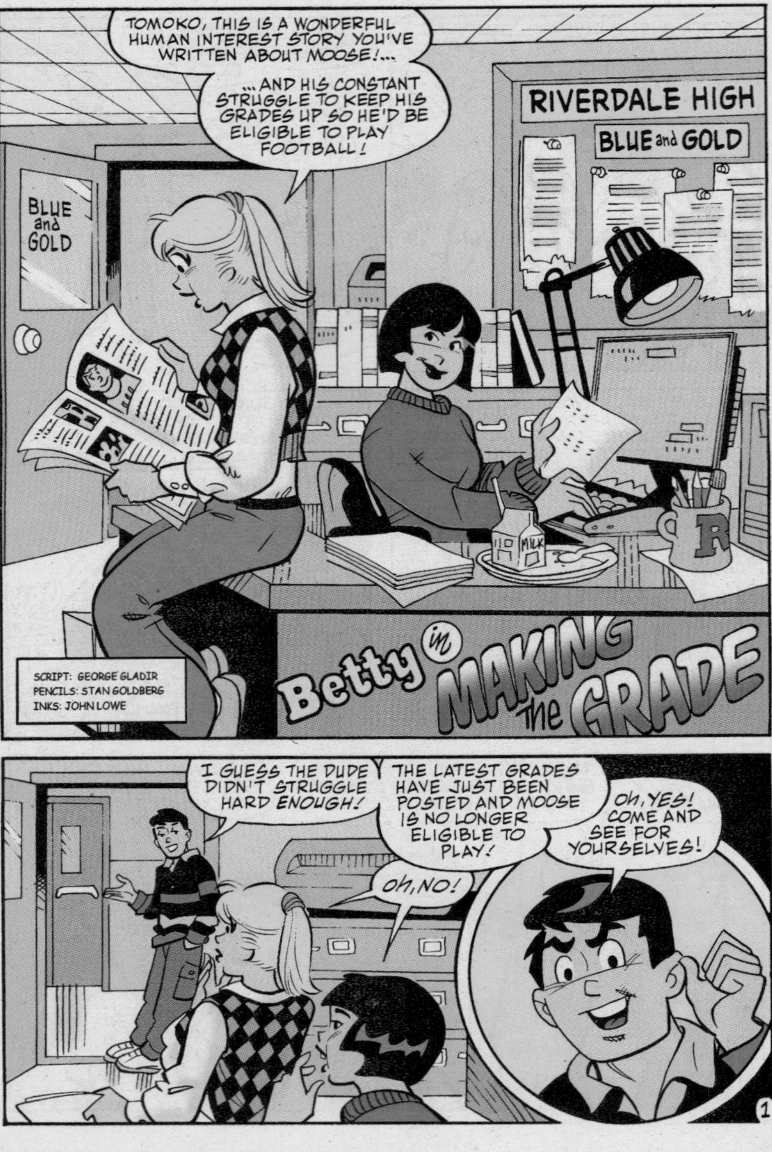
TOMOKO, THIS IS A WONDERFUL HUMAN INTEREST STORY YOU'VE WRITTEN ABOUT MOOSE!...
...AND HIS CONSTANT STRUGGLE TO KEEP HIS GRADES UP SO HE'D BE ELIGIBLE TO PLAY FOOTBALL!
RIVERDALE HIGH
BLUE and GOLD
BLUE and GOLD
MILK
R
Betty in MAKING the GRADE
SCRIPT: GEORGE GLADIR
PENCILS: STAN GOLDBERG
INKS: JOHN LOWE
I GUESS THE DUDE DIDN'T STRUGGLE HARD ENOUGH!
THE LATEST GRADES HAVE JUST BEEN POSTED AND MOOSE IS NO LONGER ELIGIBLE TO PLAY!
OH, NO!
OH, YES! COME AND SEE FOR YOURSELVES!

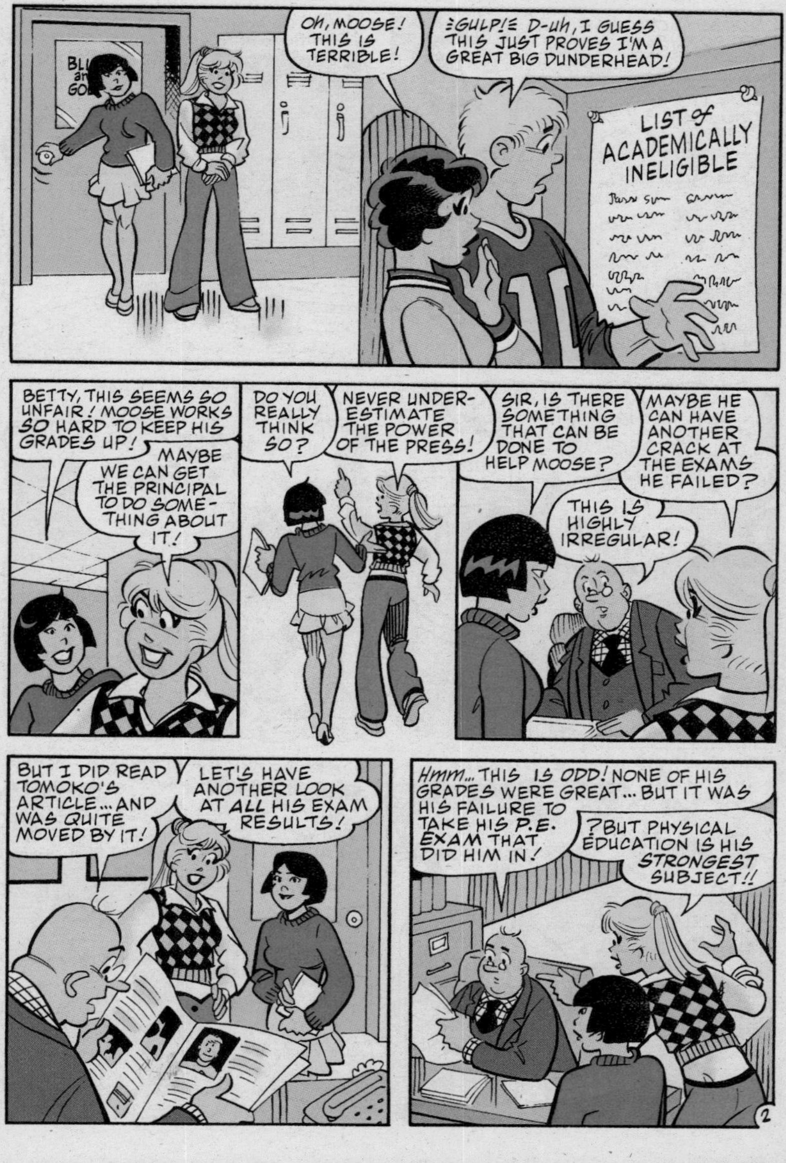

OH, MOOSE! THIS IS TERRIBLE!
GULP! D-uh, I GUESS THIS JUST PROVES I'M A GREAT BIG DUNDERHEAD!
LIST of ACADEMICALLY INELIGIBLE
BETTY, THIS SEEMS SO UNFAIR! MOOSE WORKS SO HARD TO KEEP HIS GRADES UP!
MAYBE WE CAN GET THE PRINCIPAL TO DO SOMETHING ABOUT IT!
DO YOU REALLY THINK SO?
NEVER UNDERESTIMATE THE POWER OF THE PRESS!
SIR, IS THERE SOMETHING THAT CAN BE DONE TO HELP MOOSE?
MAYBE HE CAN HAVE ANOTHER CRACK AT THE EXAMS HE FAILED?
THIS IS HIGHLY IRREGULAR!
BUT I DID READ TOMOKO'S ARTICLE... AND WAS QUITE MOVED BY IT!
LET'S HAVE ANOTHER LOOK AT ALL HIS EXAM RESULTS!
Hmm... THIS IS ODD! NONE OF HIS GRADES WERE GREAT... BUT IT WAS HIS FAILURE TO TAKE HIS P.E. EXAM THAT DID HIM IN!
?BUT PHYSICAL EDUCATION IS HIS STRONGEST SUBJECT!!
2

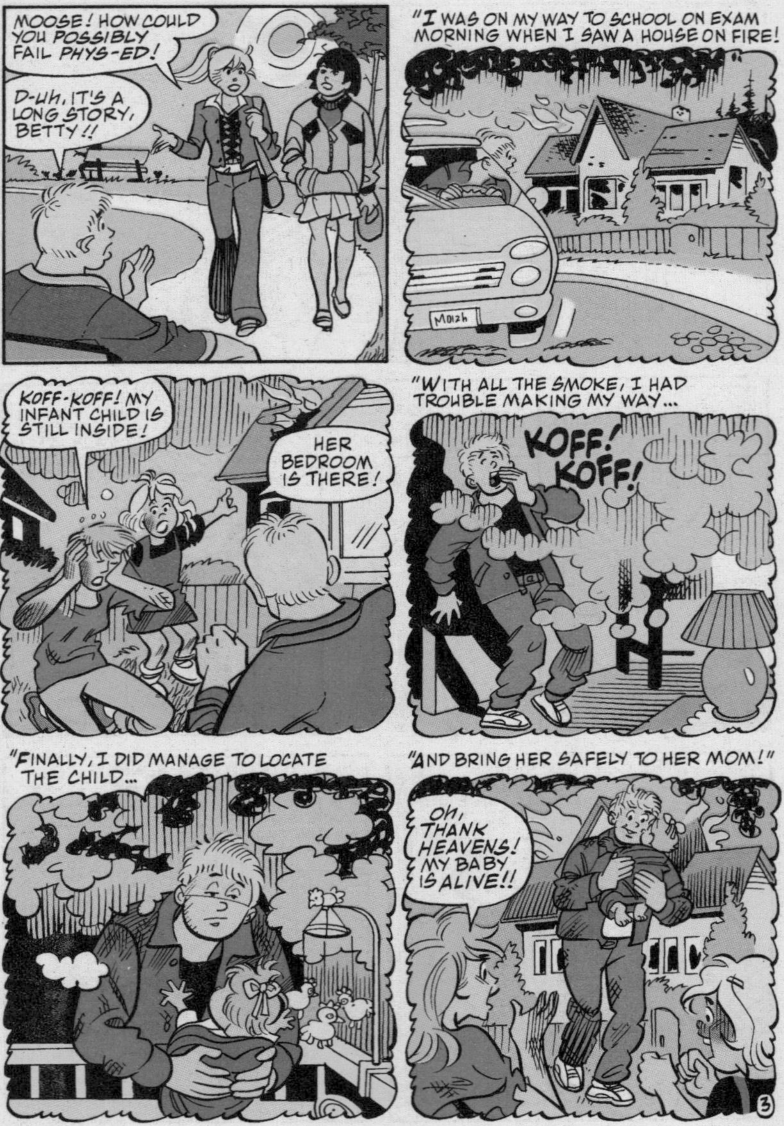
MOOSE! HOW COULD YOU POSSIBLY FAIL PHYS-ED!
D-UH, IT'S A LONG STORY, BETTY!!
"I WAS ON MY WAY TO SCHOOL ON EXAM MORNING WHEN I SAW A HOUSE ON FIRE!
MOOSE
KOFF-KOFF! MY INFANT CHILD IS STILL INSIDE!
HER BEDROOM IS THERE!
"WITH ALL THE SMOKE, I HAD TROUBLE MAKING MY WAY...
KOFF! KOFF!
"FINALLY, I DID MANAGE TO LOCATE THE CHILD...
"AND BRING HER SAFELY TO HER MOM!"
OH, THANK HEAVENS! MY BABY IS ALIVE!!
3

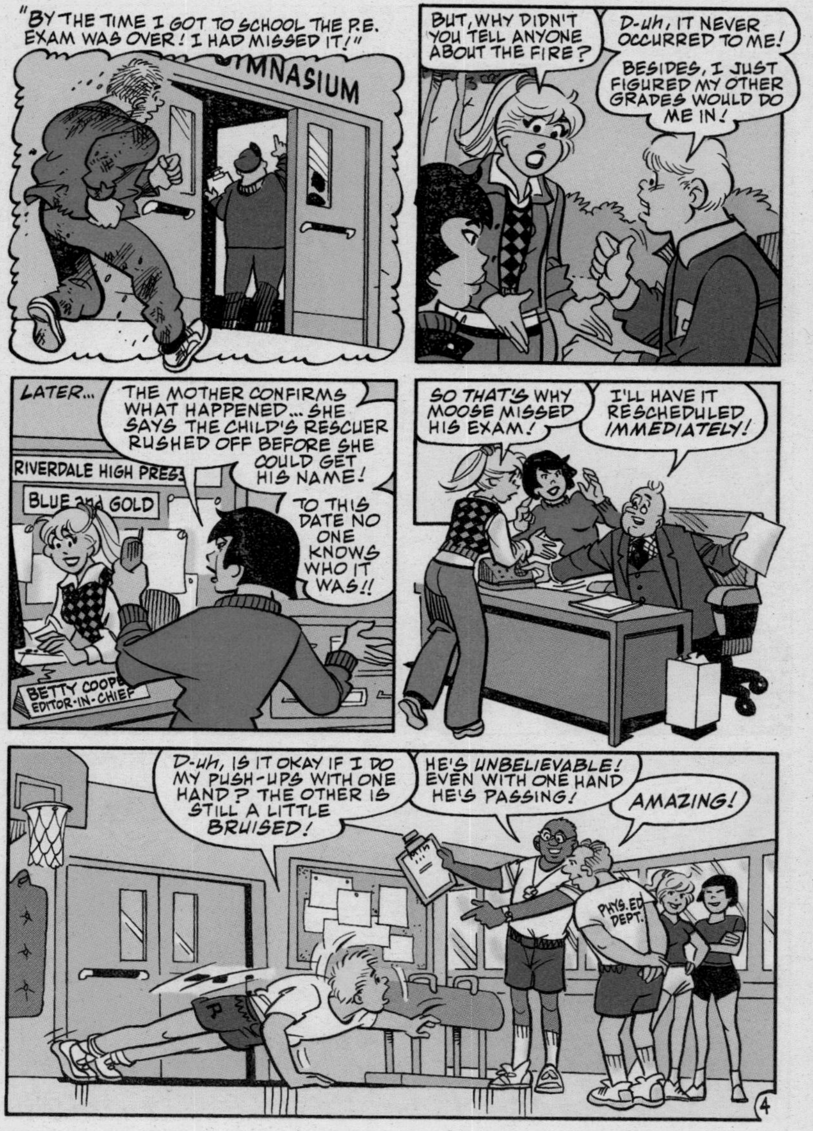

"BY THE TIME I GOT TO SCHOOL THE P.E. EXAM WAS OVER! I HAD MISSED IT!"
GYMNASIUM
BUT, WHY DIDN'T YOU TELL ANYONE ABOUT THE FIRE?
D-uh, IT NEVER OCCURRED TO ME!
BESIDES, I JUST FIGURED MY OTHER GRADES WOULD DO ME IN!
LATER...
THE MOTHER CONFIRMS WHAT HAPPENED... SHE SAYS THE CHILD'S RESCUER RUSHED OFF BEFORE SHE COULD GET HIS NAME!
TO THIS DATE NO ONE KNOWS WHO IT WAS!!
RIVERDALE HIGH PRESS
BLUE and GOLD
BETTY COOPER EDITOR-IN-CHIEF
SO THAT'S WHY MOOSE MISSED HIS EXAM!
I'LL HAVE IT RESCHEDULED IMMEDIATELY!
D-uh, IS IT OKAY IF I DO MY PUSH-UPS WITH ONE HAND? THE OTHER IS STILL A LITTLE BRUISED!
HE'S UNBELIEVABLE! EVEN WITH ONE HAND HE'S PASSING!
AMAZING!
PHYS. ED DEPT.

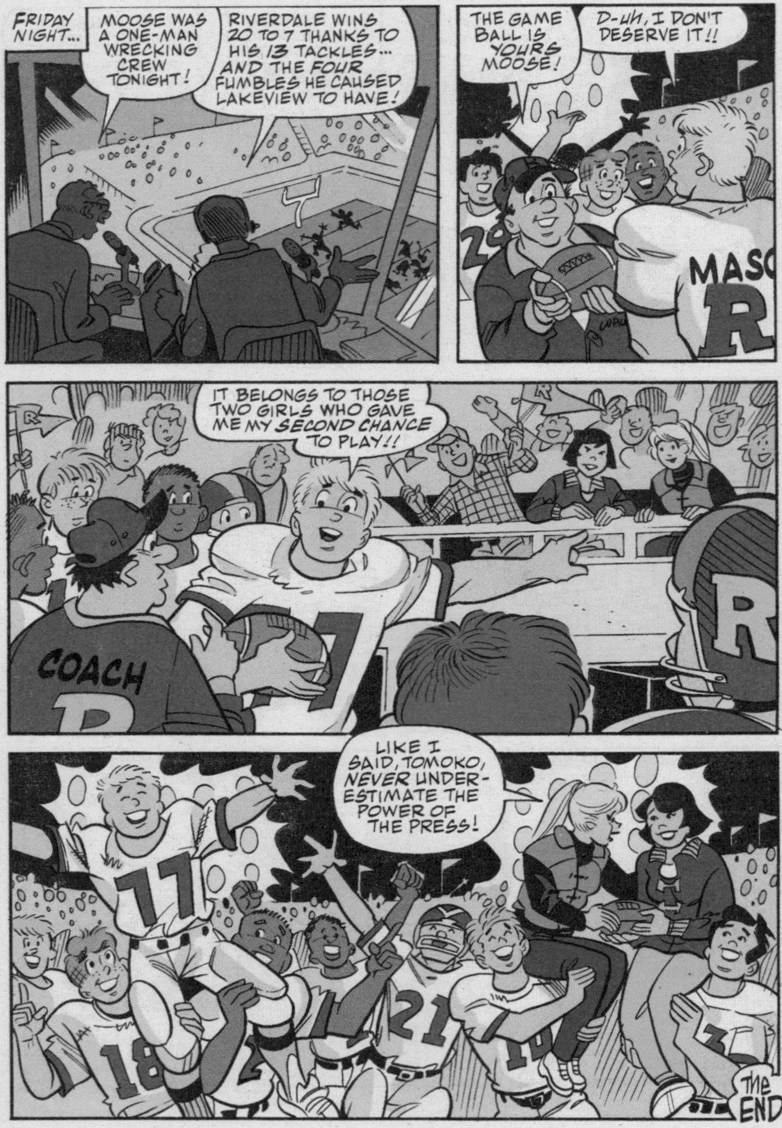
FRIDAY NIGHT...
MOOSE WAS A ONE-MAN WRECKING CREW TONIGHT!
RIVERDALE WINS 20 TO 7 THANKS TO HIS 13 TACKLES... AND THE FOUR FUMBLES HE CAUSED LAKEVIEW TO HAVE!
THE GAME BALL IS YOURS MOOSE!
D-UH, I DON'T DESERVE IT!!
MASC
IT BELONGS TO THOSE TWO GIRLS WHO GAVE ME MY SECOND CHANCE TO PLAY!!
COACH
LIKE I SAID, TOMOKO, NEVER UNDER-ESTIMATE THE POWER OF THE PRESS!
THE END

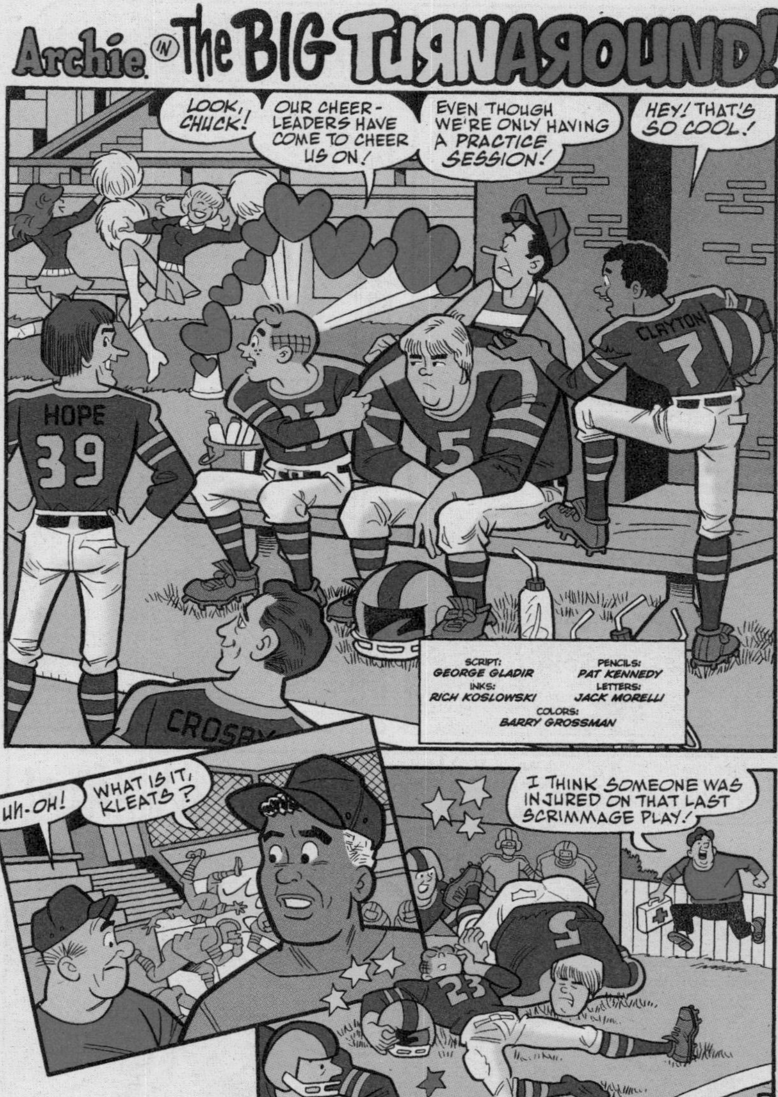
Archie in The BIG TURNAROUND!
LOOK, CHUCK!
OUR CHEER-LEADERS HAVE COME TO CHEER US ON!
EVEN THOUGH WE'RE ONLY HAVING A PRACTICE SESSION!
HEY! THAT'S SO COOL!
HOPE 39
CLAYTON 7
CROSBY
SCRIPT: GEORGE GLADIR
PENCILS: PAT KENNEDY
INKS: RICH KOSLOWSKI
LETTERS: JACK MORELLI
COLORS: BARRY GROSSMAN
UH-OH!
WHAT IS IT, KLEATS?
I THINK SOMEONE WAS INJURED ON THAT LAST SCRIMMAGE PLAY!

WHAT'S WRONG, ARCHIE?

I THINK I SPRAINED MY WRIST!

IT SHOULD BE OKAY BY FRIDAY WHEN WE PLAY CLOVER HIGH!

NO! WE CAN'T RISK FURTHER INJURY BY HAVING YOU PLAY SO SOON!

BESIDES, CLOVER SHOULD BE A PUSHOVER!

IT'S THE FOLLOWING WEEK'S GAME AGAINST POWERHOUSE CENTRAL WHEN WE REALLY NEED YOU AT QUARTERBACK!

YEAH, YOUR WRIST SHOULD BE OKAY BY THEN!

HERE COMES WEATHERBEE!

NO DOUBT TO REMIND US WHAT A STAR PLAYER HE WAS WHEN HE PLAYED FOR RIVERDALE! AGAIN!

GENTLEMEN, I BRING YOU SAD TIDINGS!

NO! IS BEAZLY SERVING LIVER AGAIN?! AGHK!

BECAUSE OF ACADEMIC DEFICIENCIES, MOOSE WILL NOT BE ALLOWED TO PLAY!

WHAT?!

Z

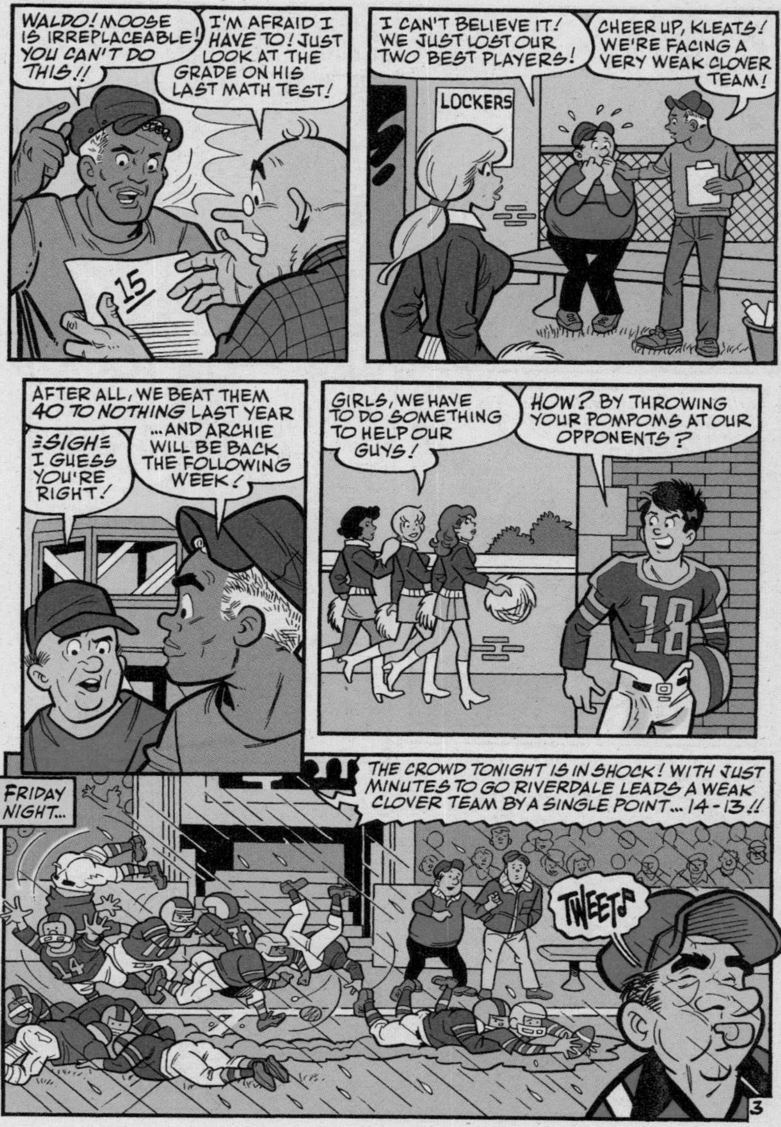

WALDO! MOOSE IS IRREPLACEABLE! YOU CAN'T DO THIS!!
I'M AFRAID I HAVE TO! JUST LOOK AT THE GRADE ON HIS LAST MATH TEST!
15
I CAN'T BELIEVE IT! WE JUST LOST OUR TWO BEST PLAYERS!
LOCKERS
CHEER UP, KLEATS! WE'RE FACING A VERY WEAK CLOVER TEAM!
AFTER ALL, WE BEAT THEM 40 TO NOTHING LAST YEAR ...AND ARCHIE WILL BE BACK THE FOLLOWING WEEK!
SIGH I GUESS YOU'RE RIGHT!
GIRLS, WE HAVE TO DO SOMETHING TO HELP OUR GUYS!
HOW? BY THROWING YOUR POMPOMS AT OUR OPPONENTS?
18
FRIDAY NIGHT...
THE CROWD TONIGHT IS IN SHOCK! WITH JUST MINUTES TO GO RIVERDALE LEADS A WEAK CLOVER TEAM BY A SINGLE POINT... 14-13!!
TWEET

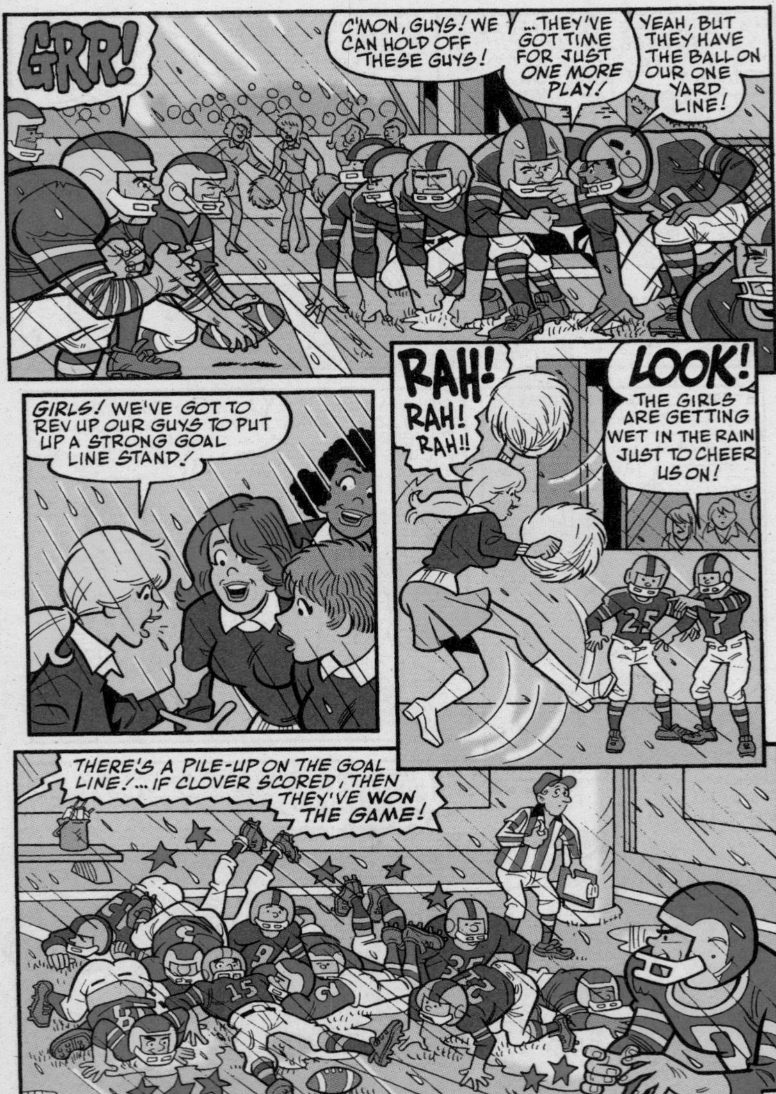
GRR!
C'MON, GUYS! WE CAN HOLD OFF THESE GUYS!
...THEY'VE GOT TIME FOR JUST ONE MORE PLAY!
YEAH, BUT THEY HAVE THE BALL ON OUR ONE YARD LINE!
GIRLS! WE'VE GOT TO REV UP OUR GUYS TO PUT UP A STRONG GOAL LINE STAND!
RAH! RAH! RAH!!
LOOK! THE GIRLS ARE GETTING WET IN THE RAIN JUST TO CHEER US ON!
THERE'S A PILE-UP ON THE GOAL LINE! ...IF CLOVER SCORED, THEN THEY'VE WON THE GAME!
4

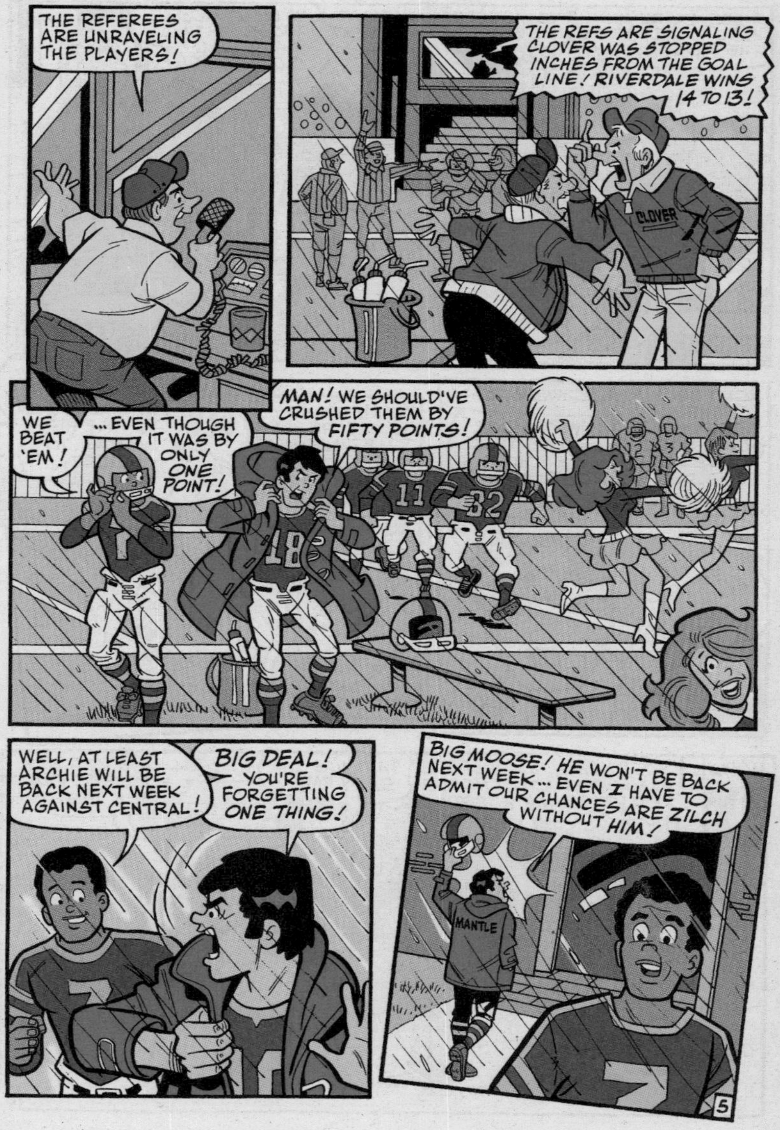
THE REFEREES ARE UNRAVELING THE PLAYERS!
THE REFS ARE SIGNALING CLOVER WAS STOPPED INCHES FROM THE GOAL LINE! RIVERDALE WINS 14 TO 13!
CLOVER
WE BEAT 'EM!
...EVEN THOUGH IT WAS BY ONLY ONE POINT!
MAN! WE SHOULD'VE CRUSHED THEM BY FIFTY POINTS!
WELL, AT LEAST ARCHIE WILL BE BACK NEXT WEEK AGAINST CENTRAL!
BIG DEAL! YOU'RE FORGETTING ONE THING!
BIG MOOSE! HE WON'T BE BACK NEXT WEEK... EVEN I HAVE TO ADMIT OUR CHANCES ARE ZILCH WITHOUT HIM!
MANTLE

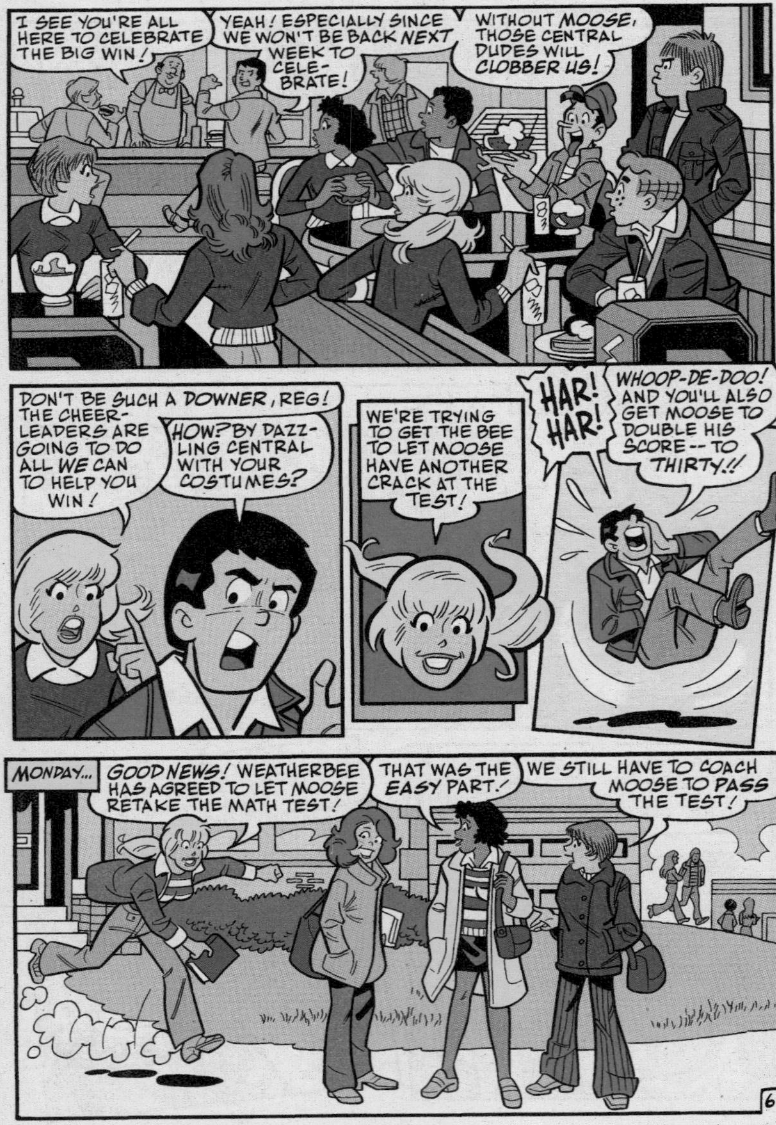

I SEE YOU'RE ALL HERE TO CELEBRATE THE BIG WIN!
YEAH! ESPECIALLY SINCE WE WON'T BE BACK NEXT WEEK TO CELE-BRATE!
WITHOUT MOOSE, THOSE CENTRAL DUDES WILL CLOBBER US!
DON'T BE SUCH A DOWNER, REG! THE CHEER-LEADERS ARE GOING TO DO ALL WE CAN TO HELP YOU WIN!
HOW? BY DAZZ-LING CENTRAL WITH YOUR COSTUMES?
WE'RE TRYING TO GET THE BEE TO LET MOOSE HAVE ANOTHER CRACK AT THE TEST!
HAR! HAR!
WHOOP-DE-DOO! AND YOU'LL ALSO GET MOOSE TO DOUBLE HIS SCORE -- TO THIRTY!!
MONDAY...
GOOD NEWS! WEATHERBEE HAS AGREED TO LET MOOSE RETAKE THE MATH TEST!
THAT WAS THE EASY PART!
WE STILL HAVE TO COACH MOOSE TO PASS THE TEST!
6

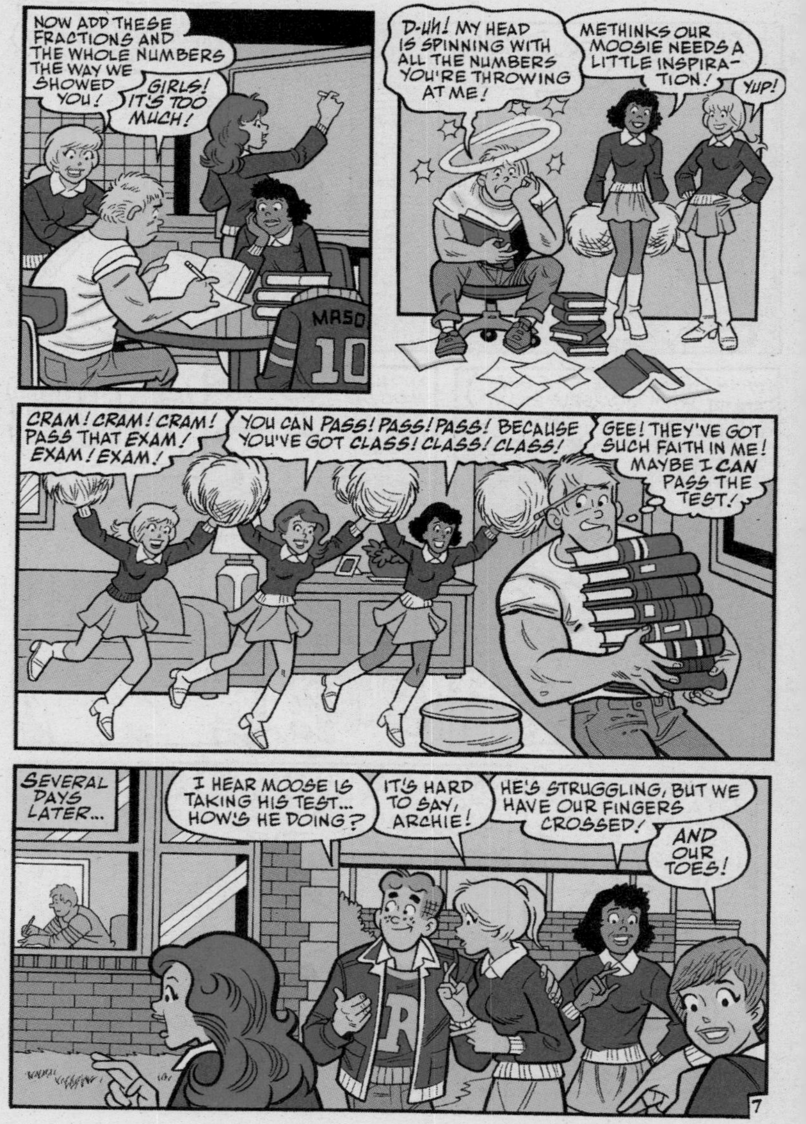
NOW ADD THESE FRACTIONS AND THE WHOLE NUMBERS THE WAY WE SHOWED YOU!
GIRLS! IT'S TOO MUCH!
MASO 10
D-UH! MY HEAD IS SPINNING WITH ALL THE NUMBERS YOU'RE THROWING AT ME!
METHINKS OUR MOOSIE NEEDS A LITTLE INSPIRA-TION!
YUP!
CRAM! CRAM! CRAM! PASS THAT EXAM! EXAM! EXAM!
YOU CAN PASS! PASS! PASS! BECAUSE YOU'VE GOT CLASS! CLASS! CLASS!
GEE! THEY'VE GOT SUCH FAITH IN ME! MAYBE I CAN PASS THE TEST!
SEVERAL DAYS LATER...
I HEAR MOOSE IS TAKING HIS TEST... HOW'S HE DOING?
IT'S HARD TO SAY, ARCHIE!
HE'S STRUGGLING, BUT WE HAVE OUR FINGERS CROSSED!
AND OUR TOES!

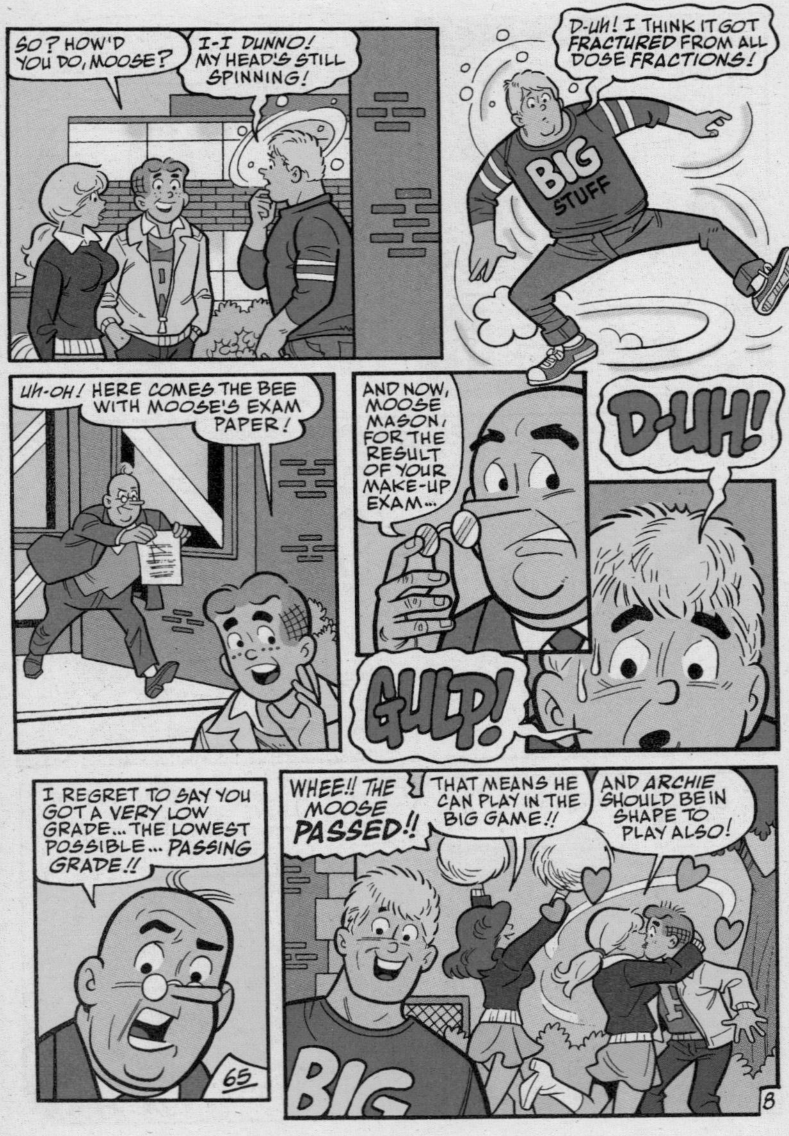
SO? HOW'D YOU DO, MOOSE?
I-I DUNNO! MY HEAD'S STILL SPINNING!
D-UH! I THINK IT GOT FRACTURED FROM ALL DOSE FRACTIONS!
BIG STUFF
UH-OH! HERE COMES THE BEE WITH MOOSE'S EXAM PAPER!
AND NOW, MOOSE MASON, FOR THE RESULT OF YOUR MAKE-UP EXAM...
D-UH!
GULP!
I REGRET TO SAY YOU GOT A VERY LOW GRADE... THE LOWEST POSSIBLE... PASSING GRADE!!
WHEE!! THE MOOSE PASSED!!
THAT MEANS HE CAN PLAY IN THE BIG GAME!!
AND ARCHIE SHOULD BE IN SHAPE TO PLAY ALSO!
BIG
65
8

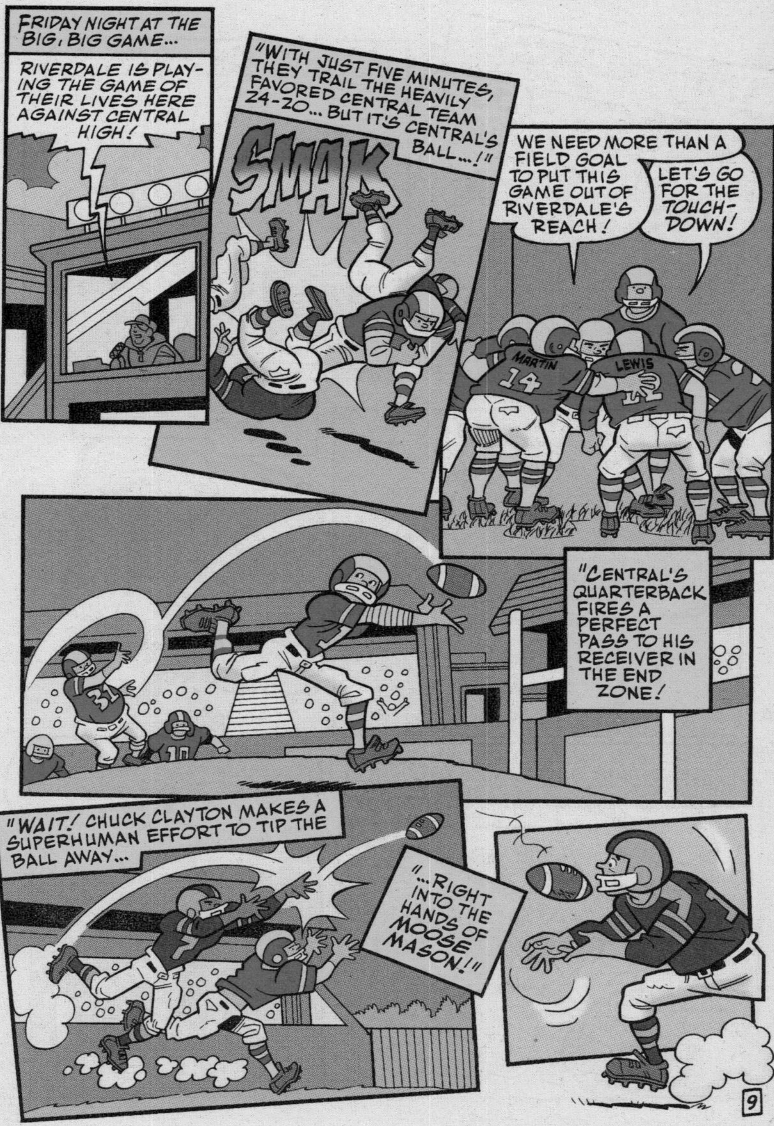

FRIDAY NIGHT AT THE BIG, BIG GAME...
RIVERDALE IS PLAYING THE GAME OF THEIR LIVES HERE AGAINST CENTRAL HIGH!
"WITH JUST FIVE MINUTES, THEY TRAIL THE HEAVILY FAVORED CENTRAL TEAM 24-20... BUT IT'S CENTRAL'S BALL...!"
SMAK
WE NEED MORE THAN A FIELD GOAL TO PUT THIS GAME OUT OF RIVERDALE'S REACH!
LET'S GO FOR THE TOUCH-DOWN!
MARTIN
14
LEWIS
12
"CENTRAL'S QUARTERBACK FIRES A PERFECT PASS TO HIS RECEIVER IN THE END ZONE!
"WAIT! CHUCK CLAYTON MAKES A SUPERHUMAN EFFORT TO TIP THE BALL AWAY...
"...RIGHT INTO THE HANDS OF MOOSE MASON!"

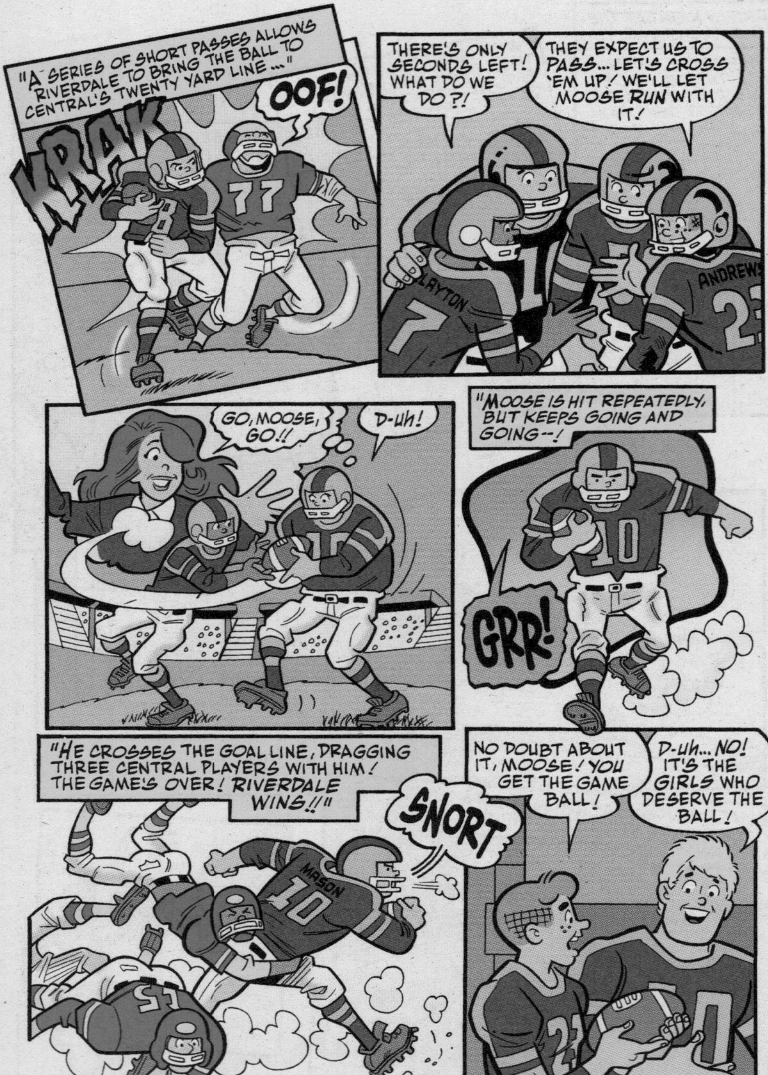
"A SERIES OF SHORT PASSES ALLOWS RIVERDALE TO BRING THE BALL TO CENTRAL'S TWENTY YARD LINE ..."
KRAK
OOF!
THERE'S ONLY SECONDS LEFT! WHAT DO WE DO?!
THEY EXPECT US TO PASS... LET'S CROSS 'EM UP! WE'LL LET MOOSE RUN WITH IT!
GO, MOOSE, GO!!
D-uh!
"MOOSE IS HIT REPEATEDLY, BUT KEEPS GOING AND GOING--!
GRR!
"HE CROSSES THE GOAL LINE, DRAGGING THREE CENTRAL PLAYERS WITH HIM! THE GAME'S OVER! RIVERDALE WINS!!"
SNORT
NO DOUBT ABOUT IT, MOOSE! YOU GET THE GAME BALL!
D-uh... NO! IT'S THE GIRLS WHO DESERVE THE BALL!

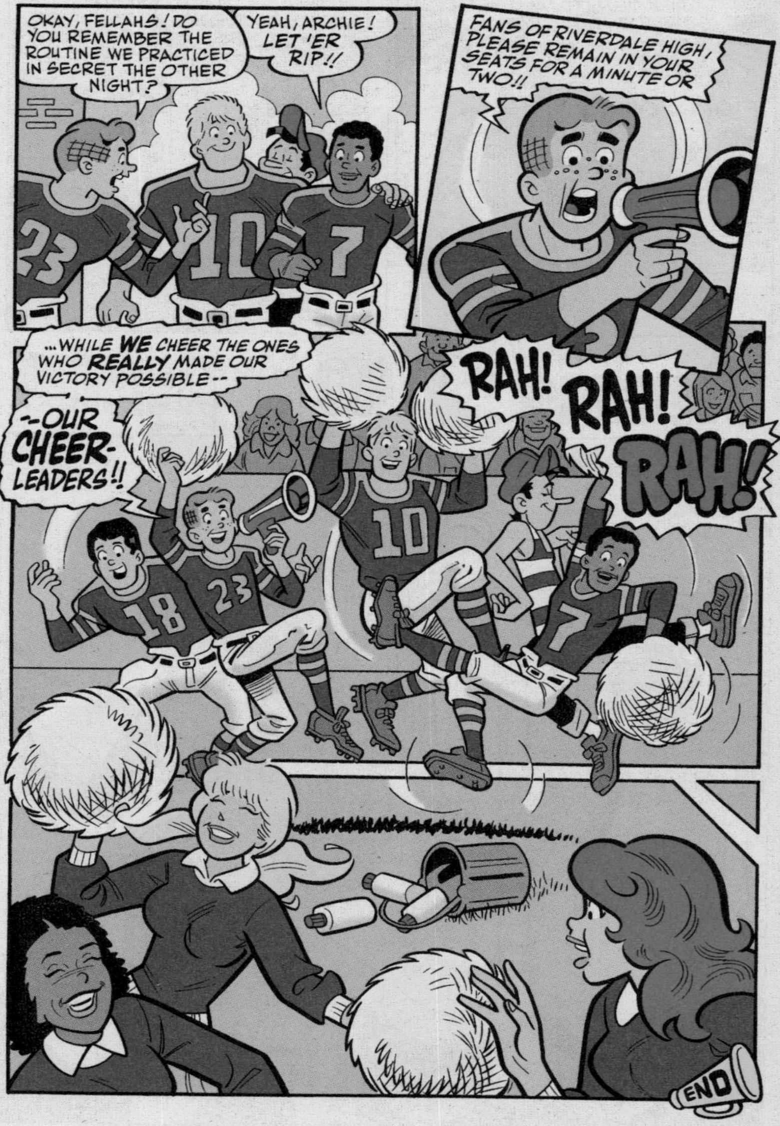
OKAY, FELLAHS! DO YOU REMEMBER THE ROUTINE WE PRACTICED IN SECRET THE OTHER NIGHT?
YEAH, ARCHIE! LET 'ER RIP!!
FANS OF RIVERDALE HIGH, PLEASE REMAIN IN YOUR SEATS FOR A MINUTE OR TWO!!
...WHILE WE CHEER THE ONES WHO REALLY MADE OUR VICTORY POSSIBLE--
--OUR CHEER-LEADERS!!
RAH! RAH! RAH!
END

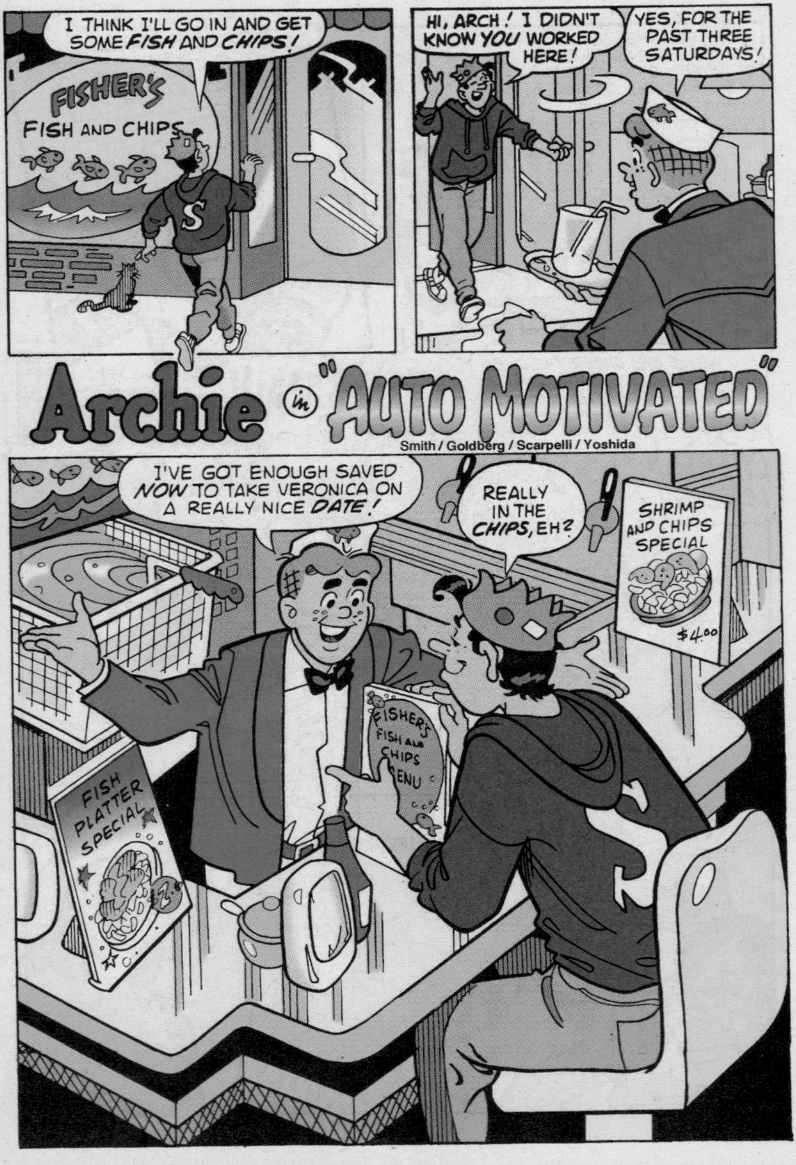
I THINK I'LL GO IN AND GET SOME FISH AND CHIPS!
FISHER'S
FISH AND CHIPS
HI, ARCH! I DIDN'T KNOW YOU WORKED HERE!
YES, FOR THE PAST THREE SATURDAYS!
Archie in "AUTO MOTIVATED"
Smith / Goldberg / Scarpelli / Yoshida
I'VE GOT ENOUGH SAVED NOW TO TAKE VERONICA ON A REALLY NICE DATE!
REALLY IN THE CHIPS, EH?
SHRIMP AND CHIPS SPECIAL
$4.00
FISHER'S FISH AND CHIPS MENU
FISH PLATTER SPECIAL

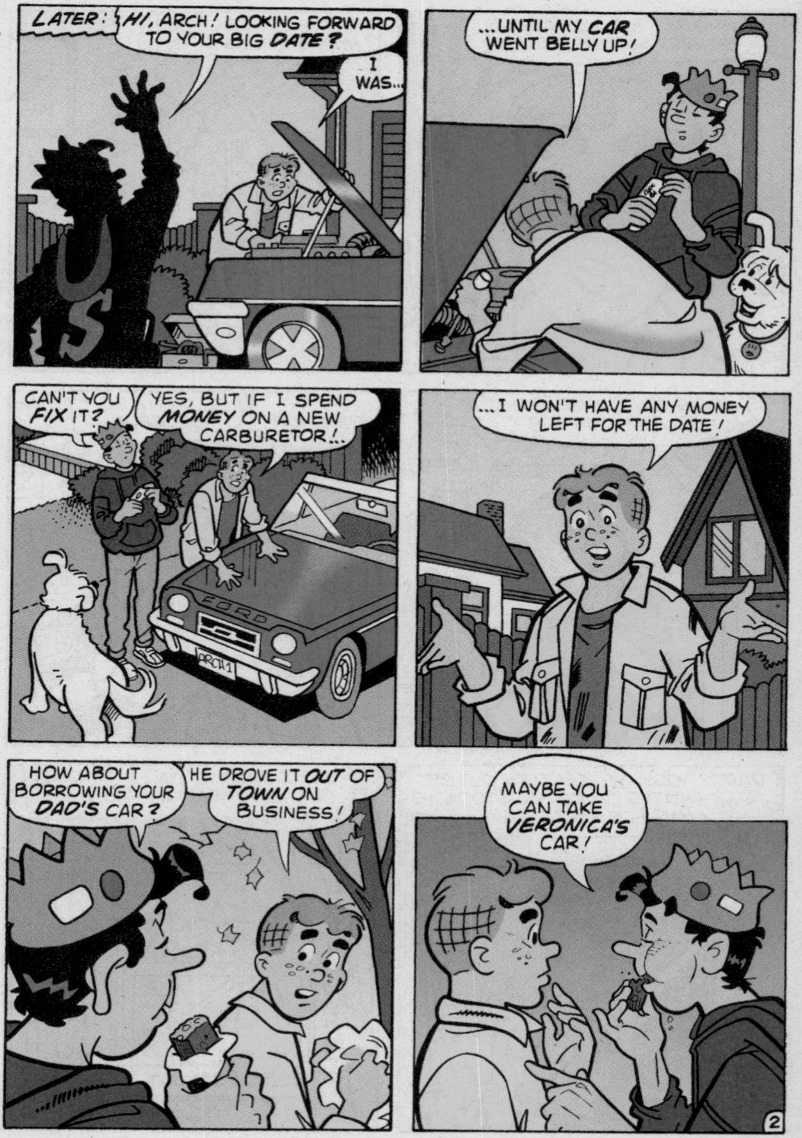

LATER:
HI, ARCH! LOOKING FORWARD TO YOUR BIG DATE?
I WAS...
...UNTIL MY CAR WENT BELLY UP!
CAN'T YOU FIX IT?
YES, BUT IF I SPEND MONEY ON A NEW CARBURETOR!..
FORD
ARCH 1
...I WON'T HAVE ANY MONEY LEFT FOR THE DATE!
HOW ABOUT BORROWING YOUR DAD'S CAR?
HE DROVE IT OUT OF TOWN ON BUSINESS!
MAYBE YOU CAN TAKE VERONICA'S CAR!
2

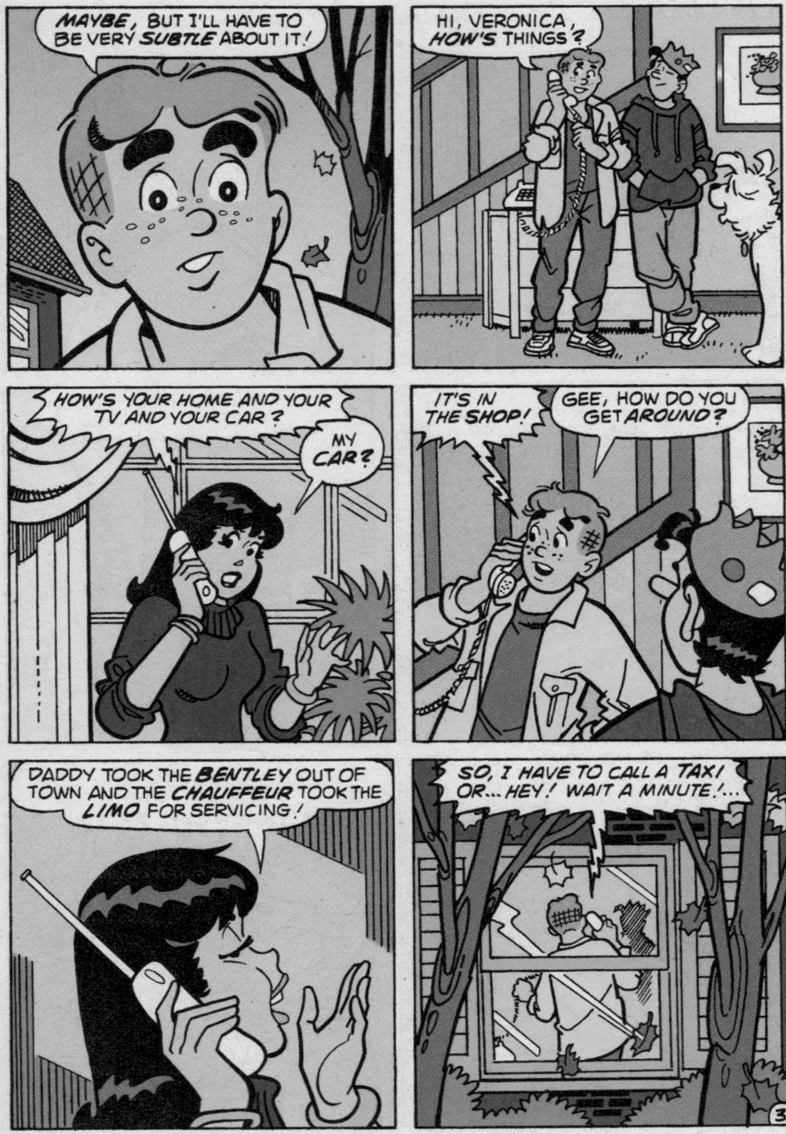
MAYBE, BUT I'LL HAVE TO BE VERY SUBTLE ABOUT IT!
HI, VERONICA, HOW'S THINGS?
HOW'S YOUR HOME AND YOUR TV AND YOUR CAR?
MY CAR?
IT'S IN THE SHOP!
GEE, HOW DO YOU GET AROUND?
DADDY TOOK THE BENTLEY OUT OF TOWN AND THE CHAUFFEUR TOOK THE LIMO FOR SERVICING!
SO, I HAVE TO CALL A TAXI OR... HEY! WAIT A MINUTE!...
3

IS THERE SOMETHING WRONG WITH *YOUR* CAR?

MY CAR...ER... NO... NOT A *THING!*

WHAT DID SHE *SAY?*

SHE SAYS SHE HAS TO TRAVEL BY *TAXI!*

I CAN'T AFFORD THAT OR TO RENT A *CAR!*

THEN I GUESS HIRING A *LIMO* IS DEFINITELY OUT!

LATER... YOU LOOK DEPRESSED, ARCHIE! WHAT'S WRONG?

FISH & CHIPS (L) LOBST SHRIMP PLATTER (L) TUNA

I HAVE A BIG PROBLEM, MR. FISHER!

FISH PLATTER SPECIAL!

I NEED A *CAR* FOR *TONIGHT,* I CAN'T AFFORD TO FIX MINE, I CAN'T BORROW ONE...

FISHER'S FISH AND CHIPS

AND I CAN'T AFFORD TO *RENT* ONE!

NO *PROBLEM!*

SHR ROLL

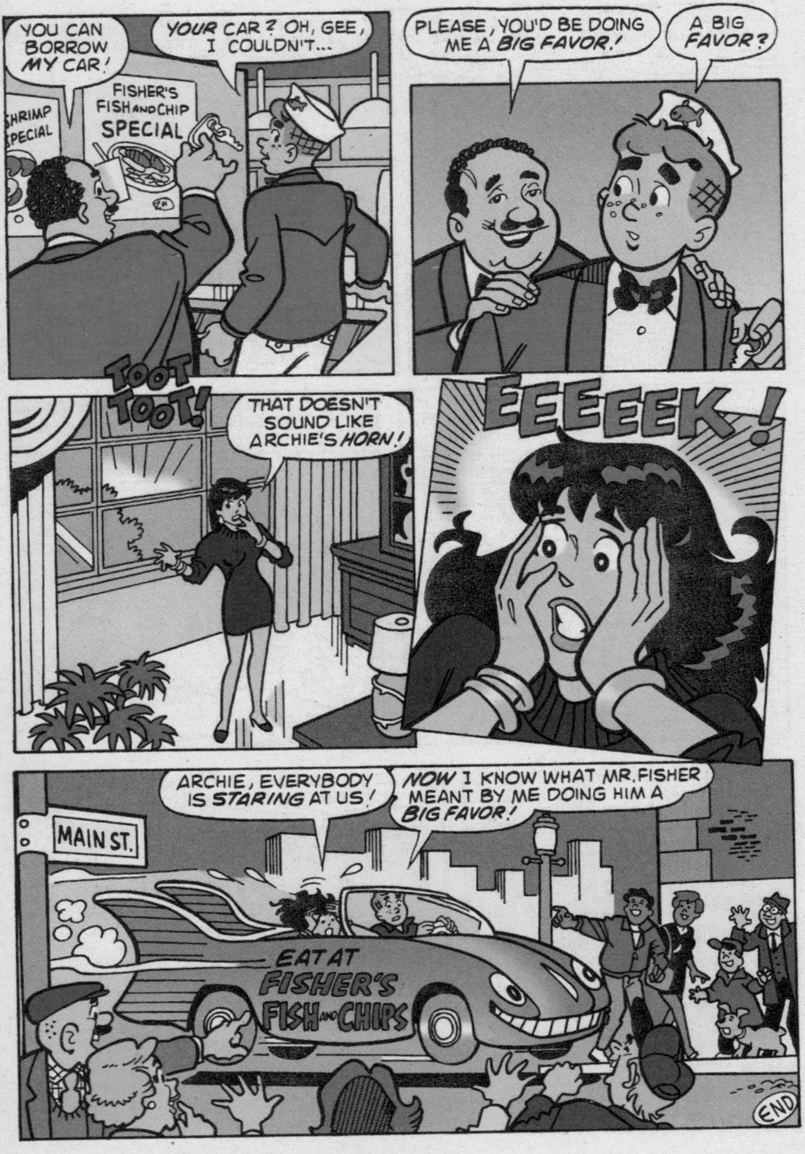
YOU CAN BORROW MY CAR!
YOUR CAR? OH, GEE, I COULDN'T...
SHRIMP SPECIAL
FISHER'S FISH AND CHIP SPECIAL
PLEASE, YOU'D BE DOING ME A BIG FAVOR!
A BIG FAVOR?
TOOT TOOT!
THAT DOESN'T SOUND LIKE ARCHIE'S HORN!
EEEEEK!
ARCHIE, EVERYBODY IS STARING AT US!
NOW I KNOW WHAT MR. FISHER MEANT BY ME DOING HIM A BIG FAVOR!
MAIN ST.
EAT AT FISHER'S FISH AND CHIPS
END

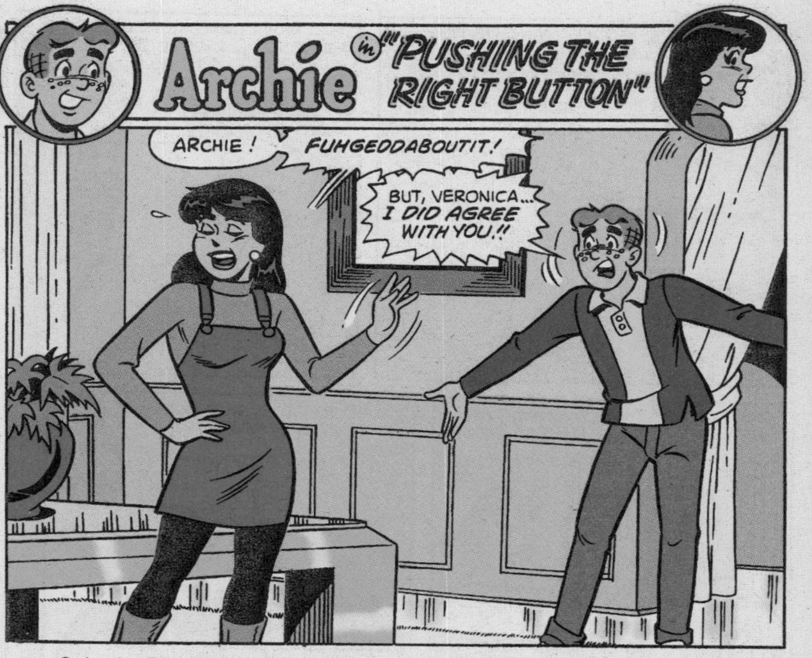
Archie in "PUSHING THE RIGHT BUTTON"
ARCHIE! FUHGEDDABOUTIT!
BUT, VERONICA... I DID AGREE WITH YOU!!

Script: Joe Edwards / Pencils: Fernando Ruiz / Inks: Jon D'Agostino / Letters: Bill Yoshida

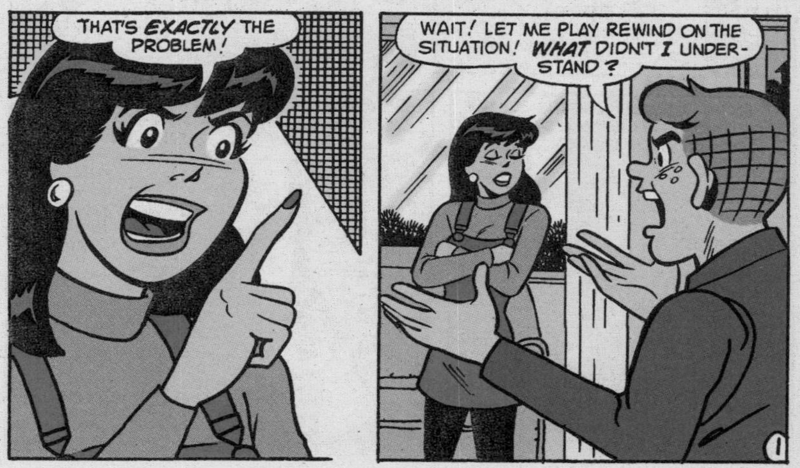
THAT'S EXACTLY THE PROBLEM!
WAIT! LET ME PLAY REWIND ON THE SITUATION! WHAT DIDN'T I UNDER-STAND?
1

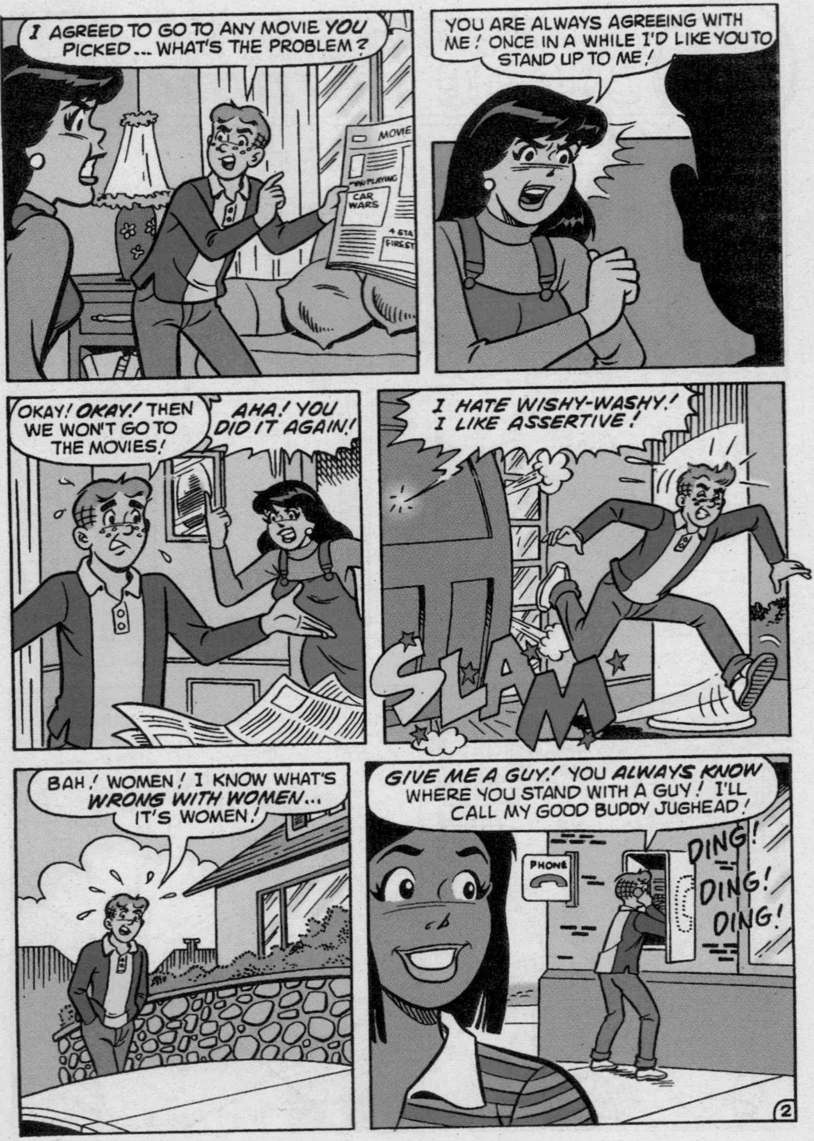
I AGREED TO GO TO ANY MOVIE YOU PICKED... WHAT'S THE PROBLEM?
MOVIE
NOW PLAYING
CAR WARS
YOU ARE ALWAYS AGREEING WITH ME! ONCE IN A WHILE I'D LIKE YOU TO STAND UP TO ME!
OKAY! OKAY! THEN WE WON'T GO TO THE MOVIES!
AHA! YOU DID IT AGAIN!
I HATE WISHY-WASHY! I LIKE ASSERTIVE!
SLAM
BAH! WOMEN! I KNOW WHAT'S WRONG WITH WOMEN... IT'S WOMEN!
GIVE ME A GUY! YOU ALWAYS KNOW WHERE YOU STAND WITH A GUY! I'LL CALL MY GOOD BUDDY JUGHEAD!
PHONE
DING! DING! DING!

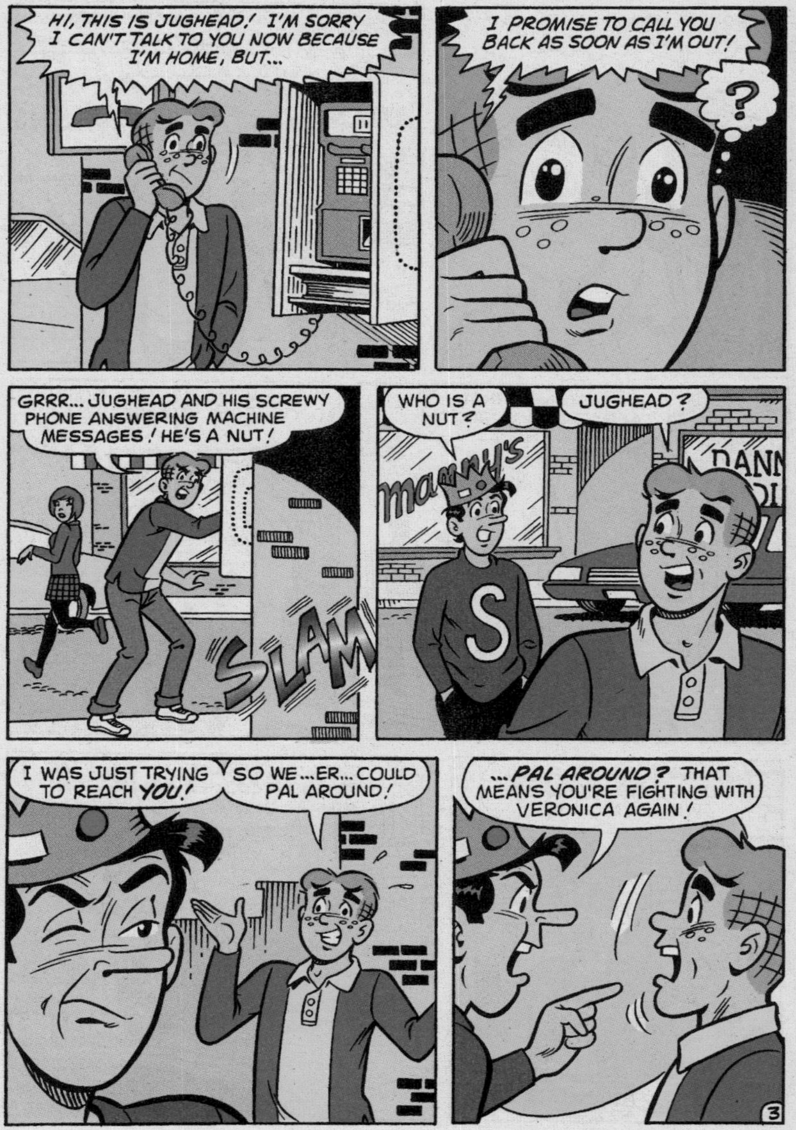
HI, THIS IS JUGHEAD! I'M SORRY I CAN'T TALK TO YOU NOW BECAUSE I'M HOME, BUT...
I PROMISE TO CALL YOU BACK AS SOON AS I'M OUT!
?
GRRR... JUGHEAD AND HIS SCREWY PHONE ANSWERING MACHINE MESSAGES! HE'S A NUT!
SLAM
WHO IS A NUT?
JUGHEAD?
I WAS JUST TRYING TO REACH YOU!
SO WE...ER...COULD PAL AROUND!
...PAL AROUND? THAT MEANS YOU'RE FIGHTING WITH VERONICA AGAIN!
3

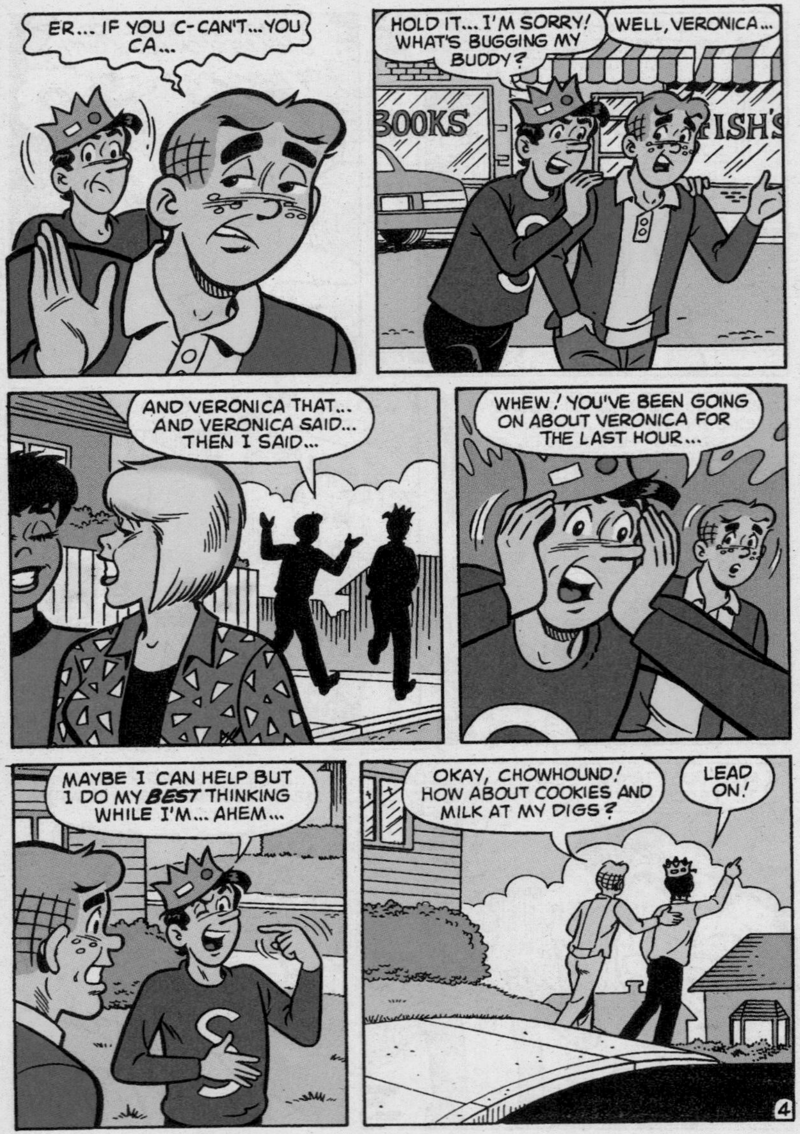
ER... IF YOU C-CAN'T...YOU CA...
HOLD IT... I'M SORRY! WHAT'S BUGGING MY BUDDY?
WELL, VERONICA...
BOOKS
ISH'S
AND VERONICA THAT... AND VERONICA SAID... THEN I SAID...
WHEW! YOU'VE BEEN GOING ON ABOUT VERONICA FOR THE LAST HOUR...
MAYBE I CAN HELP BUT I DO MY *BEST* THINKING WHILE I'M... AHEM...
OKAY, CHOWHOUND! HOW ABOUT COOKIES AND MILK AT MY DIGS?
LEAD ON!
4

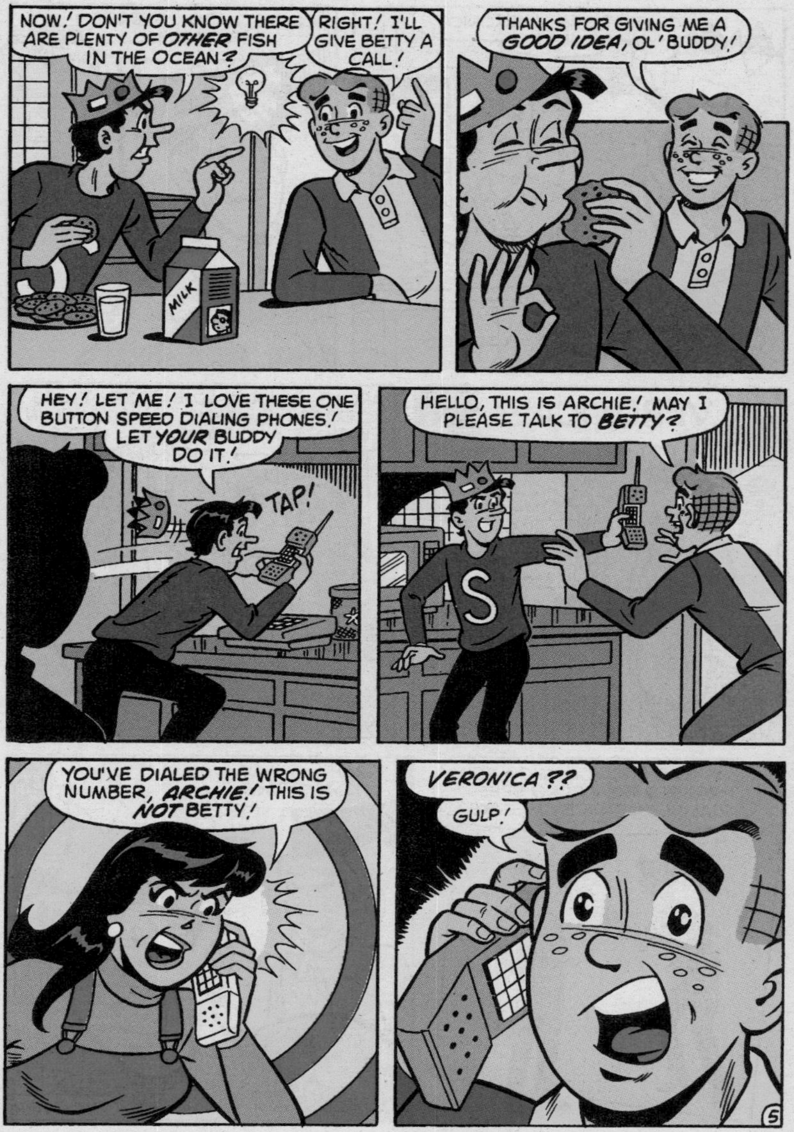

NOW! DON'T YOU KNOW THERE ARE PLENTY OF OTHER FISH IN THE OCEAN?
RIGHT! I'LL GIVE BETTY A CALL!
MILK
THANKS FOR GIVING ME A GOOD IDEA, OL' BUDDY!
HEY! LET ME! I LOVE THESE ONE BUTTON SPEED DIALING PHONES! LET YOUR BUDDY DO IT!
TAP!
HELLO, THIS IS ARCHIE! MAY I PLEASE TALK TO BETTY?
YOU'VE DIALED THE WRONG NUMBER, ARCHIE! THIS IS NOT BETTY!
VERONICA??
GULP!
5

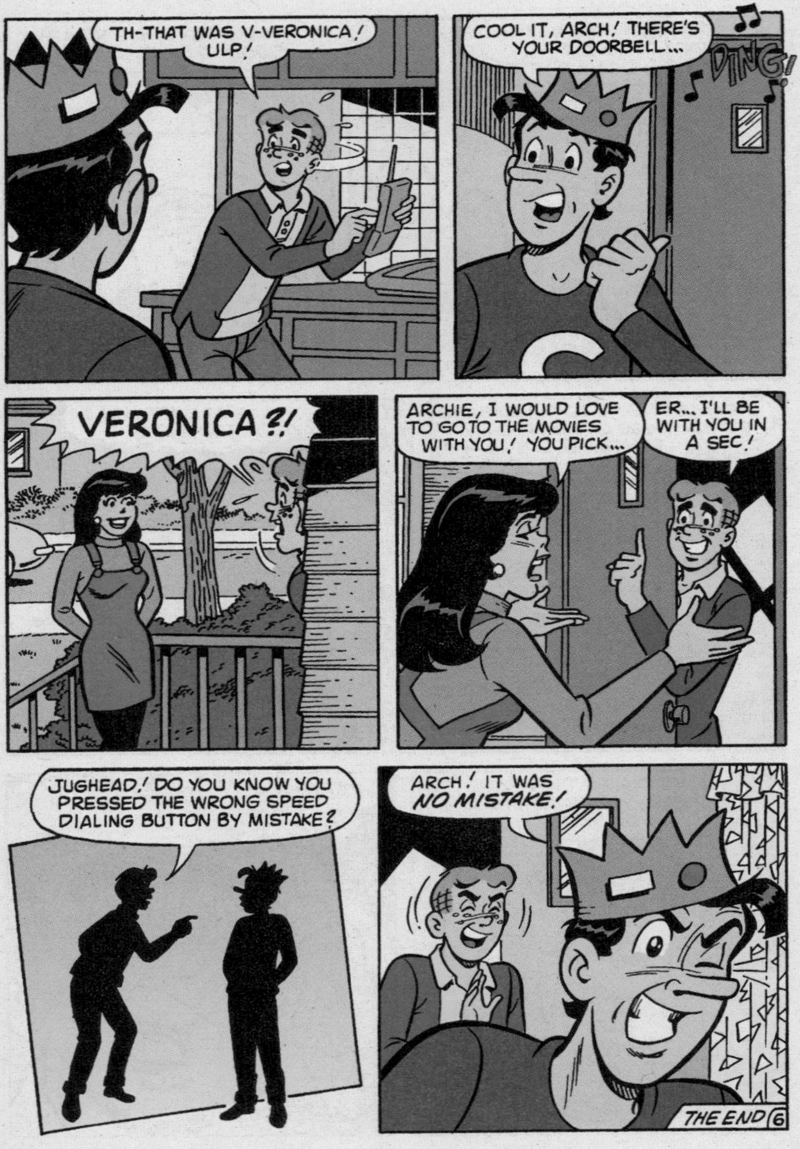

TH-THAT WAS V-VERONICA! ULP!
COOL IT, ARCH! THERE'S YOUR DOORBELL...
DING!
VERONICA?!
ARCHIE, I WOULD LOVE TO GO TO THE MOVIES WITH YOU! YOU PICK...
ER... I'LL BE WITH YOU IN A SEC!
JUGHEAD! DO YOU KNOW YOU PRESSED THE WRONG SPEED DIALING BUTTON BY MISTAKE?
ARCH! IT WAS NO MISTAKE!
THE END
6

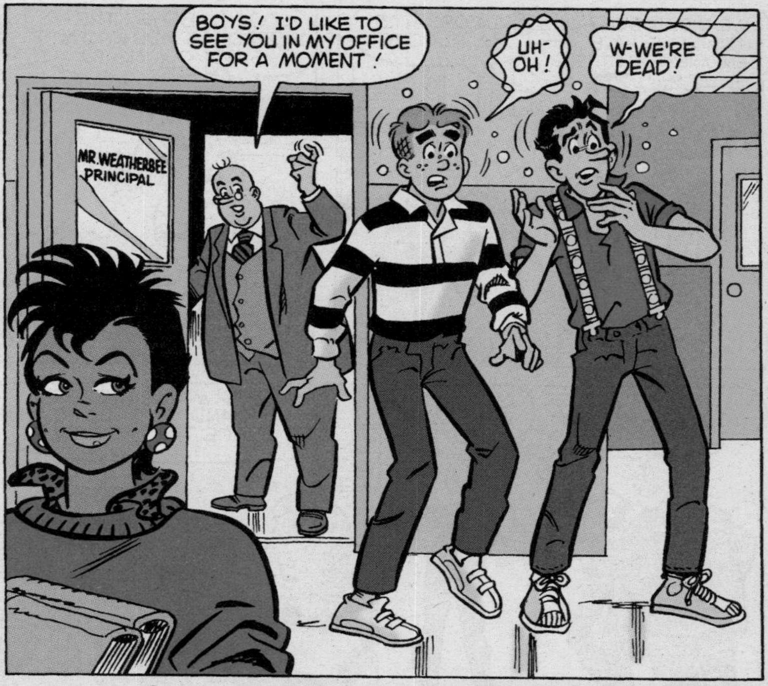
MR. WEATHERBEE
PRINCIPAL
BOYS! I'D LIKE TO SEE YOU IN MY OFFICE FOR A MOMENT!
UH-OH!
W-WE'RE DEAD!

Archie -IN- DESIGNERS' CHOICE

Script: Frank Doyle / Pencils: Stan Goldberg / Inks: Mike Esposito / Letters: Bill Yoshida

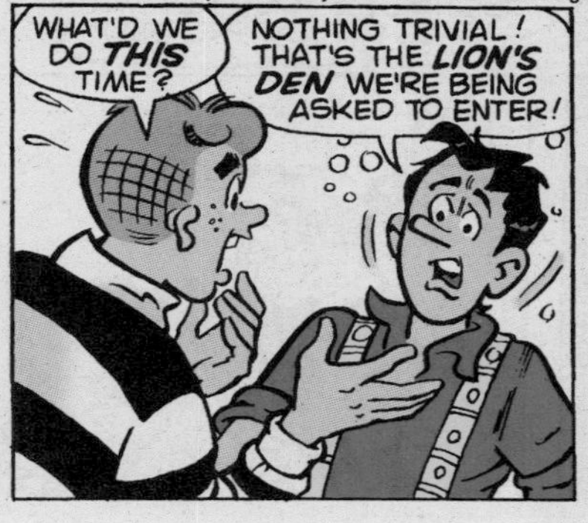
WHAT'D WE DO *THIS* TIME?
NOTHING TRIVIAL! THAT'S THE *LION'S DEN* WE'RE BEING ASKED TO ENTER!

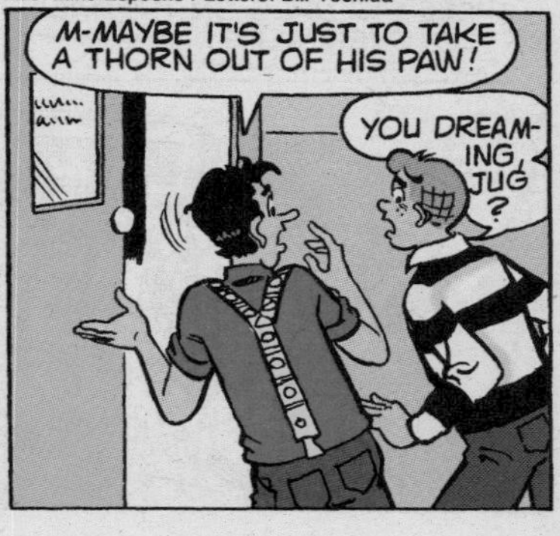
M-MAYBE IT'S JUST TO TAKE A THORN OUT OF HIS PAW!
YOU DREAMING, JUG?

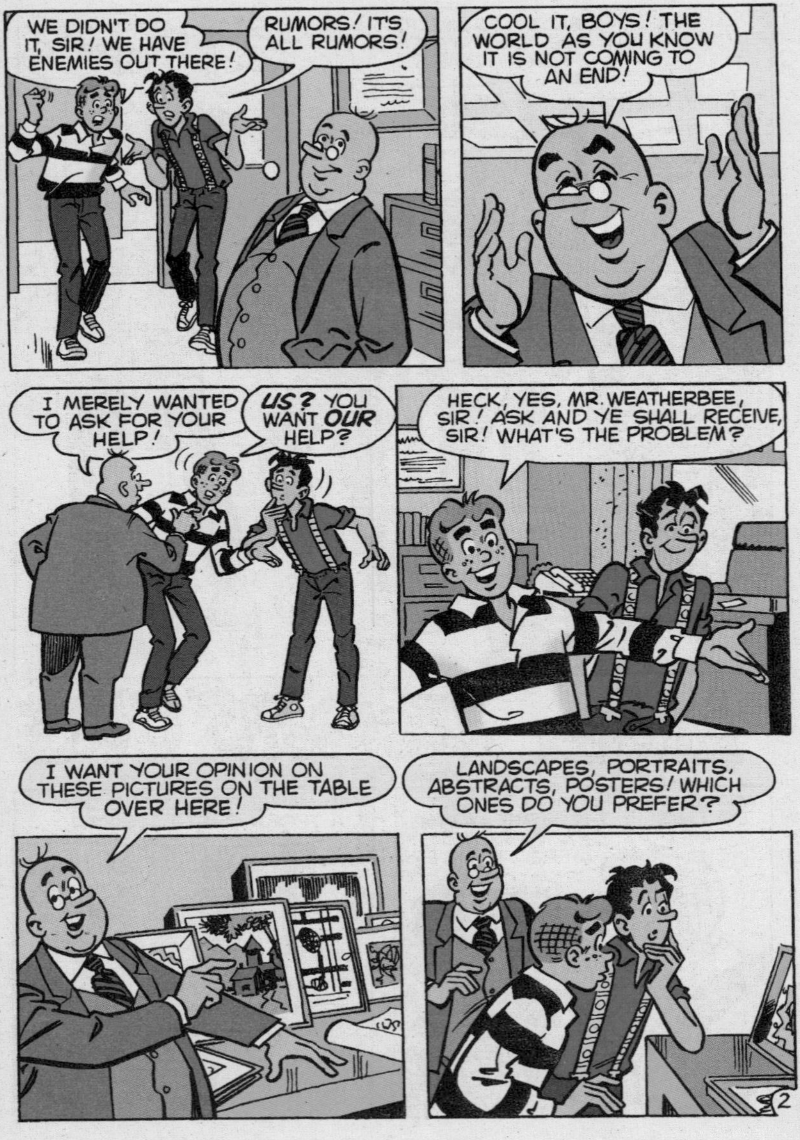
WE DIDN'T DO IT, SIR! WE HAVE ENEMIES OUT THERE!
RUMORS! IT'S ALL RUMORS!
COOL IT, BOYS! THE WORLD AS YOU KNOW IT IS NOT COMING TO AN END!
I MERELY WANTED TO ASK FOR YOUR HELP!
US? YOU WANT OUR HELP?
HECK, YES, MR. WEATHERBEE, SIR! ASK AND YE SHALL RECEIVE, SIR! WHAT'S THE PROBLEM?
I WANT YOUR OPINION ON THESE PICTURES ON THE TABLE OVER HERE!
LANDSCAPES, PORTRAITS, ABSTRACTS, POSTERS! WHICH ONES DO YOU PREFER?
2

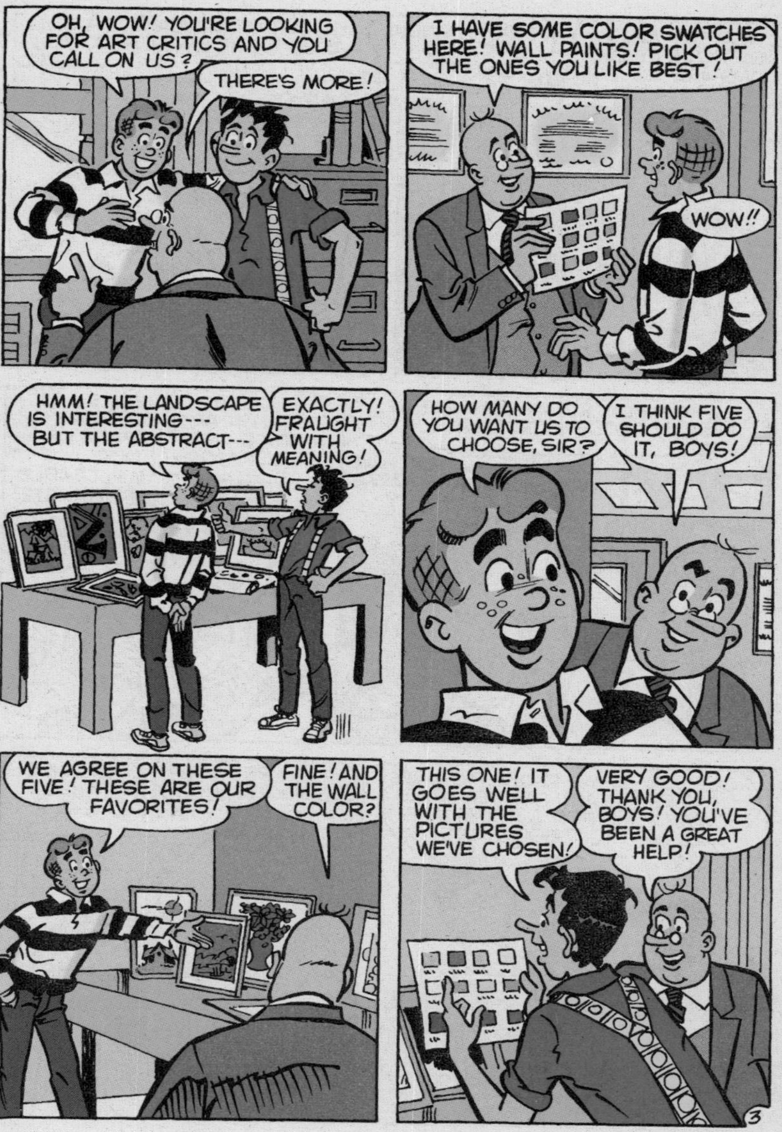
OH, WOW! YOU'RE LOOKING FOR ART CRITICS AND YOU CALL ON US?
THERE'S MORE!
I HAVE SOME COLOR SWATCHES HERE! WALL PAINTS! PICK OUT THE ONES YOU LIKE BEST!
WOW!!
HMM! THE LANDSCAPE IS INTERESTING--- BUT THE ABSTRACT---
EXACTLY! FRAUGHT WITH MEANING!
HOW MANY DO YOU WANT US TO CHOOSE, SIR?
I THINK FIVE SHOULD DO IT, BOYS!
WE AGREE ON THESE FIVE! THESE ARE OUR FAVORITES!
FINE! AND THE WALL COLOR?
THIS ONE! IT GOES WELL WITH THE PICTURES WE'VE CHOSEN!
VERY GOOD! THANK YOU, BOYS! YOU'VE BEEN A GREAT HELP!
3

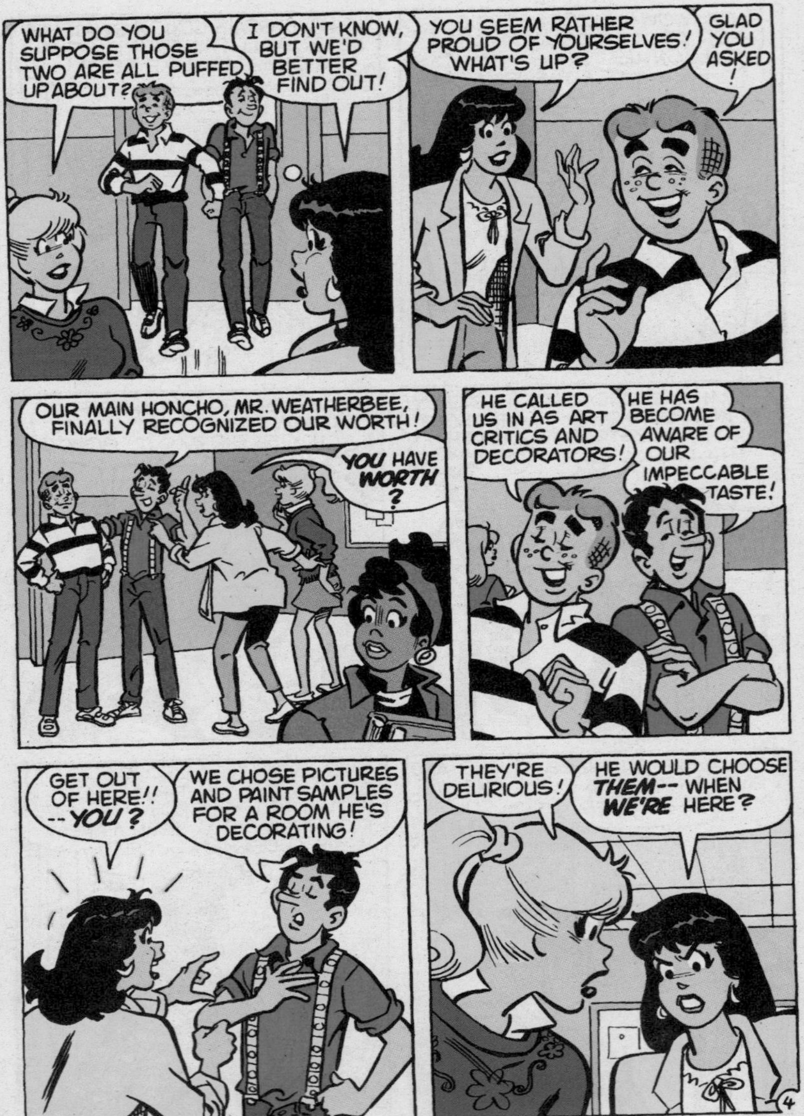
WHAT DO YOU SUPPOSE THOSE TWO ARE ALL PUFFED UP ABOUT?
I DON'T KNOW, BUT WE'D BETTER FIND OUT!
YOU SEEM RATHER PROUD OF YOURSELVES! WHAT'S UP?
GLAD YOU ASKED!
OUR MAIN HONCHO, MR. WEATHERBEE, FINALLY RECOGNIZED OUR WORTH!
YOU HAVE WORTH?
HE CALLED US IN AS ART CRITICS AND DECORATORS!
HE HAS BECOME AWARE OF OUR IMPECCABLE TASTE!
GET OUT OF HERE!! --YOU?
WE CHOSE PICTURES AND PAINT SAMPLES FOR A ROOM HE'S DECORATING!
THEY'RE DELIRIOUS!
HE WOULD CHOOSE THEM-- WHEN WE'RE HERE?
4

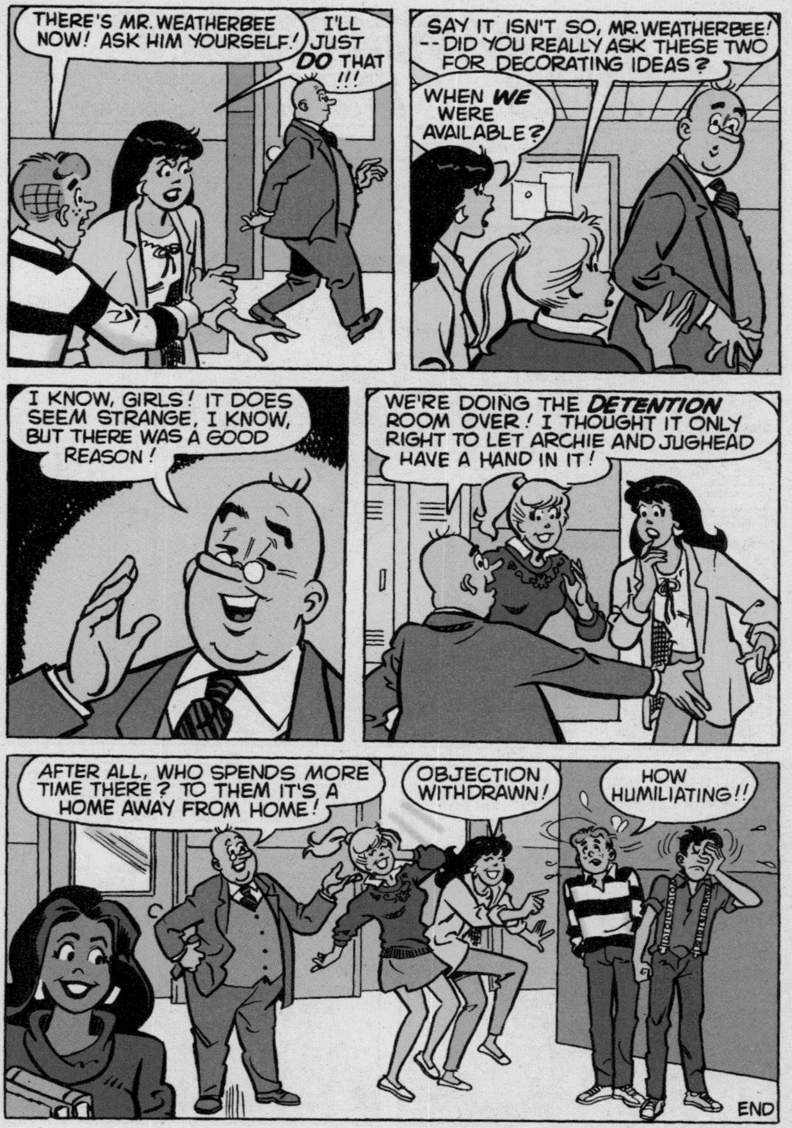
THERE'S MR. WEATHERBEE NOW! ASK HIM YOURSELF!
I'LL JUST DO THAT!!!
SAY IT ISN'T SO, MR. WEATHERBEE! --DID YOU REALLY ASK THESE TWO FOR DECORATING IDEAS?
WHEN WE WERE AVAILABLE?
I KNOW, GIRLS! IT DOES SEEM STRANGE, I KNOW, BUT THERE WAS A GOOD REASON!
WE'RE DOING THE DETENTION ROOM OVER! I THOUGHT IT ONLY RIGHT TO LET ARCHIE AND JUGHEAD HAVE A HAND IN IT!
AFTER ALL, WHO SPENDS MORE TIME THERE? TO THEM IT'S A HOME AWAY FROM HOME!
OBJECTION WITHDRAWN!
HOW HUMILIATING!!
END

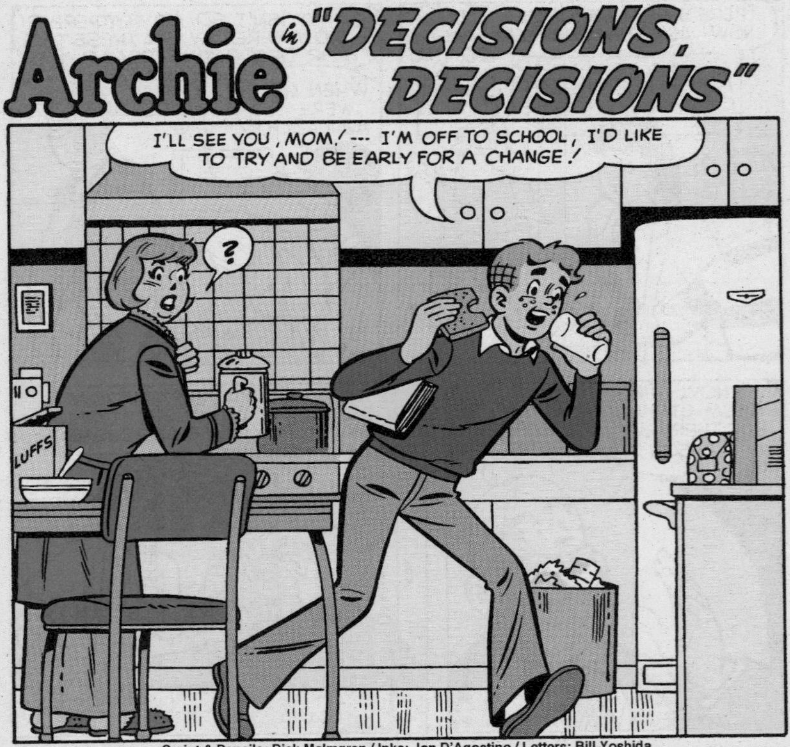
Archie in "DECISIONS, DECISIONS"
I'LL SEE YOU, MOM! --- I'M OFF TO SCHOOL, I'D LIKE TO TRY AND BE EARLY FOR A CHANGE!
?
LUFFS

Script & Pencils: Dick Malmgren / Inks: Jon D'Agostino / Letters: Bill Yoshida

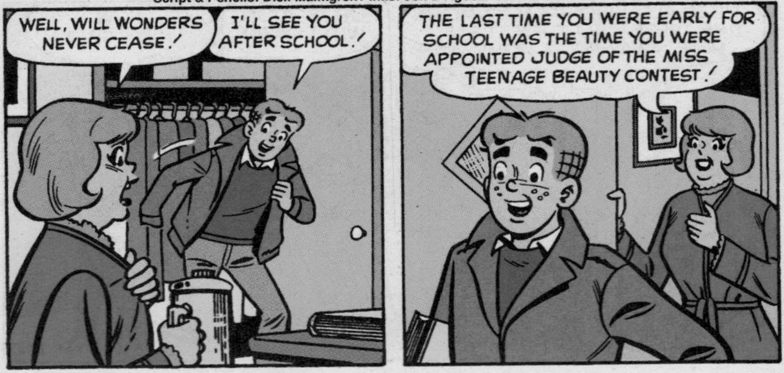
I'LL SEE YOU AFTER SCHOOL!
WELL, WILL WONDERS NEVER CEASE!
THE LAST TIME YOU WERE EARLY FOR SCHOOL WAS THE TIME YOU WERE APPOINTED JUDGE OF THE MISS TEENAGE BEAUTY CONTEST!

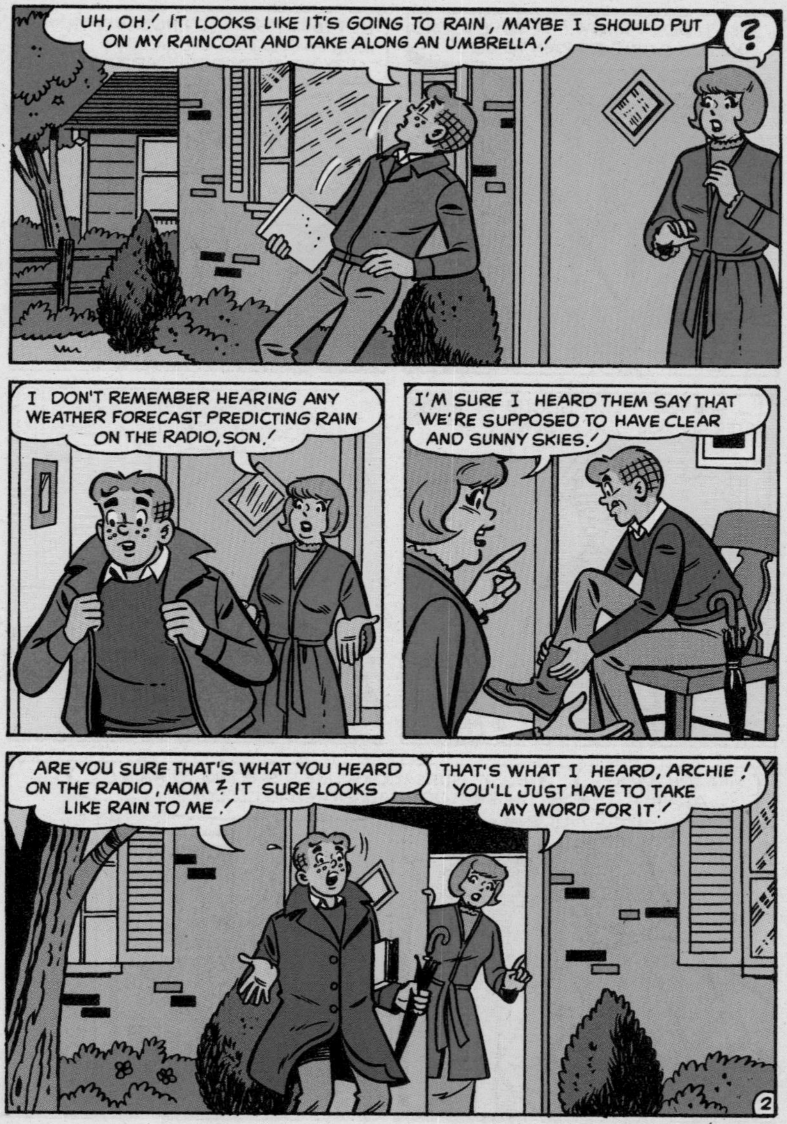
UH, OH! IT LOOKS LIKE IT'S GOING TO RAIN, MAYBE I SHOULD PUT ON MY RAINCOAT AND TAKE ALONG AN UMBRELLA!
?
I DON'T REMEMBER HEARING ANY WEATHER FORECAST PREDICTING RAIN ON THE RADIO, SON!
I'M SURE I HEARD THEM SAY THAT WE'RE SUPPOSED TO HAVE CLEAR AND SUNNY SKIES!
ARE YOU SURE THAT'S WHAT YOU HEARD ON THE RADIO, MOM? IT SURE LOOKS LIKE RAIN TO ME!
THAT'S WHAT I HEARD, ARCHIE! YOU'LL JUST HAVE TO TAKE MY WORD FOR IT!
2

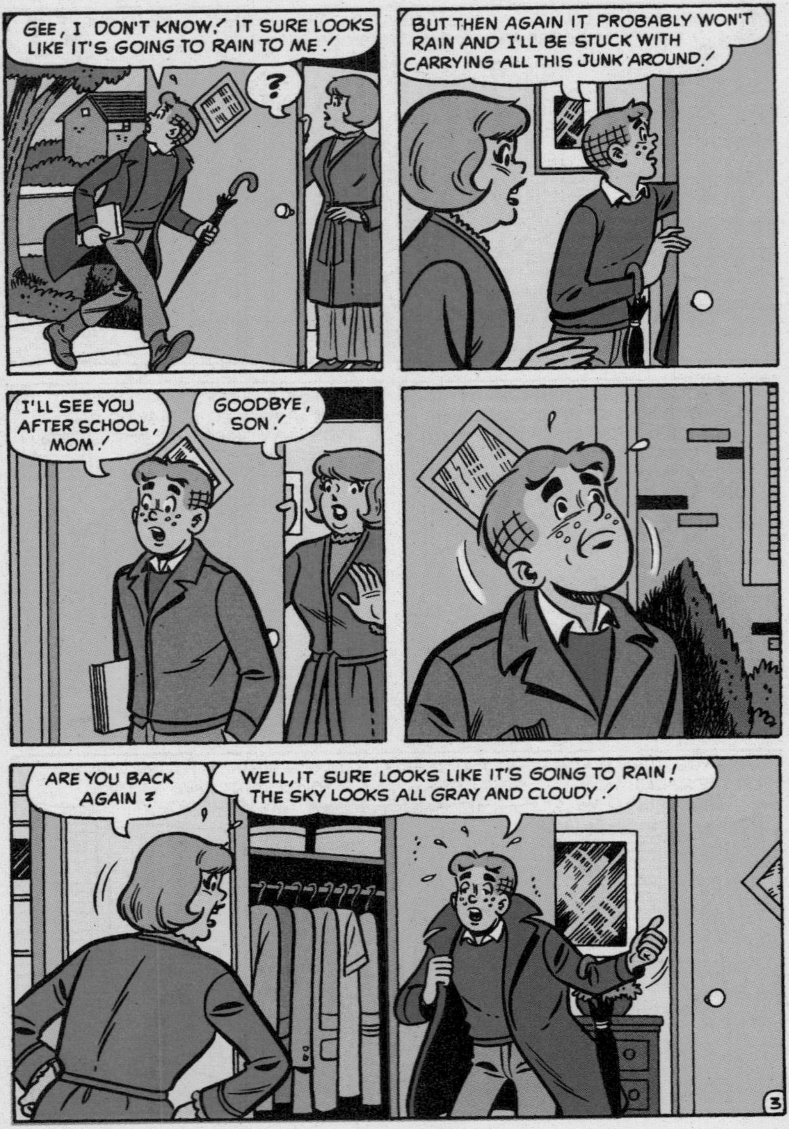

GEE, I DON'T KNOW! IT SURE LOOKS LIKE IT'S GOING TO RAIN TO ME!
?
BUT THEN AGAIN IT PROBABLY WON'T RAIN AND I'LL BE STUCK WITH CARRYING ALL THIS JUNK AROUND!
I'LL SEE YOU AFTER SCHOOL, MOM!
GOODBYE, SON!
ARE YOU BACK AGAIN ?
WELL, IT SURE LOOKS LIKE IT'S GOING TO RAIN! THE SKY LOOKS ALL GRAY AND CLOUDY!
3

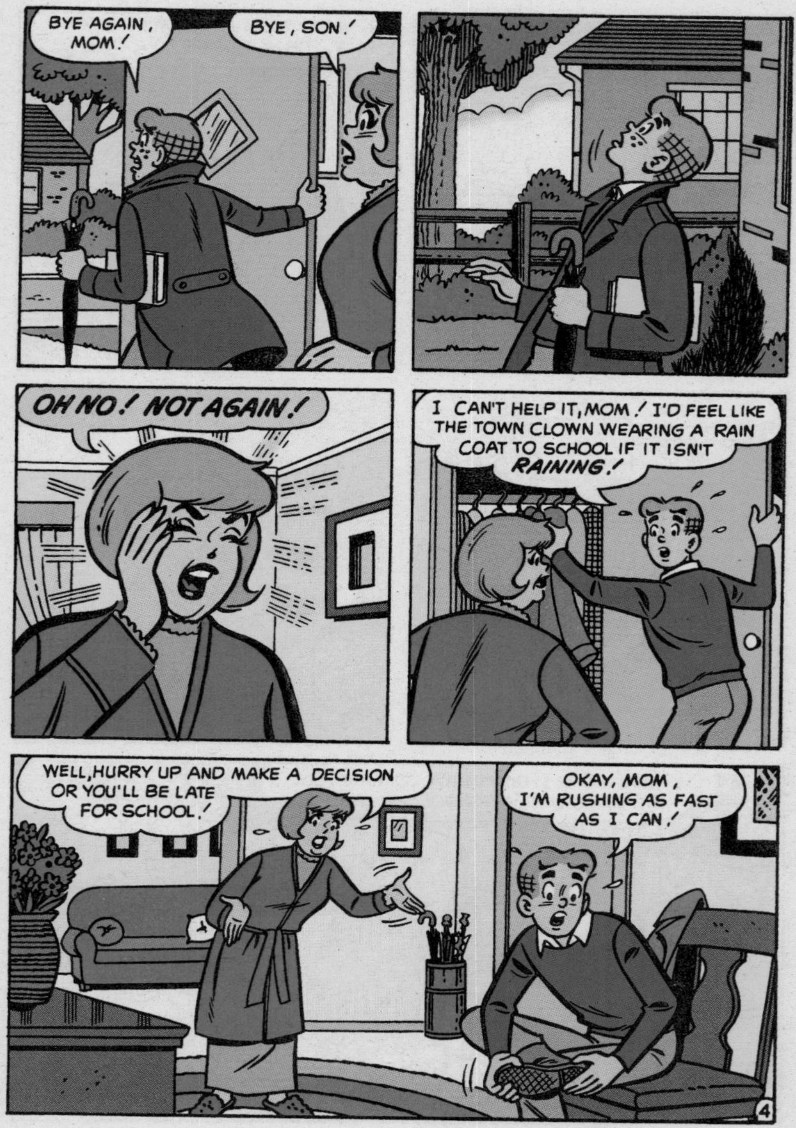
BYE AGAIN, MOM!
BYE, SON!
OH NO! NOT AGAIN!
I CAN'T HELP IT, MOM! I'D FEEL LIKE THE TOWN CLOWN WEARING A RAIN COAT TO SCHOOL IF IT ISN'T RAINING!
WELL, HURRY UP AND MAKE A DECISION OR YOU'LL BE LATE FOR SCHOOL!
OKAY, MOM, I'M RUSHING AS FAST AS I CAN!
4

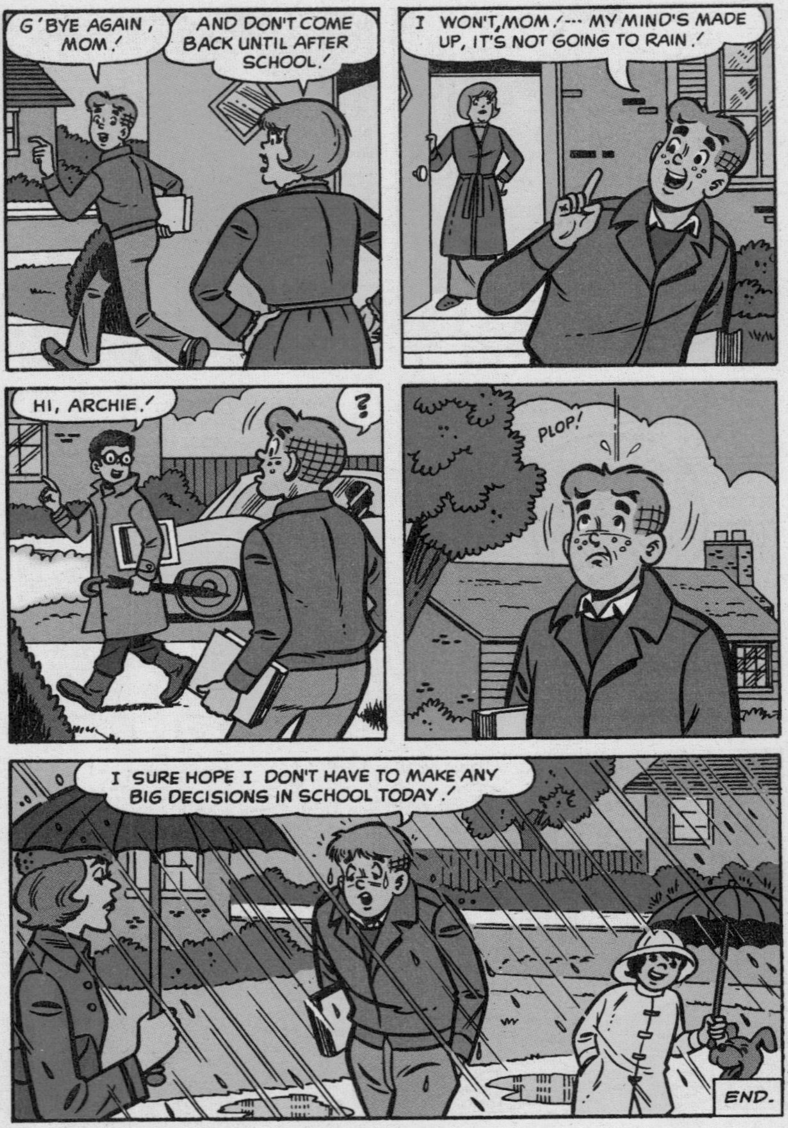
G'BYE AGAIN, MOM!
AND DON'T COME BACK UNTIL AFTER SCHOOL!
I WON'T, MOM!--- MY MIND'S MADE UP, IT'S NOT GOING TO RAIN!
HI, ARCHIE!
?
PLOP!
I SURE HOPE I DON'T HAVE TO MAKE ANY BIG DECISIONS IN SCHOOL TODAY!
END.

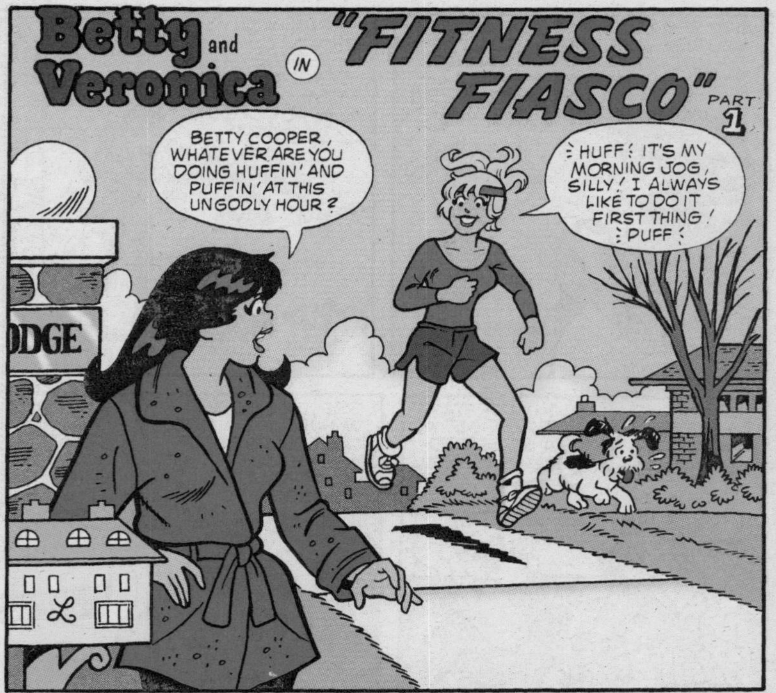
Betty and Veronica
IN
"FITNESS FIASCO" PART 1
BETTY COOPER, WHATEVER ARE YOU DOING HUFFIN' AND PUFFIN' AT THIS UNGODLY HOUR?
:HUFF: IT'S MY MORNING JOG, SILLY! I ALWAYS LIKE TO DO IT FIRST THING! :PUFF:
ODGE

Script: Golliher / Pencils: DeCarlo & Parent / Inks: Scarpelli / Letters: Yoshida

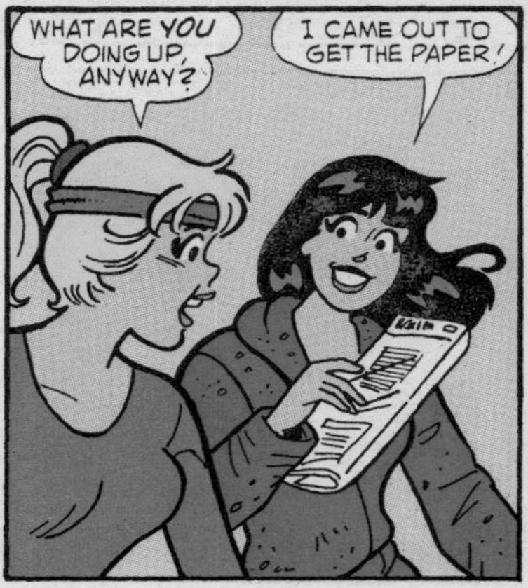
WHAT ARE YOU DOING UP, ANYWAY?
I CAME OUT TO GET THE PAPER!

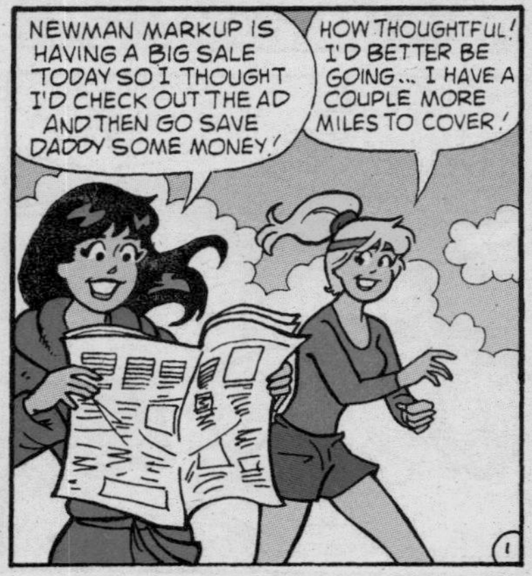
NEWMAN MARKUP IS HAVING A BIG SALE TODAY SO I THOUGHT I'D CHECK OUT THE AD AND THEN GO SAVE DADDY SOME MONEY!
HOW THOUGHTFUL! I'D BETTER BE GOING... I HAVE A COUPLE MORE MILES TO COVER!
1

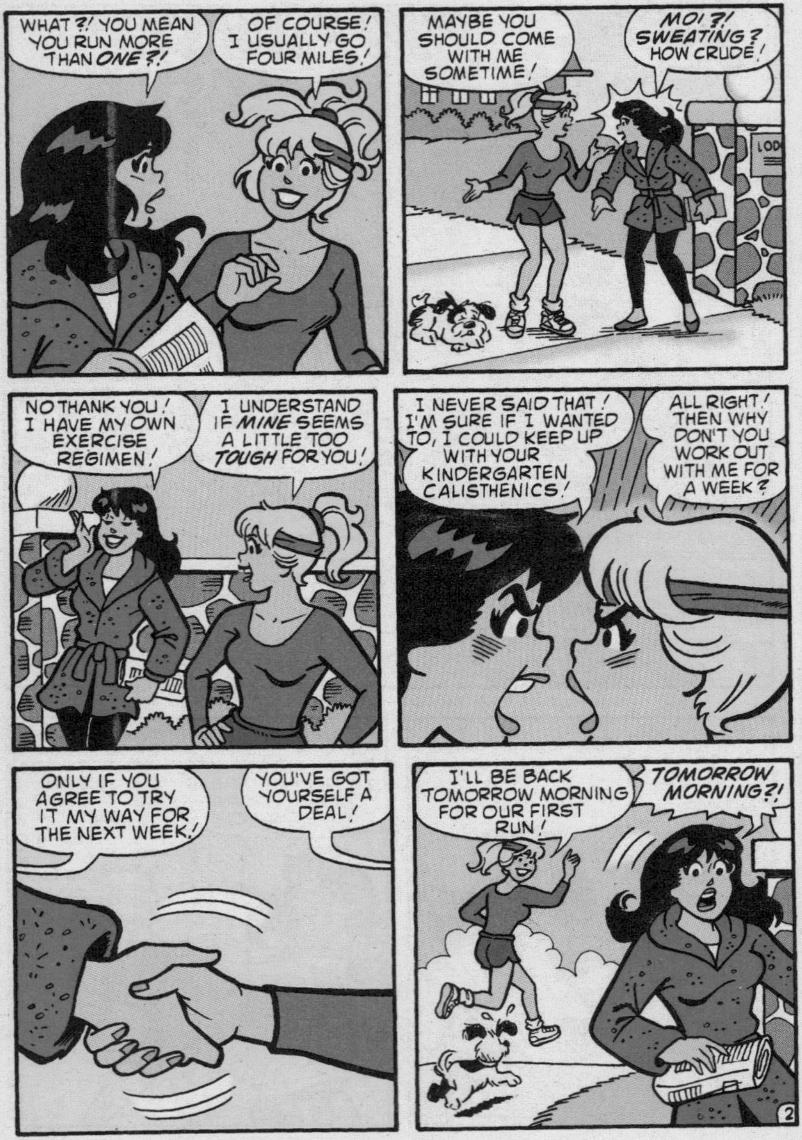
WHAT?! YOU MEAN YOU RUN MORE THAN *ONE*?!
OF COURSE! I USUALLY GO FOUR MILES!
MAYBE YOU SHOULD COME WITH ME SOMETIME!
MOI?! SWEATING? HOW CRUDE!
NO THANK YOU! I HAVE MY OWN EXERCISE REGIMEN!
I UNDERSTAND IF *MINE* SEEMS A LITTLE TOO *TOUGH* FOR YOU!
I NEVER SAID THAT! I'M SURE IF I WANTED TO, I COULD KEEP UP WITH YOUR KINDERGARTEN CALISTHENICS!
ALL RIGHT! THEN WHY DON'T YOU WORK OUT WITH ME FOR A WEEK?
ONLY IF YOU AGREE TO TRY IT MY WAY FOR THE NEXT WEEK!
YOU'VE GOT YOURSELF A DEAL!
I'LL BE BACK TOMORROW MORNING FOR OUR FIRST RUN!
TOMORROW MORNING?!
2

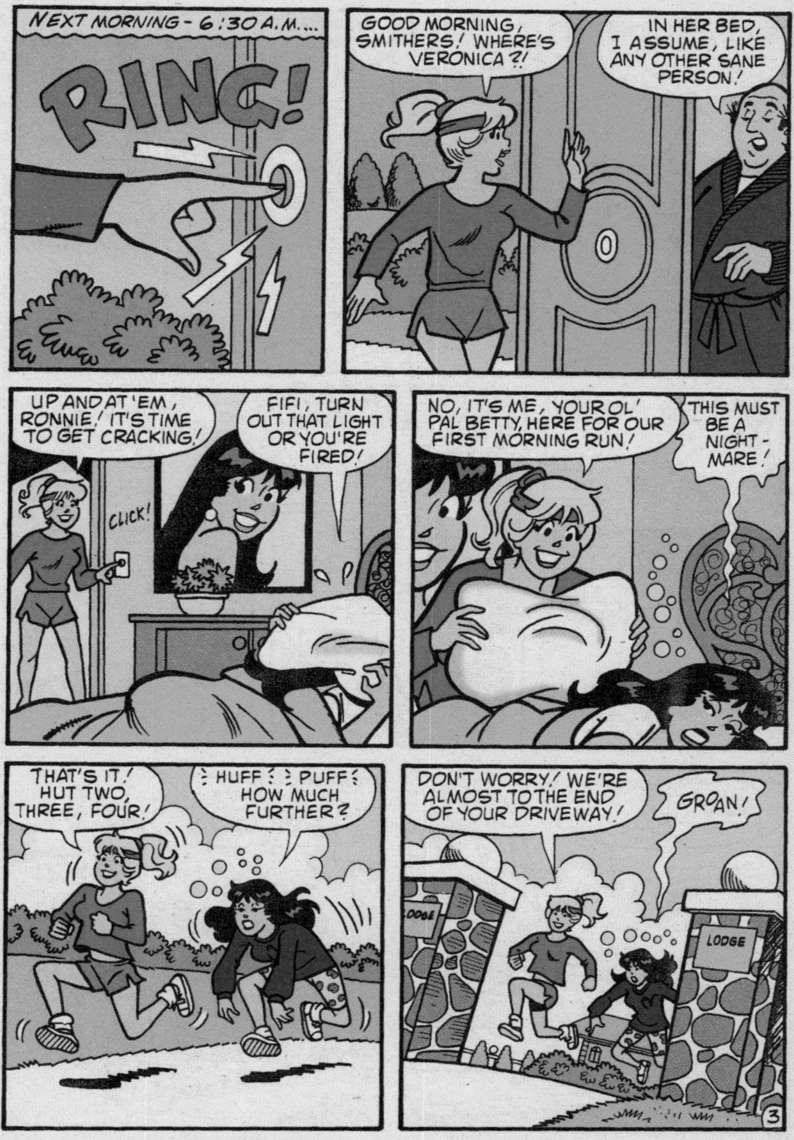
NEXT MORNING - 6:30 A.M. ...
RING!
GOOD MORNING, SMITHERS! WHERE'S VERONICA ?!
IN HER BED, I ASSUME, LIKE ANY OTHER SANE PERSON!
UP AND AT 'EM, RONNIE! IT'S TIME TO GET CRACKING!
CLICK!
FIFI, TURN OUT THAT LIGHT OR YOU'RE FIRED!
NO, IT'S ME, YOUR OL' PAL BETTY, HERE FOR OUR FIRST MORNING RUN!
THIS MUST BE A NIGHT-MARE!
THAT'S IT! HUT TWO, THREE, FOUR!
HUFF PUFF HOW MUCH FURTHER?
DON'T WORRY! WE'RE ALMOST TO THE END OF YOUR DRIVEWAY!
GROAN!
LODGE
LODGE
3

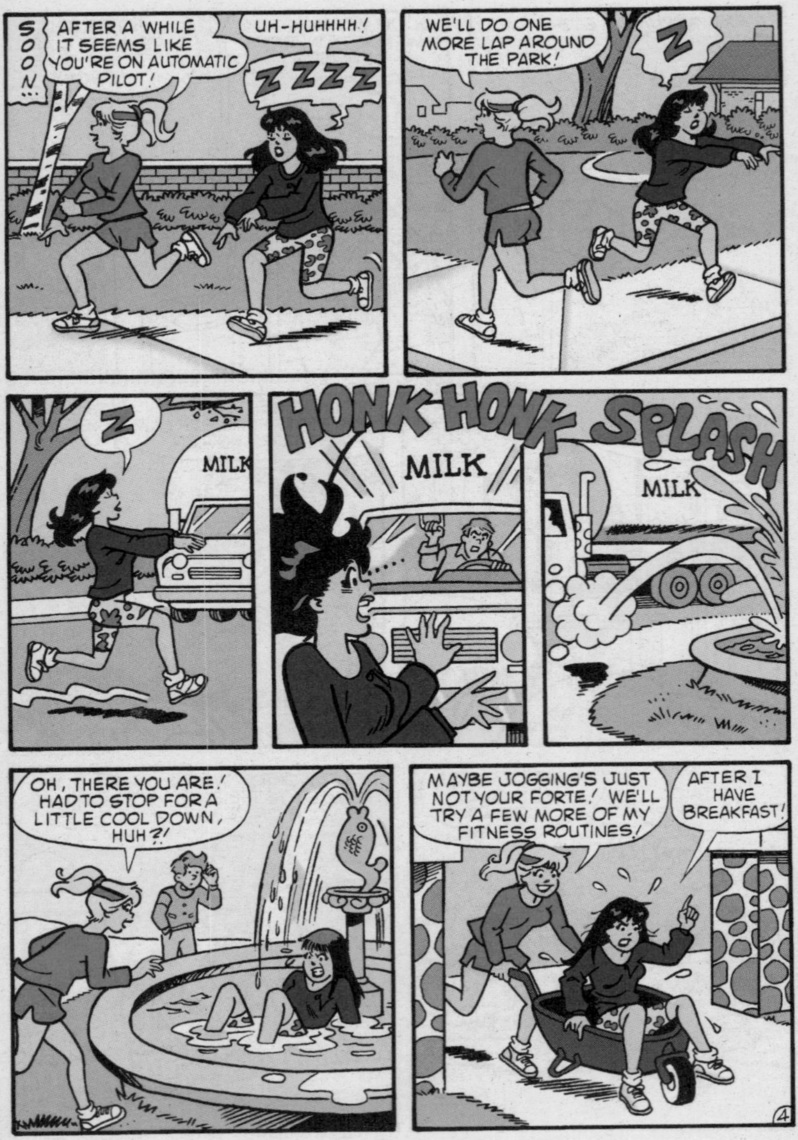
SOON...
AFTER A WHILE IT SEEMS LIKE YOU'RE ON AUTOMATIC PILOT!
UH-HUHHHH!
ZZZZ
WE'LL DO ONE MORE LAP AROUND THE PARK!
Z
Z
MILK
HONK HONK
MILK
SPLASH
MILK
OH, THERE YOU ARE! HAD TO STOP FOR A LITTLE COOL DOWN, HUH?!
MAYBE JOGGING'S JUST NOT YOUR FORTE! WE'LL TRY A FEW MORE OF MY FITNESS ROUTINES!
AFTER I HAVE BREAKFAST!
4

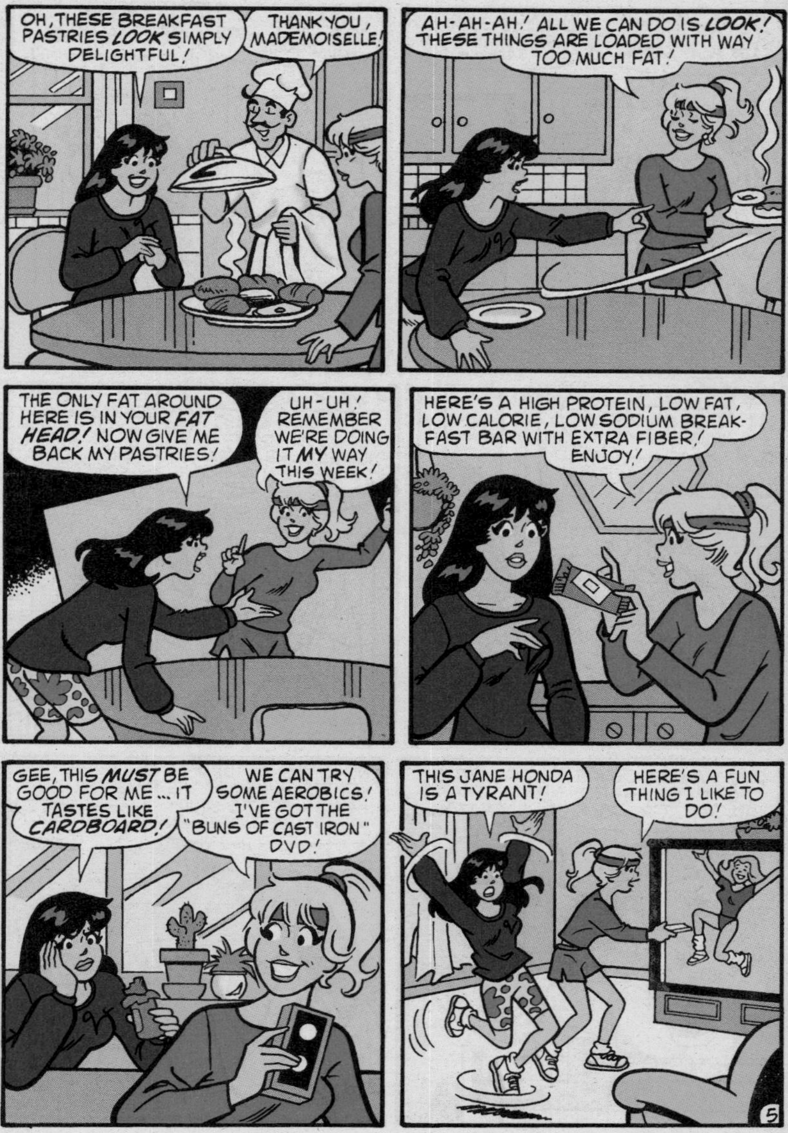
OH, THESE BREAKFAST PASTRIES *LOOK* SIMPLY DELIGHTFUL!
THANK YOU, MADEMOISELLE!
AH-AH-AH! ALL WE CAN DO IS *LOOK*! THESE THINGS ARE LOADED WITH WAY TOO MUCH FAT!
THE ONLY FAT AROUND HERE IS IN YOUR *FAT HEAD!* NOW GIVE ME BACK MY PASTRIES!
UH-UH! REMEMBER WE'RE DOING IT *MY* WAY THIS WEEK!
HERE'S A HIGH PROTEIN, LOW FAT, LOW CALORIE, LOW SODIUM BREAK-FAST BAR WITH EXTRA FIBER! ENJOY!
GEE, THIS *MUST* BE GOOD FOR ME... IT TASTES LIKE *CARDBOARD*!
WE CAN TRY SOME AEROBICS! I'VE GOT THE "BUNS OF CAST IRON" DVD!
THIS JANE HONDA IS A TYRANT!
HERE'S A FUN THING I LIKE TO DO!
5

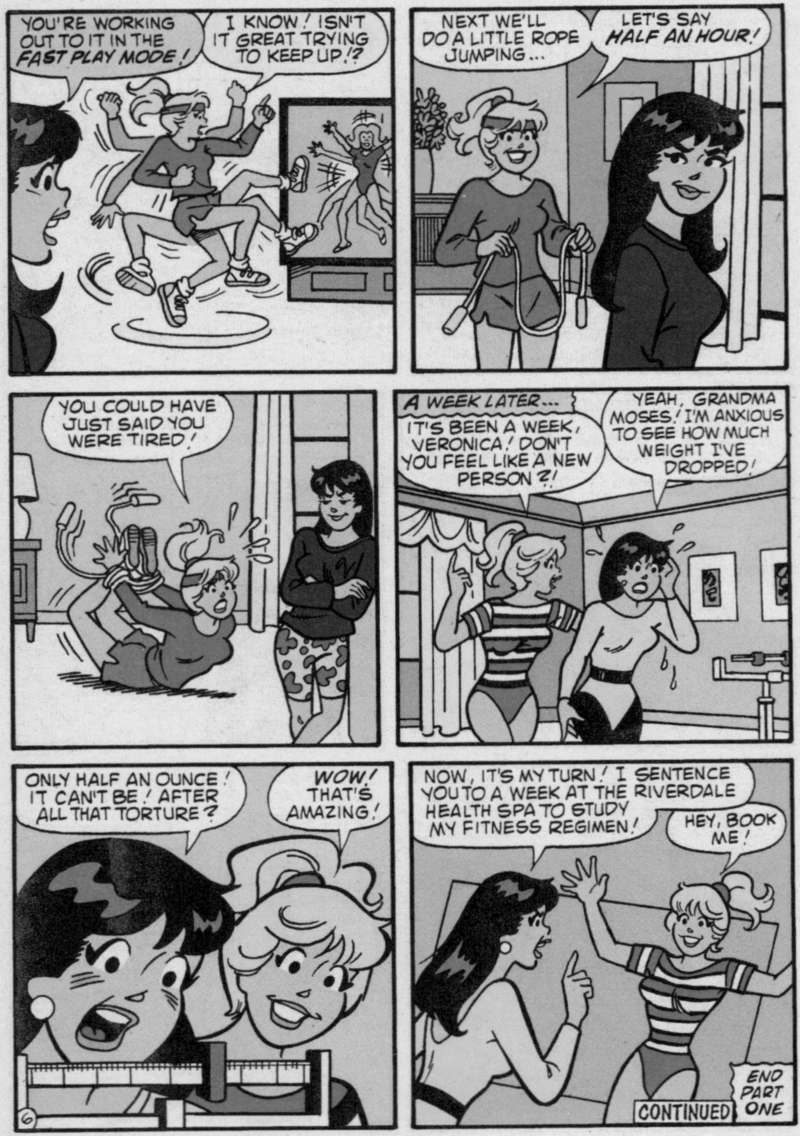

YOU'RE WORKING OUT TO IT IN THE FAST PLAY MODE!
I KNOW! ISN'T IT GREAT TRYING TO KEEP UP!?
NEXT WE'LL DO A LITTLE ROPE JUMPING...
LET'S SAY HALF AN HOUR!
YOU COULD HAVE JUST SAID YOU WERE TIRED!
A WEEK LATER...
IT'S BEEN A WEEK, VERONICA! DON'T YOU FEEL LIKE A NEW PERSON?!
YEAH, GRANDMA MOSES! I'M ANXIOUS TO SEE HOW MUCH WEIGHT I'VE DROPPED!
ONLY HALF AN OUNCE! IT CAN'T BE! AFTER ALL THAT TORTURE?
WOW! THAT'S AMAZING!
NOW, IT'S MY TURN! I SENTENCE YOU TO A WEEK AT THE RIVERDALE HEALTH SPA TO STUDY MY FITNESS REGIMEN!
HEY, BOOK ME!
END PART ONE
CONTINUED
6

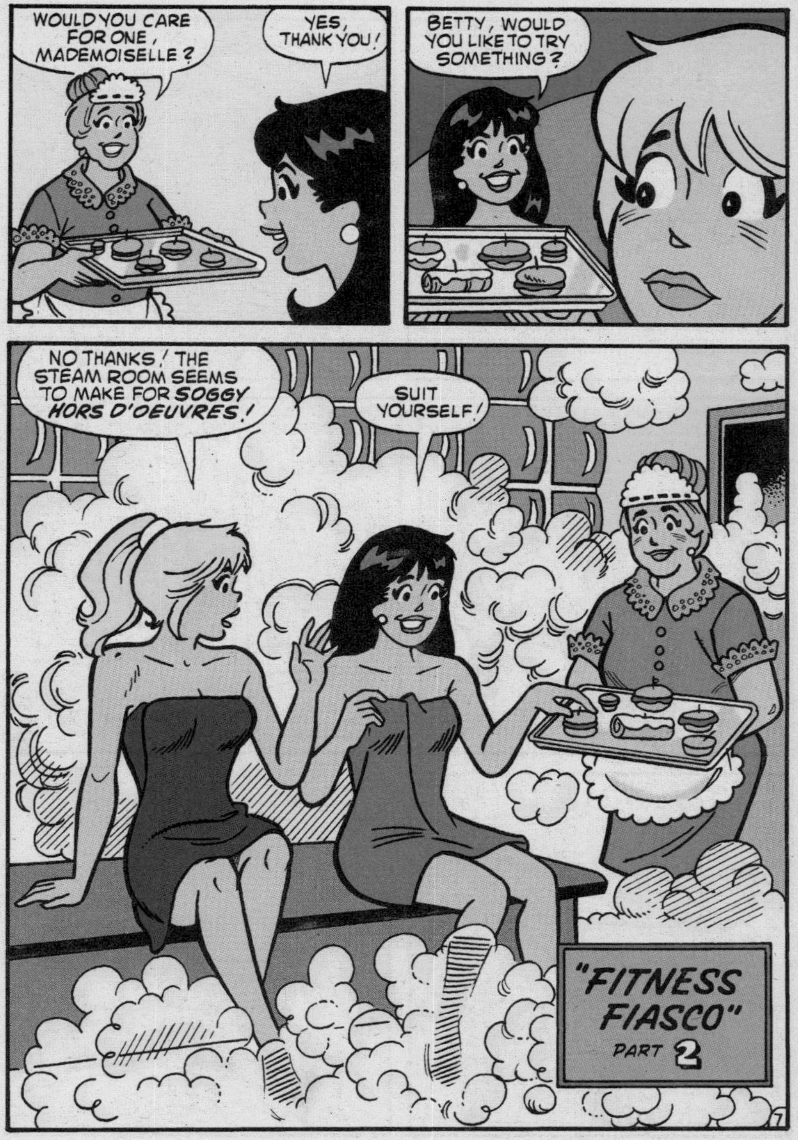

WOULD YOU CARE FOR ONE, MADEMOISELLE?
YES, THANK YOU!
BETTY, WOULD YOU LIKE TO TRY SOMETHING?
NO THANKS! THE STEAM ROOM SEEMS TO MAKE FOR SOGGY HORS D'OEUVRES!
SUIT YOURSELF!
"FITNESS FIASCO" PART 2
7

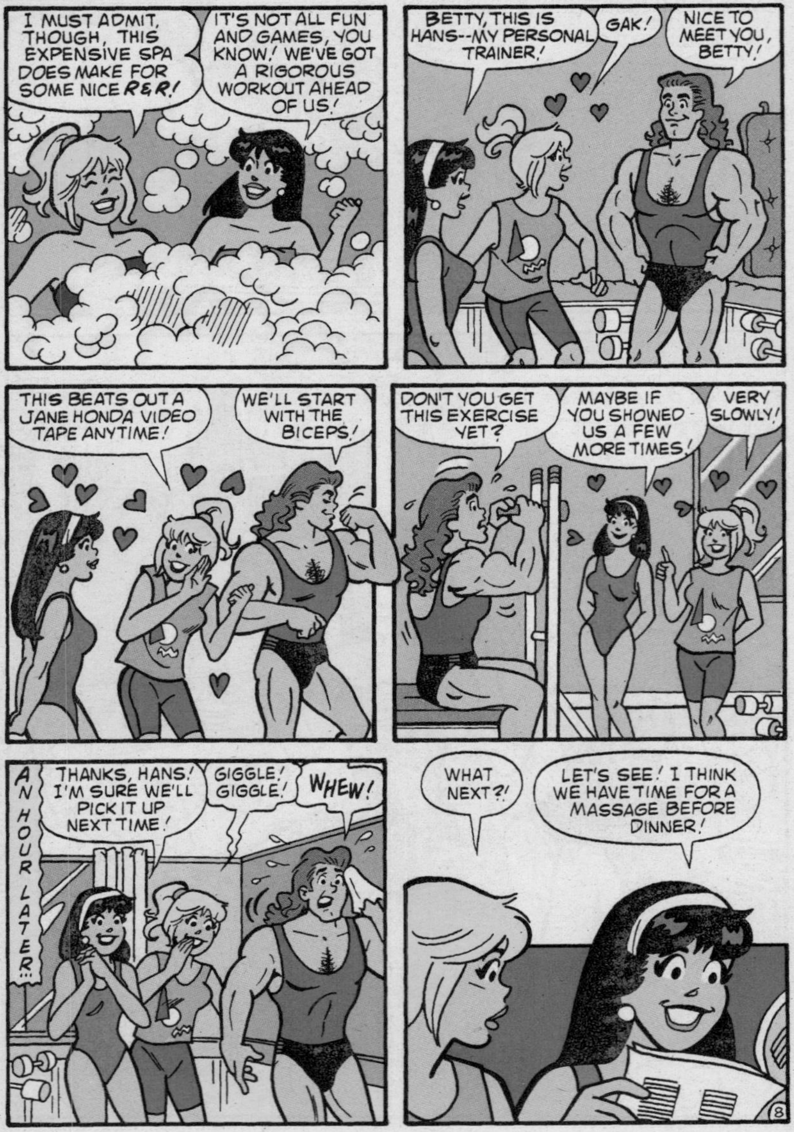
I MUST ADMIT, THOUGH, THIS EXPENSIVE SPA DOES MAKE FOR SOME NICE R&R!
IT'S NOT ALL FUN AND GAMES, YOU KNOW! WE'VE GOT A RIGOROUS WORKOUT AHEAD OF US!
BETTY, THIS IS HANS--MY PERSONAL TRAINER!
GAK!
NICE TO MEET YOU, BETTY!
THIS BEATS OUT A JANE HONDA VIDEO TAPE ANYTIME!
WE'LL START WITH THE BICEPS!
DON'T YOU GET THIS EXERCISE YET?
MAYBE IF YOU SHOWED US A FEW MORE TIMES!
VERY SLOWLY!
AN HOUR LATER...
THANKS, HANS! I'M SURE WE'LL PICK IT UP NEXT TIME!
GIGGLE! GIGGLE!
WHEW!
WHAT NEXT?!
LET'S SEE! I THINK WE HAVE TIME FOR A MASSAGE BEFORE DINNER!
8

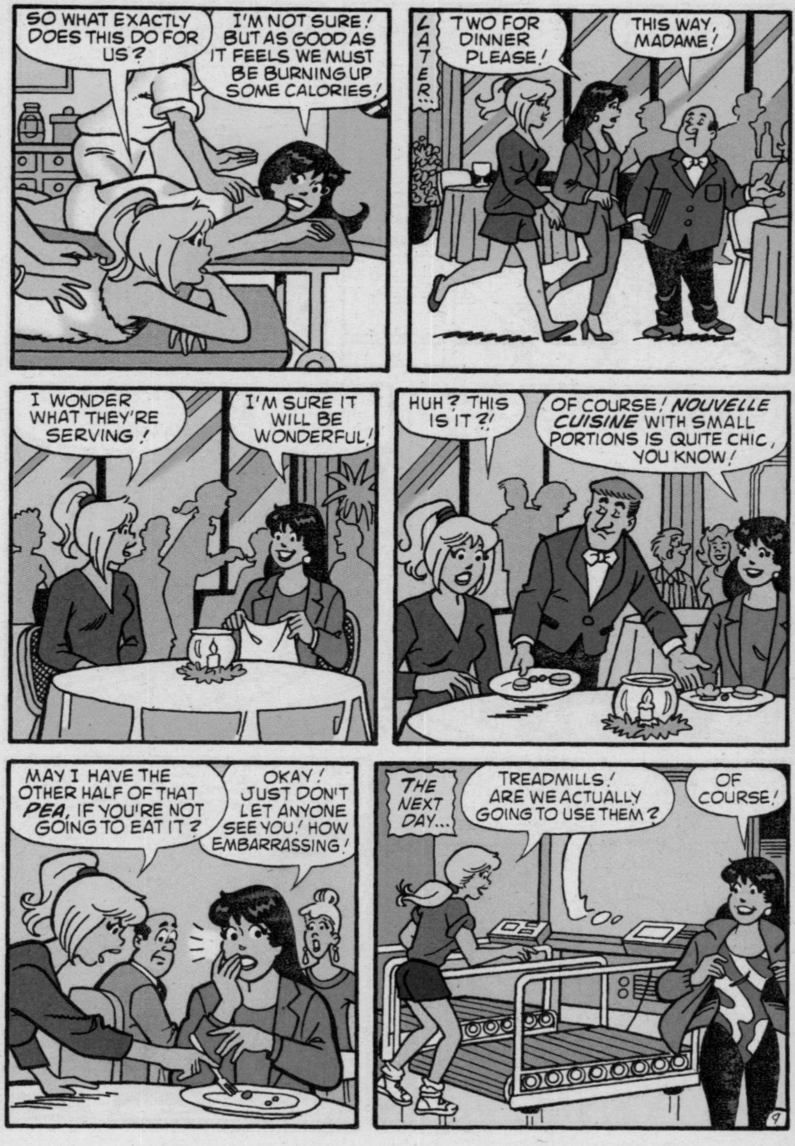
SO WHAT EXACTLY DOES THIS DO FOR US?
I'M NOT SURE! BUT AS GOOD AS IT FEELS WE MUST BE BURNING UP SOME CALORIES!
LATER...
TWO FOR DINNER PLEASE!
THIS WAY, MADAME!
I WONDER WHAT THEY'RE SERVING!
I'M SURE IT WILL BE WONDERFUL!
HUH? THIS IS IT?!
OF COURSE! NOUVELLE CUISINE WITH SMALL PORTIONS IS QUITE CHIC, YOU KNOW!
MAY I HAVE THE OTHER HALF OF THAT PEA, IF YOU'RE NOT GOING TO EAT IT?
OKAY! JUST DON'T LET ANYONE SEE YOU! HOW EMBARRASSING!
THE NEXT DAY...
TREADMILLS! ARE WE ACTUALLY GOING TO USE THEM?
OF COURSE!
9

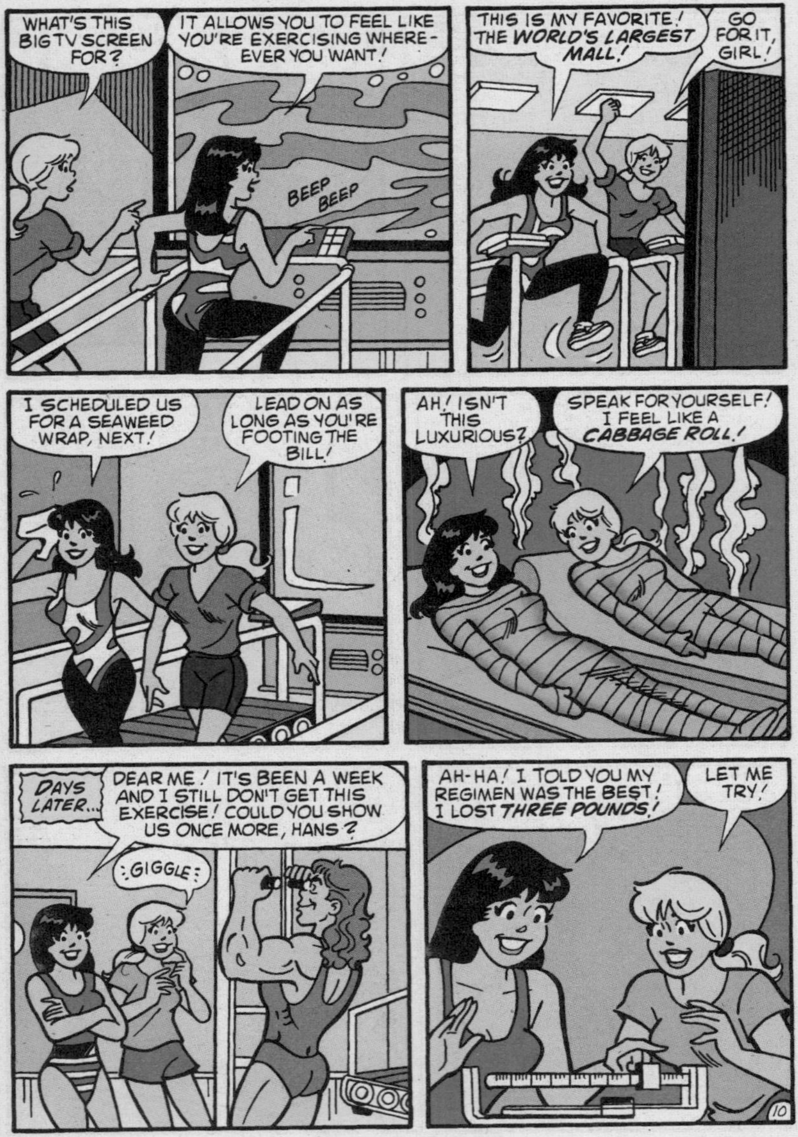
WHAT'S THIS BIG TV SCREEN FOR?
IT ALLOWS YOU TO FEEL LIKE YOU'RE EXERCISING WHERE-EVER YOU WANT!
BEEP BEEP
THIS IS MY FAVORITE! THE WORLD'S LARGEST MALL!
GO FOR IT, GIRL!
I SCHEDULED US FOR A SEAWEED WRAP, NEXT!
LEAD ON AS LONG AS YOU'RE FOOTING THE BILL!
AH! ISN'T THIS LUXURIOUS?
SPEAK FOR YOURSELF! I FEEL LIKE A CABBAGE ROLL!
DAYS LATER...
DEAR ME! IT'S BEEN A WEEK AND I STILL DON'T GET THIS EXERCISE! COULD YOU SHOW US ONCE MORE, HANS?
GIGGLE
AH-HA! I TOLD YOU MY REGIMEN WAS THE BEST! I LOST THREE POUNDS!
LET ME TRY!
10

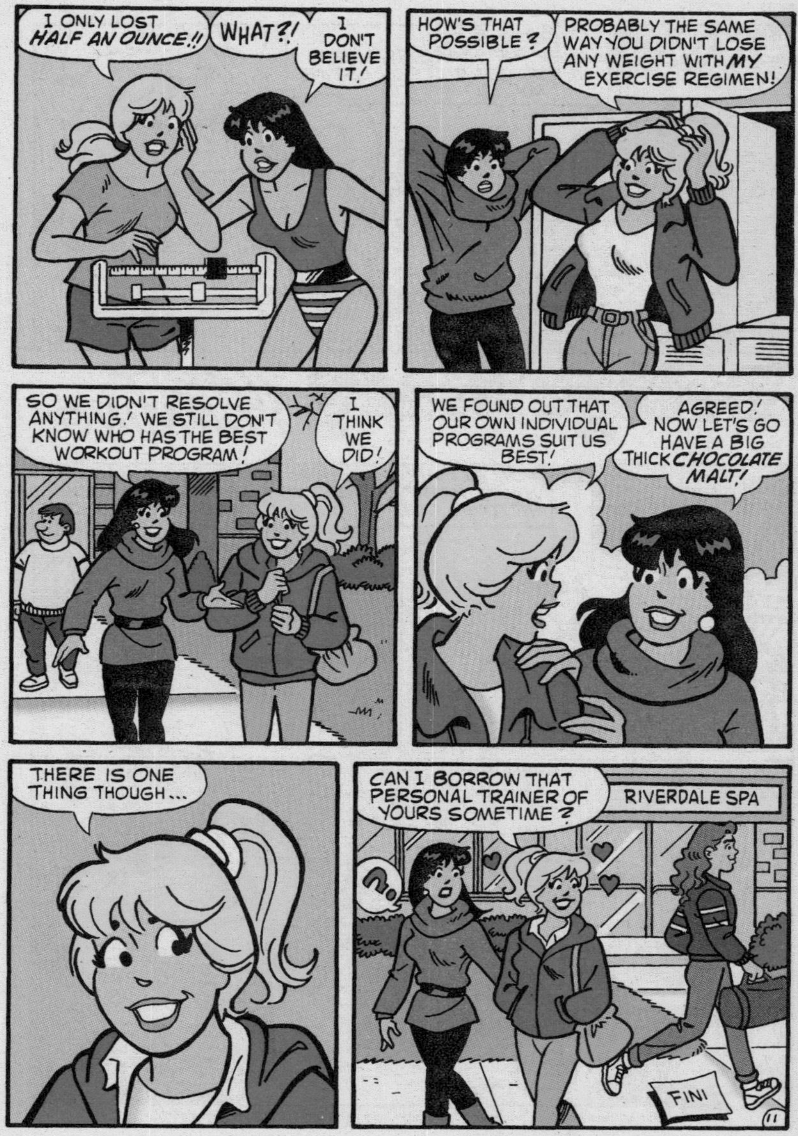
I ONLY LOST HALF AN OUNCE!!
WHAT?!
I DON'T BELIEVE IT!
HOW'S THAT POSSIBLE?
PROBABLY THE SAME WAY YOU DIDN'T LOSE ANY WEIGHT WITH MY EXERCISE REGIMEN!
SO WE DIDN'T RESOLVE ANYTHING! WE STILL DON'T KNOW WHO HAS THE BEST WORKOUT PROGRAM!
I THINK WE DID!
WE FOUND OUT THAT OUR OWN INDIVIDUAL PROGRAMS SUIT US BEST!
AGREED! NOW LET'S GO HAVE A BIG THICK CHOCOLATE MALT!
THERE IS ONE THING THOUGH...
CAN I BORROW THAT PERSONAL TRAINER OF YOURS SOMETIME?
RIVERDALE SPA
?
FINI
11

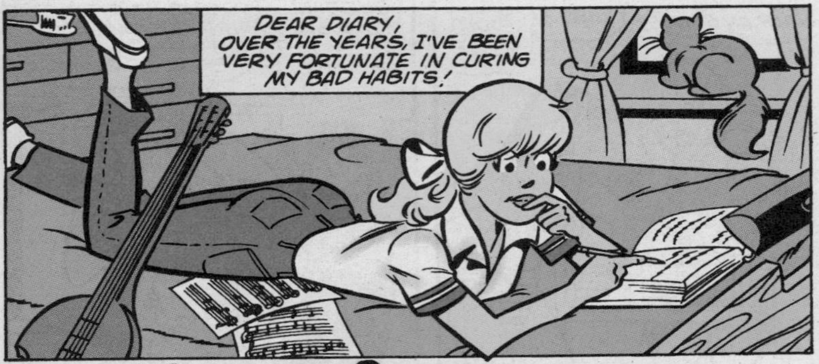
DEAR DIARY, OVER THE YEARS, I'VE BEEN VERY FORTUNATE IN CURING MY BAD HABITS!

Betty's Diary "HABIT FORMING"

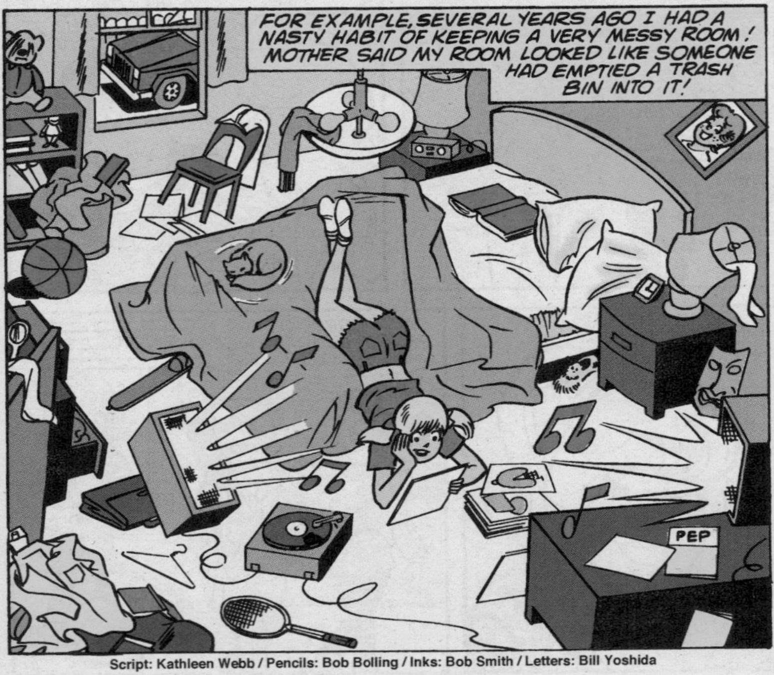
FOR EXAMPLE, SEVERAL YEARS AGO I HAD A NASTY HABIT OF KEEPING A VERY MESSY ROOM! MOTHER SAID MY ROOM LOOKED LIKE SOMEONE HAD EMPTIED A TRASH BIN INTO IT!
PEP

Script: Kathleen Webb / Pencils: Bob Bolling / Inks: Bob Smith / Letters: Bill Yoshida

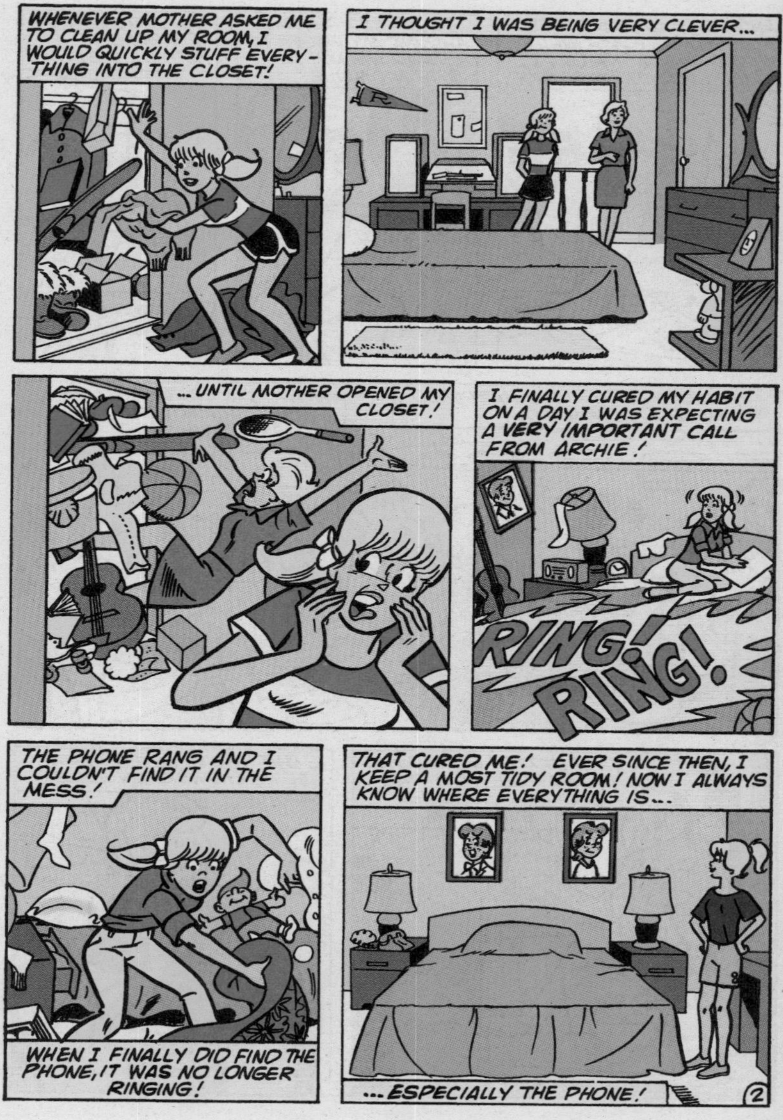
WHENEVER MOTHER ASKED ME TO CLEAN UP MY ROOM, I WOULD QUICKLY STUFF EVERY-THING INTO THE CLOSET!
I THOUGHT I WAS BEING VERY CLEVER...
... UNTIL MOTHER OPENED MY CLOSET!
I FINALLY CURED MY HABIT ON A DAY I WAS EXPECTING A VERY IMPORTANT CALL FROM ARCHIE!
RING! RING!
THE PHONE RANG AND I COULDN'T FIND IT IN THE MESS!
WHEN I FINALLY DID FIND THE PHONE, IT WAS NO LONGER RINGING!
THAT CURED ME! EVER SINCE THEN, I KEEP A MOST TIDY ROOM! NOW I ALWAYS KNOW WHERE EVERYTHING IS...
... ESPECIALLY THE PHONE!
2

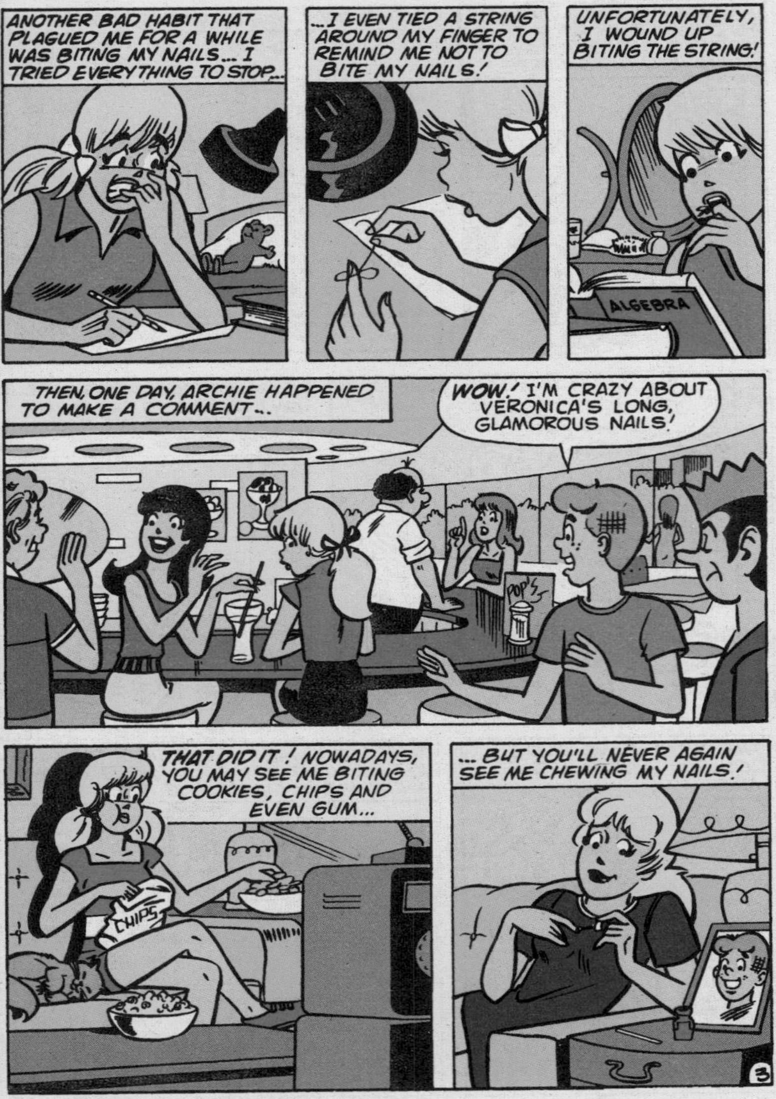

ANOTHER BAD HABIT THAT PLAGUED ME FOR A WHILE WAS BITING MY NAILS... I TRIED EVERYTHING TO STOP...
...I EVEN TIED A STRING AROUND MY FINGER TO REMIND ME NOT TO BITE MY NAILS!
UNFORTUNATELY, I WOUND UP BITING THE STRING!
ALGEBRA
THEN, ONE DAY, ARCHIE HAPPENED TO MAKE A COMMENT...
WOW! I'M CRAZY ABOUT VERONICA'S LONG, GLAMOROUS NAILS!
POP'S
THAT DID IT! NOWADAYS, YOU MAY SEE ME BITING COOKIES, CHIPS AND EVEN GUM...
CHIPS
... BUT YOU'LL NEVER AGAIN SEE ME CHEWING MY NAILS!
3

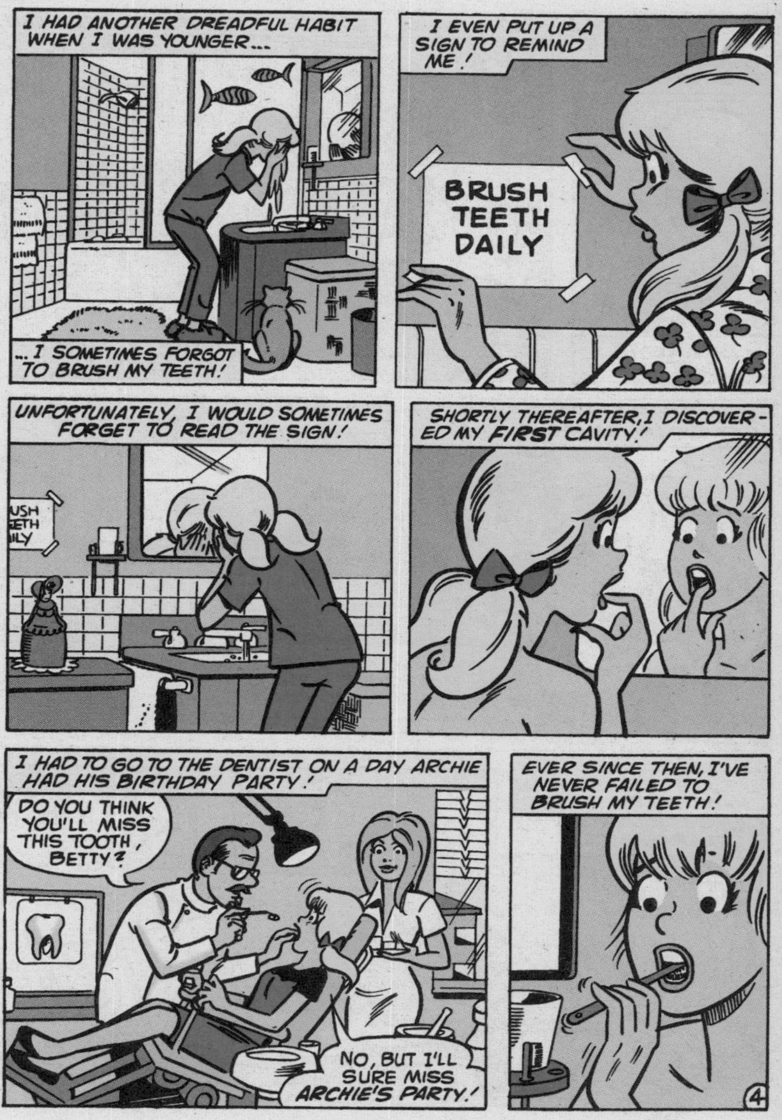
I HAD ANOTHER DREADFUL HABIT WHEN I WAS YOUNGER...
...I SOMETIMES FORGOT TO BRUSH MY TEETH!
I EVEN PUT UP A SIGN TO REMIND ME!
BRUSH TEETH DAILY
UNFORTUNATELY, I WOULD SOMETIMES FORGET TO READ THE SIGN!
SHORTLY THEREAFTER, I DISCOVERED MY FIRST CAVITY!
I HAD TO GO TO THE DENTIST ON A DAY ARCHIE HAD HIS BIRTHDAY PARTY!
DO YOU THINK YOU'LL MISS THIS TOOTH, BETTY?
NO, BUT I'LL SURE MISS ARCHIE'S PARTY!
EVER SINCE THEN, I'VE NEVER FAILED TO BRUSH MY TEETH!
4

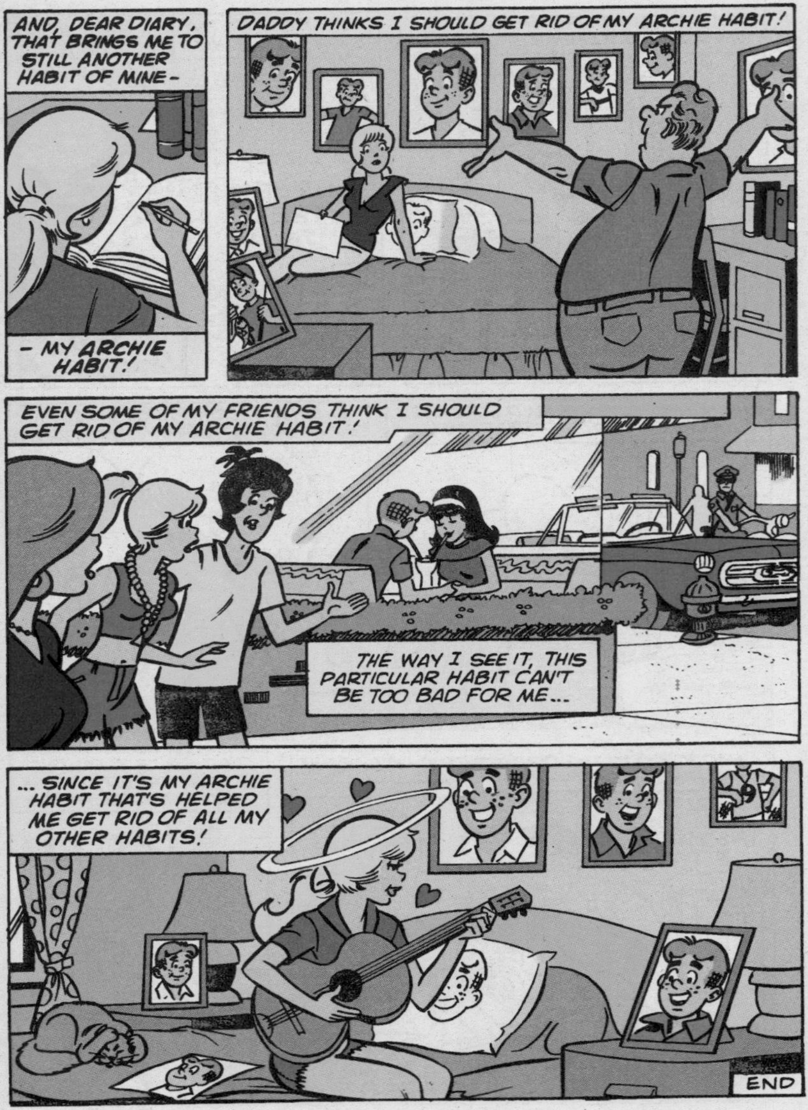
AND, DEAR DIARY, THAT BRINGS ME TO STILL ANOTHER HABIT OF MINE -
- MY ARCHIE HABIT!
DADDY THINKS I SHOULD GET RID OF MY ARCHIE HABIT!
EVEN SOME OF MY FRIENDS THINK I SHOULD GET RID OF MY ARCHIE HABIT!
THE WAY I SEE IT, THIS PARTICULAR HABIT CAN'T BE TOO BAD FOR ME...
... SINCE IT'S MY ARCHIE HABIT THAT'S HELPED ME GET RID OF ALL MY OTHER HABITS!
END

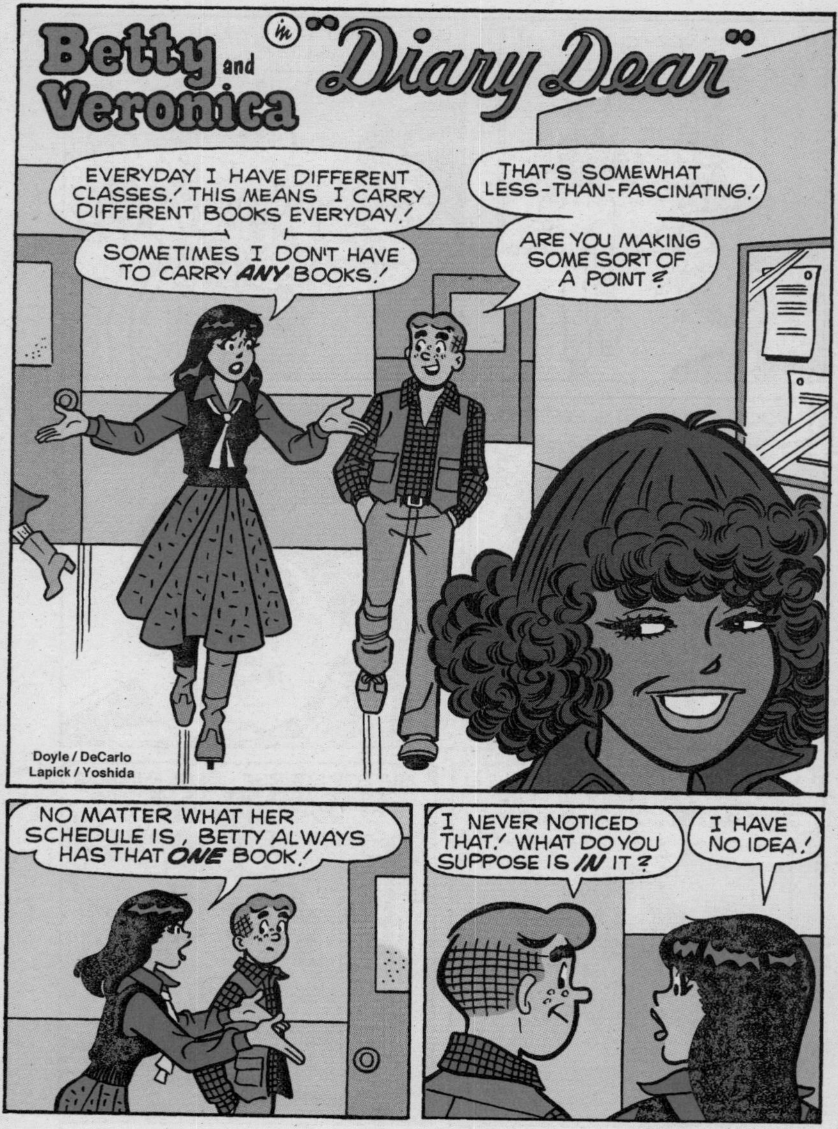
Betty and Veronica in "Diary Dear"
EVERYDAY I HAVE DIFFERENT CLASSES! THIS MEANS I CARRY DIFFERENT BOOKS EVERYDAY!
SOMETIMES I DON'T HAVE TO CARRY ANY BOOKS!
THAT'S SOMEWHAT LESS-THAN-FASCINATING!
ARE YOU MAKING SOME SORT OF A POINT?
Doyle / DeCarlo
Lapick / Yoshida
NO MATTER WHAT HER SCHEDULE IS, BETTY ALWAYS HAS THAT ONE BOOK!
I NEVER NOTICED THAT! WHAT DO YOU SUPPOSE IS IN IT?
I HAVE NO IDEA!

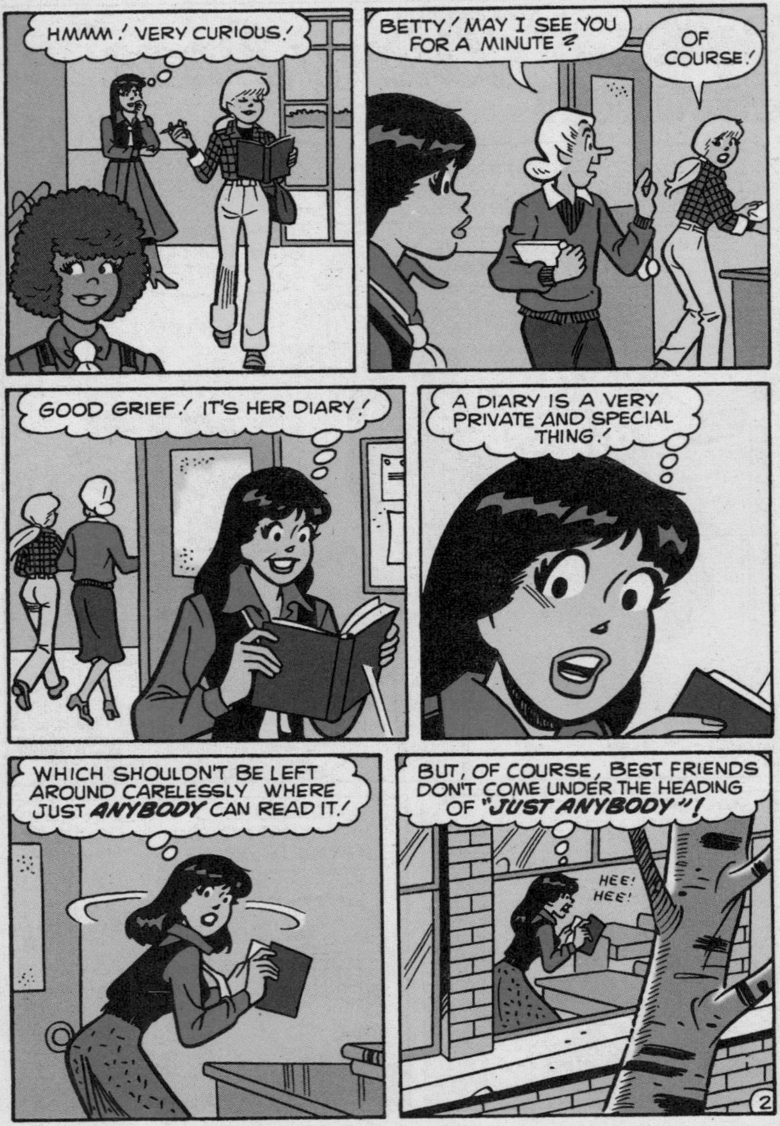

HMMM! VERY CURIOUS!
BETTY! MAY I SEE YOU FOR A MINUTE?
OF COURSE!
GOOD GRIEF! IT'S HER DIARY!
A DIARY IS A VERY PRIVATE AND SPECIAL THING!
WHICH SHOULDN'T BE LEFT AROUND CARELESSLY WHERE JUST *ANYBODY* CAN READ IT!
BUT, OF COURSE, BEST FRIENDS DON'T COME UNDER THE HEADING OF "*JUST ANYBODY*"!
HEE! HEE!
2

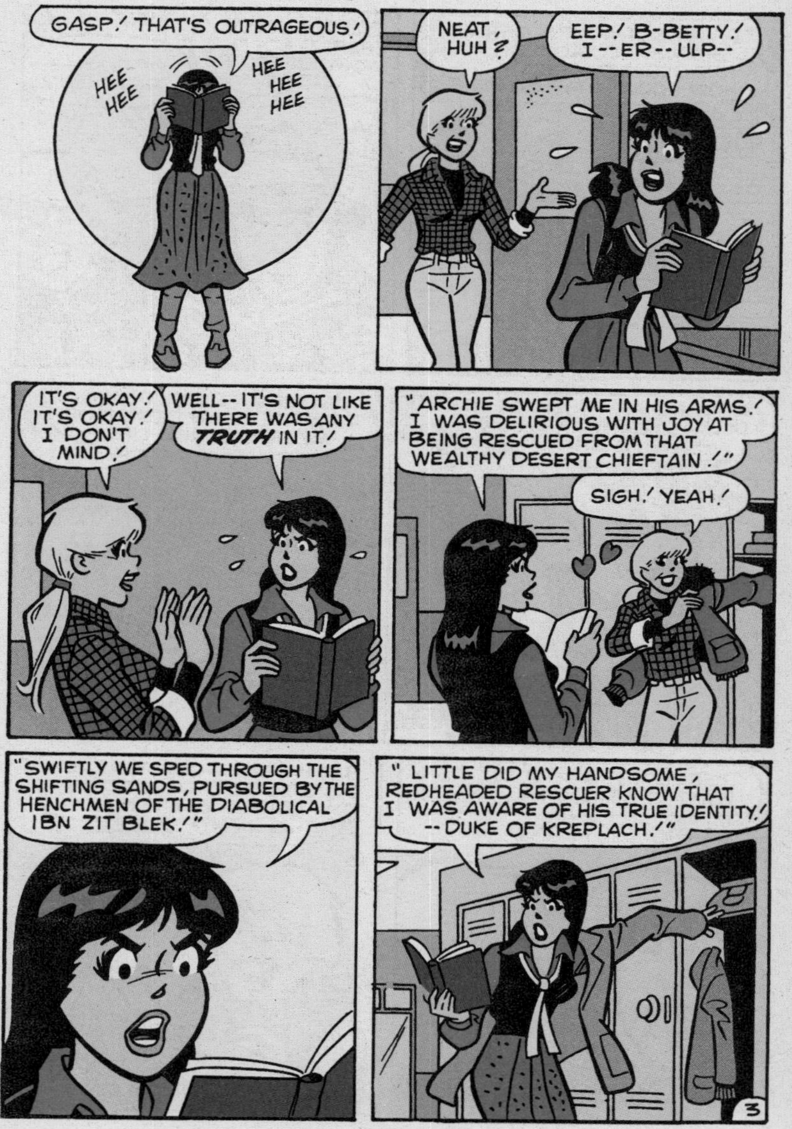

GASP! THAT'S OUTRAGEOUS!
HEE HEE
HEE HEE HEE
NEAT, HUH?
EEP! B-BETTY! I--ER--ULP--
IT'S OKAY! IT'S OKAY! I DON'T MIND!
WELL--IT'S NOT LIKE THERE WAS ANY TRUTH IN IT!
"ARCHIE SWEPT ME IN HIS ARMS! I WAS DELIRIOUS WITH JOY AT BEING RESCUED FROM THAT WEALTHY DESERT CHIEFTAIN!"
SIGH! YEAH!
"SWIFTLY WE SPED THROUGH THE SHIFTING SANDS, PURSUED BY THE HENCHMEN OF THE DIABOLICAL IBN ZIT BLEK!"
"LITTLE DID MY HANDSOME, REDHEADED RESCUER KNOW THAT I WAS AWARE OF HIS TRUE IDENTITY! --DUKE OF KREPLACH!"
3

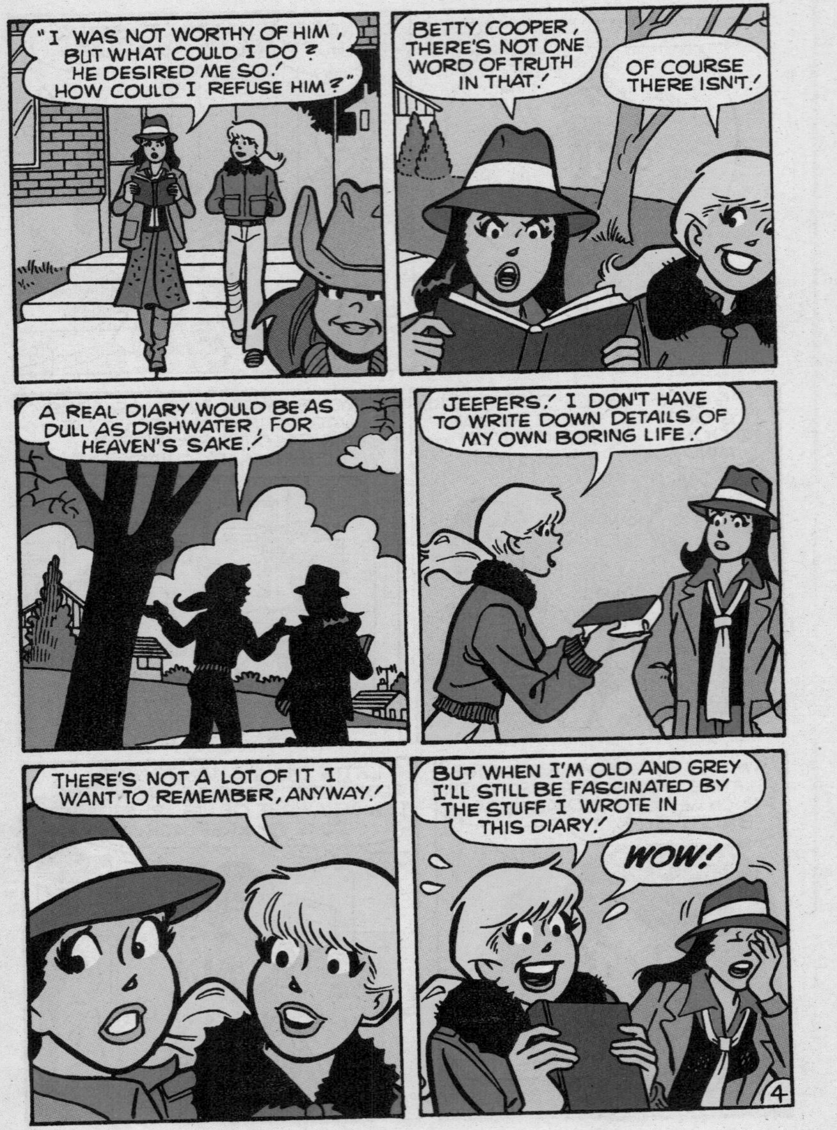
"I WAS NOT WORTHY OF HIM, BUT WHAT COULD I DO? HE DESIRED ME SO! HOW COULD I REFUSE HIM?"
BETTY COOPER, THERE'S NOT ONE WORD OF TRUTH IN THAT!
OF COURSE THERE ISN'T!
A REAL DIARY WOULD BE AS DULL AS DISHWATER, FOR HEAVEN'S SAKE!
JEEPERS! I DON'T HAVE TO WRITE DOWN DETAILS OF MY OWN BORING LIFE!
THERE'S NOT A LOT OF IT I WANT TO REMEMBER, ANYWAY!
BUT WHEN I'M OLD AND GREY I'LL STILL BE FASCINATED BY THE STUFF I WROTE IN THIS DIARY!
WOW!
4

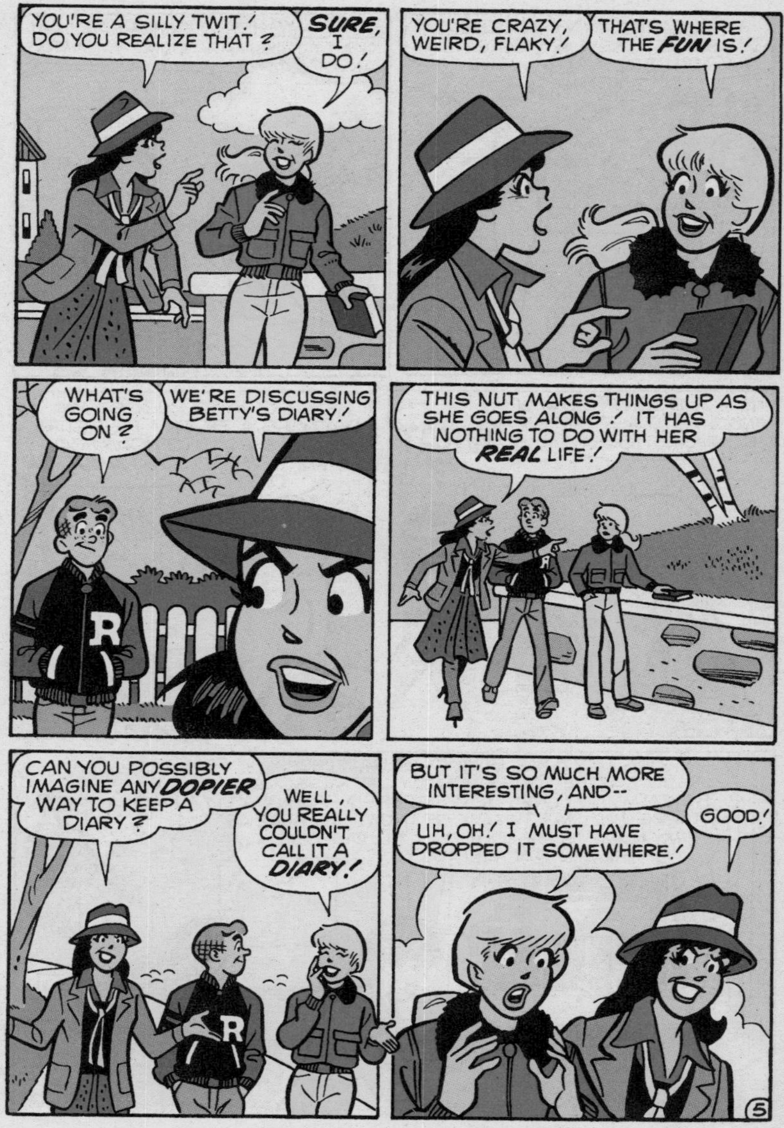
YOU'RE A SILLY TWIT! DO YOU REALIZE THAT?
SURE, I DO!
YOU'RE CRAZY, WEIRD, FLAKY!
THAT'S WHERE THE FUN IS!
WHAT'S GOING ON?
WE'RE DISCUSSING BETTY'S DIARY!
THIS NUT MAKES THINGS UP AS SHE GOES ALONG! IT HAS NOTHING TO DO WITH HER REAL LIFE!
CAN YOU POSSIBLY IMAGINE ANY DOPIER WAY TO KEEP A DIARY?
WELL, YOU REALLY COULDN'T CALL IT A DIARY!
BUT IT'S SO MUCH MORE INTERESTING, AND--
UH, OH! I MUST HAVE DROPPED IT SOMEWHERE!
GOOD!
5

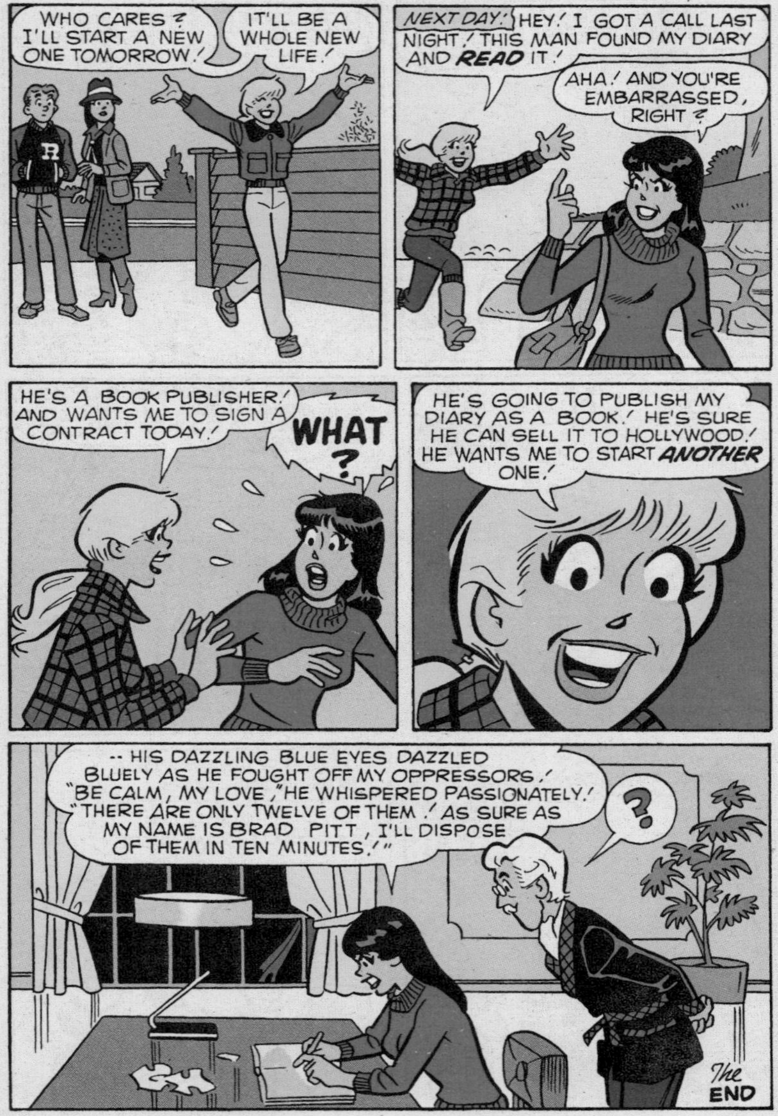
WHO CARES? I'LL START A NEW ONE TOMORROW!
IT'LL BE A WHOLE NEW LIFE!
NEXT DAY: HEY! I GOT A CALL LAST NIGHT! THIS MAN FOUND MY DIARY AND READ IT!
AHA! AND YOU'RE EMBARRASSED, RIGHT?
HE'S A BOOK PUBLISHER! AND WANTS ME TO SIGN A CONTRACT TODAY!
WHAT?
HE'S GOING TO PUBLISH MY DIARY AS A BOOK! HE'S SURE HE CAN SELL IT TO HOLLYWOOD! HE WANTS ME TO START ANOTHER ONE!
-- HIS DAZZLING BLUE EYES DAZZLED BLUELY AS HE FOUGHT OFF MY OPPRESSORS! "BE CALM, MY LOVE," HE WHISPERED PASSIONATELY! "THERE ARE ONLY TWELVE OF THEM! AS SURE AS MY NAME IS BRAD PITT, I'LL DISPOSE OF THEM IN TEN MINUTES!"
?
The END

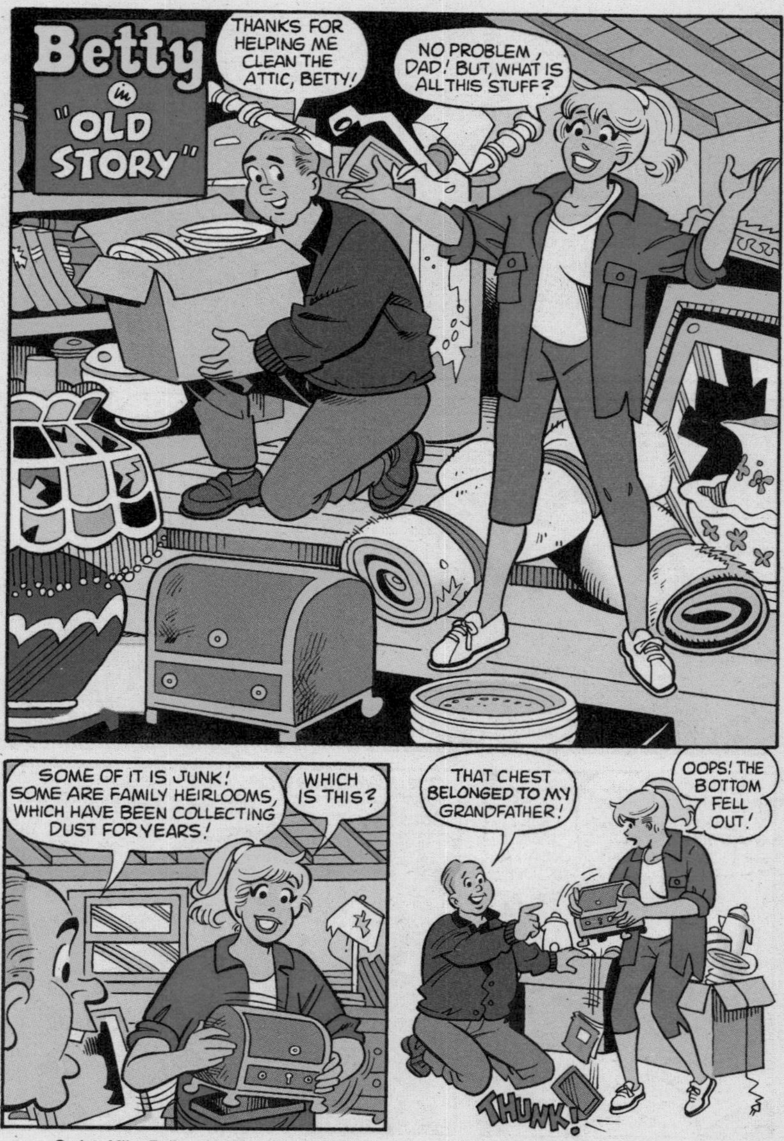
Betty
in
"OLD STORY"
THANKS FOR HELPING ME CLEAN THE ATTIC, BETTY!
NO PROBLEM, DAD! BUT, WHAT IS ALL THIS STUFF?
SOME OF IT IS JUNK! SOME ARE FAMILY HEIRLOOMS, WHICH HAVE BEEN COLLECTING DUST FOR YEARS!
WHICH IS THIS?
THAT CHEST BELONGED TO MY GRANDFATHER!
OOPS! THE BOTTOM FELL OUT!
THUNK!

Script: Mike Pellowski / Pencils: Stan Goldberg / Inks: John Lowe / Letters: Bill Yoshida

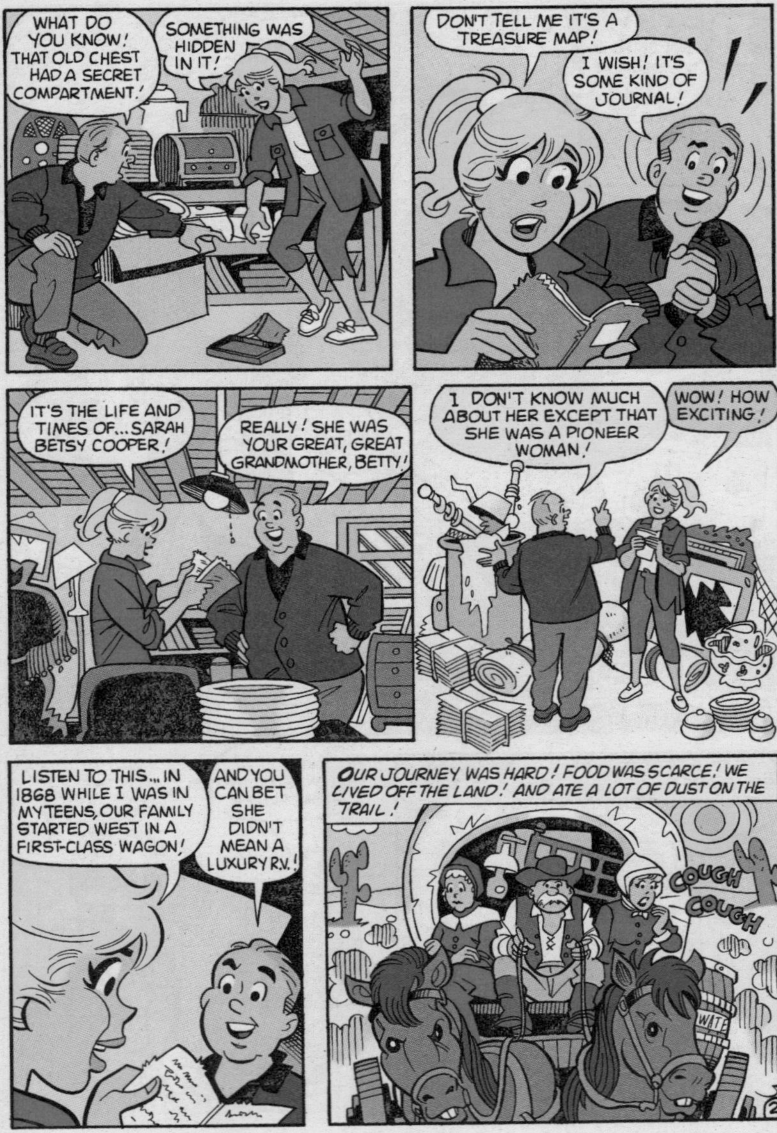
WHAT DO YOU KNOW! THAT OLD CHEST HAD A SECRET COMPARTMENT!
SOMETHING WAS HIDDEN IN IT!
DON'T TELL ME IT'S A TREASURE MAP!
I WISH! IT'S SOME KIND OF JOURNAL!
IT'S THE LIFE AND TIMES OF...SARAH BETSY COOPER!
REALLY! SHE WAS YOUR GREAT, GREAT GRANDMOTHER, BETTY!
I DON'T KNOW MUCH ABOUT HER EXCEPT THAT SHE WAS A PIONEER WOMAN!
WOW! HOW EXCITING!
LISTEN TO THIS... IN 1868 WHILE I WAS IN MY TEENS, OUR FAMILY STARTED WEST IN A FIRST-CLASS WAGON!
AND YOU CAN BET SHE DIDN'T MEAN A LUXURY R.V.!
OUR JOURNEY WAS HARD! FOOD WAS SCARCE! WE LIVED OFF THE LAND! AND ATE A LOT OF DUST ON THE TRAIL!
COUGH
COUGH
2

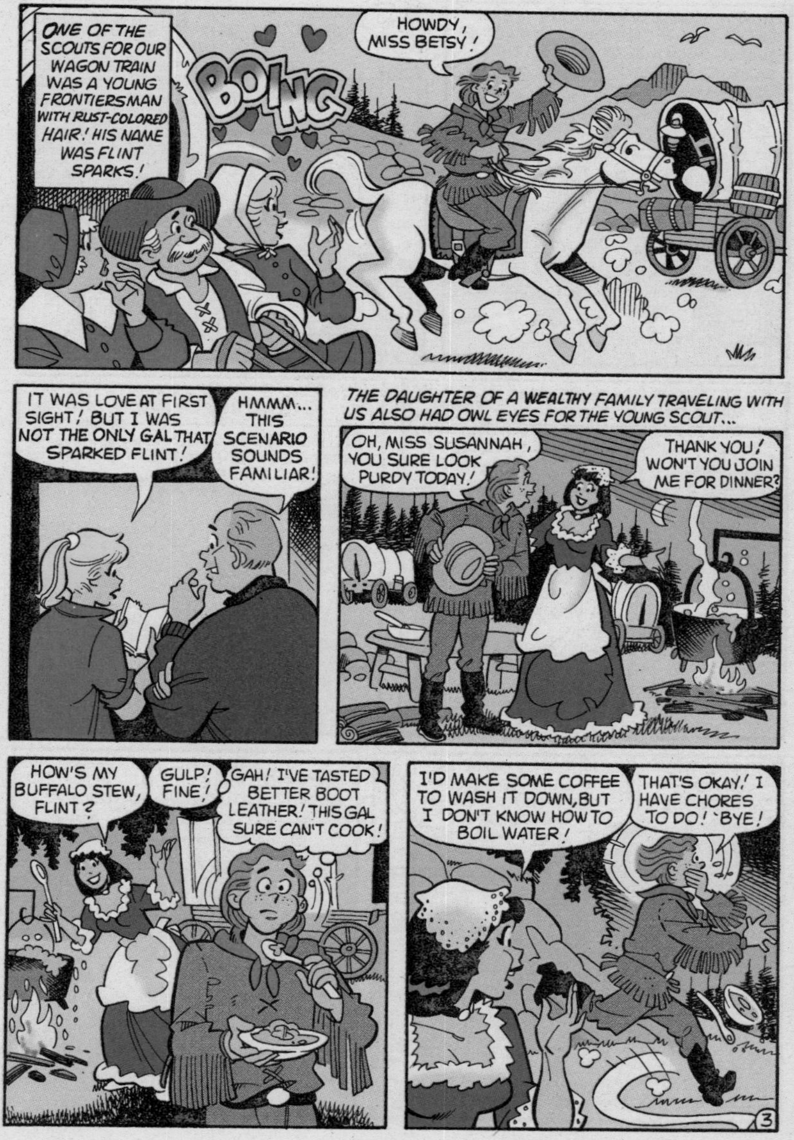
ONE OF THE SCOUTS FOR OUR WAGON TRAIN WAS A YOUNG FRONTIERSMAN WITH RUST-COLORED HAIR! HIS NAME WAS FLINT SPARKS!
BOING
HOWDY, MISS BETSY!
IT WAS LOVE AT FIRST SIGHT! BUT I WAS NOT THE ONLY GAL THAT SPARKED FLINT!
HMMM... THIS SCENARIO SOUNDS FAMILIAR!
THE DAUGHTER OF A WEALTHY FAMILY TRAVELING WITH US ALSO HAD OWL EYES FOR THE YOUNG SCOUT...
OH, MISS SUSANNAH, YOU SURE LOOK PURDY TODAY!
THANK YOU! WON'T YOU JOIN ME FOR DINNER?
HOW'S MY BUFFALO STEW, FLINT?
GULP! FINE!
GAH! I'VE TASTED BETTER BOOT LEATHER! THIS GAL SURE CAN'T COOK!
I'D MAKE SOME COFFEE TO WASH IT DOWN, BUT I DON'T KNOW HOW TO BOIL WATER!
THAT'S OKAY! I HAVE CHORES TO DO! 'BYE!
3

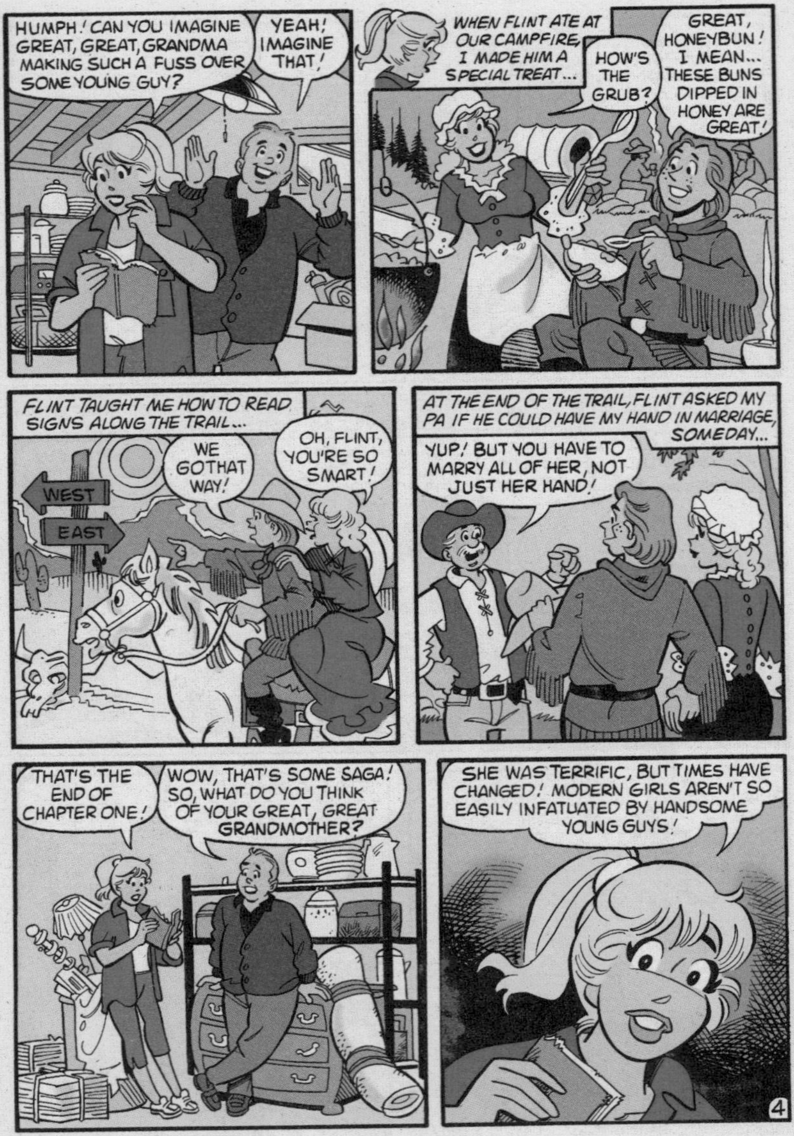
HUMPH! CAN YOU IMAGINE GREAT, GREAT, GRANDMA MAKING SUCH A FUSS OVER SOME YOUNG GUY?
YEAH! IMAGINE THAT!
WHEN FLINT ATE AT OUR CAMPFIRE, I MADE HIM A SPECIAL TREAT...
HOW'S THE GRUB?
GREAT, HONEYBUN! I MEAN... THESE BUNS DIPPED IN HONEY ARE GREAT!
FLINT TAUGHT ME HOW TO READ SIGNS ALONG THE TRAIL...
WEST
EAST
WE GOT THAT WAY!
OH, FLINT, YOU'RE SO SMART!
AT THE END OF THE TRAIL, FLINT ASKED MY PA IF HE COULD HAVE MY HAND IN MARRIAGE, SOMEDAY...
YUP! BUT YOU HAVE TO MARRY ALL OF HER, NOT JUST HER HAND!
THAT'S THE END OF CHAPTER ONE!
WOW, THAT'S SOME SAGA! SO, WHAT DO YOU THINK OF YOUR GREAT, GREAT GRANDMOTHER?
SHE WAS TERRIFIC, BUT TIMES HAVE CHANGED! MODERN GIRLS AREN'T SO EASILY INFATUATED BY HANDSOME YOUNG GUYS!
4

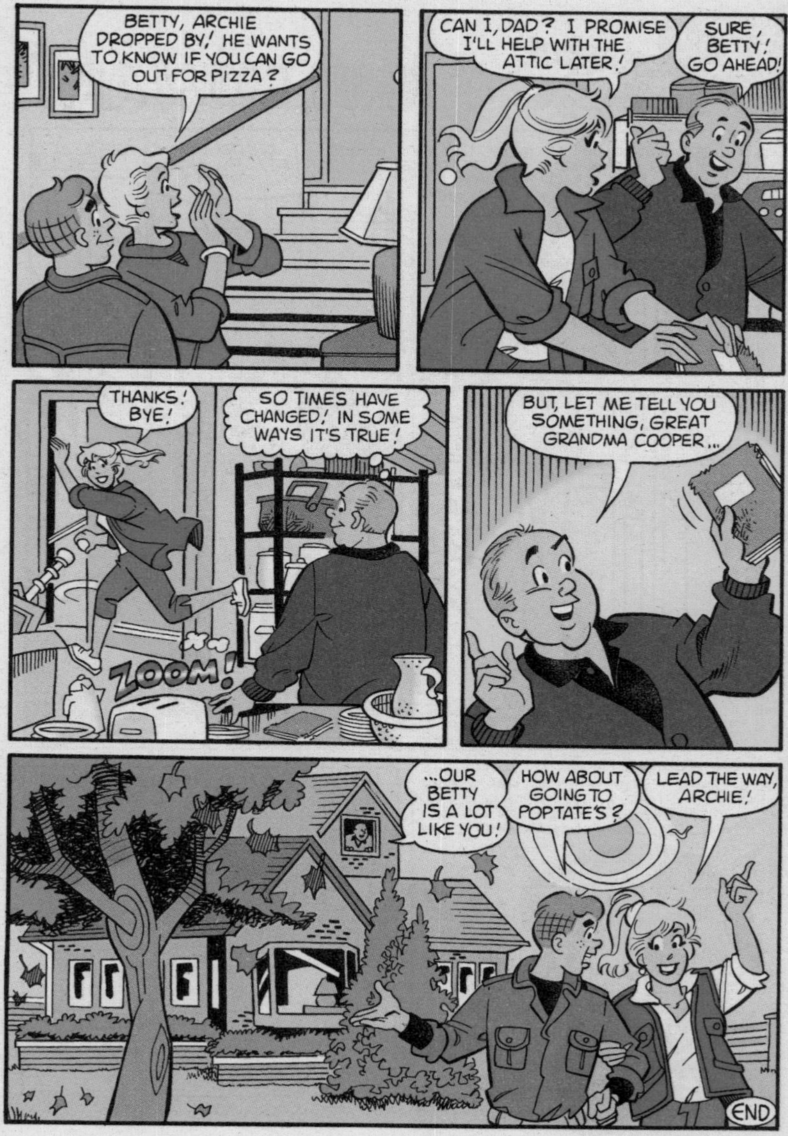
BETTY, ARCHIE DROPPED BY! HE WANTS TO KNOW IF YOU CAN GO OUT FOR PIZZA?
CAN I, DAD? I PROMISE I'LL HELP WITH THE ATTIC LATER!
SURE, BETTY! GO AHEAD!
THANKS! BYE!
SO TIMES HAVE CHANGED! IN SOME WAYS IT'S TRUE!
ZOOM!
BUT, LET ME TELL YOU SOMETHING, GREAT GRANDMA COOPER...
...OUR BETTY IS A LOT LIKE YOU!
HOW ABOUT GOING TO POP TATE'S?
LEAD THE WAY, ARCHIE!
END

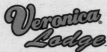

Veronica Lodge in "OUI, MON AMI"

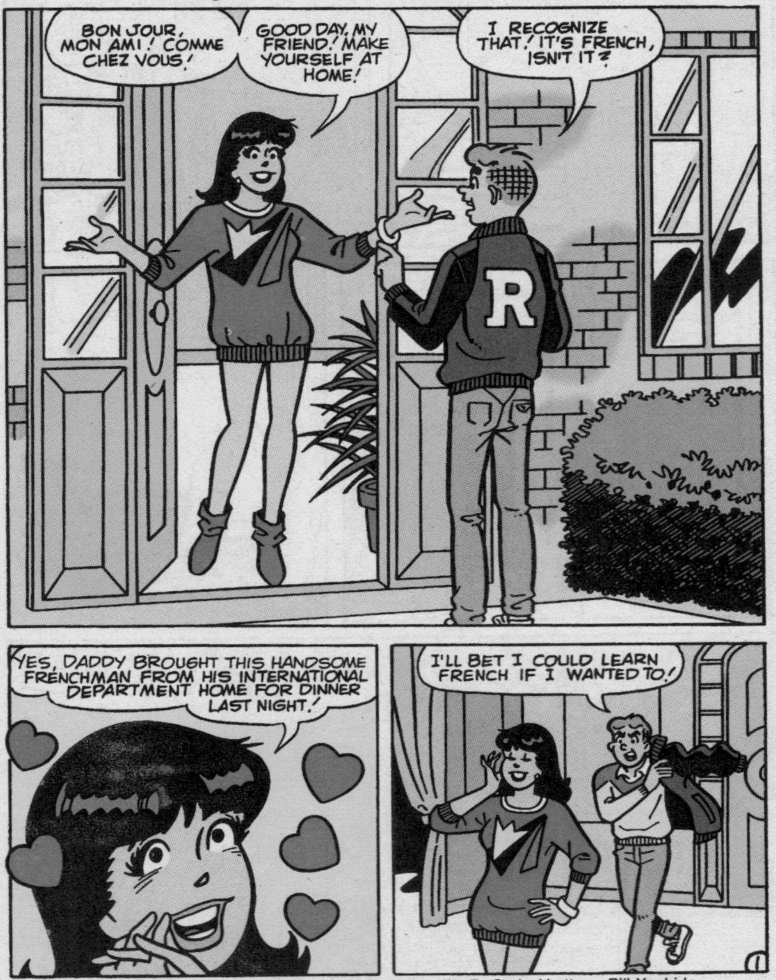

BON JOUR, MON AMI! COMME CHEZ VOUS!
GOOD DAY, MY FRIEND! MAKE YOURSELF AT HOME!
I RECOGNIZE THAT! IT'S FRENCH, ISN'T IT?
R
YES, DADDY BROUGHT THIS HANDSOME FRENCHMAN FROM HIS INTERNATIONAL DEPARTMENT HOME FOR DINNER LAST NIGHT!
I'LL BET I COULD LEARN FRENCH IF I WANTED TO!
1

Script: Jim Ruth / Pencils: Dan DeCarlo Jr. / Inks: Jim DeCarlo / Letters: Bill Yoshida

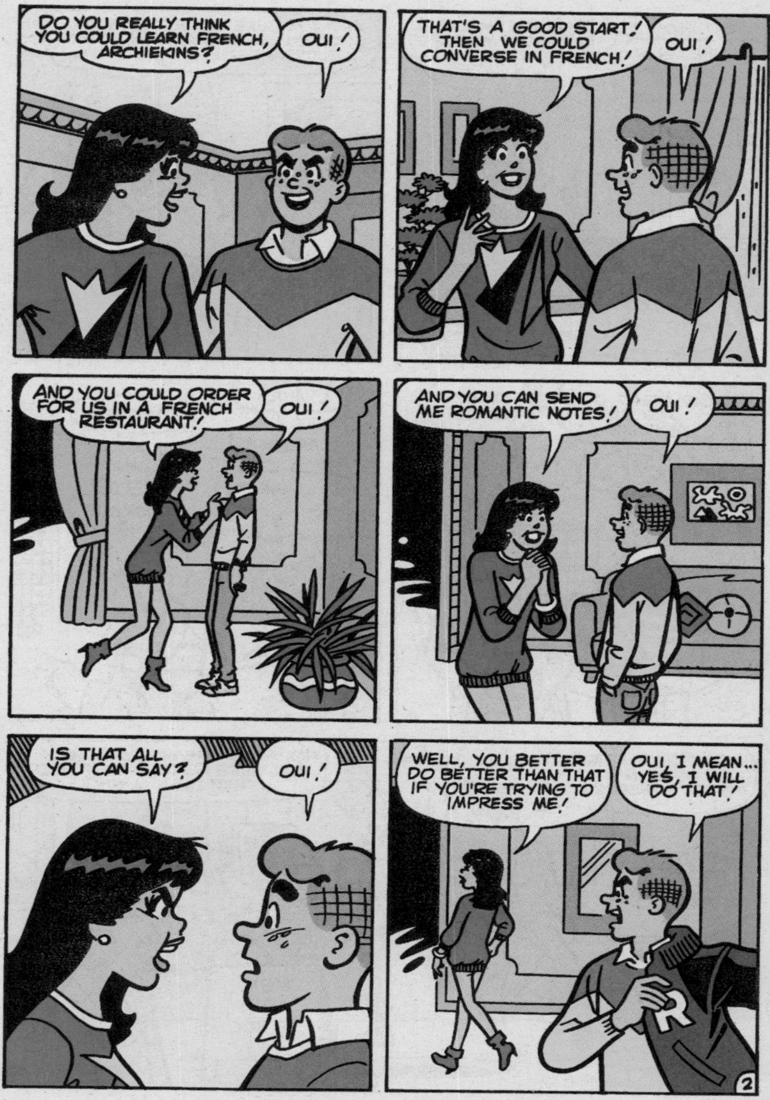
DO YOU REALLY THINK YOU COULD LEARN FRENCH, ARCHIEKINS?
OUI!
THAT'S A GOOD START! THEN WE COULD CONVERSE IN FRENCH!
OUI!
AND YOU COULD ORDER FOR US IN A FRENCH RESTAURANT!
OUI!
AND YOU CAN SEND ME ROMANTIC NOTES!
OUI!
IS THAT ALL YOU CAN SAY?
OUI!
WELL, YOU BETTER DO BETTER THAN THAT IF YOU'RE TRYING TO IMPRESS ME!
OUI, I MEAN... YES, I WILL DO THAT!
2

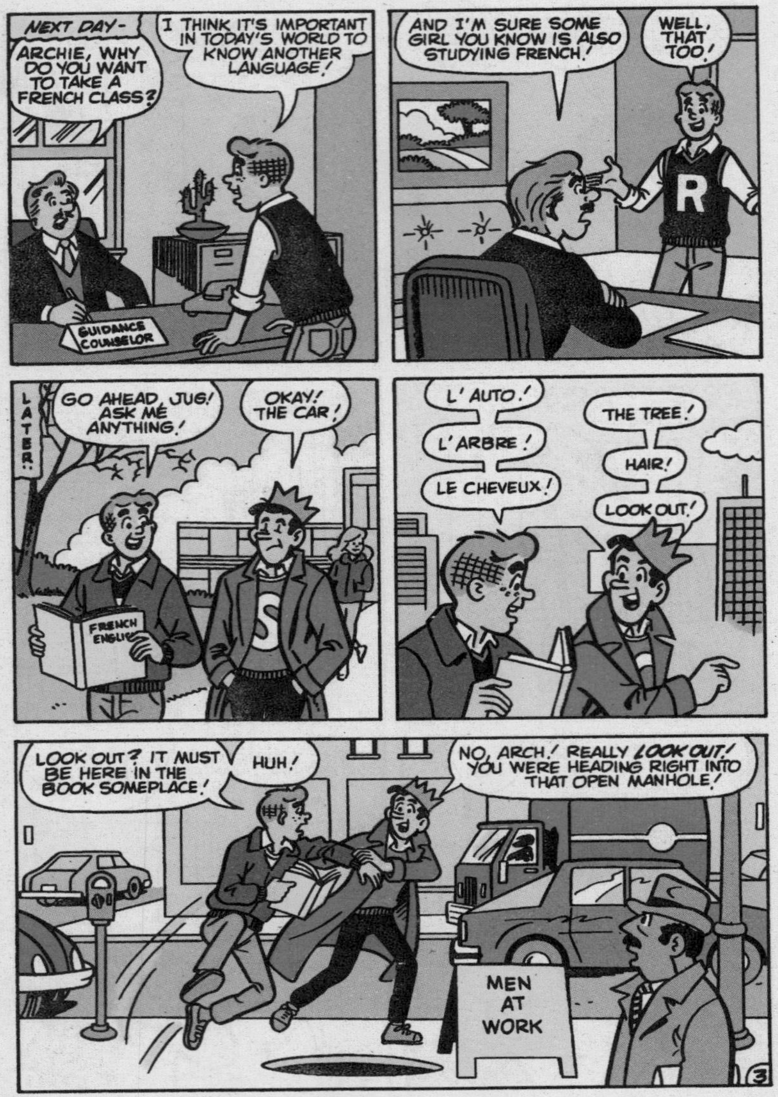
NEXT DAY-
ARCHIE, WHY DO YOU WANT TO TAKE A FRENCH CLASS?
I THINK IT'S IMPORTANT IN TODAY'S WORLD TO KNOW ANOTHER LANGUAGE!
GUIDANCE COUNSELOR
AND I'M SURE SOME GIRL YOU KNOW IS ALSO STUDYING FRENCH!
WELL, THAT TOO!
R
LATER:
GO AHEAD, JUG! ASK ME ANYTHING!
OKAY! THE CAR!
FRENCH ENGLI
S
L' AUTO!
THE TREE!
L' ARBRE!
HAIR!
LE CHEVEUX!
LOOK OUT!
LOOK OUT? IT MUST BE HERE IN THE BOOK SOMEPLACE!
HUH!
NO, ARCH! REALLY *LOOK OUT!* YOU WERE HEADING RIGHT INTO THAT OPEN MANHOLE!
MEN AT WORK
3

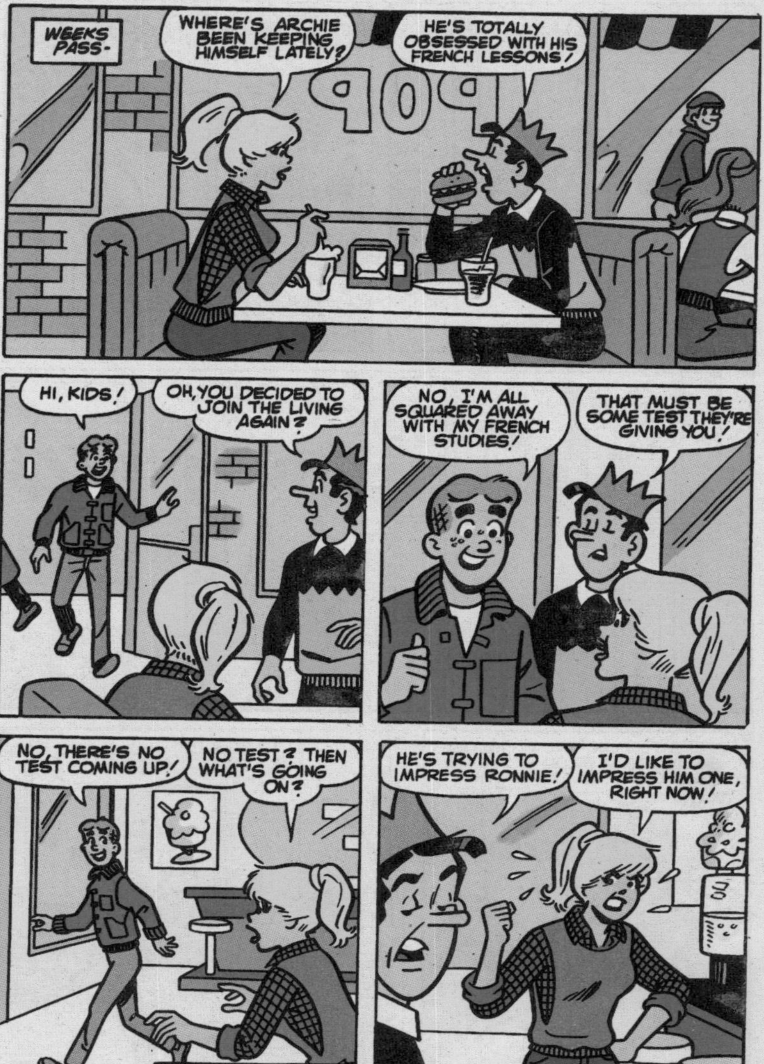
WEEKS PASS-
WHERE'S ARCHIE BEEN KEEPING HIMSELF LATELY?
HE'S TOTALLY OBSESSED WITH HIS FRENCH LESSONS!
POP
HI, KIDS!
OH, YOU DECIDED TO JOIN THE LIVING AGAIN?
NO, I'M ALL SQUARED AWAY WITH MY FRENCH STUDIES!
THAT MUST BE SOME TEST THEY'RE GIVING YOU!
NO, THERE'S NO TEST COMING UP!
NO TEST? THEN WHAT'S GOING ON?
HE'S TRYING TO IMPRESS RONNIE!
I'D LIKE TO IMPRESS HIM ONE, RIGHT NOW!
4

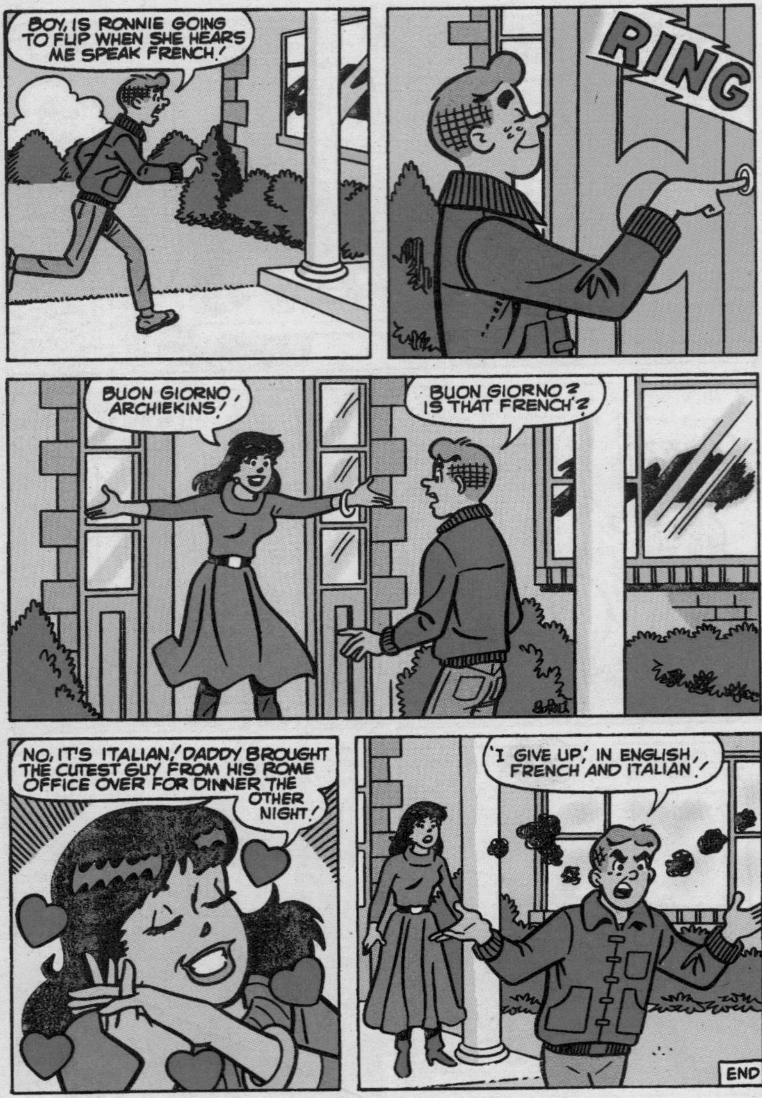
BOY, IS RONNIE GOING TO FLIP WHEN SHE HEARS ME SPEAK FRENCH!
RING
BUON GIORNO, ARCHIEKINS!
BUON GIORNO? IS THAT FRENCH?
NO, IT'S ITALIAN! DADDY BROUGHT THE CUTEST GUY FROM HIS ROME OFFICE OVER FOR DINNER THE OTHER NIGHT!
'I GIVE UP,' IN ENGLISH, FRENCH AND ITALIAN!
END

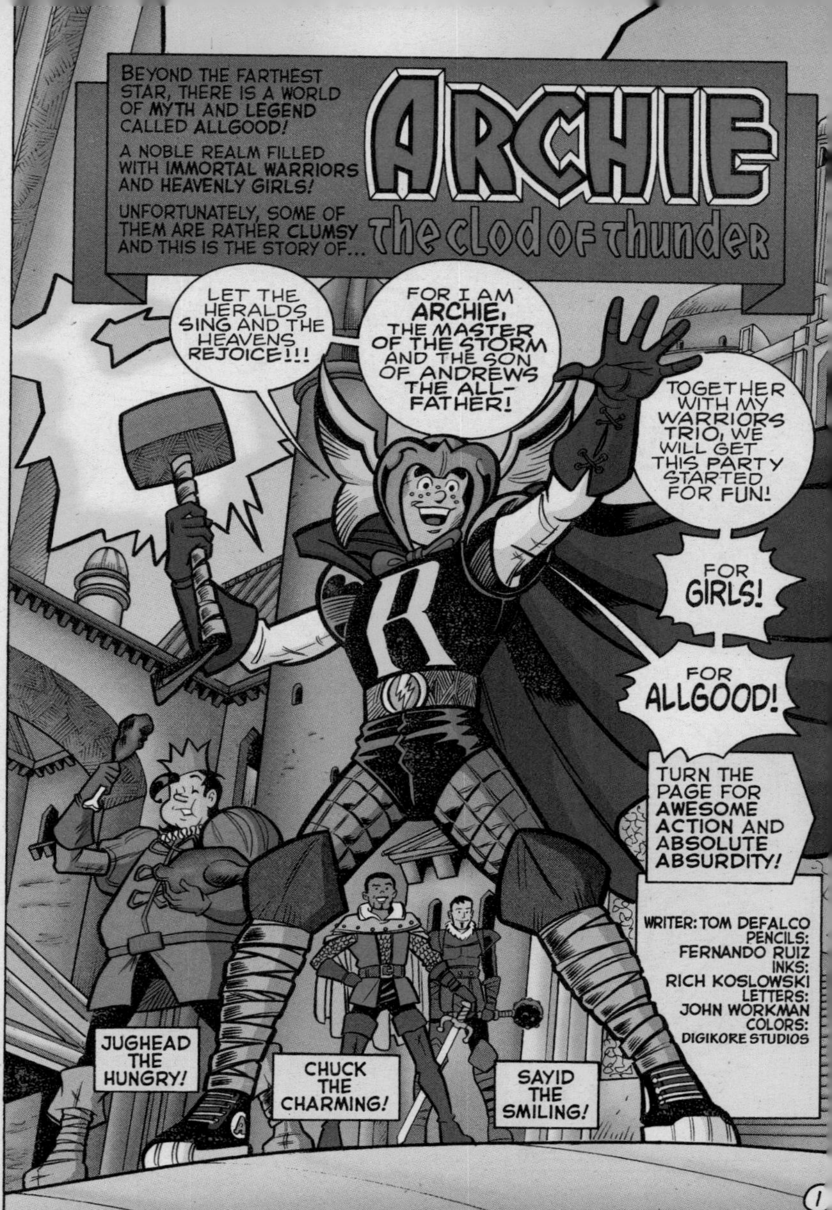

BEYOND THE FARTHEST STAR, THERE IS A WORLD OF MYTH AND LEGEND CALLED ALLGOOD!
A NOBLE REALM FILLED WITH IMMORTAL WARRIORS AND HEAVENLY GIRLS!
UNFORTUNATELY, SOME OF THEM ARE RATHER CLUMSY AND THIS IS THE STORY OF...
ARCHIE
the clod of thunder
LET THE HERALDS SING AND THE HEAVENS REJOICE!!!
FOR I AM ARCHIE, THE MASTER OF THE STORM AND THE SON OF ANDREWS THE ALL-FATHER!
TOGETHER WITH MY WARRIORS TRIO, WE WILL GET THIS PARTY STARTED FOR FUN!
FOR GIRLS!
FOR ALLGOOD!
TURN THE PAGE FOR AWESOME ACTION AND ABSOLUTE ABSURDITY!
WRITER: TOM DEFALCO PENCILS: FERNANDO RUIZ INKS: RICH KOSLOWSKI LETTERS: JOHN WORKMAN COLORS: DIGIKORE STUDIOS
JUGHEAD THE HUNGRY!
CHUCK THE CHARMING!
SAYID THE SMILING!

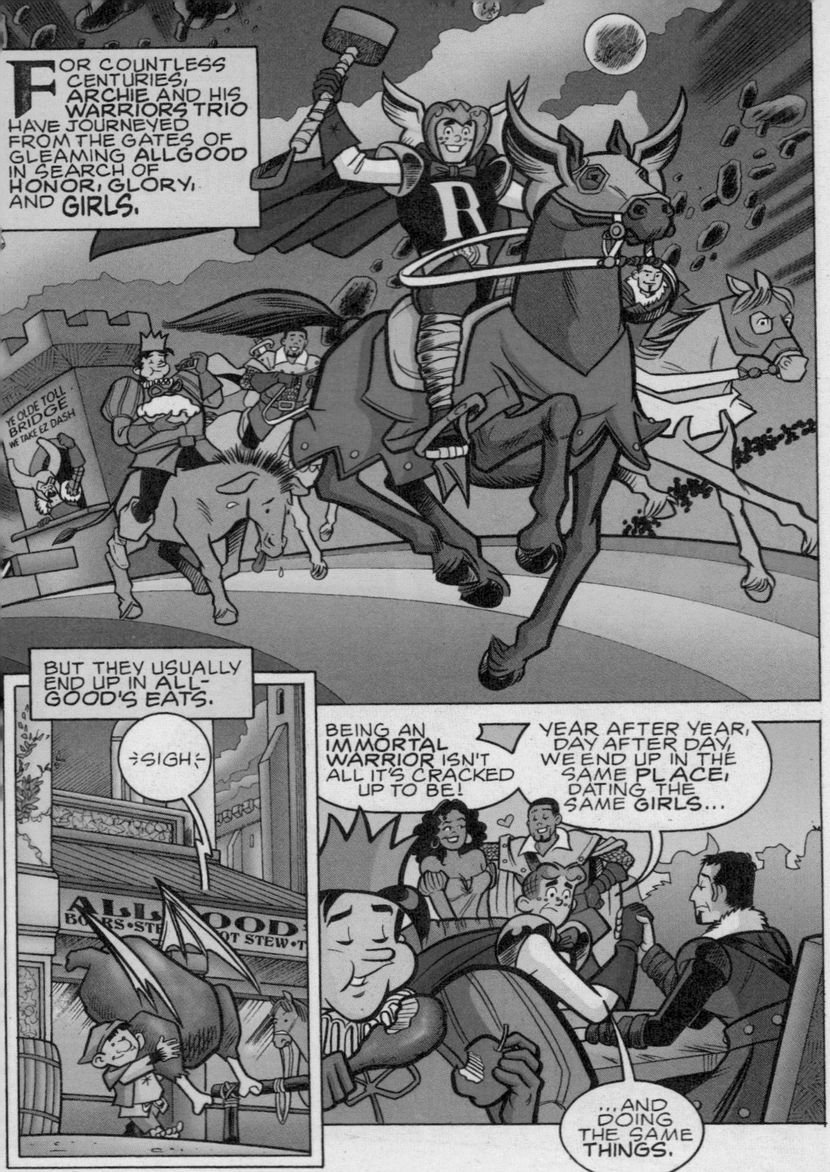

FOR COUNTLESS CENTURIES, ARCHIE AND HIS WARRIORS TRIO HAVE JOURNEYED FROM THE GATES OF GLEAMING ALLGOOD IN SEARCH OF HONOR, GLORY, AND GIRLS.
YE OLDE TOLL BRIDGE WE TAKE EZ DASH
BUT THEY USUALLY END UP IN ALL-GOOD'S EATS.
SIGH
BEING AN IMMORTAL WARRIOR ISN'T ALL IT'S CRACKED UP TO BE!
YEAR AFTER YEAR, DAY AFTER DAY, WE END UP IN THE SAME PLACE, DATING THE SAME GIRLS...
...AND DOING THE SAME THINGS.

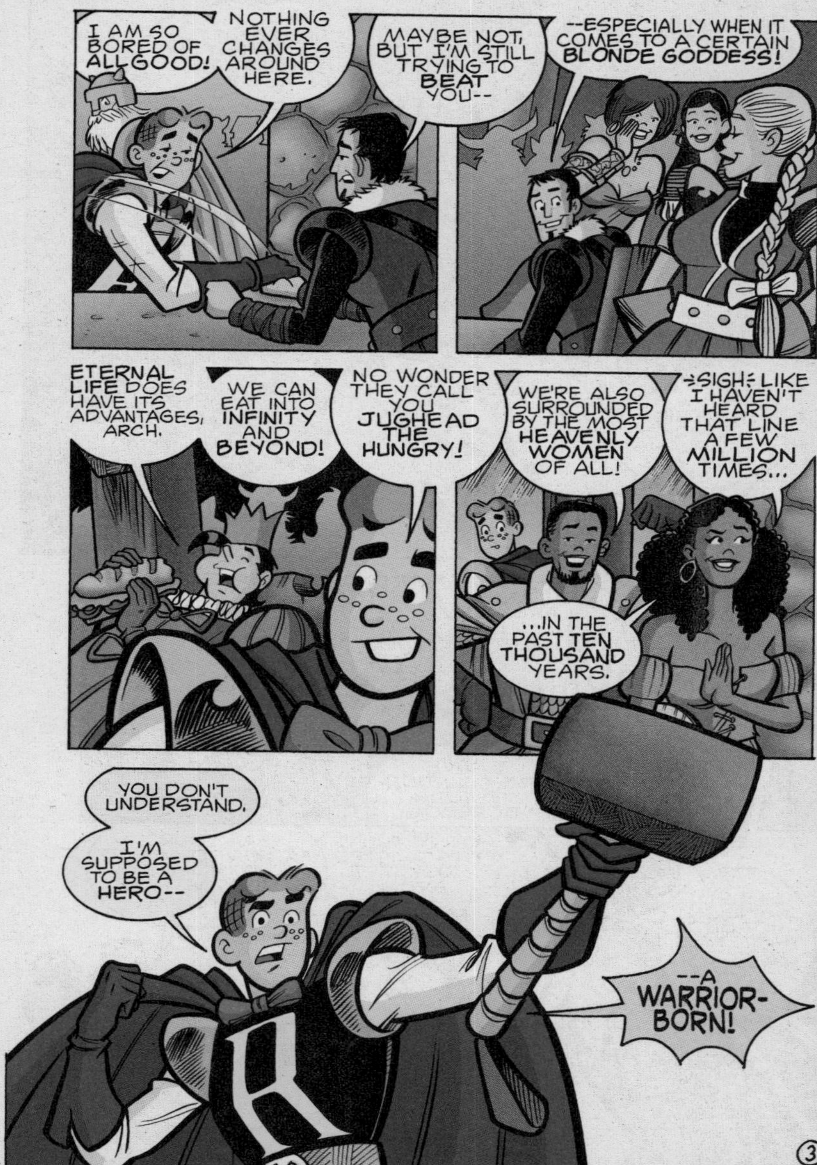
I AM SO BORED OF ALLGOOD!
NOTHING EVER CHANGES AROUND HERE.
MAYBE NOT, BUT I'M STILL TRYING TO BEAT YOU--
--ESPECIALLY WHEN IT COMES TO A CERTAIN BLONDE GODDESS!
ETERNAL LIFE DOES HAVE ITS ADVANTAGES, ARCH.
WE CAN EAT INTO INFINITY AND BEYOND!
NO WONDER THEY CALL YOU JUGHEAD THE HUNGRY!
WE'RE ALSO SURROUNDED BY THE MOST HEAVENLY WOMEN OF ALL!
=SIGH= LIKE I HAVEN'T HEARD THAT LINE A FEW MILLION TIMES...
...IN THE PAST TEN THOUSAND YEARS.
YOU DON'T UNDERSTAND.
I'M SUPPOSED TO BE A HERO--
--A WARRIOR-BORN!

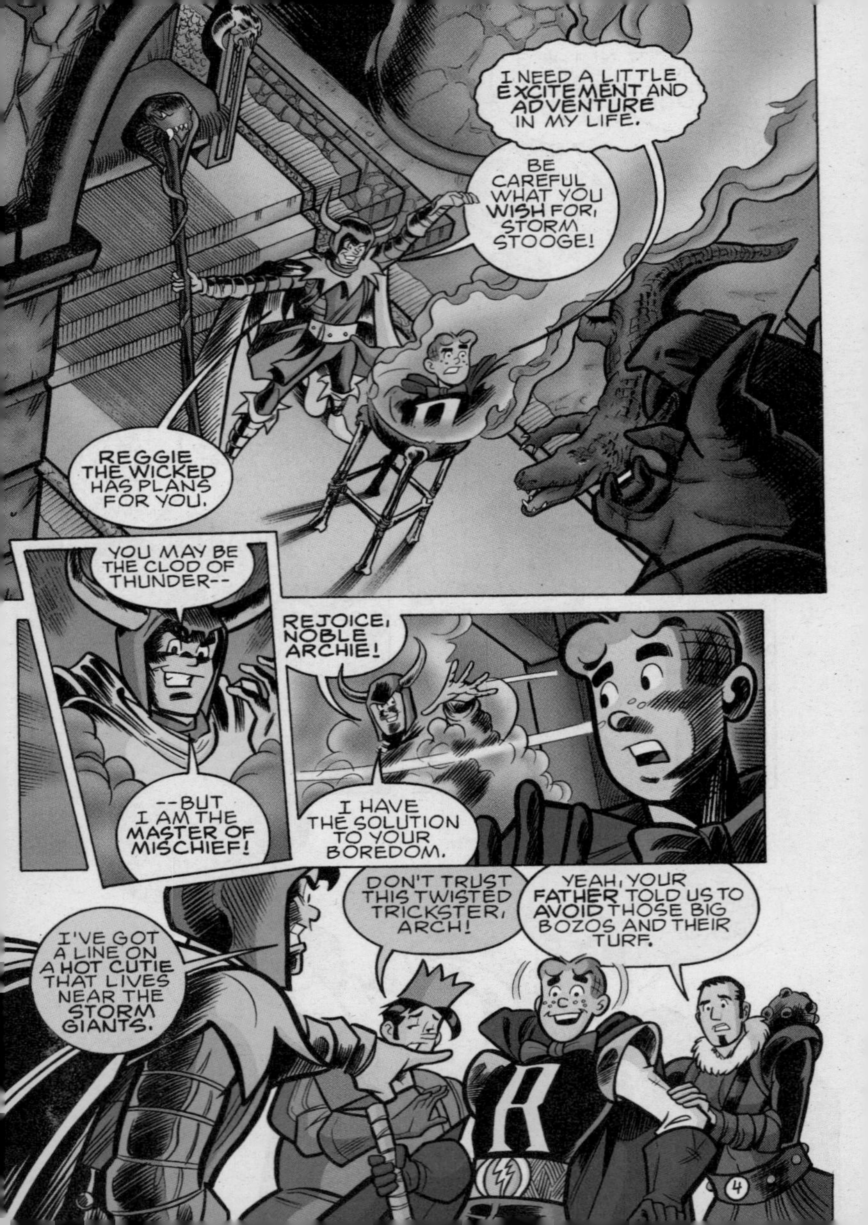
I NEED A LITTLE EXCITEMENT AND ADVENTURE IN MY LIFE.
BE CAREFUL WHAT YOU WISH FOR, STORM STOOGE!
REGGIE THE WICKED HAS PLANS FOR YOU.
YOU MAY BE THE CLOD OF THUNDER--
--BUT I AM THE MASTER OF MISCHIEF!
REJOICE, NOBLE ARCHIE!
I HAVE THE SOLUTION TO YOUR BOREDOM.
I'VE GOT A LINE ON A HOT CUTIE THAT LIVES NEAR THE STORM GIANTS.
DON'T TRUST THIS TWISTED TRICKSTER, ARCH!
YEAH, YOUR FATHER TOLD US TO AVOID THOSE BIG BOZOS AND THEIR TURF.
4

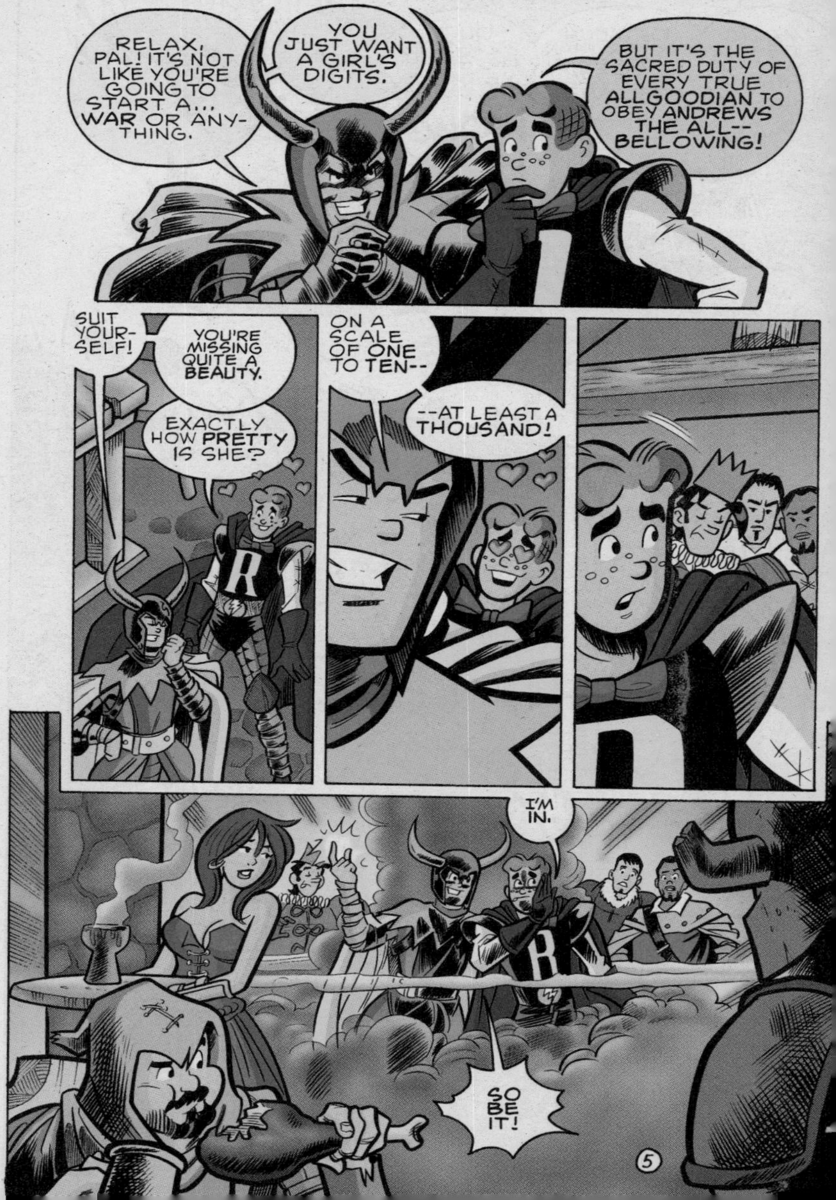
RELAX, PAL! IT'S NOT LIKE YOU'RE GOING TO START A... WAR OR ANYTHING.
YOU JUST WANT A GIRL'S DIGITS.
BUT IT'S THE SACRED DUTY OF EVERY TRUE ALLGOODIAN TO OBEY ANDREWS THE ALL--BELLOWING!
SUIT YOURSELF!
YOU'RE MISSING QUITE A BEAUTY.
EXACTLY HOW PRETTY IS SHE?
ON A SCALE OF ONE TO TEN--
--AT LEAST A THOUSAND!
I'M IN.
SO BE IT!

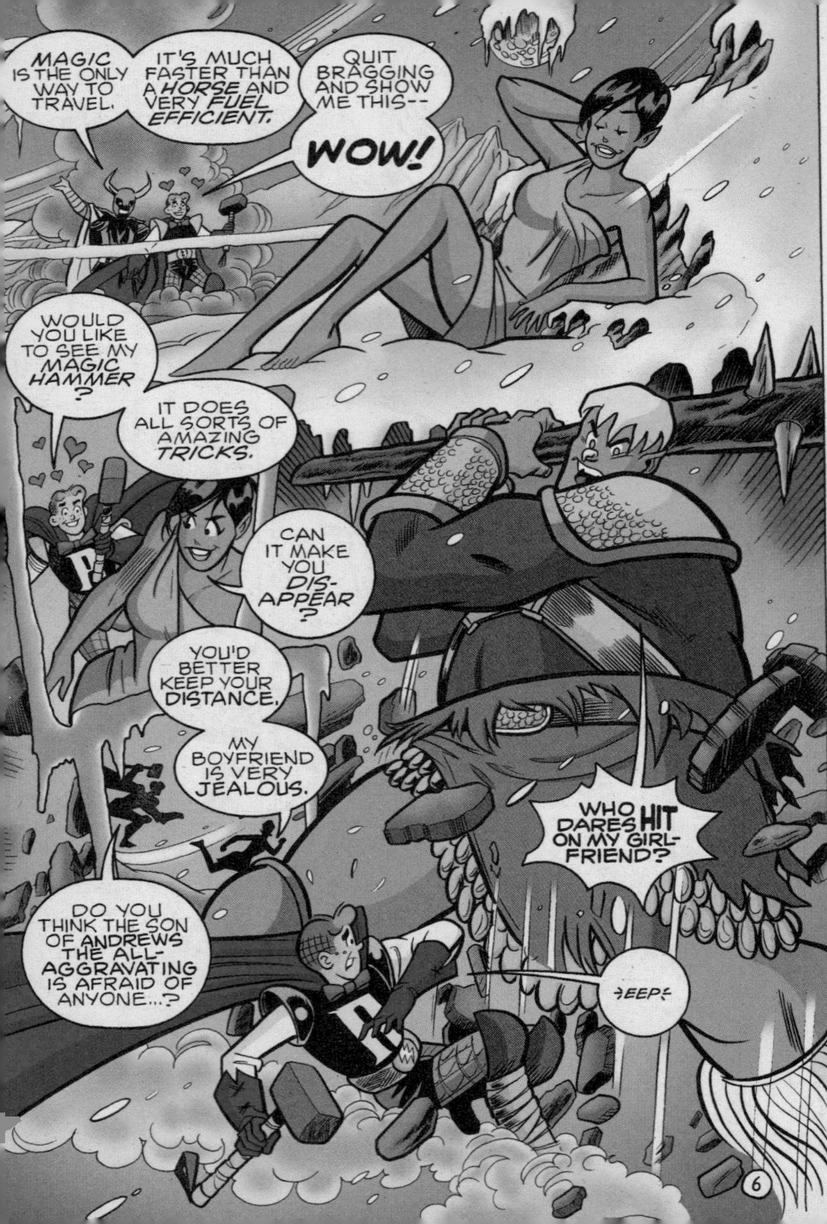
MAGIC IS THE ONLY WAY TO TRAVEL.
IT'S MUCH FASTER THAN A HORSE AND VERY FUEL EFFICIENT.
QUIT BRAGGING AND SHOW ME THIS--
WOW!
WOULD YOU LIKE TO SEE MY MAGIC HAMMER?
IT DOES ALL SORTS OF AMAZING TRICKS.
CAN IT MAKE YOU DIS-APPEAR?
YOU'D BETTER KEEP YOUR DISTANCE.
MY BOYFRIEND IS VERY JEALOUS.
WHO DARES HIT ON MY GIRL-FRIEND?
DO YOU THINK THE SON OF ANDREWS THE ALL-AGGRAVATING IS AFRAID OF ANYONE...?
EEP

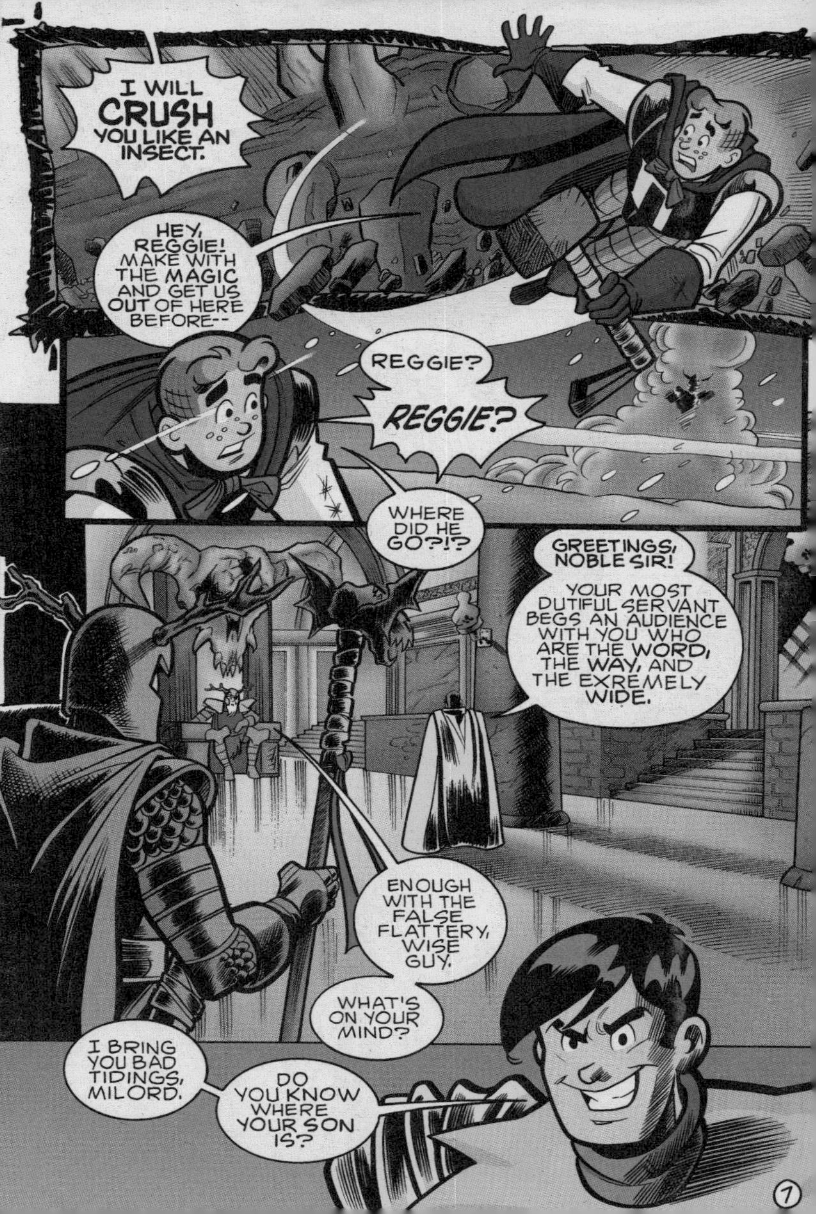
I WILL CRUSH YOU LIKE AN INSECT.
HEY, REGGIE! MAKE WITH THE MAGIC AND GET US OUT OF HERE BEFORE--
REGGIE?
REGGIE?
WHERE DID HE GO?!?
GREETINGS, NOBLE SIR!
YOUR MOST DUTIFUL SERVANT BEGS AN AUDIENCE WITH YOU WHO ARE THE WORD, THE WAY, AND THE EXREMELY WIDE.
ENOUGH WITH THE FALSE FLATTERY, WISE GUY.
WHAT'S ON YOUR MIND?
I BRING YOU BAD TIDINGS, MILORD.
DO YOU KNOW WHERE YOUR SON IS?
7

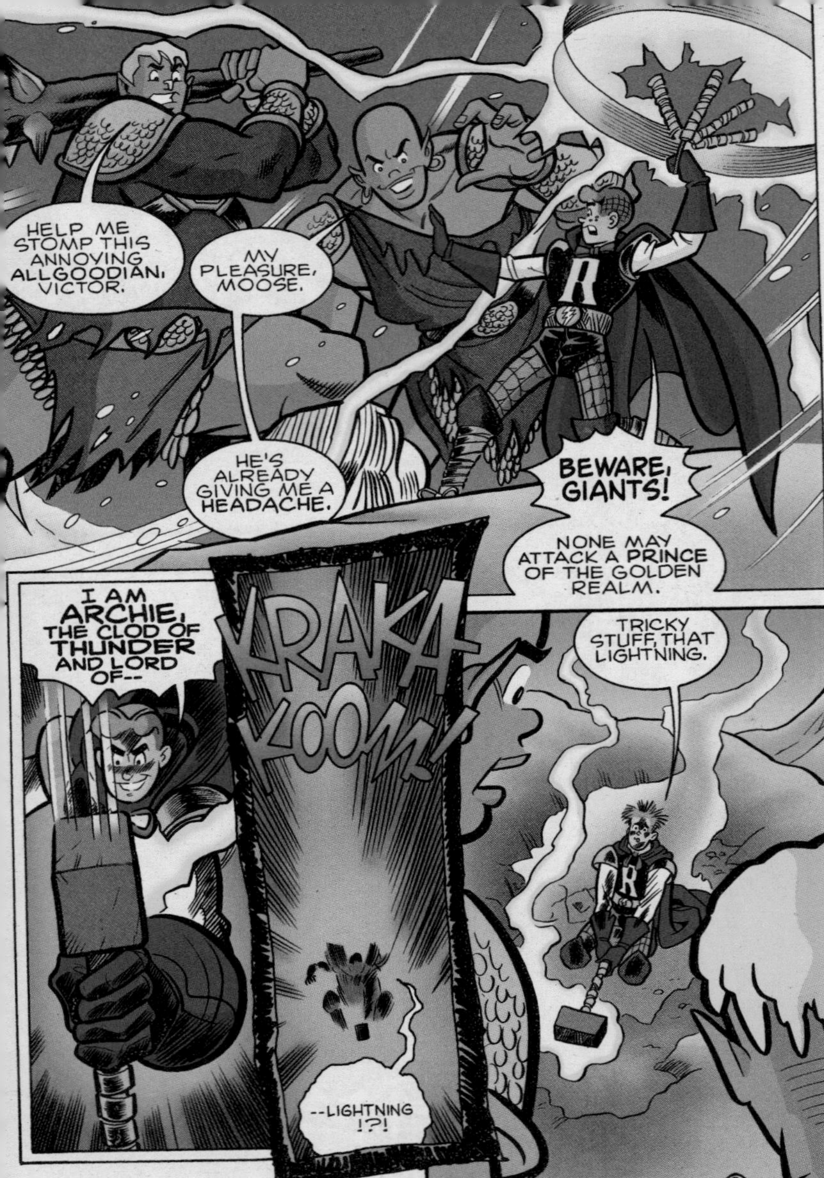
HELP ME STOMP THIS ANNOYING ALLGOODIAN, VICTOR.
MY PLEASURE, MOOSE.
HE'S ALREADY GIVING ME A HEADACHE.
BEWARE, GIANTS!
NONE MAY ATTACK A PRINCE OF THE GOLDEN REALM.
I AM ARCHIE, THE CLOD OF THUNDER AND LORD OF--
KRAKA KOOM!
--LIGHTNING !?!
TRICKY STUFF, THAT LIGHTNING.

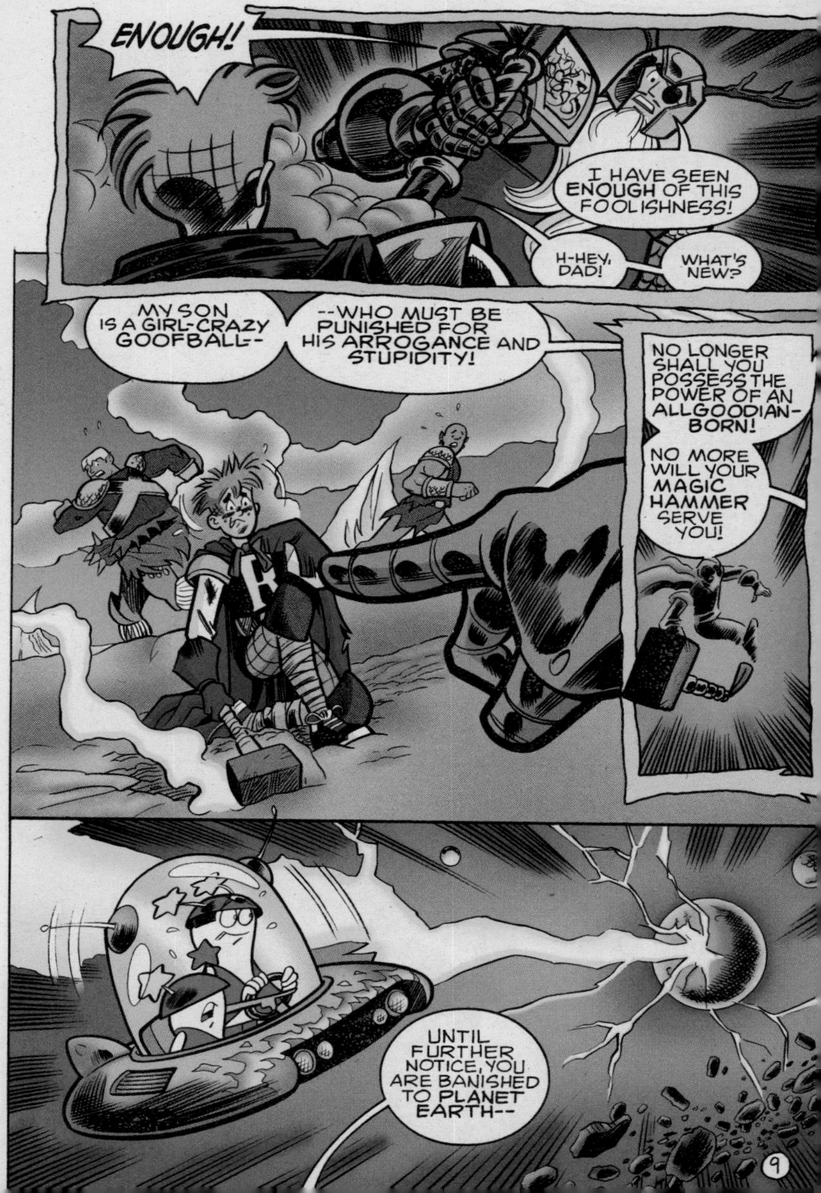
ENOUGH!
I HAVE SEEN ENOUGH OF THIS FOOLISHNESS!
H-HEY, DAD!
WHAT'S NEW?
MY SON IS A GIRL-CRAZY GOOFBALL--
--WHO MUST BE PUNISHED FOR HIS ARROGANCE AND STUPIDITY!
NO LONGER SHALL YOU POSSESS THE POWER OF AN ALLGOODIAN-BORN!
NO MORE WILL YOUR MAGIC HAMMER SERVE YOU!
UNTIL FURTHER NOTICE, YOU ARE BANISHED TO PLANET EARTH--

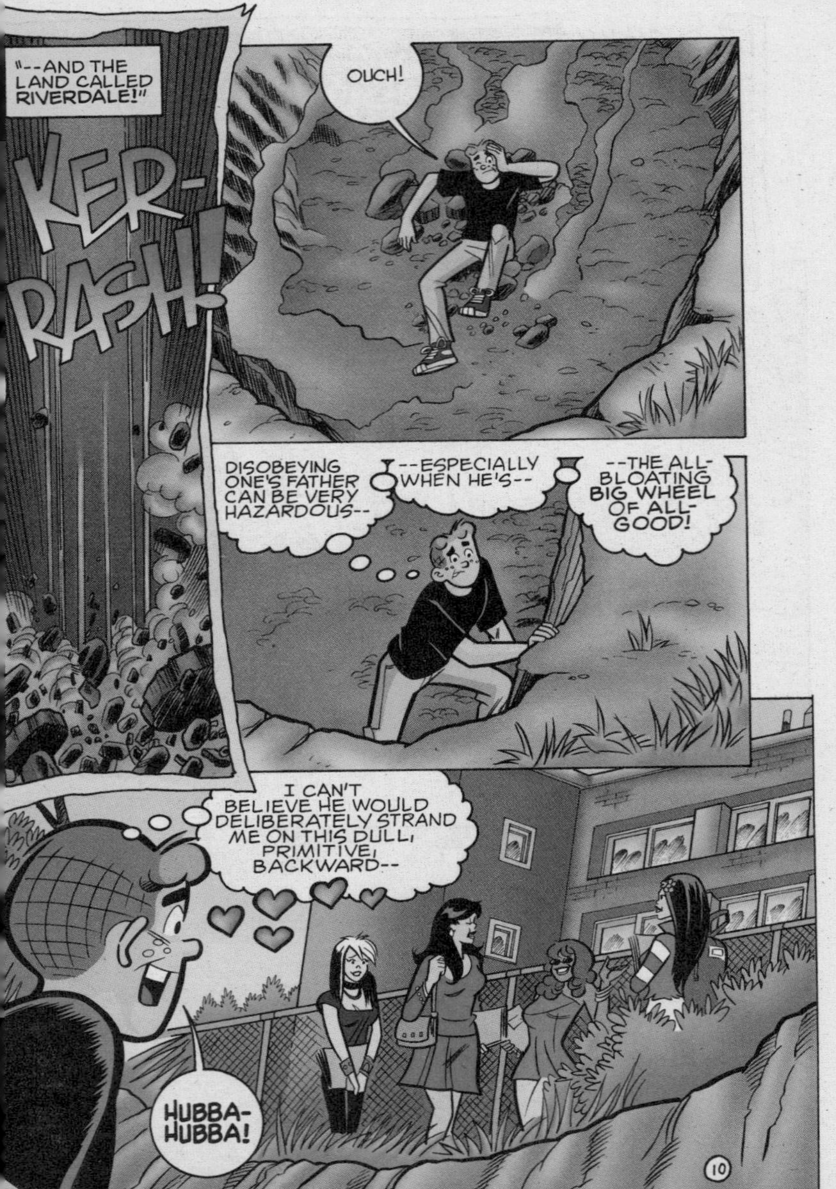
"--AND THE LAND CALLED RIVERDALE!"
KER-RASH!!
OUCH!
DISOBEYING ONE'S FATHER CAN BE VERY HAZARDOUS--
--ESPECIALLY WHEN HE'S--
--THE ALL-BLOATING BIG WHEEL OF ALL-GOOD!
I CAN'T BELIEVE HE WOULD DELIBERATELY STRAND ME ON THIS DULL, PRIMITIVE, BACKWARD--
HUBBA-HUBBA!
10

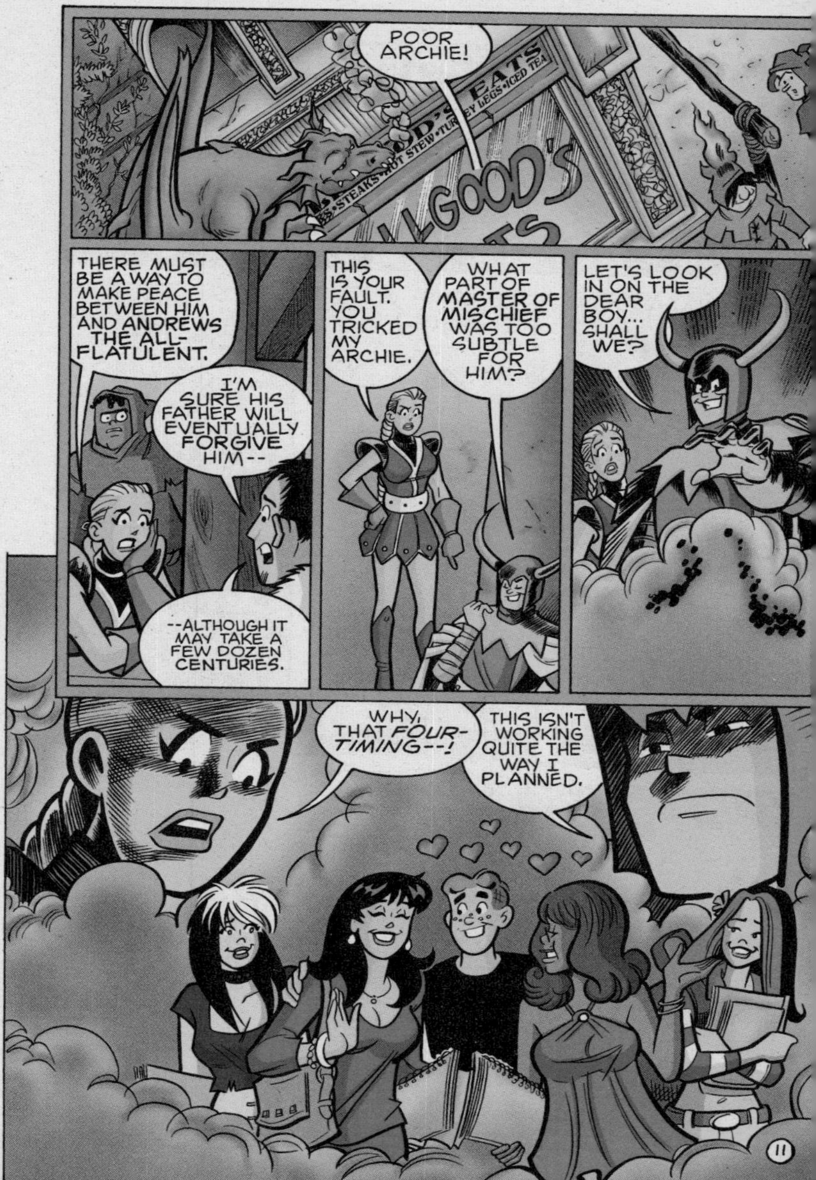
POOR ARCHIE!
EATS
STEAKS•HOT STEW•TURKEY LEGS•ICED TEA
GOOD'S
THERE MUST BE A WAY TO MAKE PEACE BETWEEN HIM AND ANDREWS THE ALL-FLATULENT.
I'M SURE HIS FATHER WILL EVENTUALLY FORGIVE HIM--
--ALTHOUGH IT MAY TAKE A FEW DOZEN CENTURIES.
THIS IS YOUR FAULT. YOU TRICKED MY ARCHIE.
WHAT PART OF MASTER OF MISCHIEF WAS TOO SUBTLE FOR HIM?
LET'S LOOK IN ON THE DEAR BOY... SHALL WE?
WHY, THAT *FOUR-TIMING*--!
THIS ISN'T WORKING QUITE THE WAY I PLANNED.

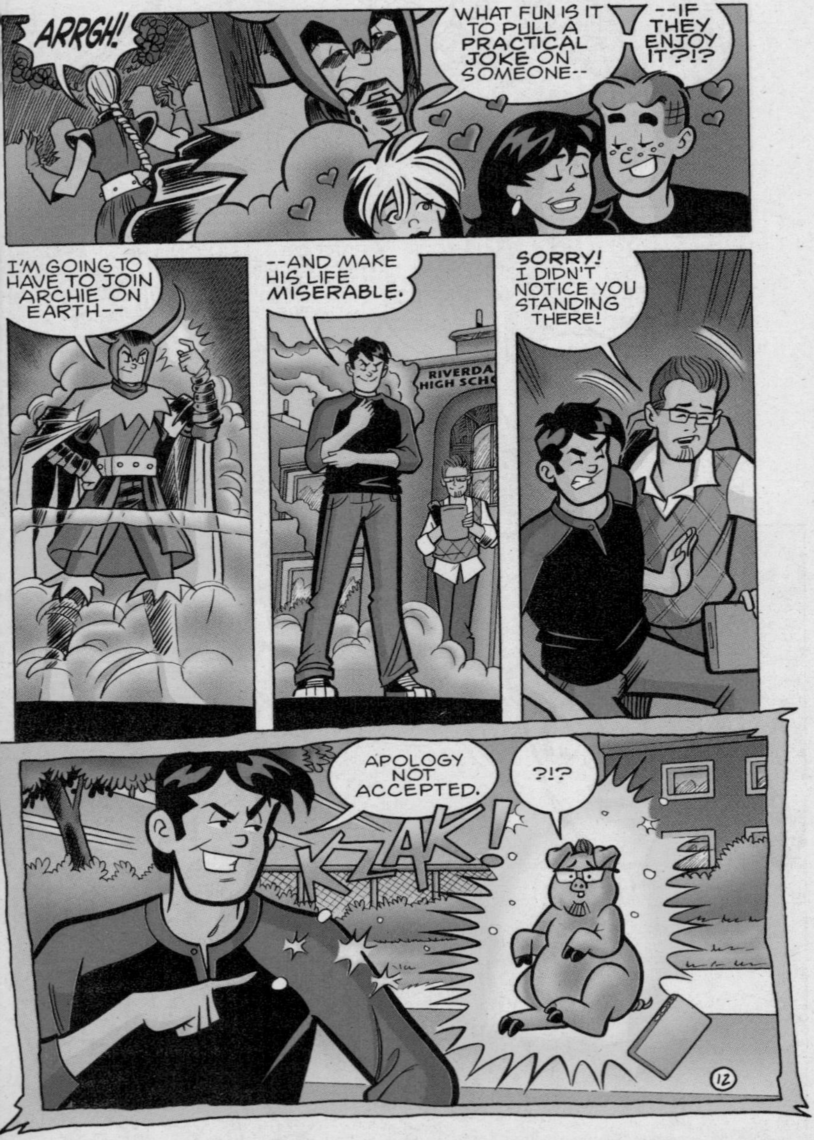
ARRGH!
WHAT FUN IS IT TO PULL A PRACTICAL JOKE ON SOMEONE--
--IF THEY ENJOY IT?!?
I'M GOING TO HAVE TO JOIN ARCHIE ON EARTH--
--AND MAKE HIS LIFE MISERABLE.
RIVERDA
HIGH SCH
SORRY! I DIDN'T NOTICE YOU STANDING THERE!
APOLOGY NOT ACCEPTED.
?!?
KZAK!
12

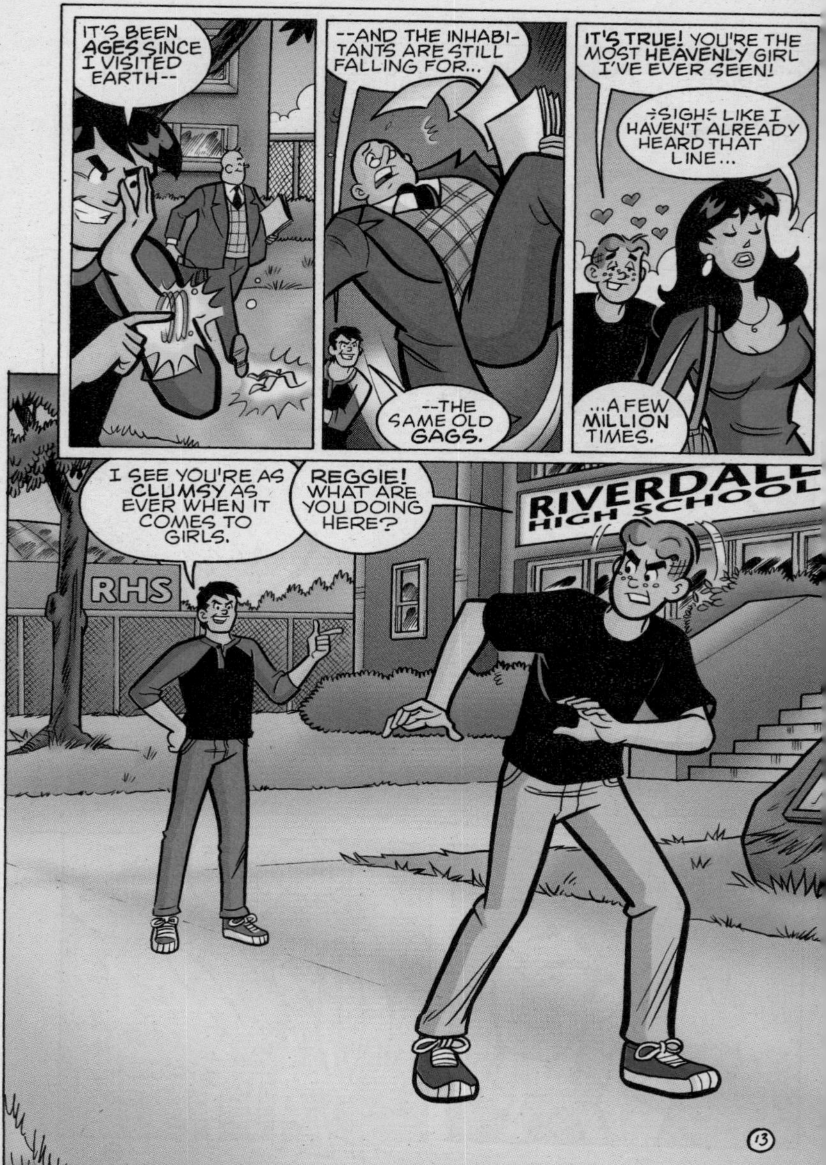

IT'S BEEN AGES SINCE I VISITED EARTH--
--AND THE INHABITANTS ARE STILL FALLING FOR...
--THE SAME OLD GAGS.
IT'S TRUE! YOU'RE THE MOST HEAVENLY GIRL I'VE EVER SEEN!
⁼SIGH⁼ LIKE I HAVEN'T ALREADY HEARD THAT LINE...
...A FEW MILLION TIMES.
I SEE YOU'RE AS CLUMSY AS EVER WHEN IT COMES TO GIRLS.
REGGIE! WHAT ARE YOU DOING HERE?
RIVERDALE HIGH SCHOOL
RHS

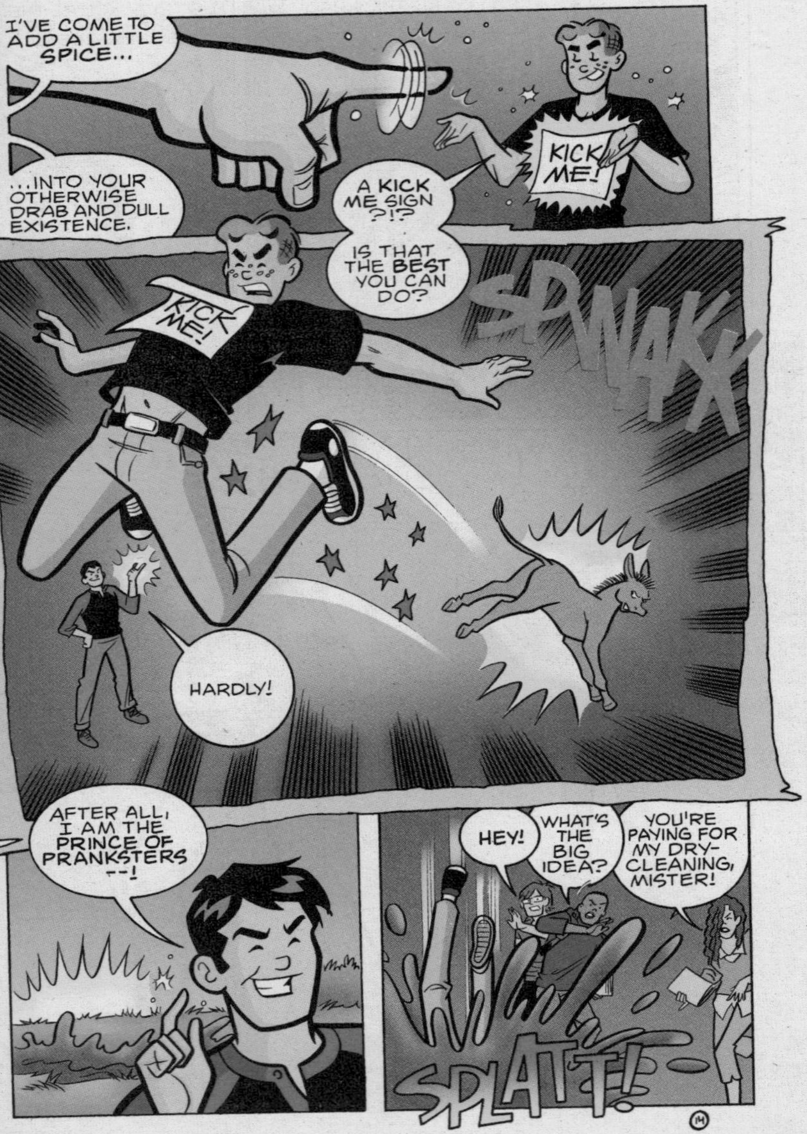
I'VE COME TO ADD A LITTLE SPICE...
...INTO YOUR OTHERWISE DRAB AND DULL EXISTENCE.
A KICK ME SIGN ?!?
KICK ME!
IS THAT THE BEST YOU CAN DO?
SPWAKK
HARDLY!
AFTER ALL, I AM THE PRINCE OF PRANKSTERS --!
HEY!
WHAT'S THE BIG IDEA?
YOU'RE PAYING FOR MY DRY-CLEANING, MISTER!
SPLATT!

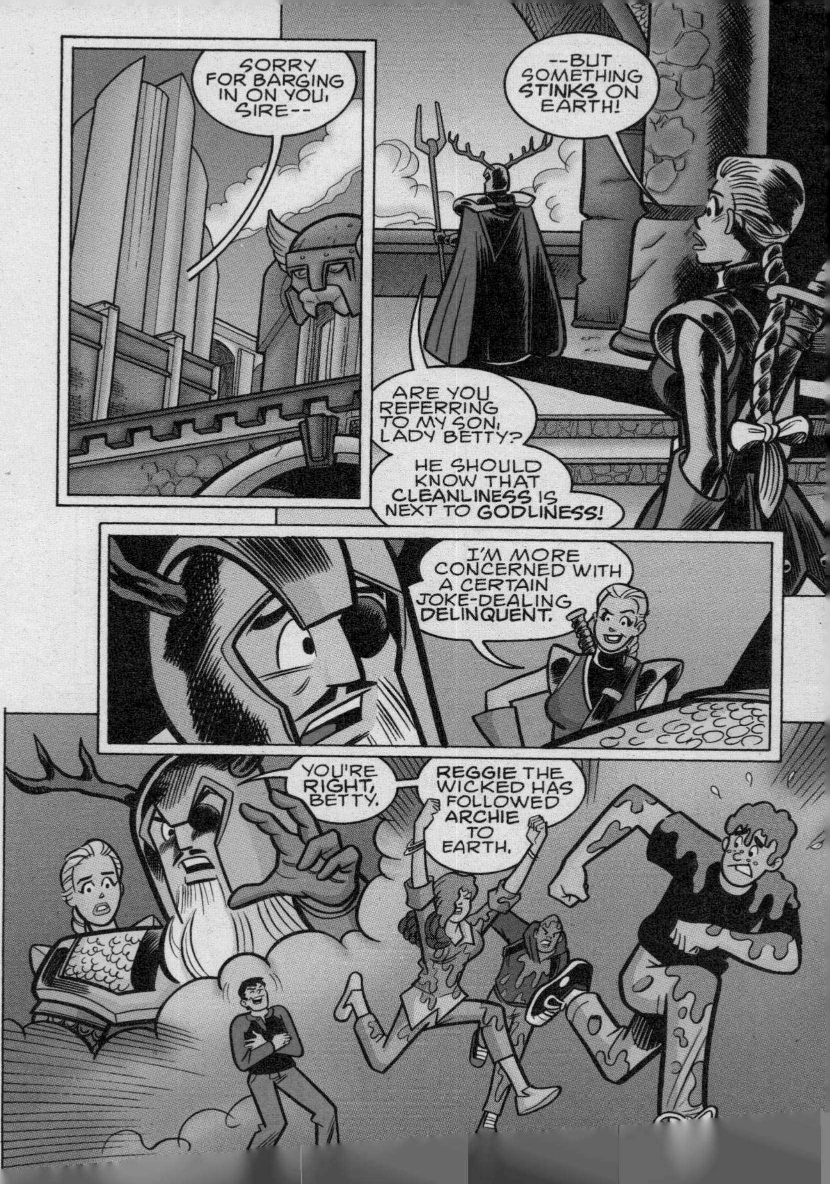
SORRY FOR BARGING IN ON YOU, SIRE--
--BUT SOMETHING STINKS ON EARTH!
ARE YOU REFERRING TO MY SON, LADY BETTY?
HE SHOULD KNOW THAT CLEANLINESS IS NEXT TO GODLINESS!
I'M MORE CONCERNED WITH A CERTAIN JOKE-DEALING DELINQUENT.
YOU'RE RIGHT, BETTY.
REGGIE THE WICKED HAS FOLLOWED ARCHIE TO EARTH.

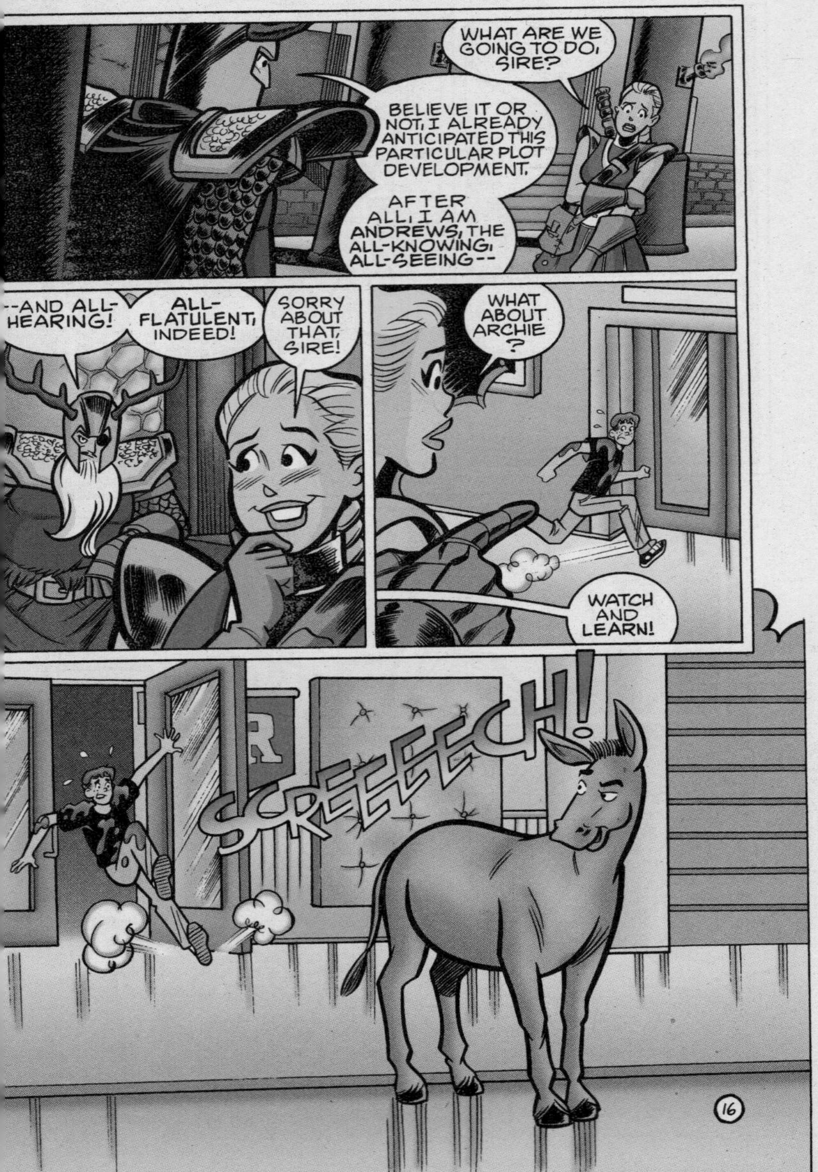
WHAT ARE WE GOING TO DO, SIRE?
BELIEVE IT OR NOT, I ALREADY ANTICIPATED THIS PARTICULAR PLOT DEVELOPMENT.
AFTER ALL, I AM ANDREWS, THE ALL-KNOWING, ALL-SEEING--
--AND ALL-HEARING!
ALL-FLATULENT, INDEED!
SORRY ABOUT THAT, SIRE!
WHAT ABOUT ARCHIE?
WATCH AND LEARN!
R
SCREEEEECH!

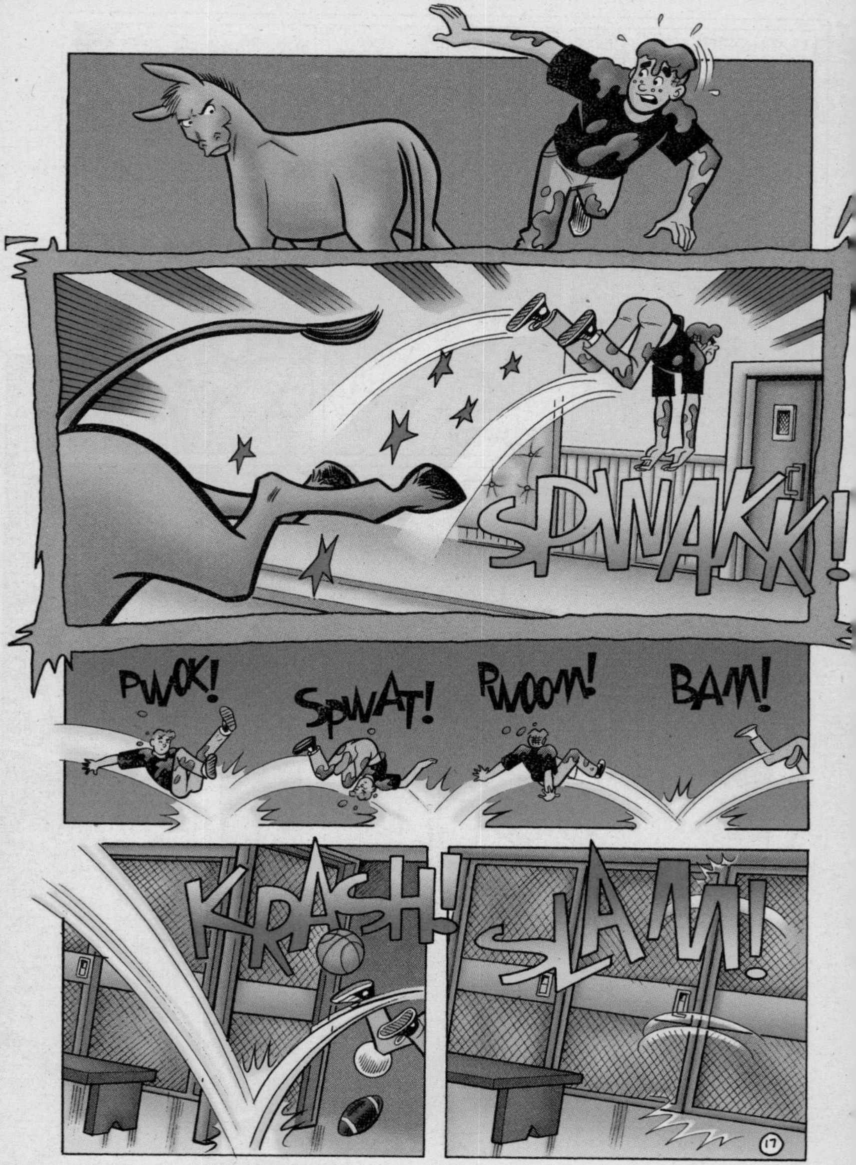
SPWAKK!
PWOK!
SPWAT!
PWOOM!
BAM!
KRASH!
SLAM!

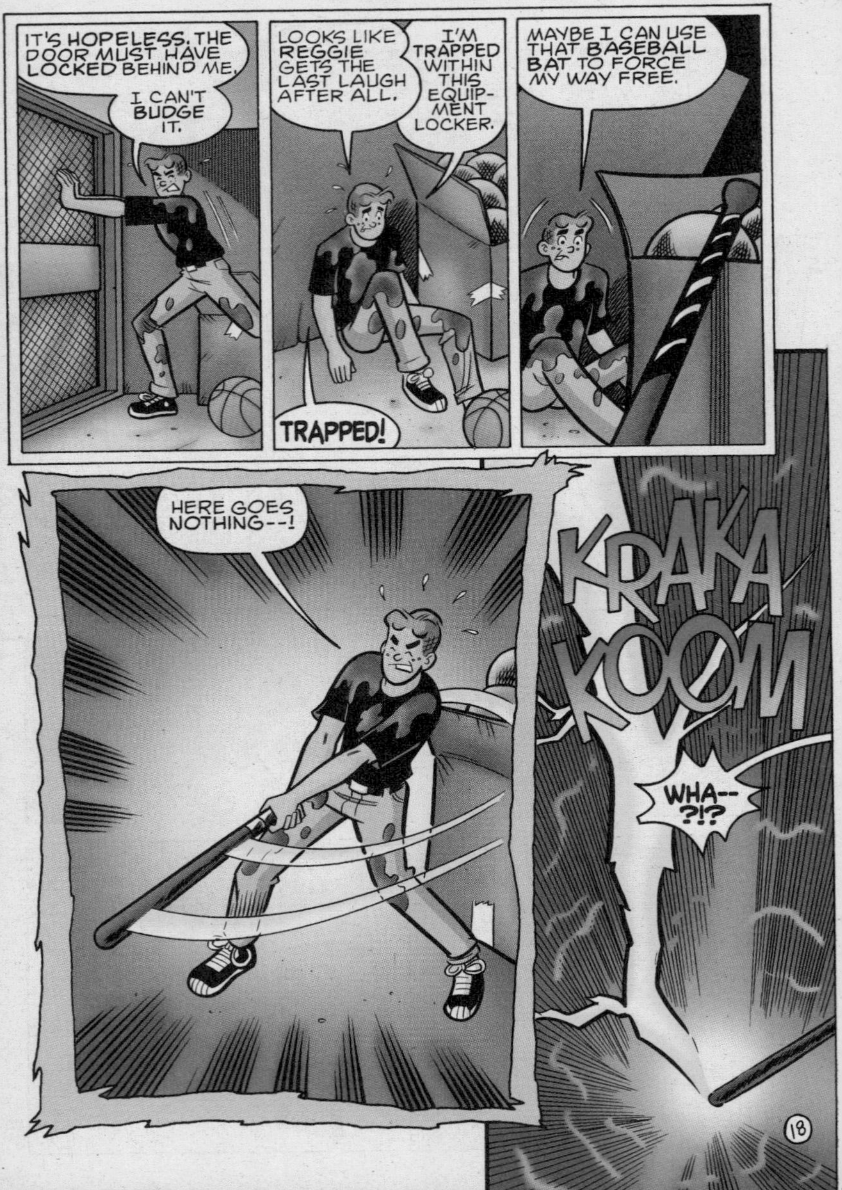
IT'S HOPELESS. THE DOOR MUST HAVE LOCKED BEHIND ME.
I CAN'T BUDGE IT.
LOOKS LIKE REGGIE GETS THE LAST LAUGH AFTER ALL.
I'M TRAPPED WITHIN THIS EQUIP-MENT LOCKER.
TRAPPED!
MAYBE I CAN USE THAT BASEBALL BAT TO FORCE MY WAY FREE.
HERE GOES NOTHING--!
KRAKA KOOM
WHA-- ?!?

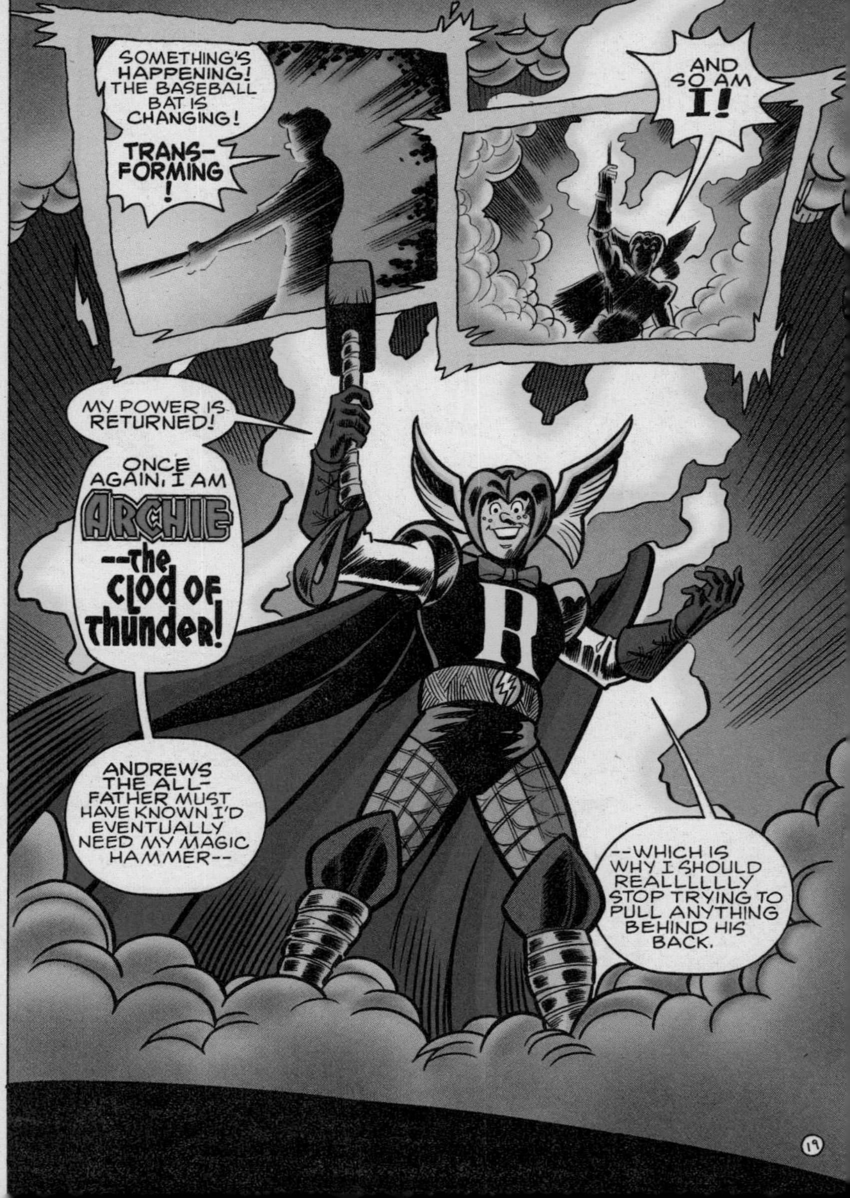
SOMETHING'S HAPPENING! THE BASEBALL BAT IS CHANGING!
TRANS-FORMING!
AND SO AM I!
MY POWER IS RETURNED!
ONCE AGAIN, I AM ARCHIE --the CLOD OF thunder!
ANDREWS THE ALL-FATHER MUST HAVE KNOWN I'D EVENTUALLY NEED MY MAGIC HAMMER--
--WHICH IS WHY I SHOULD REALLLLLLY STOP TRYING TO PULL ANYTHING BEHIND HIS BACK.

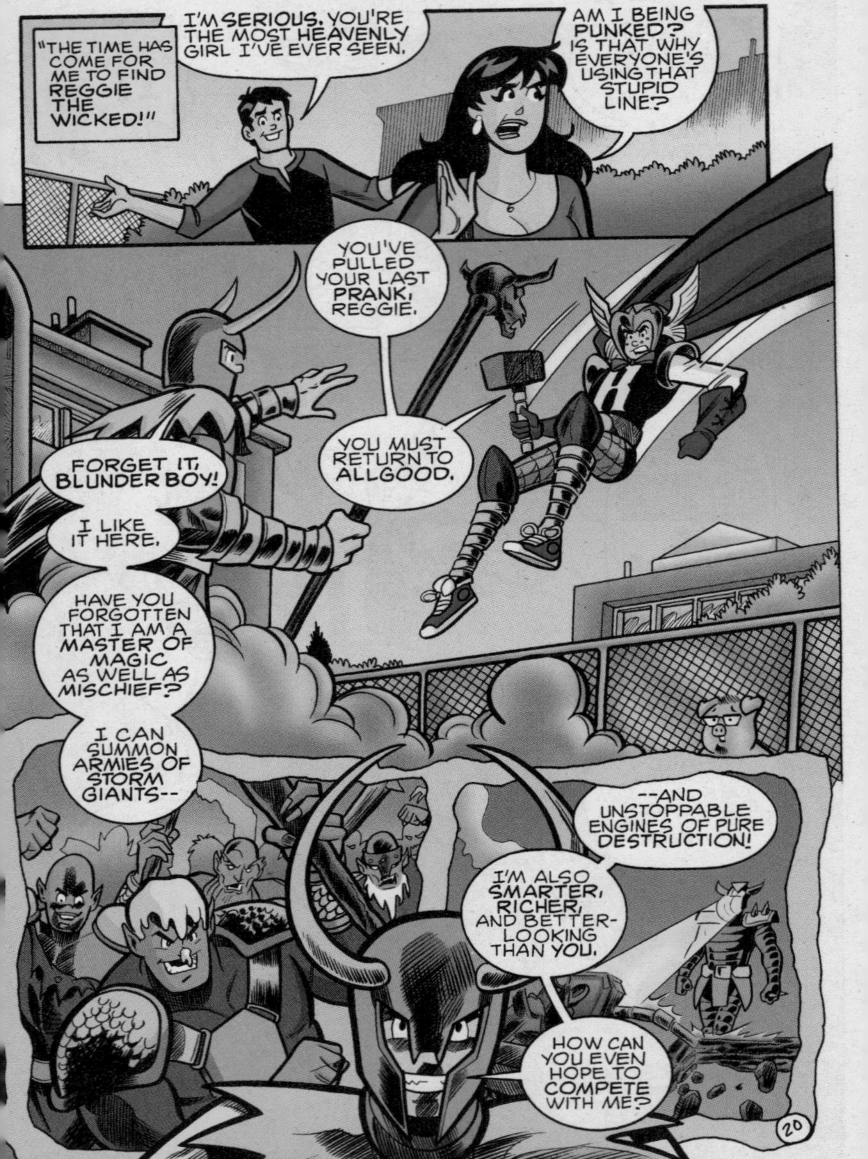
"THE TIME HAS COME FOR ME TO FIND REGGIE THE WICKED!"
I'M SERIOUS. YOU'RE THE MOST HEAVENLY GIRL I'VE EVER SEEN.
AM I BEING PUNKED? IS THAT WHY EVERYONE'S USING THAT STUPID LINE?
YOU'VE PULLED YOUR LAST PRANK, REGGIE.
YOU MUST RETURN TO ALLGOOD.
FORGET IT, BLUNDER BOY!
I LIKE IT HERE.
HAVE YOU FORGOTTEN THAT I AM A MASTER OF MAGIC AS WELL AS MISCHIEF?
I CAN SUMMON ARMIES OF STORM GIANTS--
--AND UNSTOPPABLE ENGINES OF PURE DESTRUCTION!
I'M ALSO SMARTER, RICHER, AND BETTER-LOOKING THAN YOU.
HOW CAN YOU EVEN HOPE TO COMPETE WITH ME?
20

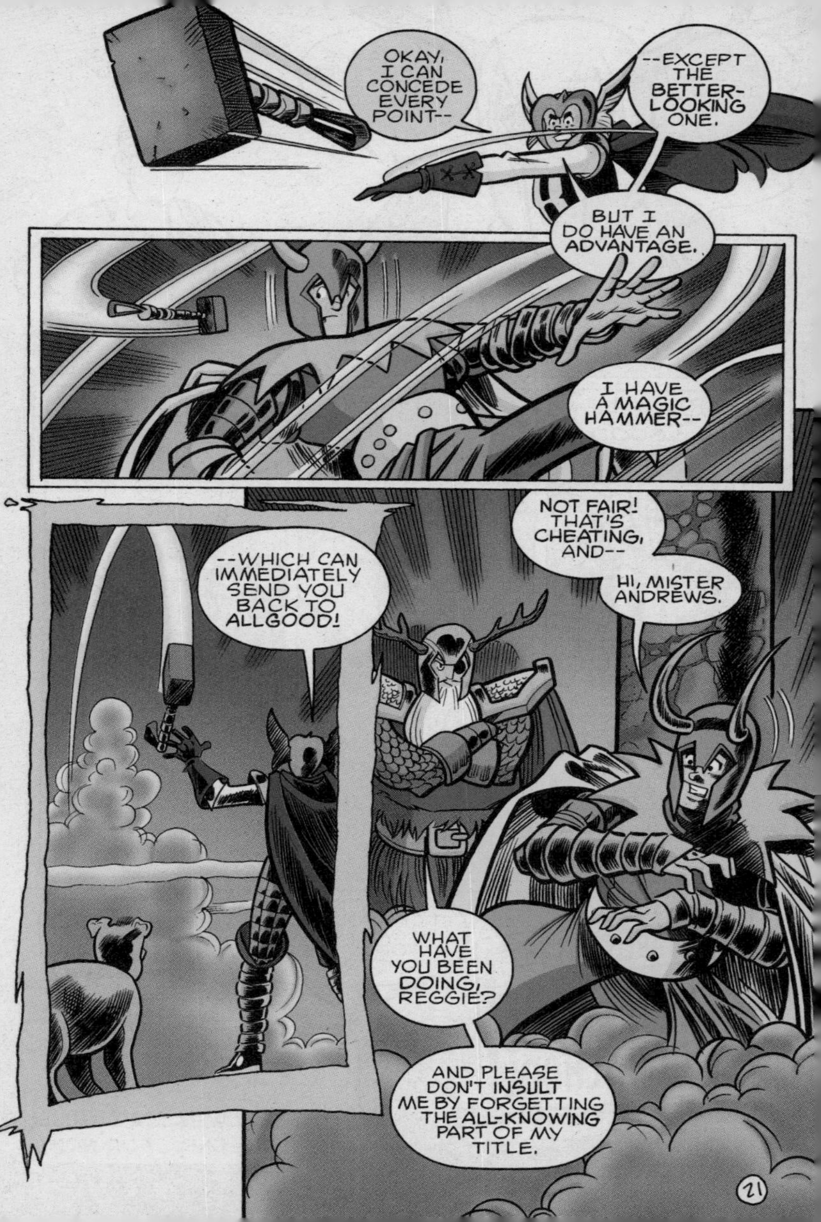
OKAY, I CAN CONCEDE EVERY POINT--
--EXCEPT THE BETTER-LOOKING ONE.
BUT I DO HAVE AN ADVANTAGE.
I HAVE A MAGIC HAMMER--
--WHICH CAN IMMEDIATELY SEND YOU BACK TO ALLGOOD!
NOT FAIR! THAT'S CHEATING, AND--
HI, MISTER ANDREWS.
WHAT HAVE YOU BEEN DOING, REGGIE?
AND PLEASE DON'T INSULT ME BY FORGETTING THE ALL-KNOWING PART OF MY TITLE.

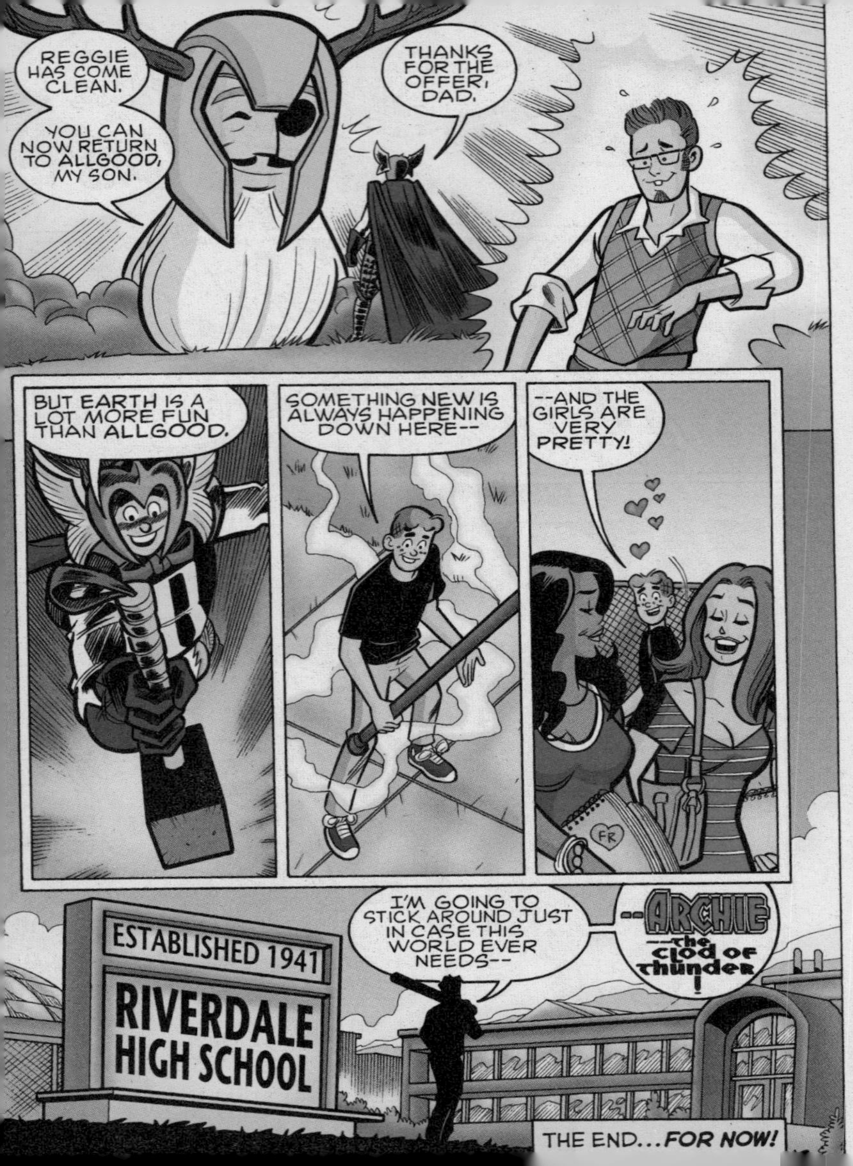

REGGIE HAS COME CLEAN.
YOU CAN NOW RETURN TO ALLGOOD, MY SON.
THANKS FOR THE OFFER, DAD.
BUT EARTH IS A LOT MORE FUN THAN ALLGOOD.
SOMETHING NEW IS ALWAYS HAPPENING DOWN HERE--
--AND THE GIRLS ARE VERY PRETTY!
FR
ESTABLISHED 1941
RIVERDALE HIGH SCHOOL
I'M GOING TO STICK AROUND JUST IN CASE THIS WORLD EVER NEEDS--
--ARCHIE
--the clod of thunder!
THE END... FOR NOW!

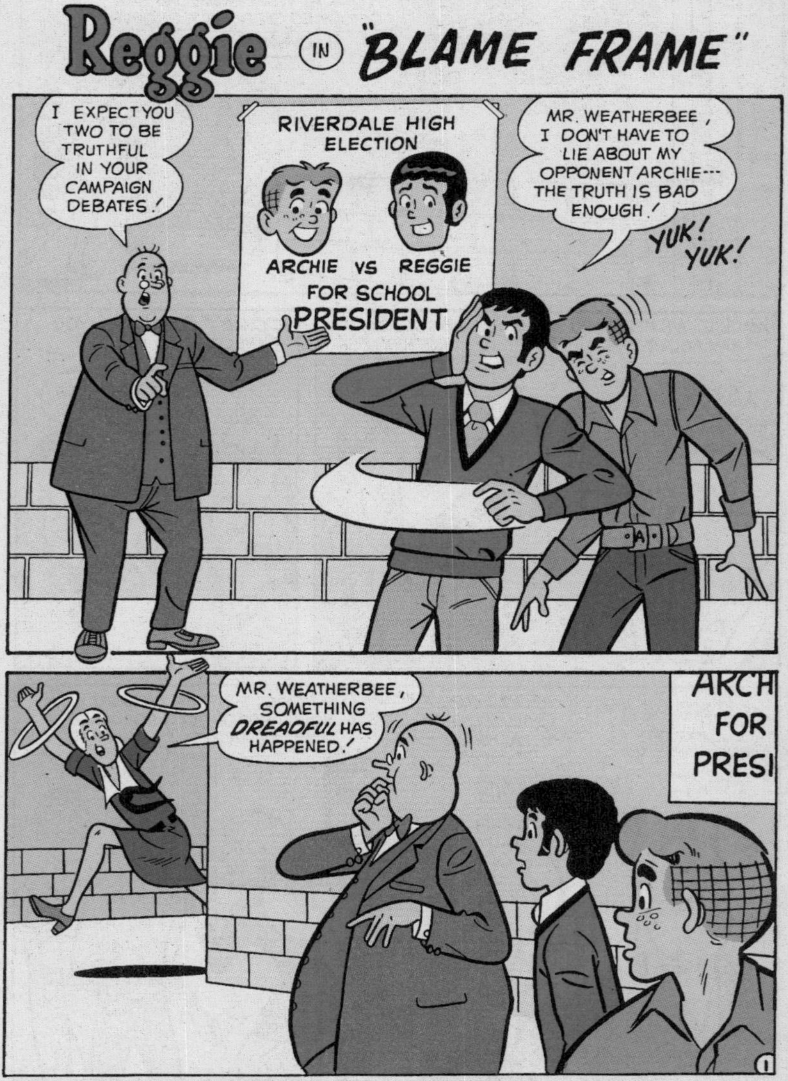
Reggie IN "BLAME FRAME"
I EXPECT YOU TWO TO BE TRUTHFUL IN YOUR CAMPAIGN DEBATES!
RIVERDALE HIGH ELECTION
ARCHIE VS REGGIE
FOR SCHOOL PRESIDENT
MR. WEATHERBEE, I DON'T HAVE TO LIE ABOUT MY OPPONENT ARCHIE--- THE TRUTH IS BAD ENOUGH!
YUK! YUK!
MR. WEATHERBEE, SOMETHING DREADFUL HAS HAPPENED!
ARCH
FOR
PRESI
1

Script: George Gladir / Pencils: Bob Bolling / Inks: Rudy Lapick / Letters: Bill Yoshida

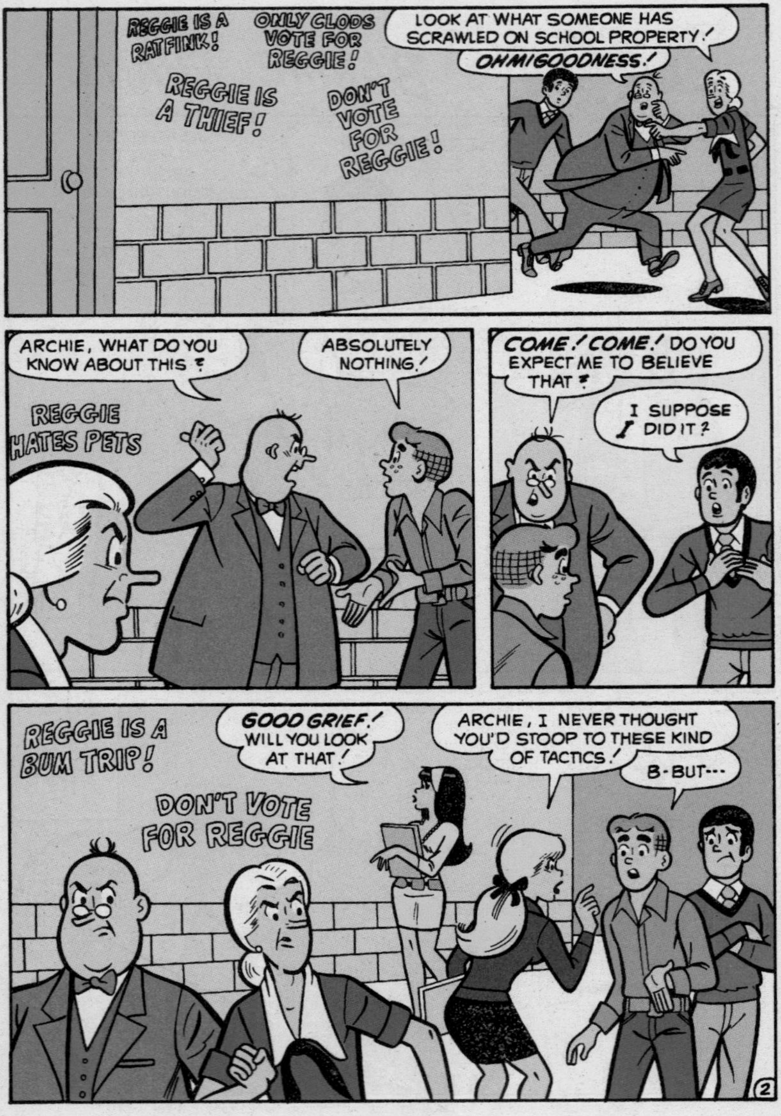
REGGIE IS A RATFINK!
ONLY CLODS VOTE FOR REGGIE!
REGGIE IS A THIEF!
DON'T VOTE FOR REGGIE!
LOOK AT WHAT SOMEONE HAS SCRAWLED ON SCHOOL PROPERTY!
OHMIGOODNESS!
ARCHIE, WHAT DO YOU KNOW ABOUT THIS?
ABSOLUTELY NOTHING!
REGGIE HATES PETS
COME! COME! DO YOU EXPECT ME TO BELIEVE THAT?
I SUPPOSE I DID IT?
REGGIE IS A BUM TRIP!
DON'T VOTE FOR REGGIE
GOOD GRIEF! WILL YOU LOOK AT THAT!
ARCHIE, I NEVER THOUGHT YOU'D STOOP TO THESE KIND OF TACTICS!
B-BUT---
2

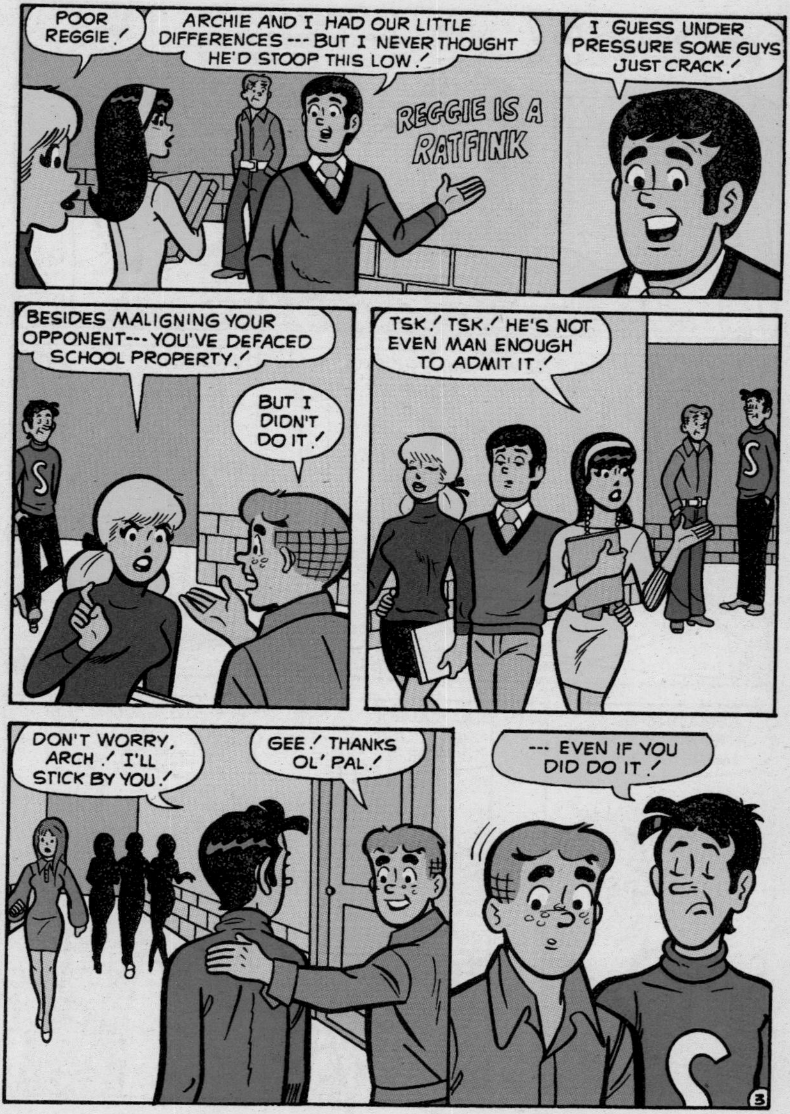
POOR REGGIE!
ARCHIE AND I HAD OUR LITTLE DIFFERENCES --- BUT I NEVER THOUGHT HE'D STOOP THIS LOW!
REGGIE IS A RATFINK
I GUESS UNDER PRESSURE SOME GUYS JUST CRACK!
BESIDES MALIGNING YOUR OPPONENT--- YOU'VE DEFACED SCHOOL PROPERTY!
BUT I DIDN'T DO IT!
TSK! TSK! HE'S NOT EVEN MAN ENOUGH TO ADMIT IT!
DON'T WORRY, ARCH! I'LL STICK BY YOU!
GEE! THANKS OL' PAL!
--- EVEN IF YOU DID DO IT!
3

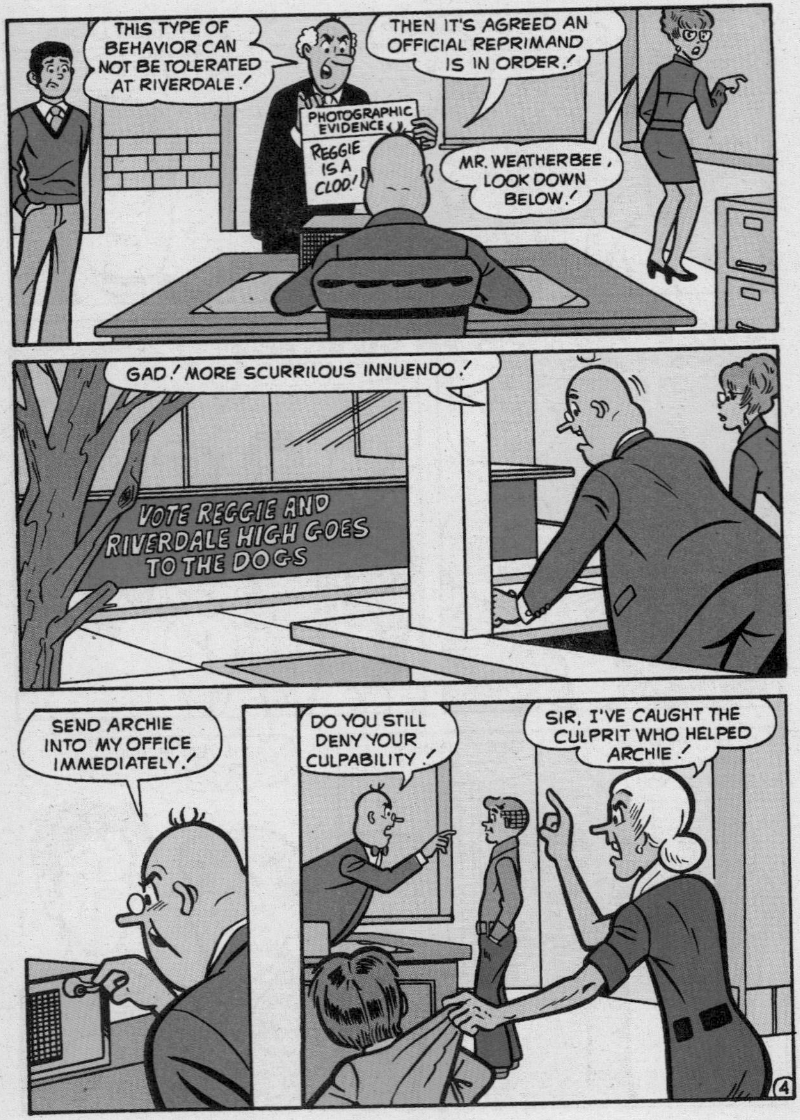
THIS TYPE OF BEHAVIOR CAN NOT BE TOLERATED AT RIVERDALE!
PHOTOGRAPHIC EVIDENCE
REGGIE IS A CLOD!
THEN IT'S AGREED AN OFFICIAL REPRIMAND IS IN ORDER!
MR. WEATHERBEE, LOOK DOWN BELOW!
GAD! MORE SCURRILOUS INNUENDO!
VOTE REGGIE AND RIVERDALE HIGH GOES TO THE DOGS
SEND ARCHIE INTO MY OFFICE IMMEDIATELY!
DO YOU STILL DENY YOUR CULPABILITY!
SIR, I'VE CAUGHT THE CULPRIT WHO HELPED ARCHIE!
4

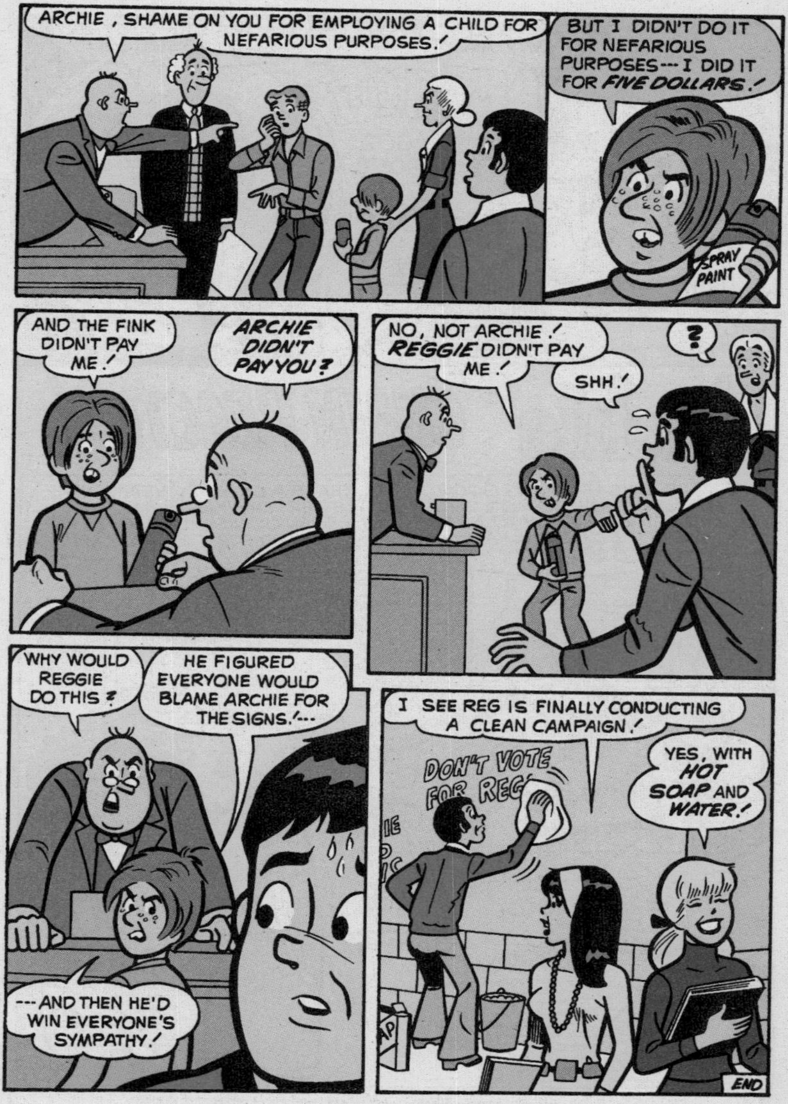

ARCHIE, SHAME ON YOU FOR EMPLOYING A CHILD FOR NEFARIOUS PURPOSES.!
BUT I DIDN'T DO IT FOR NEFARIOUS PURPOSES--- I DID IT FOR FIVE DOLLARS.!
SPRAY PAINT
AND THE FINK DIDN'T PAY ME.!
ARCHIE DIDN'T PAY YOU?
NO, NOT ARCHIE.! REGGIE DIDN'T PAY ME.!
SHH.!
?
WHY WOULD REGGIE DO THIS?
HE FIGURED EVERYONE WOULD BLAME ARCHIE FOR THE SIGNS.!---
---AND THEN HE'D WIN EVERYONE'S SYMPATHY.!
I SEE REG IS FINALLY CONDUCTING A CLEAN CAMPAIGN.!
DON'T VOTE FOR REG
YES, WITH HOT SOAP AND WATER.!
END

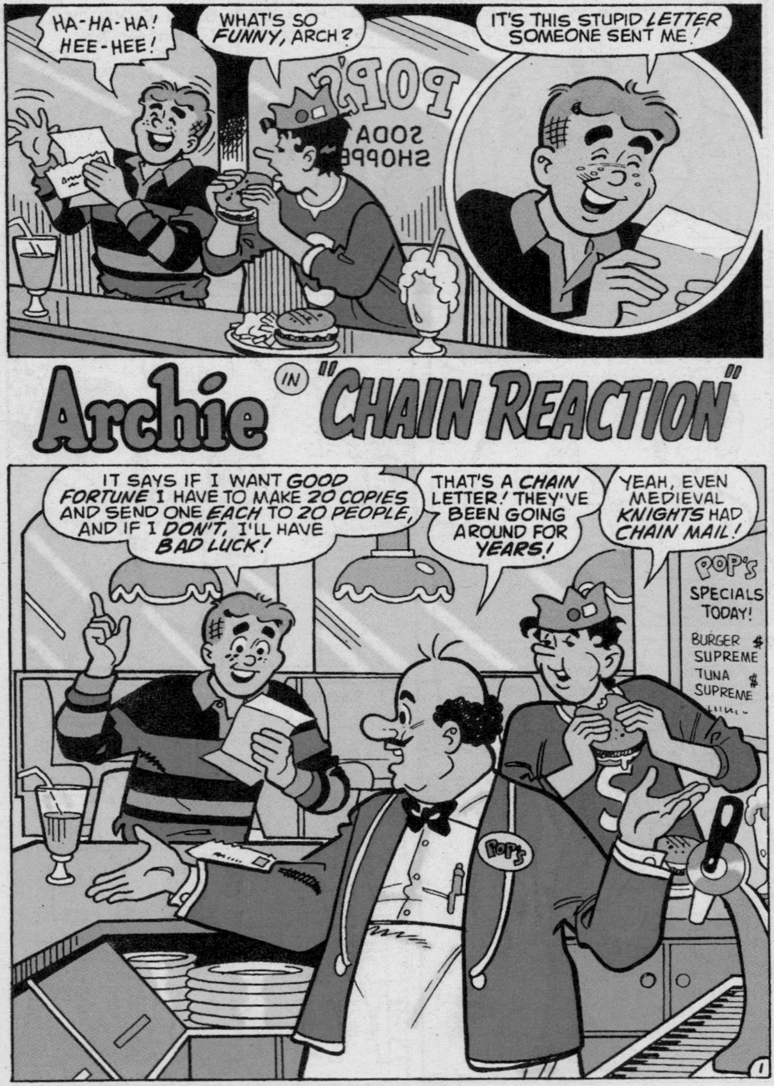
HA-HA-HA! HEE-HEE!
WHAT'S SO FUNNY, ARCH?
POP'S SODA SHOPPE
IT'S THIS STUPID LETTER SOMEONE SENT ME!
Archie IN "CHAIN REACTION"
IT SAYS IF I WANT GOOD FORTUNE I HAVE TO MAKE 20 COPIES AND SEND ONE EACH TO 20 PEOPLE, AND IF I DON'T, I'LL HAVE BAD LUCK!
THAT'S A CHAIN LETTER! THEY'VE BEEN GOING AROUND FOR YEARS!
YEAH, EVEN MEDIEVAL KNIGHTS HAD CHAIN MAIL!
POP'S SPECIALS TODAY!
BURGER SUPREME $
TUNA SUPREME $
POP'S
1

Script: Hal Smith / Pencils: Stan Goldberg / Inks: Henry Scarpelli / Letters: Bill Yoshida

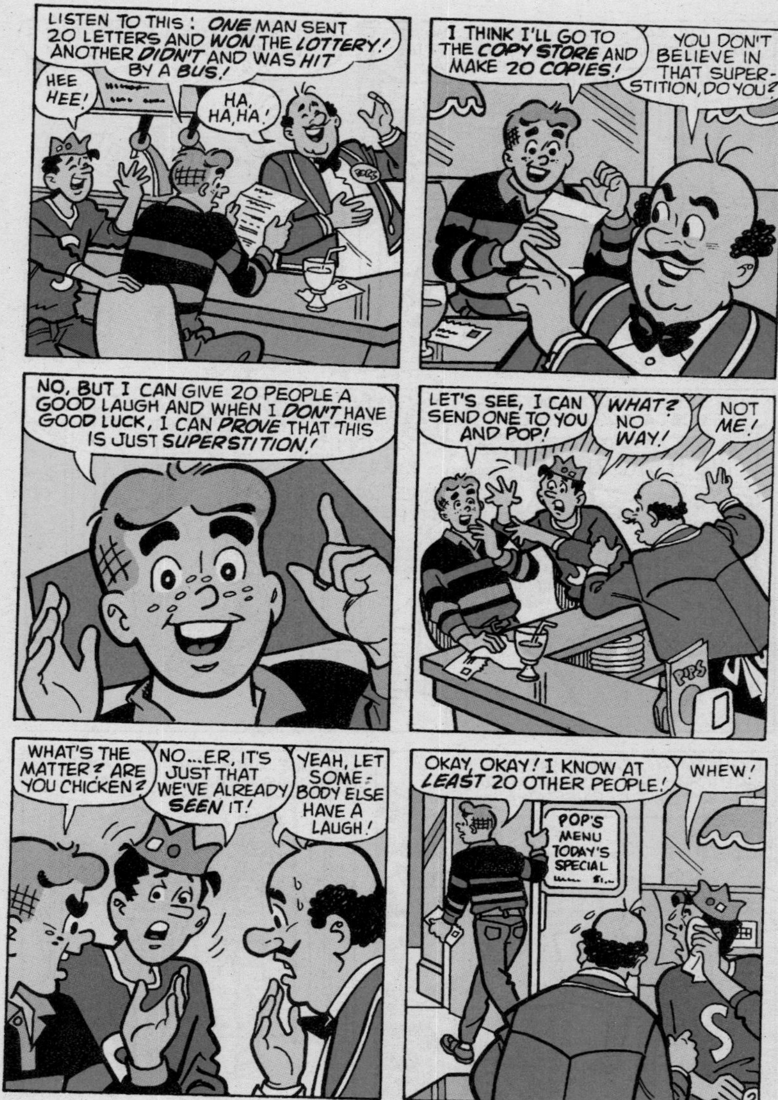
LISTEN TO THIS: ONE MAN SENT 20 LETTERS AND WON THE LOTTERY! ANOTHER DIDN'T AND WAS HIT BY A BUS!
HEE HEE!
HA, HA, HA!
I THINK I'LL GO TO THE COPY STORE AND MAKE 20 COPIES!
YOU DON'T BELIEVE IN THAT SUPER-STITION, DO YOU?
NO, BUT I CAN GIVE 20 PEOPLE A GOOD LAUGH AND WHEN I DON'T HAVE GOOD LUCK, I CAN PROVE THAT THIS IS JUST SUPERSTITION!
LET'S SEE, I CAN SEND ONE TO YOU AND POP!
WHAT? NO WAY!
NOT ME!
POP'S
WHAT'S THE MATTER? ARE YOU CHICKEN?
NO...ER, IT'S JUST THAT WE'VE ALREADY SEEN IT!
YEAH, LET SOME-BODY ELSE HAVE A LAUGH!
OKAY, OKAY! I KNOW AT LEAST 20 OTHER PEOPLE!
WHEW!
POP'S MENU TODAY'S SPECIAL
2

THE NEXT DAY...

HI, ARCH! WIN ANYTHING YET?

NO... I... WHAT'S THAT ON THE SIDEWALK?

OH, WOW! IT'S A TWENTY DOLLAR BILL!

BOY! THAT'S LUCKY!

THAT DOESN'T PROVE ANYTHING! IT'S JUST A COINCIDENCE!

RIVERDALE DEP

CLANG WHOOOFF CLANG

RIVERDALE DEPT. STORE

WHAT?... HUH?

RIV DEP

CONGRATULATIONS, SIR! YOU'RE OUR MILLIONTH CUSTOMER! YOU WIN A $1,000 GIFT CERTIFICATE!

1,000,000 CUSTOMER

DIRECTORY
FIRST FLOOR

GEE, ARCH, THAT WAS REALLY...

DON'T SAY IT!

3

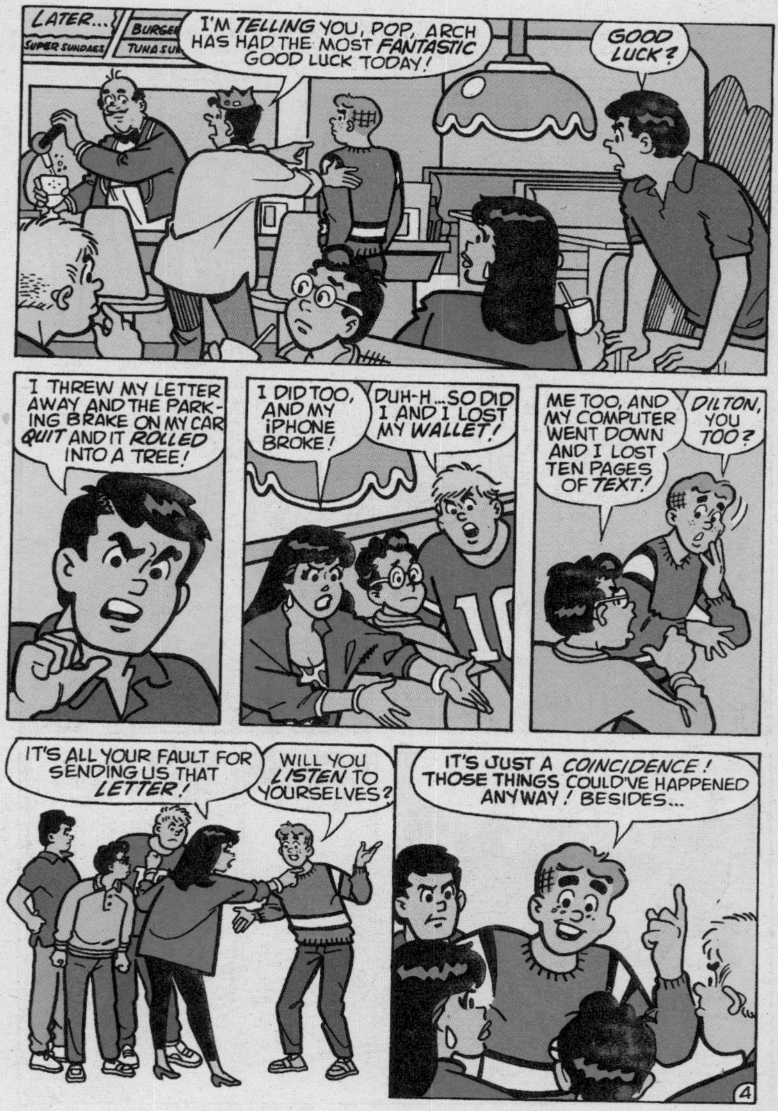
LATER...
BURGER
SUPER SUNDAES
TUNA SUB
I'M TELLING YOU, POP, ARCH HAS HAD THE MOST FANTASTIC GOOD LUCK TODAY!
GOOD LUCK?
I THREW MY LETTER AWAY AND THE PARK-ING BRAKE ON MY CAR QUIT AND IT ROLLED INTO A TREE!
I DID TOO, AND MY iPHONE BROKE!
DUH-H... SO DID I AND I LOST MY WALLET!
ME TOO, AND MY COMPUTER WENT DOWN AND I LOST TEN PAGES OF TEXT!
DILTON, YOU TOO?
IT'S ALL YOUR FAULT FOR SENDING US THAT LETTER!
WILL YOU LISTEN TO YOURSELVES?
IT'S JUST A COINCIDENCE! THOSE THINGS COULD'VE HAPPENED ANYWAY! BESIDES...
4

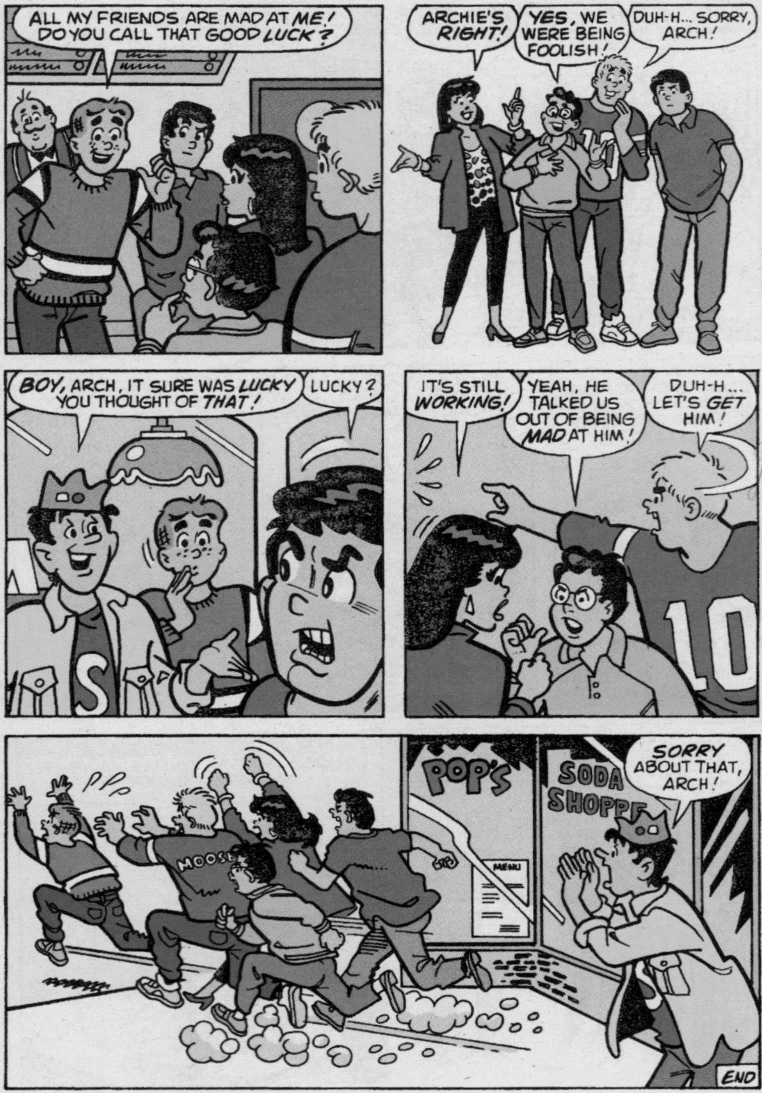
ALL MY FRIENDS ARE MAD AT ME! DO YOU CALL THAT GOOD LUCK?
ARCHIE'S RIGHT!
YES, WE WERE BEING FOOLISH!
DUH-H... SORRY, ARCH!
BOY, ARCH, IT SURE WAS LUCKY YOU THOUGHT OF THAT!
LUCKY?
IT'S STILL WORKING!
YEAH, HE TALKED US OUT OF BEING MAD AT HIM!
DUH-H... LET'S GET HIM!
POP'S
SODA SHOPPE
MENU
MOOSE
SORRY ABOUT THAT, ARCH!
END

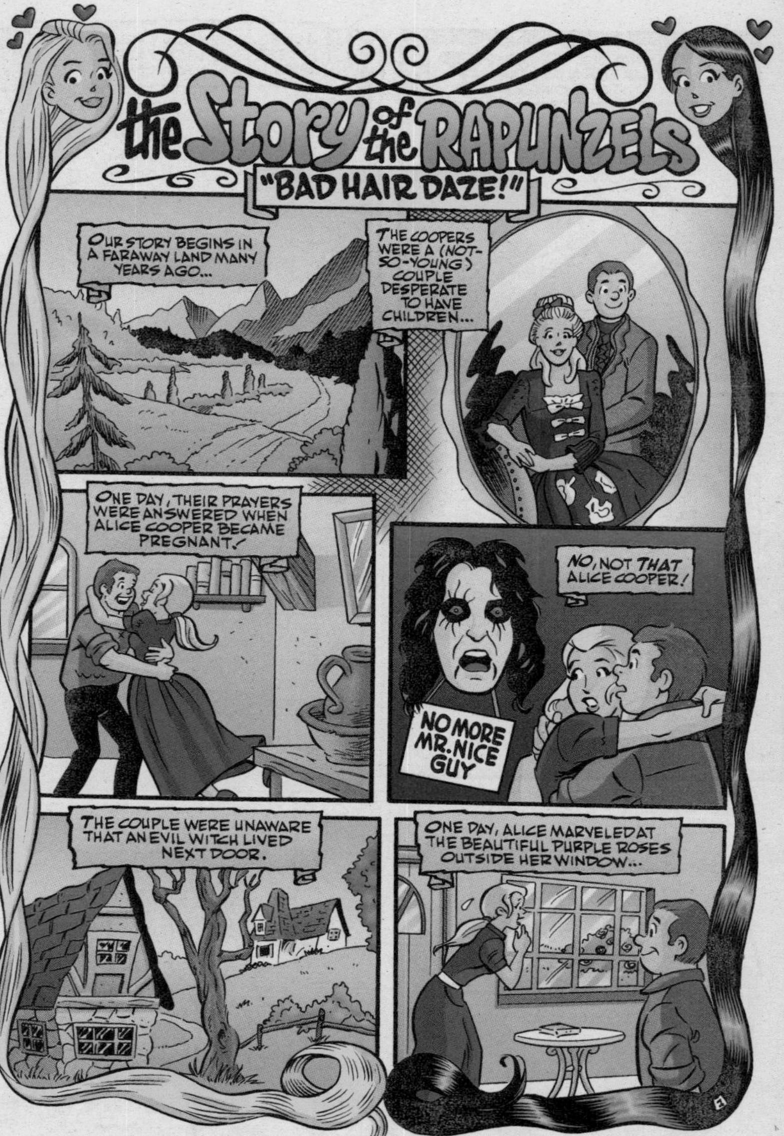
the Story of the RAPUNZELS
"BAD HAIR DAZE!"
OUR STORY BEGINS IN A FARAWAY LAND MANY YEARS AGO...
THE COOPERS WERE A (NOT-SO-YOUNG) COUPLE DESPERATE TO HAVE CHILDREN...
ONE DAY, THEIR PRAYERS WERE ANSWERED WHEN ALICE COOPER BECAME PREGNANT!
NO, NOT THAT ALICE COOPER!
NO MORE MR. NICE GUY
THE COUPLE WERE UNAWARE THAT AN EVIL WITCH LIVED NEXT DOOR.
ONE DAY, ALICE MARVELED AT THE BEAUTIFUL PURPLE ROSES OUTSIDE HER WINDOW...

Script: Dan Parent Pencils: Jeff Shultz Inks: Bob Smith Letters: Jack Morelli Colors: Digikore Studios

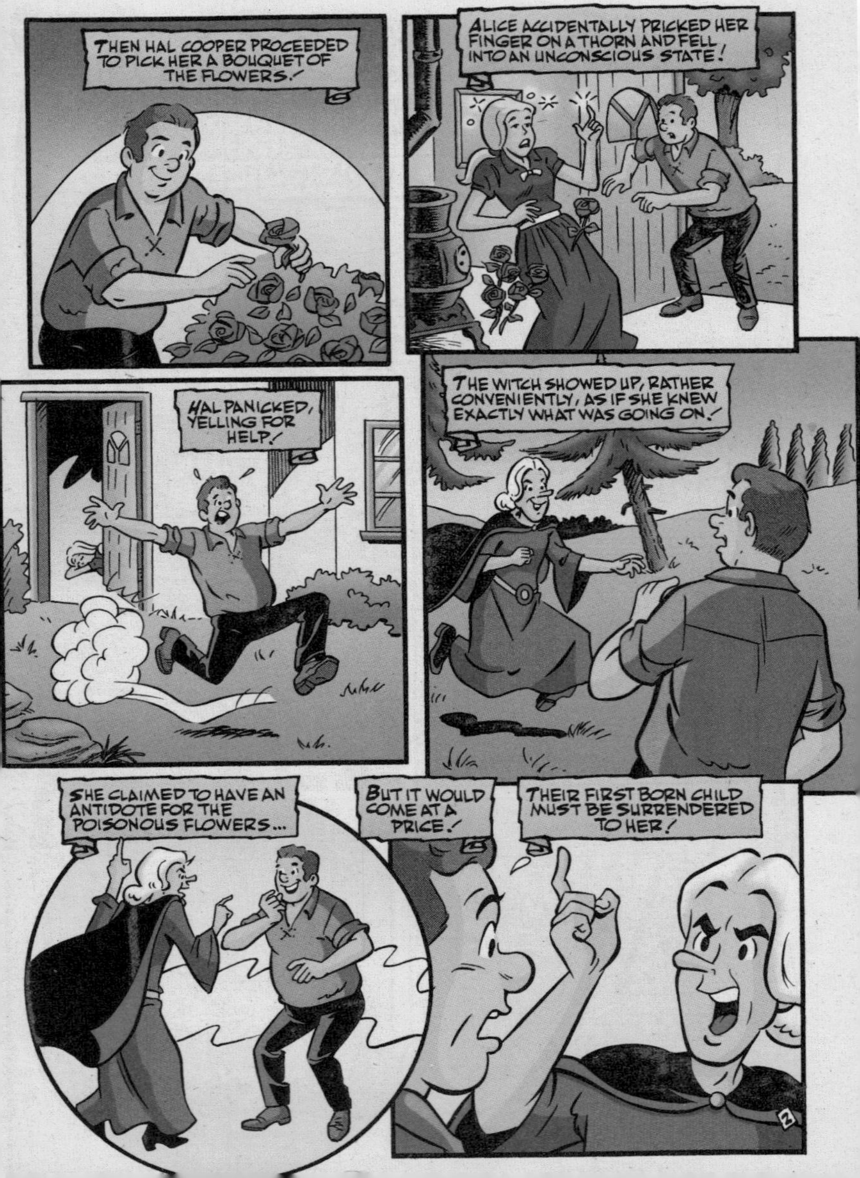
THEN HAL COOPER PROCEEDED TO PICK HER A BOUQUET OF THE FLOWERS.
ALICE ACCIDENTALLY PRICKED HER FINGER ON A THORN AND FELL INTO AN UNCONSCIOUS STATE!
HAL PANICKED, YELLING FOR HELP!
THE WITCH SHOWED UP, RATHER CONVENIENTLY, AS IF SHE KNEW EXACTLY WHAT WAS GOING ON!
SHE CLAIMED TO HAVE AN ANTIDOTE FOR THE POISONOUS FLOWERS...
BUT IT WOULD COME AT A PRICE!
THEIR FIRST BORN CHILD MUST BE SURRENDERED TO HER!
2

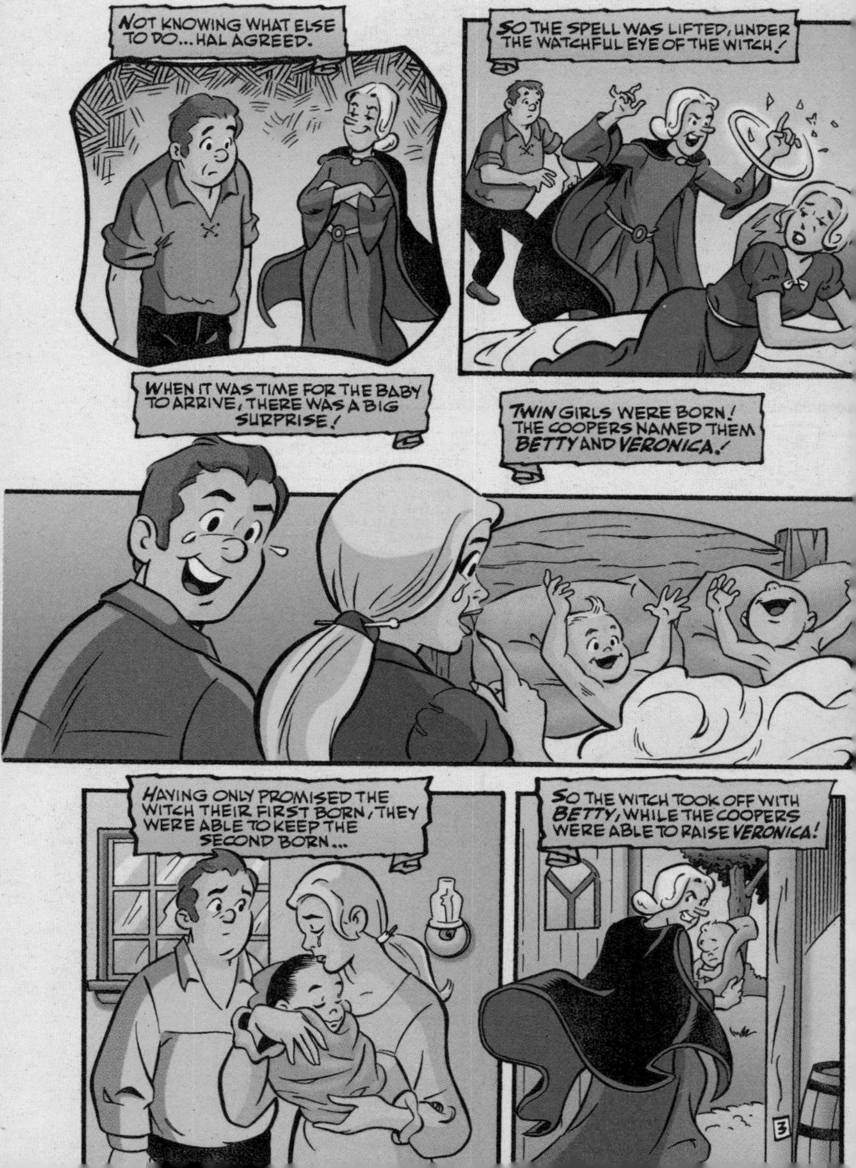
NOT KNOWING WHAT ELSE TO DO... HAL AGREED.
SO THE SPELL WAS LIFTED, UNDER THE WATCHFUL EYE OF THE WITCH!
WHEN IT WAS TIME FOR THE BABY TO ARRIVE, THERE WAS A BIG SURPRISE!
TWIN GIRLS WERE BORN! THE COOPERS NAMED THEM BETTY AND VERONICA!
HAVING ONLY PROMISED THE WITCH THEIR FIRST BORN, THEY WERE ABLE TO KEEP THE SECOND BORN...
SO THE WITCH TOOK OFF WITH BETTY, WHILE THE COOPERS WERE ABLE TO RAISE VERONICA!
3

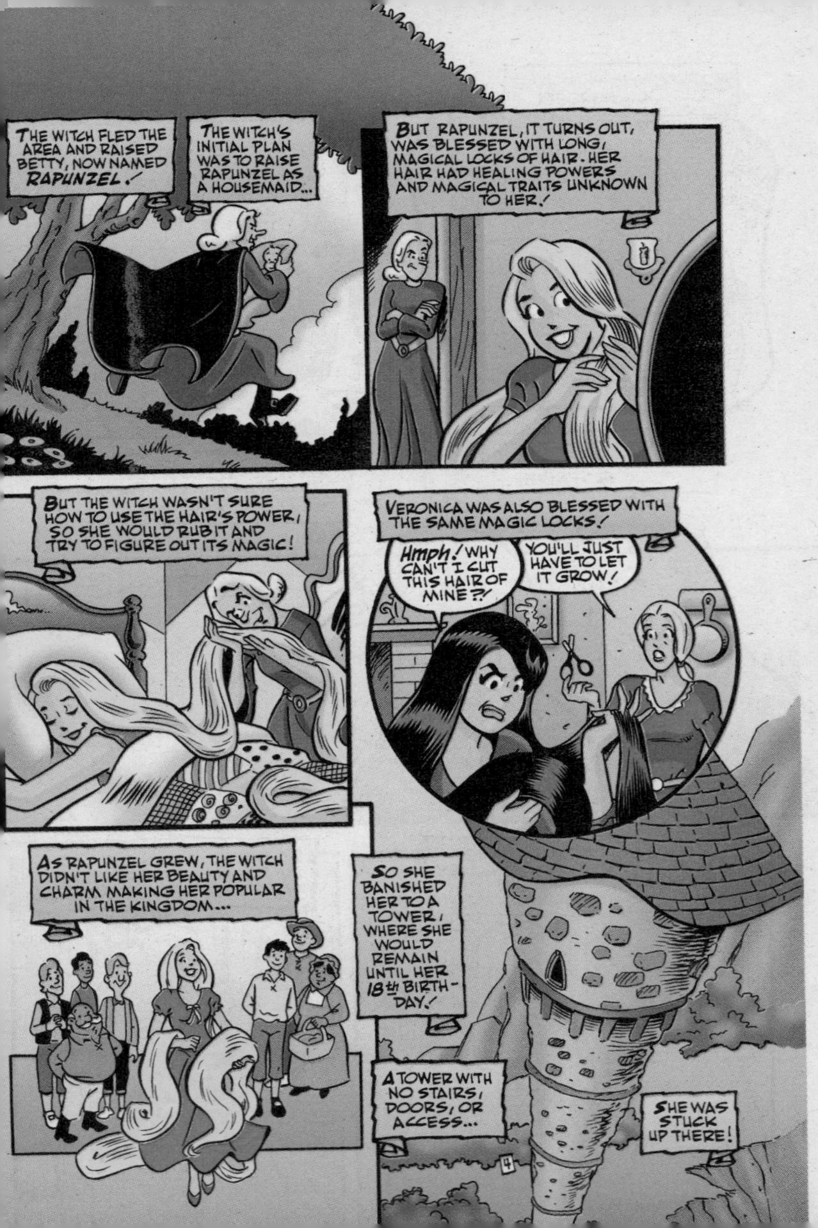
THE WITCH FLED THE AREA AND RAISED BETTY, NOW NAMED RAPUNZEL!
THE WITCH'S INITIAL PLAN WAS TO RAISE RAPUNZEL AS A HOUSEMAID...
BUT RAPUNZEL, IT TURNS OUT, WAS BLESSED WITH LONG, MAGICAL LOCKS OF HAIR. HER HAIR HAD HEALING POWERS AND MAGICAL TRAITS UNKNOWN TO HER!
BUT THE WITCH WASN'T SURE HOW TO USE THE HAIR'S POWER, SO SHE WOULD RUB IT AND TRY TO FIGURE OUT ITS MAGIC!
VERONICA WAS ALSO BLESSED WITH THE SAME MAGIC LOCKS!
Hmph! WHY CAN'T I CUT THIS HAIR OF MINE?!
YOU'LL JUST HAVE TO LET IT GROW!
AS RAPUNZEL GREW, THE WITCH DIDN'T LIKE HER BEAUTY AND CHARM MAKING HER POPULAR IN THE KINGDOM...
SO SHE BANISHED HER TO A TOWER, WHERE SHE WOULD REMAIN UNTIL HER 18th BIRTHDAY!
A TOWER WITH NO STAIRS, DOORS, OR ACCESS...
SHE WAS STUCK UP THERE!
4

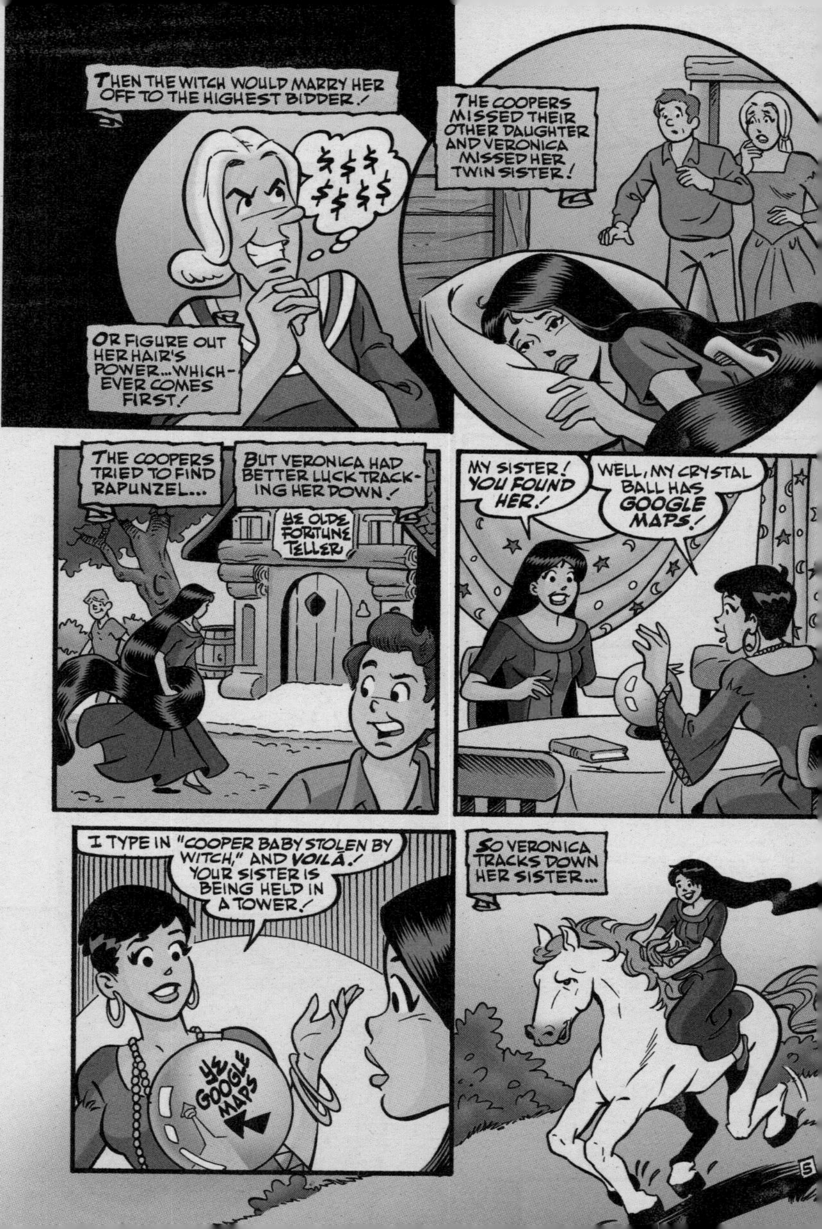
THEN THE WITCH WOULD MARRY HER OFF TO THE HIGHEST BIDDER!
$$$ $$$$
OR FIGURE OUT HER HAIR'S POWER...WHICH-EVER COMES FIRST!
THE COOPERS MISSED THEIR OTHER DAUGHTER AND VERONICA MISSED HER TWIN SISTER!
THE COOPERS TRIED TO FIND RAPUNZEL...
BUT VERONICA HAD BETTER LUCK TRACK-ING HER DOWN!
YE OLDE FORTUNE TELLER
MY SISTER! YOU FOUND HER!
WELL, MY CRYSTAL BALL HAS GOOGLE MAPS!
I TYPE IN "COOPER BABY STOLEN BY WITCH," AND VOILÀ! YOUR SISTER IS BEING HELD IN A TOWER!
YE GOOGLE MAPS
SO VERONICA TRACKS DOWN HER SISTER...
5

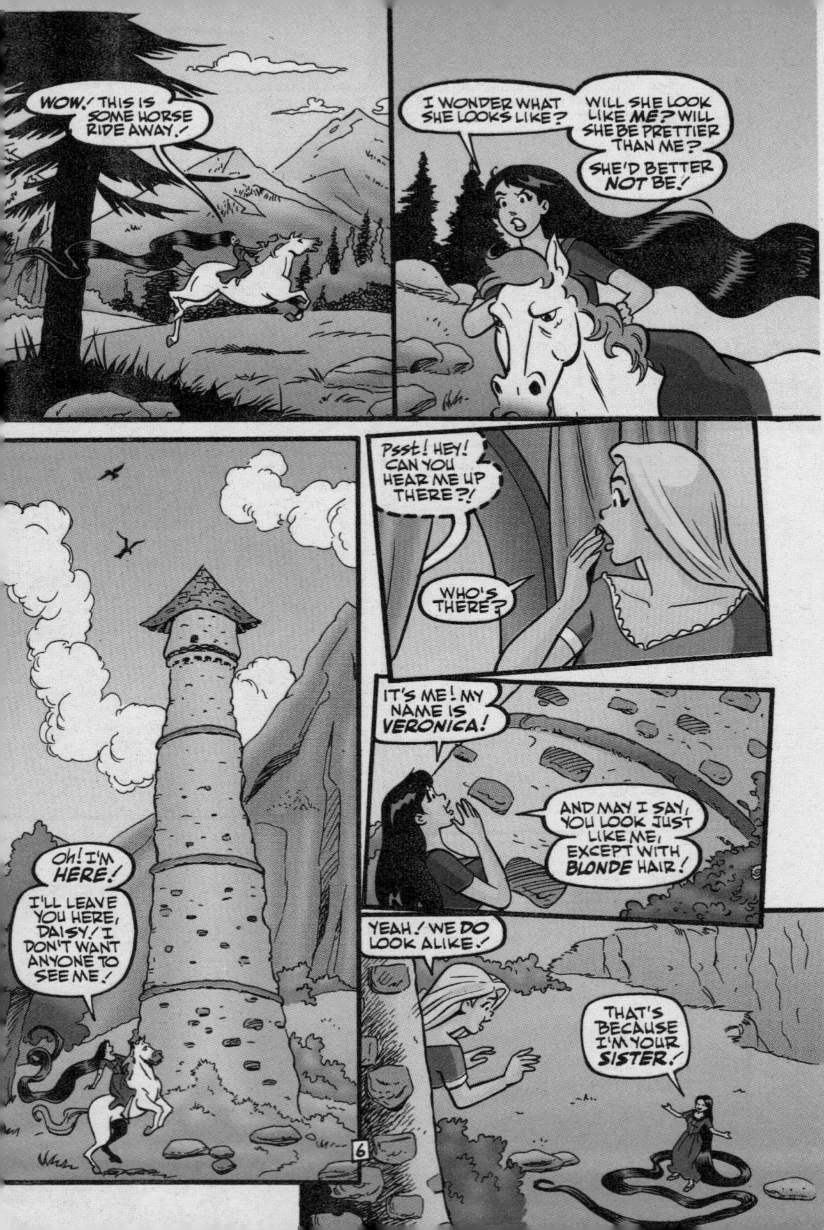
WOW! THIS IS SOME HORSE RIDE AWAY!
I WONDER WHAT SHE LOOKS LIKE?
WILL SHE LOOK LIKE ME? WILL SHE BE PRETTIER THAN ME?
SHE'D BETTER NOT BE!
Oh! I'M HERE!
I'LL LEAVE YOU HERE, DAISY! I DON'T WANT ANYONE TO SEE ME!
Psst! HEY! CAN YOU HEAR ME UP THERE?!
WHO'S THERE?
IT'S ME! MY NAME IS VERONICA!
AND MAY I SAY, YOU LOOK JUST LIKE ME, EXCEPT WITH BLONDE HAIR!
YEAH! WE DO LOOK ALIKE!
THAT'S BECAUSE I'M YOUR SISTER!
6

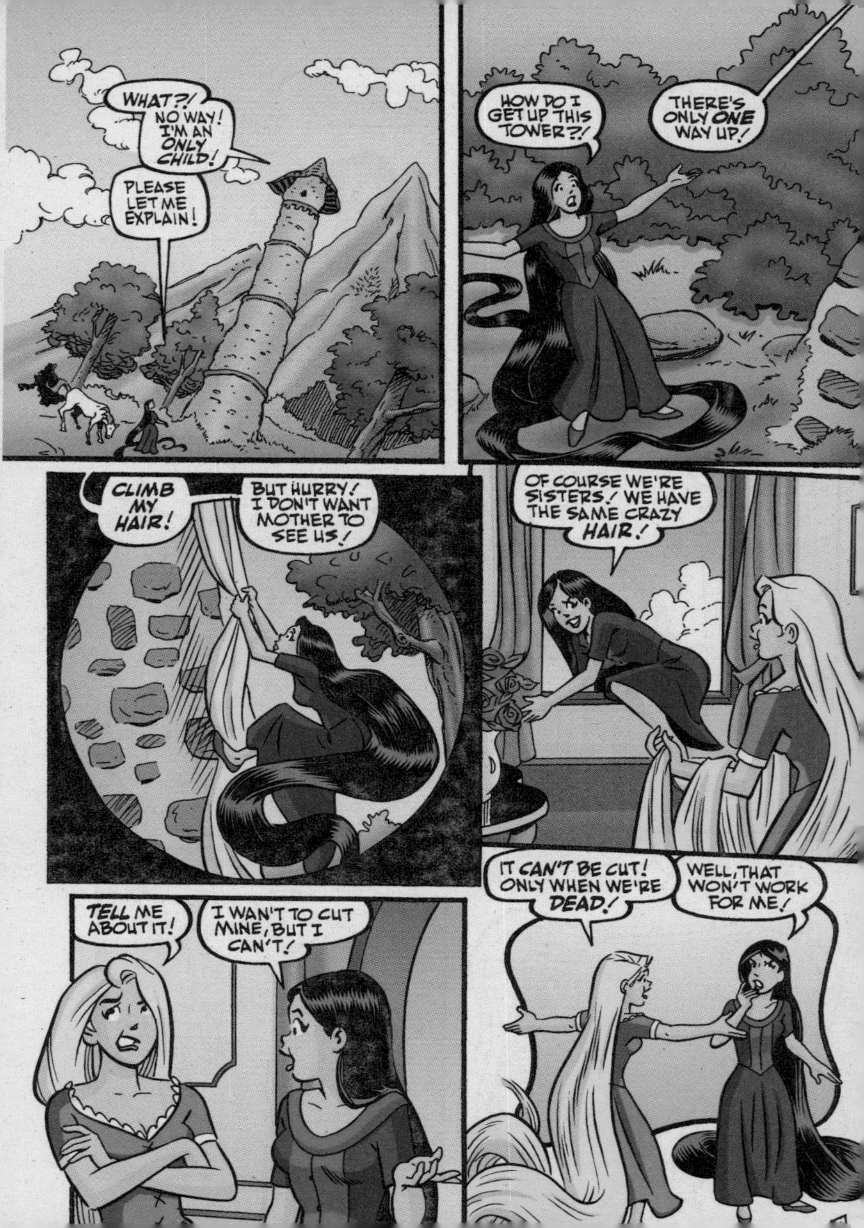
WHAT?! NO WAY! I'M AN ONLY CHILD!
PLEASE LET ME EXPLAIN!
HOW DO I GET UP THIS TOWER?!
THERE'S ONLY ONE WAY UP!
CLIMB MY HAIR!
BUT HURRY! I DON'T WANT MOTHER TO SEE US!
OF COURSE WE'RE SISTERS! WE HAVE THE SAME CRAZY HAIR!
TELL ME ABOUT IT!
I WAN'T TO CUT MINE, BUT I CAN'T!
IT CAN'T BE CUT! ONLY WHEN WE'RE DEAD!
WELL, THAT WON'T WORK FOR ME!

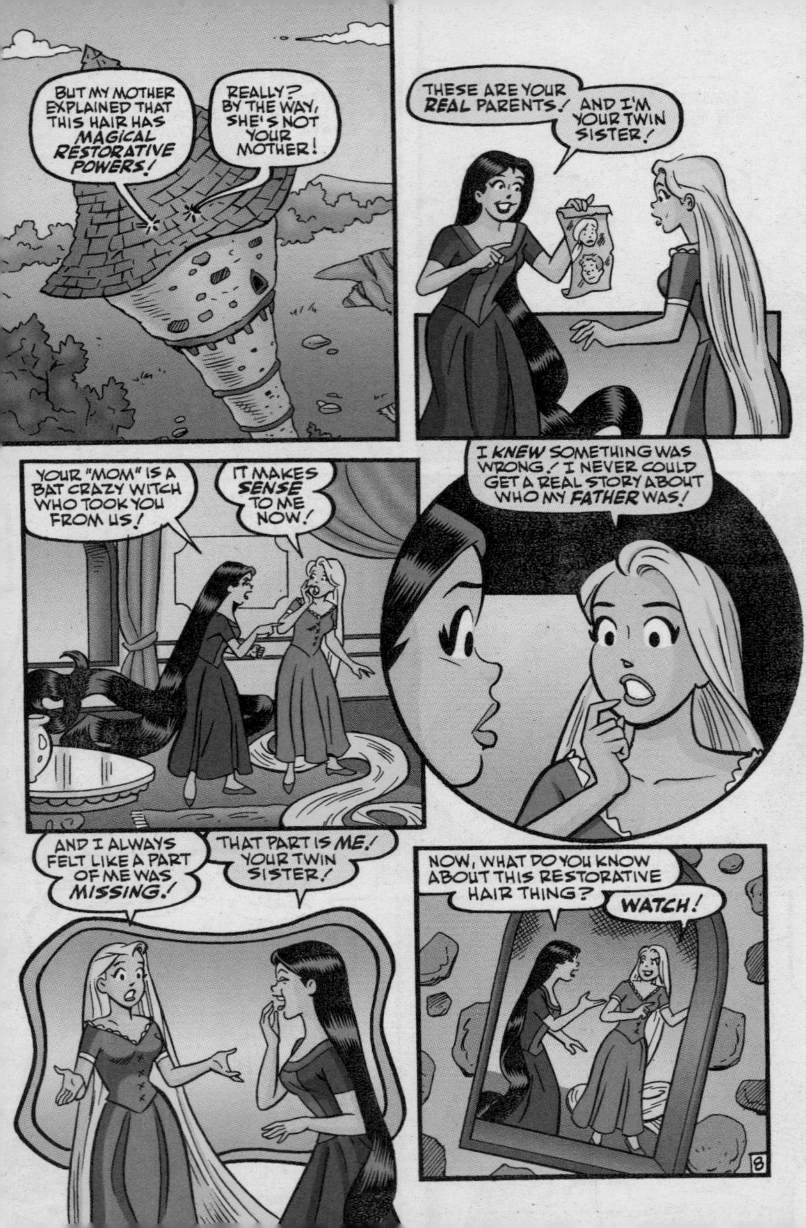

BUT MY MOTHER EXPLAINED THAT THIS HAIR HAS MAGICAL RESTORATIVE POWERS!
REALLY? BY THE WAY, SHE'S NOT YOUR MOTHER!
THESE ARE YOUR REAL PARENTS!
AND I'M YOUR TWIN SISTER!
YOUR "MOM" IS A BAT CRAZY WITCH WHO TOOK YOU FROM US!
IT MAKES SENSE TO ME NOW!
I KNEW SOMETHING WAS WRONG! I NEVER COULD GET A REAL STORY ABOUT WHO MY FATHER WAS!
AND I ALWAYS FELT LIKE A PART OF ME WAS MISSING!
THAT PART IS ME! YOUR TWIN SISTER!
NOW, WHAT DO YOU KNOW ABOUT THIS RESTORATIVE HAIR THING?
WATCH!
8

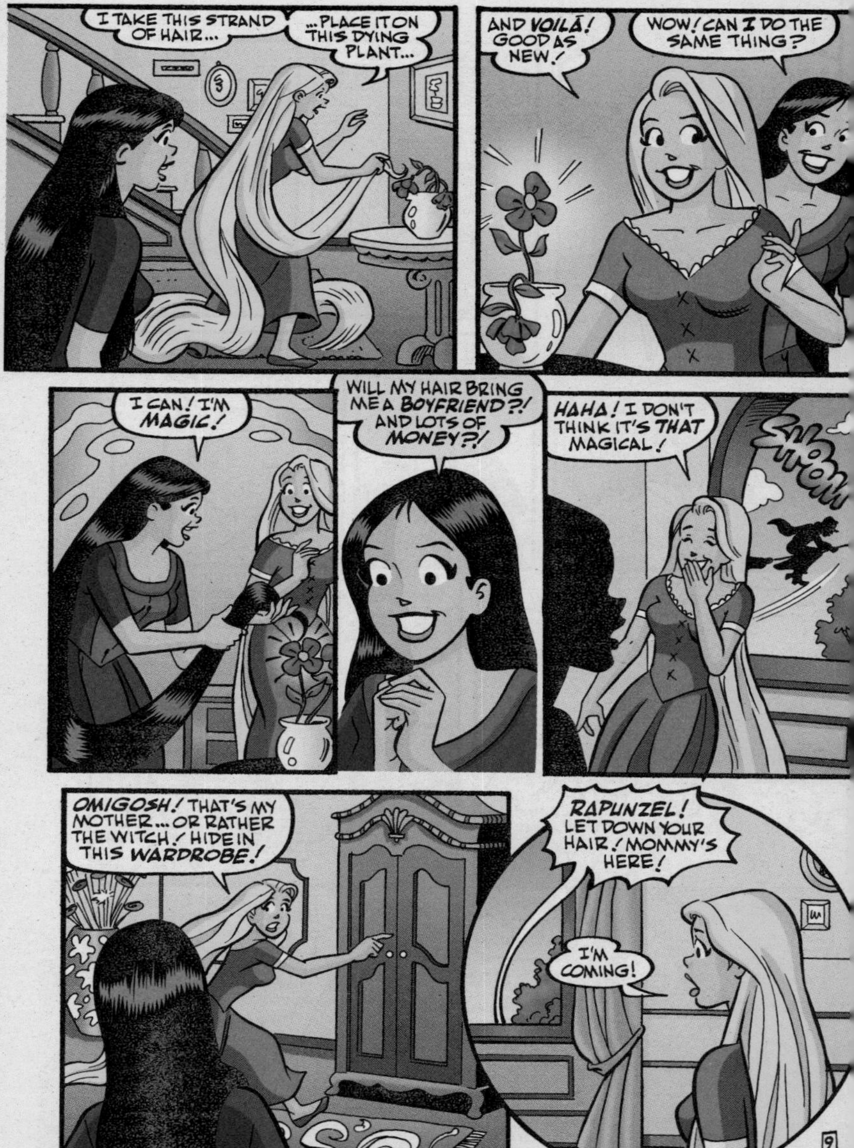
I TAKE THIS STRAND OF HAIR...
...PLACE IT ON THIS DYING PLANT...
AND VOILÀ! GOOD AS NEW!
WOW! CAN I DO THE SAME THING?
I CAN! I'M MAGIC!
WILL MY HAIR BRING ME A BOYFRIEND?! AND LOTS OF MONEY?!
HAHA! I DON'T THINK IT'S THAT MAGICAL!
SHOOM
OMIGOSH! THAT'S MY MOTHER... OR RATHER THE WITCH! HIDE IN THIS WARDROBE!
RAPUNZEL! LET DOWN YOUR HAIR! MOMMY'S HERE!
I'M COMING!

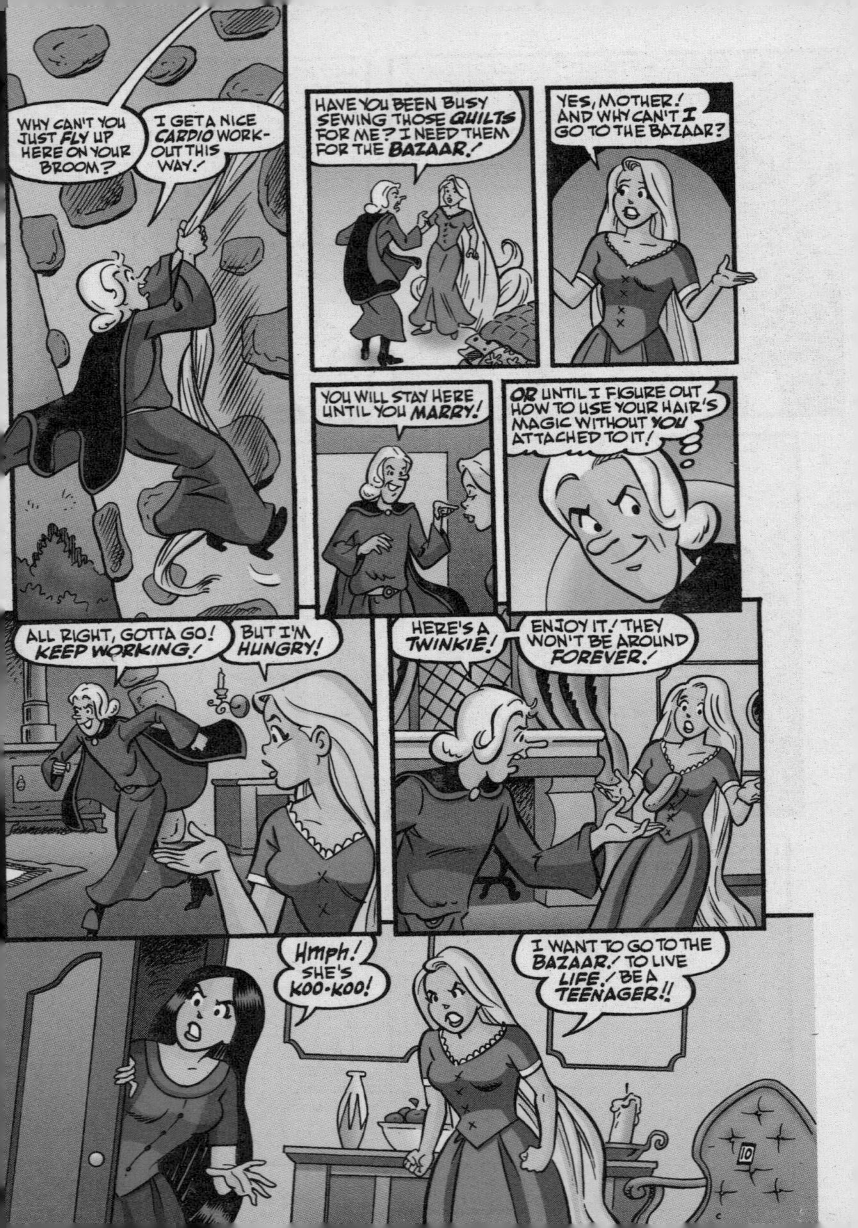
WHY CAN'T YOU JUST FLY UP HERE ON YOUR BROOM?
I GET A NICE CARDIO WORK-OUT THIS WAY!
HAVE YOU BEEN BUSY SEWING THOSE QUILTS FOR ME? I NEED THEM FOR THE BAZAAR!
YES, MOTHER! AND WHY CAN'T I GO TO THE BAZAAR?
YOU WILL STAY HERE UNTIL YOU MARRY!
OR UNTIL I FIGURE OUT HOW TO USE YOUR HAIR'S MAGIC WITHOUT YOU ATTACHED TO IT!
ALL RIGHT, GOTTA GO! KEEP WORKING!
BUT I'M HUNGRY!
HERE'S A TWINKIE!
ENJOY IT! THEY WON'T BE AROUND FOREVER!
Hmph! SHE'S KOO-KOO!
I WANT TO GO TO THE BAZAAR! TO LIVE LIFE! BE A TEENAGER!!
10

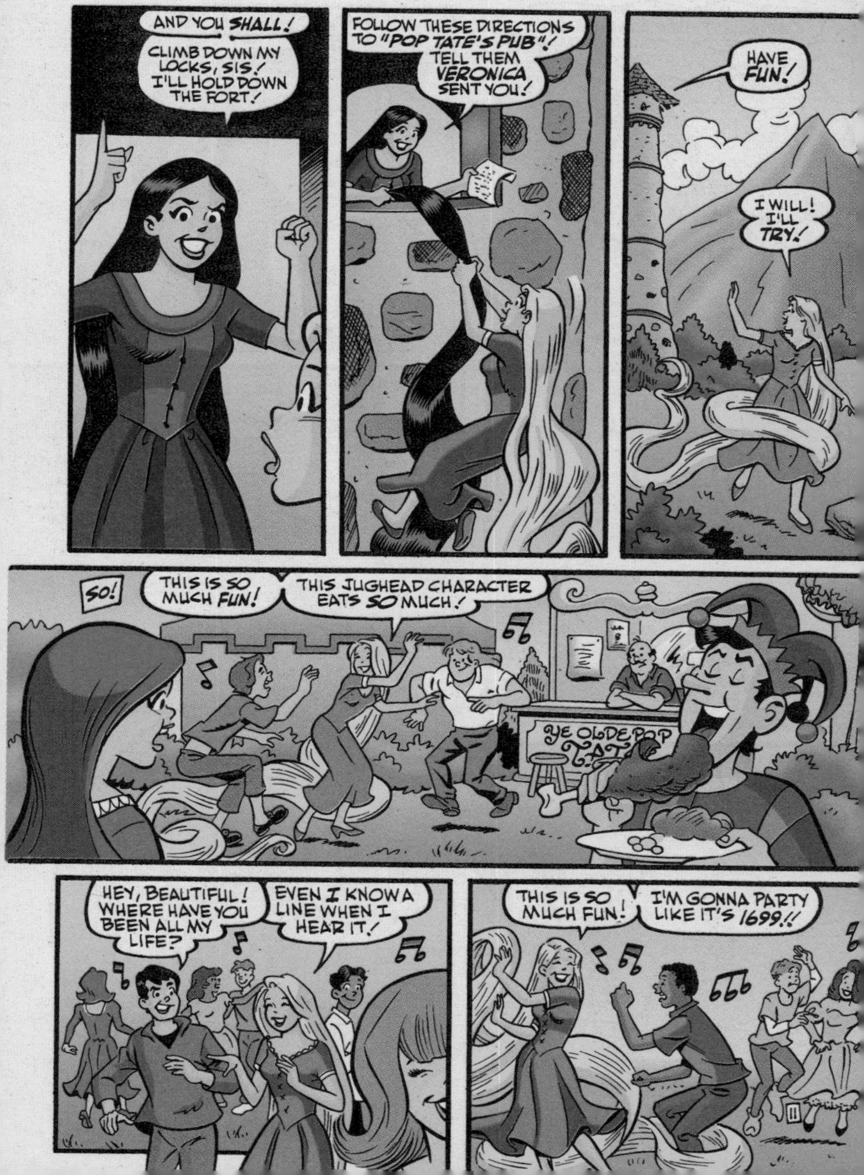
AND YOU SHALL!
CLIMB DOWN MY LOCKS, SIS! I'LL HOLD DOWN THE FORT!
FOLLOW THESE DIRECTIONS TO "POP TATE'S PUB"! TELL THEM VERONICA SENT YOU!
HAVE FUN!
I WILL! I'LL TRY!
SO!
THIS IS SO MUCH FUN!
THIS JUGHEAD CHARACTER EATS SO MUCH!
YE OLDE POP TATE
HEY, BEAUTIFUL! WHERE HAVE YOU BEEN ALL MY LIFE?
EVEN I KNOW A LINE WHEN I HEAR IT!
THIS IS SO MUCH FUN!
I'M GONNA PARTY LIKE IT'S 1699!!

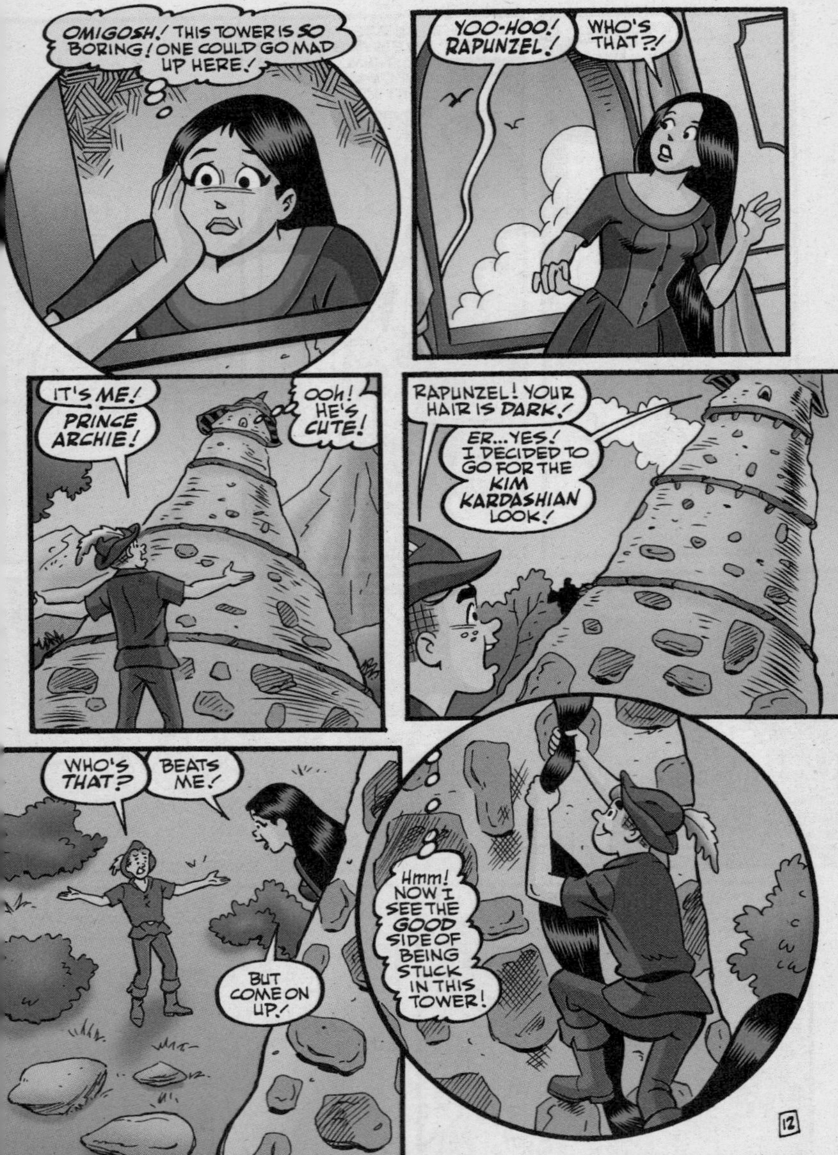
OMIGOSH! THIS TOWER IS SO BORING! ONE COULD GO MAD UP HERE!
YOO-HOO! RAPUNZEL!
WHO'S THAT?!
IT'S ME! PRINCE ARCHIE!
Ooh! HE'S CUTE!
RAPUNZEL! YOUR HAIR IS DARK!
ER...YES! I DECIDED TO GO FOR THE KIM KARDASHIAN LOOK!
WHO'S THAT?
BEATS ME!
BUT COME ON UP!
Hmm! NOW I SEE THE GOOD SIDE OF BEING STUCK IN THIS TOWER!
12

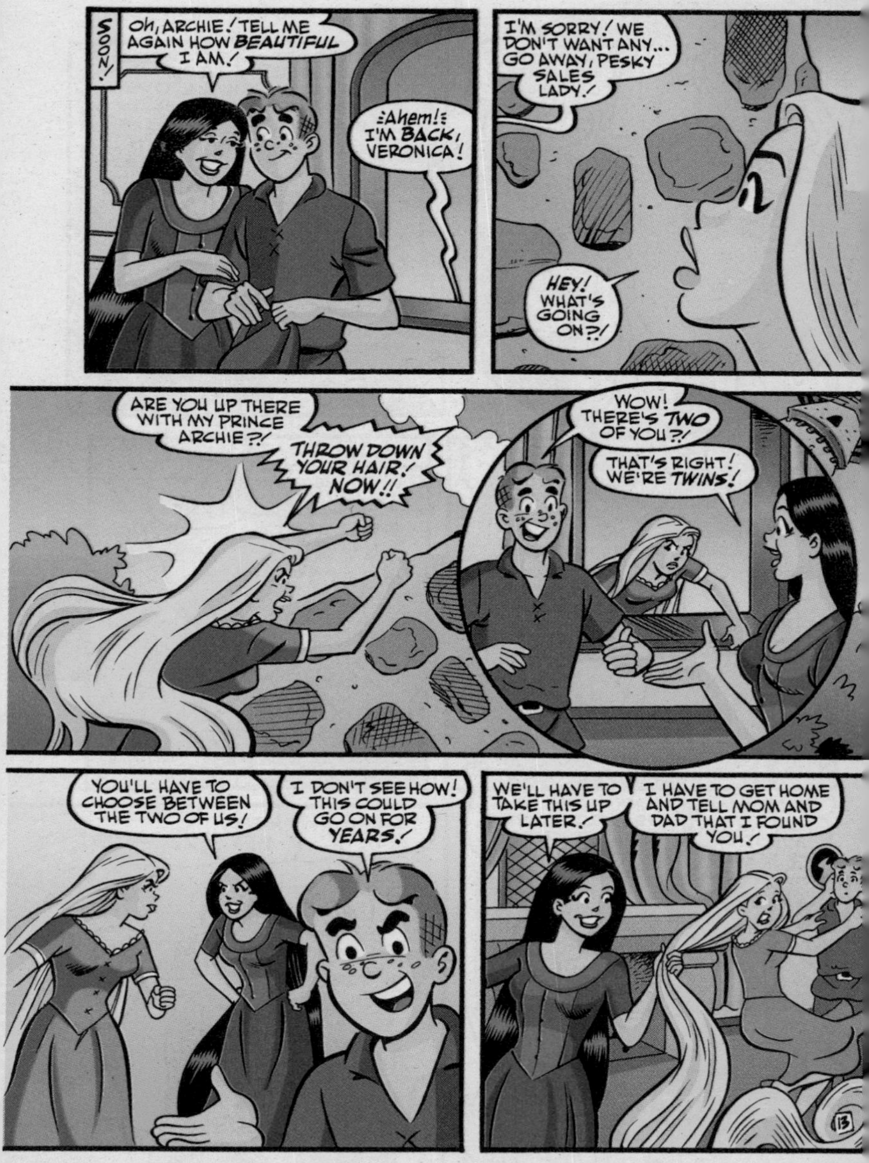
SOON!
OH, ARCHIE! TELL ME AGAIN HOW *BEAUTIFUL* I AM!
Ahem! I'M *BACK*, VERONICA!
I'M SORRY! WE DON'T WANT ANY... GO AWAY, PESKY SALES LADY!
HEY! WHAT'S GOING ON?!
ARE YOU UP THERE WITH MY PRINCE ARCHIE?!
THROW DOWN YOUR HAIR! NOW!!
WOW! THERE'S *TWO* OF YOU?!
THAT'S RIGHT! WE'RE *TWINS*!
YOU'LL HAVE TO CHOOSE BETWEEN THE TWO OF US!
I DON'T SEE HOW! THIS COULD GO ON FOR *YEARS*!
WE'LL HAVE TO TAKE THIS UP LATER!
I HAVE TO GET HOME AND TELL MOM AND DAD THAT I FOUND YOU!
13

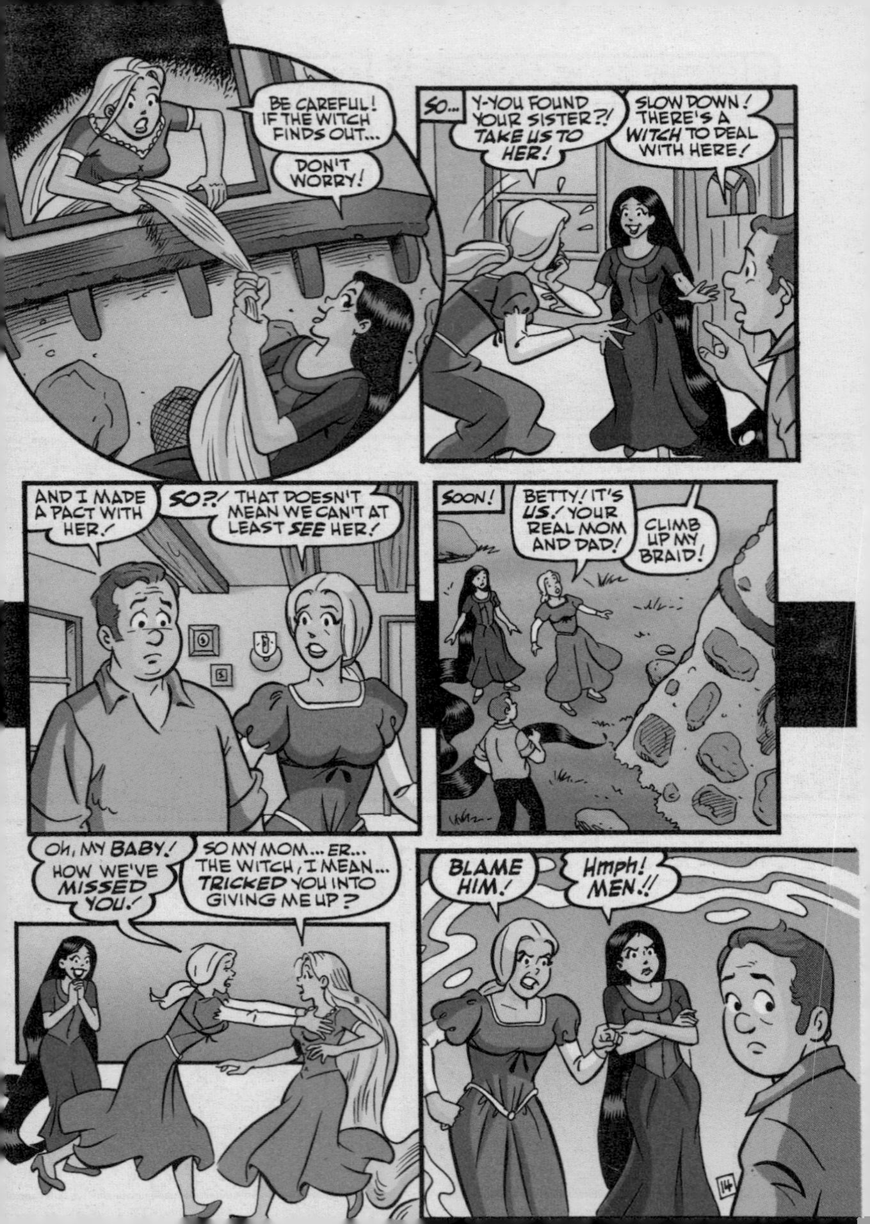

BE CAREFUL! IF THE WITCH FINDS OUT...
DON'T WORRY!
SO...
Y-YOU FOUND YOUR SISTER?! TAKE US TO HER!
SLOW DOWN! THERE'S A WITCH TO DEAL WITH HERE!
AND I MADE A PACT WITH HER!
SO?! THAT DOESN'T MEAN WE CAN'T AT LEAST SEE HER!
SOON!
BETTY! IT'S US! YOUR REAL MOM AND DAD!
CLIMB UP MY BRAID!
Oh, MY BABY! HOW WE'VE MISSED YOU!
SO MY MOM... ER... THE WITCH, I MEAN... TRICKED YOU INTO GIVING ME UP?
BLAME HIM!
Hmph! MEN!!
14

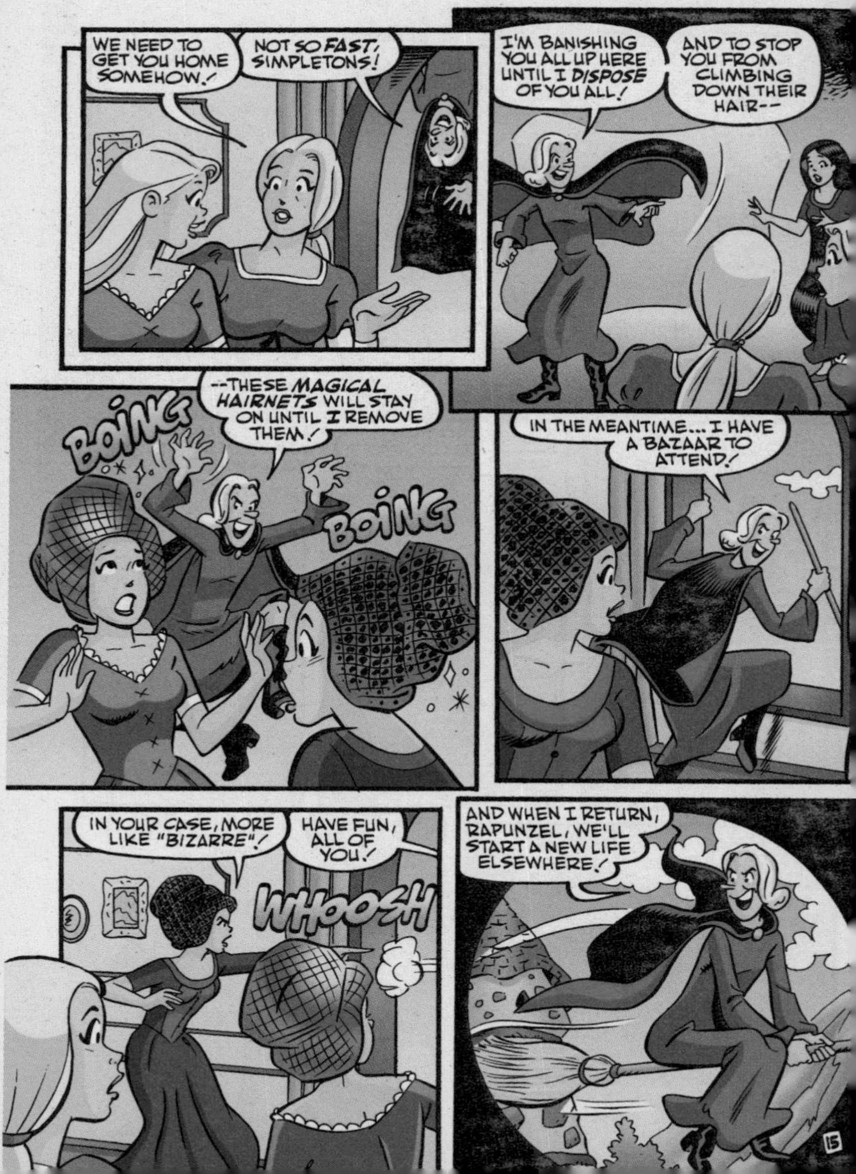
WE NEED TO GET YOU HOME SOMEHOW.!
NOT SO FAST, SIMPLETONS!
I'M BANISHING YOU ALL UP HERE UNTIL I DISPOSE OF YOU ALL!
AND TO STOP YOU FROM CLIMBING DOWN THEIR HAIR--
--THESE MAGICAL HAIRNETS WILL STAY ON UNTIL I REMOVE THEM!
BOING
BOING
IN THE MEANTIME... I HAVE A BAZAAR TO ATTEND!
IN YOUR CASE, MORE LIKE "BIZARRE"!
HAVE FUN, ALL OF YOU!
WHOOSH
AND WHEN I RETURN, RAPUNZEL, WE'LL START A NEW LIFE ELSEWHERE!
15

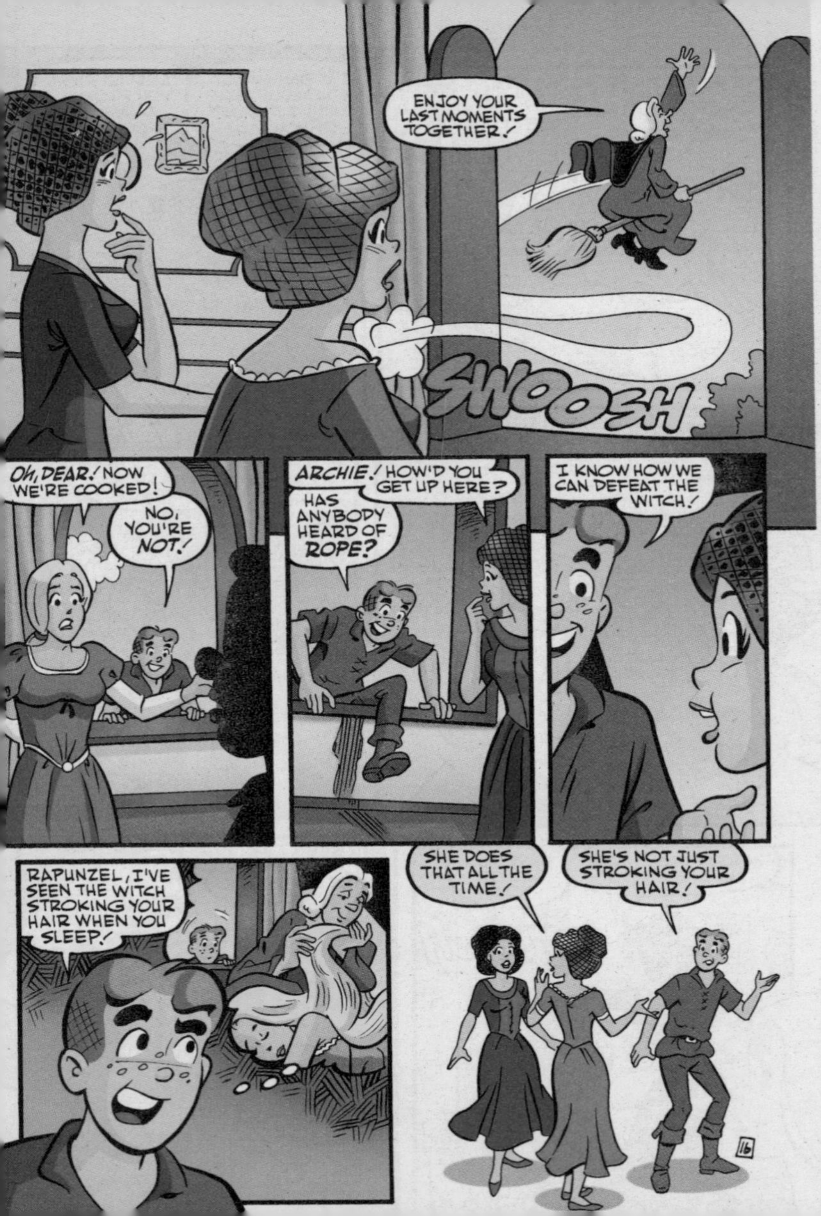
ENJOY YOUR LAST MOMENTS TOGETHER!
SWOOSH
OH, DEAR! NOW WE'RE COOKED!
NO, YOU'RE NOT!
ARCHIE! HOW'D YOU GET UP HERE?
HAS ANYBODY HEARD OF ROPE?
I KNOW HOW WE CAN DEFEAT THE WITCH!
RAPUNZEL, I'VE SEEN THE WITCH STROKING YOUR HAIR WHEN YOU SLEEP!
SHE DOES THAT ALL THE TIME!
SHE'S NOT JUST STROKING YOUR HAIR!
16

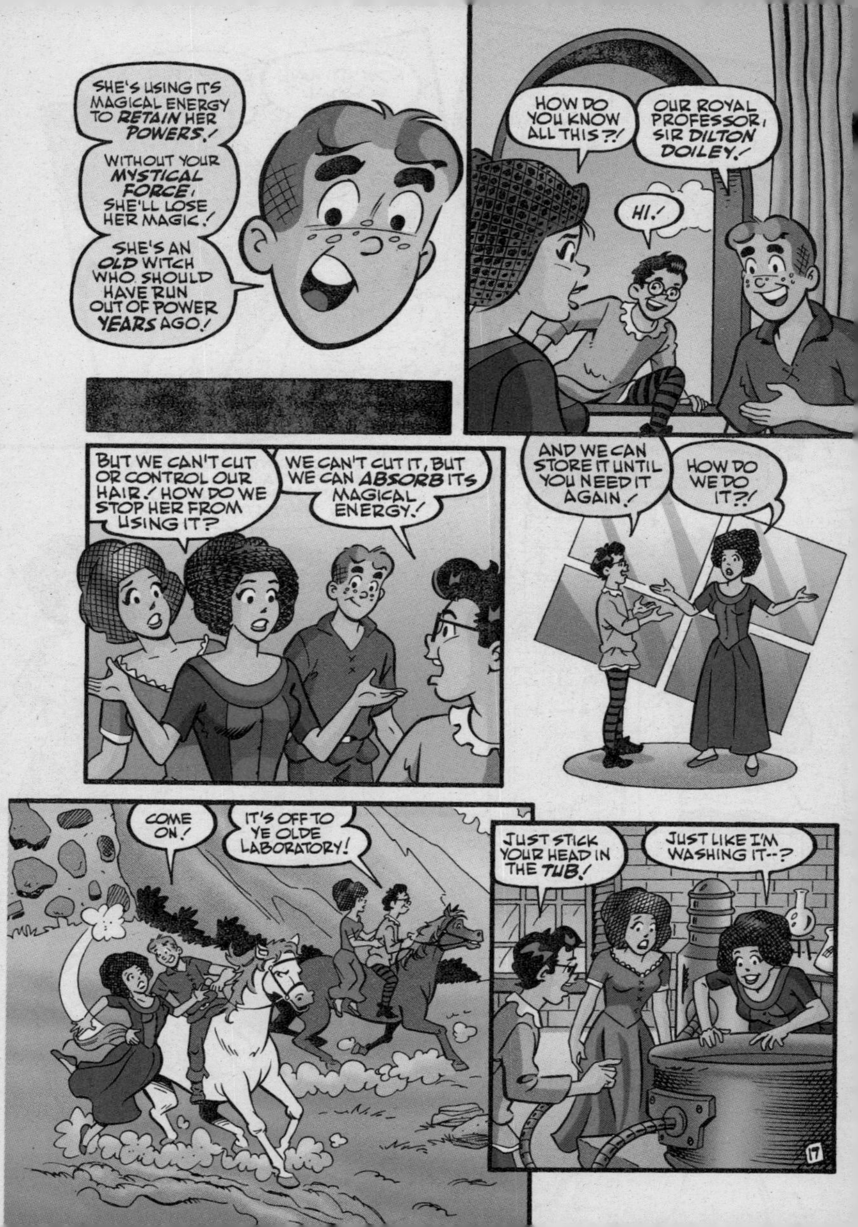
SHE'S USING IT'S MAGICAL ENERGY TO RETAIN HER POWERS!
WITHOUT YOUR MYSTICAL FORCE, SHE'LL LOSE HER MAGIC!
SHE'S AN OLD WITCH WHO SHOULD HAVE RUN OUT OF POWER YEARS AGO!
HOW DO YOU KNOW ALL THIS?!
OUR ROYAL PROFESSOR, SIR DILTON DOILEY!
HI!
[redacted]
BUT WE CAN'T CUT OR CONTROL OUR HAIR! HOW DO WE STOP HER FROM USING IT?
WE CAN'T CUT IT, BUT WE CAN ABSORB ITS MAGICAL ENERGY!
AND WE CAN STORE IT UNTIL YOU NEED IT AGAIN!
HOW DO WE DO IT?!
COME ON!
IT'S OFF TO YE OLDE LABORATORY!
JUST STICK YOUR HEAD IN THE TUB!
JUST LIKE I'M WASHING IT--?
17

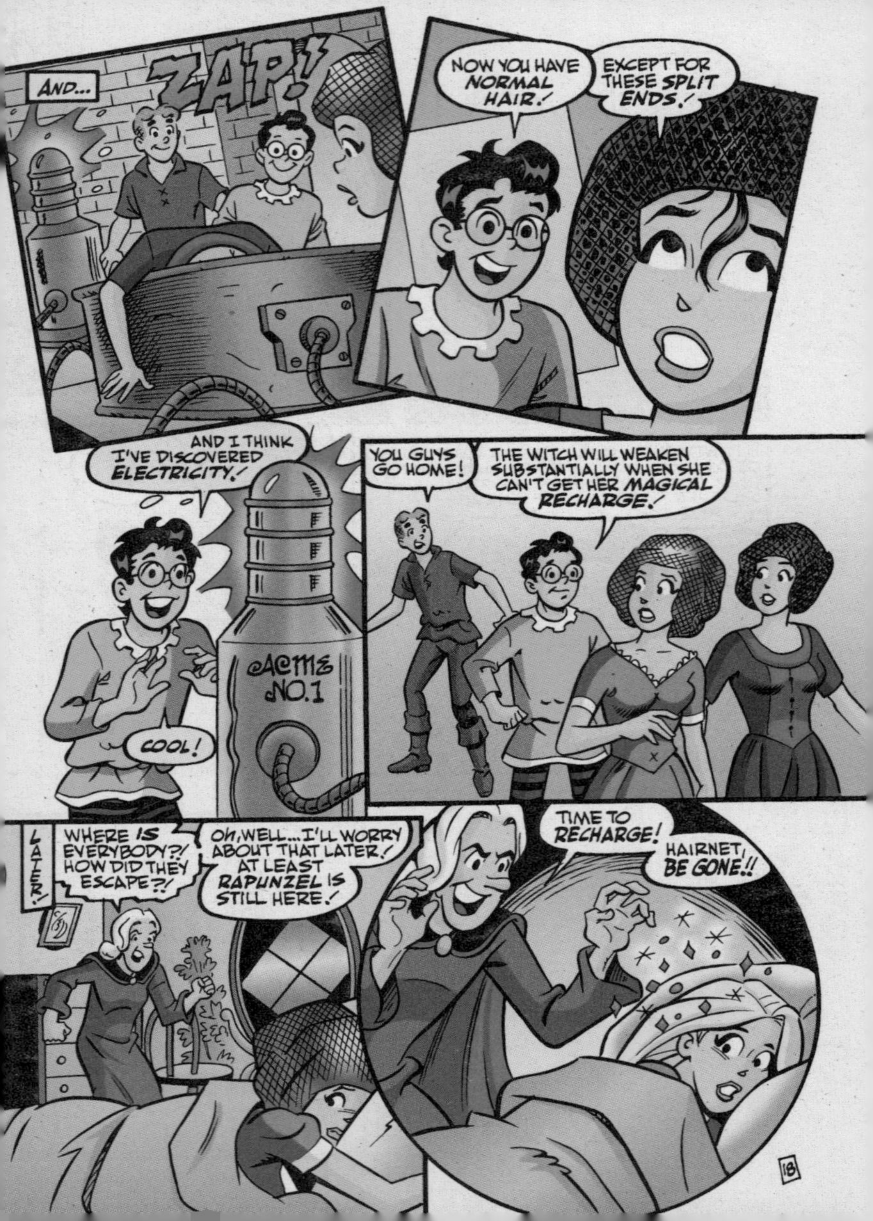
AND...
ZAP!
NOW YOU HAVE NORMAL HAIR!
EXCEPT FOR THESE SPLIT ENDS!
AND I THINK I'VE DISCOVERED ELECTRICITY!
COOL!
ACME NO.1
YOU GUYS GO HOME!
THE WITCH WILL WEAKEN SUBSTANTIALLY WHEN SHE CAN'T GET HER MAGICAL RECHARGE!
LATER!
WHERE IS EVERYBODY?! HOW DID THEY ESCAPE?!
OH, WELL... I'LL WORRY ABOUT THAT LATER! AT LEAST RAPUNZEL IS STILL HERE!
TIME TO RECHARGE!
HAIRNET, BE GONE!!
18

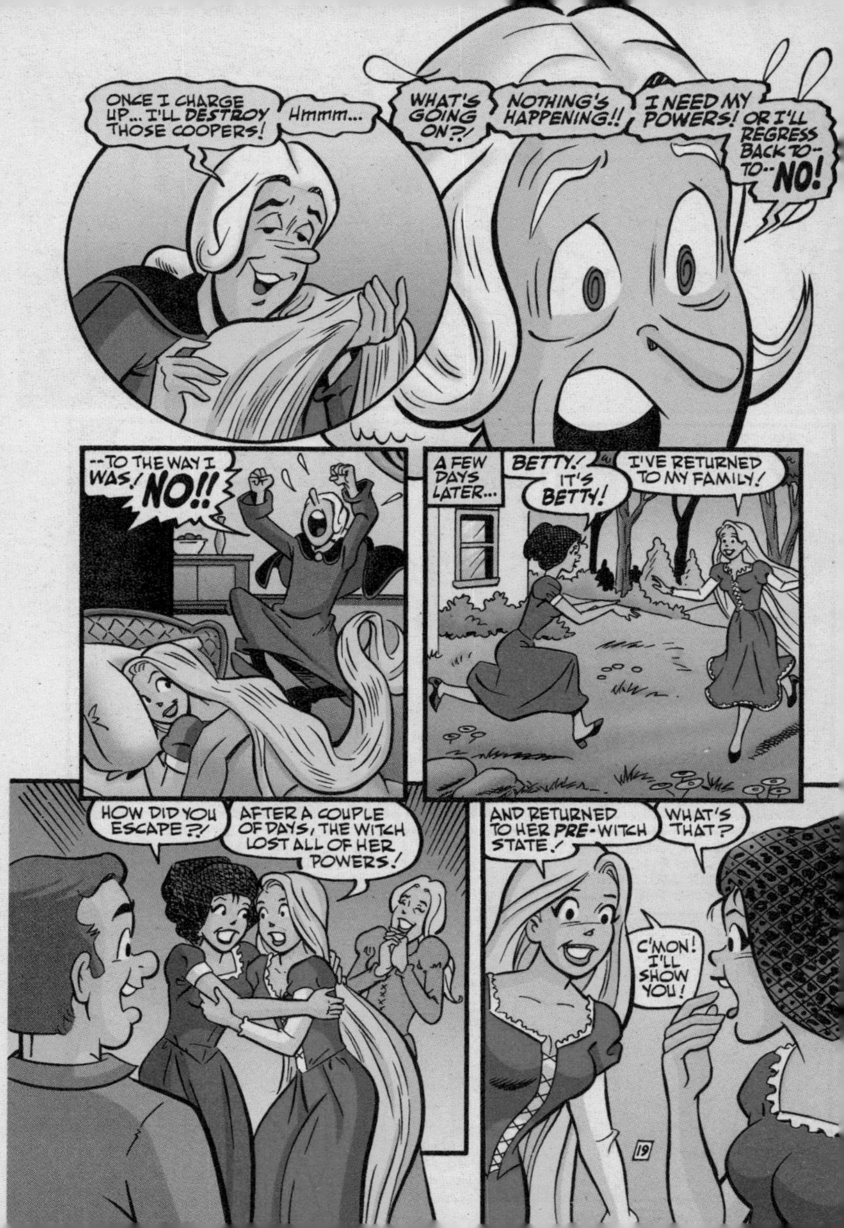
ONCE I CHARGE UP... I'LL DESTROY THOSE COOPERS!
Hmmm...
WHAT'S GOING ON?!
NOTHING'S HAPPENING!!
I NEED MY POWERS! OR I'LL REGRESS BACK TO-- TO-- NO!
--TO THE WAY I WAS! NO!!
A FEW DAYS LATER...
BETTY! IT'S BETTY!
I'VE RETURNED TO MY FAMILY!
HOW DID YOU ESCAPE?!
AFTER A COUPLE OF DAYS, THE WITCH LOST ALL OF HER POWERS!
AND RETURNED TO HER PRE-WITCH STATE!
WHAT'S THAT?
C'MON! I'LL SHOW YOU!
19

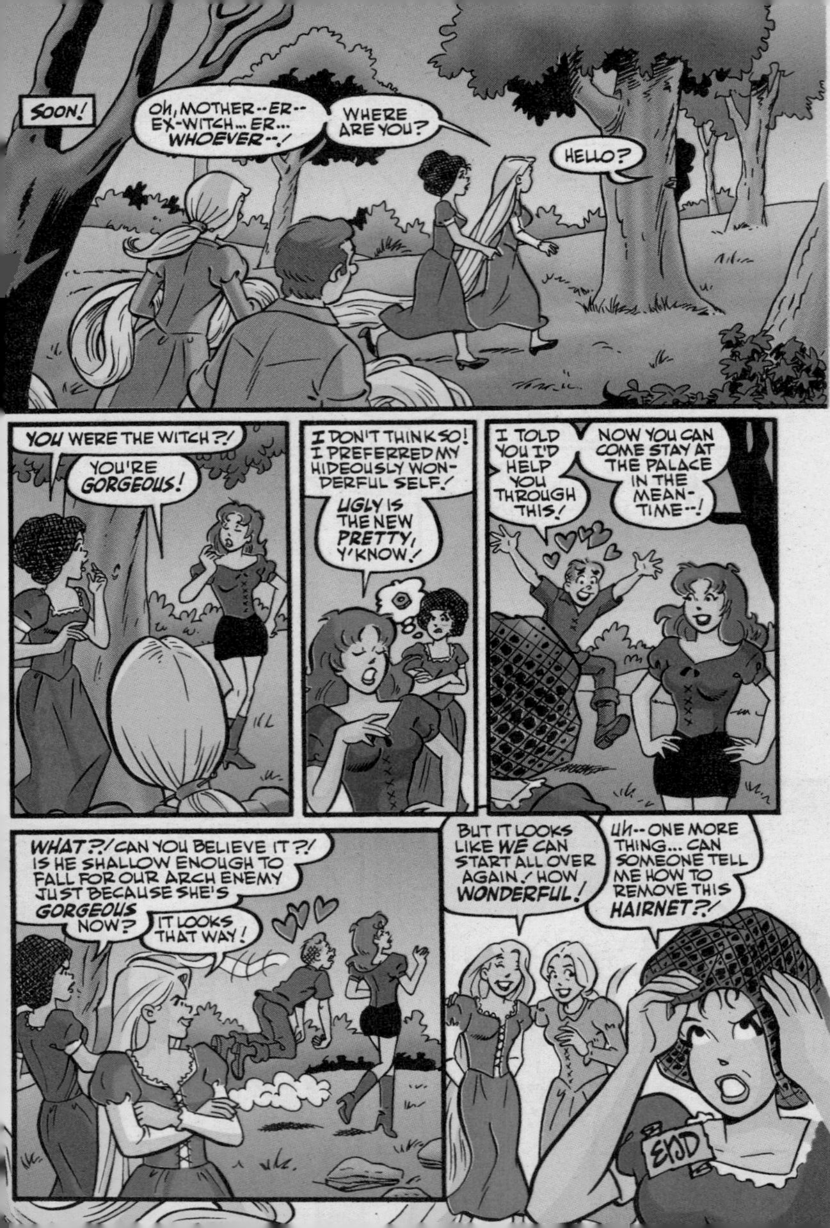
SOON!
OH, MOTHER--ER--EX-WITCH... ER... WHOEVER--!
WHERE ARE YOU?
HELLO?
YOU WERE THE WITCH?!
YOU'RE GORGEOUS!
I DON'T THINK SO! I PREFERRED MY HIDEOUSLY WONDERFUL SELF!
UGLY IS THE NEW PRETTY, Y'KNOW!
I TOLD YOU I'D HELP YOU THROUGH THIS!
NOW YOU CAN COME STAY AT THE PALACE IN THE MEANTIME--!
WHAT?! CAN YOU BELIEVE IT?! IS HE SHALLOW ENOUGH TO FALL FOR OUR ARCH ENEMY JUST BECAUSE SHE'S GORGEOUS NOW?
IT LOOKS THAT WAY!
BUT IT LOOKS LIKE WE CAN START ALL OVER AGAIN! HOW WONDERFUL!
UH-- ONE MORE THING... CAN SOMEONE TELL ME HOW TO REMOVE THIS HAIRNET?!
END

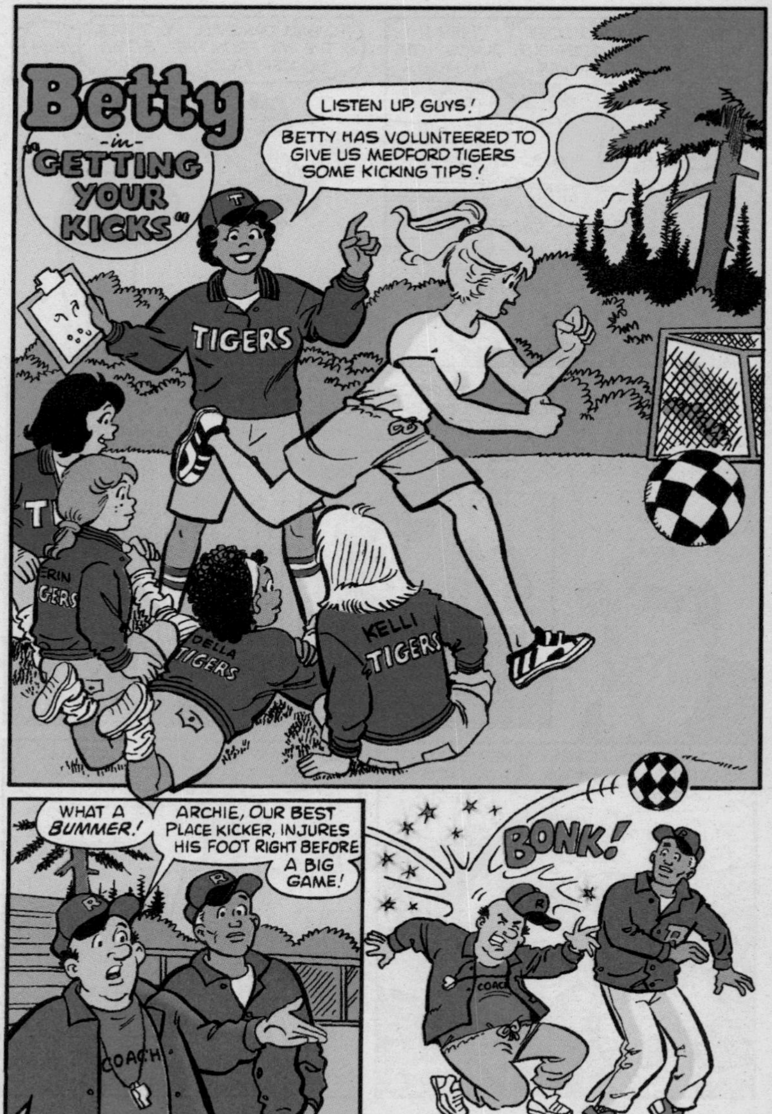
Betty
-in-
"GETTING YOUR KICKS"
LISTEN UP, GUYS!
BETTY HAS VOLUNTEERED TO GIVE US MEDFORD TIGERS SOME KICKING TIPS!
TIGERS
ERIN
DELLA TIGERS
KELLI TIGERS
WHAT A BUMMER!
ARCHIE, OUR BEST PLACE KICKER, INJURES HIS FOOT RIGHT BEFORE A BIG GAME!
COACH
BONK!
COACH

Script: George Gladir / Pencils: Stan Goldberg / Inks: Mike Esposito / Letters: Bill Yoshida

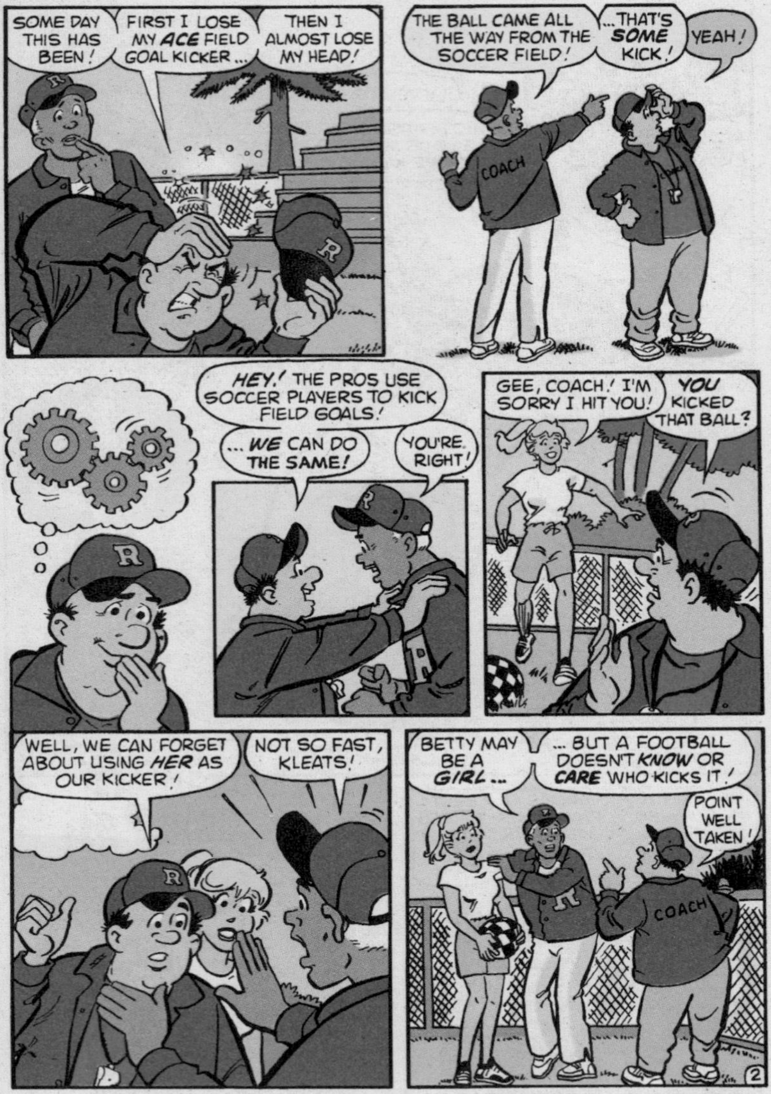

SOME DAY THIS HAS BEEN!
FIRST I LOSE MY ACE FIELD GOAL KICKER...
THEN I ALMOST LOSE MY HEAD!
THE BALL CAME ALL THE WAY FROM THE SOCCER FIELD!
...THAT'S SOME KICK!
YEAH!
COACH
HEY! THE PROS USE SOCCER PLAYERS TO KICK FIELD GOALS!
...WE CAN DO THE SAME!
YOU'RE RIGHT!
GEE, COACH! I'M SORRY I HIT YOU!
YOU KICKED THAT BALL?
WELL, WE CAN FORGET ABOUT USING HER AS OUR KICKER!
NOT SO FAST, KLEATS!
BETTY MAY BE A GIRL...
...BUT A FOOTBALL DOESN'T KNOW OR CARE WHO KICKS IT!
POINT WELL TAKEN!
COACH
2

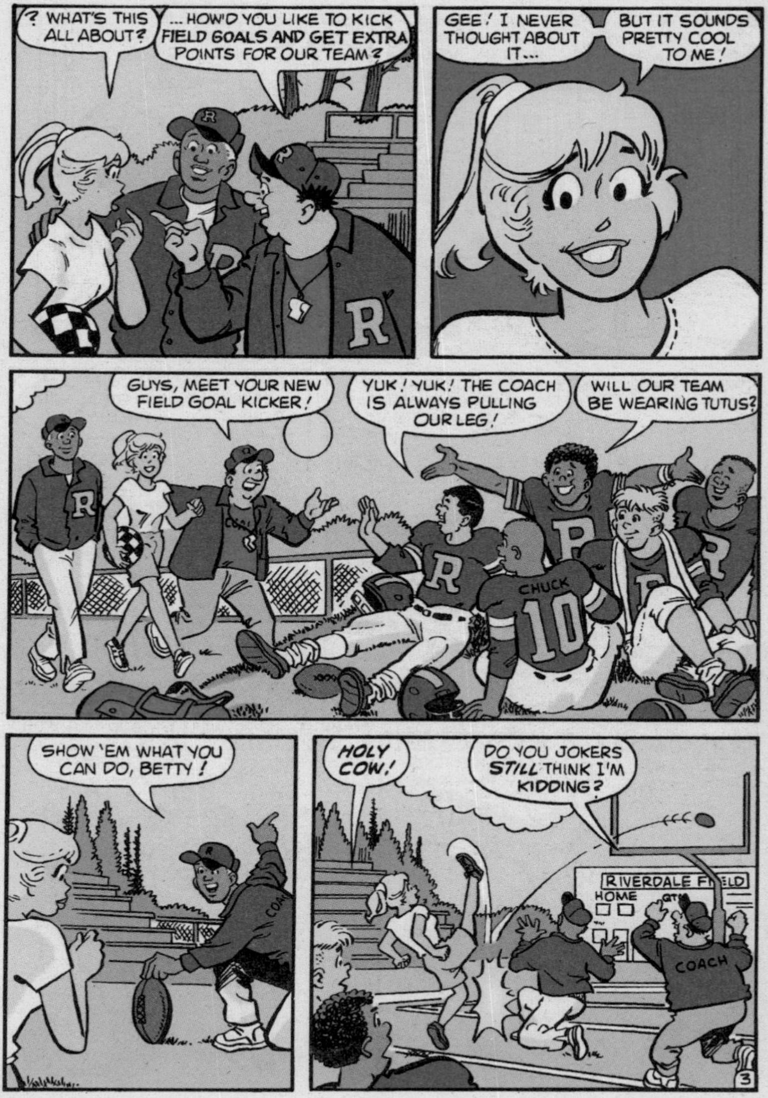
? WHAT'S THIS ALL ABOUT?
... HOW'D YOU LIKE TO KICK FIELD GOALS AND GET EXTRA POINTS FOR OUR TEAM?
GEE! I NEVER THOUGHT ABOUT IT...
BUT IT SOUNDS PRETTY COOL TO ME!
GUYS, MEET YOUR NEW FIELD GOAL KICKER!
YUK! YUK! THE COACH IS ALWAYS PULLING OUR LEG!
WILL OUR TEAM BE WEARING TUTUS?
CHUCK
10
SHOW 'EM WHAT YOU CAN DO, BETTY!
HOLY COW!
DO YOU JOKERS STILL THINK I'M KIDDING?
RIVERDALE FIELD
HOME
COACH
3

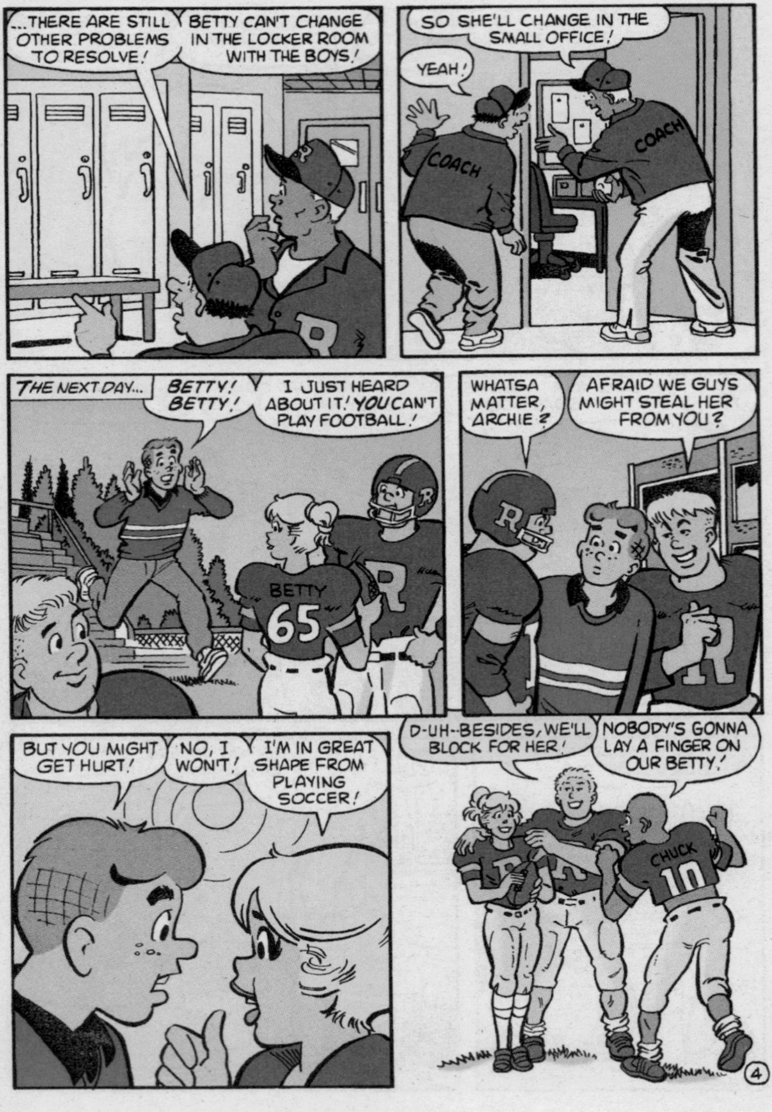
...THERE ARE STILL OTHER PROBLEMS TO RESOLVE!
BETTY CAN'T CHANGE IN THE LOCKER ROOM WITH THE BOYS!
SO SHE'LL CHANGE IN THE SMALL OFFICE!
YEAH!
COACH
COACH
THE NEXT DAY...
BETTY! BETTY!
I JUST HEARD ABOUT IT! YOU CAN'T PLAY FOOTBALL!
BETTY
65
WHATSA MATTER, ARCHIE?
AFRAID WE GUYS MIGHT STEAL HER FROM YOU?
BUT YOU MIGHT GET HURT!
NO, I WON'T!
I'M IN GREAT SHAPE FROM PLAYING SOCCER!
D-UH--BESIDES, WE'LL BLOCK FOR HER!
NOBODY'S GONNA LAY A FINGER ON OUR BETTY!
CHUCK
10
4

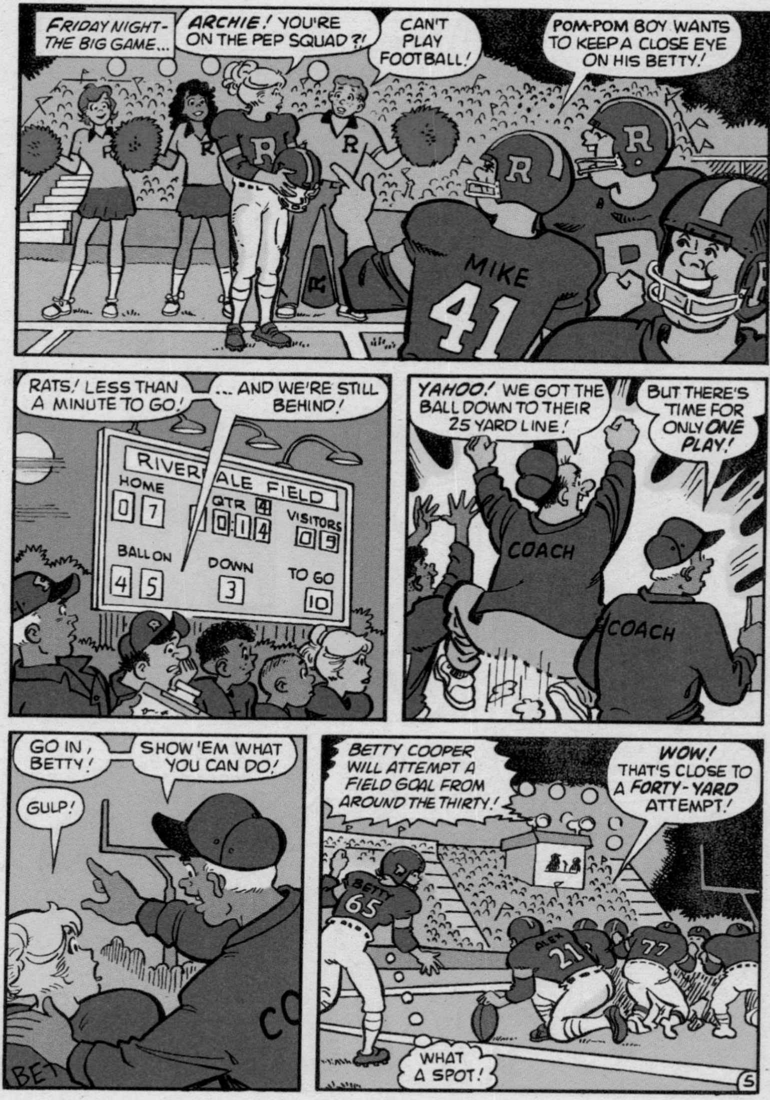
FRIDAY NIGHT- THE BIG GAME...
ARCHIE! YOU'RE ON THE PEP SQUAD?!
CAN'T PLAY FOOTBALL!
POM-POM BOY WANTS TO KEEP A CLOSE EYE ON HIS BETTY!
MIKE 41
RATS! LESS THAN A MINUTE TO GO!
... AND WE'RE STILL BEHIND!
RIVERDALE FIELD
HOME 07
QTR 4
0:14
VISITORS 09
BALL ON 45
DOWN 3
TO GO 10
YAHOO! WE GOT THE BALL DOWN TO THEIR 25 YARD LINE!
BUT THERE'S TIME FOR ONLY ONE PLAY!
COACH
COACH
GO IN, BETTY!
SHOW 'EM WHAT YOU CAN DO!
GULP!
BETTY COOPER WILL ATTEMPT A FIELD GOAL FROM AROUND THE THIRTY!
WOW! THAT'S CLOSE TO A FORTY-YARD ATTEMPT!
BETTY 65
ALEX 21
77
WHAT A SPOT!

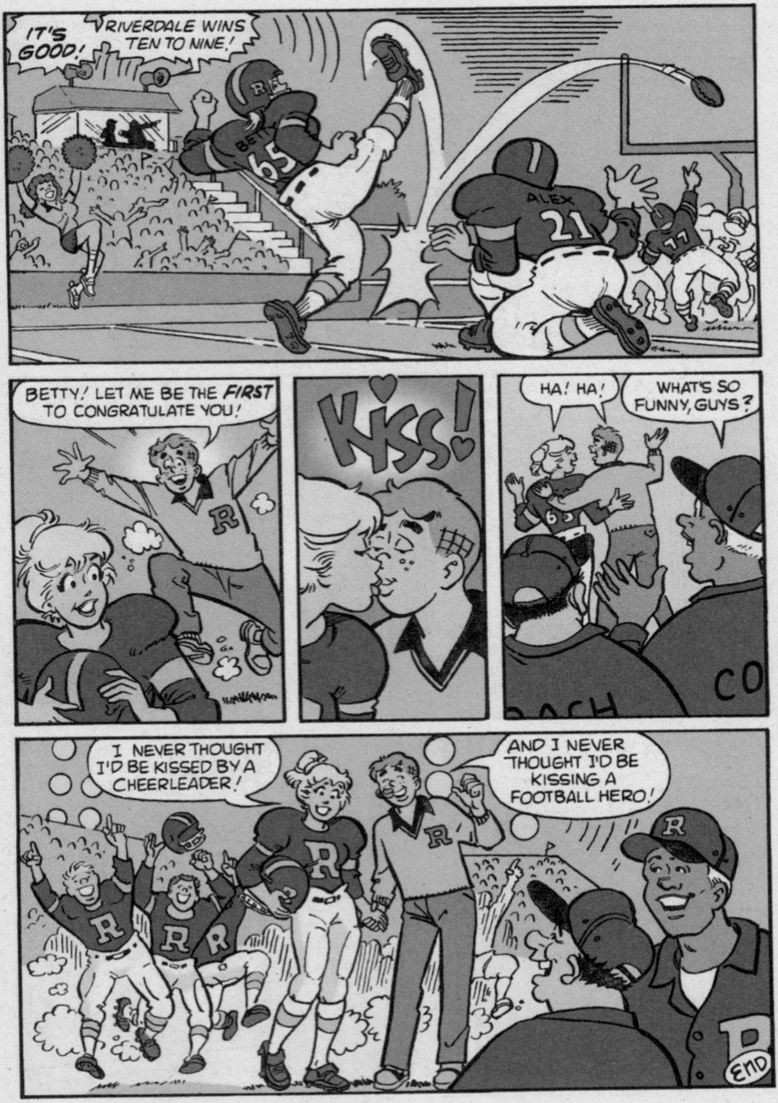
IT'S GOOD!
RIVERDALE WINS TEN TO NINE!
BETTY
65
ALEX
21
77
BETTY! LET ME BE THE FIRST TO CONGRATULATE YOU!
KISS!
HA! HA!
WHAT'S SO FUNNY, GUYS?
I NEVER THOUGHT I'D BE KISSED BY A CHEERLEADER!
AND I NEVER THOUGHT I'D BE KISSING A FOOTBALL HERO!
END

Betty and Veronica in "IT'S IN THE BAG"

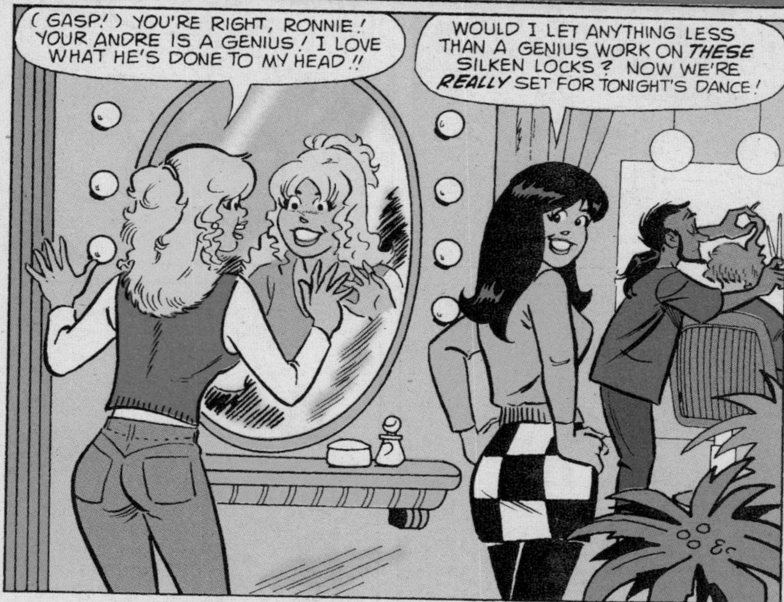

(GASP!) YOU'RE RIGHT, RONNIE! YOUR ANDRE IS A GENIUS! I LOVE WHAT HE'S DONE TO MY HEAD!!
WOULD I LET ANYTHING LESS THAN A GENIUS WORK ON *THESE* SILKEN LOCKS? NOW WE'RE *REALLY* SET FOR TONIGHT'S DANCE!

Script: Frank Doyle / Pencils: Dan DeCarlo / Inks: Mike Esposito / Letters: Bill Yoshida

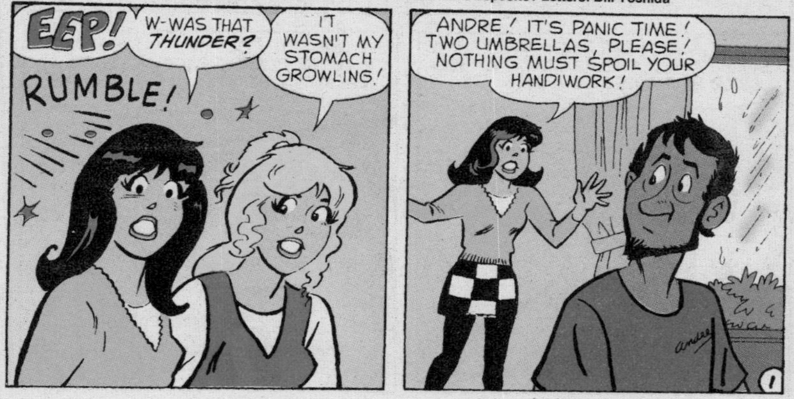

EEP!
W-WAS THAT *THUNDER?*
RUMBLE!
IT WASN'T MY STOMACH GROWLING!
ANDRE! IT'S PANIC TIME! TWO UMBRELLAS, PLEASE! NOTHING MUST SPOIL YOUR HANDIWORK!

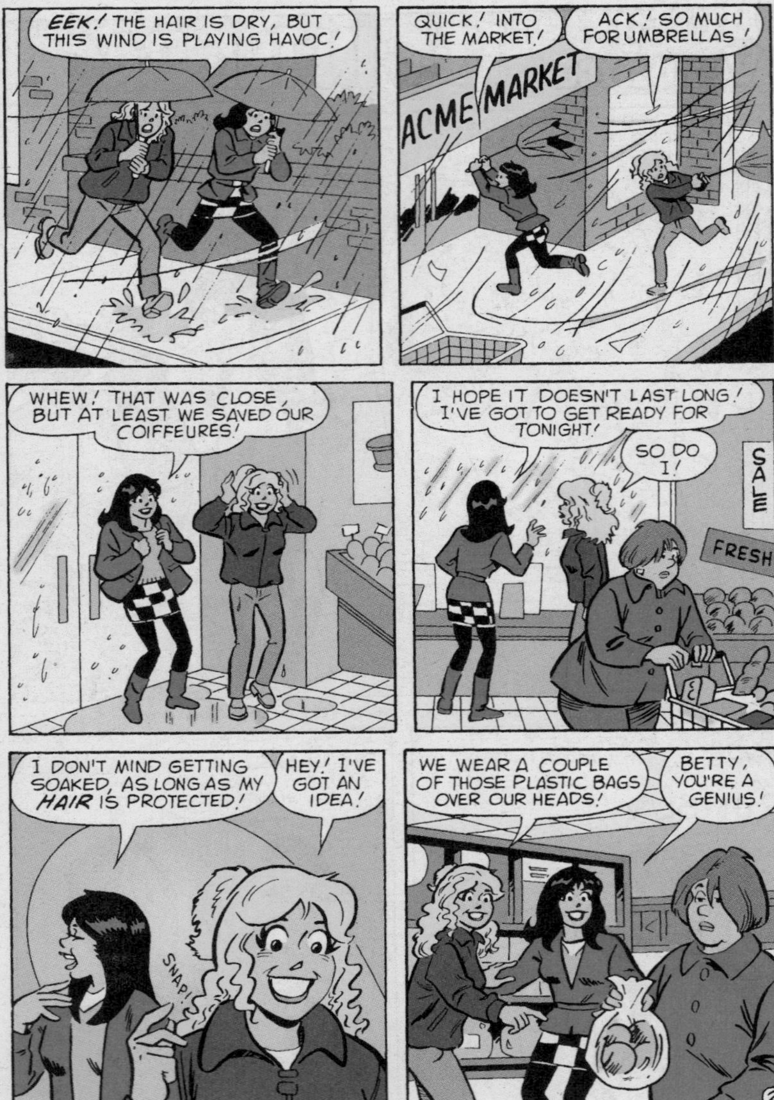
EEK! THE HAIR IS DRY, BUT THIS WIND IS PLAYING HAVOC!
QUICK! INTO THE MARKET!
ACK! SO MUCH FOR UMBRELLAS!
ACME MARKET
WHEW! THAT WAS CLOSE, BUT AT LEAST WE SAVED OUR COIFFEURES!
I HOPE IT DOESN'T LAST LONG! I'VE GOT TO GET READY FOR TONIGHT!
SO DO I!
SALE
FRESH
I DON'T MIND GETTING SOAKED, AS LONG AS MY HAIR IS PROTECTED!
HEY! I'VE GOT AN IDEA!
SNAP!
WE WEAR A COUPLE OF THOSE PLASTIC BAGS OVER OUR HEADS!
BETTY, YOU'RE A GENIUS!
2

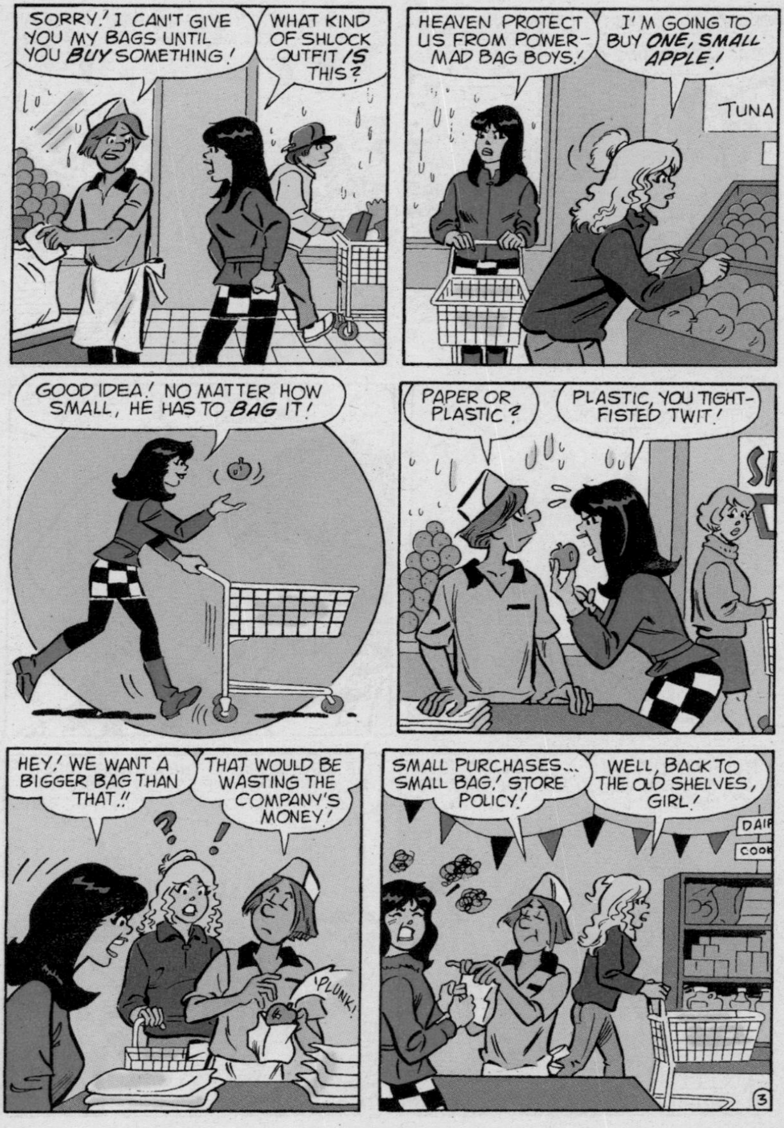
SORRY! I CAN'T GIVE YOU MY BAGS UNTIL YOU BUY SOMETHING!
WHAT KIND OF SHLOCK OUTFIT IS THIS?
HEAVEN PROTECT US FROM POWER-MAD BAG BOYS!
I'M GOING TO BUY ONE, SMALL APPLE!
TUNA
GOOD IDEA! NO MATTER HOW SMALL, HE HAS TO BAG IT!
PAPER OR PLASTIC?
PLASTIC, YOU TIGHT-FISTED TWIT!
HEY! WE WANT A BIGGER BAG THAN THAT!!
THAT WOULD BE WASTING THE COMPANY'S MONEY!
PLUNK!
SMALL PURCHASES... SMALL BAG! STORE POLICY!
WELL, BACK TO THE OLD SHELVES, GIRL!
3

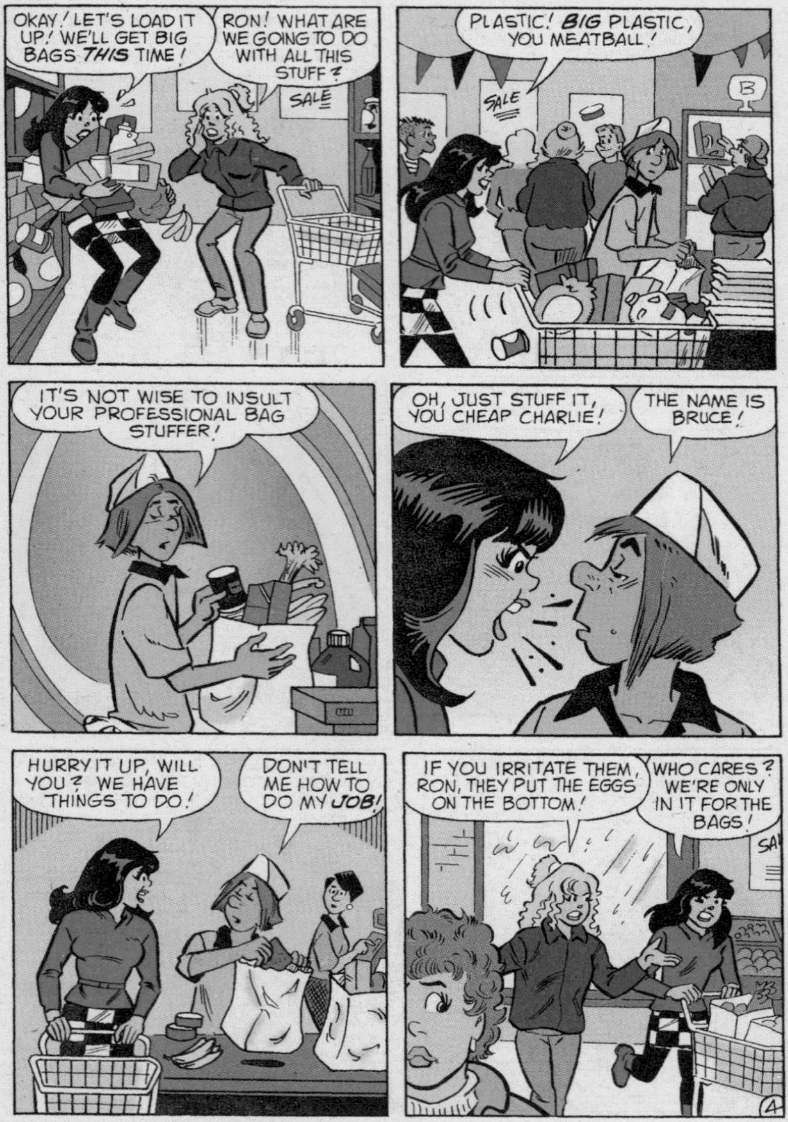
OKAY! LET'S LOAD IT UP! WE'LL GET BIG BAGS THIS TIME!
RON! WHAT ARE WE GOING TO DO WITH ALL THIS STUFF?
SALE
PLASTIC! BIG PLASTIC, YOU MEATBALL!
SALE
B
IT'S NOT WISE TO INSULT YOUR PROFESSIONAL BAG STUFFER!
OH, JUST STUFF IT, YOU CHEAP CHARLIE!
THE NAME IS BRUCE!
HURRY IT UP, WILL YOU? WE HAVE THINGS TO DO!
DON'T TELL ME HOW TO DO MY JOB!
IF YOU IRRITATE THEM, RON, THEY PUT THE EGGS ON THE BOTTOM!
WHO CARES? WE'RE ONLY IN IT FOR THE BAGS!
4

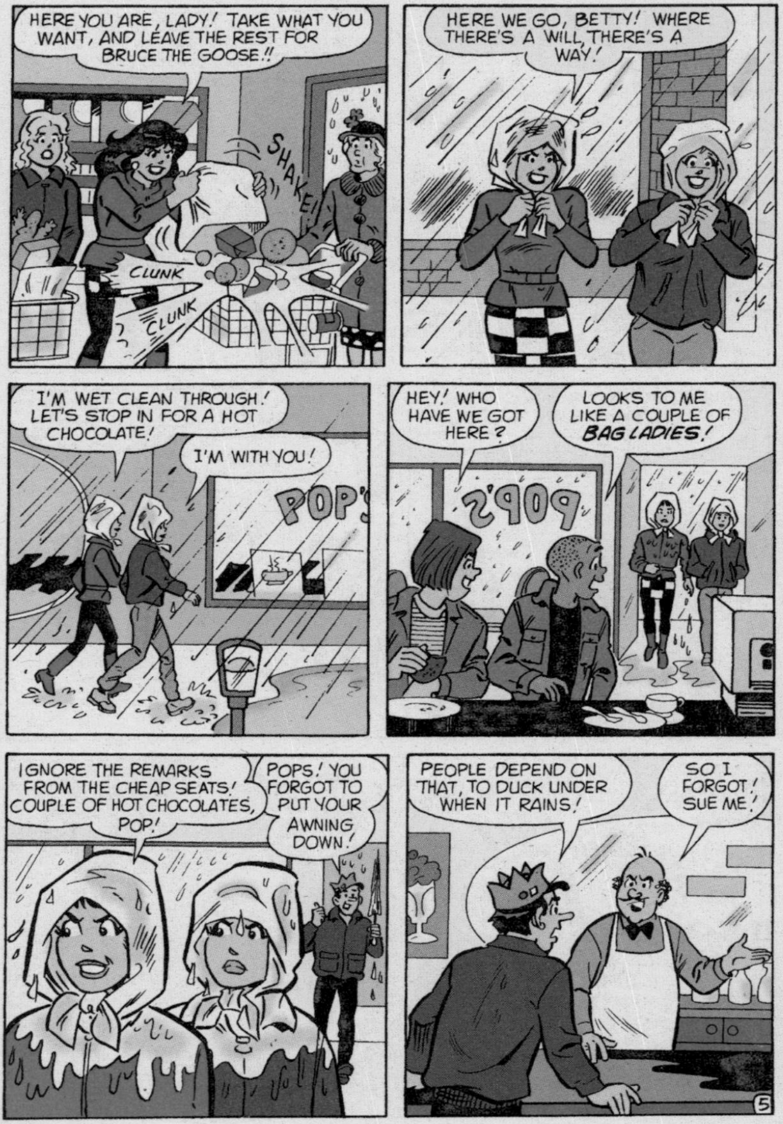
HERE YOU ARE, LADY! TAKE WHAT YOU WANT, AND LEAVE THE REST FOR BRUCE THE GOOSE!!
SHAKE!
CLUNK
CLUNK
HERE WE GO, BETTY! WHERE THERE'S A WILL, THERE'S A WAY!
I'M WET CLEAN THROUGH! LET'S STOP IN FOR A HOT CHOCOLATE!
I'M WITH YOU!
POP'S
HEY! WHO HAVE WE GOT HERE?
LOOKS TO ME LIKE A COUPLE OF BAG LADIES!
IGNORE THE REMARKS FROM THE CHEAP SEATS! COUPLE OF HOT CHOCOLATES, POP!
POPS! YOU FORGOT TO PUT YOUR AWNING DOWN!
PEOPLE DEPEND ON THAT, TO DUCK UNDER WHEN IT RAINS!
SO I FORGOT! SUE ME!
5

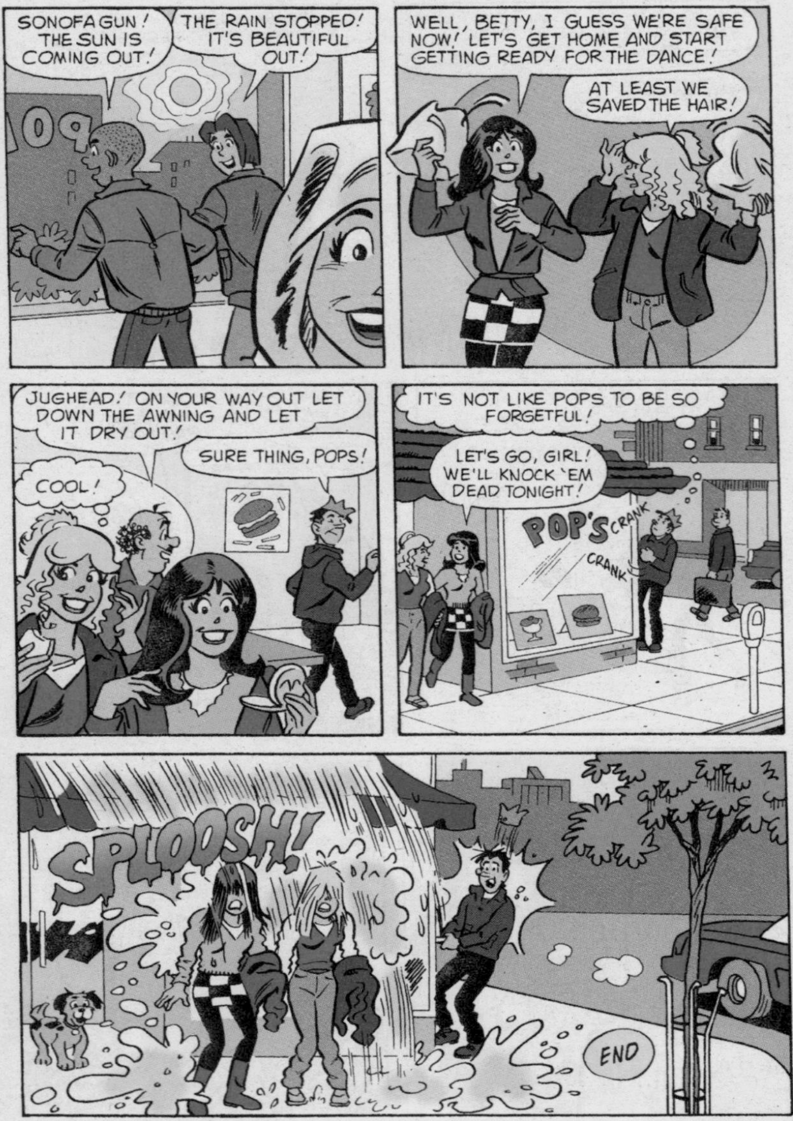
SONOFAGUN! THE SUN IS COMING OUT!
THE RAIN STOPPED! IT'S BEAUTIFUL OUT!
WELL, BETTY, I GUESS WE'RE SAFE NOW! LET'S GET HOME AND START GETTING READY FOR THE DANCE!
AT LEAST WE SAVED THE HAIR!
JUGHEAD! ON YOUR WAY OUT LET DOWN THE AWNING AND LET IT DRY OUT!
COOL!
SURE THING, POPS!
IT'S NOT LIKE POPS TO BE SO FORGETFUL!
LET'S GO, GIRL! WE'LL KNOCK 'EM DEAD TONIGHT!
POP'S
CRANK
CRANK
SPLOOSH!
END

Archie in "No Help Wanted"

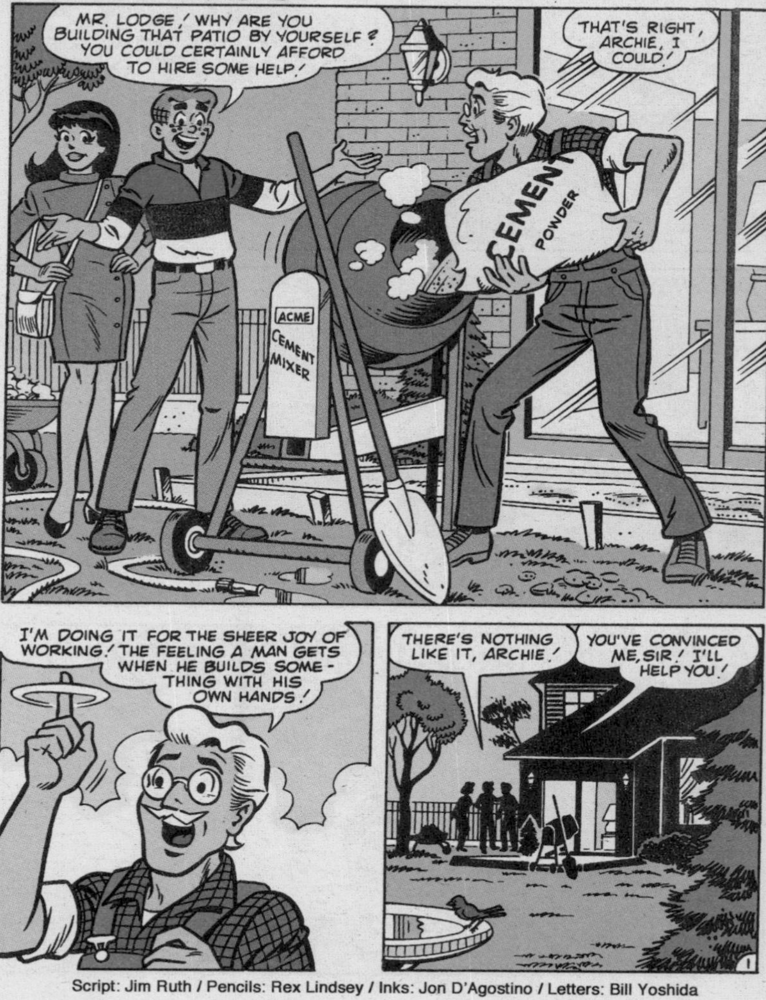

MR. LODGE! WHY ARE YOU BUILDING THAT PATIO BY YOURSELF? YOU COULD CERTAINLY AFFORD TO HIRE SOME HELP!
THAT'S RIGHT, ARCHIE, I COULD!
CEMENT POWDER
ACME CEMENT MIXER
I'M DOING IT FOR THE SHEER JOY OF WORKING! THE FEELING A MAN GETS WHEN HE BUILDS SOME-THING WITH HIS OWN HANDS!
THERE'S NOTHING LIKE IT, ARCHIE!
YOU'VE CONVINCED ME, SIR! I'LL HELP YOU!
1

Script: Jim Ruth / Pencils: Rex Lindsey / Inks: Jon D'Agostino / Letters: Bill Yoshida

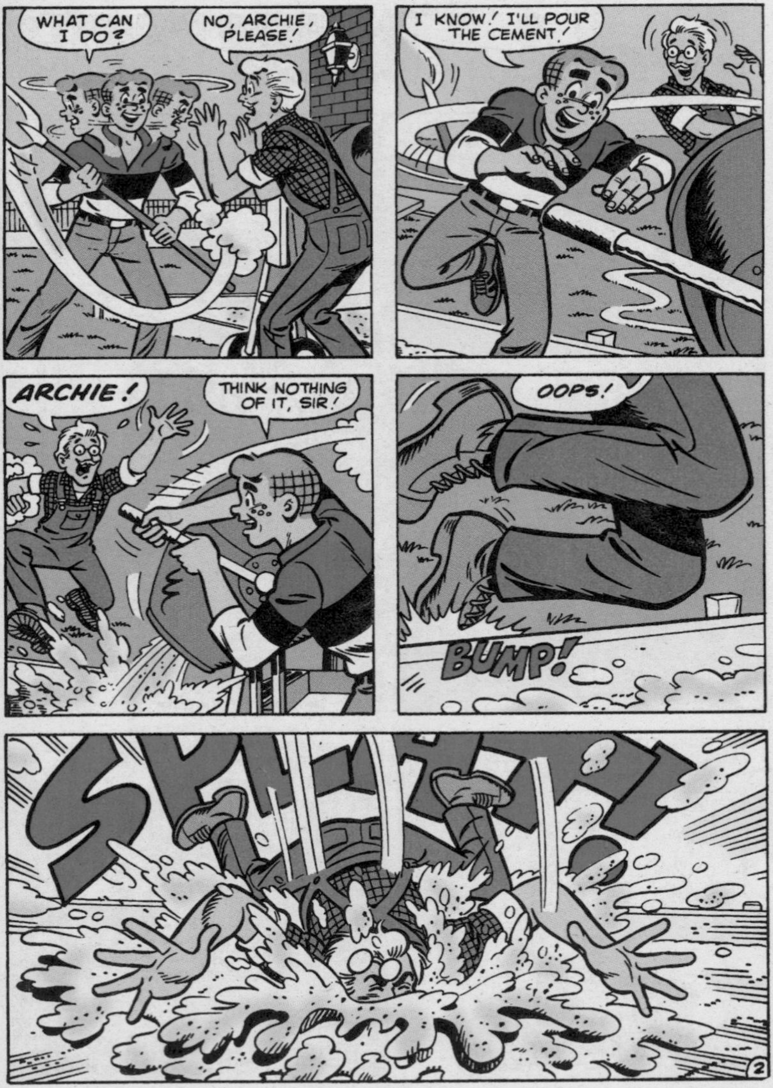
WHAT CAN I DO?
NO, ARCHIE, PLEASE!
I KNOW! I'LL POUR THE CEMENT!
ARCHIE!
THINK NOTHING OF IT, SIR!
OOPS!
BUMP!
2

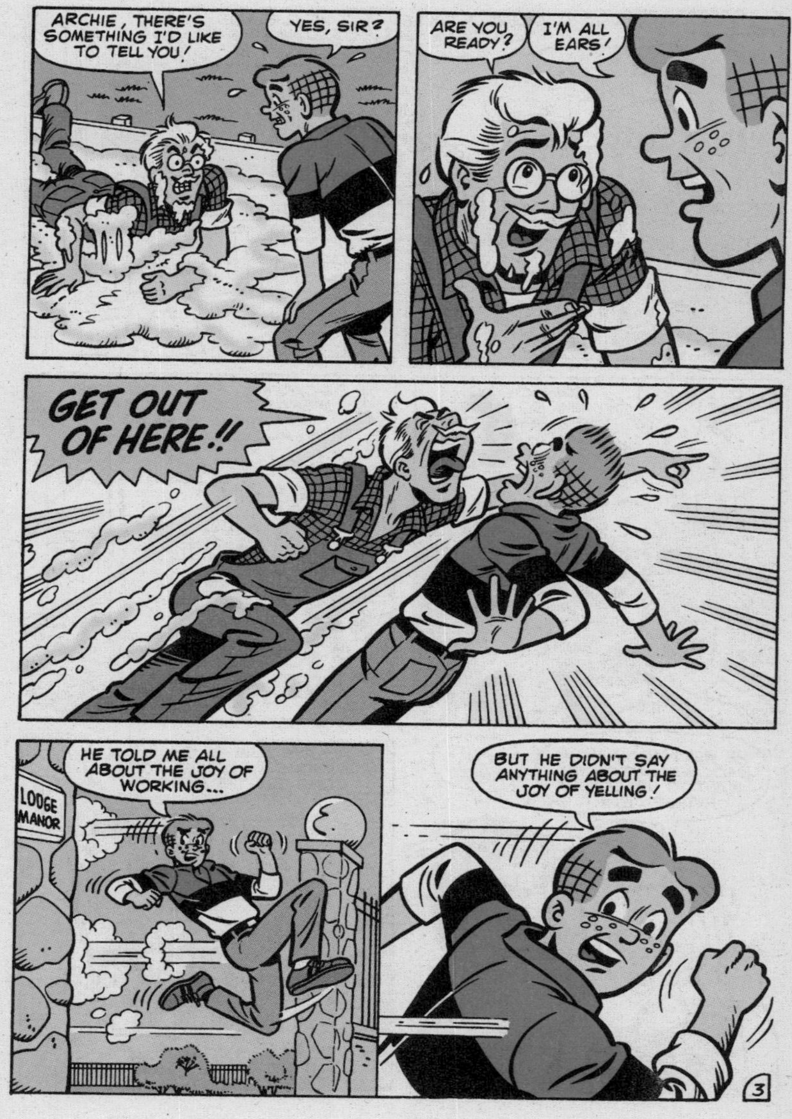
ARCHIE, THERE'S SOMETHING I'D LIKE TO TELL YOU!
YES, SIR?
ARE YOU READY?
I'M ALL EARS!
GET OUT OF HERE!!
HE TOLD ME ALL ABOUT THE JOY OF WORKING...
LODGE MANOR
BUT HE DIDN'T SAY ANYTHING ABOUT THE JOY OF YELLING!
3

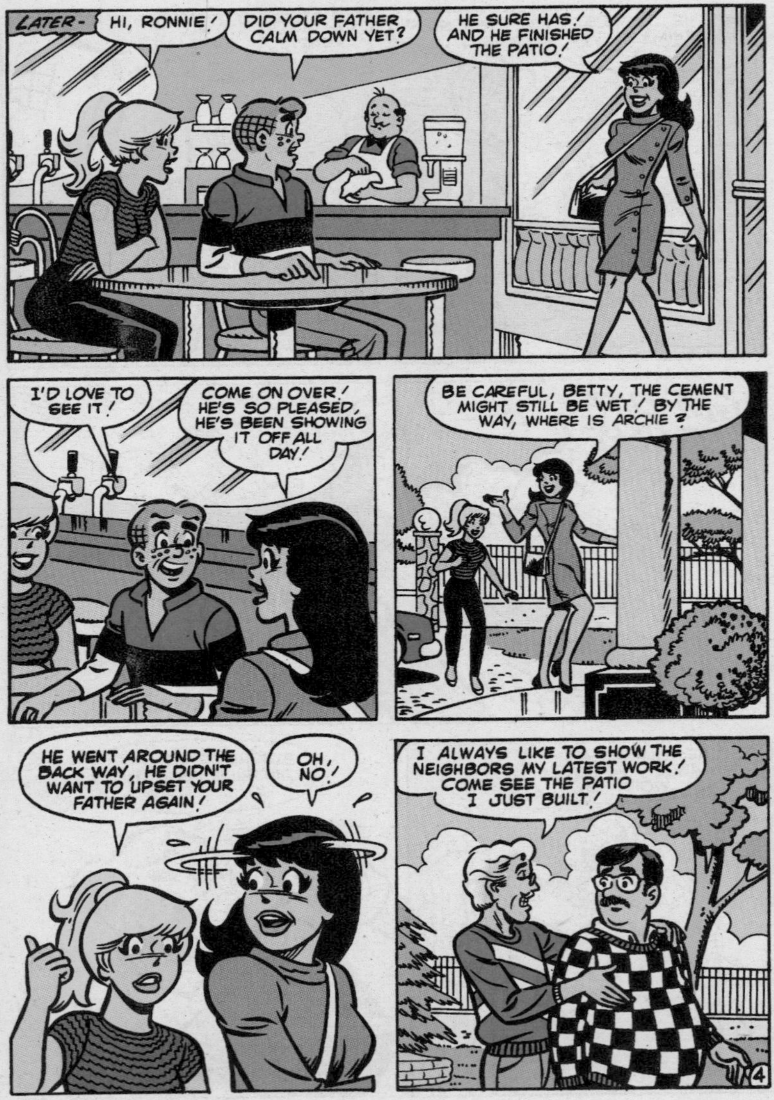
LATER-
HI, RONNIE!
DID YOUR FATHER CALM DOWN YET?
HE SURE HAS! AND HE FINISHED THE PATIO!
I'D LOVE TO SEE IT!
COME ON OVER! HE'S SO PLEASED, HE'S BEEN SHOWING IT OFF ALL DAY!
BE CAREFUL, BETTY, THE CEMENT MIGHT STILL BE WET! BY THE WAY, WHERE IS ARCHIE?
HE WENT AROUND THE BACK WAY, HE DIDN'T WANT TO UPSET YOUR FATHER AGAIN!
OH, NO!
I ALWAYS LIKE TO SHOW THE NEIGHBORS MY LATEST WORK! COME SEE THE PATIO I JUST BUILT!
4

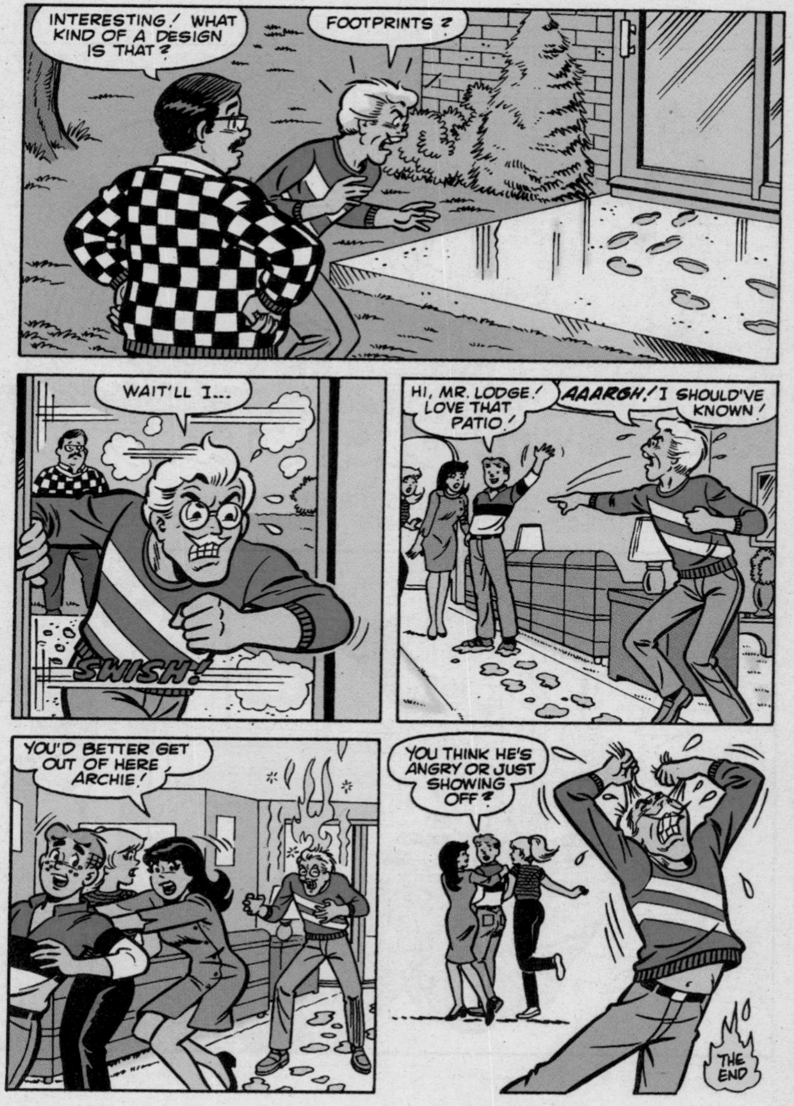
INTERESTING! WHAT KIND OF A DESIGN IS THAT?
FOOTPRINTS?
WAIT'LL I...
SWISH!
HI, MR. LODGE! LOVE THAT PATIO!
AAARGH! I SHOULD'VE KNOWN!
YOU'D BETTER GET OUT OF HERE, ARCHIE!
YOU THINK HE'S ANGRY OR JUST SHOWING OFF?
THE END

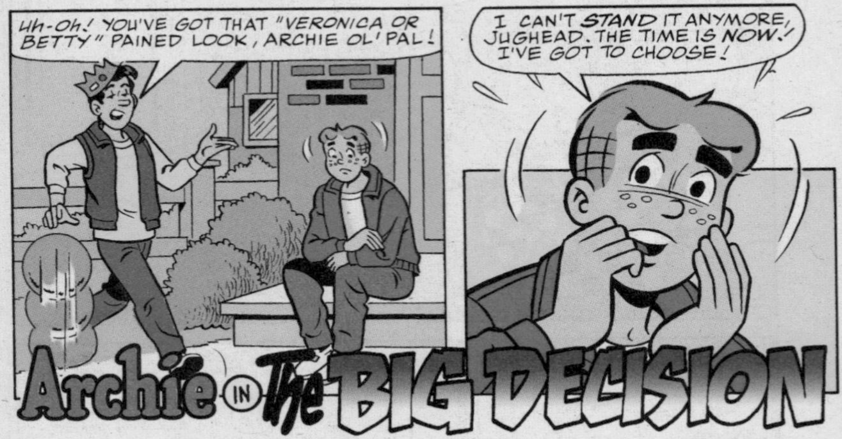
Uh-Oh! YOU'VE GOT THAT "VERONICA OR BETTY" PAINED LOOK, ARCHIE OL' PAL!
I CAN'T STAND IT ANYMORE, JUGHEAD. THE TIME IS NOW! I'VE GOT TO CHOOSE!
Archie IN The BIG DECISION

SCRIPT: BARBARA SLATE PENCILS: TIM KENNEDY INKS: JON D'AGOSTINO
COLORS: BARRY GROSSMAN LETTERS: JACK MORELLI

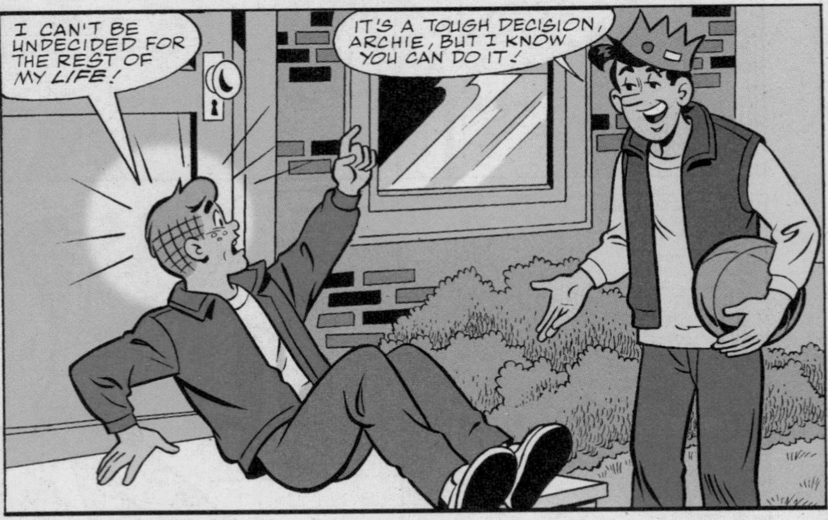
I CAN'T BE UNDECIDED FOR THE REST OF MY LIFE!
IT'S A TOUGH DECISION, ARCHIE, BUT I KNOW YOU CAN DO IT!

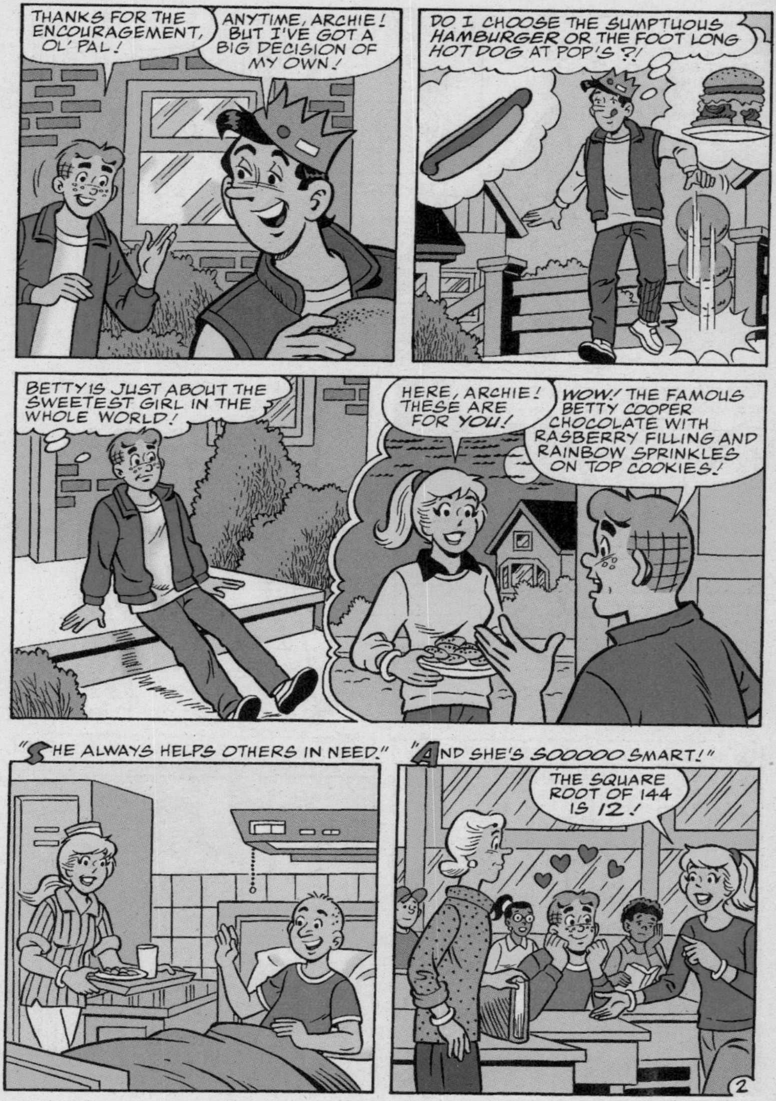
THANKS FOR THE ENCOURAGEMENT, OL' PAL!
ANYTIME, ARCHIE! BUT I'VE GOT A BIG DECISION OF MY OWN!
DO I CHOOSE THE SUMPTUOUS HAMBURGER OR THE FOOT LONG HOT DOG AT POP'S ?!
BETTY IS JUST ABOUT THE SWEETEST GIRL IN THE WHOLE WORLD!
HERE, ARCHIE! THESE ARE FOR YOU!
WOW! THE FAMOUS BETTY COOPER CHOCOLATE WITH RASBERRY FILLING AND RAINBOW SPRINKLES ON TOP COOKIES!
"SHE ALWAYS HELPS OTHERS IN NEED."
"AND SHE'S SOOOOOO SMART!"
THE SQUARE ROOT OF 144 IS 12!

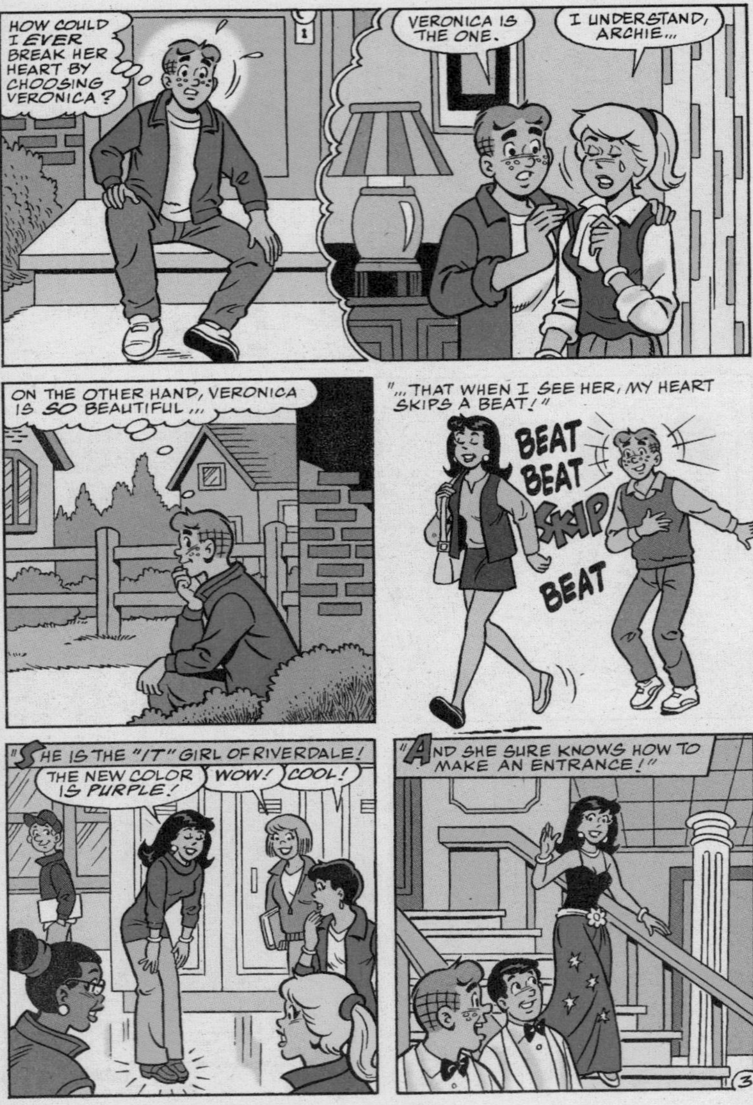
HOW COULD I EVER BREAK HER HEART BY CHOOSING VERONICA?
VERONICA IS THE ONE.
I UNDERSTAND, ARCHIE...
ON THE OTHER HAND, VERONICA IS SO BEAUTIFUL...
"...THAT WHEN I SEE HER, MY HEART SKIPS A BEAT!"
BEAT
BEAT
SKIP
BEAT
"SHE IS THE "IT" GIRL OF RIVERDALE!
THE NEW COLOR IS PURPLE!
WOW!
COOL!
"AND SHE SURE KNOWS HOW TO MAKE AN ENTRANCE!"
3

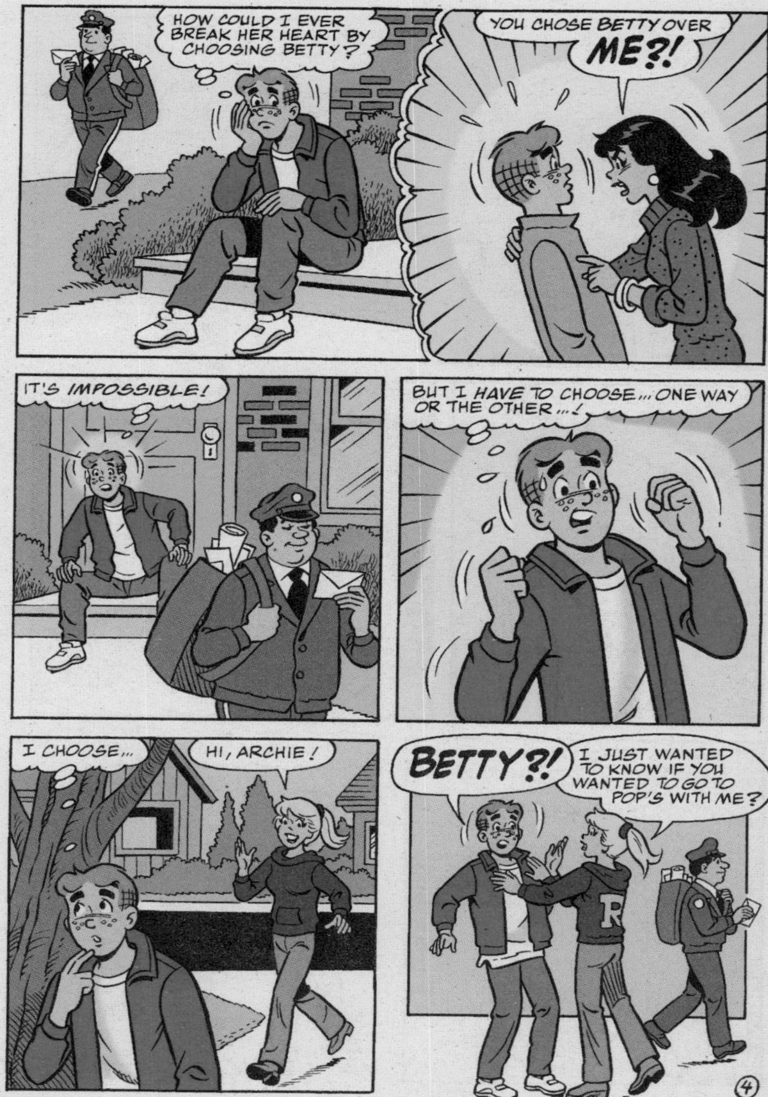
HOW COULD I EVER BREAK HER HEART BY CHOOSING BETTY?
YOU CHOSE BETTY OVER ME?!
IT'S IMPOSSIBLE!
BUT I HAVE TO CHOOSE... ONE WAY OR THE OTHER...!
I CHOOSE...
HI, ARCHIE!
BETTY?!
I JUST WANTED TO KNOW IF YOU WANTED TO GO TO POP'S WITH ME?

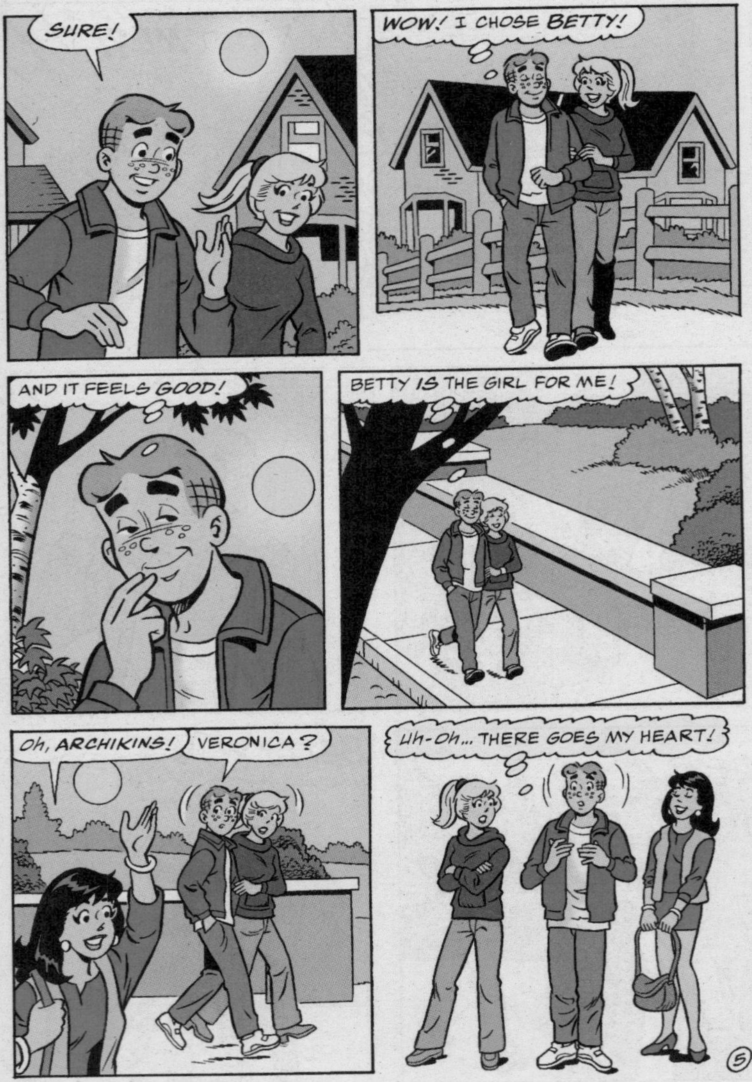
SURE!
WOW! I CHOSE BETTY!
AND IT FEELS GOOD!
BETTY IS THE GIRL FOR ME!
Oh, ARCHIKINS!
VERONICA?
Uh-Oh... THERE GOES MY HEART!
5

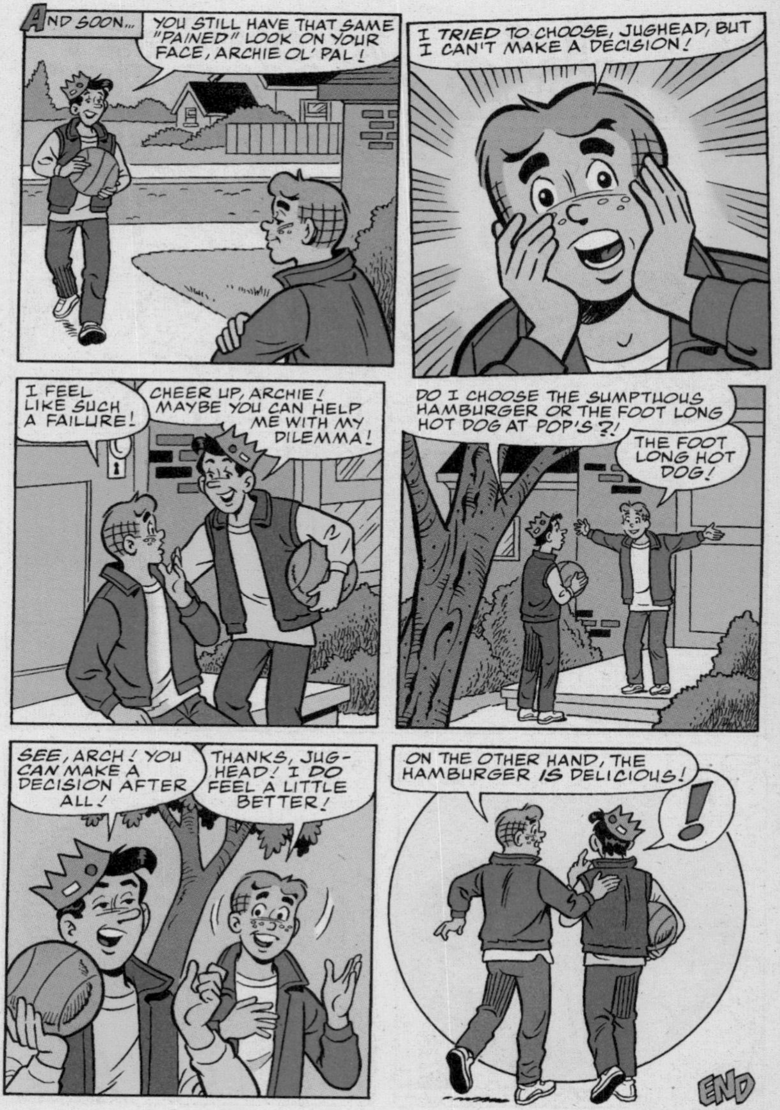
AND SOON...
YOU STILL HAVE THAT SAME "PAINED" LOOK ON YOUR FACE, ARCHIE OL' PAL!
I TRIED TO CHOOSE, JUGHEAD, BUT I CAN'T MAKE A DECISION!
I FEEL LIKE SUCH A FAILURE!
CHEER UP, ARCHIE! MAYBE YOU CAN HELP ME WITH MY DILEMMA!
DO I CHOOSE THE SUMPTUOUS HAMBURGER OR THE FOOT LONG HOT DOG AT POP'S ?!
THE FOOT LONG HOT DOG!
SEE, ARCH! YOU CAN MAKE A DECISION AFTER ALL!
THANKS, JUG-HEAD! I DO FEEL A LITTLE BETTER!
ON THE OTHER HAND, THE HAMBURGER IS DELICIOUS!
!
END

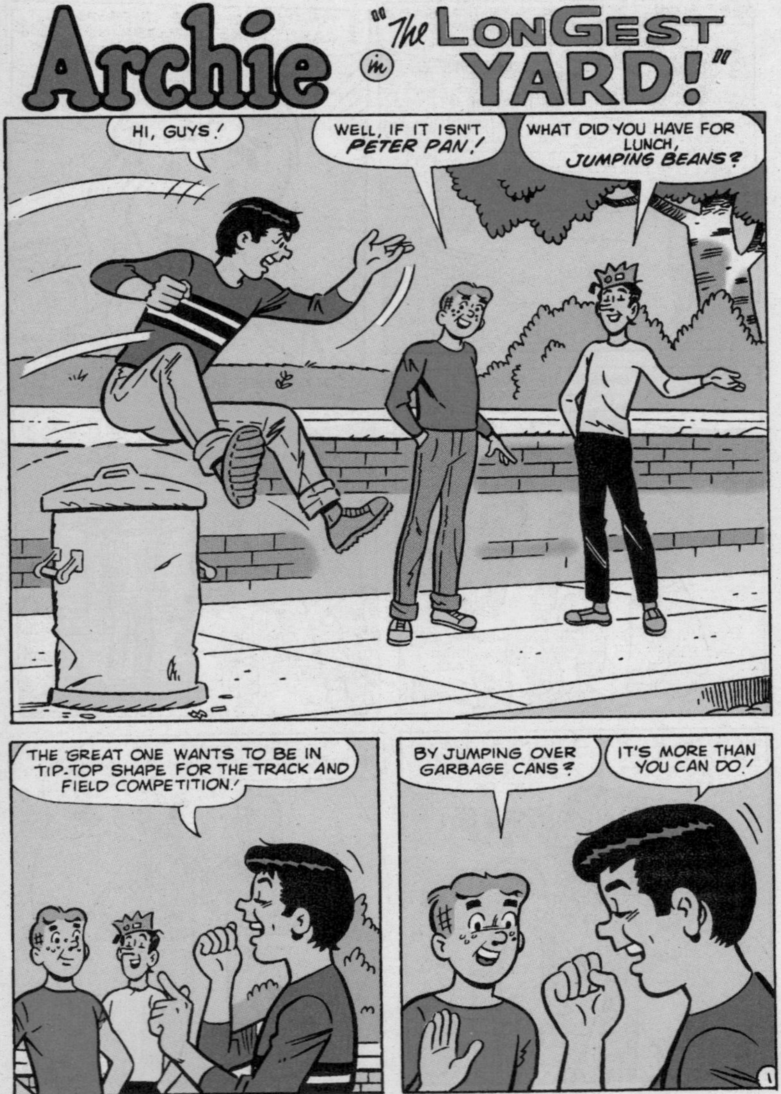
Archie in "The Longest Yard!"
HI, GUYS!
WELL, IF IT ISN'T PETER PAN!
WHAT DID YOU HAVE FOR LUNCH, JUMPING BEANS?
THE GREAT ONE WANTS TO BE IN TIP-TOP SHAPE FOR THE TRACK AND FIELD COMPETITION!
BY JUMPING OVER GARBAGE CANS?
IT'S MORE THAN YOU CAN DO!
1

Script: Dick Malmgren / Pencils: Chic Stone / Inks: Rudy Lapick / Letters: Bill Yoshida

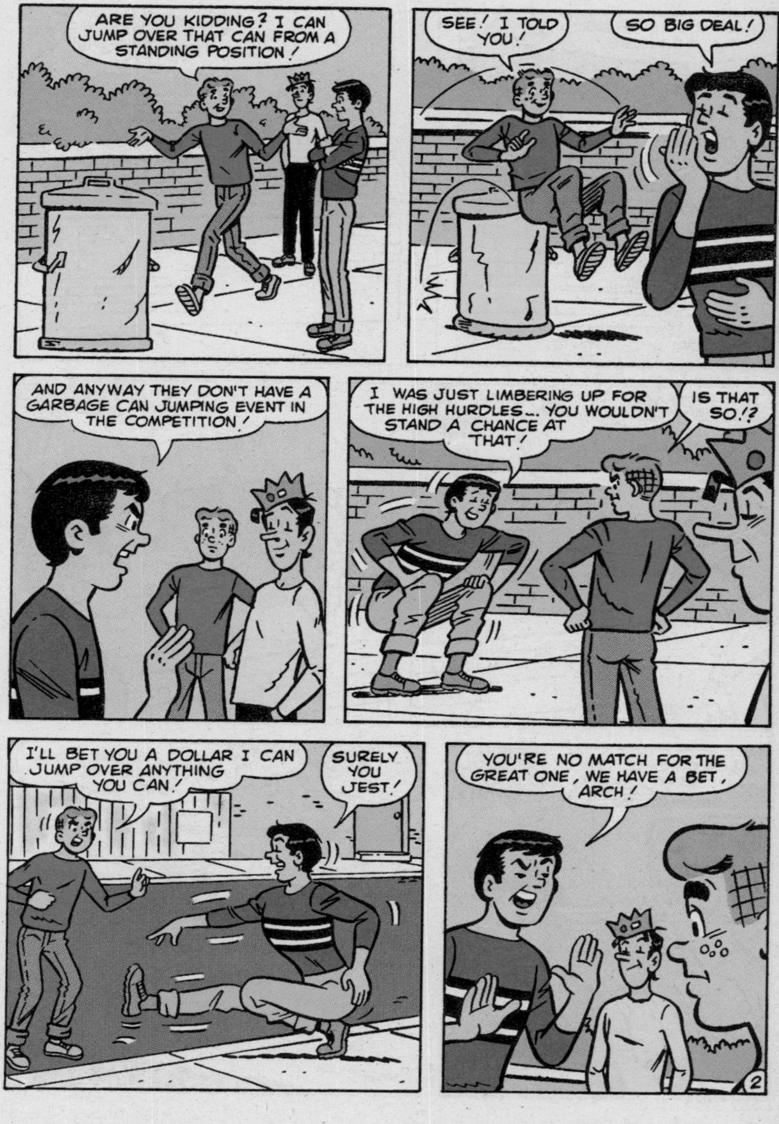
ARE YOU KIDDING? I CAN JUMP OVER THAT CAN FROM A STANDING POSITION!
SEE! I TOLD YOU!
SO BIG DEAL!
AND ANYWAY THEY DON'T HAVE A GARBAGE CAN JUMPING EVENT IN THE COMPETITION!
I WAS JUST LIMBERING UP FOR THE HIGH HURDLES... YOU WOULDN'T STAND A CHANCE AT THAT!
IS THAT SO!?
I'LL BET YOU A DOLLAR I CAN JUMP OVER ANYTHING YOU CAN!
SURELY YOU JEST!
YOU'RE NO MATCH FOR THE GREAT ONE, WE HAVE A BET, ARCH!
2

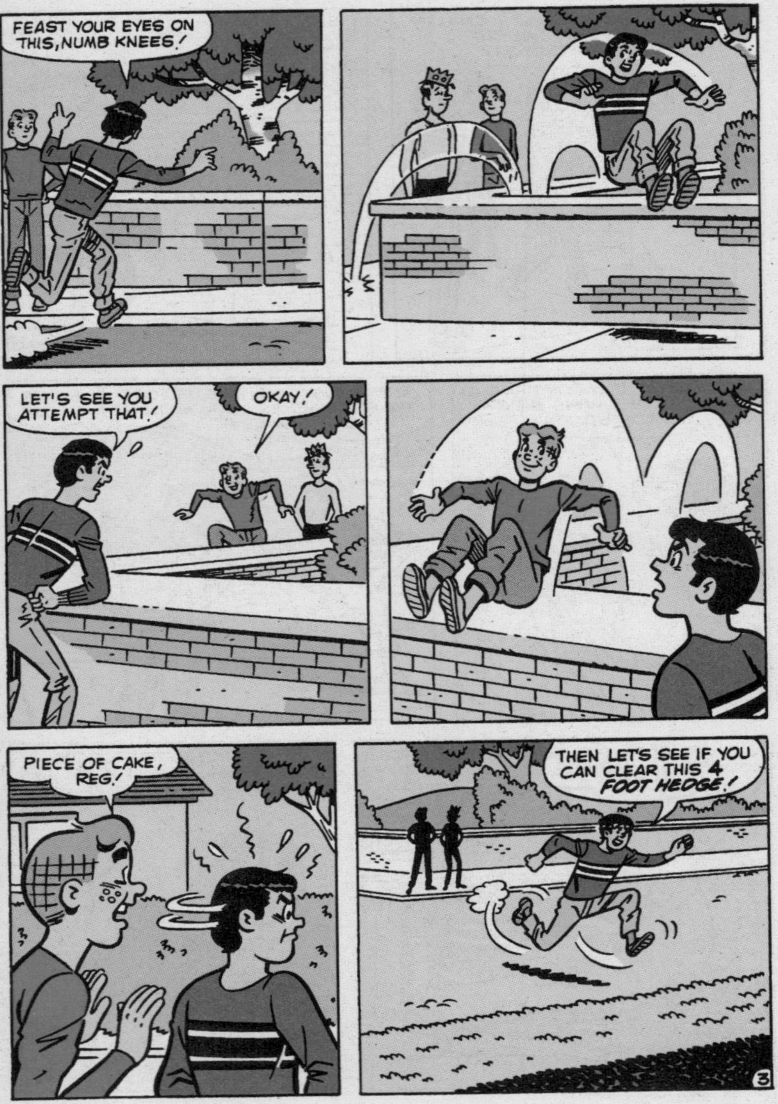
FEAST YOUR EYES ON THIS, NUMB KNEES!
LET'S SEE YOU ATTEMPT THAT!
OKAY!
PIECE OF CAKE, REG!
THEN LET'S SEE IF YOU CAN CLEAR THIS 4 FOOT HEDGE!
3

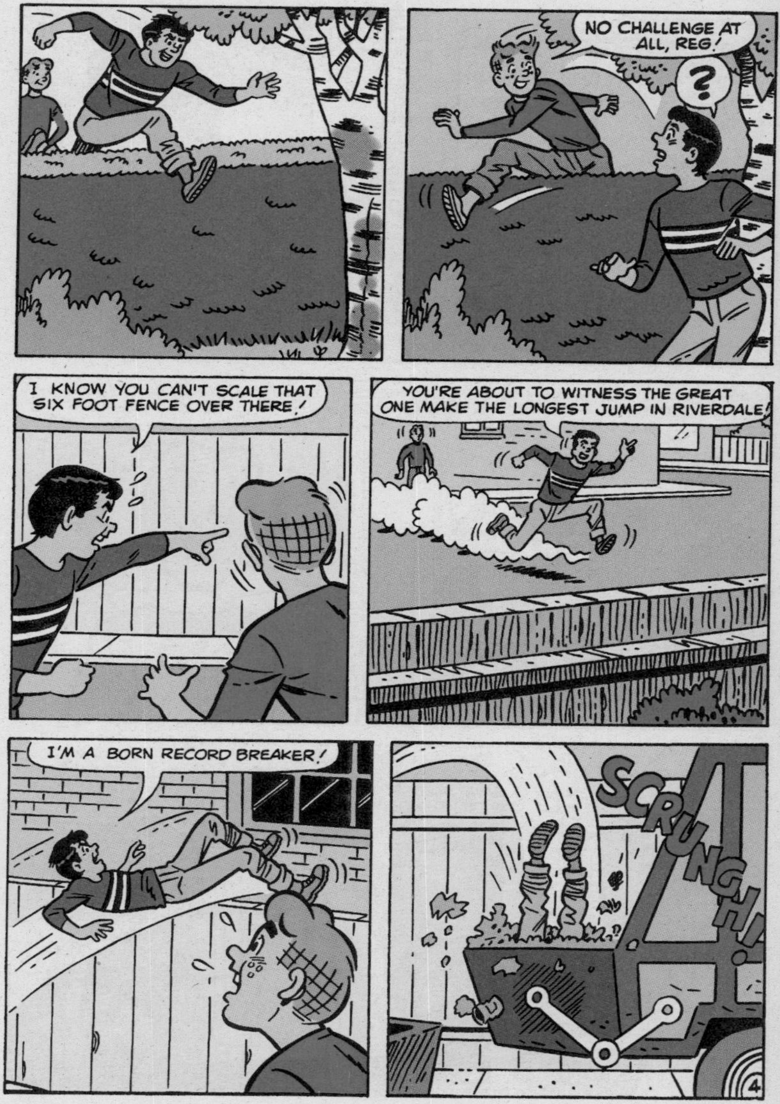
NO CHALLENGE AT ALL, REG!
?
I KNOW YOU CAN'T SCALE THAT SIX FOOT FENCE OVER THERE!
YOU'RE ABOUT TO WITNESS THE GREAT ONE MAKE THE LONGEST JUMP IN RIVERDALE!
I'M A BORN RECORD BREAKER!
SCRUNGH!
4

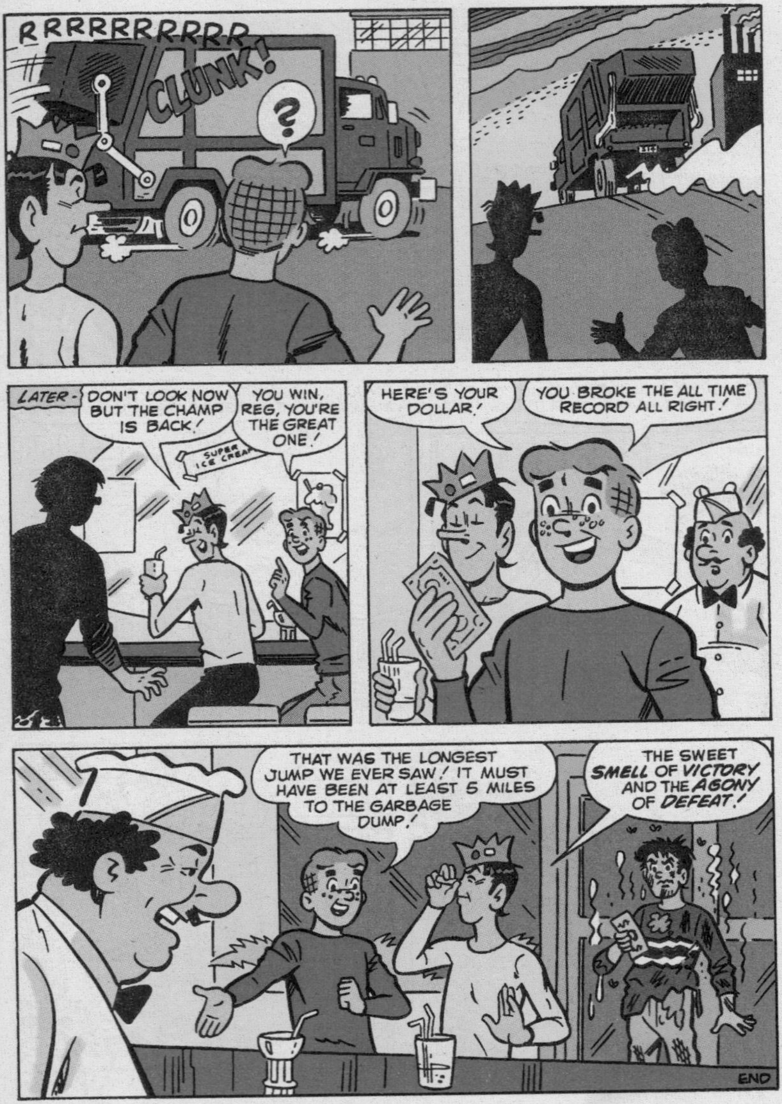
RRRRRRRRRR
CLUNK!
?
LATER-
DON'T LOOK NOW BUT THE CHAMP IS BACK!
YOU WIN, REG, YOU'RE THE GREAT ONE!
SUPER ICE CREAM
HERE'S YOUR DOLLAR!
YOU BROKE THE ALL TIME RECORD ALL RIGHT!
THAT WAS THE LONGEST JUMP WE EVER SAW! IT MUST HAVE BEEN AT LEAST 5 MILES TO THE GARBAGE DUMP!
THE SWEET SMELL OF VICTORY AND THE AGONY OF DEFEAT!
END

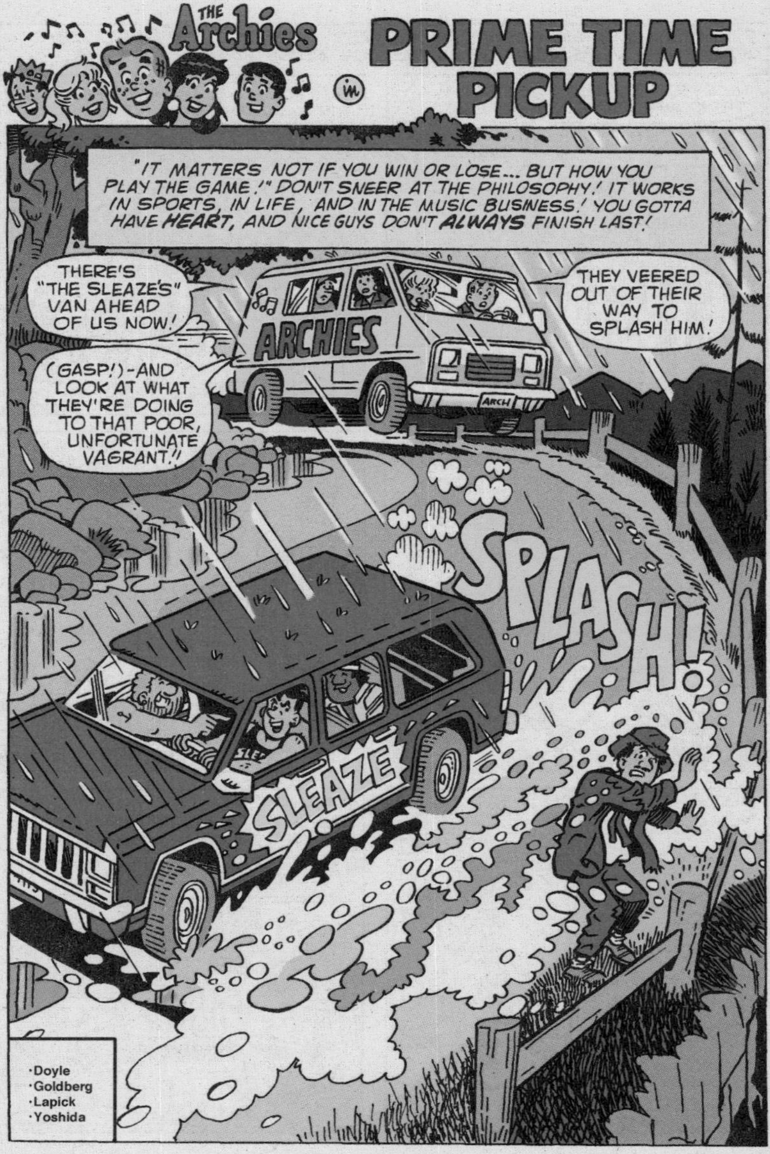

THE Archies
in
PRIME TIME PICKUP
"IT MATTERS NOT IF YOU WIN OR LOSE... BUT HOW YOU PLAY THE GAME!" DON'T SNEER AT THE PHILOSOPHY! IT WORKS IN SPORTS, IN LIFE, AND IN THE MUSIC BUSINESS! YOU GOTTA HAVE HEART, AND NICE GUYS DON'T ALWAYS FINISH LAST!
THERE'S "THE SLEAZE'S" VAN AHEAD OF US NOW!
(GASP!)-AND LOOK AT WHAT THEY'RE DOING TO THAT POOR, UNFORTUNATE VAGRANT!!
THEY VEERED OUT OF THEIR WAY TO SPLASH HIM!
ARCHIES
SPLASH!
SLEAZE
·Doyle
·Goldberg
·Lapick
·Yoshida

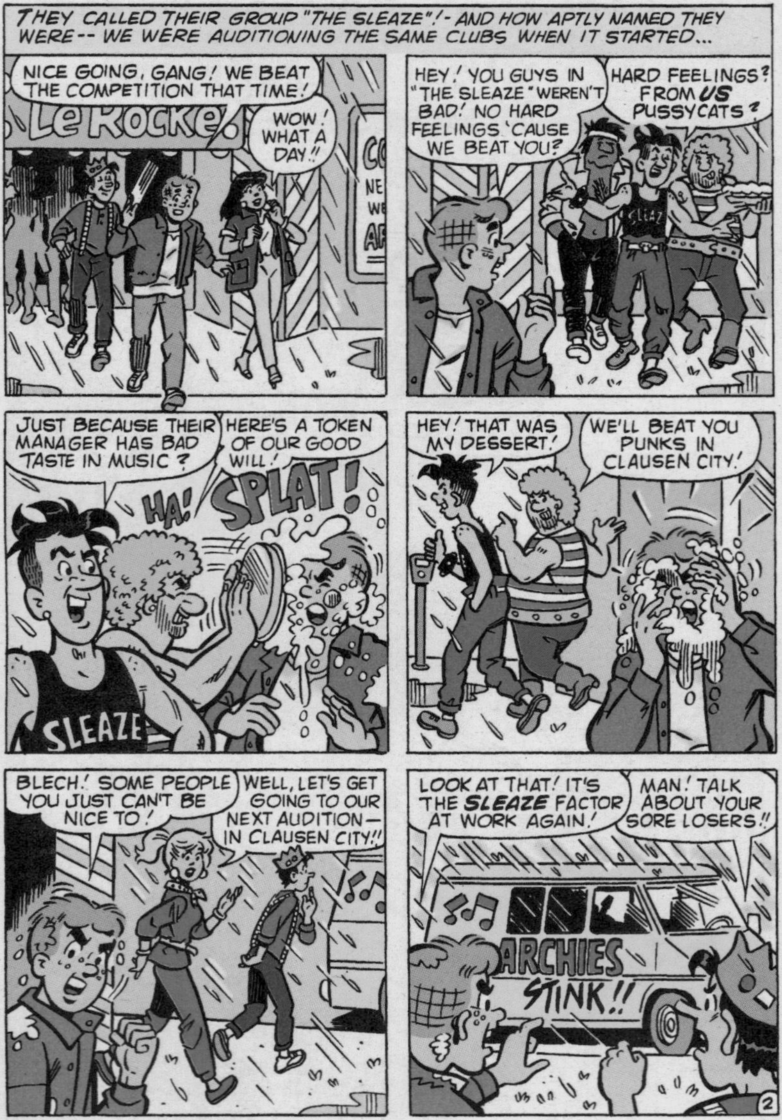

THEY CALLED THEIR GROUP "THE SLEAZE"!- AND HOW APTLY NAMED THEY WERE-- WE WERE AUDITIONING THE SAME CLUBS WHEN IT STARTED...
NICE GOING, GANG! WE BEAT THE COMPETITION THAT TIME!
LE ROCKE
WOW! WHAT A DAY!!
HEY! YOU GUYS IN "THE SLEAZE" WEREN'T BAD! NO HARD FEELINGS 'CAUSE WE BEAT YOU?
HARD FEELINGS? FROM US PUSSYCATS?
SLEAZ
JUST BECAUSE THEIR MANAGER HAS BAD TASTE IN MUSIC?
HERE'S A TOKEN OF OUR GOOD WILL!
HA!
SPLAT!
SLEAZE
HEY! THAT WAS MY DESSERT!
WE'LL BEAT YOU PUNKS IN CLAUSEN CITY!
BLECH! SOME PEOPLE YOU JUST CAN'T BE NICE TO!
WELL, LET'S GET GOING TO OUR NEXT AUDITION— IN CLAUSEN CITY!!
LOOK AT THAT! IT'S THE SLEAZE FACTOR AT WORK AGAIN!
MAN! TALK ABOUT YOUR SORE LOSERS!!
ARCHIES STINK!!
2

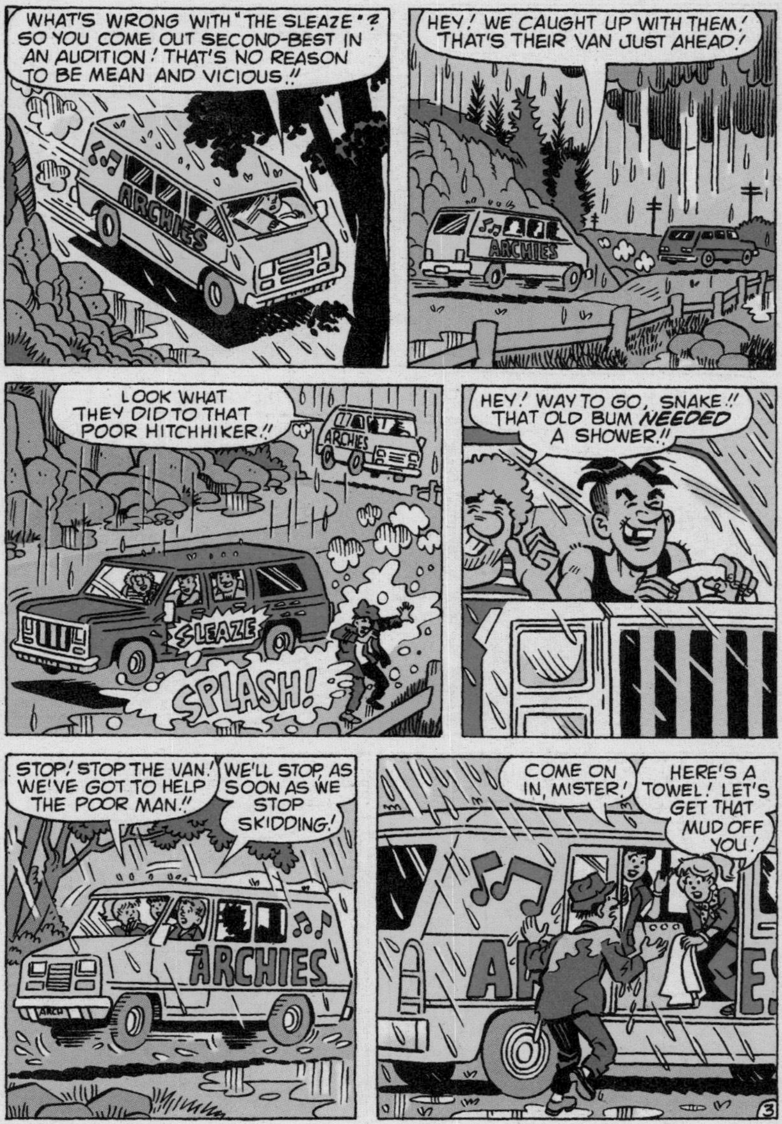
WHAT'S WRONG WITH "THE SLEAZE"? SO YOU COME OUT SECOND-BEST IN AN AUDITION! THAT'S NO REASON TO BE MEAN AND VICIOUS!!
ARCHIES
HEY! WE CAUGHT UP WITH THEM! THAT'S THEIR VAN JUST AHEAD!
ARCHIES
LOOK WHAT THEY DID TO THAT POOR HITCHHIKER!!
ARCHIES
SLEAZE
SPLASH!
HEY! WAY TO GO, SNAKE!! THAT OLD BUM NEEDED A SHOWER!!
STOP! STOP THE VAN! WE'VE GOT TO HELP THE POOR MAN!!
WE'LL STOP AS SOON AS WE STOP SKIDDING!
ARCHIES
COME ON IN, MISTER!
HERE'S A TOWEL! LET'S GET THAT MUD OFF YOU!
3

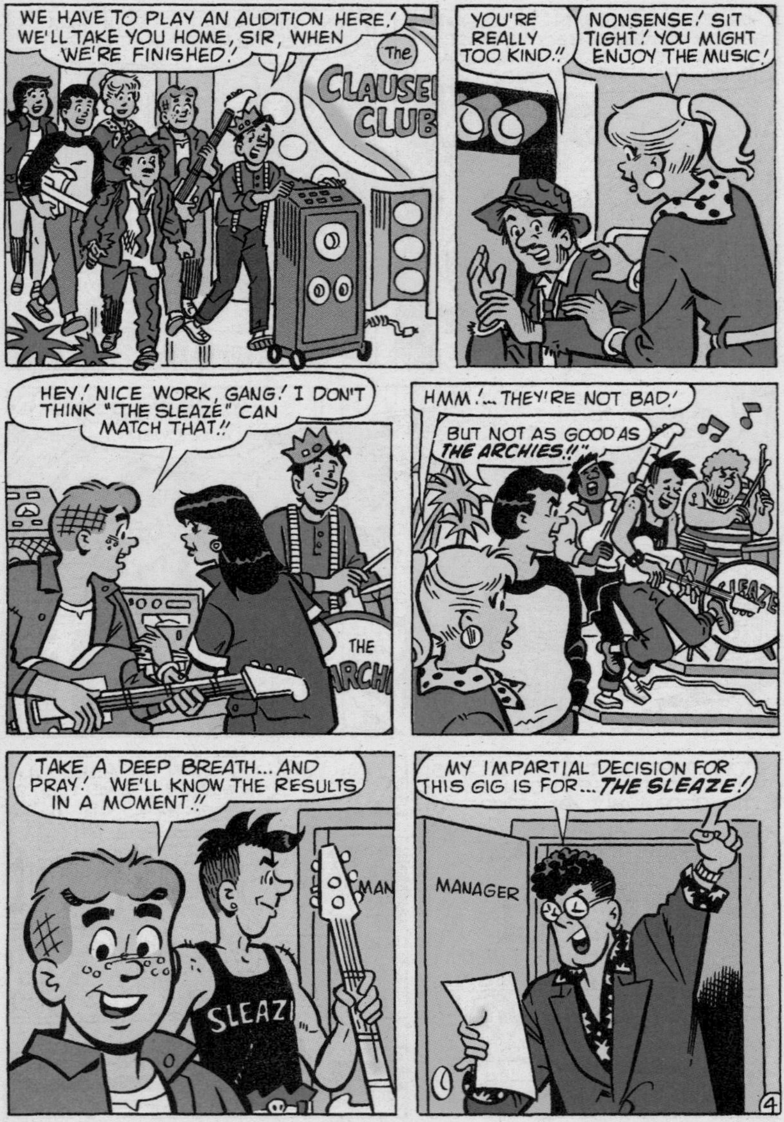
WE HAVE TO PLAY AN AUDITION HERE! WE'LL TAKE YOU HOME, SIR, WHEN WE'RE FINISHED!
The CLAUSEI CLUB
YOU'RE REALLY TOO KIND!!
NONSENSE! SIT TIGHT! YOU MIGHT ENJOY THE MUSIC!
HEY! NICE WORK, GANG! I DON'T THINK "THE SLEAZE" CAN MATCH THAT!!
THE ARCHI
HMM!... THEY'RE NOT BAD!
BUT NOT AS GOOD AS THE ARCHIES!!"
SLEAZE
TAKE A DEEP BREATH... AND PRAY! WE'LL KNOW THE RESULTS IN A MOMENT!!
MAN
SLEAZI
MY IMPARTIAL DECISION FOR THIS GIG IS FOR... THE SLEAZE!
MANAGER
4

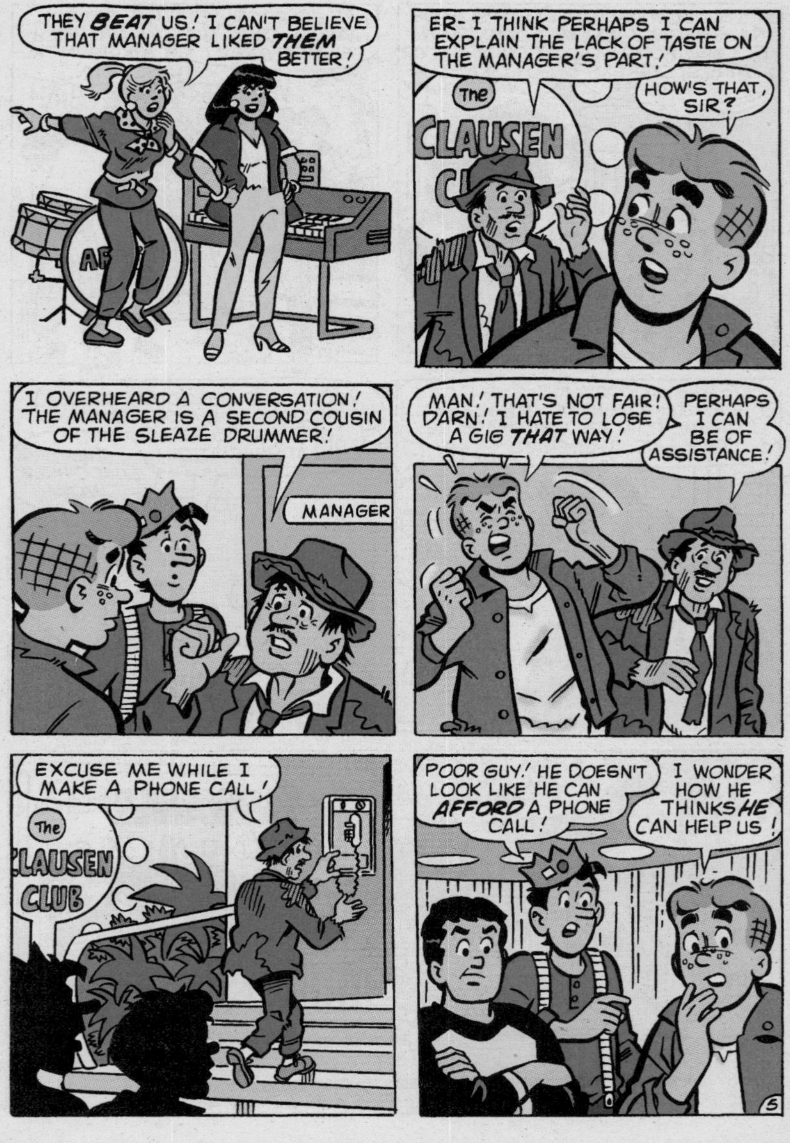
THEY BEAT US! I CAN'T BELIEVE THAT MANAGER LIKED THEM BETTER!
ER- I THINK PERHAPS I CAN EXPLAIN THE LACK OF TASTE ON THE MANAGER'S PART!
The CLAUSEN CL
HOW'S THAT, SIR?
I OVERHEARD A CONVERSATION! THE MANAGER IS A SECOND COUSIN OF THE SLEAZE DRUMMER!
MANAGER
MAN! THAT'S NOT FAIR! DARN! I HATE TO LOSE A GIG THAT WAY!
PERHAPS I CAN BE OF ASSISTANCE!
EXCUSE ME WHILE I MAKE A PHONE CALL!
The CLAUSEN CLUB
POOR GUY! HE DOESN'T LOOK LIKE HE CAN AFFORD A PHONE CALL!
I WONDER HOW HE THINKS HE CAN HELP US!
5

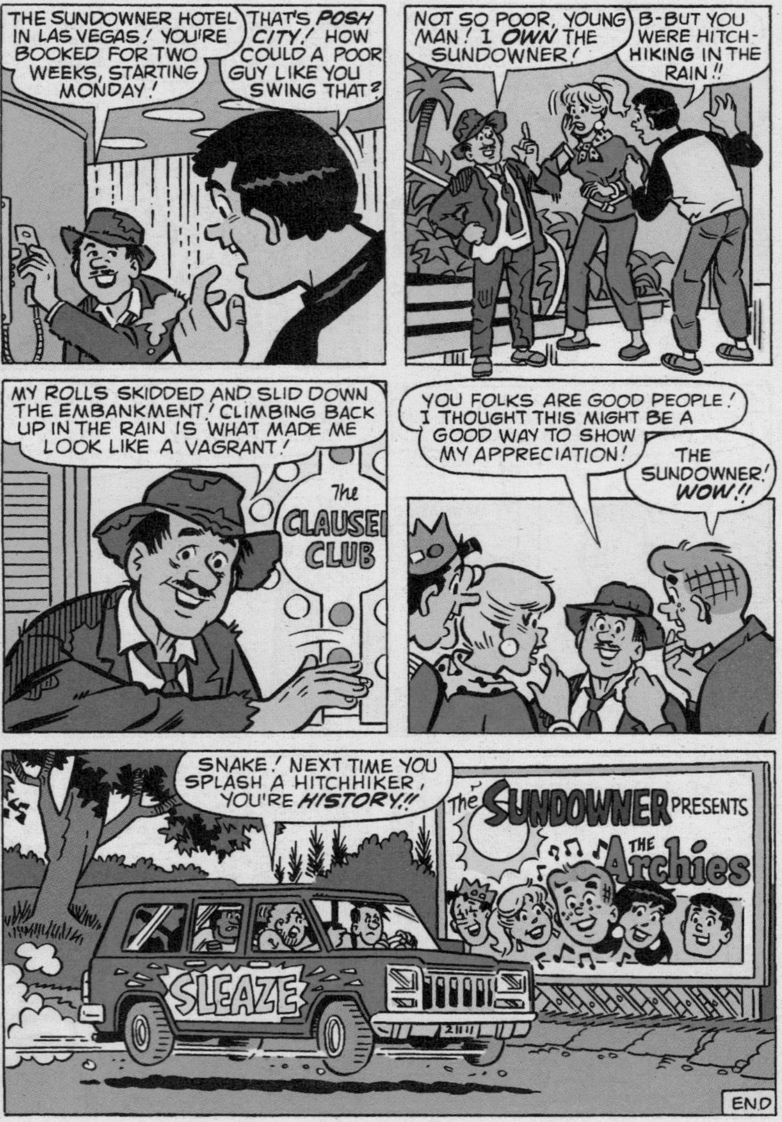
THE SUNDOWNER HOTEL IN LAS VEGAS! YOU'RE BOOKED FOR TWO WEEKS, STARTING MONDAY!
THAT'S POSH CITY! HOW COULD A POOR GUY LIKE YOU SWING THAT?
NOT SO POOR, YOUNG MAN! I OWN THE SUNDOWNER!
B-BUT YOU WERE HITCH-HIKING IN THE RAIN!!
MY ROLLS SKIDDED AND SLID DOWN THE EMBANKMENT! CLIMBING BACK UP IN THE RAIN IS WHAT MADE ME LOOK LIKE A VAGRANT!
The CLAUSE CLUB
YOU FOLKS ARE GOOD PEOPLE! I THOUGHT THIS MIGHT BE A GOOD WAY TO SHOW MY APPRECIATION!
THE SUNDOWNER! WOW!!
SNAKE! NEXT TIME YOU SPLASH A HITCHHIKER, YOU'RE HISTORY!!
The SUNDOWNER PRESENTS THE Archies
SLEAZE
END

Archie in "OUT STANDING"

Malmgren / Lindsey / D'Agostino / Yoshida

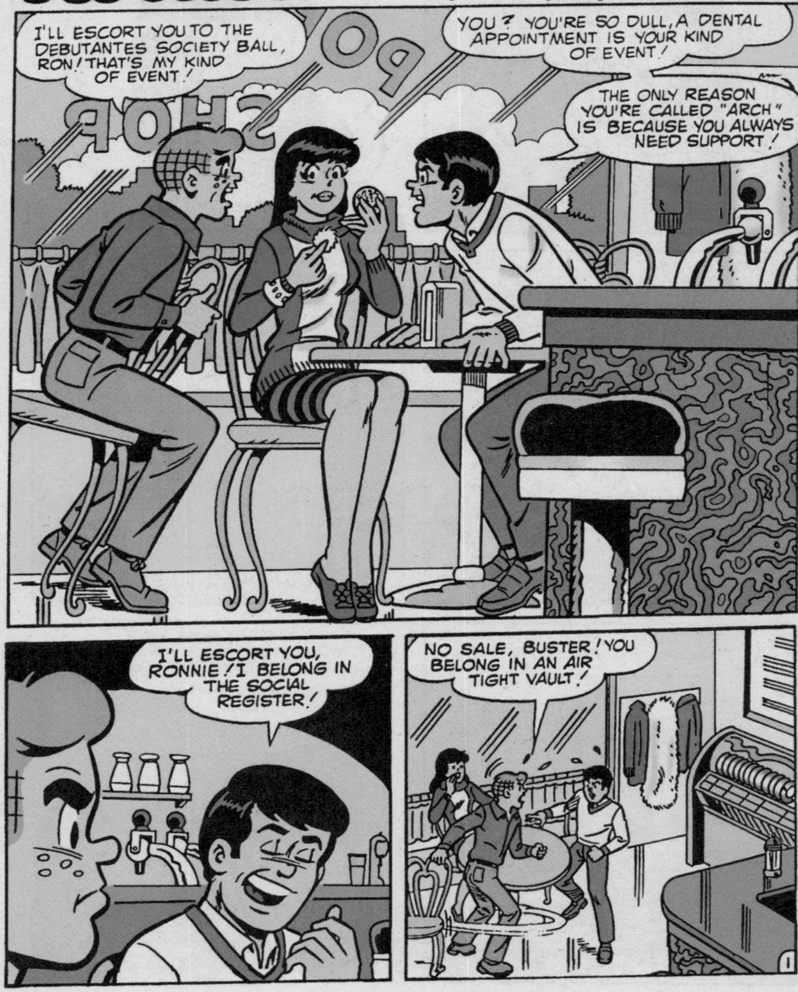
I'LL ESCORT YOU TO THE DEBUTANTES SOCIETY BALL, RON! THAT'S MY KIND OF EVENT!
YOU? YOU'RE SO DULL, A DENTAL APPOINTMENT IS YOUR KIND OF EVENT!
THE ONLY REASON YOU'RE CALLED "ARCH" IS BECAUSE YOU ALWAYS NEED SUPPORT!
I'LL ESCORT YOU, RONNIE! I BELONG IN THE SOCIAL REGISTER!
NO SALE, BUSTER! YOU BELONG IN AN AIR TIGHT VAULT!
1

FELLOWS, PLEASE! I CAN ONLY HAVE ONE ESCORT TO THE BALL!

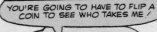

YOU'RE GOING TO HAVE TO FLIP A COIN TO SEE WHO TAKES ME!

OKAY, HEADS I WIN, TAILS YOU LOSE!

YOU MEAN TAILS I WIN! I'M WISE TO YOU!

HAVE IT YOUR WAY!

IT'S TAILS! I WIN! I'M RONNIE'S ESCORT!

WHY, THAT FINK MUST HAVE SWITCHED COINS ON ME! THAT WAS MY TWO HEADED COIN!

2

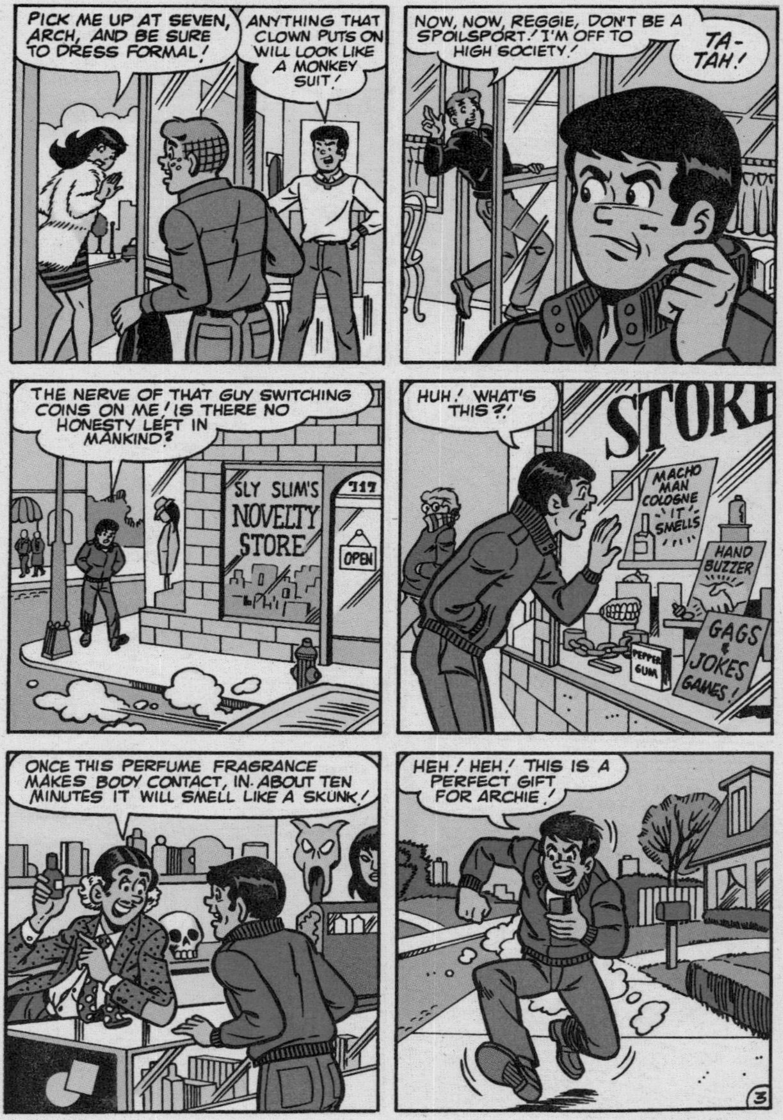
PICK ME UP AT SEVEN, ARCH, AND BE SURE TO DRESS FORMAL!
ANYTHING THAT CLOWN PUTS ON WILL LOOK LIKE A MONKEY SUIT!
NOW, NOW, REGGIE, DON'T BE A SPOILSPORT! I'M OFF TO HIGH SOCIETY!
TA-TAH!
THE NERVE OF THAT GUY SWITCHING COINS ON ME! IS THERE NO HONESTY LEFT IN MANKIND?
SLY SLIM'S NOVELTY STORE
717
OPEN
HUH! WHAT'S THIS?!
STORE
MACHO MAN COLOGNE IT SMELLS
HAND BUZZER
PEPPER GUM
GAGS & JOKES GAMES!
ONCE THIS PERFUME FRAGRANCE MAKES BODY CONTACT, IN ABOUT TEN MINUTES IT WILL SMELL LIKE A SKUNK!
HEH! HEH! THIS IS A PERFECT GIFT FOR ARCHIE!
3

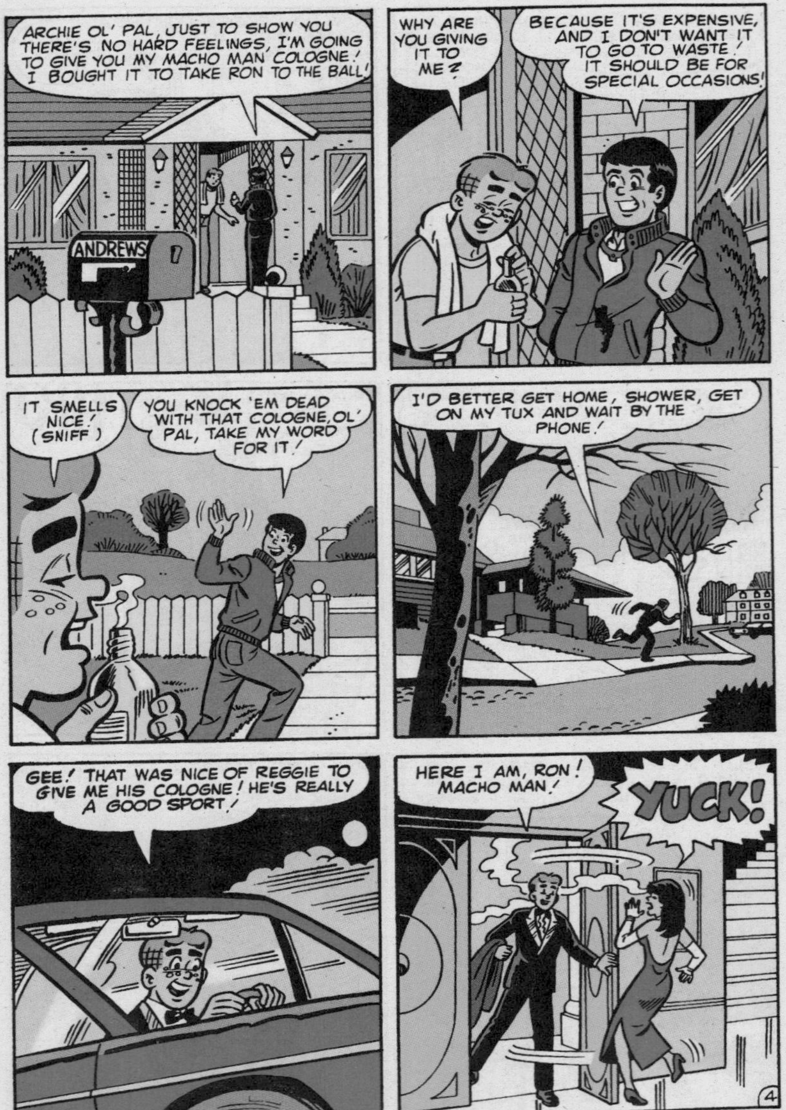
ARCHIE OL' PAL, JUST TO SHOW YOU THERE'S NO HARD FEELINGS, I'M GOING TO GIVE YOU MY MACHO MAN COLOGNE! I BOUGHT IT TO TAKE RON TO THE BALL!
ANDREWS
WHY ARE YOU GIVING IT TO ME?
BECAUSE IT'S EXPENSIVE, AND I DON'T WANT IT TO GO TO WASTE! IT SHOULD BE FOR SPECIAL OCCASIONS!
IT SMELLS NICE! (SNIFF)
YOU KNOCK 'EM DEAD WITH THAT COLOGNE, OL' PAL, TAKE MY WORD FOR IT!
I'D BETTER GET HOME, SHOWER, GET ON MY TUX AND WAIT BY THE PHONE!
GEE! THAT WAS NICE OF REGGIE TO GIVE ME HIS COLOGNE! HE'S REALLY A GOOD SPORT!
HERE I AM, RON! MACHO MAN!
YUCK!
4

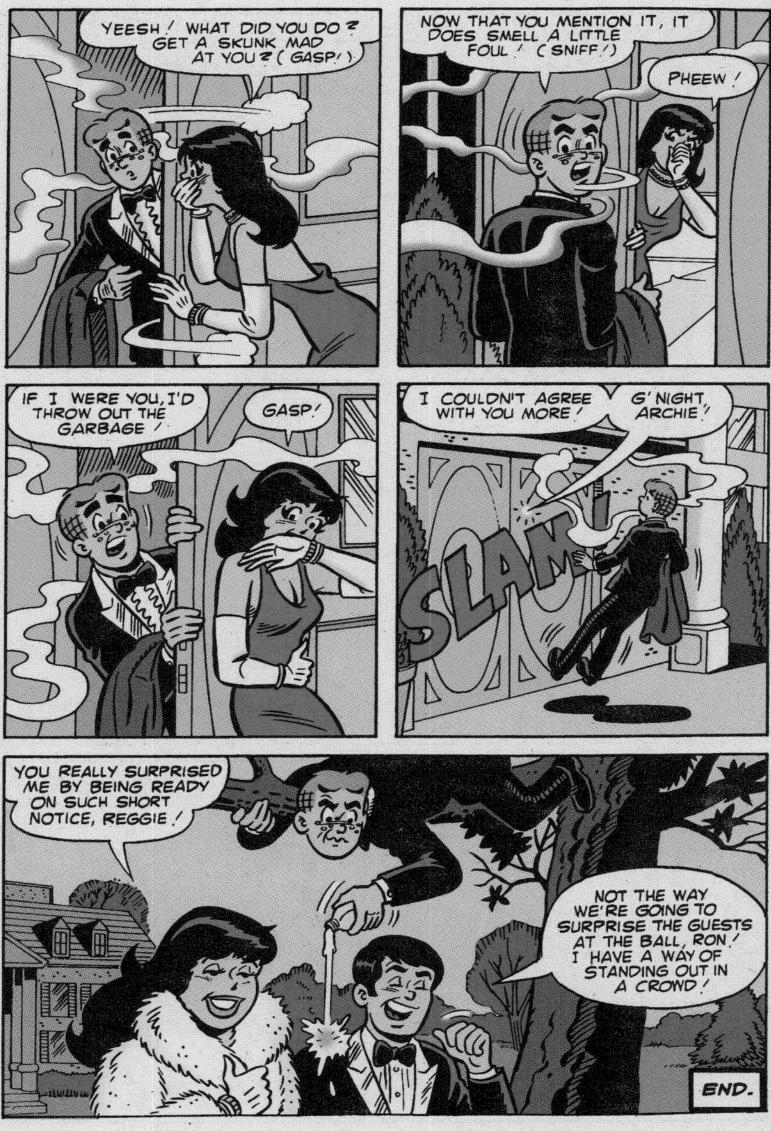
YEESH! WHAT DID YOU DO? GET A SKUNK MAD AT YOU? (GASP!)
NOW THAT YOU MENTION IT, IT DOES SMELL A LITTLE FOUL! (SNIFF!)
PHEEW!
IF I WERE YOU, I'D THROW OUT THE GARBAGE!
GASP!
I COULDN'T AGREE WITH YOU MORE!
G' NIGHT, ARCHIE!
SLAM
YOU REALLY SURPRISED ME BY BEING READY ON SUCH SHORT NOTICE, REGGIE!
NOT THE WAY WE'RE GOING TO SURPRISE THE GUESTS AT THE BALL, RON! I HAVE A WAY OF STANDING OUT IN A CROWD!
END.

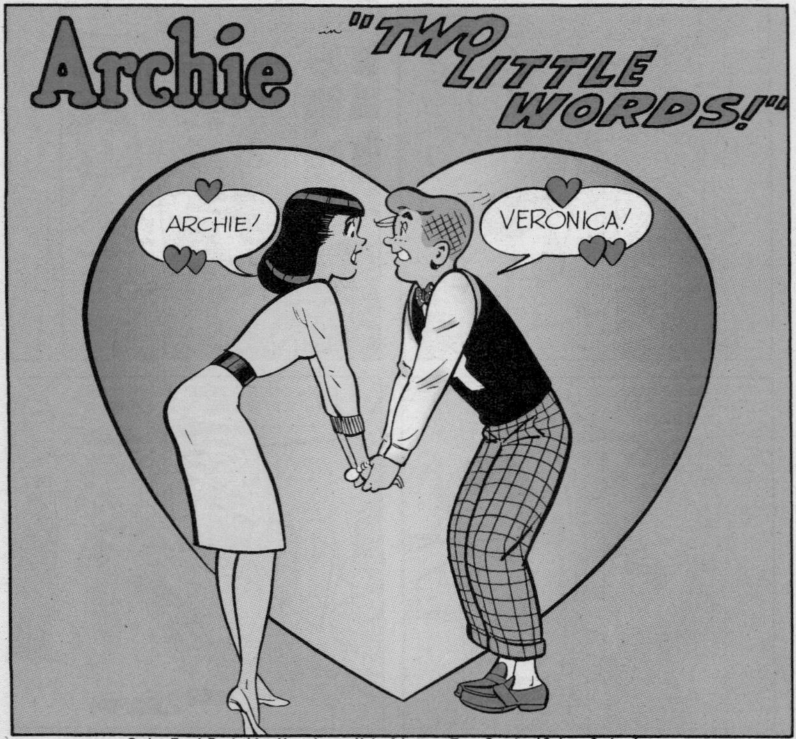
Archie
-in-
"TWO LITTLE WORDS!"
ARCHIE!
VERONICA!

Script: Frank Doyle / Art: Harry Lucey / Inks & Letters: Terry Szenics / Colors: Carlos Antunes

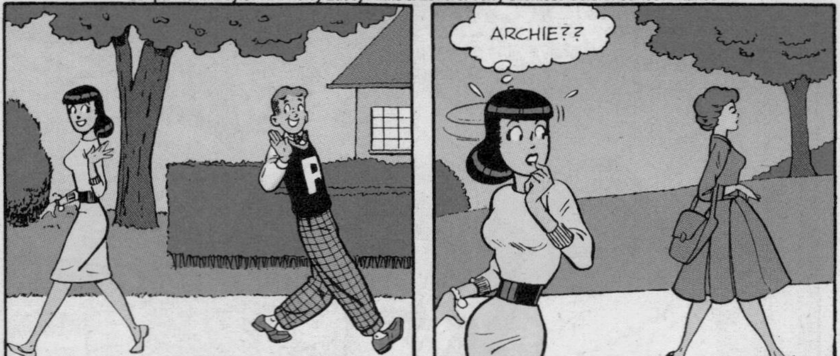
ARCHIE??

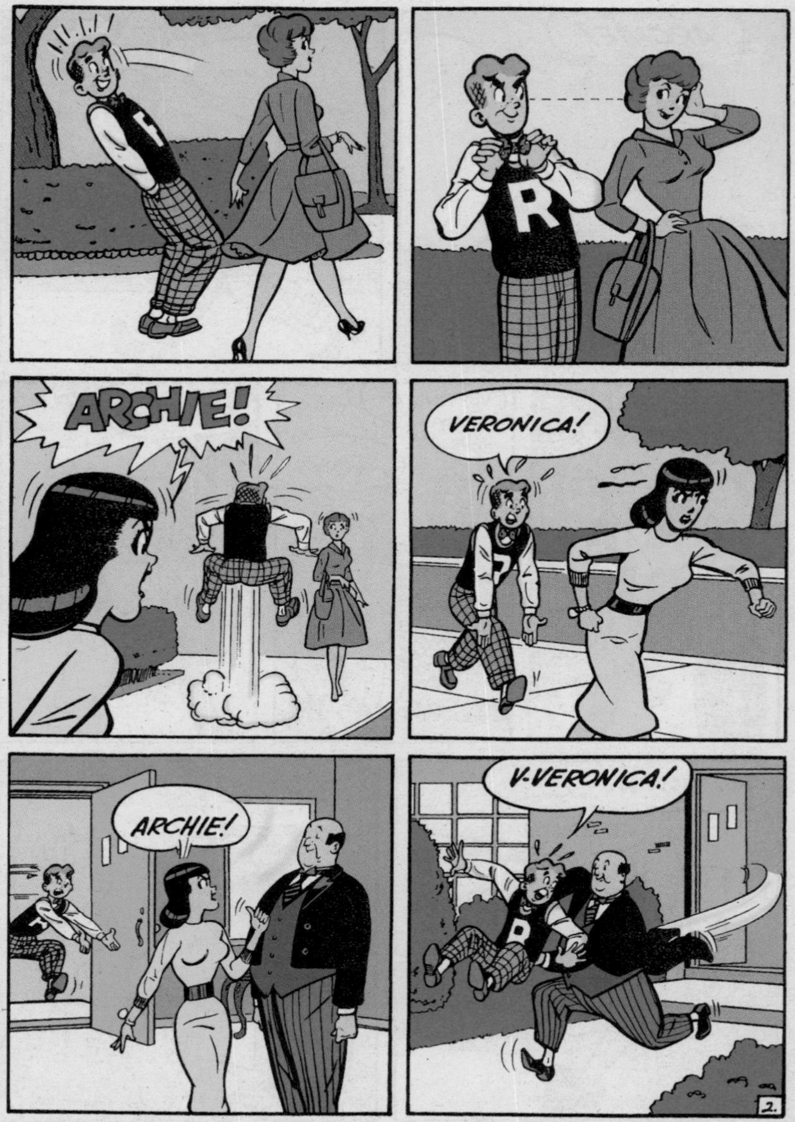
ARCHIE!
VERONICA!
ARCHIE!
V-VERONICA!
2.

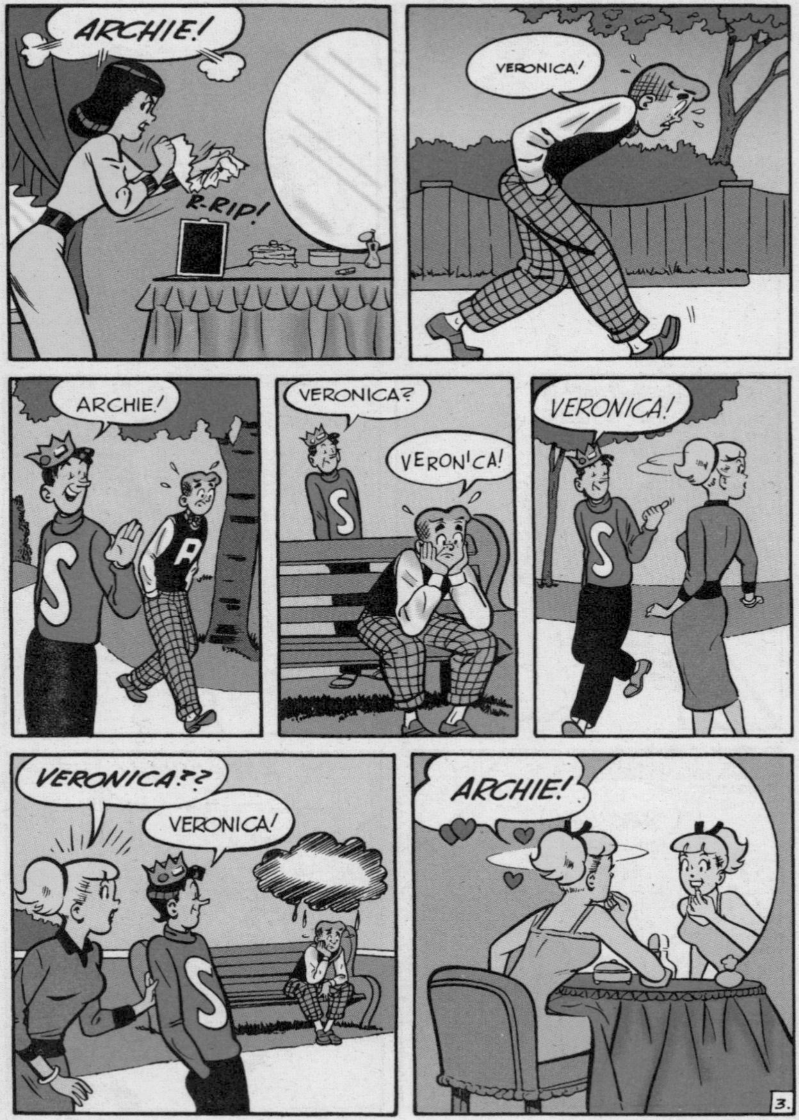
ARCHIE!
R-RIP!
VERONICA!
ARCHIE!
VERONICA?
VERONICA!
VERONICA!
VERONICA??
VERONICA!
ARCHIE!
3.

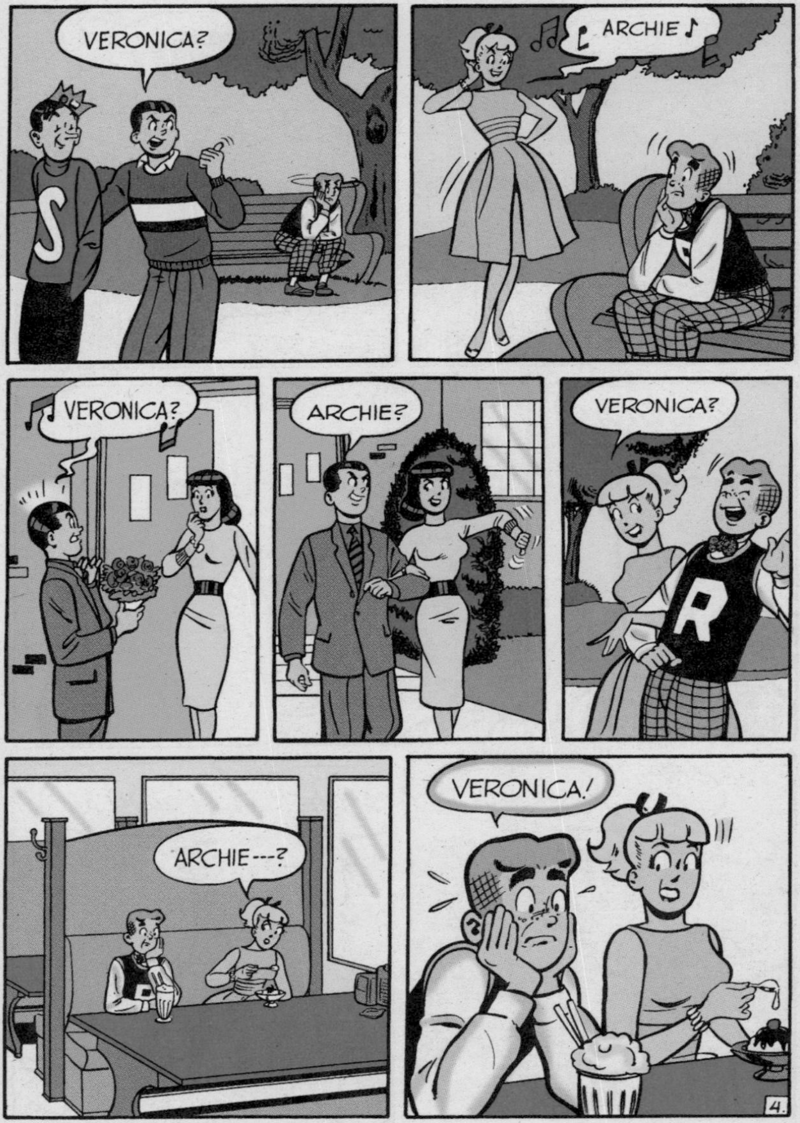
VERONICA?
ARCHIE
VERONICA?
ARCHIE?
VERONICA?
ARCHIE---?
VERONICA!
4.

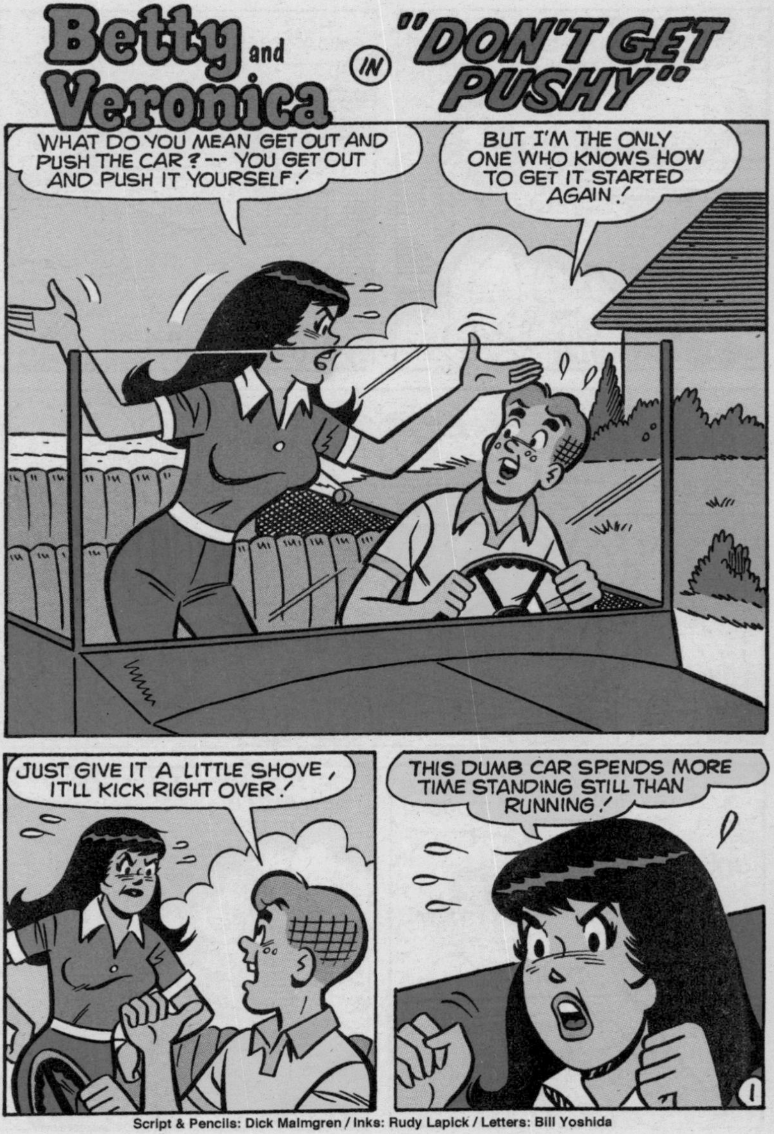
Betty and Veronica IN "DON'T GET PUSHY"
WHAT DO YOU MEAN GET OUT AND PUSH THE CAR ? --- YOU GET OUT AND PUSH IT YOURSELF !
BUT I'M THE ONLY ONE WHO KNOWS HOW TO GET IT STARTED AGAIN !
JUST GIVE IT A LITTLE SHOVE , IT'LL KICK RIGHT OVER !
THIS DUMB CAR SPENDS MORE TIME STANDING STILL THAN RUNNING !
1

Script & Pencils: Dick Malmgren / Inks: Rudy Lapick / Letters: Bill Yoshida

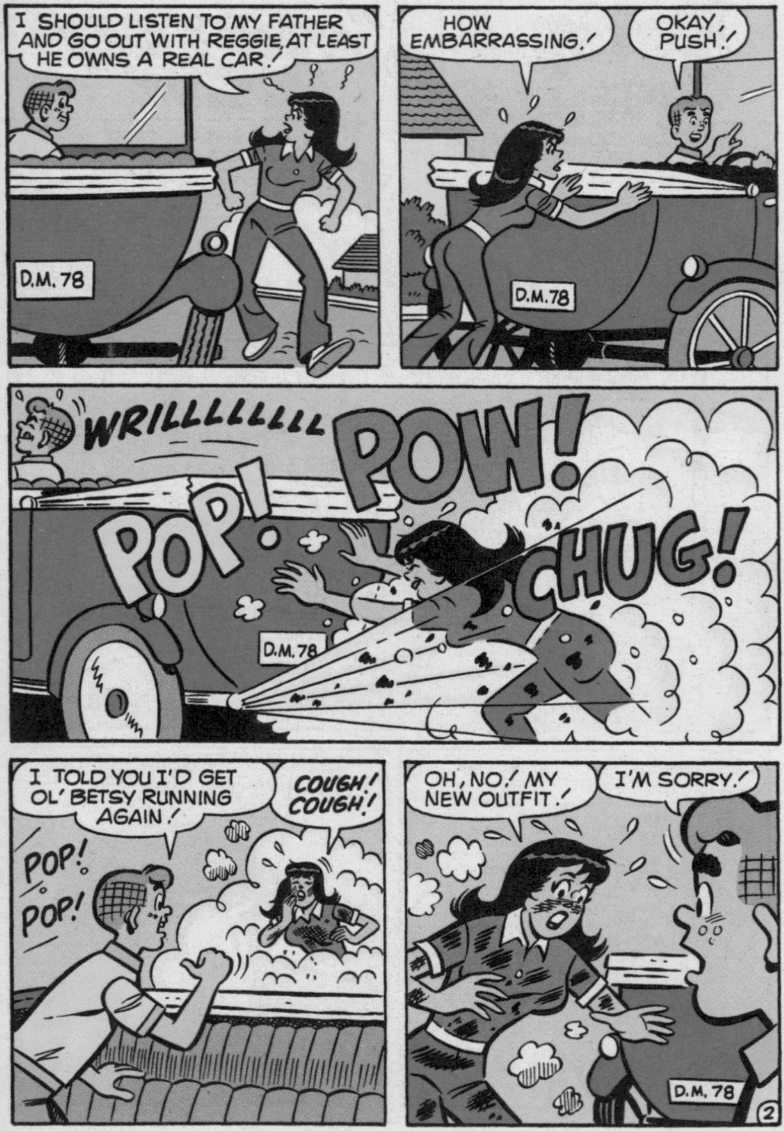
I SHOULD LISTEN TO MY FATHER AND GO OUT WITH REGGIE, AT LEAST HE OWNS A REAL CAR!
D.M. 78
HOW EMBARRASSING!
OKAY, PUSH!
D.M. 78
WRILLLLLLLL
POW!
POP!
CHUG!
D.M. 78
I TOLD YOU I'D GET OL' BETSY RUNNING AGAIN!
COUGH! COUGH!
POP!
POP!
OH, NO! MY NEW OUTFIT!
I'M SORRY!
D.M. 78
2

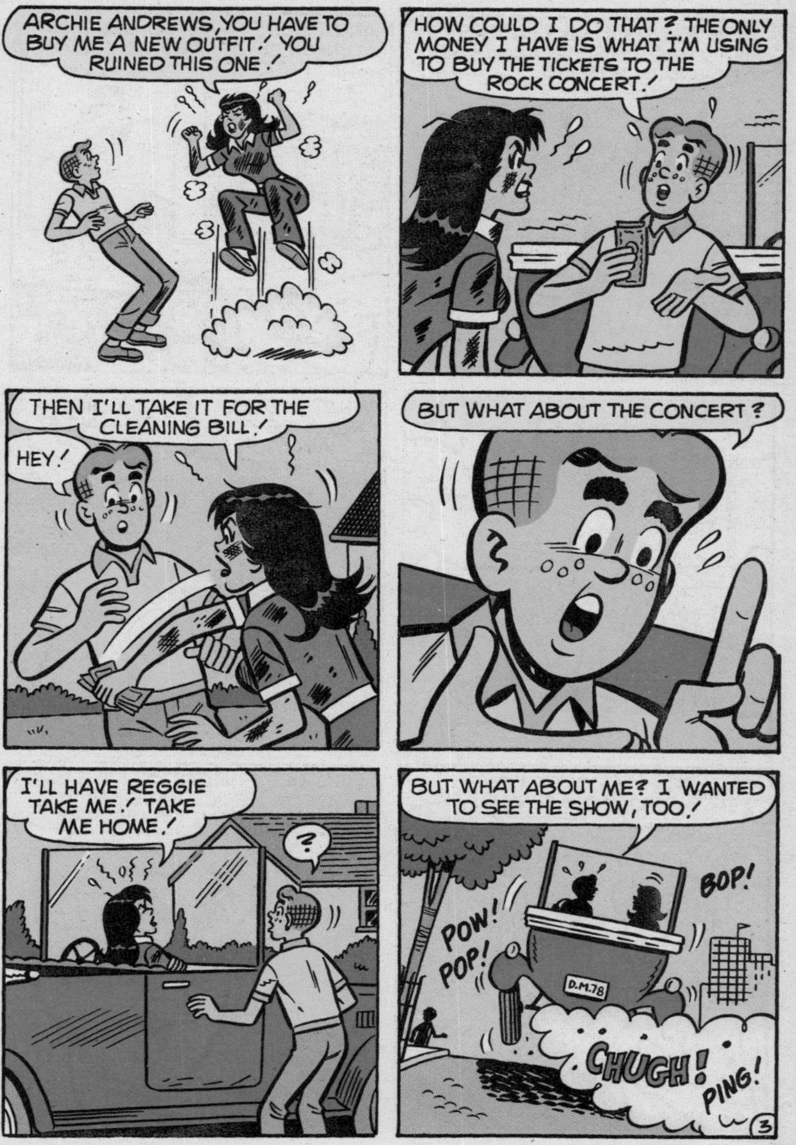
ARCHIE ANDREWS, YOU HAVE TO BUY ME A NEW OUTFIT! YOU RUINED THIS ONE!
HOW COULD I DO THAT? THE ONLY MONEY I HAVE IS WHAT I'M USING TO BUY THE TICKETS TO THE ROCK CONCERT!
THEN I'LL TAKE IT FOR THE CLEANING BILL!
HEY!
BUT WHAT ABOUT THE CONCERT?
I'LL HAVE REGGIE TAKE ME! TAKE ME HOME!
?
BUT WHAT ABOUT ME? I WANTED TO SEE THE SHOW, TOO!
BOP!
POW!
POP!
D.M.78
CHUGH!
PING!
3

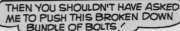

THEN YOU SHOULDN'T HAVE ASKED ME TO PUSH THIS BROKEN DOWN BUNDLE OF BOLTS!

POW!

POW!

BOP!

AND I DON'T WANT TO SEE THIS CLUNKER ON MY PROPERTY AGAIN! IS THAT CLEAR?

MUMBLE! GRUMBLE!

?

SLAM!

WHAT ARE YOU SO UPTIGHT ABOUT?

VERONICA--- SHE MAKES ME MAD!

SHE TOOK MY TICKET MONEY FOR THE ROCK CONCERT!

WHAT FOR?

BECAUSE SHE GOT A LITTLE BLACK SOOT ON HER CLOTHES FROM THE EXHAUST OF MY CAR!

4

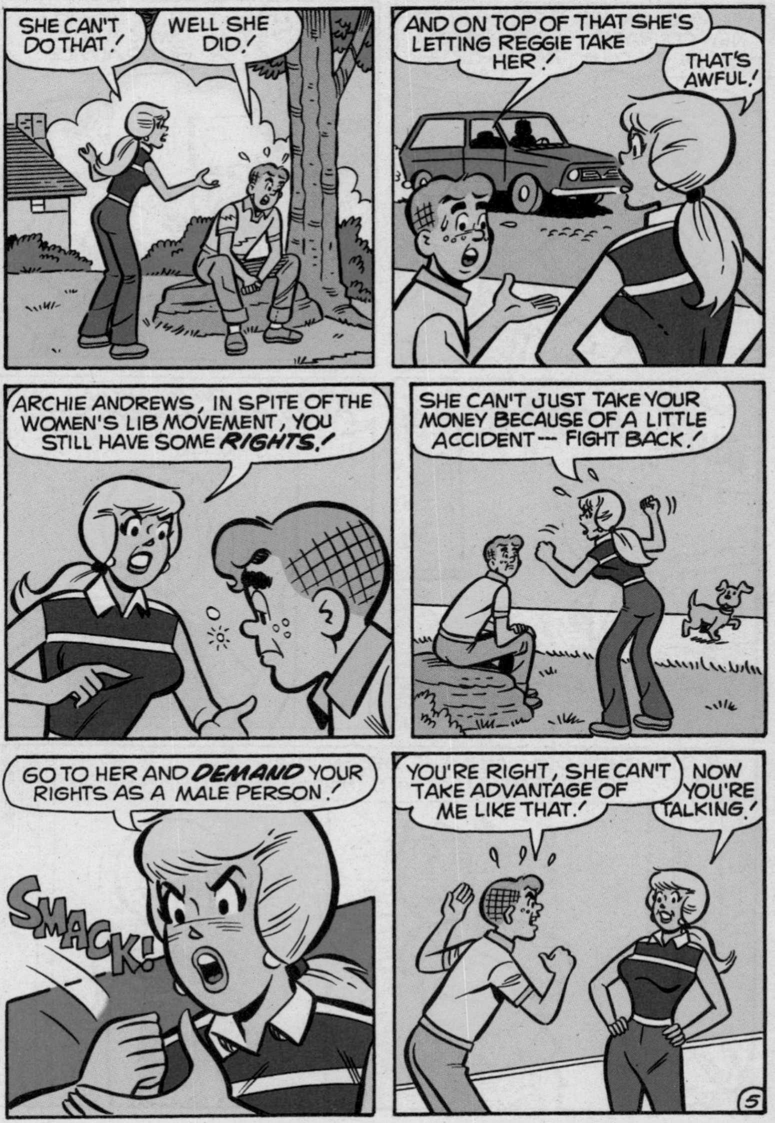
SHE CAN'T DO THAT!
WELL SHE DID!
AND ON TOP OF THAT SHE'S LETTING REGGIE TAKE HER!
THAT'S AWFUL!
ARCHIE ANDREWS, IN SPITE OF THE WOMEN'S LIB MOVEMENT, YOU STILL HAVE SOME RIGHTS!
SHE CAN'T JUST TAKE YOUR MONEY BECAUSE OF A LITTLE ACCIDENT --- FIGHT BACK!
GO TO HER AND DEMAND YOUR RIGHTS AS A MALE PERSON!
SMACK!
YOU'RE RIGHT, SHE CAN'T TAKE ADVANTAGE OF ME LIKE THAT!
NOW YOU'RE TALKING!
5

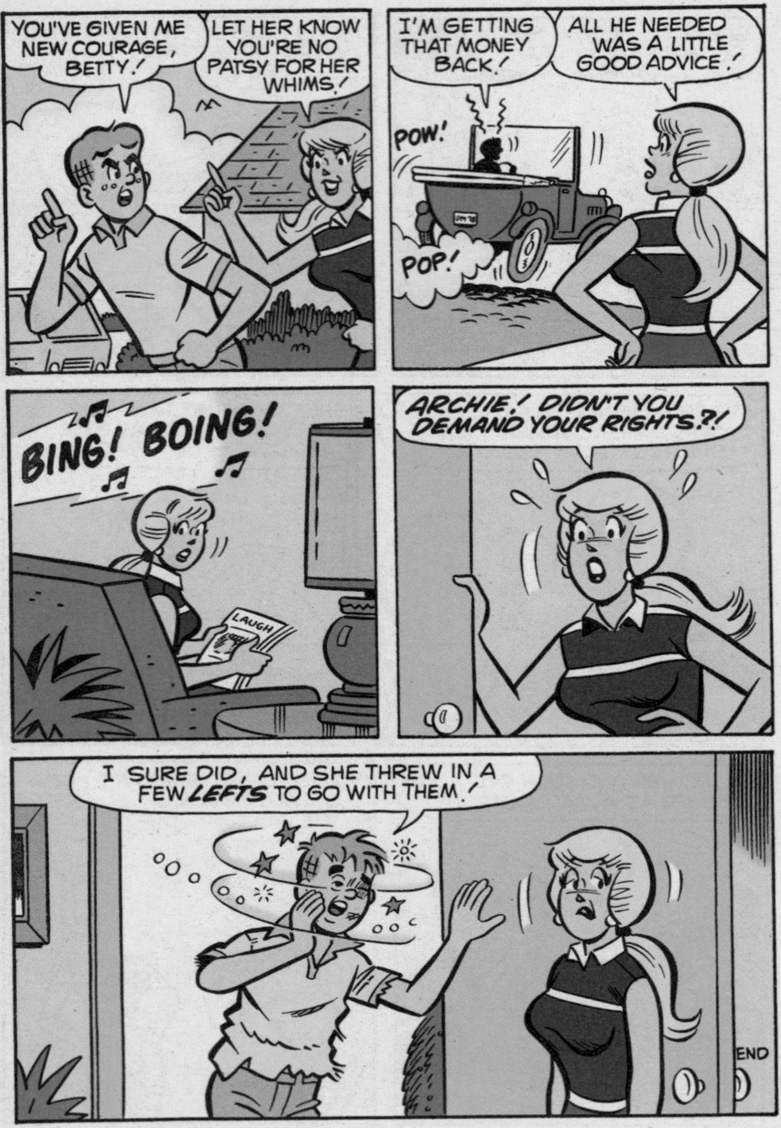

YOU'VE GIVEN ME NEW COURAGE, BETTY!
LET HER KNOW YOU'RE NO PATSY FOR HER WHIMS!
I'M GETTING THAT MONEY BACK!
ALL HE NEEDED WAS A LITTLE GOOD ADVICE!
POW!
POP!
BING! BOING!
LAUGH
ARCHIE! DIDN'T YOU DEMAND YOUR RIGHTS?!
I SURE DID, AND SHE THREW IN A FEW LEFTS TO GO WITH THEM!
END

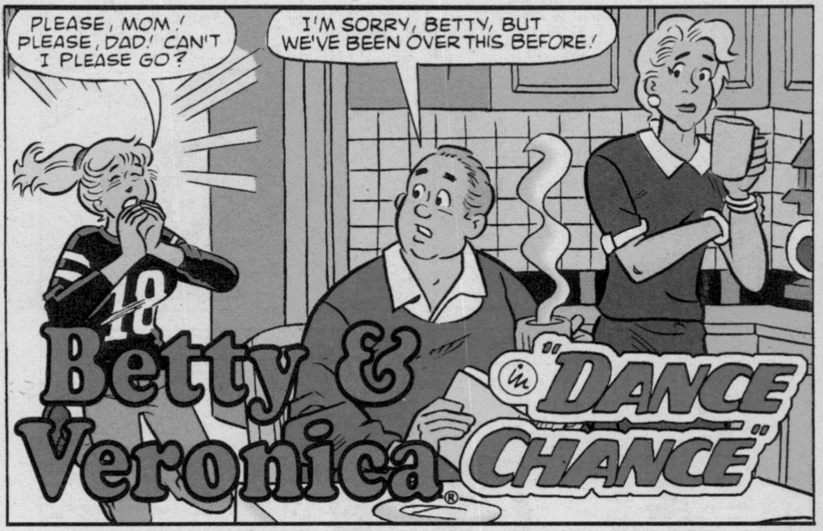
PLEASE, MOM! PLEASE, DAD! CAN'T I PLEASE GO?
I'M SORRY, BETTY, BUT WE'VE BEEN OVER THIS BEFORE!
Betty & Veronica®
in "DANCE CHANCE"

SCRIPT: MIKE PELLOWSKI PENCILS: TIM KENNEDY INKS: RUDY LAPICK
COLORS: BARRY GROSSMAN LETTERS: BILL YOSHIDA

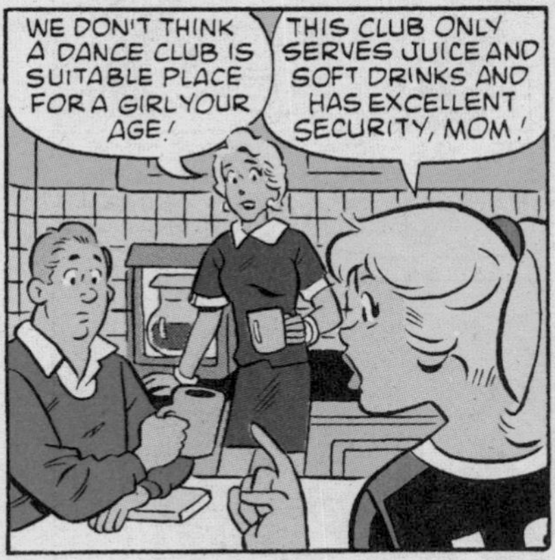
WE DON'T THINK A DANCE CLUB IS SUITABLE PLACE FOR A GIRL YOUR AGE!
THIS CLUB ONLY SERVES JUICE AND SOFT DRINKS AND HAS EXCELLENT SECURITY, MOM!

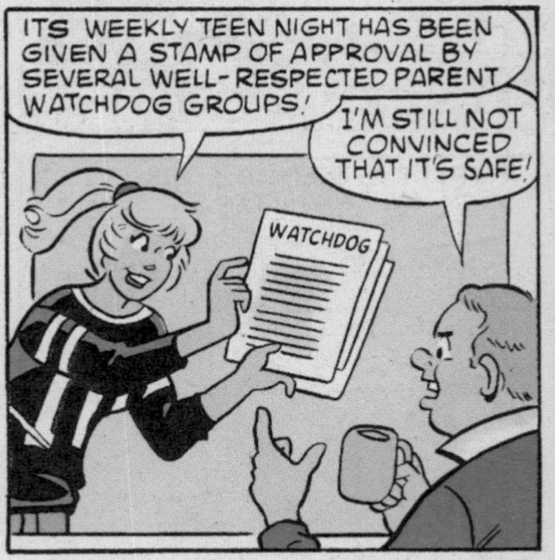
ITS WEEKLY TEEN NIGHT HAS BEEN GIVEN A STAMP OF APPROVAL BY SEVERAL WELL-RESPECTED PARENT WATCHDOG GROUPS!
I'M STILL NOT CONVINCED THAT IT'S SAFE!
WATCHDOG

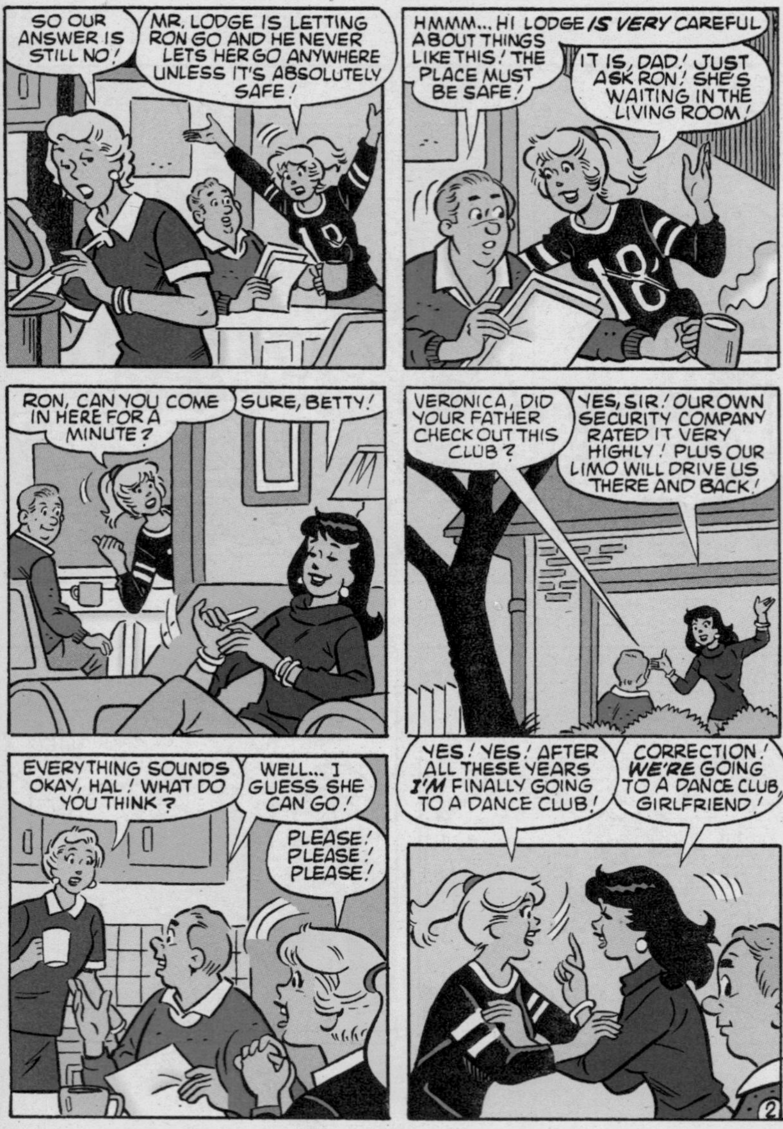
SO OUR ANSWER IS STILL NO!
MR. LODGE IS LETTING RON GO AND HE NEVER LETS HER GO ANYWHERE UNLESS IT'S ABSOLUTELY SAFE!
HMMM... HI LODGE IS VERY CAREFUL ABOUT THINGS LIKE THIS! THE PLACE MUST BE SAFE!
IT IS, DAD! JUST ASK RON! SHE'S WAITING IN THE LIVING ROOM!
RON, CAN YOU COME IN HERE FOR A MINUTE?
SURE, BETTY!
VERONICA, DID YOUR FATHER CHECK OUT THIS CLUB?
YES, SIR! OUR OWN SECURITY COMPANY RATED IT VERY HIGHLY! PLUS OUR LIMO WILL DRIVE US THERE AND BACK!
EVERYTHING SOUNDS OKAY, HAL! WHAT DO YOU THINK?
WELL... I GUESS SHE CAN GO!
PLEASE! PLEASE! PLEASE!
YES! YES! AFTER ALL THESE YEARS I'M FINALLY GOING TO A DANCE CLUB!
CORRECTION! WE'RE GOING TO A DANCE CLUB, GIRLFRIEND!
2

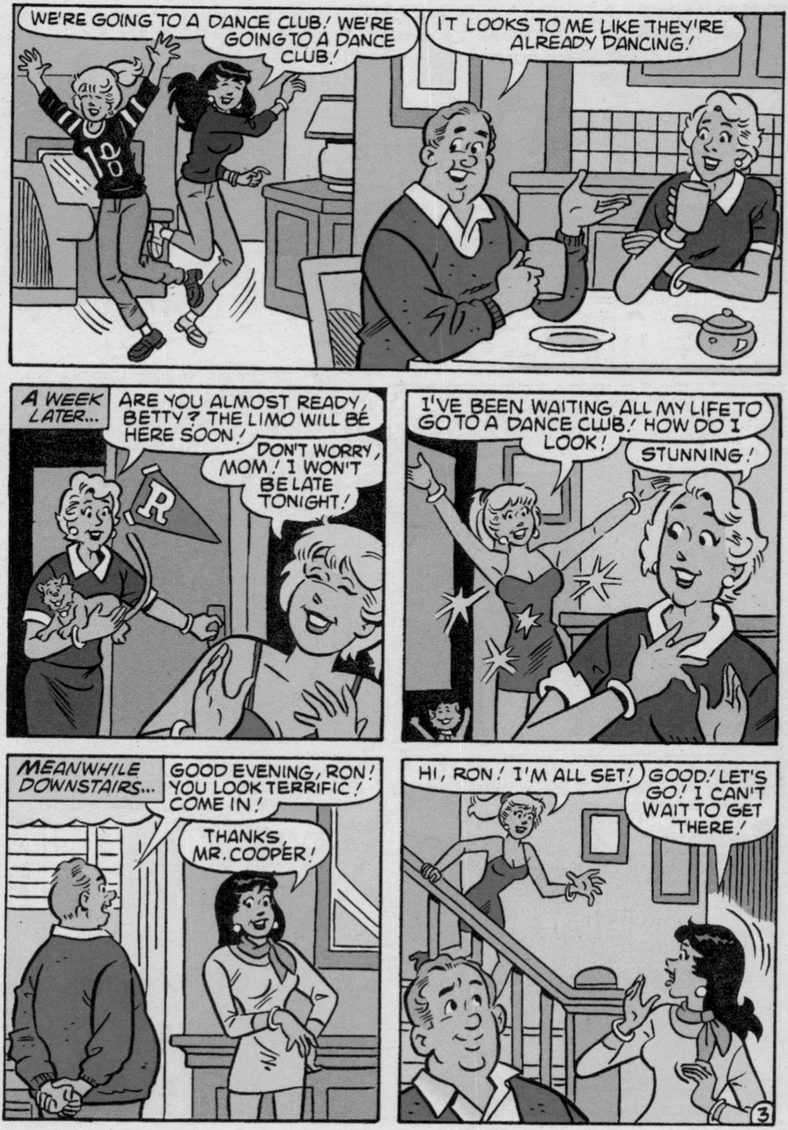
WE'RE GOING TO A DANCE CLUB! WE'RE GOING TO A DANCE CLUB!
IT LOOKS TO ME LIKE THEY'RE ALREADY DANCING!
A WEEK LATER...
ARE YOU ALMOST READY, BETTY? THE LIMO WILL BE HERE SOON!
DON'T WORRY, MOM! I WON'T BE LATE TONIGHT!
I'VE BEEN WAITING ALL MY LIFE TO GO TO A DANCE CLUB! HOW DO I LOOK!
STUNNING!
MEANWHILE DOWNSTAIRS...
GOOD EVENING, RON! YOU LOOK TERRIFIC! COME IN!
THANKS, MR. COOPER!
HI, RON! I'M ALL SET!
GOOD! LET'S GO! I CAN'T WAIT TO GET THERE!
3

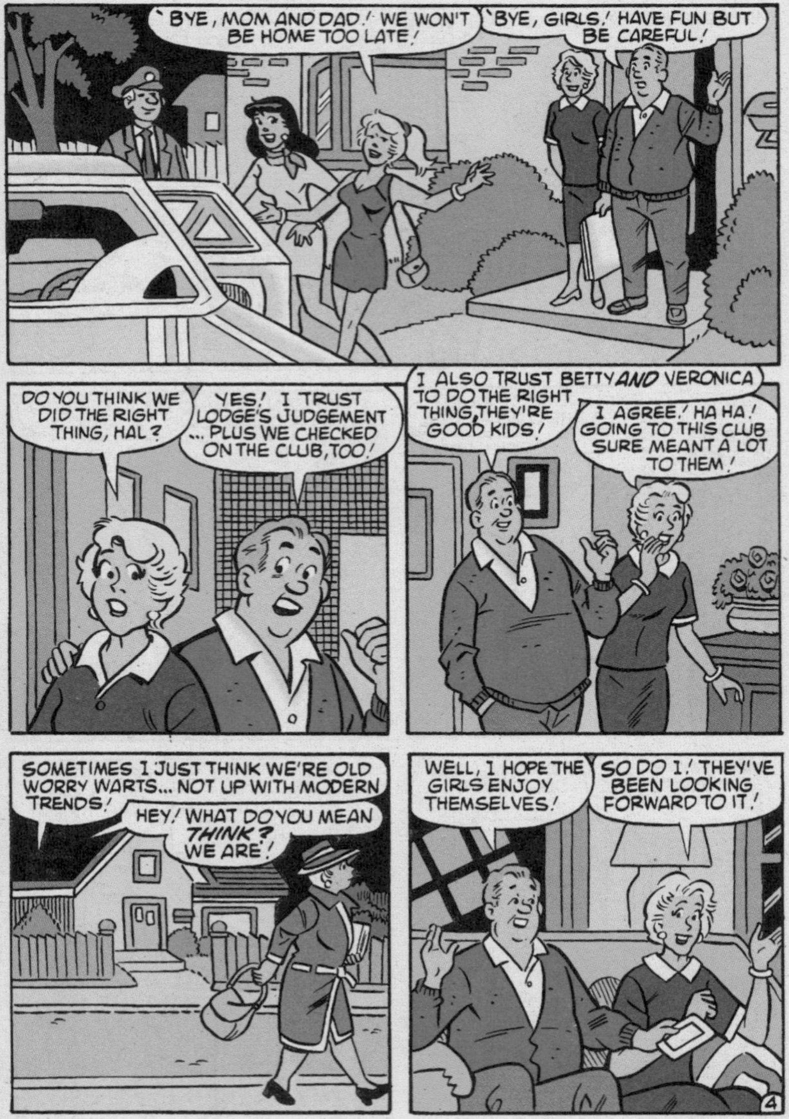
`BYE, MOM AND DAD! WE WON'T BE HOME TOO LATE!
`BYE, GIRLS! HAVE FUN BUT BE CAREFUL!
DO YOU THINK WE DID THE RIGHT THING, HAL?
YES! I TRUST LODGE'S JUDGEMENT ... PLUS WE CHECKED ON THE CLUB, TOO!
I ALSO TRUST BETTY AND VERONICA TO DO THE RIGHT THING. THEY'RE GOOD KIDS!
I AGREE! HA HA! GOING TO THIS CLUB SURE MEANT A LOT TO THEM!
SOMETIMES I JUST THINK WE'RE OLD WORRY WARTS... NOT UP WITH MODERN TRENDS!
HEY! WHAT DO YOU MEAN THINK? WE ARE!
WELL, I HOPE THE GIRLS ENJOY THEMSELVES!
SO DO I! THEY'VE BEEN LOOKING FORWARD TO IT!
4

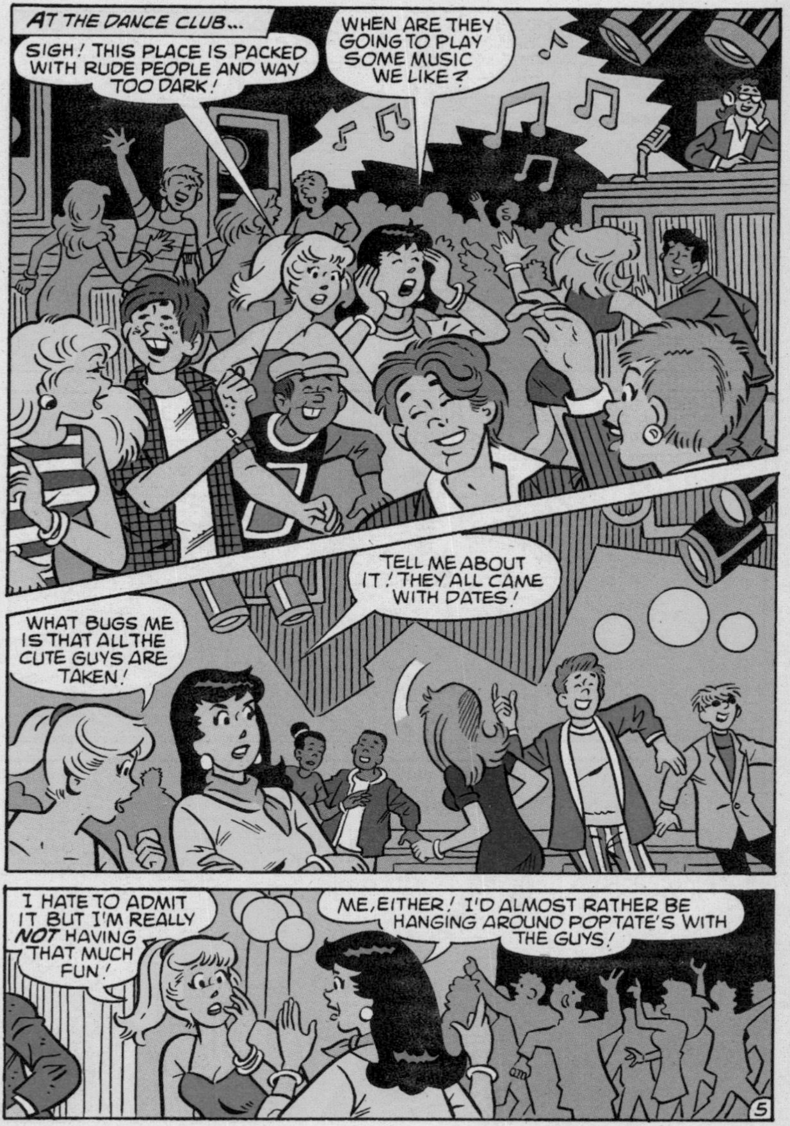

AT THE DANCE CLUB...
SIGH! THIS PLACE IS PACKED WITH RUDE PEOPLE AND WAY TOO DARK!
WHEN ARE THEY GOING TO PLAY SOME MUSIC WE LIKE?
WHAT BUGS ME IS THAT ALL THE CUTE GUYS ARE TAKEN!
TELL ME ABOUT IT! THEY ALL CAME WITH DATES!
I HATE TO ADMIT IT BUT I'M REALLY NOT HAVING THAT MUCH FUN!
ME, EITHER! I'D ALMOST RATHER BE HANGING AROUND POPTATE'S WITH THE GUYS!
5

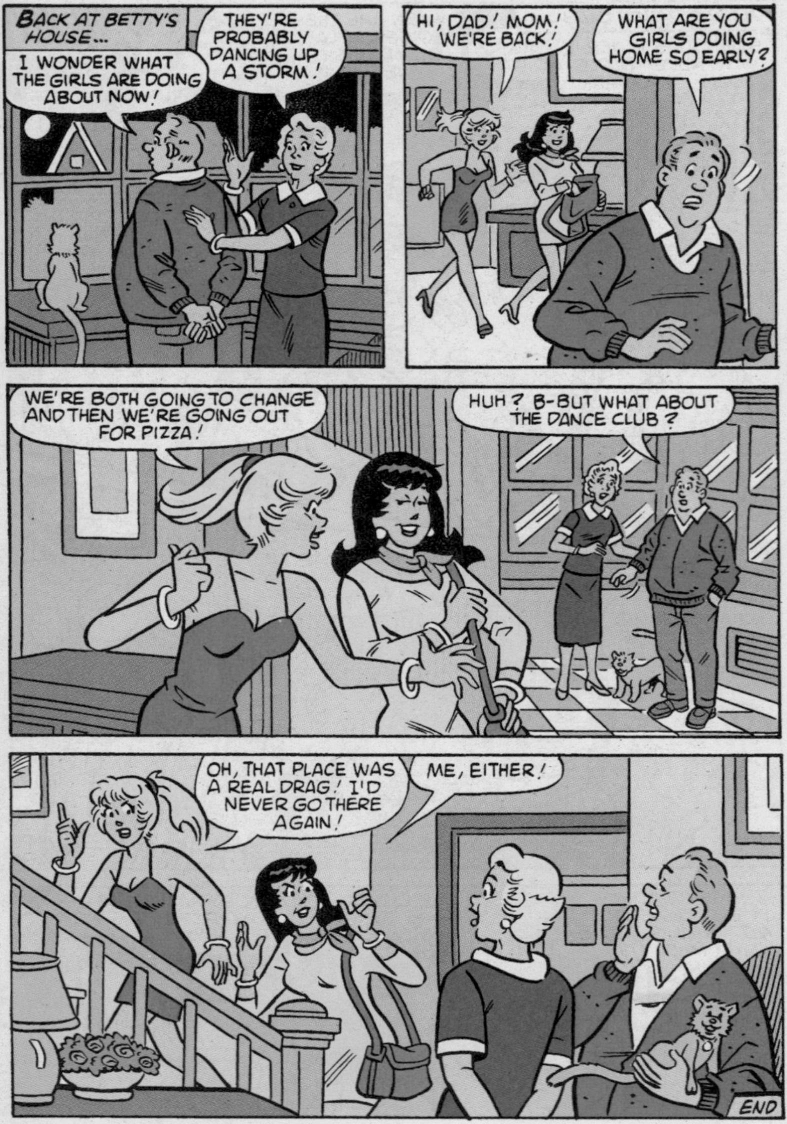
BACK AT BETTY'S HOUSE...
I WONDER WHAT THE GIRLS ARE DOING ABOUT NOW!
THEY'RE PROBABLY DANCING UP A STORM!
HI, DAD! MOM! WE'RE BACK!
WHAT ARE YOU GIRLS DOING HOME SO EARLY?
WE'RE BOTH GOING TO CHANGE AND THEN WE'RE GOING OUT FOR PIZZA!
HUH? B-BUT WHAT ABOUT THE DANCE CLUB?
OH, THAT PLACE WAS A REAL DRAG! I'D NEVER GO THERE AGAIN!
ME, EITHER!
END

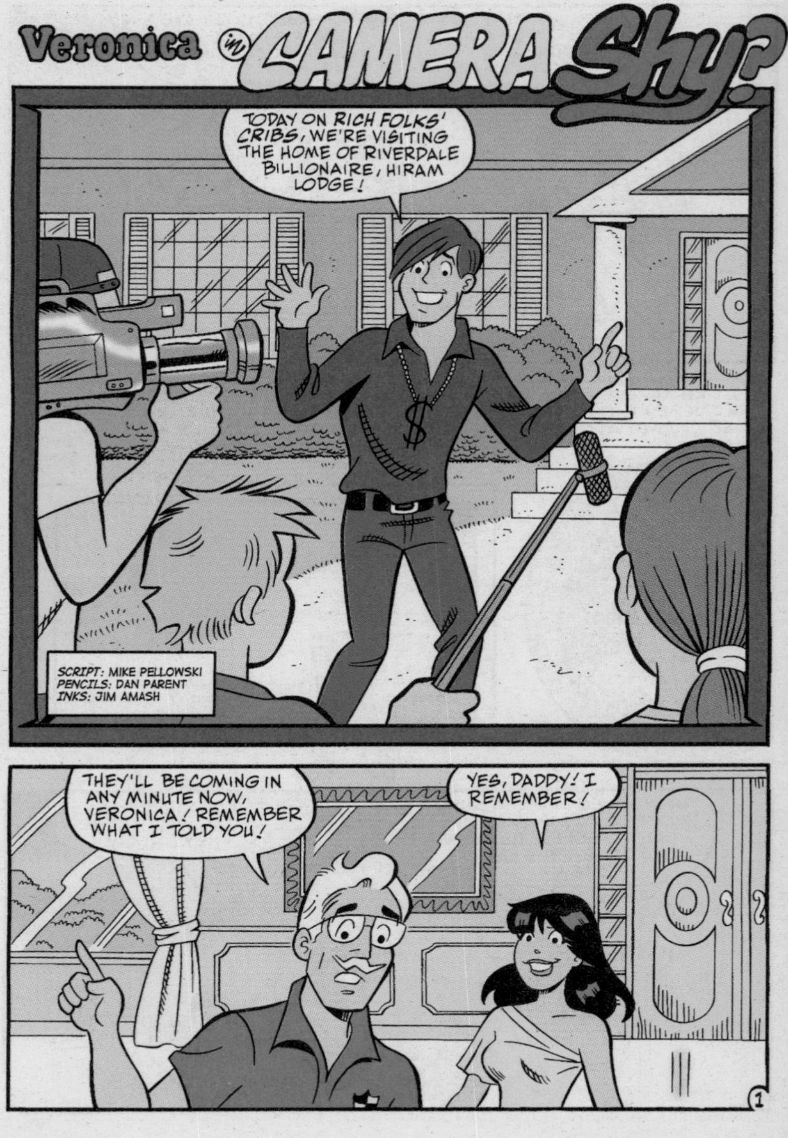
Veronica in CAMERA Shy?
TODAY ON RICH FOLKS' CRIBS, WE'RE VISITING THE HOME OF RIVERDALE BILLIONAIRE, HIRAM LODGE!
SCRIPT: MIKE PELLOWSKI
PENCILS: DAN PARENT
INKS: JIM AMASH
THEY'LL BE COMING IN ANY MINUTE NOW, VERONICA! REMEMBER WHAT I TOLD YOU!
YES, DADDY! I REMEMBER!
1

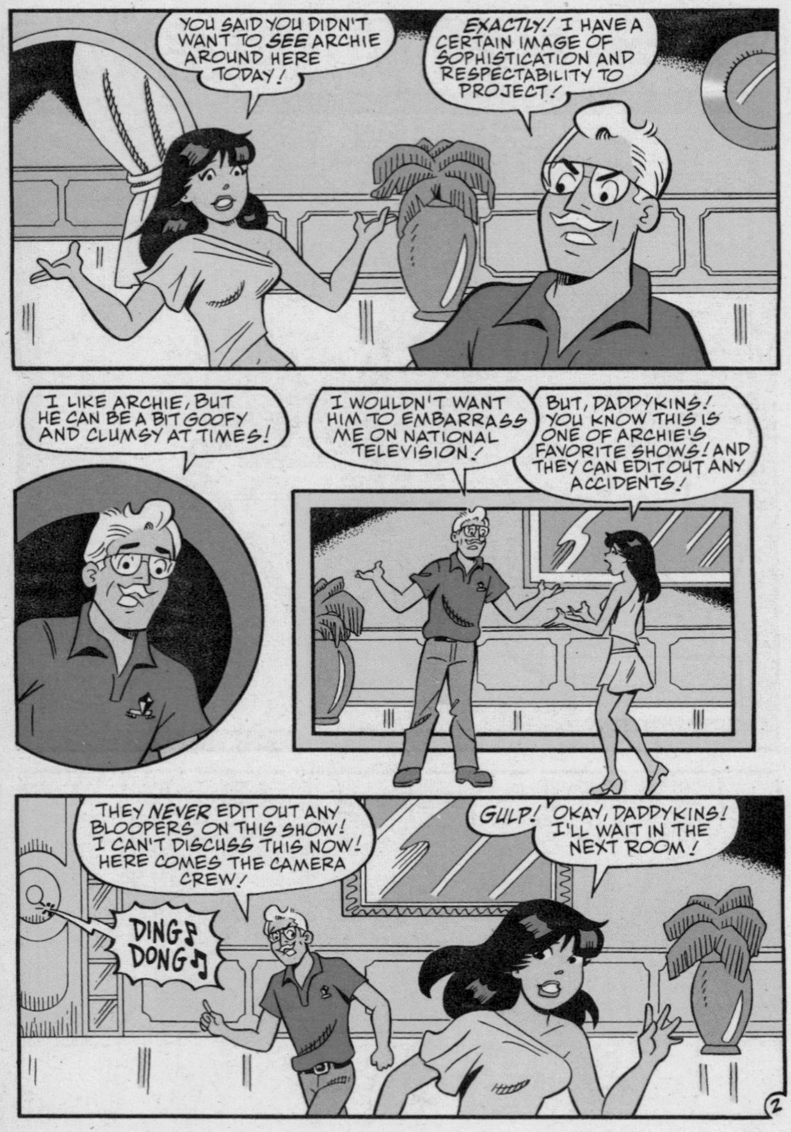
YOU SAID YOU DIDN'T WANT TO *SEE* ARCHIE AROUND HERE TODAY!
EXACTLY! I HAVE A CERTAIN IMAGE OF SOPHISTICATION AND RESPECTABILITY TO PROJECT!
I LIKE ARCHIE, BUT HE CAN BE A BIT GOOFY AND CLUMSY AT TIMES!
I WOULDN'T WANT HIM TO EMBARRASS ME ON NATIONAL TELEVISION!
BUT, DADDYKINS! YOU KNOW THIS IS ONE OF ARCHIE'S FAVORITE SHOWS! AND THEY CAN EDIT OUT ANY ACCIDENTS!
THEY *NEVER* EDIT OUT ANY BLOOPERS ON THIS SHOW! I CAN'T DISCUSS THIS NOW! HERE COMES THE CAMERA CREW!
DING DONG
GULP!
OKAY, DADDYKINS! I'LL WAIT IN THE NEXT ROOM!
2

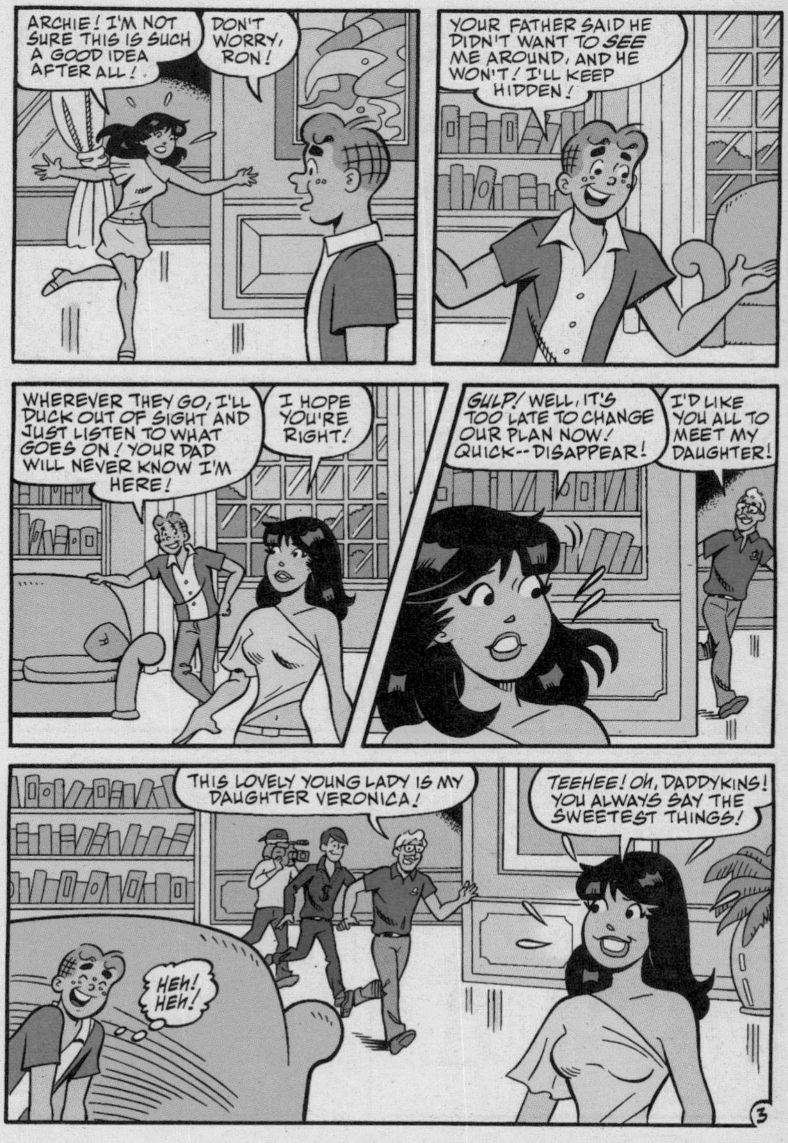
ARCHIE! I'M NOT SURE THIS IS SUCH A GOOD IDEA AFTER ALL!
DON'T WORRY, RON!
YOUR FATHER SAID HE DIDN'T WANT TO SEE ME AROUND, AND HE WON'T! I'LL KEEP HIDDEN!
WHEREVER THEY GO, I'LL DUCK OUT OF SIGHT AND JUST LISTEN TO WHAT GOES ON! YOUR DAD WILL NEVER KNOW I'M HERE!
I HOPE YOU'RE RIGHT!
GULP! WELL, IT'S TOO LATE TO CHANGE OUR PLAN NOW! QUICK--DISAPPEAR!
I'D LIKE YOU ALL TO MEET MY DAUGHTER!
THIS LOVELY YOUNG LADY IS MY DAUGHTER VERONICA!
TEEHEE! OH, DADDYKINS! YOU ALWAYS SAY THE SWEETEST THINGS!
HEH! HEH!
3

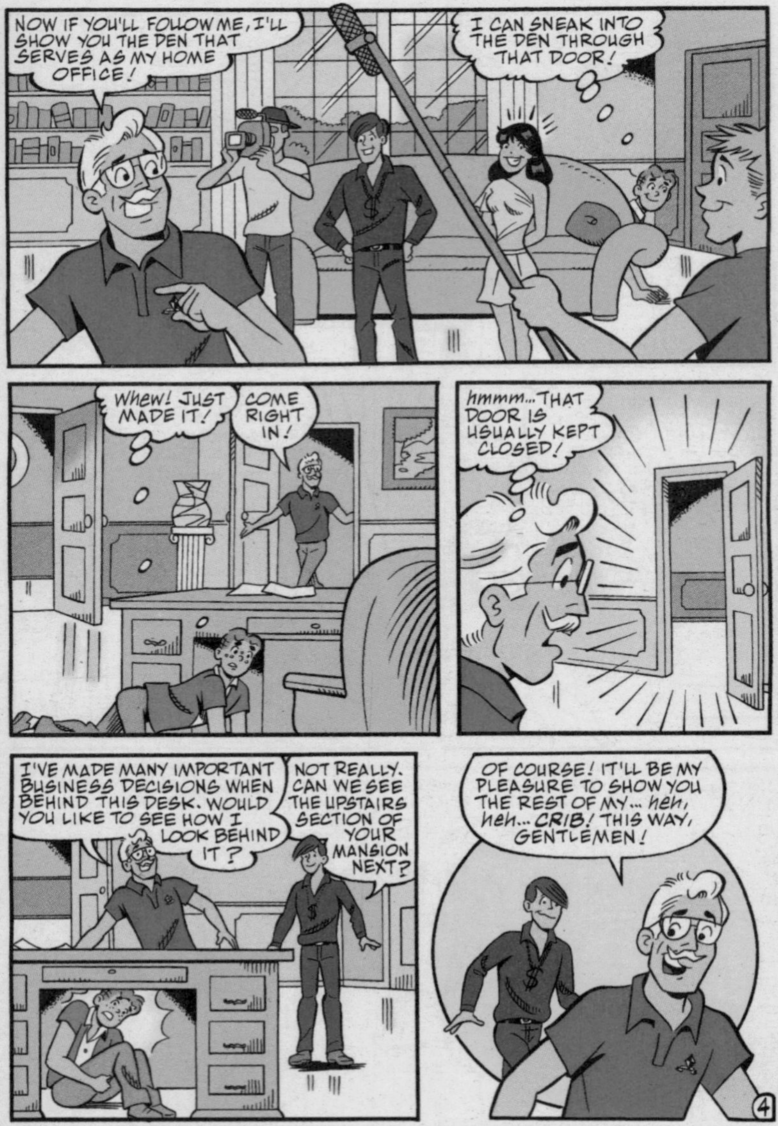
NOW IF YOU'LL FOLLOW ME, I'LL SHOW YOU THE DEN THAT SERVES AS MY HOME OFFICE!
I CAN SNEAK INTO THE DEN THROUGH THAT DOOR!
Whew! JUST MADE IT!
COME RIGHT IN!
hmmm... THAT DOOR IS USUALLY KEPT CLOSED!
I'VE MADE MANY IMPORTANT BUSINESS DECISIONS WHEN BEHIND THIS DESK. WOULD YOU LIKE TO SEE HOW I LOOK BEHIND IT?
NOT REALLY. CAN WE SEE THE UPSTAIRS SECTION OF YOUR MANSION NEXT?
OF COURSE! IT'LL BE MY PLEASURE TO SHOW YOU THE REST OF MY... heh, heh... CRIB! THIS WAY, GENTLEMEN!
4

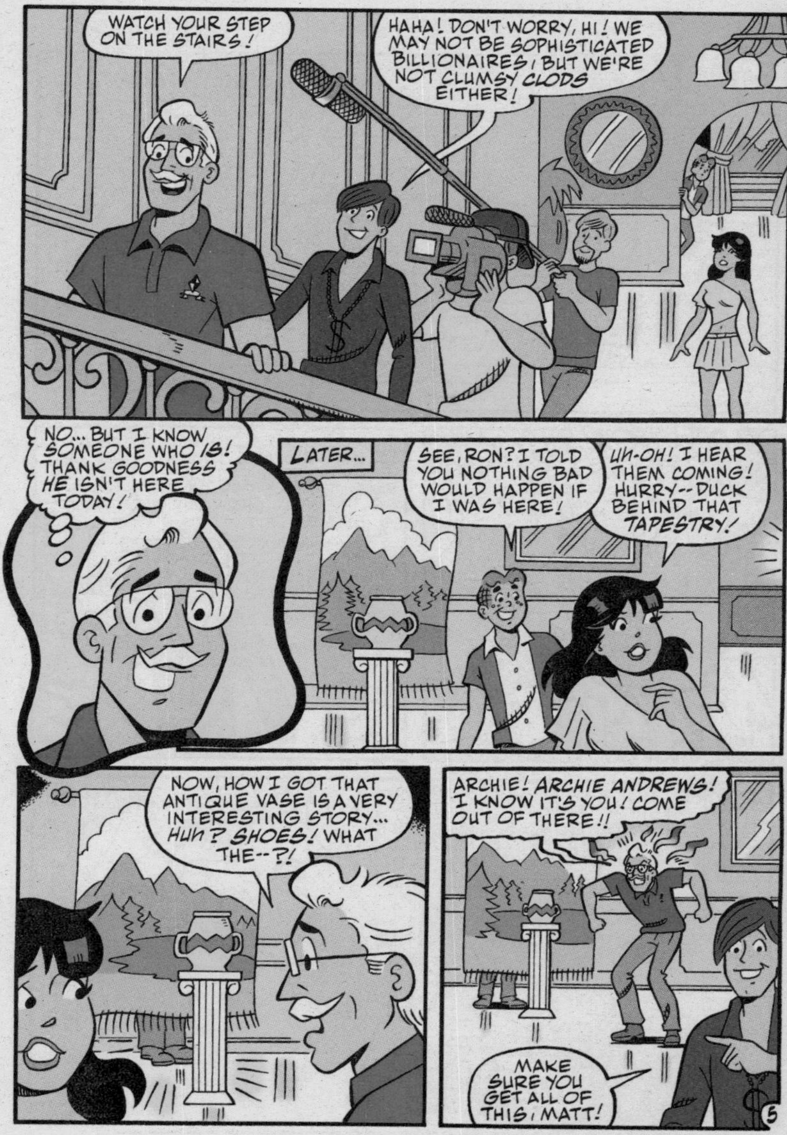
WATCH YOUR STEP ON THE STAIRS!
HAHA! DON'T WORRY, HI! WE MAY NOT BE SOPHISTICATED BILLIONAIRES, BUT WE'RE NOT CLUMSY CLODS EITHER!
NO... BUT I KNOW SOMEONE WHO IS! THANK GOODNESS HE ISN'T HERE TODAY!
LATER...
SEE, RON? I TOLD YOU NOTHING BAD WOULD HAPPEN IF I WAS HERE!
UH-OH! I HEAR THEM COMING! HURRY--DUCK BEHIND THAT TAPESTRY!
NOW, HOW I GOT THAT ANTIQUE VASE IS A VERY INTERESTING STORY... HUH? SHOES! WHAT THE--?!
ARCHIE! ARCHIE ANDREWS! I KNOW IT'S YOU! COME OUT OF THERE!!
MAKE SURE YOU GET ALL OF THIS, MATT!

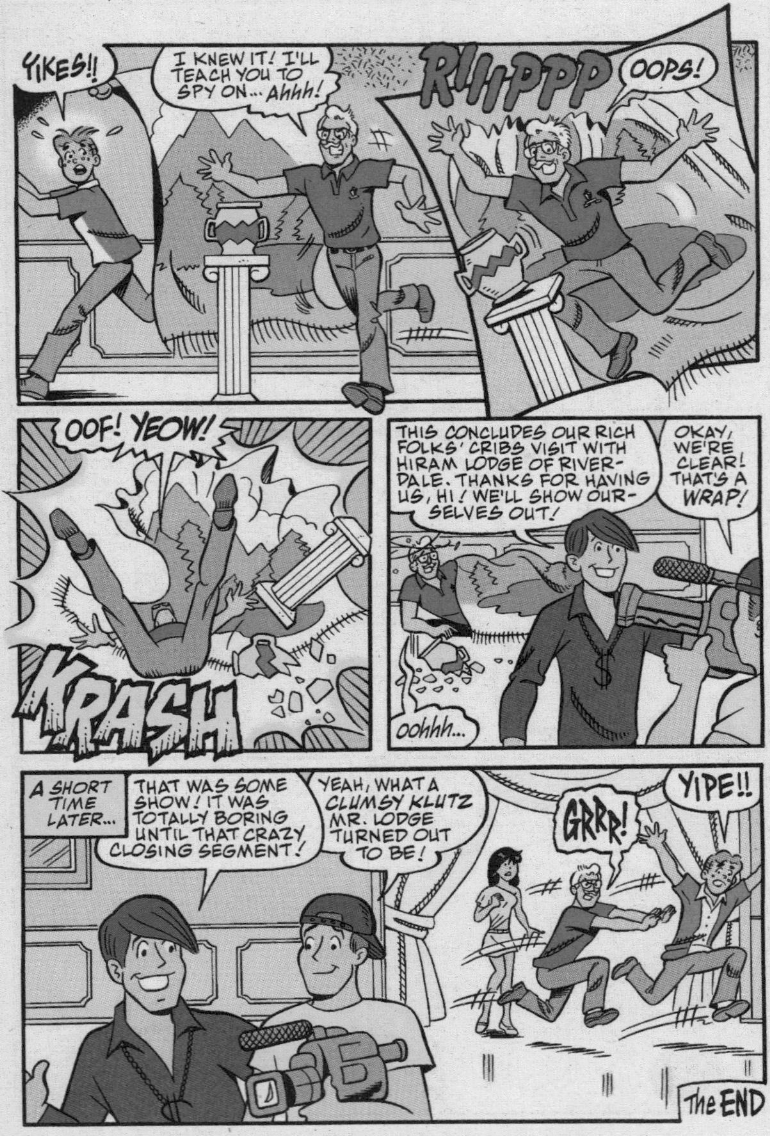
YIKES!!
I KNEW IT! I'LL TEACH YOU TO SPY ON... Ahhh!
RIIIPPPP
OOPS!
OOF! YEOW!
KRASH
THIS CONCLUDES OUR RICH FOLKS' CRIBS VISIT WITH HIRAM LODGE OF RIVER-DALE. THANKS FOR HAVING US, HI! WE'LL SHOW OUR-SELVES OUT!
OKAY, WE'RE CLEAR! THAT'S A WRAP!
oohhh...
A SHORT TIME LATER...
THAT WAS SOME SHOW! IT WAS TOTALLY BORING UNTIL THAT CRAZY CLOSING SEGMENT!
YEAH, WHAT A CLUMSY KLUTZ MR. LODGE TURNED OUT TO BE!
GRRR!
YIPE!!
The END

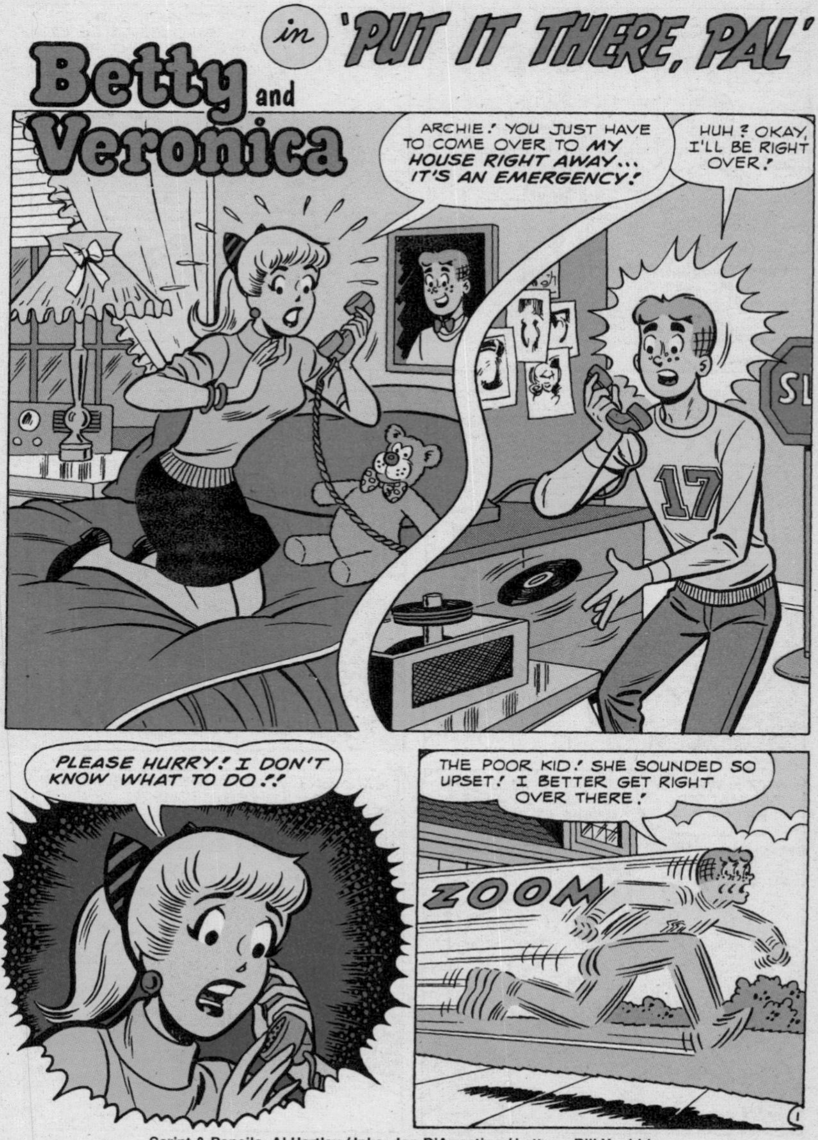
Betty and Veronica
in 'PUT IT THERE, PAL'
ARCHIE! YOU JUST HAVE TO COME OVER TO MY HOUSE RIGHT AWAY... IT'S AN EMERGENCY!
HUH? OKAY, I'LL BE RIGHT OVER!
17
PLEASE HURRY! I DON'T KNOW WHAT TO DO!!
THE POOR KID! SHE SOUNDED SO UPSET! I BETTER GET RIGHT OVER THERE!
ZOOM
1

Script & Pencils: Al Hartley / Inks: Jon D'Agostino / Letters: Bill Yoshida

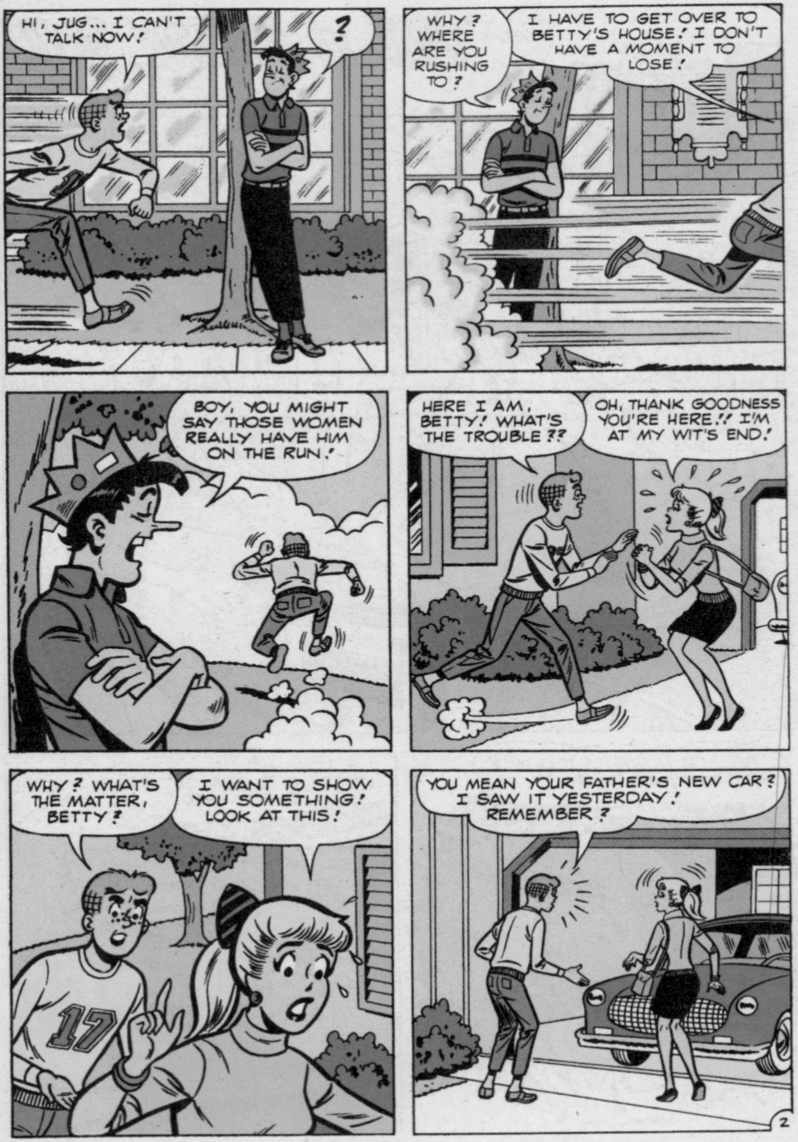
HI, JUG... I CAN'T TALK NOW!
?
WHY? WHERE ARE YOU RUSHING TO?
I HAVE TO GET OVER TO BETTY'S HOUSE! I DON'T HAVE A MOMENT TO LOSE!
BOY, YOU MIGHT SAY THOSE WOMEN REALLY HAVE HIM ON THE RUN!
HERE I AM, BETTY! WHAT'S THE TROUBLE??
OH, THANK GOODNESS YOU'RE HERE!! I'M AT MY WIT'S END!
WHY? WHAT'S THE MATTER, BETTY?
I WANT TO SHOW YOU SOMETHING! LOOK AT THIS!
YOU MEAN YOUR FATHER'S NEW CAR? I SAW IT YESTERDAY! REMEMBER?
17
2

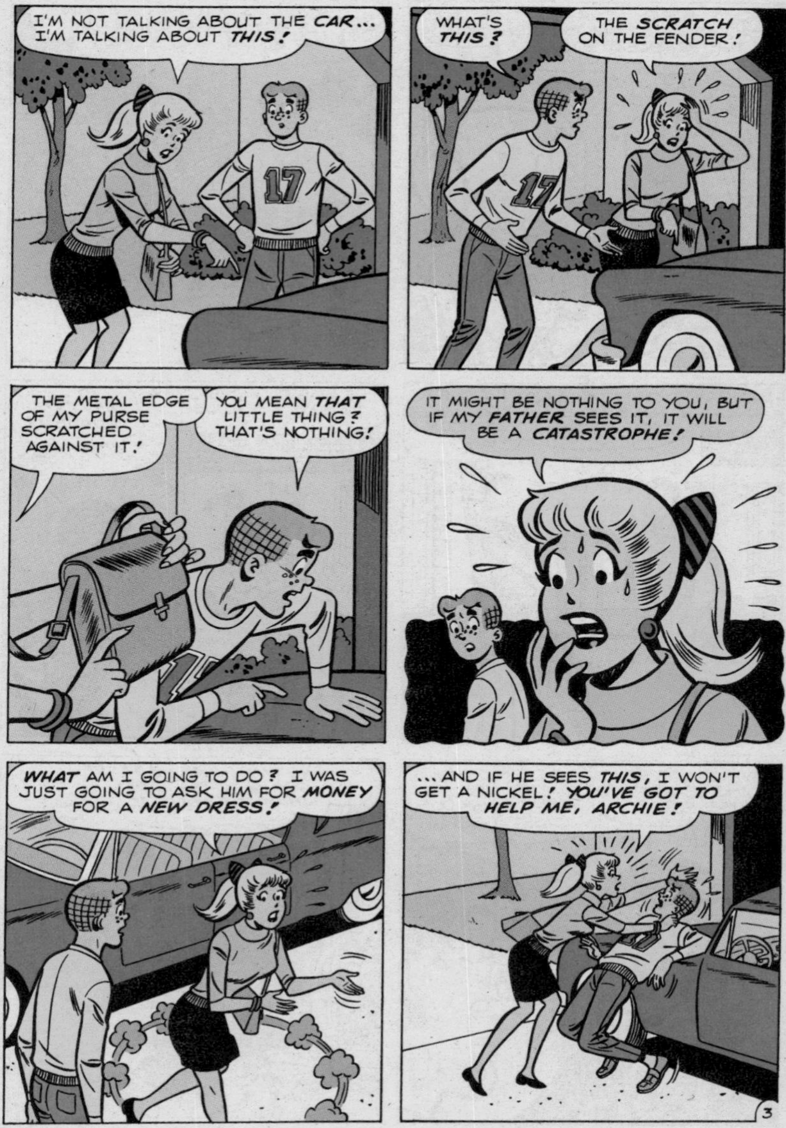
I'M NOT TALKING ABOUT THE CAR... I'M TALKING ABOUT THIS!
WHAT'S THIS?
THE SCRATCH ON THE FENDER!
THE METAL EDGE OF MY PURSE SCRATCHED AGAINST IT!
YOU MEAN THAT LITTLE THING? THAT'S NOTHING!
IT MIGHT BE NOTHING TO YOU, BUT IF MY FATHER SEES IT, IT WILL BE A CATASTROPHE!
WHAT AM I GOING TO DO? I WAS JUST GOING TO ASK HIM FOR MONEY FOR A NEW DRESS!
...AND IF HE SEES THIS, I WON'T GET A NICKEL! YOU'VE GOT TO HELP ME, ARCHIE!
3

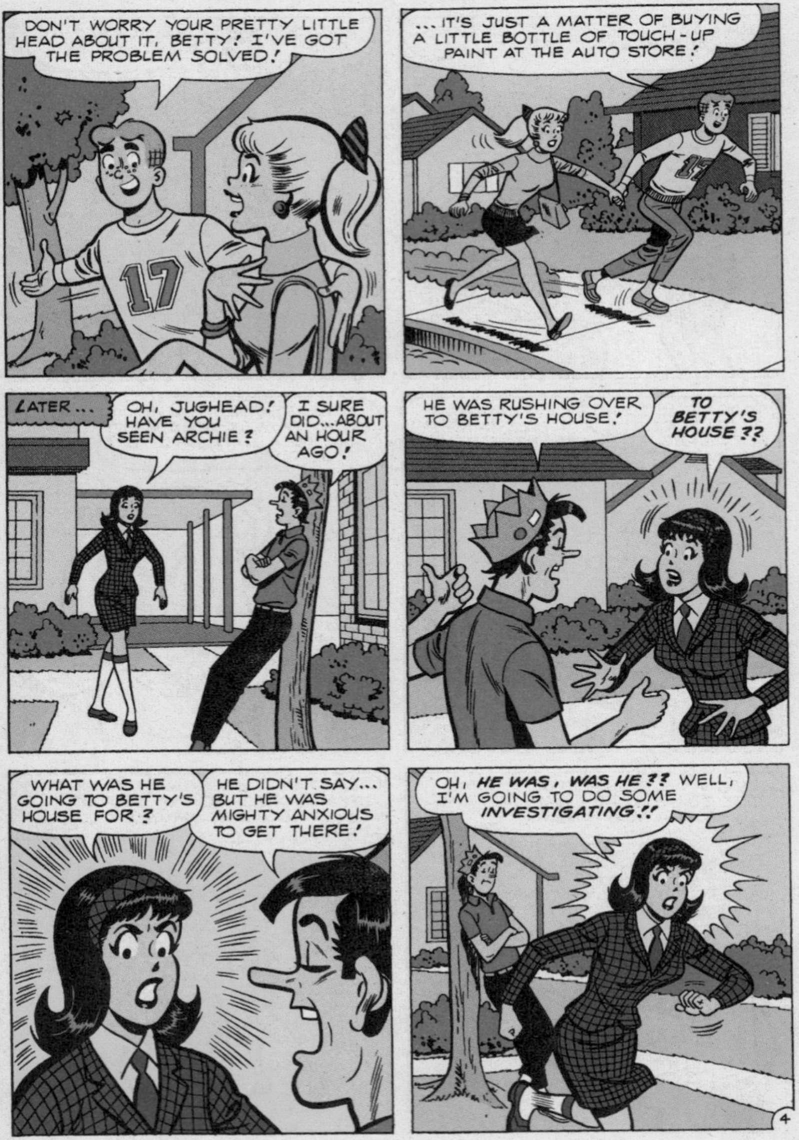
DON'T WORRY YOUR PRETTY LITTLE HEAD ABOUT IT, BETTY! I'VE GOT THE PROBLEM SOLVED!
... IT'S JUST A MATTER OF BUYING A LITTLE BOTTLE OF TOUCH-UP PAINT AT THE AUTO STORE!
LATER...
OH, JUGHEAD! HAVE YOU SEEN ARCHIE?
I SURE DID... ABOUT AN HOUR AGO!
HE WAS RUSHING OVER TO BETTY'S HOUSE!
TO BETTY'S HOUSE??
WHAT WAS HE GOING TO BETTY'S HOUSE FOR?
HE DIDN'T SAY... BUT HE WAS MIGHTY ANXIOUS TO GET THERE!
OH, HE WAS, WAS HE?? WELL, I'M GOING TO DO SOME INVESTIGATING!!
4

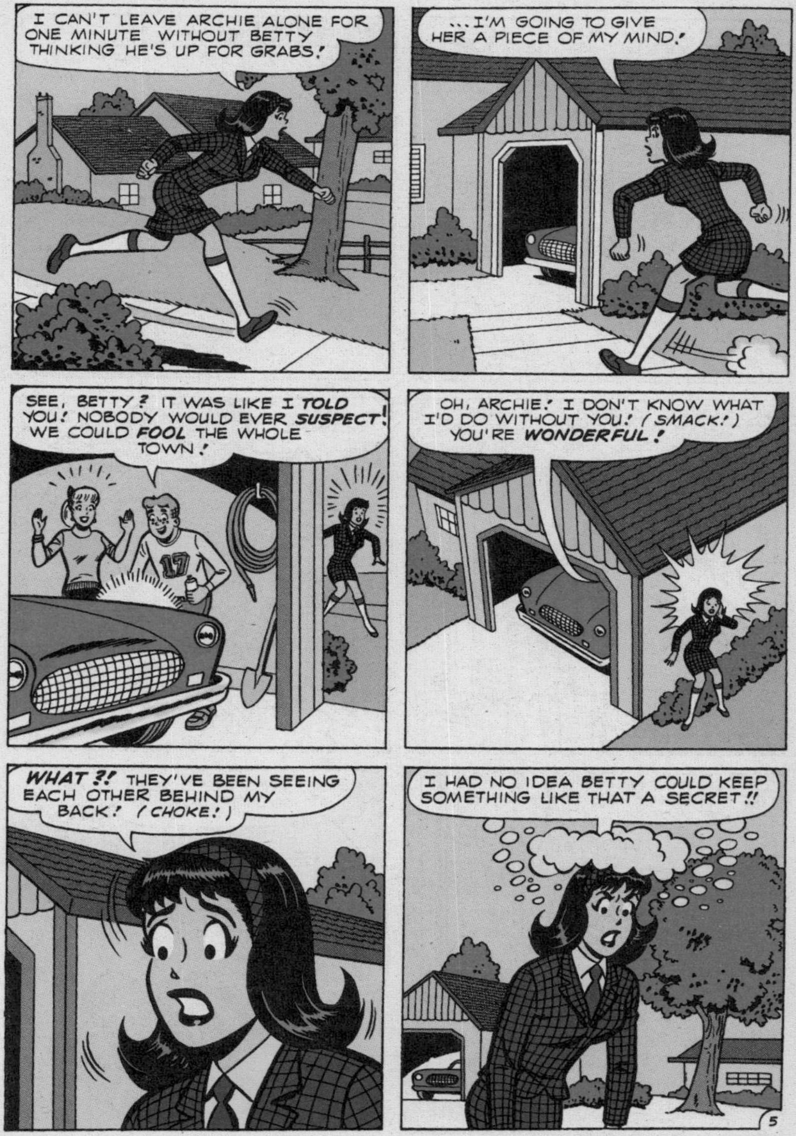
I CAN'T LEAVE ARCHIE ALONE FOR ONE MINUTE WITHOUT BETTY THINKING HE'S UP FOR GRABS!
...I'M GOING TO GIVE HER A PIECE OF MY MIND!
SEE, BETTY? IT WAS LIKE I TOLD YOU! NOBODY WOULD EVER SUSPECT! WE COULD FOOL THE WHOLE TOWN!
OH, ARCHIE! I DON'T KNOW WHAT I'D DO WITHOUT YOU! (SMACK!) YOU'RE WONDERFUL!
WHAT ?! THEY'VE BEEN SEEING EACH OTHER BEHIND MY BACK! (CHOKE!)
I HAD NO IDEA BETTY COULD KEEP SOMETHING LIKE THAT A SECRET!!
5

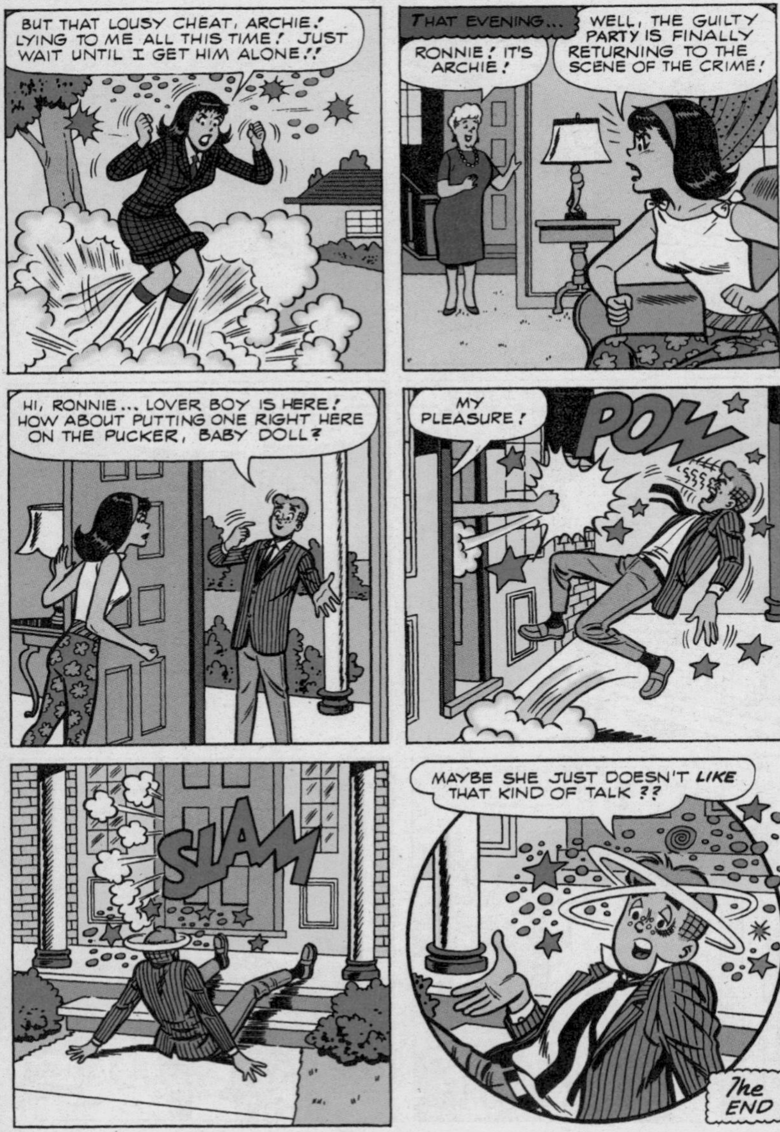

BUT THAT LOUSY CHEAT, ARCHIE! LYING TO ME ALL THIS TIME! JUST WAIT UNTIL I GET HIM ALONE!!
THAT EVENING...
RONNIE! IT'S ARCHIE!
WELL, THE GUILTY PARTY IS FINALLY RETURNING TO THE SCENE OF THE CRIME!
HI, RONNIE... LOVER BOY IS HERE! HOW ABOUT PUTTING ONE RIGHT HERE ON THE PUCKER, BABY DOLL?
MY PLEASURE!
POW
SLAM
MAYBE SHE JUST DOESN'T LIKE THAT KIND OF TALK ??
The END

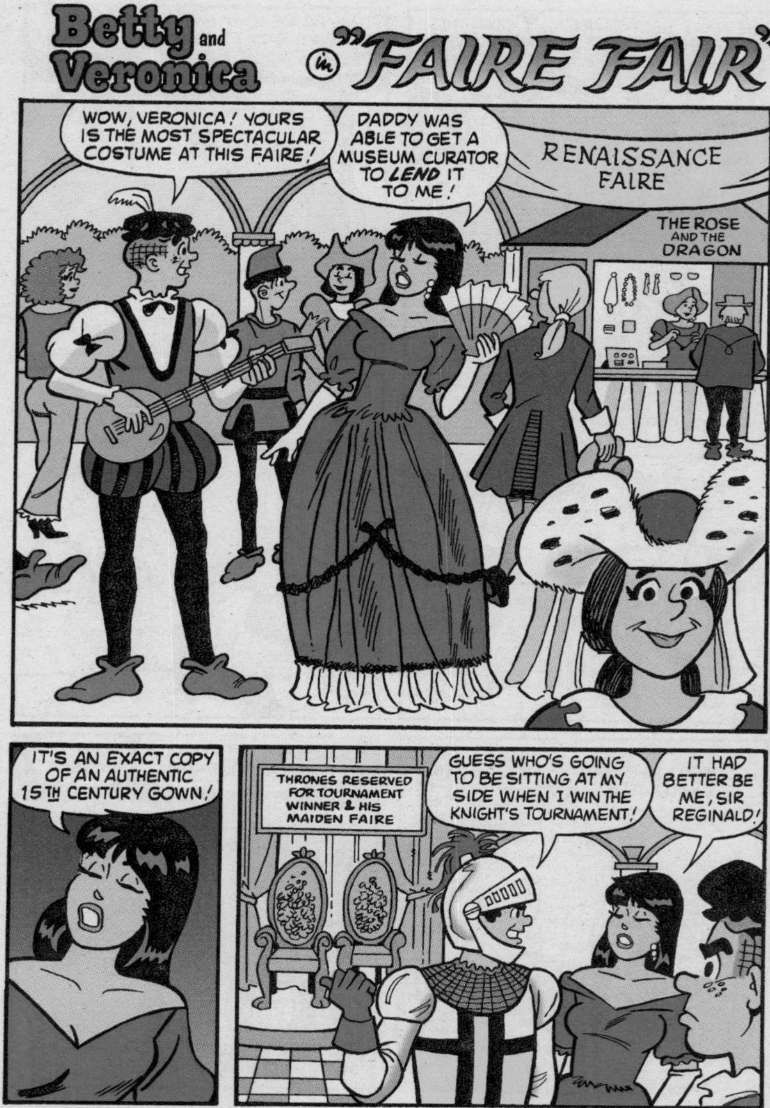
Betty and Veronica in "FAIRE FAIR"
WOW, VERONICA! YOURS IS THE MOST SPECTACULAR COSTUME AT THIS FAIRE!
DADDY WAS ABLE TO GET A MUSEUM CURATOR TO LEND IT TO ME!
RENAISSANCE FAIRE
THE ROSE AND THE DRAGON
IT'S AN EXACT COPY OF AN AUTHENTIC 15TH CENTURY GOWN!
THRONES RESERVED FOR TOURNAMENT WINNER & HIS MAIDEN FAIRE
GUESS WHO'S GOING TO BE SITTING AT MY SIDE WHEN I WIN THE KNIGHT'S TOURNAMENT!
IT HAD BETTER BE ME, SIR REGINALD!

Script: George Gladir / Pencils: Dan DeCarlo / Inks: Henry Scarpelli / Letters: Bill Yoshida

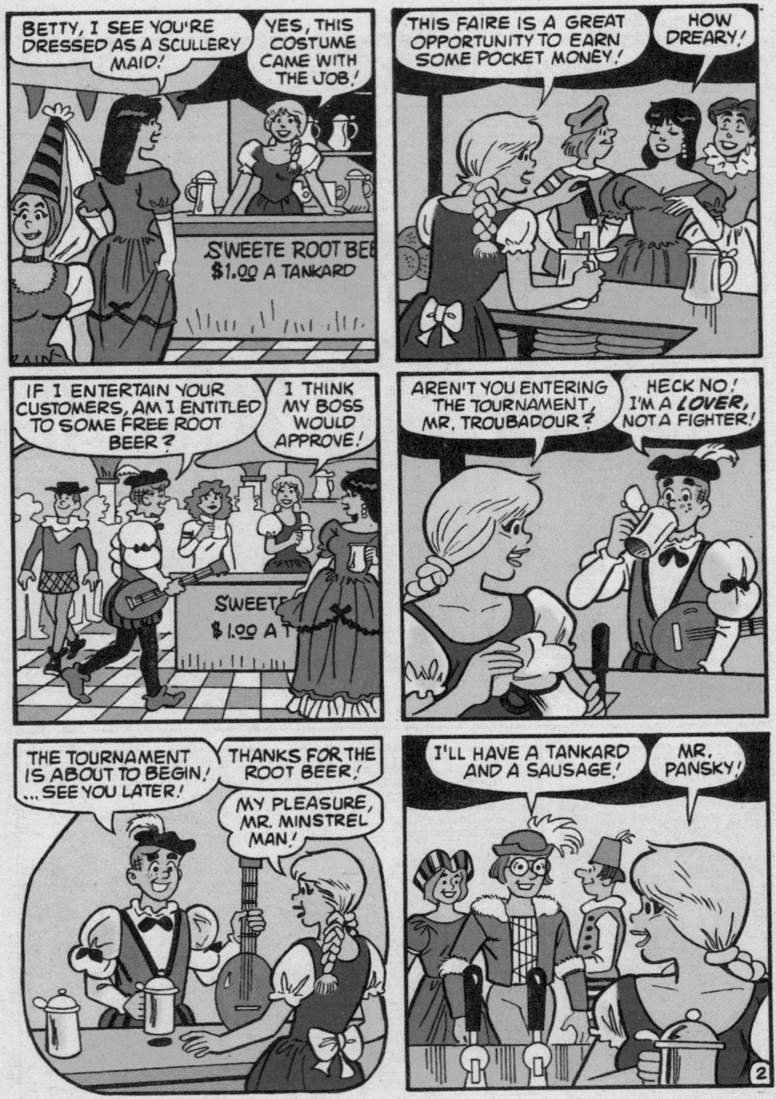
BETTY, I SEE YOU'RE DRESSED AS A SCULLERY MAID!
YES, THIS COSTUME CAME WITH THE JOB!
SWEETE ROOT BEE
$1.00 A TANKARD
THIS FAIRE IS A GREAT OPPORTUNITY TO EARN SOME POCKET MONEY!
HOW DREARY!
IF I ENTERTAIN YOUR CUSTOMERS, AM I ENTITLED TO SOME FREE ROOT BEER?
I THINK MY BOSS WOULD APPROVE!
SWEETE
$1.00 A T
AREN'T YOU ENTERING THE TOURNAMENT, MR. TROUBADOUR?
HECK NO! I'M A LOVER, NOT A FIGHTER!
THE TOURNAMENT IS ABOUT TO BEGIN! ...SEE YOU LATER!
THANKS FOR THE ROOT BEER!
MY PLEASURE, MR. MINSTREL MAN!
I'LL HAVE A TANKARD AND A SAUSAGE!
MR. PANSKY!
2

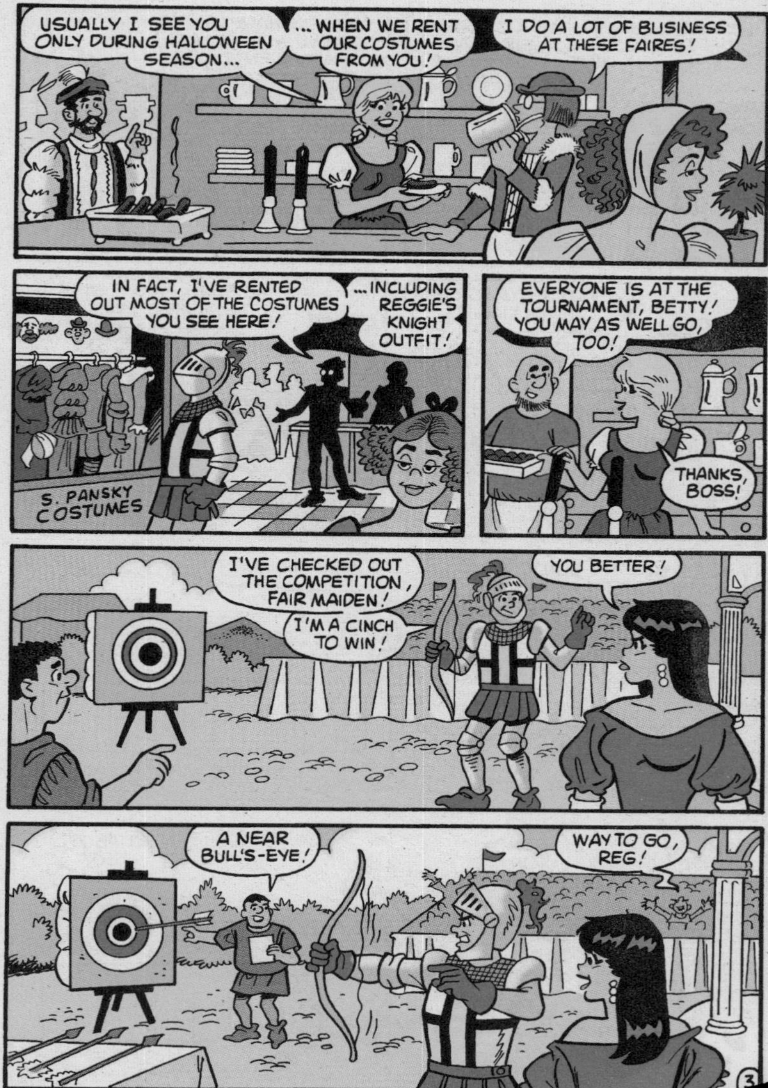
USUALLY I SEE YOU ONLY DURING HALLOWEEN SEASON...
...WHEN WE RENT OUR COSTUMES FROM YOU!
I DO A LOT OF BUSINESS AT THESE FAIRES!
IN FACT, I'VE RENTED OUT MOST OF THE COSTUMES YOU SEE HERE!
...INCLUDING REGGIE'S KNIGHT OUTFIT!
S. PANSKY COSTUMES
EVERYONE IS AT THE TOURNAMENT, BETTY! YOU MAY AS WELL GO, TOO!
THANKS, BOSS!
I'VE CHECKED OUT THE COMPETITION, FAIR MAIDEN!
I'M A CINCH TO WIN!
YOU BETTER!
A NEAR BULL'S-EYE!
WAY TO GO, REG!
3

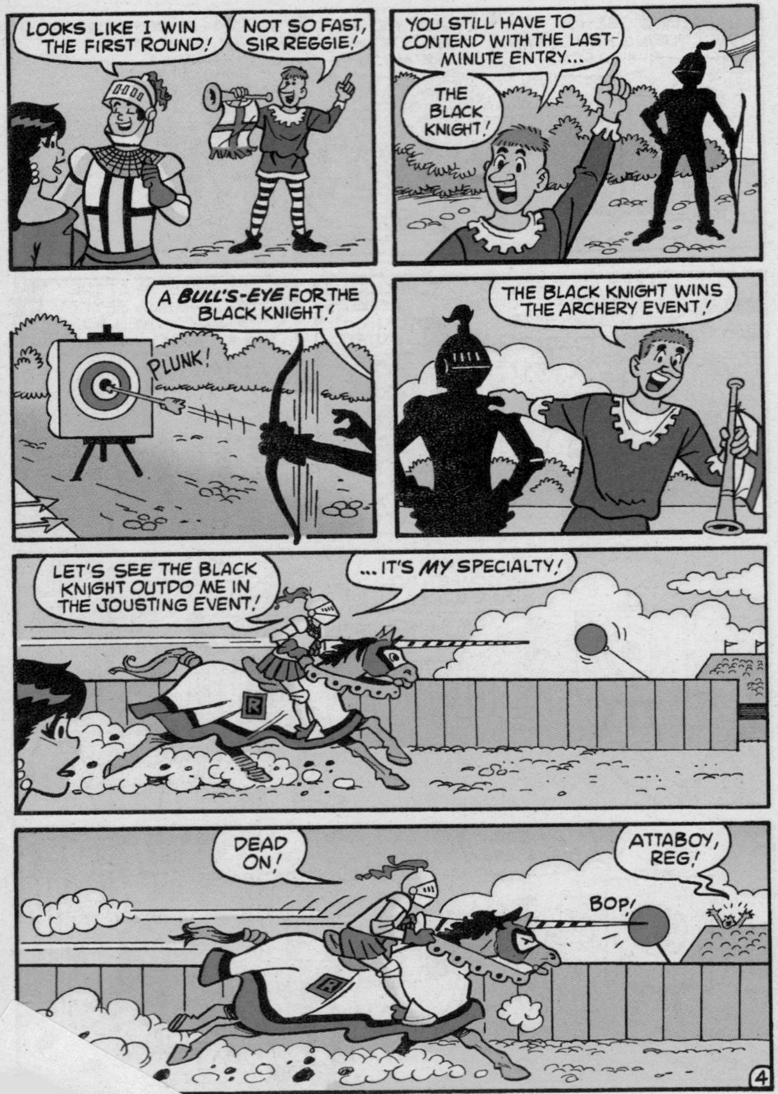
LOOKS LIKE I WIN THE FIRST ROUND!
NOT SO FAST, SIR REGGIE!
YOU STILL HAVE TO CONTEND WITH THE LAST-MINUTE ENTRY...
THE BLACK KNIGHT!
A BULL'S-EYE FOR THE BLACK KNIGHT!
PLUNK!
THE BLACK KNIGHT WINS THE ARCHERY EVENT!
LET'S SEE THE BLACK KNIGHT OUTDO ME IN THE JOUSTING EVENT!
...IT'S MY SPECIALTY!
R
DEAD ON!
ATTABOY, REG!
BOP!
R
4

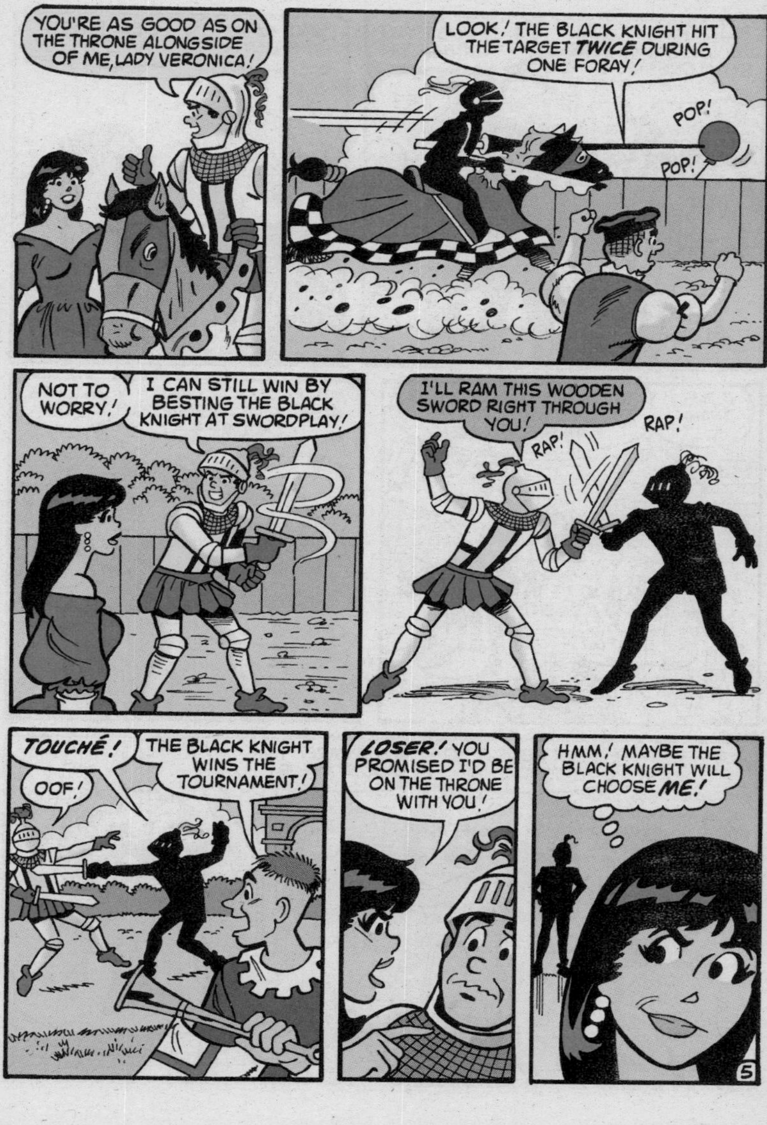
YOU'RE AS GOOD AS ON THE THRONE ALONGSIDE OF ME, LADY VERONICA!
LOOK! THE BLACK KNIGHT HIT THE TARGET TWICE DURING ONE FORAY!
POP!
POP!
NOT TO WORRY!
I CAN STILL WIN BY BESTING THE BLACK KNIGHT AT SWORDPLAY!
I'LL RAM THIS WOODEN SWORD RIGHT THROUGH YOU!
RAP!
RAP!
TOUCHÉ!
OOF!
THE BLACK KNIGHT WINS THE TOURNAMENT!
LOSER! YOU PROMISED I'D BE ON THE THRONE WITH YOU!
HMM! MAYBE THE BLACK KNIGHT WILL CHOOSE ME!
5

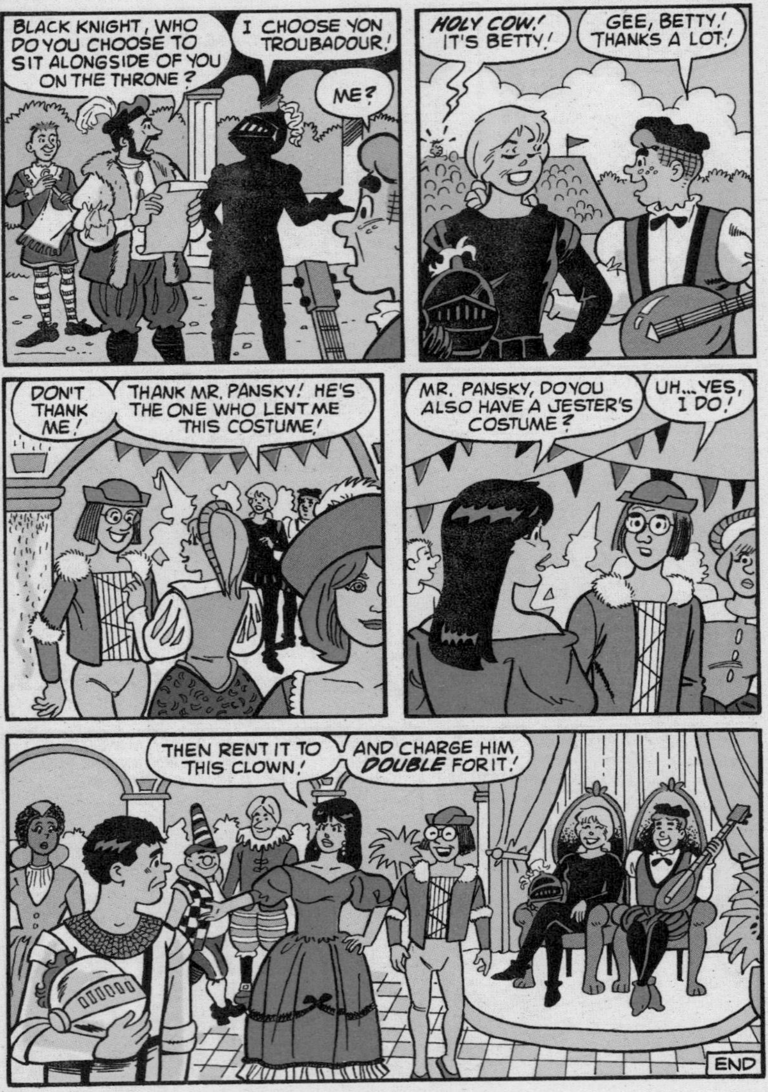
BLACK KNIGHT, WHO DO YOU CHOOSE TO SIT ALONGSIDE OF YOU ON THE THRONE?
I CHOOSE YON TROUBADOUR!
ME?
HOLY COW! IT'S BETTY!
GEE, BETTY! THANKS A LOT!
DON'T THANK ME!
THANK MR. PANSKY! HE'S THE ONE WHO LENT ME THIS COSTUME!
MR. PANSKY, DO YOU ALSO HAVE A JESTER'S COSTUME?
UH... YES, I DO!
THEN RENT IT TO THIS CLOWN!
AND CHARGE HIM DOUBLE FOR IT!
END

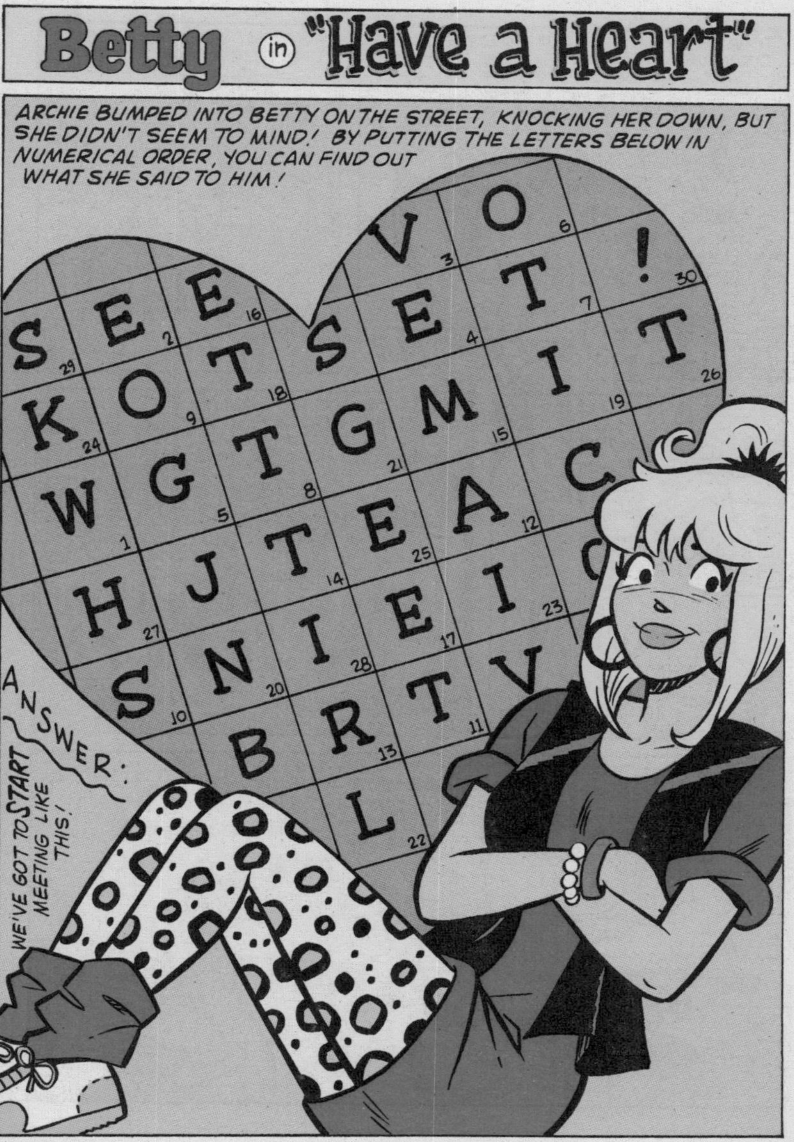

Betty in "Have a Heart"
ARCHIE BUMPED INTO BETTY ON THE STREET, KNOCKING HER DOWN, BUT SHE DIDN'T SEEM TO MIND! BY PUTTING THE LETTERS BELOW IN NUMERICAL ORDER, YOU CAN FIND OUT WHAT SHE SAID TO HIM!
ANSWER:
WE'VE GOT TO START MEETING LIKE THIS!

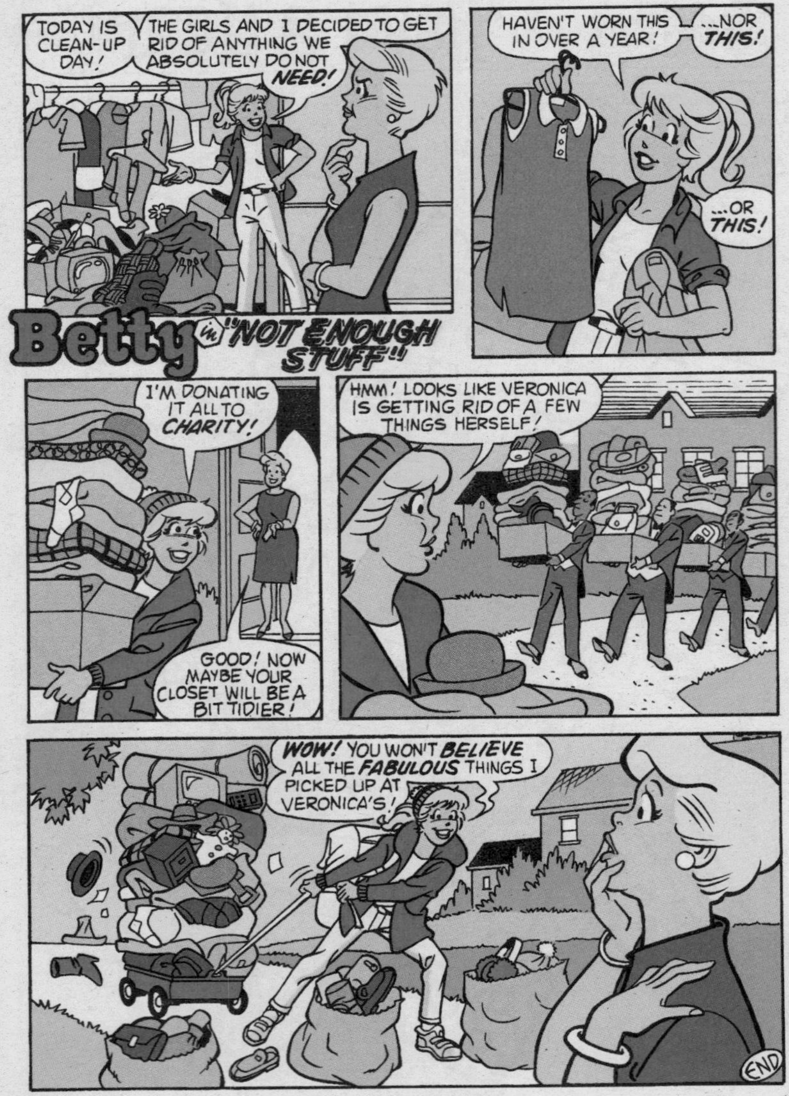
TODAY IS CLEAN-UP DAY!
THE GIRLS AND I DECIDED TO GET RID OF ANYTHING WE ABSOLUTELY DO NOT NEED!
HAVEN'T WORN THIS IN OVER A YEAR!
...NOR THIS!
...OR THIS!
Betty in "NOT ENOUGH STUFF!"
I'M DONATING IT ALL TO CHARITY!
GOOD! NOW MAYBE YOUR CLOSET WILL BE A BIT TIDIER!
HMM! LOOKS LIKE VERONICA IS GETTING RID OF A FEW THINGS HERSELF!
WOW! YOU WON'T BELIEVE ALL THE FABULOUS THINGS I PICKED UP AT VERONICA'S!
END

Archie MEDIUM RARE
PART I
AH, YES! YES! I FEEL IT SO STRONGLY! EMANATIONS FROM THE SPIRIT WORLD-- POWERFUL--- DEMANDING!-- IS IT YOU, AGATHA? ARE YOU READY TO COME OVER?
WHO'S AGATHA?
SSSH!
Doyle
Goldberg
Lapick
Yoshida

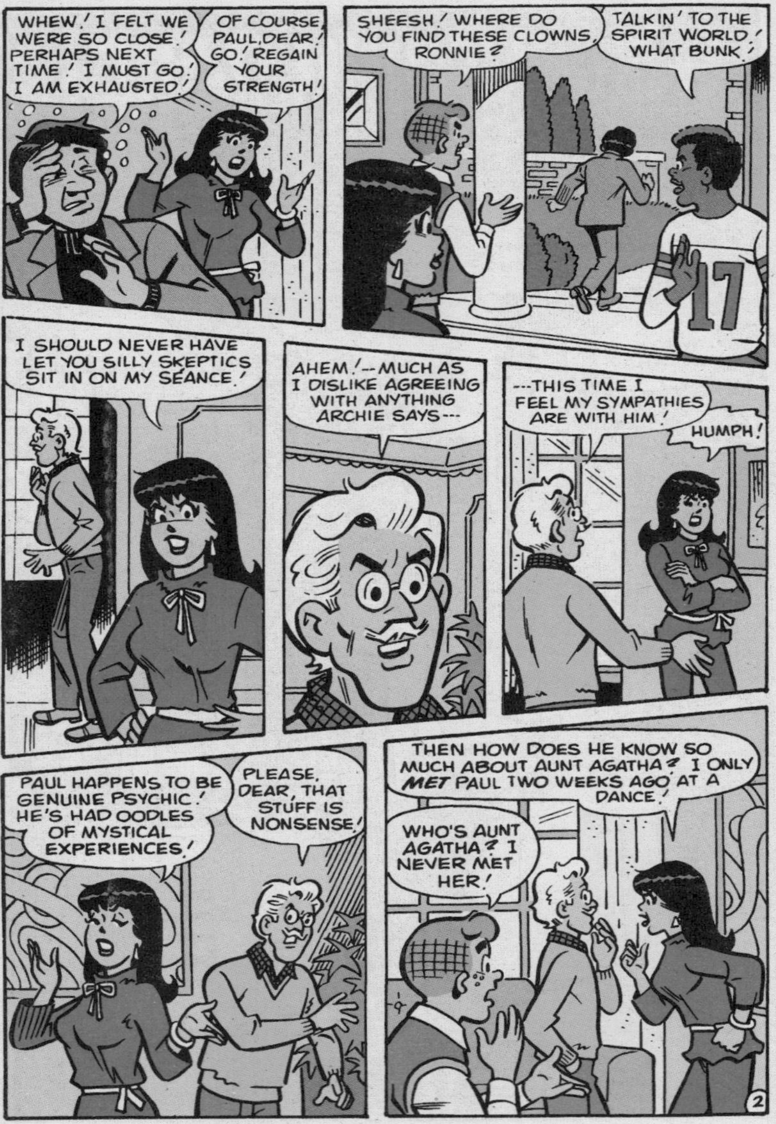

WHEW! I FELT WE WERE SO CLOSE! PERHAPS NEXT TIME! I MUST GO! I AM EXHAUSTED!
OF COURSE PAUL, DEAR! GO! REGAIN YOUR STRENGTH!
SHEESH! WHERE DO YOU FIND THESE CLOWNS, RONNIE?
TALKIN' TO THE SPIRIT WORLD! WHAT BUNK!
17
I SHOULD NEVER HAVE LET YOU SILLY SKEPTICS SIT IN ON MY SÉANCE!
AHEM!--MUCH AS I DISLIKE AGREEING WITH ANYTHING ARCHIE SAYS---
---THIS TIME I FEEL MY SYMPATHIES ARE WITH HIM!
HUMPH!
PAUL HAPPENS TO BE GENUINE PSYCHIC! HE'S HAD OODLES OF MYSTICAL EXPERIENCES!
PLEASE, DEAR, THAT STUFF IS NONSENSE!
THEN HOW DOES HE KNOW SO MUCH ABOUT AUNT AGATHA? I ONLY MET PAUL TWO WEEKS AGO AT A DANCE!
WHO'S AUNT AGATHA? I NEVER MET HER!
2

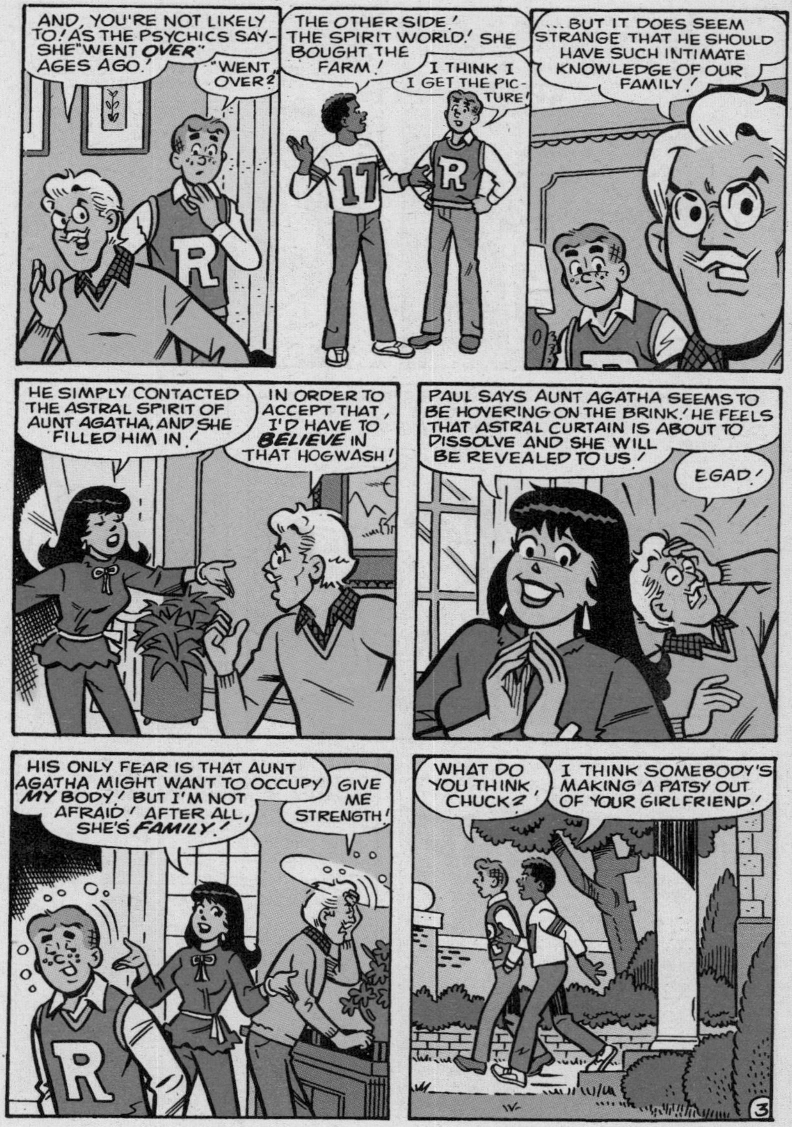
AND, YOU'RE NOT LIKELY TO! AS THE PSYCHICS SAY- SHE "WENT OVER" AGES AGO!
"WENT OVER?"
THE OTHER SIDE! THE SPIRIT WORLD! SHE BOUGHT THE FARM!
I THINK I I GET THE PICTURE!
...BUT IT DOES SEEM STRANGE THAT HE SHOULD HAVE SUCH INTIMATE KNOWLEDGE OF OUR FAMILY!
HE SIMPLY CONTACTED THE ASTRAL SPIRIT OF AUNT AGATHA, AND SHE FILLED HIM IN!
IN ORDER TO ACCEPT THAT, I'D HAVE TO BELIEVE IN THAT HOGWASH!
PAUL SAYS AUNT AGATHA SEEMS TO BE HOVERING ON THE BRINK! HE FEELS THAT ASTRAL CURTAIN IS ABOUT TO DISSOLVE AND SHE WILL BE REVEALED TO US!
EGAD!
HIS ONLY FEAR IS THAT AUNT AGATHA MIGHT WANT TO OCCUPY MY BODY! BUT I'M NOT AFRAID! AFTER ALL, SHE'S FAMILY!
GIVE ME STRENGTH!
WHAT DO YOU THINK, CHUCK?
I THINK SOMEBODY'S MAKING A PATSY OUT OF YOUR GIRLFRIEND!
3

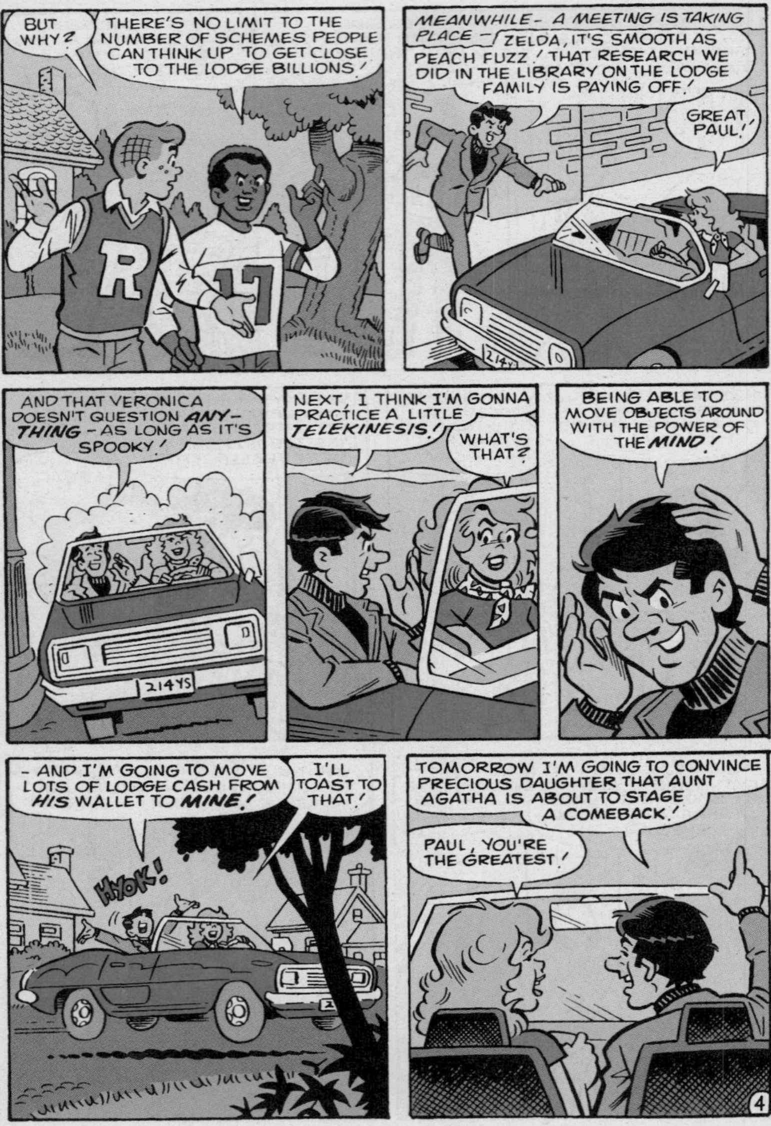
BUT WHY?
THERE'S NO LIMIT TO THE NUMBER OF SCHEMES PEOPLE CAN THINK UP TO GET CLOSE TO THE LODGE BILLIONS!
MEANWHILE - A MEETING IS TAKING PLACE -
ZELDA, IT'S SMOOTH AS PEACH FUZZ! THAT RESEARCH WE DID IN THE LIBRARY ON THE LODGE FAMILY IS PAYING OFF!
GREAT, PAUL!
AND THAT VERONICA DOESN'T QUESTION ANY-THING - AS LONG AS IT'S SPOOKY!
214YS
NEXT, I THINK I'M GONNA PRACTICE A LITTLE TELEKINESIS!
WHAT'S THAT?
BEING ABLE TO MOVE OBJECTS AROUND WITH THE POWER OF THE MIND!
- AND I'M GOING TO MOVE LOTS OF LODGE CASH FROM HIS WALLET TO MINE!
I'LL TOAST TO THAT!
HYOK!
TOMORROW I'M GOING TO CONVINCE PRECIOUS DAUGHTER THAT AUNT AGATHA IS ABOUT TO STAGE A COMEBACK!
PAUL, YOU'RE THE GREATEST!

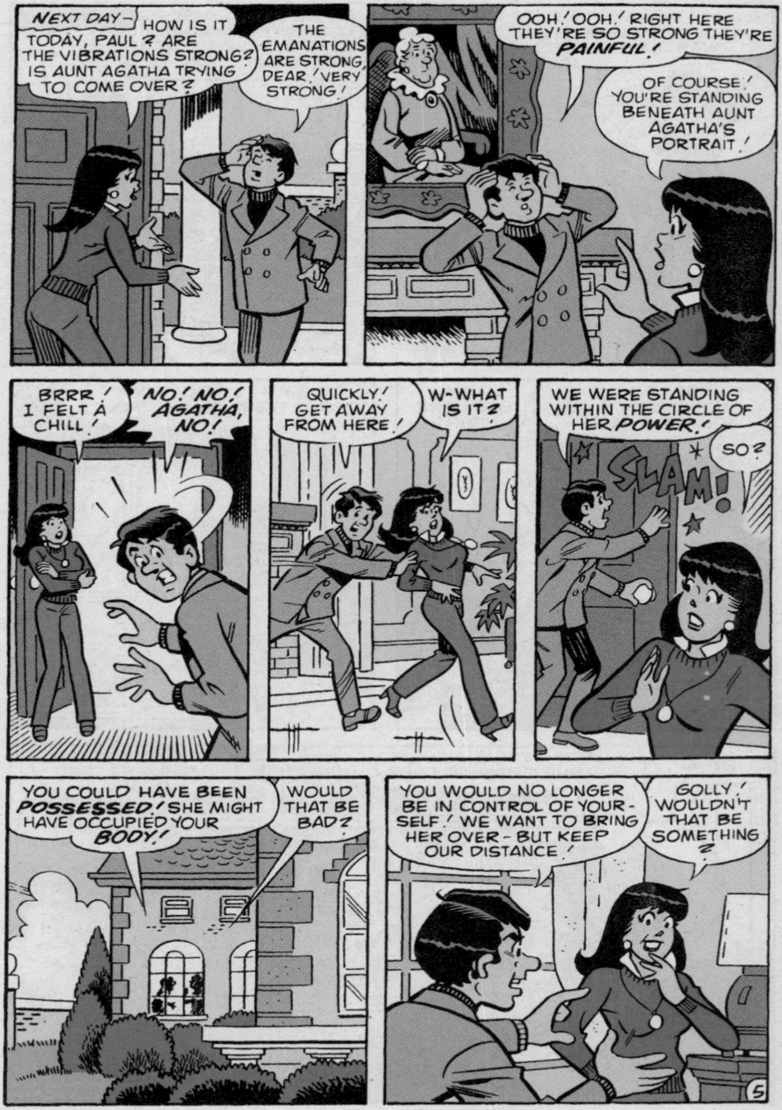
NEXT DAY–
HOW IS IT TODAY, PAUL? ARE THE VIBRATIONS STRONG? IS AUNT AGATHA TRYING TO COME OVER?
THE EMANATIONS ARE STRONG, DEAR! VERY STRONG!
OOH! OOH! RIGHT HERE THEY'RE SO STRONG THEY'RE PAINFUL!
OF COURSE! YOU'RE STANDING BENEATH AUNT AGATHA'S PORTRAIT!
BRRR! I FELT A CHILL!
NO! NO! AGATHA, NO!
QUICKLY! GET AWAY FROM HERE!
W-WHAT IS IT?
WE WERE STANDING WITHIN THE CIRCLE OF HER POWER!
SO?
SLAM!
YOU COULD HAVE BEEN POSSESSED! SHE MIGHT HAVE OCCUPIED YOUR BODY!
WOULD THAT BE BAD?
YOU WOULD NO LONGER BE IN CONTROL OF YOURSELF! WE WANT TO BRING HER OVER – BUT KEEP OUR DISTANCE!
GOLLY! WOULDN'T THAT BE SOMETHING?
5

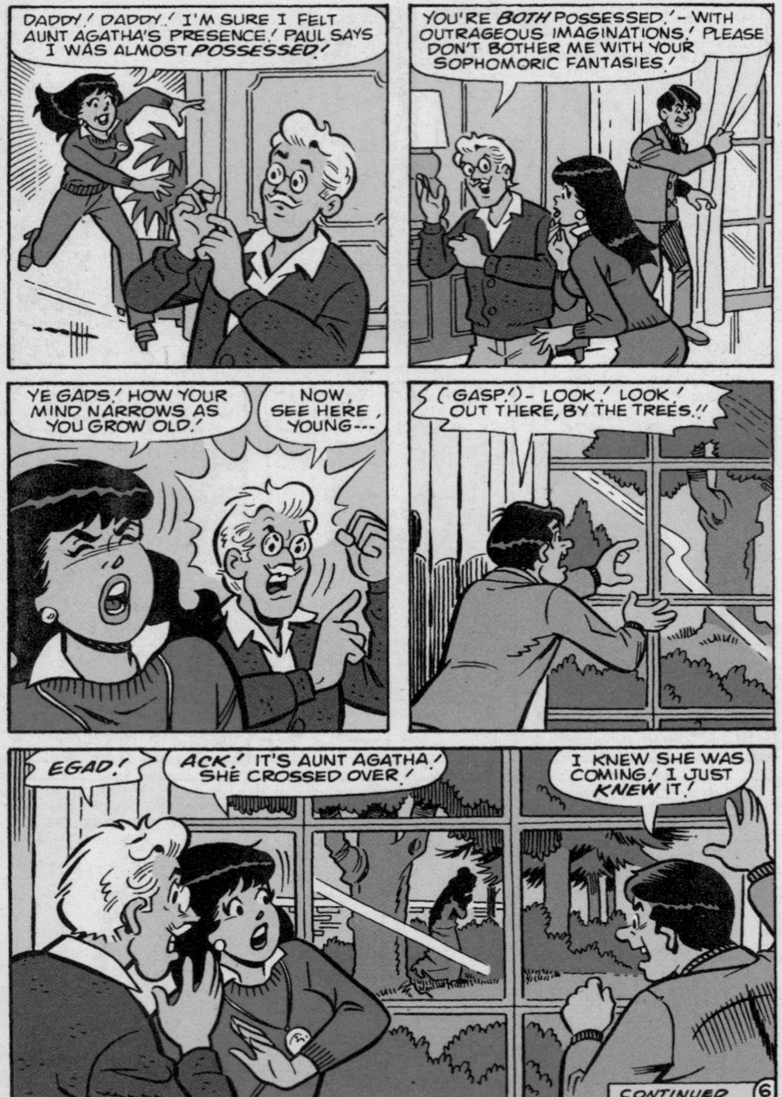
DADDY! DADDY! I'M SURE I FELT AUNT AGATHA'S PRESENCE! PAUL SAYS I WAS ALMOST POSSESSED!
YOU'RE BOTH POSSESSED! - WITH OUTRAGEOUS IMAGINATIONS! PLEASE DON'T BOTHER ME WITH YOUR SOPHOMORIC FANTASIES!
YE GADS! HOW YOUR MIND NARROWS AS YOU GROW OLD!
NOW, SEE HERE, YOUNG---
(GASP!) - LOOK! LOOK! OUT THERE, BY THE TREES!!
EGAD!
ACK! IT'S AUNT AGATHA! SHE CROSSED OVER!
I KNEW SHE WAS COMING! I JUST KNEW IT!
CONTINUED
6

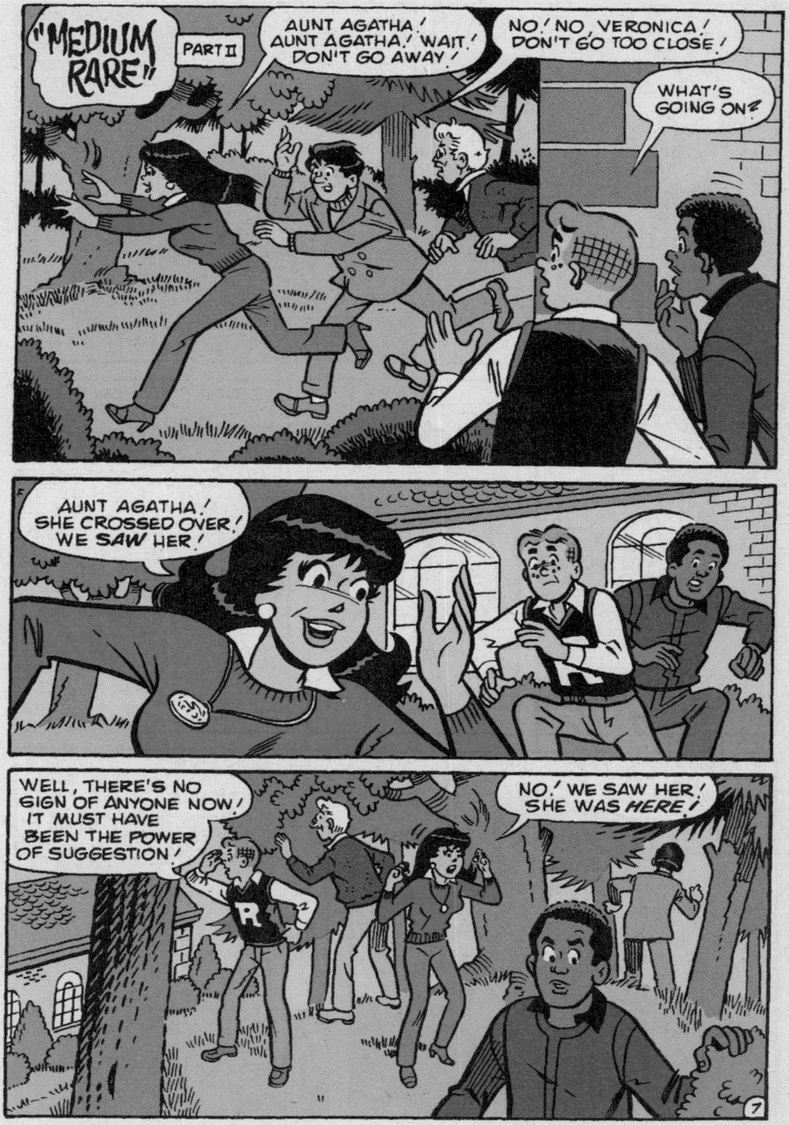
"MEDIUM RARE"
PART II
AUNT AGATHA! AUNT AGATHA! WAIT! DON'T GO AWAY!
NO! NO, VERONICA! DON'T GO TOO CLOSE!
WHAT'S GOING ON?
AUNT AGATHA! SHE CROSSED OVER! WE SAW HER!
WELL, THERE'S NO SIGN OF ANYONE NOW! IT MUST HAVE BEEN THE POWER OF SUGGESTION!
NO! WE SAW HER! SHE WAS HERE!
7

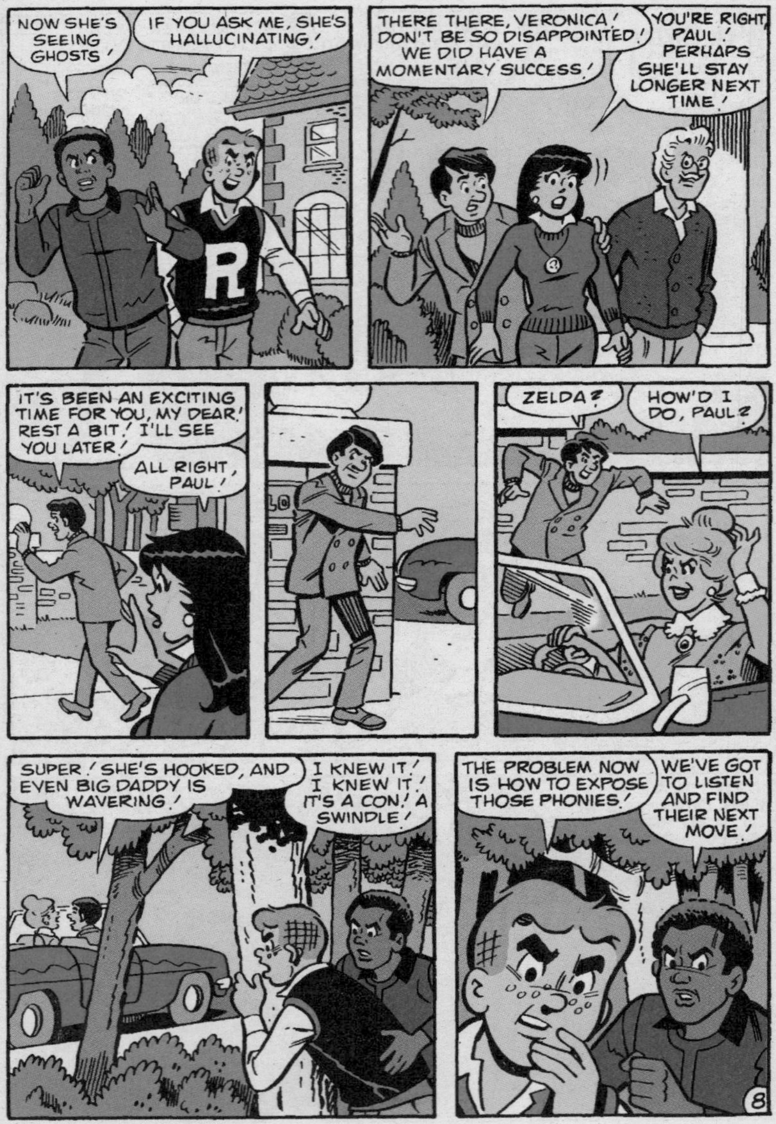
NOW SHE'S SEEING GHOSTS!
IF YOU ASK ME, SHE'S HALLUCINATING!
THERE THERE, VERONICA! DON'T BE SO DISAPPOINTED! WE DID HAVE A MOMENTARY SUCCESS!
YOU'RE RIGHT, PAUL! PERHAPS SHE'LL STAY LONGER NEXT TIME!
IT'S BEEN AN EXCITING TIME FOR YOU, MY DEAR! REST A BIT! I'LL SEE YOU LATER!
ALL RIGHT, PAUL!
ZELDA?
HOW'D I DO, PAUL?
SUPER! SHE'S HOOKED, AND EVEN BIG DADDY IS WAVERING!
I KNEW IT! I KNEW IT! IT'S A CON! A SWINDLE!
THE PROBLEM NOW IS HOW TO EXPOSE THOSE PHONIES!
WE'VE GOT TO LISTEN AND FIND THEIR NEXT MOVE!
8

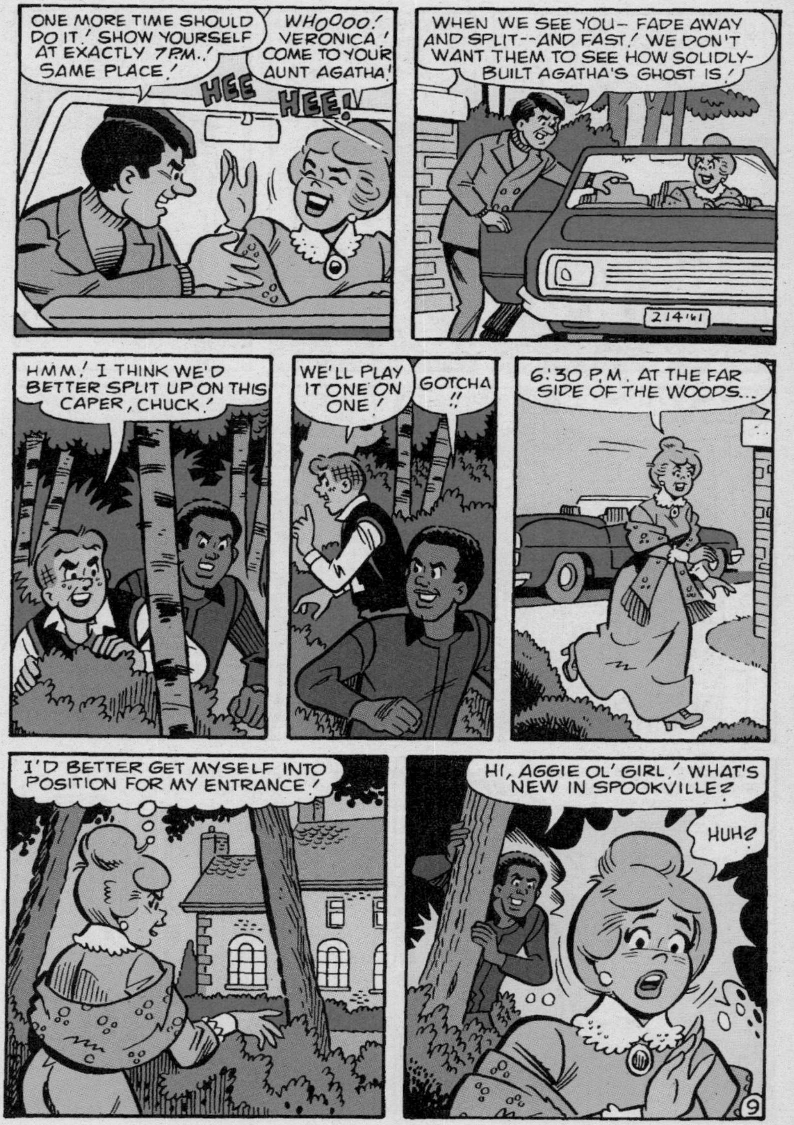
ONE MORE TIME SHOULD DO IT! SHOW YOURSELF AT EXACTLY 7P.M.! SAME PLACE!
WHOOOOO! VERONICA! COME TO YOUR AUNT AGATHA!
HEE
HEE!
WHEN WE SEE YOU– FADE AWAY AND SPLIT--AND FAST! WE DON'T WANT THEM TO SEE HOW SOLIDLY-BUILT AGATHA'S GHOST IS!
HMM! I THINK WE'D BETTER SPLIT UP ON THIS CAPER, CHUCK!
WE'LL PLAY IT ONE ON ONE!
GOTCHA!!
6:30 P.M. AT THE FAR SIDE OF THE WOODS...
I'D BETTER GET MYSELF INTO POSITION FOR MY ENTRANCE!
HI, AGGIE OL' GIRL! WHAT'S NEW IN SPOOKVILLE?
HUH?

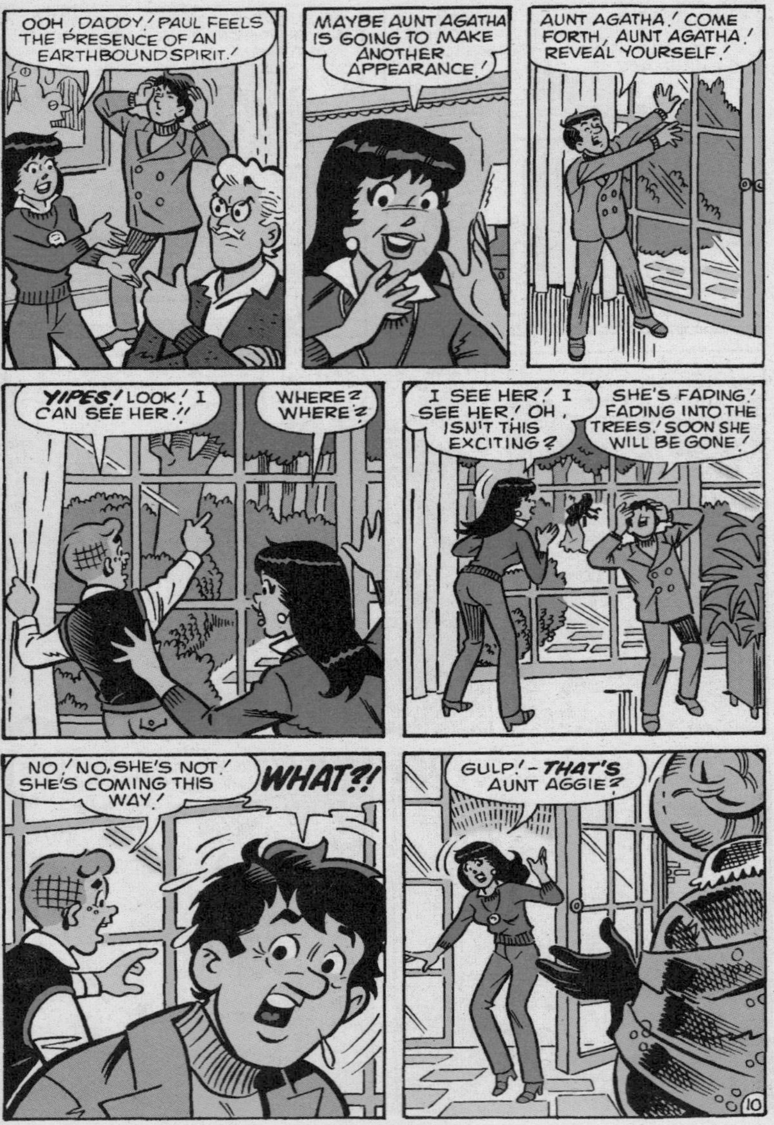
OOH, DADDY! PAUL FEELS THE PRESENCE OF AN EARTHBOUND SPIRIT!
MAYBE AUNT AGATHA IS GOING TO MAKE ANOTHER APPEARANCE!
AUNT AGATHA! COME FORTH, AUNT AGATHA! REVEAL YOURSELF!
YIPES! LOOK! I CAN SEE HER!!
WHERE? WHERE?
I SEE HER! I SEE HER! OH, ISN'T THIS EXCITING?
SHE'S FADING! FADING INTO THE TREES! SOON SHE WILL BE GONE!
NO! NO, SHE'S NOT! SHE'S COMING THIS WAY!
WHAT?!
GULP! - THAT'S AUNT AGGIE?
10

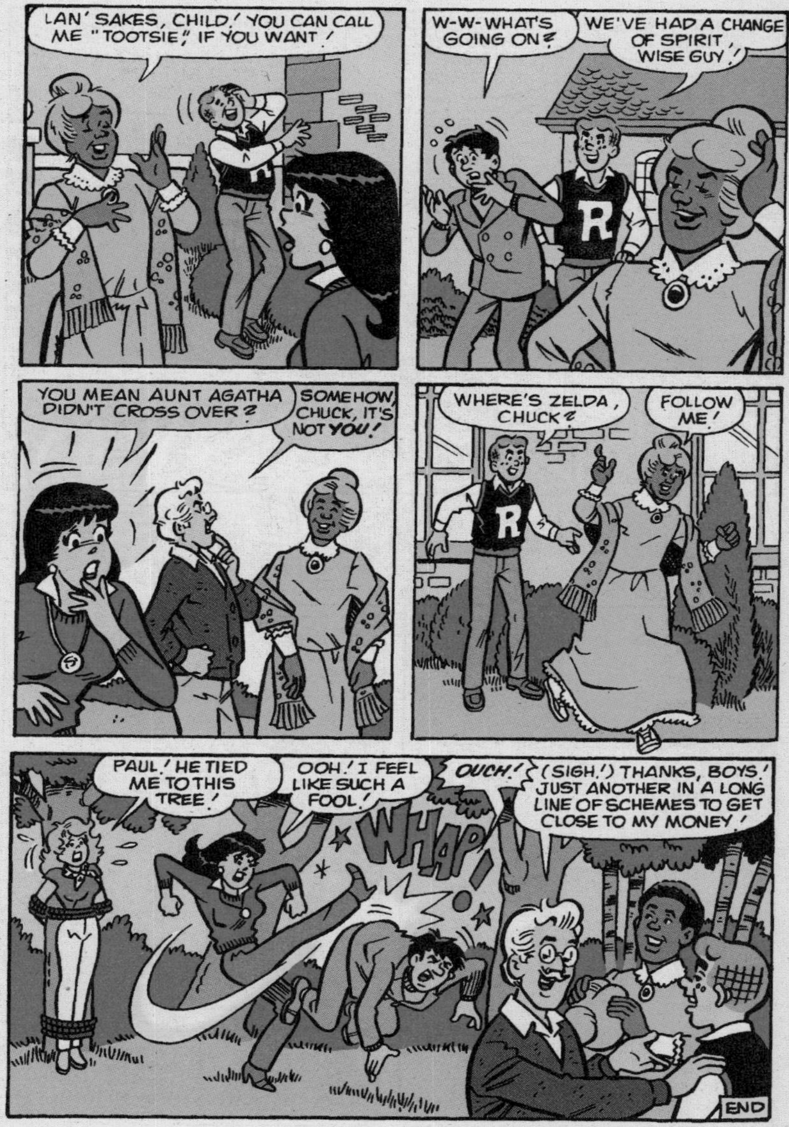
LAN' SAKES, CHILD! YOU CAN CALL ME "TOOTSIE," IF YOU WANT!
W-W-WHAT'S GOING ON?
WE'VE HAD A CHANGE OF SPIRIT, WISE GUY!
YOU MEAN AUNT AGATHA DIDN'T CROSS OVER?
SOMEHOW, CHUCK, IT'S NOT YOU!
WHERE'S ZELDA, CHUCK?
FOLLOW ME!
PAUL! HE TIED ME TO THIS TREE!
OOH! I FEEL LIKE SUCH A FOOL!
WHAP!
OUCH!
(SIGH!) THANKS, BOYS! JUST ANOTHER IN A LONG LINE OF SCHEMES TO GET CLOSE TO MY MONEY!
END

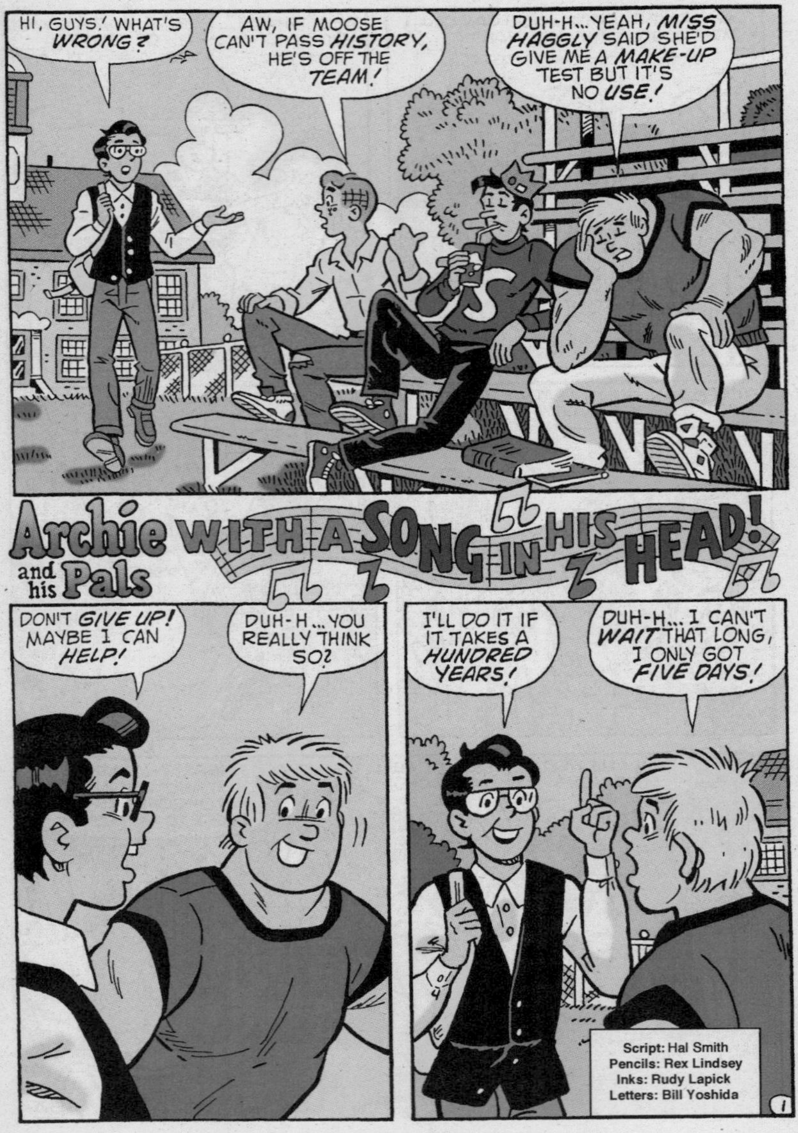
HI, GUYS! WHAT'S WRONG?
AW, IF MOOSE CAN'T PASS HISTORY, HE'S OFF THE TEAM!
DUH-H...YEAH, MISS HAGGLY SAID SHE'D GIVE ME A MAKE-UP TEST BUT IT'S NO USE!
Archie and his Pals
WITH A SONG IN HIS HEAD!
DON'T GIVE UP! MAYBE I CAN HELP!
DUH-H...YOU REALLY THINK SO?
I'LL DO IT IF IT TAKES A HUNDRED YEARS!
DUH-H... I CAN'T WAIT THAT LONG, I ONLY GOT FIVE DAYS!
Script: Hal Smith
Pencils: Rex Lindsey
Inks: Rudy Lapick
Letters: Bill Yoshida
1

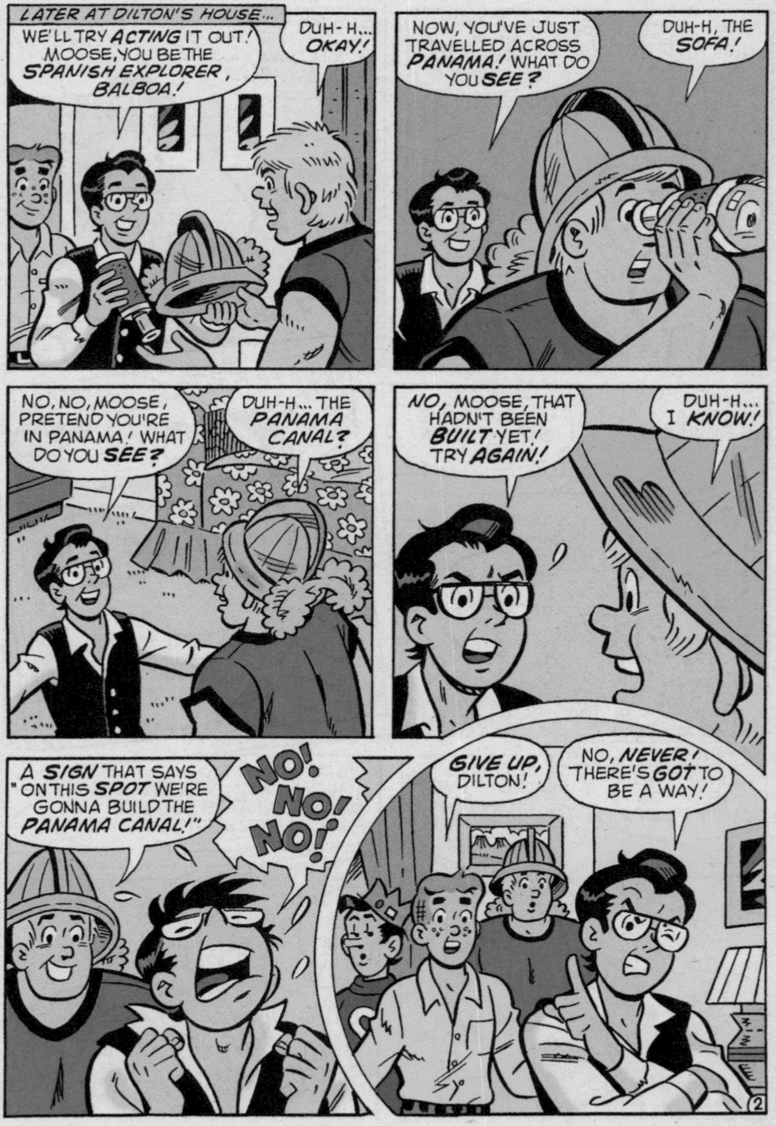
LATER AT DILTON'S HOUSE...
WE'LL TRY ACTING IT OUT! MOOSE, YOU BE THE SPANISH EXPLORER, BALBOA!
DUH-H... OKAY!
NOW, YOU'VE JUST TRAVELLED ACROSS PANAMA! WHAT DO YOU SEE?
DUH-H, THE SOFA!
NO, NO, MOOSE, PRETEND YOU'RE IN PANAMA! WHAT DO YOU SEE?
DUH-H... THE PANAMA CANAL?
NO, MOOSE, THAT HADN'T BEEN BUILT YET! TRY AGAIN!
DUH-H... I KNOW!
A SIGN THAT SAYS "ON THIS SPOT WE'RE GONNA BUILD THE PANAMA CANAL!"
NO! NO! NO!
GIVE UP, DILTON!
NO, NEVER! THERE'S GOT TO BE A WAY!
2

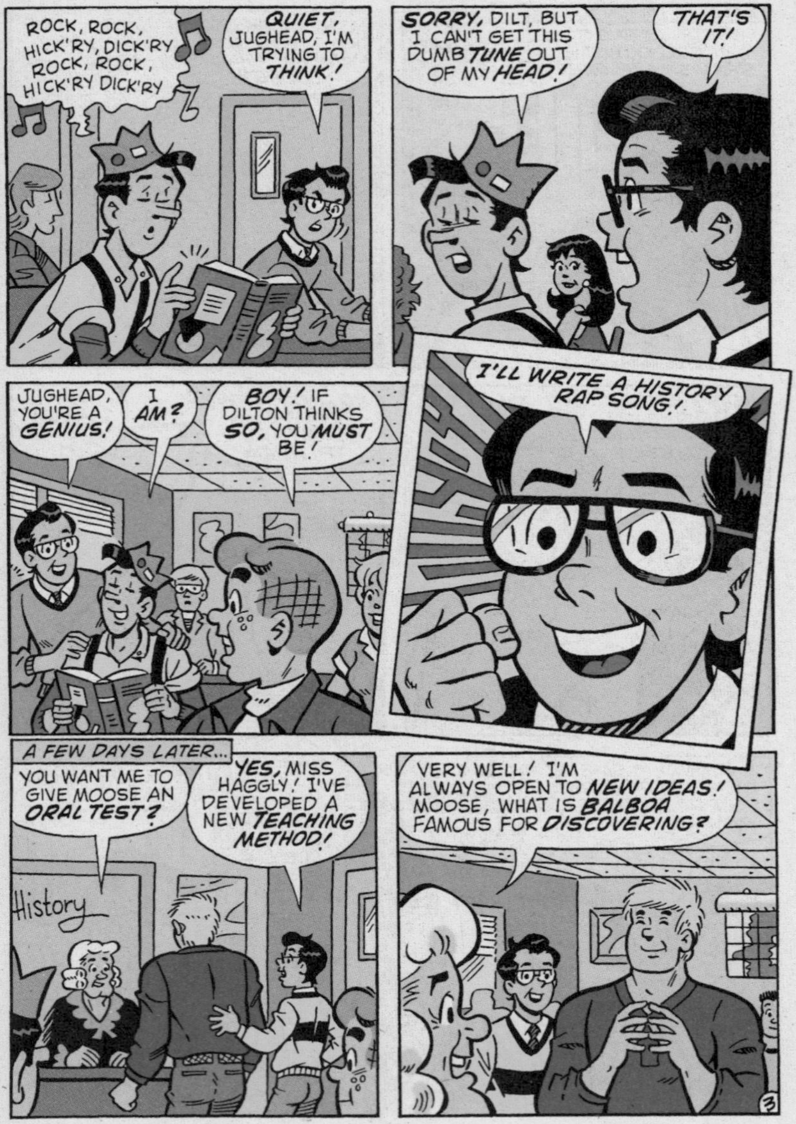
ROCK, ROCK, HICK'RY, DICK'RY ROCK, ROCK, HICK'RY DICK'RY
QUIET, JUGHEAD, I'M TRYING TO THINK!
SORRY, DILT, BUT I CAN'T GET THIS DUMB TUNE OUT OF MY HEAD!
THAT'S IT!
JUGHEAD, YOU'RE A GENIUS!
I AM?
BOY! IF DILTON THINKS SO, YOU MUST BE!
I'LL WRITE A HISTORY RAP SONG!
A FEW DAYS LATER...
YOU WANT ME TO GIVE MOOSE AN ORAL TEST?
YES, MISS HAGGLY! I'VE DEVELOPED A NEW TEACHING METHOD!
History
VERY WELL! I'M ALWAYS OPEN TO NEW IDEAS! MOOSE, WHAT IS BALBOA FAMOUS FOR DISCOVERING?
3

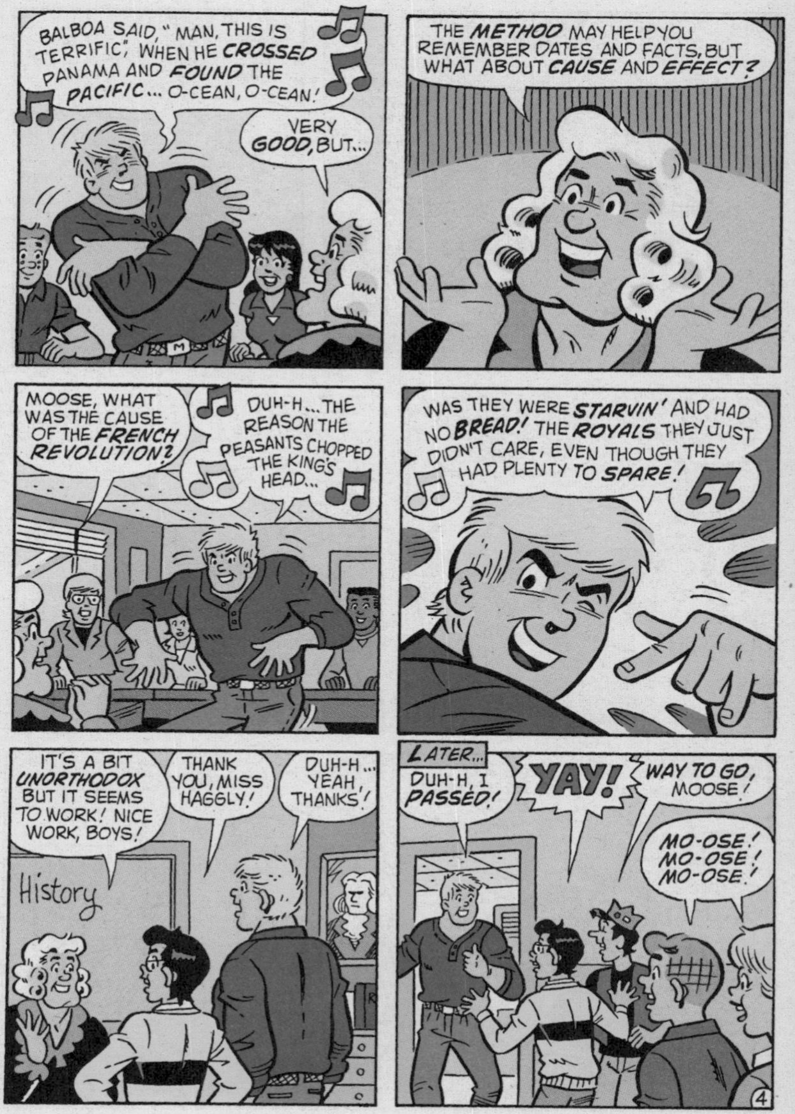

BALBOA SAID, " MAN, THIS IS TERRIFIC", WHEN HE CROSSED PANAMA AND FOUND THE PACIFIC... O-CEAN, O-CEAN!
VERY GOOD, BUT...
THE METHOD MAY HELP YOU REMEMBER DATES AND FACTS, BUT WHAT ABOUT CAUSE AND EFFECT?
MOOSE, WHAT WAS THE CAUSE OF THE FRENCH REVOLUTION?
DUH-H... THE REASON THE PEASANTS CHOPPED THE KING'S HEAD...
WAS THEY WERE STARVIN' AND HAD NO BREAD! THE ROYALS THEY JUST DIDN'T CARE, EVEN THOUGH THEY HAD PLENTY TO SPARE!
IT'S A BIT UNORTHODOX BUT IT SEEMS TO WORK! NICE WORK, BOYS!
THANK YOU, MISS HAGGLY!
DUH-H... YEAH, THANKS!
History
LATER...
DUH-H, I PASSED!
YAY!
WAY TO GO, MOOSE!
MO-OSE! MO-OSE! MO-OSE!

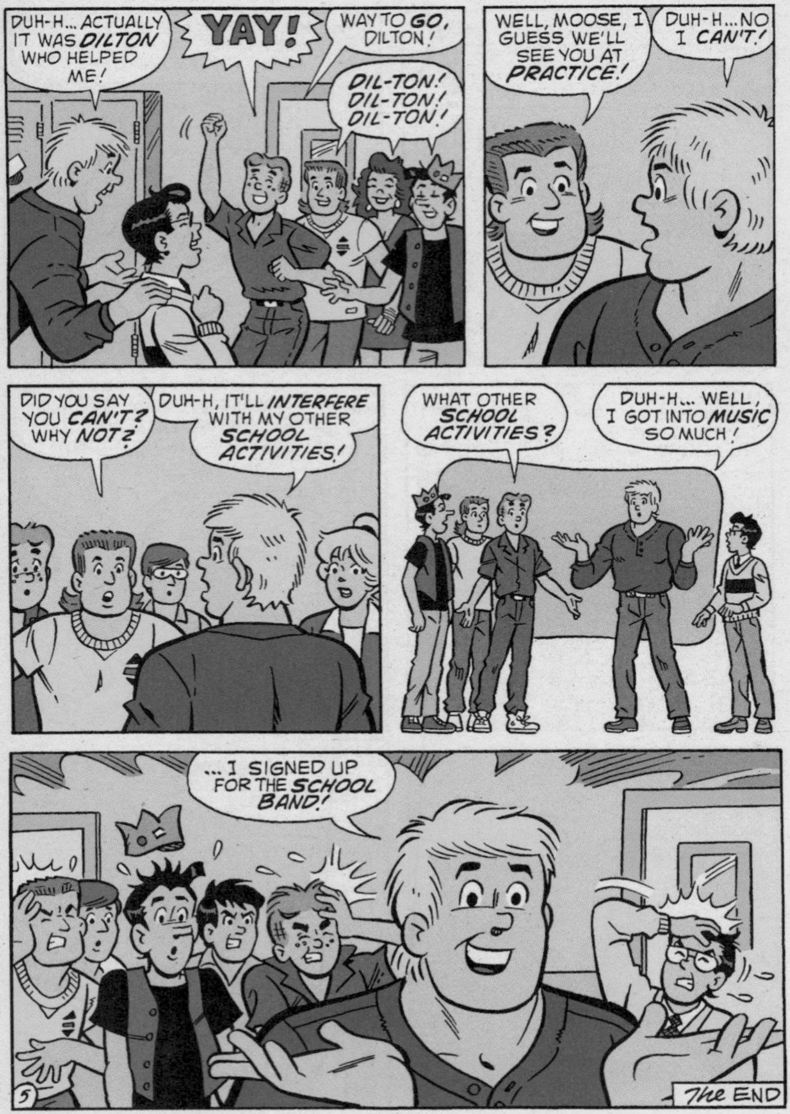
DUH-H... ACTUALLY IT WAS DILTON WHO HELPED ME!
YAY!
WAY TO GO, DILTON!
DIL-TON! DIL-TON! DIL-TON!
WELL, MOOSE, I GUESS WE'LL SEE YOU AT PRACTICE!
DUH-H...NO I CAN'T!
DID YOU SAY YOU CAN'T? WHY NOT?
DUH-H, IT'LL INTERFERE WITH MY OTHER SCHOOL ACTIVITIES!
WHAT OTHER SCHOOL ACTIVITIES?
DUH-H... WELL, I GOT INTO MUSIC SO MUCH!
...I SIGNED UP FOR THE SCHOOL BAND!
5
The END

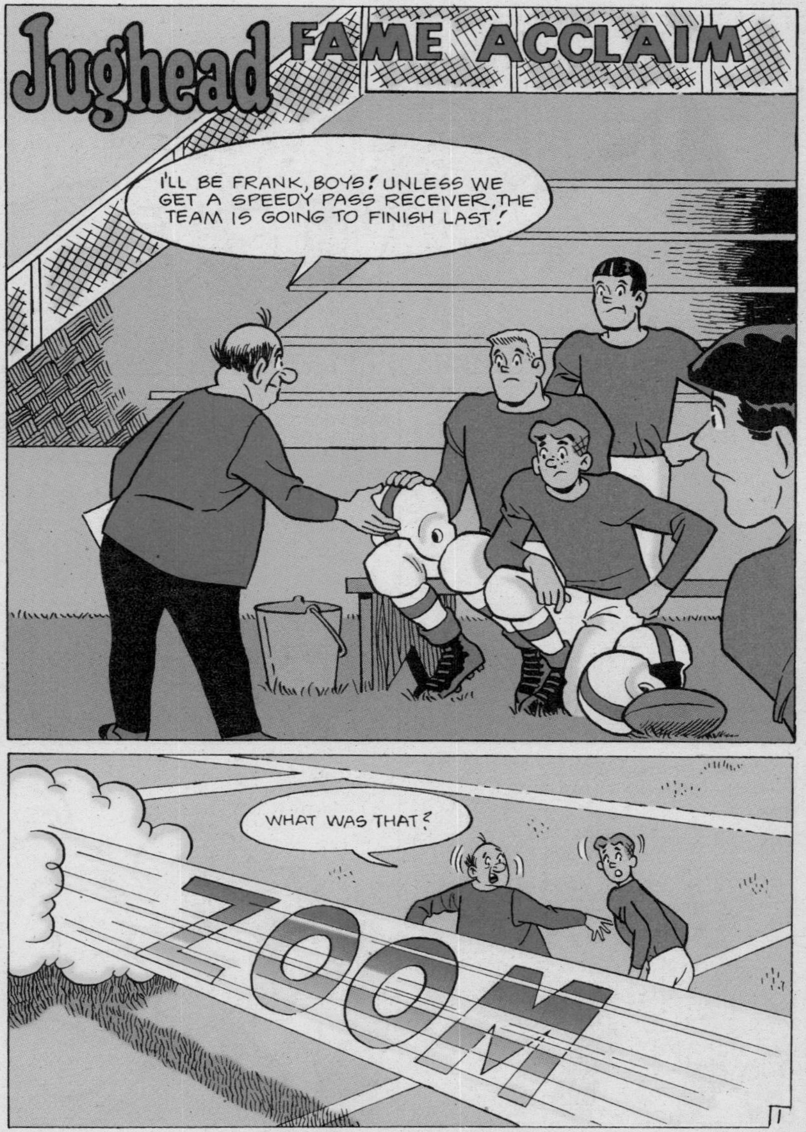
Jughead
FAME ACCLAIM
I'LL BE FRANK, BOYS! UNLESS WE GET A SPEEDY PASS RECEIVER, THE TEAM IS GOING TO FINISH LAST!
WHAT WAS THAT?
ZOOM

Script: George Gladir / Art & Letters: Samm Schwartz

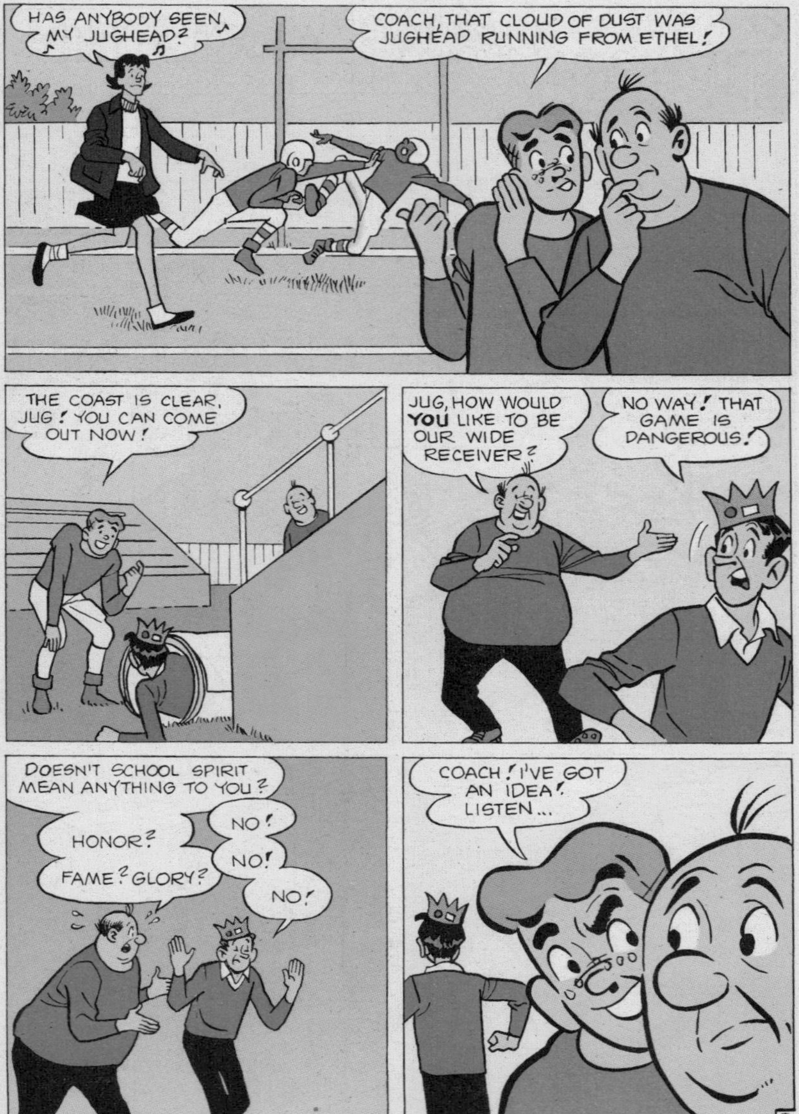
HAS ANYBODY SEEN MY JUGHEAD?
COACH, THAT CLOUD OF DUST WAS JUGHEAD RUNNING FROM ETHEL!
THE COAST IS CLEAR, JUG! YOU CAN COME OUT NOW!
JUG, HOW WOULD **YOU** LIKE TO BE OUR WIDE RECEIVER?
NO WAY! THAT GAME IS DANGEROUS!
DOESN'T SCHOOL SPIRIT MEAN ANYTHING TO YOU?
NO!
HONOR?
NO!
FAME? GLORY?
NO!
COACH! I'VE GOT AN IDEA! LISTEN...
2

DOES ALL THE HAMBURGERS YOU CAN EAT AT POP TATE'S MEAN ANYTHING TO YOU?

AS I WAS SAYING.. WHAT DO I HAVE TO DO?

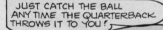

JUST CATCH THE BALL ANY TIME THE QUARTERBACK THROWS IT TO YOU!

RUN OUT, JUG, LIKE ETHEL'S AFTER YOU AND CATCH THE PASS I THROW!

THUNK!

JUST WHAT I NEED! A BUTTERFINGERED PASS DROPPER!

COOL IT! I'VE GOT AN IDEA!

WHAT ARE YOU DOING?

MAKING SURE HE'LL NEVER DROP ANOTHER PASS!

3

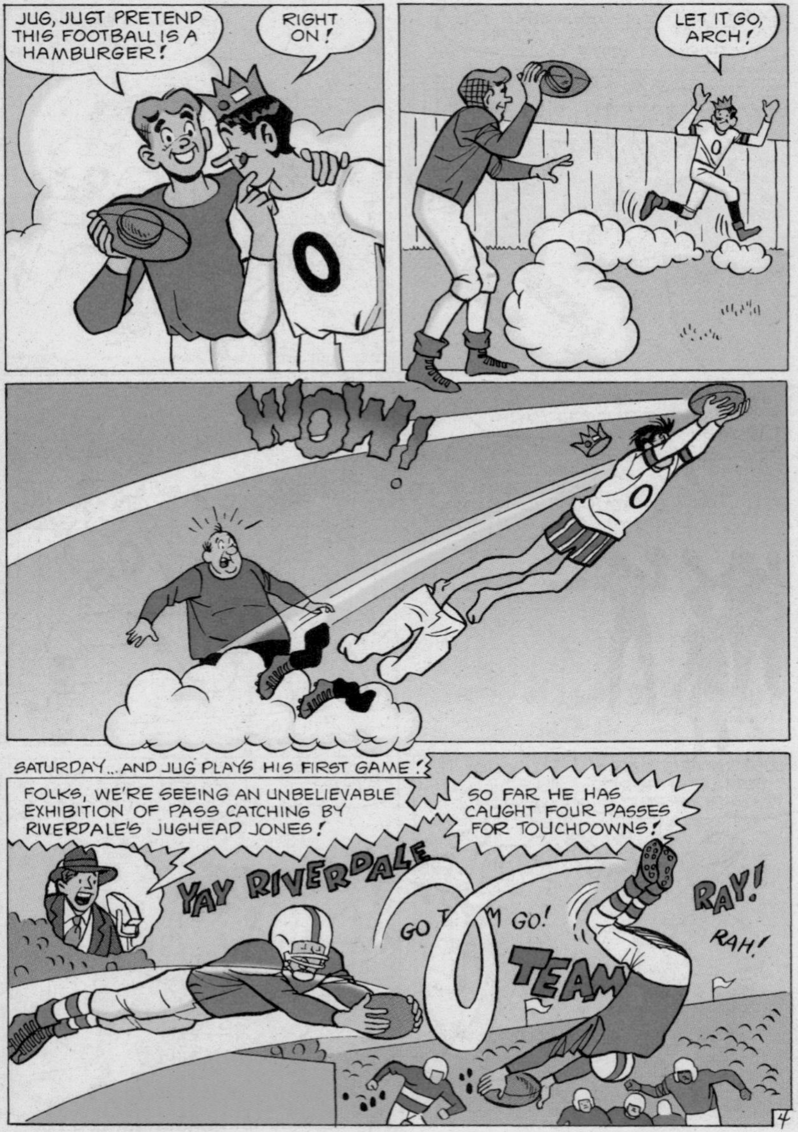

JUG, JUST PRETEND THIS FOOTBALL IS A HAMBURGER!
RIGHT ON!
LET IT GO, ARCH!
WOW!
SATURDAY... AND JUG PLAYS HIS FIRST GAME!
FOLKS, WE'RE SEEING AN UNBELIEVABLE EXHIBITION OF PASS CATCHING BY RIVERDALE'S JUGHEAD JONES!
SO FAR HE HAS CAUGHT FOUR PASSES FOR TOUCHDOWNS!
YAY RIVERDALE
RAY!
RAH!
TEAM

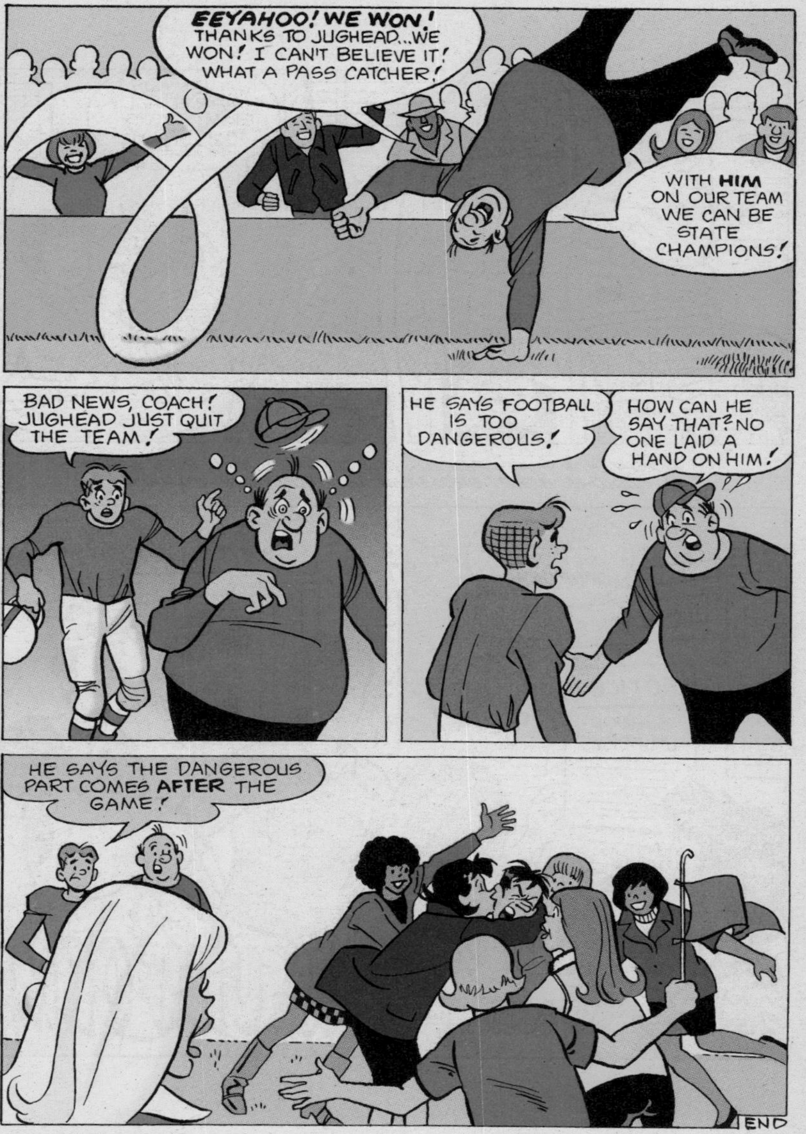
EEYAHOO! WE WON! THANKS TO JUGHEAD...WE WON! I CAN'T BELIEVE IT! WHAT A PASS CATCHER!
WITH HIM ON OUR TEAM WE CAN BE STATE CHAMPIONS!
BAD NEWS, COACH! JUGHEAD JUST QUIT THE TEAM!
HE SAYS FOOTBALL IS TOO DANGEROUS!
HOW CAN HE SAY THAT? NO ONE LAID A HAND ON HIM!
HE SAYS THE DANGEROUS PART COMES AFTER THE GAME!
END

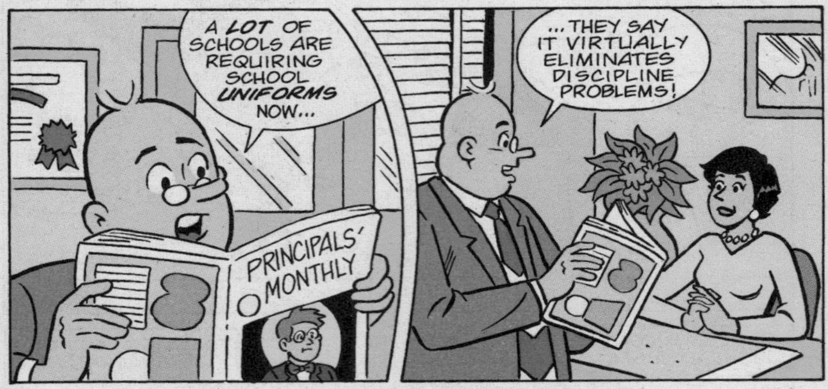
A LOT OF SCHOOLS ARE REQUIRING SCHOOL UNIFORMS NOW...
PRINCIPALS' MONTHLY
...THEY SAY IT VIRTUALLY ELIMINATES DISCIPLINE PROBLEMS!

SCRIPT: HAL SMITH PENCILS: BILL GOLLIHER INKS: RUDY LAPICK
COLORS: BARRY GROSSMAN LETTERS: VICKIE WILLIAMS

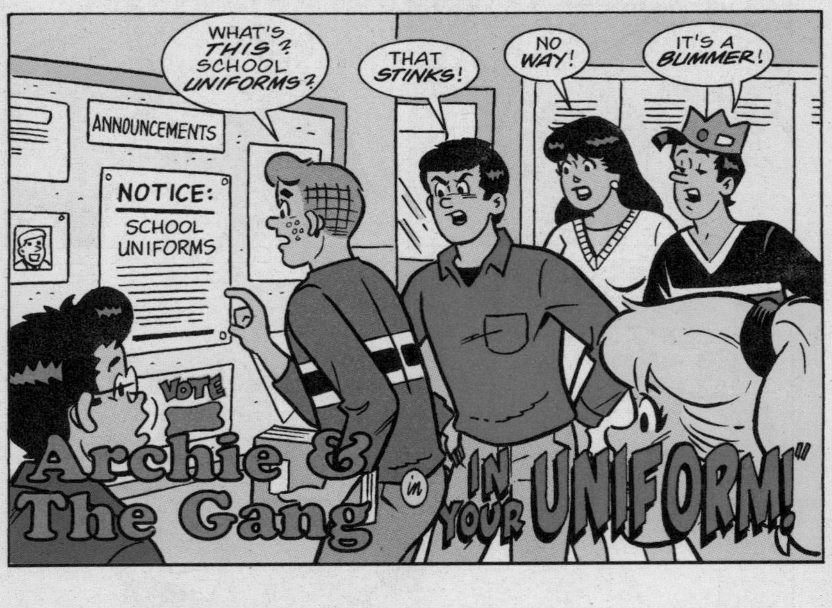
WHAT'S THIS? SCHOOL UNIFORMS?
THAT STINKS!
NO WAY!
IT'S A BUMMER!
ANNOUNCEMENTS
NOTICE:
SCHOOL UNIFORMS
VOTE
Archie & The Gang
in
"IN YOUR UNIFORM!"

WHAT'S THAT *COMMOTION* OUTSIDE?

NO WAY!

UNIFORMS UNFAIR!

DON'T STIFLE CREATIVITY!

NO UNIFORMS!

NO UNIFORMS

DON'T BE "CLOTHES" MINDED!

UNIFORMS ARE A NO-NO!

LOOKS AS IF YOUR UNIFORM PLAN IS BEING SHUT *DOWN!*

TUT, TUT, TUT,...

UNIFORM UNFAIR

I KNOW HOW TO HANDLE *THIS!*

STUDENTS! STUDENTS!

I HAVE A *PROPOSAL* FOR YOU!

NIFORMS NFAIR!

UNIF NO WAY!

I'LL LET YOU *DESIGN* YOUR *OWN* UNIFORMS!

DON'T "CLOT

FREE

YOU WILL?

NO UNI

②

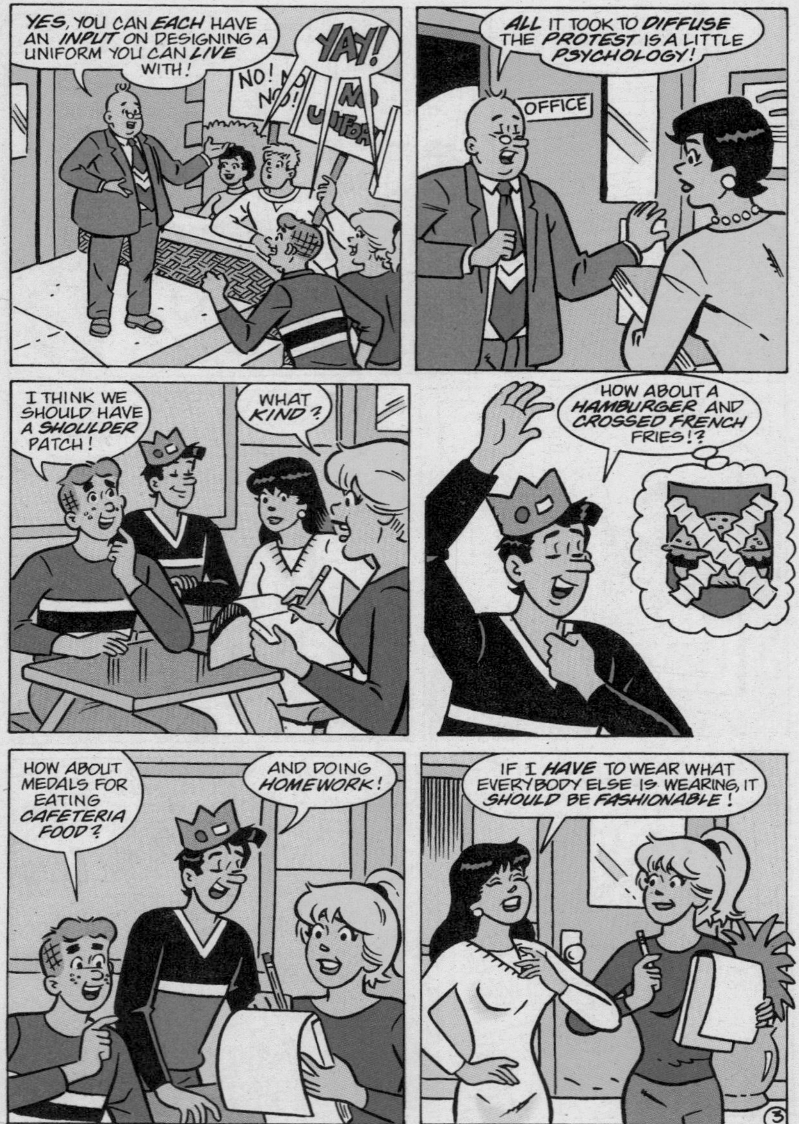
YES, YOU CAN EACH HAVE AN INPUT ON DESIGNING A UNIFORM YOU CAN LIVE WITH!
YAY!
NO! NO NO!
NO UNIFORM
ALL IT TOOK TO DIFFUSE THE PROTEST IS A LITTLE PSYCHOLOGY!
OFFICE
I THINK WE SHOULD HAVE A SHOULDER PATCH!
WHAT KIND?
HOW ABOUT A HAMBURGER AND CROSSED FRENCH FRIES!?
HOW ABOUT MEDALS FOR EATING CAFETERIA FOOD?
AND DOING HOMEWORK!
IF I HAVE TO WEAR WHAT EVERYBODY ELSE IS WEARING, IT SHOULD BE FASHIONABLE!
3

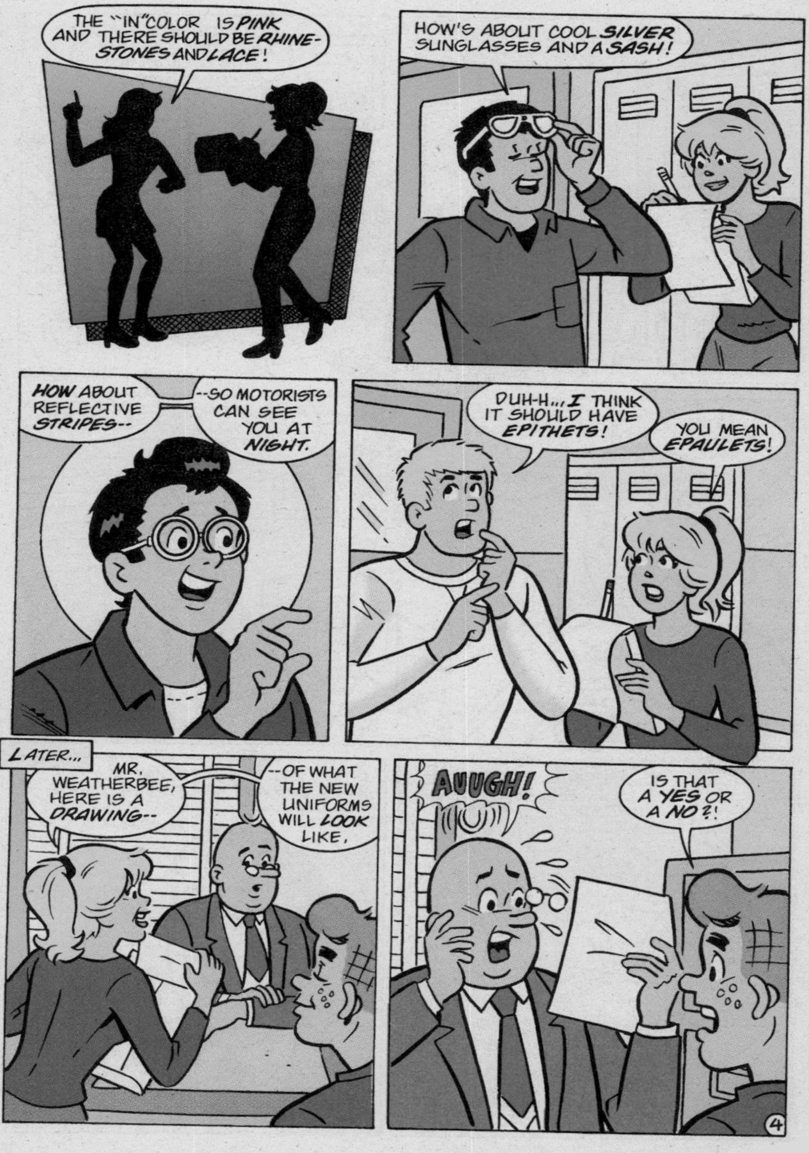

THE "IN" COLOR IS PINK AND THERE SHOULD BE RHINE-STONES AND LACE!
HOW'S ABOUT COOL SILVER SUNGLASSES AND A SASH!
HOW ABOUT REFLECTIVE STRIPES--
--SO MOTORISTS CAN SEE YOU AT NIGHT.
DUH-H..., I THINK IT SHOULD HAVE EPITHETS!
YOU MEAN EPAULETS!
LATER...
MR. WEATHERBEE, HERE IS A DRAWING--
--OF WHAT THE NEW UNIFORMS WILL LOOK LIKE.
AUUGH!
IS THAT A YES OR A NO?!
4

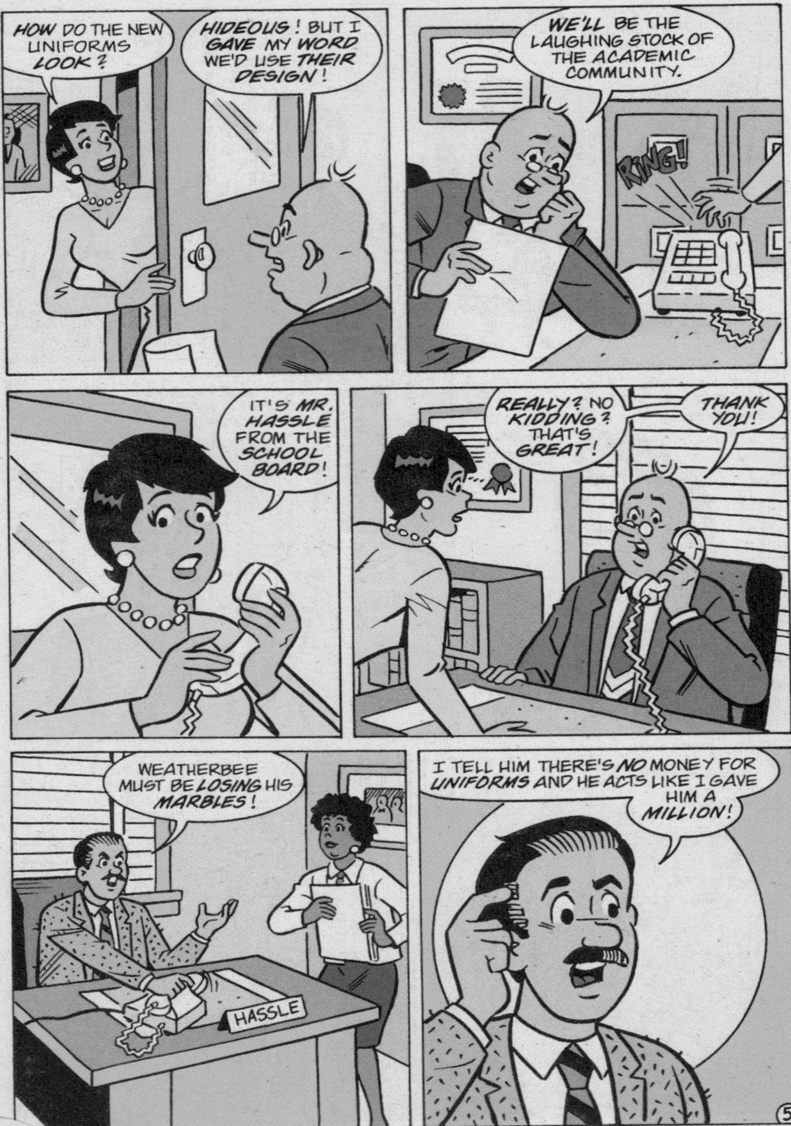
HOW DO THE NEW UNIFORMS LOOK?
HIDEOUS! BUT I GAVE MY WORD WE'D USE THEIR DESIGN!
WE'LL BE THE LAUGHING STOCK OF THE ACADEMIC COMMUNITY.
RING!
IT'S MR. HASSLE FROM THE SCHOOL BOARD!
REALLY? NO KIDDING? THAT'S GREAT!
THANK YOU!
WEATHERBEE MUST BE LOSING HIS MARBLES!
HASSLE
I TELL HIM THERE'S NO MONEY FOR UNIFORMS AND HE ACTS LIKE I GAVE HIM A MILLION!

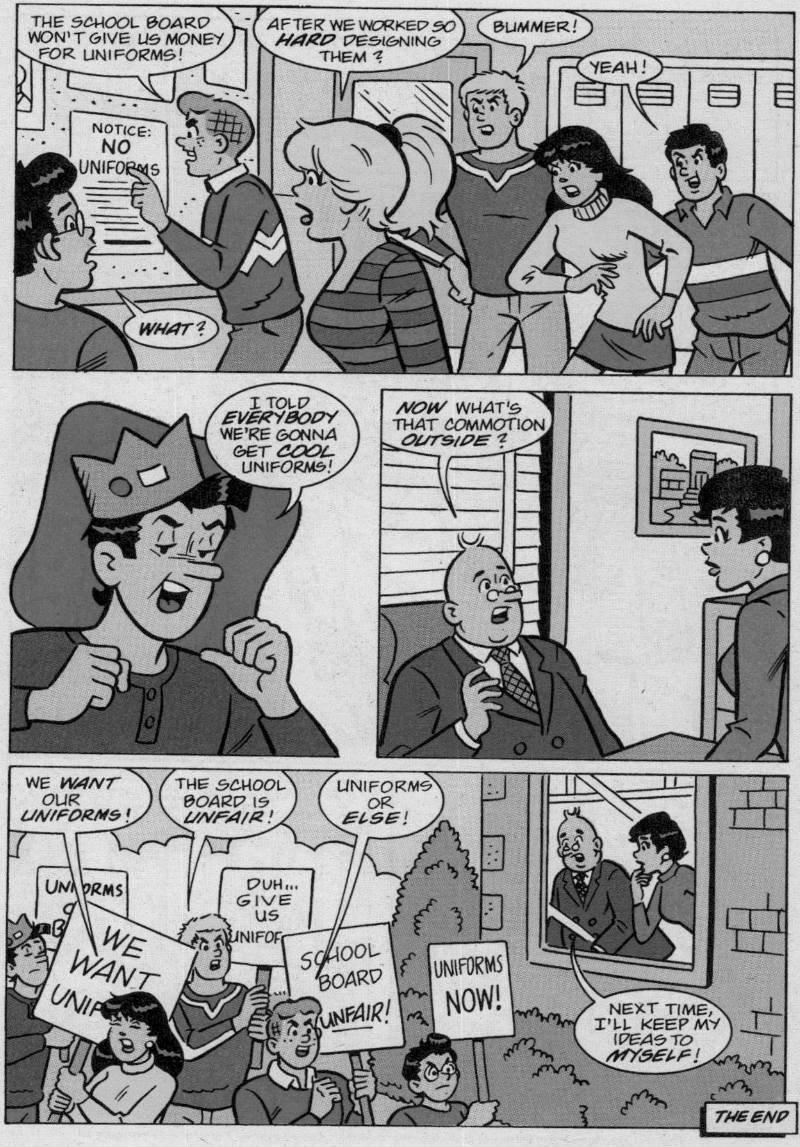

THE SCHOOL BOARD WON'T GIVE US MONEY FOR UNIFORMS!
NOTICE: NO UNIFORMS
WHAT?
AFTER WE WORKED SO HARD DESIGNING THEM?
BUMMER!
YEAH!
I TOLD EVERYBODY WE'RE GONNA GET COOL UNIFORMS!
NOW WHAT'S THAT COMMOTION OUTSIDE?
WE WANT OUR UNIFORMS!
THE SCHOOL BOARD IS UNFAIR!
UNIFORMS OR ELSE!
WE WANT UNIF
DUH... GIVE US UNIFOR
SCHOOL BOARD UNFAIR!
UNIFORMS NOW!
NEXT TIME, I'LL KEEP MY IDEAS TO MYSELF!
THE END

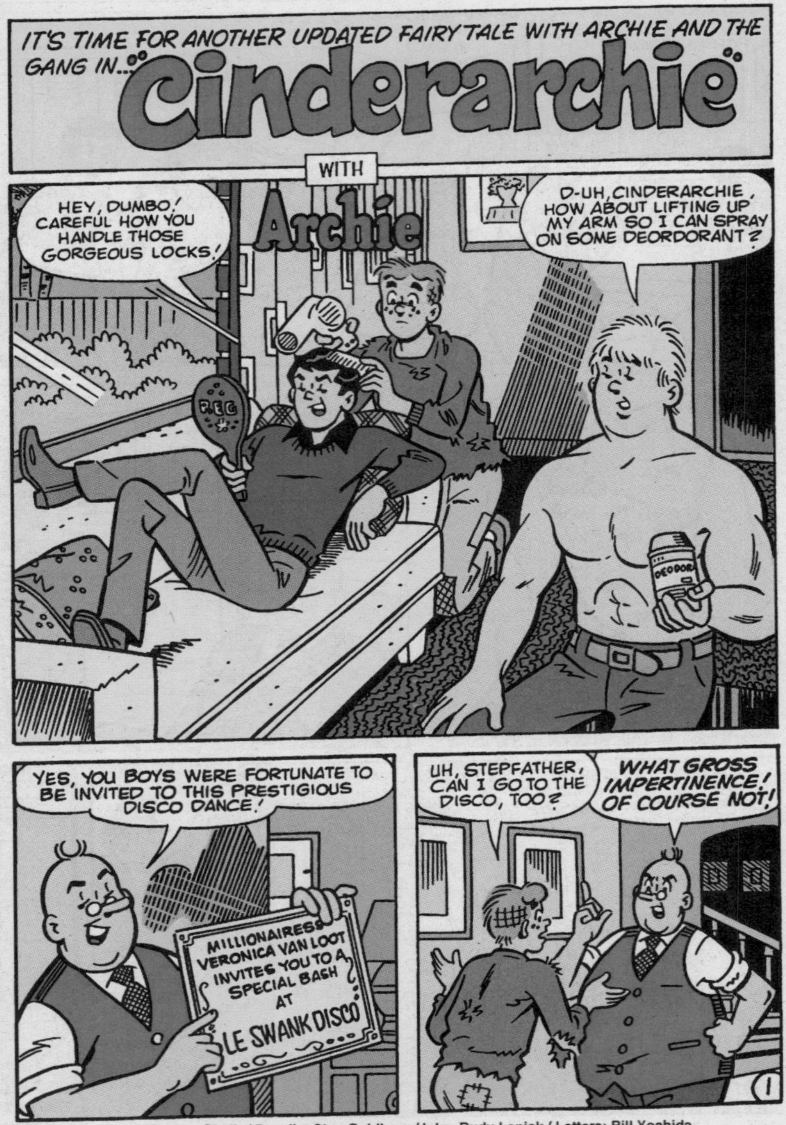
IT'S TIME FOR ANOTHER UPDATED FAIRY TALE WITH ARCHIE AND THE GANG IN...
Cinderarchie
WITH
Archie
HEY, DUMBO! CAREFUL HOW YOU HANDLE THOSE GORGEOUS LOCKS!
D-UH, CINDERARCHIE, HOW ABOUT LIFTING UP MY ARM SO I CAN SPRAY ON SOME DEORDORANT?
REG
YES, YOU BOYS WERE FORTUNATE TO BE INVITED TO THIS PRESTIGIOUS DISCO DANCE!
MILLIONAIRESS VERONICA VAN LOOT INVITES YOU TO A SPECIAL BASH AT LE SWANK DISCO
UH, STEPFATHER, CAN I GO TO THE DISCO, TOO?
WHAT GROSS IMPERTINENCE! OF COURSE NOT!
1

Script: George Gladir / Pencils: Stan Goldberg / Inks: Rudy Lapick / Letters: Bill Yoshida

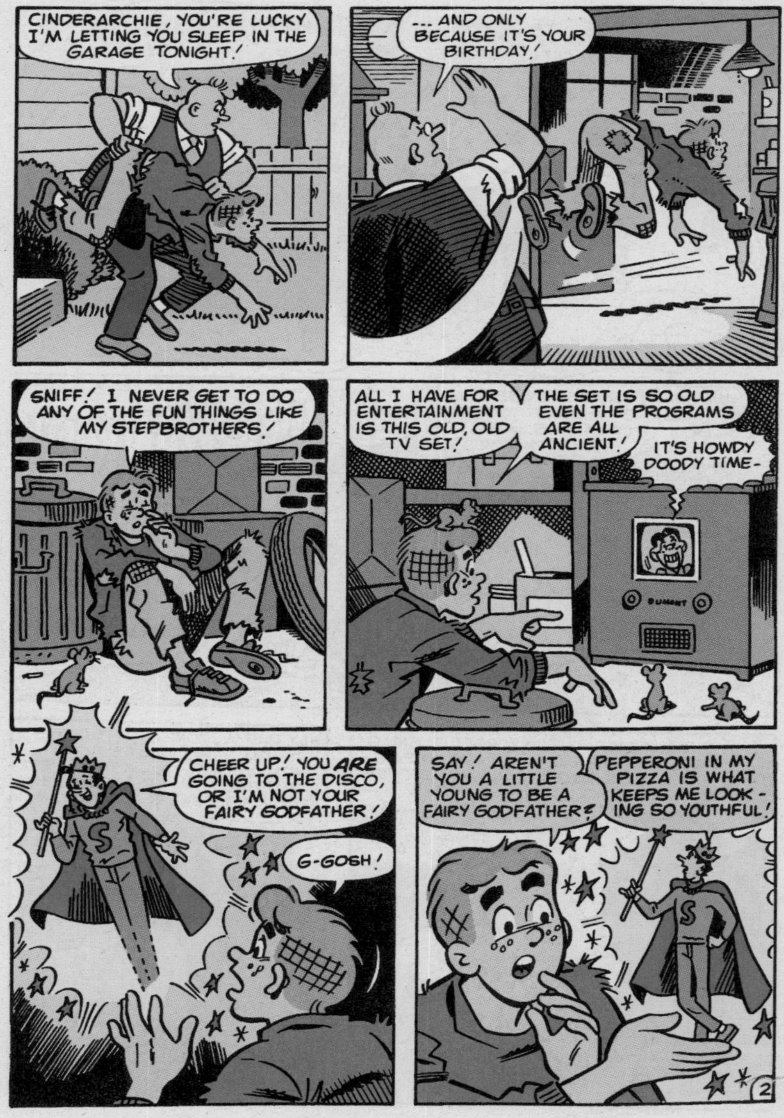
CINDERARCHIE, YOU'RE LUCKY I'M LETTING YOU SLEEP IN THE GARAGE TONIGHT!
...AND ONLY BECAUSE IT'S YOUR BIRTHDAY!
SNIFF! I NEVER GET TO DO ANY OF THE FUN THINGS LIKE MY STEPBROTHERS!
ALL I HAVE FOR ENTERTAINMENT IS THIS OLD, OLD TV SET!
THE SET IS SO OLD EVEN THE PROGRAMS ARE ALL ANCIENT!
IT'S HOWDY DOODY TIME-
CHEER UP! YOU ARE GOING TO THE DISCO, OR I'M NOT YOUR FAIRY GODFATHER!
G-GOSH!
SAY! AREN'T YOU A LITTLE YOUNG TO BE A FAIRY GODFATHER?
PEPPERONI IN MY PIZZA IS WHAT KEEPS ME LOOKING SO YOUTHFUL!
2

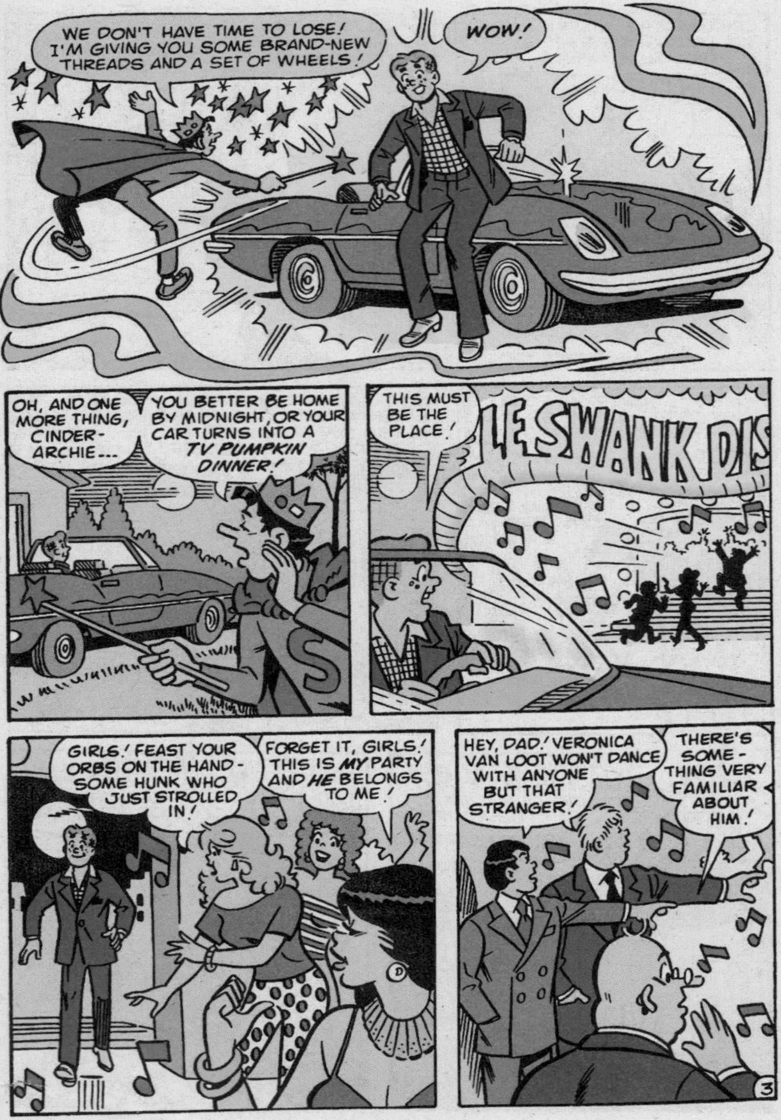
WE DON'T HAVE TIME TO LOSE! I'M GIVING YOU SOME BRAND-NEW THREADS AND A SET OF WHEELS!
WOW!
OH, AND ONE MORE THING, CINDER-ARCHIE...
YOU BETTER BE HOME BY MIDNIGHT, OR YOUR CAR TURNS INTO A TV PUMPKIN DINNER!
THIS MUST BE THE PLACE!
LE SWANK DIS
GIRLS! FEAST YOUR ORBS ON THE HANDSOME HUNK WHO JUST STROLLED IN!
FORGET IT, GIRLS! THIS IS MY PARTY AND HE BELONGS TO ME!
HEY, DAD! VERONICA VAN LOOT WON'T DANCE WITH ANYONE BUT THAT STRANGER!
THERE'S SOMETHING VERY FAMILIAR ABOUT HIM!
3

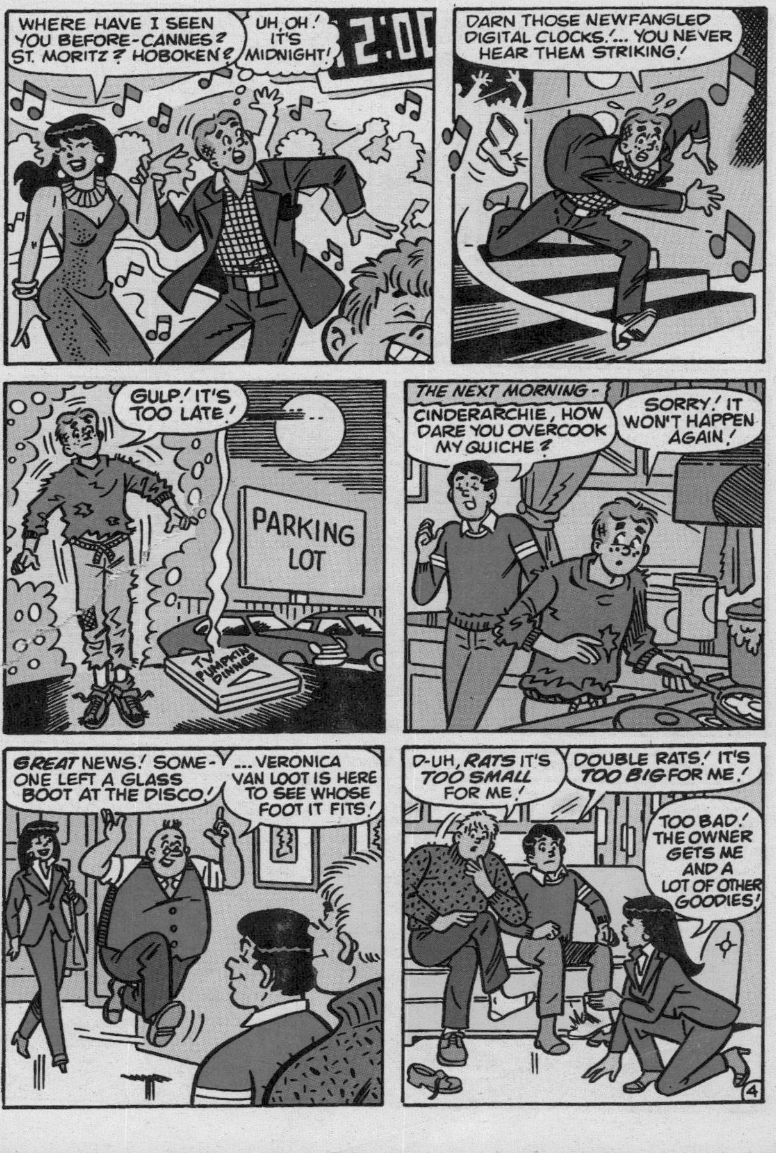
WHERE HAVE I SEEN YOU BEFORE-CANNES? ST. MORITZ? HOBOKEN?
UH, OH! IT'S MIDNIGHT!
DARN THOSE NEWFANGLED DIGITAL CLOCKS!... YOU NEVER HEAR THEM STRIKING!
GULP! IT'S TOO LATE!
PARKING LOT
TV PUMPKIN DINNER
THE NEXT MORNING-
CINDERARCHIE, HOW DARE YOU OVERCOOK MY QUICHE?
SORRY! IT WON'T HAPPEN AGAIN!
GREAT NEWS! SOME-ONE LEFT A GLASS BOOT AT THE DISCO!
...VERONICA VAN LOOT IS HERE TO SEE WHOSE FOOT IT FITS!
D-UH, RATS IT'S TOO SMALL FOR ME!
DOUBLE RATS! IT'S TOO BIG FOR ME!
TOO BAD! THE OWNER GETS ME AND A LOT OF OTHER GOODIES!
4

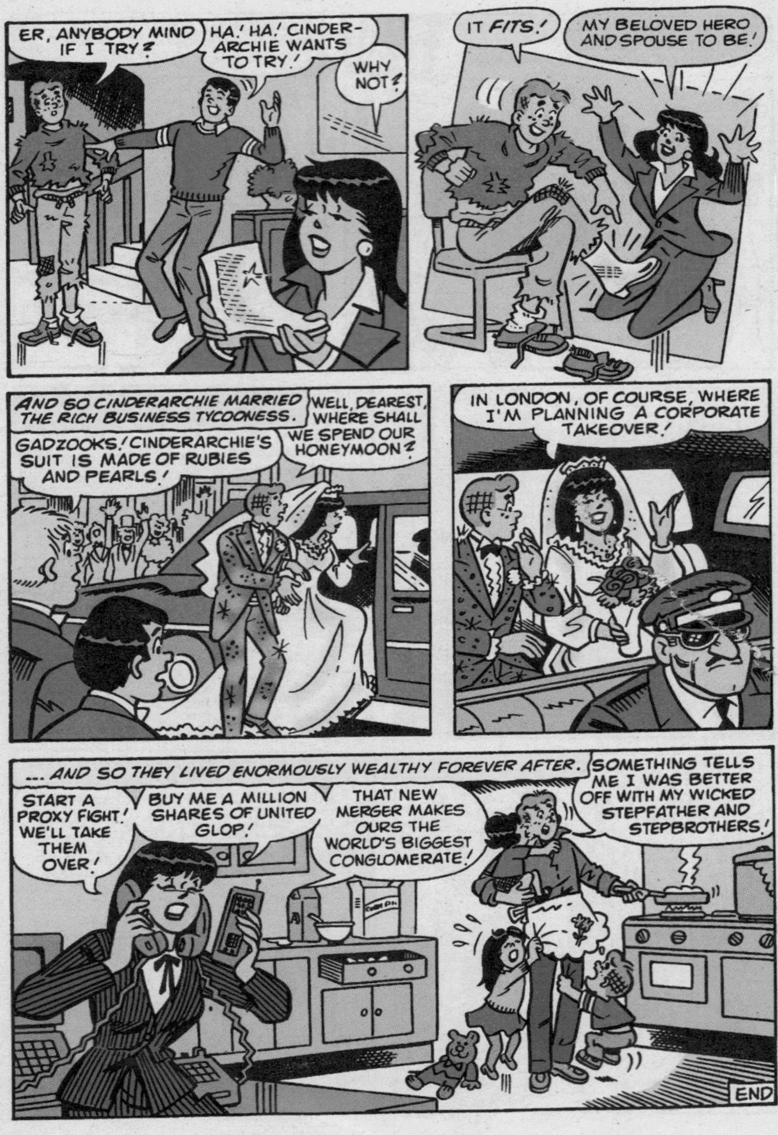

ER, ANYBODY MIND IF I TRY?
HA! HA! CINDER-ARCHIE WANTS TO TRY!
WHY NOT?
IT FITS!
MY BELOVED HERO AND SPOUSE TO BE!
AND SO CINDERARCHIE MARRIED THE RICH BUSINESS TYCOONESS.
GADZOOKS! CINDERARCHIE'S SUIT IS MADE OF RUBIES AND PEARLS!
WELL, DEAREST, WHERE SHALL WE SPEND OUR HONEYMOON?
IN LONDON, OF COURSE, WHERE I'M PLANNING A CORPORATE TAKEOVER!
... AND SO THEY LIVED ENORMOUSLY WEALTHY FOREVER AFTER.
START A PROXY FIGHT! WE'LL TAKE THEM OVER!
BUY ME A MILLION SHARES OF UNITED GLOP!
THAT NEW MERGER MAKES OURS THE WORLD'S BIGGEST CONGLOMERATE!
SOMETHING TELLS ME I WAS BETTER OFF WITH MY WICKED STEPFATHER AND STEPBROTHERS!
END